Albert Wendt is of the Aiga Sa-Tuaopepe of Lefaga, the Aiga Sa-Maualaivao of Malie and the Aiga Sa-Patu of Vaiala of Samoa. He first came to New Zealand in 1952, where he went to high school, teachers training college and university. Later he was Principal of Samoa College and Pro-Vice-Chancellor and Professor of Pacific Literature at the University of the South Pacific. At present he is Professor of English at the University of Auckland. He has published numerous novels and poems as well as short stories.

the mango's
KISS

A novel by Albert Wendt

V
VINTAGE

National Library of New Zealand Cataloguing-in-Publication Data

Wendt, Albert, 1939-

The mango's kiss / Albert Wendt.

I. Title.

ISBN 1-86941-580-9

NZ823.2—dc 21

A VINTAGE BOOK

published by

Random House New Zealand

18 Poland Road, Glenfield, Auckland, New Zealand

www.randomhouse.co.nz

First published 2003

ISBN 1 86941 580 9

Design: Elin Termannsen

Cover design: Katy Yiakmis

Printed in Australia by Griffin Press

For all my Aiga for their alofa and support

CONTENTS

BOOK ONE
Daughters of the Mango Season

The Beginning, the End

Around her suddenly, the warm familiar smell of the man she'd later come to know as her father, and, as usual, she moved into it, letting it envelop her like a second skin. Down-pressing round coldness on her right cheek, radiating out across her face and down through her body to her tingling toes. She jerked away from it, hands clasped to the wet spot on her cheek. In her father's hand, at the centre of her seeing, was a round green-orange object. (A mango, she'd learn later.) From the object to his hand, to his face, she looked, recognising he was smiling. She moved closer to him, her hand taking the object, the fruit, which assumed the shape of her grip: solid, fitting, apt, balanced. Her father nuzzled his forehead against hers.

During the final moments of her dying, years later, that was how Peleiupu (or Pele, as everyone came to call her) was to recall, in slow vivid detail, that incredible dawn when her father, Mautu Tuifolau, pressed the dew-covered mango against her right cheek. At that startled moment, she was conscious for the first time she was an entity (I, me), separate from everything and everyone else — including her father, who was encouraging her, with repeated nods, to raise the fruit to her mouth and bite it. She would try, in her dying, to remember whether she'd taken that bite or what the mango had tasted like, and not be able to.

It was 1882 and she was about two (her father would tell her later), her parents' first child, and they were living in Satoa, Savai'i, where Mautu was the pastor of the Lotu Ta'iti, the only church in the village. Satoa then was an orderly collection of about thirty aiga in fale spread along the shore under palms; a trading store owned by the Englishman Barker and his Satoan wife, Poto; and a modest church constructed of bush-cut timber and sugarcane thatching with a sand floor anchored to the earth by centuries of settlement and genealogical trees rooted in the atua, and a prophecy that Satoa would one day produce an aiga of prodigies who would lead the country.

A year after the mango fruit's kiss, Peleiupu's brother Arona was born, a year later Ruta, then another sister, Naomi, and finally Iakopo, another brother.

For a surprised while Peleiupu couldn't believe she'd heard her mother, Lalaga, whispering to her father in their mosquito net: 'Iakopo is very sick!' Pretending to be asleep, Peleiupu held her breath.

'Sick from what?' he asked.

Peleiupu caught it in her mother's ragged breathing even before she released it: 'It may be . . .' She couldn't say it.

'May be what?' he whispered.

'It may be the Disease,' she admitted, finally.

There was a long pause as Mautu gathered his sleeping sheet around his shoulders. The dim light of the lamp outlined and isolated his face in the dark as he gazed at Iakopo, who was asleep in the next mosquito net. 'Are you sure?' he asked.

'It could be.'

'But he's only three!' he protested. Peleiupu turned over and, snuggling around her mother's legs, held on to them. Lalaga started caressing her face.

Mautu's predecessor had died the previous year from what everyone called the Satoan Disease which, in a matter of days, had transformed him — as it had done to its previous victims — from a handsomely robust man of exceptional physical strength into a delirious, suicidal bundle of excruciating pain, skin and bone. Some Satoans believed their Disease had been introduced into their genealogy and lives by a papalagi sailor who'd deserted his ship when it had called in to Satoa for water and fresh provisions. Others believed that a pre-Christian atua had infected a Satoan woman with it.

'I've tried everything I learned at Vaiuta,' Lalaga told Mautu. When he remained silent she added, 'I'll get the fofo in the morning.' She pulled up the side of their net, crawled into the next net, returned with Iakopo in her arms and laid him beside Peleiupu, who reached out and held his burning hand.

Peleiupu would wake periodically during the night and see her parents, sheets wrapped securely around their bodies, watching over Iakopo.

Even before the fat sun could sit safely on the sharp eastern rim of mountains, Lalaga disappeared into the village and returned a short time after with Filivai, the most skilled fofo in Satoa. There were more skilled fofo elsewhere but they didn't understand the Satoan Disease.

Peleiupu and her brother and sisters wanted to watch Filivai treating their brother, but Lalaga got one of the older women to take them to the kitchen fale to prepare their morning meal.

'What's wrong with Iakopo?' Arona asked their minder.

'Yes, what's wrong with him?' Ruta echoed.

'He's sick, isn't he?' Naomi tugged at their minder's ie lavalava.

As she followed them towards the kitchen fale Peleiupu noticed that the others were leaving clear white footprints in the layer of dew. 'Iakopo is going to be all right,' she heard their minder reassuring the others. Peleiupu started placing her feet in their minder's footprints; she had to take longer strides to do so. One day she'd have feet as large. When she looked back at the main fale Filivai was massaging Iakopo's body, while Mautu and Lalaga watched.

At the kitchen fale Arona ran off and joined the boys who were collecting the fallen leaves and other rubbish around the compound. The women frying pancakes and corned beef over the open fire called over Naomi and Ruta, and soon their endless chatter added body to the sizzling sound of the frying. As Peleiupu helped their minder boil the large pot of water for Iakopo's bath they sang a well-known song:

The moon of the morning tide is rising	Ua oso mai le masina o le tai taeao
The year is ending	Ua i'u le tausaga
I wait for my beloved hoping he'll return.	Mo'omo'oga ia toe fo'i mai la'u pele.

When the meal was ready their minder asked five of the men and women to serve it. They took the pots and baskets of food to the main fale. The children ate, with the other young people, in the faleo'o.

Immediately after Filivai left, the minder filled the tub with warm water and got a clean towel and a piece of soap. Peleiupu and her sisters followed her to the main fale. The children sat around the tub and watched. The pain was obvious in Iakopo's face and body over which the tiny red sores that were symptomatic of the Disease were spreading rapidly, but he didn't cry as Lalaga lowered him into the bath and started soaping him. Peleiupu glanced up and saw the other women preparing a mosquito net and a bed of mats for Iakopo at the far end of the fale.

Lalaga laid Iakopo in her lap and dried him with the towel. She beckoned to Peleiupu, who uncorked the bottle of coconut oil and, pouring the smooth liquid into her hands, rubbed it over her brother's body. Long firm stroke after stroke after stroke relaxed Iakopo's pain eventually and he started to fall asleep.

'Can we do it next time?' Ruta asked Lalaga, who nodded.

Gingerly so as not to wake him, Naomi put on Iakopo's singlet, Ruta combed his hair, Peleiupu wrapped him in a clean sleeping sheet, and Lalaga carried him around the tapa-cloth curtain that now hung across the fale to his bed. Peleiupu and her sisters lowered the net around him, anchored it to the floor with the large smooth stones they used for the purpose, and sat with Lalaga around the net. Through the white mesh of netting their brother looked as if he were cocooned in a fine mist. Mosquitoes zinged at the edge of their attention.

By evening everyone in Satoa knew about Iakopo, and in their evening lotu pleaded with God to save their pastor's son from the Disease.

To many Satoan elders, everything about their pastor was *heavy*: his appearance, mannerisms, speech, and the reassuring but pompous aura of impregnable confidence that he exuded. It was as if Mautu had been born an adult; had missed out on his childhood. They had heard that their pastor had succeeded at theological college because he had been utterly trustworthy and solid in everything, the epitome of Christian respectability, who would maintain and strengthen tradition. The Satoan elders admired him for that, and for his down-to-earth sermons, which echoed the values of his missionary teachers: hard work, cleanliness, thrift, honesty and the determination to conquer the Devil, who lived in the pagan darkness that still covered much of Samoa and the Pacific.

So they viewed Iakopo's illness as the first real attack on their pastor's solidity. The Disease had selected their pastor's son, and they watched how Mautu would survive it. Some were even willing to wager that he wouldn't.

During their lotu, Lalaga assured Mautu and their household that Iakopo was going to recover. But before the lotu was over, Iakopo was screaming with pain. Mautu sent two youths to fetch Filivai.

While they waited, Lalaga clasped her son to her body. 'Shhh, you'll be all right!' she crooned into his hair as she rocked back and forth. Mautu dabbed at Iakopo's burning forehead with a wet cloth.

Filivai scrambled through the curtain and Lalaga handed Iakopo to her. When Naomi and Ruta started whimpering, Peleiupu took them out to the paepae where they sat and watched the stars, which looked like luminous pebbles breaking up out of the dark lake of sky.

'Is Iakopo going to die?' Arona asked Peleiupu.

'Is he?' chorused Ruta and Naomi.

'God will save him,' Peleiupu tried to comfort them. She then wound her arms around her sisters and pulled them in to her sides. The stars looked so far away, lost in the dark emptiness, but they were hanging on to their meagre light. Hanging on.

For almost two weeks the female elders took turns, in groups, helping Lalaga and Filivai care for Iakopo. They watched over him at night while Lalaga and Mautu tried to rest. Each aiga sent people to help in the cooking and caring for the elders and visitors. Because Lalaga was busy with Iakopo, Mautu ran their school on his own. His lessons were punctuated with lengthening stretches of unexpected silence and desperate attempts to remember what he'd just said. Sometimes his voice broke, and his students heard him swallowing back the pain. They behaved around him as if he were as fragile as eggshell. The care of Mautu's and Lalaga's children was left to the other women in their household.

With almost clinical detachment the Satoans watched their pastor shedding his solidity as the Disease sucked in Iakopo's beauty, and the fofo and Mautu's prayers failed to arrest the inward contraction, until, on Sunday in the pulpit in his now ill-fitting white suit, he looked like a butterfly cocoon collapsing in on itself.

'This morning I stand before you not understanding our God's sense of justice,' Mautu started his sermon. 'I have not chosen a text or prepared a sermon.' There was a tense pause as he tried to gather his strength and control his trembling. 'Though many of you have told me I shouldn't be afraid for my son because his illness is God's way of testing my faith, I am mortally afraid. My fear, born out of love for my son . . .' His voice breaking, he swallowed again. 'My fear is more real to me than anything else in my life . . .'

As Mautu spoke, Sao and some of the other elders observed that the righteous certainty was gone. Mautu was adrift in the sea of complicated greys, complex choices and unanswerable questions and contradictions; of blurred boundaries between good and evil, right and wrong; of God being not only a beneficent Creator but also an unforgiving Destroyer. And their alofa and admiration for him grew.

'What do you think?' Sao asked some of the elders as they left the church that morning.

'He will endure,' Vaomatua, his wife, replied.

'He's getting there,' a cataract-eyed sage said.

'He'll do!' someone else concluded.

Only the dumb roar of the surf breaking on the reef and the breeze clattering through the palms framed the silence that rang in Peleiupu's hearing when she woke. She sat up and looked around. In the shifting light from the lamp beside Iakopo's mosquito net she observed that everyone, including the two women who were supposed to be caring for Iakopo, was asleep. She raised the side of her net, hesitated and looked down at Lalaga, who was snoring almost inaudibly beside her, reached down and caressed her mother's forehead, and then slid noiselessly out of the net and crawled across the mats into Iakopo's net.

The previous night, as she had lain in bed trying not to listen to the fofo treating Iakopo's pain, she had decided finally, and had been surprised she wasn't afraid of her decision. It had nothing to do with what was right and wrong. 'Why is God not ending my brother's pain?' she'd asked Lalaga, who'd reached across and brushed her hair from her face.

'God's justice is beyond our understanding,' her mother had said.

'You're just repeating what Mautu says!'

The light and the whiteness of the pillows accentuated the emaciated condition of Iakopo's face. Only the skin was preventing the skull from erupting into the open; his eyes had retreated deeply into their sockets; almost all his hair was gone. He looked like the eighty-six-year-old deacon who'd died the year before. She could barely hear Iakopo's breathing, but at least he was momentarily free of the pain. Was that ripe mango she could smell?

She reached out and, with her fingers, delicately traced and read the contours of his face and the pulse beating irregularly at the side of his neck, while the night watched and waited. Then she pinched his nostrils shut and held her grip, fearlessly. The pulse in his neck eased away as she held and held . . .

My brother, my beloved brother.

At dawn, when Lalaga's muted wailing fished them out of their dark sleep, Peleiupu was prepared for it. For a while she lay still and watched. Their household operated to routines and practices laid down by Lalaga and tradition. Mautu was embracing Lalaga, trying to ease her grief. Filivai and two other women untied Iakopo's net and started washing his body. The rest of the people untied their nets, rolled up the sleeping mats and stored them on the rafters. Then the males hurried off to prepare the food for the mourners; some of them would go off to dig Iakopo's grave. Some of the women were cleaning the fale, ringing the posts with good mats and preparing the thick bed of fine mats for Iakopo's body. Peleiupu rolled out of the net, got up and untied it from the rafters. Then she woke the other children and untied their net. 'What's happening?' Arona asked, alarmed.

'Our brother has gone to God,' she told him, imitating their father.

She stood alone while the other children rushed into Lalaga's arms. When Filivai reached out to her, Peleiupu edged away and to her father who, though only two paces away, was alone, gazing up into the eastern sky as the sun singed it with a golden fire. When Peleiupu placed her hands on his shoulders, his right arm swept her in to his side. Together they watched the sun rising. Rising. And in its light Peleiupu saw her healing fingers exploring and reading Iakopo's face and the final horizon of his short life.

A short while later when the deacons, led by Sao, the tuua, arrived and they discussed Iakopo's funeral, they were surprised when Mautu ignored the church requirement that pastors should not conduct the funeral services of their own kin and insisted that he was going to do it.

'It is as if he's not the father!' a young deacon protested as they left the pastor's house.

'He is,' Sao remarked. 'He's just trying to hide his grief. We all do it at times like this.'

When the deacon continued his accusation, Sao silenced him with one wave of his hand.

The sun climbed into the white sky and a fierce heat started gripping Satoa. No one minded, though, because there'd be no work that day. They were all getting ready for Iakopo's funeral.

After she helped her sisters dress, Peleiupu went to her father. She got him his shaving gear and a basin of water. After he had shaved, slowly, cutting himself several times, she got him his clothes, fan, hymn book and Bible, and, when he was dressed, took him to sit beside Iakopo's body.

Dressed in his Sunday clothes, Iakopo was covered up to his neck in ie toga. 'Are you all right?' Peleiupu asked Lalaga, who nodded once. She led her mother to sit beside Iakopo's head, with Arona, Ruta and Naomi. Peleiupu sat down beside her father.

They were ready.

The deacons and other elders arrived first and occupied the main posts; the church choir came as a group and sat in rows across the centre of the fale; the rest of Satoa took up the remainder of the space and spilled out over the paepae to the shade of the breadfruit and mango trees outside.

There was no ornate, poetic or lengthy welcome from Mautu. 'We are gathered here today to farewell Iakopo,' was all he said. 'He has gone to be with our Maker.' He paused, no sign of grief. 'Let us pray. Our Heavenly Father, thank you for this glorious morning. It is an apt day for Iakopo's journey towards you, to be with you, forever.' He paused again. 'Thank you for ending his pain, his suffering. Amen.'

Most people were left suspended, having expected a longer, more anguished prayer. Many kept their heads lowered, their eyes closed. A few of the elders looked at one another. Peleiupu handed Mautu the hymn book and he flipped through it quickly. Stopped. Everyone was now with him. 'Let us sing hymn number 134.'

The choirmaster stood up, raised his arms, sang the first line of the hymn — *Let us praise the Lord for His Love* — and then the choir and mourners joined him.

> . . . for this life is one of sorrow and pain
> This earth a place of sin we need to be freed from.
> Lord, give us the courage and the strength . . .

They were further surprised when Mautu said, 'There will be no sermon, for Iakopo was only a child. Suffice to say, in witness, that he was a happy and honest boy.' He swallowed and straightened up again. 'Yes, he is fortunate to be with God.' He bent forward, kissed his son on the forehead, and then backed away. Lalaga and their children followed. Peleiupu would never forget the cold sweaty feel of her brother's forehead when she kissed it. That memory would almost choke her every time she attended a funeral and kissed the corpse farewell. The choir started singing another hymn. The rest of the congregation began coming forward to farewell Iakopo.

Only when Filivai and two other women started wrapping the body in mats did Lalaga weep openly. Arona, Ruta, Naomi and many of their household joined her. When the wrapping was finished and tied with sinnet, Sao encouraged the weeping to end. 'It is enough: there is no need to be sorrowful. Iakopo is lucky to be free of this life. He is with God.'

Two young men carried the body as they moved towards the grave site behind the church, with Mautu and Sao leading the procession. A generous breeze, heavy with the tang of the sea, cooled them in the noonday heat. Peleiupu walked in her father's shadow, holding Lalaga's hand. A kingfisher shot from the heads of the mango trees and across the church. A good omen, Peleiupu thought, remembering that Mautu had once told them that the kingfisher had been an atua in pre-Christian times. Casually she noted that the mango trees were bare of fruit.

The air smelled of newly turned earth drying in the sun. Mautu and Lalaga stood at the head of the open grave. The congregation ringed the grave or sat on nearby graves; many of the children perched on the frangipani trees. Using ropes, the pall-bearers slowly lowered the body into the earth. With the sun caught in the large beads of sweat on his brow, Mautu uttered the shortest and most surprising prayer any of them would ever hear: 'Thank you, God. Amen.' Sao and a few of the elders interpreted it as a statement of defiance and were shocked. The rest believed Mautu was too grief-stricken to say any more.

Picking up a handful of earth, Mautu sprinkled it over the body. Lalaga and her children did the same. Many of the mourners threw flowers taken from the wreaths or from nearby trees and plants, and called, 'Farewell, Iakopo. May your journey end well.'

The men who'd dug the grave moved forward to fill it. Mautu waved them away, took a spade from one of them, and, scooping up earth, hurled it into the grave.

His family and the other Satoans watched him bury his son, one spadeful after another, with silent tears washing down his face. His tears mixed with the earth that was staining his white suit until he stood, arms crossed over the wet handle of the spade, which he had stabbed into the head of the remaining mound of earth, head bowed, alone and apart from them. Nobody knew what to do.

Peleiupu broke from the group and went to him. She held his hand and started leading him home.

'Mautu has buried his former self with his son,' Sao would say later.

'He and his family are now of us, of Satoa, of our eleele. Our Disease has made sure of that,' another matai would say.

'Yes, they have paid at last to be of us,' the elders agreed.

It was 1889.

The Trader

According to Satoan oral history the first papalagi ship to break into their bay was in 1827. (They'd seen papalagi in other villages before then.) Since then other ships had called in, but it was only Barker who had come in his schooner every three months or so to trade his cargo of axes, bushknives, nails, cloth and other papalagi goods for copra. They began referring to him affectionately as 'our papalagi'. Sometimes, when there was war between the country's political factions and Satoa allied itself to one of the factions, Barker brought rifles and ammunition, dynamite and other weapons, and with expert skill showed them how to use them. One time he taught the matai how to use a compass and sextant, then a telescope, a clock, and soap. Another time his cook taught the women how to bake bread, cook stew, and roast stuffed chicken. He took huge delight in introducing papalagi technology, ideas, fashions and fads to Satoa, despite his own constant complaints that papalagi civilisation was corrupt and evil and the missionaries were 'castrating' the native peoples. The Satoans, who'd converted to Christianity overnight because their tamaaiga had ordered them to do so, feigned shock at his attack on the new religion, and kept expecting their new atua to strike him down dead.

A bulky man with a bushy beard, wild blond hair and massive hands, which the Satoans believed had killed many people, Barker would stay for a week or so along with his crew, and some of his men would acquire wives, but Barker avoided Satoan women. Not that he wasn't tempted. However business, he claimed, was business, and better without your clients' women (and the possibility of jealous Satoan men).

Just before Christmas, during the sixth year of Barker's visits, an unexpected storm had swept his schooner onto the reef. It sank with everything he owned. Barker and two of his crew were rescued by Sao and members of his aiga. Within a month he had married Poto, Sao's eldest daughter. (It was good business to marry into the leading aiga, he'd later admit to Mautu.) She'd already eloped with two men but both relationships had failed, so Sao didn't mind her being the first Satoan to marry a papalagi. Using Poto's large and influential aiga, Barker collected, cut and dried a rich harvest of copra, built a fautasi and used it to transport the copra to Apia. There he sold it, and was soon back with a new cargo of goods to trade, and three other varieties of mango, which he planted behind their home.

Poto also soon proved to be a shrewd and efficient businesswoman. She got her father to allocate them a large area of land and, again using their aiga's strong and fit young men, Barker cleared the bush and planted the first commercial plantation of coconut trees in Satoa. They built a store in the middle of their aiga's compound and Barker left the running of it to Poto. Attached to it, at the back, were three large rooms in which they lived with the numerous children she produced, one every year. Physically, Barker and his children were the most distinct of Satoans: they were all blond-haired, with deeply tanned bodies and blue-green eyes that everyone referred to as cats' eyes. Some of the children had freckles, which the Satoans called tae lago, flyshit.

The Satoans did not express their condemnation, openly, of Barker as an atheist, a non-believer, but Poto knew it was there and felt humiliated, and told him so, repeatedly. However, despite her nagging accusation that he was a disgrace to his 'wonderful Christian race', and Sao's curt instructions that he attend church, Barker refused to do so. He boasted openly of having no need for Christianity (or Jehovah). He stopped working on Sundays only when Sao and the matai fono threatened to banish him from Satoa if he continued. He also drank his home-made whisky secretly so as not to bring the wrath of the fono upon his aiga. He knew — and was pleased — that Sao and the fono were afraid of him because, even though they knew he was distilling whisky, they didn't order him to stop.

'You're trying to corrupt me with the Devil's water!' Poto rejected his attempts to entice her to be his drinking partner. (Later on in their life she'd take the occasional secret nip to 'warm her blood'.)

When other matai pointed to his son-in-law's 'uncivilised ways' Sao excused him by saying, wistfully, 'What do you expect from a papalagi?' Then he said, 'He is useful, though, to our village.'

At first Poto was ashamed of being married to a papalagi because the Satoans viewed papalagi as strange, inferior creatures. However, as they prospered and she gained power and status, she came to admire and love her husband. She claimed publicly that she loved his 'strange and independent pagan papalagi ways'.

About every four months Barker took his fautasi to Apia to sell his copra and bought goods for their store. He was now trading all over Savai'i. Poto accompanied him sometimes, to learn to trade. Here again she was a quick and perceptive learner.

He always took any Satoans who wanted to visit Apia. Since he had first settled in Satoa Mautu had made only one trip with Barker, so Lalaga and their aiga and many of the Satoans were surprised when, soon after Iakopo's death, Mautu again accompanied Barker, and on their return began spending much of his time at Barker's home. At first they believed Mautu was trying to persuade Barker, the defiant atheist, to return to the church.

It was late afternoon and overcast, dark clouds trailing their immense shadows across the bay. You could see the luminous joy in his eyes, Peleiupu observed as Mautu danced into the fale holding a calico-wrapped parcel. She rushed to him as he sat down beside Lalaga who, caught in his strange luminosity, stopped weaving. A bemused smile on his lips, Mautu kept gazing down at the parcel, and waited. Their other children were soon around him too. Peleiupu glanced up. The clouds were breaking out of the bay into the open sea.

Carefully he unwrapped the parcel while they watched. Then, for a breathless moment, they gazed down at its contents as if they were admiring a newborn baby asleep in its swaddling clothes. It was a book: a thick, black book with gold-edged pages and expensive binding.

'It's a gift from Barker,' Mautu said.

'It is a beautiful gift,' Lalaga sighed. Peleiupu managed to stop herself from caressing the book.

'What book is it?' asked Arona. The others looked at him.

'It's a Bible!' Naomi belittled him.

'I know it's a Bible!' Arona tried to rescue himself.

'And it's in English,' Peleiupu added.

'Barker told me he has no further need for it,' Mautu told Lalaga. 'Once upon a time he used to go.'

'To church?' Lalaga asked. He nodded. 'But why doesn't he go any more?'

'I don't know.' When Mautu started rewrapping the parcel, Peleiupu asked if she could do it and he handed it to her. Ruta reached out to intercept it, but Mautu ignored her. 'Let Pele do it,' he said. Peleiupu took her time rewrapping the Bible. 'He's teaching me English as well,' Mautu said.

'What is English?' Naomi asked.

'It's the language of the papalagi.' Arona got his own back.

'And the missionaries?' asked Ruta.

'Yes,' Lalaga replied.

'And God?' asked Naomi. The children were puzzled when their parents started laughing.

'You children ask a lot of questions!' Mautu exclaimed.

'English is the language of the English who live in England,' Peleiupu explained to her brother and sisters and was embarrassed (and annoyed) when the adults laughed some more. She turned her back on them and looked out at the bay: the dark clouds were banking up against the horizon and being forced up into the drizzling sky.

From that time on, whenever Mautu was free at night he sat in the light of the lamp, reading and repeating words, then whole sentences, from the English Bible. His sounds, unintelligible to them, were like incantations cast to dispel the darkness. Sometimes the children sat around him and listened until they got bored or fell asleep, then they were put into their nets. He started teaching them some of the English words.

As his English improved, he returned from his lessons with Barker carrying more books, and at night was soon reading parts of those to Lalaga and their children and others in their household who wanted to listen. During school he also read to his students, who listened politely even though they didn't understand English. Whenever a story enthralled him, he translated it aloud to his listeners, and they loved it. So he did more and more and more of that. Fairytales, fables, parables, adventures, descriptions of other lands, other seas, other sciences, other minds and eyes and dreams. His readings became a treasure house to feed the curiosity and imagination, until their home was full of listeners every night, none of his students stayed away from school, and the church was crammed full every Sunday.

At first the Satoans — particularly Sao and the deacons — were upset with him for spending so much time with Barker, their papalagi but a pagan. However, as time passed and they saw no harmful effects on Mautu, they accepted it. Finally they encouraged him enthusiastically when his sermons became fabulous stories about God's territories beyond the reefs; about courageous papalagi missionaries conquering the savage kingdoms of darkest Africa and Asia; about evil and miserly papalagi millionaires and kings seeing the Light and giving their wealth to the poor; about papalagi explorers traversing the deserts and the lands of ice and snow, defeating heathen armies and destroying their idolatrous gods; about miraculous sciences, such as alchemy, that produced gold from worthless matter; about astrology, which explained your fate in the patterns of the stars; about the Church's valiant fight against slavery, heathenism, cannibalism and more. It was all irrefutable proof of God's existence and beneficence and mana. Yes, their pastor had been freed by his son's death, then freed further by the knowledge he was acquiring from those books. He was now capable of making them believe anything.

Many would remember him for the rest of their lives, up there in his pulpit clothed with the intense morning light, his eyes afire with the new vision, his vibrant voice reaching into their hearts and souls and setting them alight.

Early in their friendship, Mautu sensed that Barker didn't want to visit his home, so he didn't invite him. However, whenever he stayed away for more than a day, Barker sent one of his children to fetch him. As Mautu's English improved and he could converse in it for long periods, Barker's need for his company seemed to deepen, for in Satoa no one else spoke English, and Barker refused to learn Samoan properly.

At this time Mautu started taking the eleven-year-old Peleiupu almost everywhere he went, including Barker's home. It was as if Peleiupu's presence were his protection.

On Peleiupu's first visit with Mautu to Barker's they stopped at the front door and she almost choked with the stench of flying-fox and unwashed bodies and mould that surged from the room. She coughed politely and tried to ignore it.

'Don't be afraid,' Mautu whispered. She followed him into the gloom.

He sat down in the cane chair by the door and she sat cross-legged on the floor at his feet. 'He'll be here soon,' he told her.

Her eyes quickly adjusted to the gloom. On the large bed at the far side was a jumble of clothes, books and other paraphernalia. Above it, against the wall, were shelves that were cluttered with more books, jars and strange implements she'd not seen before. Chairs, tables and a tangle of iron boxes and tools were scattered around the room. Never before had Peleiupu seen such wealth, but she thought it was a pity not one window was open to let out the sickening smell, which her father didn't seem to notice. With a few more visits she too would get used to the smell.

Then the back door was pulled open and Barker, a looming shadow outlined momentarily against the daylight behind him, thrust himself into the room. Immediately Peleiupu recognised the source of the flying-fox smell.

'Greetings, Reverend Pastor and daughter!' He greeted them in English.

'Good morning, Mr Barker!' Mautu replied slowly in English as Barker wove through the clutter and sank into the throne-like chair opposite them.

'Excellent English, Mr Mautu,' Barker exclaimed, smiling. 'Excellent!'

Mautu and Peleiupu watched while he used the front end of his stained shirt to wipe the sweat off his hands, face and beard, and finally off his bulging neck, all the while congratulating Mautu on the quality of his English. Afraid yet fascinated by Barker, Peleiupu wanted to be invisible. However, as the two men talked, with Barker saying most, his heavy hands sweeping through the air, she lost her fear and her fascination intensified. This was the first papalagi she'd seen up close. Like other Satoan children she was convinced that papalagi of Barker's size were creatures to be avoided. Possessors of strange powers, knowledge and secrets, they had to be respected but were also uncivilised, pagan and cruel. The missionaries were the only civilised papalagi in Samoa. She was also captivated by the odd mixture of English and Samoan that Barker used. For instance, 'Reverend, o oe le kagaka piko sili laga English in legei akunu'u.' He paused, his face screwed up as he tried to find the Samoan to continue with. 'Ia, you are the best kaukala in English. Some day ka o i Pelekania, lo'u akunu'u agasala!'

They visited Barker again two days later. His unruly gaggle of children were milling around him and Poto. Peleiupu crouched behind Mautu's legs, afraid of the children's rudeness and their cat-like eyes, which all seemed to fasten on her at once. 'Go, go!' Poto ordered them.

They streamed past Mautu and Peleiupu, shouting and laughing and pushing one another. Tavita, the oldest one and about Peleiupu's age, hesitated in front of Peleiupu, smiled and extended a ripe nonu towards her. Peleiupu moved back. 'Take it,' Poto encouraged her.

'Yes, take it,' Barker said in Samoan. 'My children are not usually generous.' Peleiupu almost snatched it out of Tavita's hand. He chortled and skipped off.

Though Barker and Mautu did most of the talking, Poto seemed to be there always, a quiet, persistent reminder they weren't alone in the world. Peleiupu sensed early that there was a deep current of affection between Barker and Poto. Later when they got up to leave, Poto gave her some sugar and flour to take home for their aiga, and lollies for herself.

It was during her seventh visit that she first observed a strange power in her vision. It scared her at first, and she would never tell anyone about it.

In the usual gloom, Barker was again in his high-backed chair, which made him appear as if he had a large hump on his shoulders, and Mautu was reading easily from the English Bible. Barker listened with his eyes half closed. Whenever Mautu stumbled over a word, Barker corrected him. Incredibly, Peleiupu saw a white glow emanating from Barker and growing until it was about a foot thick and illuminating every detail of his features and clothes. She shut her eyes tightly, but when she looked again it was still there. Now it was exposing in heightened detail Barker's fiery freckles, the black streaks of dirt and grease, the wrinkles and blue scars and bulging veins of his face and neck and arms and hands, the bristling body hair which reminded her of the fur of a dog, the black dirt lodged in his uncut fingernails, the rotting food particles and decay in his teeth, the stains and tears and holes in his clothes, the blood pulsing and cruising

through his body. And as the rhythm of Barker's breathing inhabited her, she knew —
and dreaded knowing — that the rhythm was ending, soon.

That night, in a vivid and disturbing dream, she saw his bones, like sharp coral,
breaking through his putrefying body, the flesh flaking off like tattered clothing.

She never again saw the fearful luminosity around Barker, but as she grew more
fond of him she experienced an inexplicable sadness.

The saddest times began when Mautu's love of books became more important
than talking to Barker and he stayed away from Barker's house. Barker would send
Tavita to demand that he come at once.

'You don't care for my company any more?' Barker demanded in English as soon
as they were seated. Poto was weaving a mat on the floor beside his chair. 'You don't
care any more now that you've stolen my language and books!'

'Don't be silly!' Poto tried to calm him. 'The pastor didn't come to listen to your
— your pain.'

He waved her away. 'He's stolen my language and books!'

Mautu was patient with him, reassuring him of his friendship, respect and gratitude. 'And how can I steal your English language?' he joked. 'I speak it so badly, and
it surely belongs to anyone who learns it.' He paused. 'And, Mr Barker, you can go
right ahead and steal my language, which you speak very badly!'

'Reverend, ga ou kago foa'i aku la'u English ia oe. I gave you my English!' Barker
was smiling again.

'It is a barbaric-sounding language, Mr Barker!' Mautu said in Samoan.

'It's a language that sounds like ducks quacking!' Poto remarked.

'Not as barbaric as German!' Barker laughed. Peleiupu remembered Barker telling
them that the Germans were establishing themselves in Apia at the time.

'He longs for his home in England,' Poto said to Peleiupu, again giving her food
to take home.

On their way home Peleiupu asked Mautu to tell her what Barker's anger had
been about. 'Nothing much,' he said. 'He accused me of being an ungrateful native
who steals from generous benefactors like himself and gives nothing in return.'

'But what have you stolen from him?' she asked.

'His language and some of his knowledge. But he knows that in return I have
given him my friendship. That's why his anger never lasts.' He stopped, smiling. 'He's
a very lonely person who needs company. No matter how harshly he criticises his own
kind and their way of life, he is still far away from home.' She didn't understand fully
but she would come to in the years to follow.

That night Mautu started telling his family about Barker's life.

The Son of the Earl

(In memory of Jorge Luis Borges)

'Ralph William Virgil Barker was the eldest son of the Earl of Sunderland Rollinson Barker, one of the great lords of England,' Barker began his autobiography through his loyal friend, Mautu. Through Mautu, Lalaga and their children, that autobiography would become part of the memory-bank and genealogy of Satoa, and seal Barker's right to be 'our papalagi'.

The Earl of Mall, Sunderland and the Counties of Oakridge and Brightrust, Lord of the Seven Mountains of Slye, Commander of the Queen's Stables, and the greatest deer hunter with bow and musket in the realm, was still a humble and loving husband to Lady Estelle, daughter of Lord Whiteside of Wallis, and a caring and generous father to seven children and thousands of people who lived and worked on his estates and in his villages and towns.

England was part of Great Britain, which possessed the mightiest empire the world had ever seen — an empire that stretched from Ireland, to India, to Africa, the Americas, the Caribbean, South East Asia, to even the islands of Oceania — and a navy that controlled the Seven Seas. This empire was ruled by a great and noble queen called Victoria, cousin to Barker's father. (Of the foreign powers — Germany, Britain and the United States of America — now squabbling over control of Samoa, Mautu favoured Britain, later telling his family and the Satoan elders that the Germans were still barbarians and the Americans had no history.)

Barker's mother, a most beautiful lady with the voice of a skylark (Mautu couldn't describe what kind of bird that was when Peleiupu asked), died of cholera when he was only twelve years old, and his father married a widow (whose name Barker erased from his memory), who had four children from her former marriage to a charlatan who peddled fake cures to royalty for gout and other aristocratic ailments.

His stepmother proved a cruel, uncouth, money-hungry woman who treated Barker and his four brothers and two sisters despicably, favouring her own children. (Much like the parable of Cinderella, which Barker gave Mautu to read, and which Mautu in turn translated to his children, and Peleiupu would, in years to come, retell like a fagogo to generations of her descendants.) Because of this, Barker at the tender of age of thirteen ran away to London, the largest city in the world. (He told Mautu about Dick Whittington and his cat and how Dick Whittington became the Mayor of London.) In London Barker signed as cabin boy on the good ship *Lady Mells*, sailing for the Americas.

For twenty-five years he sailed the Seven Seas, becoming an expert sailor and eventually a captain, coming across all manner of people and savages and learning many of their sciences and arts and ways, and leading a most adventurous life. (*The Adventures of Sinbad the Sailor* was a book that Mautu fell in love with, and from which at every Sunday to'ona'i he translated a story for the elders, who fell in love with the tales and took them home to their families, until the tales became part of the tapestry of stories that was Satoa.) For every scar on Barker's body there was an exciting, sometimes terrible, tale to tell, and Barker was a riveting, inspired teller of those tales.

For instance, when he was in India, the Maharajah of Bengal, who owned fabulous palaces, hundreds of wives and slaves and enormous coffers filled with diamonds and rubies and other precious stones, hired him to train his armies in the use of modern firearms and other weaponry. He was rewarded with anything he desired: wealth, pleasure, comforts befitting a prince. Indeed, he became a prince when he married Sarita, one of the Maharajah's seventy daughters, and for five blissfully happy years loved her with all his heart. During that time the Maharajah's magicians and scientists taught him astrology, mathematics, alchemy and a vast assortment of magical tricks. He also travelled the kingdom with his wife, hunting the wily and courageous tiger, the wild but dumb boar, the elusive pheasant, and other game. He learned much about the strange flora and fauna, and the cures you could make from some of the herbs and plants. He observed sorcerers using horns to charm cobras to rise up out of their baskets and dance to their music; sorcerers doing the same to inert ropes, and once the ropes were erect, their heads buried in the clouds, boys in colourful clothes would slide down the ropes from the sky; a skeletal hermit, with hair that covered nearly the whole floor of his cave, who had sat cross-legged on a bed of nails for a quarter of a century; Hindu priests who felt no pain when sharp knives and skewers were driven into various parts of their bodies; and, most incredible of all, priests who could levitate and suspend themselves two yards above the ground.

Tragically, Sarita died in an epidemic that killed half the kingdom's population. To try to forget his love for her and his grief, Barker left India, taking none of his wealth with him.

Once when they were shipwrecked on the coast of Africa, a continent misrepresented by white missionaries and explorers as being dark and savage, Zulu warriors massacred his crew. (False rumours were later spread by white missionaries and settlers that his crew were cooked and eaten.) For some mysterious reason the Zulus kept Barker alive and took him — through wild country populated by leopards, elephants, lions, rhinoceroses and other ferocious but marvellous creatures — to their King Bumbo, who weighed four hundred pounds and could crush the head of a man between his enormous hands. Once again, Barker's knowledge of firearms saved his life.

The Zulus were already far in advance of the British in their military tactics and strategies, but needed to know about modern weapons. So Barker trained King Bumbo's armies in their use, mastered the Zulu tactics, and then led the armies into battle against enemy tribes. Inexplicably, he found that he loved it, Barker confessed. The killing, the blood, the almost orgasmic euphoria of victory as he watched his attack plans succeeding, and most of all he revelled in the sexual orgies he and King Bumbo indulged in after each victory. Violence, death, blood, sex — they all seemed to go together in his new madness.

King Bumbo's territories increased tenfold while Barker led the armies of conquest. In the five years he was with them he became a Zulu even in mind and smell. Barker believed that every group of people had a unique odour that differentiated them from others. It was a mixture of genetics, diet, environment and history.

This adventure ended when his generous patron and friend died unexpectedly, poisoned by his brother Mungo. Because Mungo was jealous of Barker's influence over the tribe, he and a group of his warriors ambushed him. In a brisk skirmish Barker shot ten of them and fled. He almost died combating the harsh elements and gauntlet of ferocious creatures in the bush during the months he took to reach a missionary settlement on the Cape.

Years later, after countless adventures in Arabia (Barker gave Mautu *The Arabian Nights* to read, and though Mautu loved the stories he didn't want his family to read them), Ceylon, Madagascar, China (Mautu loved the chronicles of Marco Polo and retold those in elaborate detail to his family), Barker found himself stranded in America, where the natives were coloured red like the earth of the vast plains over which they roamed on their fast ponies hunting the buffalo, the most courageous animal on earth, an animal that provided them with almost everything they needed — food, clothing, courage, stamina, and their religion.

He lived with the warrior tribe called the Sioux, fighting as one of their braves, conquering other tribes, until he came to hate the savage in his soul and caught a ship to Hawaii. There he built his own schooner and set himself up as a trader.

While with the Sioux he had learned much about the land, and loving and caring for that land and the environment and the creatures and spirits that lived in it. He would never forget one event he witnessed. The shaman of his tribe, after a period of fasting and eating a special mushroom, changed into a golden eagle and flew over the mountains into the heartland of an enemy tribe who'd raided their village recently and killed his children. He returned with the soul of the enemy chief trapped in a small reed basket. After shedding his eagle form, the shaman opened the basket and the vapour inside smoked up and out of it. It resumed the shape of the enemy chief, whom the shaman then clubbed to death.

In his travels Barker observed and heard of creatures not found in Europe or Oceania, Mautu told his spellbound family. For example, in a group of islands known as the Maldives, while his ship was anchored in an uninhabited bay during a peaceful moon-bright night, a creature surfaced out of the dark water. In the moonlight it looked as if its top half were that of a woman with long black hair and perfectly formed breasts, and its bottom half was that of a giant fish. As it swam towards them they hauled anchor and fled. The creature chased them to the reef entrance.

Later, when he told other captains about it, they said it was a mermaid, a legendary creature who was searching constantly for men to love and to free her from the sea. The oldest captain, a black man with gold teeth, told him that some mermaids in their loneliness were known to get themselves deliberately snared in fishing nets. When they were pulled aboard they flapped across the deck with their clumsy fish tails, pleading to be held. Once men took pity and held them they gasped for air. To be saved, they had to be thrown overboard again, into their natural element. One captain, who was notorious for his unusual sexual tastes, built a large tank and filled it with seawater. He then offered a large price for a mermaid and when he got one he put her in the tank. She was a beautiful red-haired creature, who danced and sang in the depths to impress her master. When he joined her in the water she wove her songs and body around him, and he started teaching her 'the sinful ways of the flesh'. When Mautu told his family this part of the story, he simply said, 'While he was wrestling playfully with her, she dragged him down into the bottom of the tank. He drowned before she realised he was totally out of his element.'

Another creature was a unicorn. The Maharajah of Bengal's most learned magician had told him it existed but could only be captured by a virgin. It was like a pony but with the front legs of a deer, the beard of a goat and — most astounding of all — one long conical horn protruding from its forehead. The magician claimed that he, through the eyes of his virgin daughter, had seen it grazing in the palace gardens one overcast morning before anyone else was awake. It glowed like snow; its body was like water shimmering in the noonday light. As he had observed it he had experienced a profound thirst to know the essence of life, the whatever-it-was that gave life to all living things, and he felt utterly alone, abandoned.

In India, too, it was believed that an indestructible being known as the O, or Bodiless One, lived in a tower at the foot of the Himalayas, guarded by priests who killed anyone who tried to enter. The tower's interior was tiered with a spiral staircase consisting of 9999 steps.

The O took the form of the staircase and then, as it ascended to the topmost step and the brilliantly clean air of the Himalayas, the O assumed the colour of purity, the feel of a baby's breath, and the sound of a newly born butterfly's wings. It was believed that one day, when humankind was worthy of the O, it would leave the tower and make humans immortal with its kiss of purity.

In the swamps near the ancient South American city of the Inca king there lived a gigantic bird that had a wingspan of five yards and a long sword-like beak. It was called a swordswan. It laid thirteen eggs once a year, but when the eggs hatched it devoured twelve of its young and abandoned the last one, a female, in the nest. To save the orphan, the Inca king's priests took it into the palace and, nursing it carefully, tried instilling in it the instinct to save its young. In spring they released it into the swamps. But once again the king would be disappointed. It was a long tradition in the king's family never to give up hoping that the swordswan would one day learn to love its young.

In the middle of Africa, in the wet humid jungles that were rarely penetrated by humans, lived families of creatures that resembled humans. These massive beasts shook the earth and jungle with their bellowing and chest-drumming. Gorillas, they were called. Fierce in appearance and sound, but gentle in soul and nature. Like humans, they lived in societies according to rules evolved over hundreds of years.

Australia was a continent inhabited by a most varied and unusual menagerie of creatures, many of them found nowhere else in the world. Hundreds of animals known as kangaroos roamed the land. They had a unique way of bearing their young: they conceived then bore them in pouches around their stomachs.

Mautu explained to his family that Barker could spend days describing a menagerie of beings that would frighten, astound and delight them, and that he, Mautu, would describe more in the nights ahead.

For ten years before deciding to settle in Samoa, Barker traded in most of the islands of Oceania — hundreds of islands scattered like abandoned hopes across the Pacific. Islands with such exotically musical names as Nukuhiva, Tahiti, Moorea, Moruroa, Tuamotu, Uea, Futuna, Efate, Aotearoa, Hawaii, Oahu, Maui, Molokai, Malaita, Bellona, Lifu, Mangaia, Aitutaki, Rarotonga, Mauke, Niue, Fakaofo, Vava'u, Ha'apai, Olosega, Tutuila, Manu'a, Ta'u, Savai'i, Rapanui . . . like the flowers of a fabulous lei but, according to Barker, inhabited by selfish savages, cannibals, liars, thieves, and papalagi deserters and drunkards, loose women and ignorant missionaries who pretended humans didn't exist beneath their puritanical navels. Peleiupu and her sisters and brother would spend the next few days making up rhymes using the names of the islands, and reciting them aloud.

In his twenty-five years of sailing Barker didn't experience any serious illness. It was as if he were blessed with an invisible armour, a magic shield against disease and death. He survived wars and storms, saw hundreds die in plagues and epidemics of cholera, leprosy, whooping cough, syphilis, influenza, beriberi, mumps, smallpox, diarrhoea, tuberculosis and other known and unknown diseases, but not once was he infected by them.

During the first night of Barker's autobiography, as narrated by Mautu to his family, Mautu ended by saying that Barker, his noble friend, was a truly civilised man even though he denied God, and an aristocratic member of the English race that now ruled most of the earth and were winning souls of pagans for God. Though Barker was disavowing this grand mission for himself, he would one day see the Light — God always favoured the sheep-who-has-gone-astray — and return to the Church to help fulfil Queen Victoria's Christian plan for the empire.

The Missionaries, Marriage

and Children

Mautu taught the older students, and in the days before Barker intruded into his life his lessons were severe, unimaginative and therefore boring — but pity the inattentive student. (Even his children feared him during classes because to prove his impartiality, he treated them more harshly.) His capacity for teaching was enormous — sometimes his classes lasted all afternoon and his students staggered home mentally battered to families who were annoyed with their pastor for keeping their children away from their afternoon chores. But none questioned him.

Those students, who were also members of his household, continued their lessons in Bible reading after evening lotu and serving the meal, with Mautu laboriously correcting their errors. But when exhausted or angry he never shouted at any student. A cold lowering of his voice, a pronounced frown, a sharp clicking of his tongue was enough to frighten the culprit into obedience.

Lalaga was the more imaginative and dynamic teacher. Small, quick and of strong nerves, she worked from the first light until late at night, with the hems of her starched dresses whispering around her ankles. The students enjoyed her classes, and whenever they were bored she told them stories from the Bible.

As a student at Vaiuta she had modelled her behaviour on Miss Beth (Misi Peta) their papalagi missionary teacher. A frail middle-aged Englishwoman, with skin the hazy, milky colour of smoke, Misi Peta had timetabled every waking minute of her students' lives, and each activity was a lesson in godliness, frugality, cleanliness, punctuality and good Christian living.

They woke at 5.30 am to the jangling of a hand-bell, which Misi Peta told them had been bequeathed to her by her beloved mentor, Misi Isapela. After lotu, which usually ended with a prayer by Misi Peta admonishing students who'd committed misdemeanours, they went out to the grounds to pick up the fallen leaves and other rubbish. Then it was cold showers at 7 am and a breakfast of orange-leaf tea and home-baked bread or fa'alifu. The students were rostered to cook and serve meals, and their first lesson began at 8am.

Misi Peta taught the whole group, aided by two graduates. Apart from the three Rs and Bible knowledge they learned sewing, embroidering, cooking, weaving and first aid. Misi Peta was always nearby with her precise instructions and meticulous demonstrations, her untiring inspiration. Endless work was a supreme virtue — armour against the temptations that arose out of indolence. Samoans, she emphasised, had to learn that. You were far more than a Samoan girl from the village, you were a Christian aspiring to love God and His Holy Son, Jesus; a Christian who would one day serve God more devotedly through your pastor husband. You were a child of the Light that the courageous John Williams, whom she'd known personally, had brought to Samoa.

Though they were in awe of her, there was that permanent wall of aloofness between Misi Peta and her students — a fear of skin touching skin, of their glimpsing who she really was, of what she referred to as 'our savage and evil instincts gaining control'. There was a proper time and place for everything, and a correct Christian woman's way of doing those things. Moderation should govern one's appetites so whenever their laughter or singing or dancing became immoderate in her measure Misi Peta promptly corrected them. Bible class on Sundays was devoted to students rising and, in moderate, matter-of-fact, respectful language, confessing the 'sins' they'd committed that week. Misi Peta forgave them, always.

With her senior students, Misi Peta often talked of love, passion, 'the weaknesses of the flesh' and self-control. Love and affection between a man and a woman were not to be displayed publicly; ladies were to be ladies even in their sleep; the flesh was weak and had to be policed constantly; and a good Christian wife was to obey and serve her husband unquestioningly, bear him many children as was her duty to God, and devote her life to performing good deeds and serving her community and God. Though she described Solomon as a king who'd given way to the temptations of the flesh, she loved reciting his psalms to them, her face flushed red, her trembling upper lip beaded with sweat, her voice hoarse with emotion.

In Samoa many people were still pagan, their eyes clouded over with the Darkness, and it was the duty of every Vaiuta graduate to save those pagans for God and His Church, she exhorted them. Lalaga was to recall that she never once saw Misi Peta in anything less than black shoes and starched dresses that covered her from neck to ankle. On Saturdays when the whole school in their sailor suits marched in double file to Mulinu'u, where they fished the reef and mudflats for seafood, Misi Peta never entered the water. She sat in the shade, fanning herself and reading poetry. Her love of poetry was perhaps the one thing that Misi Peta could be accused of being immoderate about. She tried to conceal it but she recited poems during her lessons, after lotu, during church services, used them to correct their behaviour with, and she made them memorise many of her favourites. Lalaga could still recite some of them. For instance:

Let me sleep in the loving arms of our Lord,
Let His light shine upon my sinful soul,
Let Him bring the gentle rain of His love
To quench my spiritual thirst . . .

It was rumoured that Misi Peta also wrote her own poems in the black notebooks she kept locked in her study. But for most of the time it was as if she'd been born Misi Peta: ageless, always in control of everything, untouched by the immoderate tropical sun.

And Lalaga worshipped her.

At first when Mautu went into Barker's orbit he still took his classes regularly. Noticeably, however, his lessons became stories about faraway places, and as he continued to orbit with Barker, a subject such as arithmetic became inhabited by exotic creatures, heroes and adventurers performing incredible tricks of combining, plussing, minusing, and sailing in magical ships to fabulous lands. For instance, there was a hero called One-Plus which could stretch its body to fit any shape, distance or size, and which could, with its plus factor, add to itself any other creature. In one adventure, One-Plus used its plus factor to add all the Pacific Ocean to itself and was thus able to reach the kingdom of All-Plus, inhabited by creatures called Ever-Happy Positives. The mirror image of All-Plus was the kingdom of Ever-Unhappy Negatives, ruled by King Minus who, with his touch, could make things disappear.

Eyes aflame, Mautu laughed, joked and gesticulated wildly as he told his tales. Soon his stories merged into one golden stream that wove its compelling, healing, dazzling way through the enraptured imaginations of his students. Within six months Lalaga was losing students to her ever-storytelling husband.

However, as he spent more and more time with his books and Barker, he began to neglect his classes. So Lalaga, in the spirit of Misi Peta and aided by her older students, who were training for entry into Vaiuta, assumed the responsibility of teaching all the students. She revelled in her work; it was her duty to bring the virtues of Vaiuta and Misi Peta to Satoa. Soon she was also taking classes in cooking, first aid, hygiene and sanitation for her students' mothers and other women. The more she worked, the happier she was.

When Mautu started neglecting their household as well, Lalaga took charge of that, and within a brisk time the lives of their children and the other members of their household ticked to her punctual timetable. Soon their home, church, school and the surrounding area were always trim, tidy and clean like her starched dresses, and, through her classes with the women, her cleanliness spread through the village.

It was a cold evening, the fale blinds were drawn, blocking out the wind that was sweeping in from the sea, everyone had bathed earlier than usual and the mosquito nets were up. The lamp in the centre of the fale flickered and cast a swimming light over everything. Mautu called his children into the side of the fale where he slept with Lalaga. He drew the curtain to separate them from the rest of the household, lit a lamp and, after looking at each child, declared, 'Up till now I've given you the new knowledge in a very disorderly fashion, and in Samoan. An important part of the treasure is the language in which it is coming to me: English. Tonight I am going to start teaching you that language.'

'Yes, yes!' Peleiupu said. The others agreed eagerly.

The wind hummed and clattered around the fale as if it wanted to enter and participate in the lesson. Opening the English Bible, Mautu said, '"In the Beginning . . . " Repeat!'

'"In the Beginning"', chorused his children, led by Peleiupu.

'". . . was the Word . . . "'

'". . . was the Word . . . "'

'". . . and the Word . . . "'

'". . . and the Word . . . "'

'". . . was with God . . . "'

'". . . was with God . . . "'

'Once again!' he instructed them.

As their lesson continued and their tongues struggled to fit the new language it was as if the whole fale and the light were being named by another system of shaping and inventing. The wind slowed down, wrapped itself around the fale, held its breath and listened. Ruta and Naomi fell asleep and Peleiupu and Arona carried them to their mosquito nets.

Three nights later Lalaga joined the lesson around the lamp. 'The village will notice you are favouring your children,' she told him. He didn't seem to hear her. He opened the Bible and started the lesson.

She didn't mention it to him again. Worried about the transformation he was undergoing and the effect it was having on their children, she participated from then on in the English lessons. She noticed that Peleiupu was swallowing up the new language avidly, easily, at a pace she herself had to struggle to keep up with. And when the other children fell asleep where they sat and Mautu started drowsing off, Peleiupu was stridently awake and wanting more. More.

Lalaga believed Mautu was on the most important journey of his life (and, consequently, theirs): a journey into regions she was frightened to contemplate, away from the realities she cherished because they tied her securely to the earth's pulse. But because he wasn't aware he was taking their children with him, she feared for their safety and wished Barker (and his difficult language) had not entered their lives.

When Mautu stopped teaching his afternoon classes altogether, Lalaga used that time to try and influence their children away from Mautu's journey. She was harder on them, gave them more difficult schoolwork, punished them often, insisted at home that they do most of the chores and no one was to help them. They deferred to her, and did everything perfectly, without complaining. Especially Peleiupu, who did most of the work and rallied her brother and sisters whenever they threatened to rebel against their mother. It was as though Peleiupu had decided (on behalf of the others) that Lalaga's taxing lessons and demands were the price they had to pay for the wonderful education their father was giving them.

Lalaga harboured fears she was afraid to admit to herself but which made her observe, vigilantly, every change in her children. The first fear concerned the history of abnormalities in her aiga.

Earlier that century a cousin, so it was whispered, had been born with six toes on his right foot and a large black patch of pig's fur on the nape of his neck: a result, so everyone said, of his father's adulterous ways. He spurned his father, and eventually in his adulthood went mad and rushed through their village ripping with his nails at the fur on his neck and crying, 'I'm a pig! I'm a pig!'

Before him, a female ancestor in her fifth year had sprouted a large hump on her back — the result, so rumour had it, of her father's insatiable appetite for cooked human flesh. In her fiftieth year, after a granddaughter was born with a similar hump, she stabbed sticks into her father's grave and into the holes poured boiling water, cursing, 'You cannibal! Take that, you cannibal!'

Another ali'i ancestor and head of their aiga was disgraced by his eldest son's cowardice in battle so he cursed him, invoking a ferocious aiga aitu to inhabit his son's centre and remind him that he'd sired a coward. The aitu, who also felt disgraced, went further and burst open the son's insides, revealing to all that the youth was without a liver, the organ where courage resided.

Most frightening of all to Lalaga, because it was recent and concerned people she loved profoundly, was the fate of her two brothers, who had been groomed by her parents and the papalagi missionaries for the ministry.

Just before graduating, the eldest, Mose, had been found wandering through the missionary settlement, boasting loudly about the size of his manhood, and cursing God for denying him indiscriminate use of it. Their distressed parents took him home where at least once a month, despite their vigilance, he broke out of their fale and paraded his erectness through the shocked village. He hanged himself a year later, on Christmas Eve, after their father had chastised him for tearing out the first page of Ecclesiastes and eating it.

Ionatana, Lalaga's second brother, had lasted one year at the theological college, returned home and told their enraged father he didn't want to be a pastor. Their father refused to talk to him for week after week after week. Eventually Ionatana disappeared from their village, and Lalaga hadn't seen him since. She'd heard he was living in Apia and working for a German trading company.

She missed her brothers deeply. She'd loved them intensely, so when they'd both denied God and their duty to serve Him, she suspected she was tainted by the same madness. Not only was she afraid of the curse — the strain of insanity that seemed inherent in her aiga — reappearing in her children, she was also frightened of what they may have inherited from Mautu and his aiga.

Four months before Lalaga had graduated from Vaiuta her parents had visited Misi Peta and spent a long time talking in her office. Eventually Misi Peta had sent for Lalaga. She was drenched with sweat before she reached the office.

As she entered the room, head bowed, she caught the sound of a fly — an almost inaudible buzzing like a small finger twirling gently in her left ear. She was to remember that throughout her life every time she entered a place in which she didn't feel secure. She sat down beside Talaola, her mother, by the door, clasped her hands in her lap and gazed down at them.

'Lalaga,' Misi Peta started in her slow deliberate Samoan, 'now you are in your twenties, your parents, with God's guidance, have reached an important decision concerning your future and your life.' Lalaga continued staring at her hands. 'You have spent nearly three years with us, learning the ways of God as laid down in His Holy

Book. You have been a very obedient and diligent student, a credit to your people and aiga. Now your life as a student and girl must give way to your life as a woman, and a woman of God who, in His wisdom, has chosen you to spread His Word, His message, throughout this country, which in large measure is still pagan.' She paused, and Lalaga could feel those intensely blue eyes focused on her. 'Lalaga, your parents have chosen a servant of God — he will finish his training at Salua at the end of this year — to be your husband. I want to congratulate your parents for coming to that wise decision . . .'

As Misi Peta went on, Lalaga grew more bewildered. Becoming a woman, an adult and a wife and mother, and all at once, was too sudden, too overwhelming a transformation for a girl — yes, she was still a girl. And the responsibility of being a pastor's wife and spreading God's Word made it even more harassingly unbelievable. She had always accepted that her husband would be chosen by her parents but she couldn't believe that choice was being made now.

'We know, Lalaga, that you will make an excellent missionary. All you need to remember is that our Heavenly Father will always be with you. Be a good, loving wife to your husband and God and the people you are going to serve. Live by the Christian ways and rules of conduct of your school.' Misi Peta got up. 'I will leave you now to talk to your parents.' As she passed Lalaga she patted her head. Lalaga would always cherish that first and last touch of Misi Peta's blessing.

Lalaga's compact physique, the quickness of her movements and gestures and the melodious way she spoke reflected her father, Malaetasi, a small but tenacious matai, the first in their aiga to become literate, who had spent a large part of his adult life trying unsuccessfully to get one of his sons to be a pastor. In bitter desperation he had accepted the second option: his youngest daughter (and his favourite) was to be a pastor's wife. From him, Lalaga had inherited a quiet, relentless tenacity, realism and practicality. You never gave up on, or into, anything.

Her mother, Talaola, on the other hand, was illiterate, accepted most things and people for what they were, and was loved for her talent as a storyteller and her capacity to forgive others. From her, Lalaga derived an indomitable solidity, and the will to forage for what was enduring and good. Although at times Lalaga was ashamed of her mother's illiteracy, lack of sophistication, and what Misi Peta called 'superstitious and uncivilised ways', she loved her more than anyone else.

'He is a good person, a student at Salua,' Malaetasi said. Lalaga looked at her mother, who nodded. 'I have talked with his teachers, especially Misi Simaila, the papalagi missionary, about him. They agree he is an excellent pastor. He is from a good Christian aiga, too. Lotu Ta'iti, like us. His father is one of the ali'i of Fagaloto.

Excellent lineage.' He paused, waiting for Lalaga to reply. She didn't; she was trying to accept the unreality of the future being mapped out for her.

'It will be an honour for our two aiga to be united through your marriage. And a greater honour for my daughter to continue serving God in the work as a pastor's wife.'

Lalaga looked at Talaola, who rarely said anything when her husband was present. Talaola coughed and said, 'Your father, who has cared for and loved you all your life, is correct in his decision. As you know, I am an ignorant person, so I am very proud to have an educated daughter, one chosen by our Heavenly Father to do His work. And even prouder that my daughter is marrying an educated man.'

Rising slowly to his feet, Malaetasi said, 'When we leave here the tulafale of our aiga and I will visit his aiga and arrange everything.' He left the room quickly.

'There is nothing to be afraid of,' Talaola said, placing her hand over Lalaga's. Lalaga nodded once. Her mother's smell reminded her of dew-wet earth drying in the morning sun. 'We are all very proud of you,' Talaola whispered. Lalaga found herself gazing into her reflection in the tears in her mother's eyes.

As soon as she entered her dormitory Sinaula, her best friend, and the rest of her graduating class hemmed her in, wanting to know what had happened. From past experience she knew she had to tell them immediately or they'd continue embarrassing her. So she did.

'What's his name?' Sinaula asked. 'Yes!' the others chorused. She told them.

'How do you feel about marrying someone you've not even met?' someone asked. Lalaga shrugged her shoulders.

'We have no choice in the matter!' Sinaula reminded them. 'We are not papalagi, who are free to marry who they want and for love.'

'No, we're not papalagi,' Lalaga emphasised. 'But I'm sure my parents and Misi Peta have chosen a man I will respect.'

'Yes, a good servant of God!' Sinaula stopped the others' embarrassing curiosity. 'And Lalaga is lucky she's getting married. We're still waiting for our choices to be made for us.' The others nodded. 'Anyway, if you don't know who you're marrying, you may be in for pleasant surprises!' she added. Some of the others laughed.

'You may also be in for unpleasant surprises!' a pessimist offered. Lalaga glanced at Sinaula.

'As a pastor Lalaga's husband will have to behave,' Sinaula declared. The pessimist had to agree. Sinaula had a way of ultimately getting her way with the other students.

The others dispersed soon after. Sinaula sat holding Lalaga's arm. 'I'm sure it'll be all right,' she said. 'Most of the Vaiuta women have married pastors who were chosen for them. That's how my parents married — and they're still together, despite the fact that my mother bosses him around.'

During the day the others kidded her about the kind of man Mautu was going to be, and she tried not to get annoyed. Sometimes she dreaded how and what Mautu was going to be and had to consult Sinaula, who consoled her with alluring pictures of an ideal marriage, ideal 'touching of bodies', ideal children.

It was during arithmetic class that Sinaula came in and said something to their teacher. 'Misi Peta wants to see you in her office,' their teacher called to Lalaga. She knew, and her heart threatened to clog her throat. She rose unsteadily to her feet and, head bowed, headed for the door. Sinaula brushed her shoulder gently as she hurried past.

Her feet were leading her. She kept swallowing back. No one in the corridor, streaks of sunlight striped the floor ahead. She watched her feet treading on the light, disturbing the almost invisible particles of dust that rose slowly into the air.

She stopped in the open doorway. 'Come in,' Misi Peta called. Lalaga's right foot was the first to step over the threshold.

She refused to look at anyone, focusing her attention on the area directly in front of her feet.

'Sit down over there,' a male papalagi voice invited her. She caught his hand pointing at the chair near the door. She sat down. Ahead at the corner of her vision was the outline of Misi Simaila, sitting in the cane chair behind Misi Peta's desk. Misi Simaila was a regular visitor to Vaiuta. In the right-hand corner, facing the missionaries, was a young man, immense and in a white shirt and ie lavalava. Her heart was like a live bird trapped at the back of her mouth. For the rest of their meeting most of her attention would be on him.

'Thank you for coming,' Misi Simaila said in Samoan. His accent was less pronounced than Misi Peta's. Lalaga forced her vision to inch up. Misi Simaila appeared to have no flesh on his skeleton. 'Let us pray,' he declared. Bluish veins, a network of them, were visible through his jade-white skin, and his green eyes were embedded deeply in their sockets. Lalaga knew from his previous visits that, despite his austere appearance, he was kind and gentle — the first papalagi she hadn't been afraid of. Misi Simaila's prayer was short and uttered precisely. He finished, pursed his thin lips and said in Samoan, 'It is good that we are meeting here today . . .' From there Lalaga would hear only bits of Misi Simaila's conversation; her attention was now on Mautu, on the huge sweep of his shoulders and head, the square bulky forehead, the downcast eyes. '. . . We know, Mautu and Lalaga,' she heard Misi Simaila saying, 'that you will be happy together and that your children will be exceptional children of the Light . . .'

Misi Peta spoke as soon as Misi Simaila had finished. Lalaga heard little of what she said either. A cool sweat was growing, comforting her unease. '. . . Now we want you to meet Mautu,' Misi Peta declared. Immediately Lalaga's sweat turned cold. She was on her trembling legs and being dragged by her precocious feet towards Mautu, who was standing and trying not to look at her. Her feet took her into his shadow and his coconut-oil scent.

She couldn't look up at his face. All she saw was his large feet with uncut nails under which black dirt was embedded, feet with the small toes flaring outwards, with healed sore scars and bulging veins, feet that seemed anchored to the floor with a force that couldn't be severed. Tentatively she extended her right hand, and for an instant her hand was drowned in his smothering grip. She pulled it out quickly and almost ran back to her seat.

'Congratulations!' Misi Simaila said, smiling.

Back in Malaelua she soon discovered she had no say in her marriage arrangements. She wanted Sinaula to be her bridesmaid. Her father and the elders agreed but they also decided there were to be five others representing the important branches of their aiga. Behind the scenes her aunts, the most vocal and bullying being Gutu, her father's oldest sister, and the other women argued about who those were to be, almost resulting in a physical fight between Gutu and two of her younger sisters. Malaetasi again had to rule. Next, those same aunts and their husbands argued over who was to provide her wedding dress, so her father ruled that she was to have three. After another long debate about the wedding cake, during which his sisters again quarrelled — they each wanted to provide the cake — Malaetasi again had to rule that Talaola's aiga was to do it. His sisters wept bitterly. When they calmed down, which didn't take long, they insisted that the cake be at least ten tiers high, befitting the status of the Malaetasi and their aiga. Lalaga watched her poor mother fuming but knew she wouldn't say anything publicly.

The guest list offered another opportunity for squabbling. It was unanimous that the list would include Misi Peta, Misi Simaila, Lalaga's and Mautu's other teachers and their wives, their pastor and the other Lotu Ta'iti pastors and their wives from the neighbouring villages, the wedding party's parents and their friends, and Mautu's aiga. But problems arose when Malaetasi ruled to invite only the matai, deacons and their wives of Malaelua, and the main matai of their aiga throughout Samoa. He was reminded, especially by the vocal Gutu, of others and more others. 'What's going to happen when other relatives and friends hear they haven't been invited?' she argued. 'What are people going to say about our aiga — that we're mean and poor nobodies!'

Until in a suppressed rage Malaetasi declared, 'Invite the lot!' and stormed out of the fale, muttering that he was going out to try to find enough food to feed 'the hungry multitudes.' The list would continue expanding until anyone who wanted to come could come. You couldn't turn anyone away, anyway — it was mean to do so, and the Aiga Malaetasi was the most generous aiga in Samoa. God would provide, Gutu kept chorusing.

Fed up with the endless work and the squabbling, Lalaga simply wanted her wedding to be over with. 'Why do we have to go through all this?' she asked her mother.

'Because it's important to your aiga, because you're marrying a Man of God,' she replied.

'But you didn't get married in church at first,' Lalaga reminded her.

A long pause. 'No, but your father and I are not educated — and we were young, we still followed pagan ways. Later when your father wanted to be a deacon we got married in church.'

Sinaula and her mother arrived three days before the wedding, and Sinaula took control of Lalaga and the tasks she had to perform. For instance, after the young men cut coconut fronds and timber from the bush, she and the other women helped them build long shelters on the malae for the wedding feast. Sinaula organised the women and they decorated the church, tidied the church grounds and the whole Malaetasi compound; they gathered flowers and made ula for the wedding party and main guests. Lalaga envied Sinaula for the way men, while appearing to be distancing themselves, were all attracted to her. 'They're all crazy about you!' she whispered to her friend.

A week before Christmas, 1879, the wedding took place. It was a day without the threat of rain — an auspicious day for her wedding, her mother had whispered to her before they left their fale for the church. In the bright light at the end of the long aisle that divided the packed congregation stood Misi Simaila and their pastor. Misi Simaila glowed in his white suit and looked as if he were going to disintegrate at any moment. To steady her trembling, Lalaga gazed only at Misi Simaila, focused on his vibrant smile, his transparent, infectious happiness, and clung to her father's arm as they walked up the mat-covered aisle, feeling as if she were wading through thick liquid heat that smelled richly of frangipani.

At the end of the aisle to her left stood Sinaula and her bridesmaids; to her right, Mautu and his groomsmen. Lalaga and her father stopped between the two groups. Misi Simaila stepped forward. Her father handed her to Mautu, who held her hand carefully, gingerly.

'We are gathered here this beautiful morning . . .' Misi Simaila began in Samoan.

Lalaga concentrated on Misi Simaila's facial expressions, voice and gestures but didn't hear much of what he was saying. She knew the wedding service by heart, having learnt it at Vaiuta. Once when she gazed up at the light behind Misi Simaila she wished it would absorb her unto itself and she'd be free. Drops of sweat trickling down her back returned her to the present and she glanced up at Misi Simaila to find him gesturing to her and Mautu to step forward. She refused to look at Mautu as his trembling fingers sheathed the ring around her finger. She refused to look up at him when he lifted her veil, hesitated, pushed his face at hers and pecked her on the cheek.

The wedding dress clung wetly to her as they walked back down the aisle. This time she looked around and smiled at everyone: Misi Peta and her mother grinning and weeping; her father trying to look stern, unmoved; Aunt Gutu smiling and calling, 'Be happy, Lalaga!'; the friends she'd known all her life — some crying openly, some waving, some avoiding looking at her as if they didn't want to say goodbye.

For a moment the light blinded her when they emerged from the church into the crowd, which clapped and called out their congratulations. Waves of children lapped around her and the wedding party. She bent down and kissed many of the children.

The wedding dress was a heavy wet skin that squished around her when they crossed the malae to the main fale. There, Mautu and the bridesmaids and groomsmen were served fresh green coconuts and cake, while Lalaga, helped by Sinaula and directed by the over-efficient Gutu, changed into her second wedding dress, behind the curtain that had been strung across the fale. 'How is it?' Sinaula whispered.

'I'm going to survive,' she replied, and when Sinaula looked questioningly at her, smiled and repeated, 'Yes, I'm going to survive.'

When they emerged from behind the curtain Lalaga looked directly at Mautu for the first time. He smiled but looked away. One of the bridesmaids handed her a coconut, she raised it to her lips and drank long and deep, paused, took a deep breath and took another long drink, yet another and another until the nut was empty, and her whole breath and body were saturated with a defiant coolness. She sat down in the chair beside Mautu, pressed her knee against his and, almost as if she were doing it accidentally, placed her hand on his arm, which lay on his thigh. He didn't move a muscle, or indicate that he knew she was touching him. So she pressed harder, and continued gazing at his profile. Eventually he turned and looked across at her. When she smiled, he smiled back but again looked away.

As with everything else, Gutu had taken charge of the wedding feast. She told everyone weddings were a papalagi institution and their aiga would show their ignorance if they didn't do everything properly, correctly, according to the papalagi way. So immediately in front of the fale, in the shelter for the wedding party, a long table (made up of two tables borrowed from the pastor) had been set with chairs (borrowed from around the village), white tablecloths and knives and forks and expensive dinner plates and glasses (the first to be seen in Satoa), with the largest ten-tiered wedding cake ever seen in Satoa dominating everything. Women trained by Gutu as waitresses over a severe three days were fanning the flies away from the food at the main table. Eyes as sharp as newly honed knives, but with a wide smile fixed on her round face, Gutu moved about welcoming the guests and supervising the ushers, who were seating them on the mats beside the long rows of food in the other shelters. No chairs or expensive cutlery or crockery for them — just plain fingers, palm-leaf containers and foodmats.

In the neighbouring fale and circling the malae in the shade were those who'd come with the guests — hundreds of them. The hungry air was thick with the smell of umu-cooked pork, chicken, fish, palusami, faiai, taro, ota, faiai fe'e, povi masima, pisupo and other dishes. Throughout the previous night nearly all the aiga in Malaelua had made umu for the feast. 'Are you hungry?' Lalaga asked Mautu.

Nodding, he said, 'Yes, and you?'

'Yes, I'm hungry too.' She felt his hand descending on hers and clasping it. She looked away from him.

Once she and Mautu were seated at the main table, she again felt she was being watched by everyone and tried to focus only on Mautu, who kept smiling at her. Their pastor said grace, blessing the wedding feast and their marriage, and then everyone started eating.

For their wedding night her aiga had prepared the small fale by the sea: a new mosquito net, a soft bed of mats, new pillows and sleeping sheets, a lamp, lowered blinds whispering almost inaudibly as the inquisitive sea breeze poked its wispy fingers through them. For a long moment before she said goodbye to Sinaula, who had accompanied her to the fale, she stood on the paepae gazing out at the sea. The breeze was saturated with the smell of decaying coral. As the darkness broke out of the heart of the horizon and spread like soft mud across the sky, the evening chorus of cicadas started.

'Thank you for everything,' she said. Sinaula put an arm around her shoulders.

'It was a beautiful wedding,' said Sinaula.

'Yes, but I'm glad it's over,' she replied. A flying-fox broke out of the heads of the mango trees by the fale and started flying along the shore. 'We'll always be sisters, won't we?' she heard herself saying. She turned and held on to Sinaula.

'If you ever need me, I'll come, Lalaga,' Sinaula whispered. 'I'm fortunate to have you as a friend — my best friend.' She paused. 'You're lucky: Mautu is a good man. You know that now, don't you?'

The darkness and the chorus of cicadas deepened. Sinaula hurried into the fale and lit the lamp. 'By the time you get up tomorrow, my mother and I will have left,' she said, her face glowing in the light of the lamp. 'Don't forget: if you ever need me, just send a message.' Before Lalaga could embrace her, Sinaula kissed her on the cheek and rushed away, up towards the main fale where the women were stringing up the mosquito nets.

In the lamplight the net shone like a large spider's web, and as the breeze nudged it, it danced almost imperceptibly. Lalaga hesitated for a while, sat down beside the net, and through a gap in the blinds watched the darkness fill the space outside. When the mosquitoes started stinging her, she lifted the side of the net, rolled onto the bed of mats and, lying on her stomach, embraced a pillow. The pillow smelled faintly of starch and coconut oil. Suddenly the cicadas' chorus was gone, and all around her in the darkness the huge sea stirred and listened.

Huufft! Someone's sharp breath blew out the lamp and she was awake, but didn't move, sensing that Mautu was lying beside her. He smelled of sweat and coconut oil. Immediately she found herself trying to suppress her frantic breathing.

'Thank you,' he whispered. 'It was a very successful day.'

'Yes,' she replied. A long pause. Though he was a few feet away his breath on her left shoulder felt like the touch of hot skin.

'Your parents and aiga have been very generous to me.' Another pause, with a single mosquito drilling at it. 'You'll . . . you'll have to help me say the things I want to say to you.'

'I need help too,' she admitted.

'You must be very tired,' he said finally.

'Yes,' she lied at once.

'Sleep then.'

They lay awake, listening and waiting for each other. They could hear the tide rising and lapping against the paepae of the fale, and at the edge of their hearing the surf pounded on the reef. When she realised her blouse was soaked with sweat she tugged it off her skin at places and let the air cool her skin. When his elbow brushed against her shoulder she jumped away from the spark.

'There is . . . there is something I want to confess,' he said. 'My flesh has been weak, sinful, since I was fifteen. I am ashamed of my sinful appetite. In me still thrives the pagan whom good missionaries like Misi Simaila are trying to drive away from our country.' There was a painful pitch in his voice. 'Even now I am trying so hard not to desire you, not to stain your purity.'

'I am your wife now,' she heard herself inviting him, discovering she wasn't afraid of his smoky odour, which now filled the net and enveloped her. She wanted to lose herself totally in it and was surprised and afraid that she was ignoring Misi Peta's cautions. She sensed him moving towards her. She reached out and felt her hands moving slowly over the heat of his chest. However, as his arms came around her, she found her invitation turning into defence, a struggle to push him away. Yes, yes, yes, she murmured in her head, yet her knees pushed at him. His weight and strength, the whole wet heat and smell of him, she wanted to absorb, become part of, yet she struggled — for Misi Peta and her whole public upbringing.

'It's a sin, a sin,' he repeated, his body a slippery insistent embrace. But he moved to counter her resistance, her scratching and pushing and knees and panting cries. 'It's wrong!' he moaned. She pushed away and allowed him to pull her blouse up and over her head. Then the heat of his chest was crushing her taut nipples and breasts and it was exquisite, the enveloping cold-hot fire of it. 'It's wrong!' he moaned, as he buried his face in her neck and his lips and wetness were a fire around every bit of her. Her knees stopped pushing and, as she stuffed the corner of her lavalava into her mouth to stifle her cries, she wound her arms around him. When his fingers danced down her stomach and between her legs and over her wetness, as if he were breathing on her, she cried Aahah . . . ah . . . ah!

He pushed her right hand down his belly. She let him, and for an instant the thick round heat of his penis repelled her, but when he pressed her fingers around it, and he murmured, 'Yes, it's good,' she clutched it. 'Uhh, uhh!' he cried as he pushed it up and down within her grip.

She loved the free-flowing wetness and heat of it, and she pushed against his fingers as he fondled and caressed her. Then she felt his whole body tensing — a wave, a cry surging up from his hips into the hard thickness of him, which jerked and jerked in her grip and he cried through his closed mouth as the warm liquid shot onto her belly. 'Forgive me, forgive me!' he murmured.

Suspended inexplicably at the height of the wave, she was puzzled and felt guilty when he rolled off her and wrapped his ie lavalava around his waist.

At dawn when she woke he was gone. She heard him in the kitchen fale and knew he was preparing the morning meal. She raised the nearest row of blinds — it was still quite chilly and dark, though the horizon line of light was expanding — and jumped down onto the beach, wrapped her ie lavalava around her shoulders, squatted and urinated. She was surprised that she was experiencing no guilt or shame, and even more surprised that she was shamelessly savouring every memory of it.

The dark warm water wove around her feet, then her legs and thighs as she waded into it. She washed the stains off her ie lavalava and then raising it to belly height, squeezed the water out of it. The water cascaded in a rope-like stream and splattered into the surface of the sea. Lalaga closed her eyes, turned her face towards the sky and sucked in large gulps of the cold air, as if she wanted to inhale everything, the whole world of smells and tastes and feelings and desire and Mautu — yes, especially Mautu.

Mautu spent the whole day in the plantation with some of the young men of her aiga, and she helped the children and women dismantle the shelters and clean up the fale and grounds.

That evening, as soon as they were alone in their fale, after the lotu and the meal and their bathing in the communal pool, during which he avoided looking at her, she blew out the lamp and got into the net. 'Are you tired from working?' she asked when he lay down beside her.

'No, just aching a bit.'

'Let me massage your back.' She was surprised by her boldness.

There was a hesitant pause, then he said, 'Yes, go ahead.'

She was shaking and could hardly hold the bottle of oil as she pulled out the coconut husk cork, poured some oil into her left hand, rubbed her hands together, and then started rubbing the oil into his shoulders. The whole slippery heat and feel of his body and the knowledge that he was also wanting her forced her to stop periodically and suck in air through her mouth. 'It's good, very good!' he kept murmuring. That made her feel bolder, so she pressed and squeezed harder as she moved methodically down his back.

'It was wrong, what I did last night,' he said out of the darkness.

'No it wasn't, we are man and wife now.' When her hands reached the top of his ie lavalava he pushed it down. The scent of the oil filled her nostrils. 'That's good,' he moaned as her hands moved over his buttocks, as she slid and slipped and kneaded.

'No!' was her automatic cry when his left hand gripped her knee. She stopped massaging. His fingers started caressing the inside of her thigh, lightly, moving upwards. She leaned forward over him, her hands pressing firmly and sliding down the backs of his thighs, more urgently as his fingers played.

When his insistent hand clasped her between her legs, and his fingers opened her wetness gently, she shivered and held on to his thighs to stop herself from falling. 'I've never told you how beautiful you are,' he said. 'I am very lucky you are my wife, Lalaga.' He was on his knees now and holding her against his body. 'Don't be afraid: as you say, we are husband and wife now.' He tightened his embrace and stilled her shaking body, nuzzling her neck with his mouth and nose. 'Here, lie back.' He lifted her easily and laid her on the mats. 'I'll massage you, get rid of your fears.'

He was so wrong, she would think afterwards — it wasn't fear, it was uncontrollable desire, lust, love, call it what you like. She helped him take off her blouse and ie lavalava. When his hands started exploring her again, they were covered with oil and she felt as if her whole outer and inner selves were being caressed by his hands. Then all of her was centred on her wetness, over which his oiled fingers were now moving with an exquisite rhythm. She stuffed the corner of her sleeping sheet into her mouth. 'It may hurt,' he whispered as he parted her legs, and she raised her knees. His thick hardness pressed against her thigh for a moment, slippery with oil, and hot. She waited for the pain she'd been told would come. Waited. At first when he surged against her there was a tightness and resistance, but she held on and, wrapping her arms around his hips and buttocks, pushed him in hard, into a widening, an expanding, an opening up of all of herself to all of him. No pain. But she wanted him to slow down as he again, like the night before, moved urgently, rapidly. 'I'm sorry, sorry,' he kept gasping into her neck as he tensed to breaking and then ejaculated into her.

She lay beside him for a long time, gazing into the darkness. Nothing was as she'd been raised to believe. She was supposed to be ashamed of the desires of the flesh; she wasn't. She was a pastor's wife and not meant to show any sexual feelings, even towards her husband — yet she'd unashamedly shown Mautu her desire and brazenly encouraged him. And despite her reminding herself that women weren't meant to experience and enjoy orgasms — yes, she could even say it — she now wanted that more than anything else with Mautu. When she heard him snoring lightly, she found she was annoyed with him for having hurried.

The next night it rained steadily. The heavy muffled sound of it made her feel as if they were caught totally within their desire for each other, and when Mautu lay beside her, she rolled him over to his stomach and started massaging him again. This time she lingered over every stroke, every circling of her hands pressing into his body, all the kneading and plucking of her fingers. She didn't even wait for him to push down his ie lavalava; she stripped it right off, trickled oil out of the bottle onto his buttocks, and massaged — long lingering caresses. A thin, endless humming issued from his clenched mouth. When his hand started exploring her thigh, she held it palm upwards and dripped oil into it. Soon every stroke of his oiled hand against her thigh took the air out of her lungs. She parted her legs more and more as his hand moved up, and she dipped her hands down into the groove between his buttocks, dipped and caressed.

'Is that all right?' he asked as his fingers moved into her wetness.

'Yes, yes!' she moaned. He rolled onto his back, and his fingers were inside her. With his other hand he took hers and wrapped it around his erectness. It was fat and pulsating as she twisted and swivelled her hand around it, learning how to make it enjoy her playing.

'Is that good?' he asked as his fingers moved in and out of her.

'Yes, yes, yes!' she cried, moving her hips rhythmically against his fingers.

When he rolled her onto her back she held onto his penis and guided it into herself in one long, smooth movement. 'Don't! Don't!' She held on to his hips, stopping him from moving. He knew and moved slowly, gently, and she responded, and then as she moved faster, her breath broke out of her mouth in ragged gasps. Up and up and up she mounted and then in one long cry exploded into the darkness and the drumming of the protecting rain.

'Is it wrong for me to enjoy it too, and to enjoy it so much?' she asked hesitantly, later. When he didn't reply, she sensed he was going to deny her, but he didn't.

'No, I don't mind,' he said, pressing his face against her shoulder. 'I like it, I like you enjoying it.'

'You mean, it adds to your enjoyment — my wanton abandonment to passion?' She asked. He laughed softly against her breast, licking the nipple once. 'You don't behave like a good pastor, do you?' she joked.

'I'm wicked like you!' he laughed. 'But God will forgive us because we love each other truthfully . . .' He stopped abruptly.

'So you love me, do you?' she asked. He nodded against her breast.

'But you've not known me very long.'

'I know what is in my heart,' he said. 'I have great love for you, Lalaga.'

For the next two weeks, while they had the fale to themselves and before they shifted to Mautu's aiga, they abandoned themselves to their enormous passion every time they were alone. Twice they even risked it during the daytime, in the fale. Three times on the excuse of getting crops they went into the plantation and, hidden in the trees, continued exploring the limits of their desire. At first they were both surprised by their boldness and shamelessness, but as they experienced no guilt they became more daring.

In public they were the model pastor and wife: self-control and moderation. It was to be that way all their lives.

Mautu divulged little about his aiga to Lalaga, but from the five visits she'd made and from what others said, she feared for her children.

In the pre-Christian religion, the holders of the Tuifolau title and Mautu's direct ancestors were the taulaaitu of the Atua Fatutapu, revered throughout the country. With the fervent consent of their converts, the missionaries banished the atua. Mautu's uncle, Tuifolau Lei'a, the atua's taulaaitu at the time, committed suicide by simply vanishing into the mountains. At the height of his priesthood Tuifolau Lei'a was loved and respected for his gift of curing most ma'i aitu and healing any malady using fofo techniques and herbal cures, but was feared for his powers of casting spells. Most effective was his ability of making victims sleep themselves to death. It was also believed he could make himself invisible, steal any person's soul, and change into any creature.

Though the people claimed publicly they no longer believed in the superstitions of 'the Days Before the Light', they believed Fatutapu was now an aitu, an evil demon and ally of Satan, and that the Aiga Tuifolau were still Fatutapu's guardians, with Mautu's sister, Lefatu, the atua's taulaaitu. Mautu neither denied nor confirmed this but Lalaga knew that whenever someone was afflicted with ma'i aitu the victim was taken (secretly) to Lefatu who, everyone believed, possessed what the missionaries branded as 'the powers of Darkness'.

Because of all this Lalaga avoided visiting Mautu's aiga.

Lalaga attributed what Mautu kept cursing, after each 'meeting of their flesh' (her description), as his 'sinful weakness' to his aiga's aitu and to his father, who'd had numerous wives, Mautu's mother being the last and only one he'd married in church. In the district he was known affectionately (but not to his face) as 'Tuifolau-ma-le-Gaau', Tuifolau-with-the-Intestine. The reference was shamefully obvious and unchristian, Lalaga thought. Over twenty-five known children were proof of the fecundity of his intestine and the fertile source of the endless tales his people told about him everywhere they went. (Only God and his closest friends knew how many other children existed.) Rumour had it that he died at eighty-eight of a heart attack while he was trying, once again, to tame his unruly intestine. Lalaga preferred to believe her Christian brethren's claim that he'd been struck down by the Almighty for his 'sins of the flesh'.

Peleiupu was now a gangly thirteen-year-old: taller than her friends, with a high pronounced forehead that was to become the most distinctive feature of her descendants, eyes as fiercely dark as cold-water springs, and fine wavy hair (Mautu refused to have it cut), which rippled behind her when she ran — and she ran almost everywhere.

She'd been born two months late but it had been an easy birth, and when the midwife was cutting the umbilical cord they'd noticed, with astonishment, a knowing smile on her face and those intense eyes examining them. The midwife predicted an exceptional intelligence, which was soon evident, and people expected her to become a precocious child. She didn't. She exercised mature control over her behaviour. Though many people were uncomfortable when she was around, feeling her observing them and uncovering to the quick of their darkness their innermost secrets and, most disconcerting of all, anticipating their thoughts and actions, no one feared her, for she exuded an aura of understanding trust — their secrets were safe with her.

They came to admire her tremendously and, when chastising their children, held her up as the ideal they should emulate. Affectionately they referred to her as 'the pastor's walking-stick' because she accompanied Mautu everywhere.

A year younger than Peleiupu, Arona was already a miniature version of his father's former build: thickset, with a square head, long muscular arms and large hands, and showing signs of developing phenomenal physical strength. He'd been conceived during the ninth devastating whooping cough epidemic since the papalagi had introduced it, which had again killed many Satoan children. So when he was born his parents were relieved that he had no physical deformities. From the day he started walking he revealed a slow, deliberate manner, and seemed indifferent to everyone but his parents and sisters.

As his strength blossomed, his appetite for everything became a ravishing hunger that frightened Lalaga in particular because she thought he had inherited it from her and Mautu. She feared that his 'appetite' would be even more demanding than theirs.

Ruta and Naomi were separated by a year but Lalaga treated them as twins. They both learned to talk early and were soon taking everywhere their endless chatter and laughter and quarrels, which ended quickly with tearful bouts of reconciliation. They became well known in Satoa for this, and adults encouraged them, good-naturedly, to show that they were especially gifted with language.

Noting every change in her children, Lalaga's concern for their safety deepened. They seemed driven by forces inherited from her and Mautu and their aiga — forces that would either turn them into exceptional people or consume them, perhaps even turning them into allies of Satan. None were going to pursue moderation. So she worked hard to protect them from themselves, but the more she did so, the more they moved into their father's orbit.

Mautu came to spend much time teaching his children but he remained unaware of what was happening to them because to him childhood was an uninteresting period, unworthy of his attention. Not that he didn't love them: they were special people with whom he wanted to share his new knowledge. Books and English were the keys to opening up their imaginations to the miraculous secrets and powers of God's magnificent universe. There were multiple dimensions to reality, to God, and the papalagi possessed many of the ways of seeing those dimensions. His children were to discover that understanding with him. As Mautu pursued his speculations and took their children with him, Lalaga wove a protective web around them all. The children went adventuring with Mautu and eventually outgrew the other Satoan children. An unbreakable bond of alofa and respect grew between them, and their devotion to their parents intensified and became one of the strengths of their lives.

Prospecting

It was mid-1893.

On his next trip into Apia with Barker, Mautu brought home a new pick, a shovel and a bushknife, which he stored in the cupboard where he kept most of his valuable possessions. Curious about what he was going to use them for, Lalaga and their children waited for him to tell them that night during their English lesson. He didn't.

Next morning, which was Tuesday, they watched to see what he was going to do. After their meal at mid-morning he put on his working ie lavalava, got out the new implements, and handed the shovel to Peleiupu.

'May I come too?' Arona asked.

'Yes, may we?' chorused Ruta and Naomi. Mautu shook his head and started towards Barker's house, which was across the malae under some breadfruit trees.

'You're too young,' Peleiupu remarked to the other children.

'So are you!' replied Ruta. Peleiupu flicked back her long mane, wheeled, and followed Mautu, carrying the shovel, like a rifle, across her shoulder.

She waited on the veranda while Mautu went in to see Barker. Three of Barker's youngest children, snotty-nosed and naked, came out and, stopping a few paces away in a group, scrutinised her. Peleiupu knew them but, as yet, she refused to befriend any of Barker's children: she considered them too rude, too forward, altogether too papalagi, even though their mother was Samoan and they couldn't speak English.

'Is it our shovel?' the second girl asked, her right forefinger drilling into her right nostril. Peleiupu shook her head once.

'Shit!' exclaimed the youngest, a chubby male monster who was fingering his penis. Pretending she had been shocked by his remark, Peleiupu turned her back on them. 'Shit!' the boy repeated. His sisters giggled, then Peleiupu heard them running off the veranda and around the corner of the house. She tried not to laugh.

When Barker and Mautu came out, Barker was wearing his black hobnailed boots. Around his waist was his cartridge belt. What he called his sun helmet was perched precariously on his huge mound of hair. Under his left arm was his canvas satchel in which, Peleiupu knew, he carried his pens, pencils and paper. His sleek rifle was in his right hand. The great adventurer that Mautu had told them about, Peleiupu thought.

'Where are we going?' she asked Mautu. He motioned with his head towards the plantations.

'It might rain,' Barker remarked in English, gazing briefly up at the dark blue clouds covering the top of the range.

Shaking his head, Mautu said, in English, 'No, it not rain. It is fine weather.'

Peleiupu's heart skipped with joy: she understood most of what they had said. Not just words any more; now sentences as well.

'Hurry! Hurry!' Barker called in Samoan to his aiga in the fale behind the house. Two of his wife's brothers, Moamoa and Tuvanu, came running carrying another pick, bushknives and what Peleiupu thought were metal frying pans without handles. 'Where the food?' Barker asked them abruptly in Samoan. Both men were middle-aged and had children. Moamoa scurried back to the fale. 'Fool!' Barker called after him. 'You can't trust these people!' Barker said in English to Mautu.

When Moamoa was back with the basket of food they started off, with Barker and Mautu leading, setting a stiff marching pace. Peleiupu almost had to run to keep up.

People in the fale they passed greeted them with invitations to stop and eat. Their group stopped briefly every time, and Mautu refused their invitations politely. A dog, fur bristling, rushed at them with ferocious barks and snapping fangs. 'Alu! Alu!' Barker barked back at it. The poor creature cringed away, its tail between its legs.

Alongside the track, which was islanded by puddles, the vegetation was still sparkling with dew, and soon their clothes were wet from it. Peleiupu felt strong, invigorated, alive with anticipation, and smashed her reflection in the puddles merrily with her feet. As they passed through the crops, trees, creepers and shrubs she imagined they were swimming through a soundless sea world of lush green, led by the courageous Captain Barker and his loyal native lieutenant, Mautu.

Suddenly, into her daydreaming came Barker's voice. 'Gold,' he said and she glanced up at his back, hoping to understand more, but Barker was speaking too fast.

They veered off the main track and crossed over creeper-covered ground through a plantation of bananas to the Satoa River. On the edge of the bank they stood and surveyed the river valley, which meandered like a gigantic centipede up through foothills to the centre range. The river was faintly brown with silt as it rippled leisurely through narrow strips of boulders, rocks and pebbles sparkling in the sun. The light breeze brought with it, from the mountains, the odour of dank, decaying vegetation.

While they watched him, Barker found a large tree trunk nearby, brushed the creepers off it, sat down, opened his canvas satchel, took out a board and spread out sheets of blank paper on it. Then, pencil poised in his right hand, he studied the terrain before them for a long, hushed while. Quietly, Peleiupu edged over and stood looking down over his shoulder at the paper. Mautu stabbed his bushknife into the soil at his feet and sat gazing at the water, dangling his legs over the riverbank. Moamoa and Tuvanu retreated into the cool shade of a clump of bananas and watched from there. Already waves of heat were brimming visibly up from the beds of boulders and stones below.

When the hand clutching the pencil moved, it was like a quick spider drawing with all its legs. Soon black lines, a whole network of them, covered the page. Peleiupu recognised it as a map of the river valley and the area around it. She had seen a sketch map in one of Mautu's books.

Barker held it up to Mautu, who came over and, studying it, said in English, 'Good, good!' Just like Barker would have said.

'I think we should start here.' Barker pointed with his pencil at the area of sand and pebbles on his map, then down at the valley. 'Then here on our next visit.' The next area was a few hundred yards upriver.

Just before they made their way down into the shallow valley Barker shook Mautu's hand and, smiling, said, 'Good luck!' Peleiupu was even more puzzled.

The river was shallow where they were; beds of stones protruded out of the water at midstream. Mautu took one of the shallow pans and squatted down in the water. Stabbing the shovel into the pulpy sand, Barker pushed down on it with his boot until the shovel head was buried. Wrenching up a shovelful of sand, he tipped it into Mautu's pan. Peleiupu, Moamoa and Tuvanu watched fascinated.

'I not know how,' Mautu said in English to Barker.

'Let me.' Barker took the panful of pebbly sand, lowered it into the water and moved it back and forth, washing out the sand until only the bits of rock and pebble were left. He then picked out some bits with his fingers and examined them. 'Nothing yet,' he said to Mautu. 'Take the other pan.' Mautu did so. Barker, in his broken

Samoan, instructed Moamoa and Tuvanu to fill the pans with the sandy material whenever he told them to do so.

Peleiupu crouched in the water in her father's shadow and observed his every move. Mautu's eyes were alive with a brightness she hadn't seen there before. The water was cool around her feet and ankles; periodically she scooped up handfuls of it and washed her face.

Relentlessly the sun pressed down. Neither man noticed it and, whenever Moamoa and Tuvanu were slow, Barker hurled orders at them. Even in her father's shadow Peleiupu found the heat becoming painful so she lay down in the water, with only her face and head above it. The cool water tingled on her body.

Periodically they shifted upriver whenever Barker gave the order.

At noon Peleiupu whispered to Mautu that she was hungry. Her father told her and the other two men to go into the shade and eat. From the healing shade of the trees, Peleiupu munched her food and watched Barker and Mautu digging and sifting, oblivious to the heat shimmering around them in visible waves like hungry swarms of mosquitoes. They seemed locked in a time they never wanted to leave.

Mautu was the first to break the spell and hurry into the shade. He ate quickly, all the time watching Barker. When he'd finished he scrambled out again.

'Lazy! Lazy!' Barker shouted over to Moamoa and Tuvanu, who got up reluctantly, cursing under their breath, and went out.

Gold, Peleiupu remembered Barker saying earlier that morning, as she watched. She fell asleep and dreamt of Mautu looming above her, his chest puffed out, his face beaming with a golden light. Then, digging his hands into the centre of his chest, he prized open his ribcage and out of the cavern of his chest gushed a river of liquid gold, in which she splashed and laughed and laughed.

They got home that evening as Lalaga was lighting the lamp. Without speaking to their inquisitive aiga they took some soap and a towel and bathed in the communal pool beside the church.

Their whole aiga were in the main fale ready for the lotu when they returned. Mautu put on a shirt. Peleiupu brought him the Bible.

Straight after their meal, during which Mautu ate as if he were caught utterly in his own thoughts, he went to where he usually slept, drew the curtain behind him, and they soon heard him snoring heavily.

Anticipating her mother's question, Peleiupu offered a vivid, matter-of-fact description of what she called 'their expedition', but omitted her speculation that Barker and Mautu were prospecting for gold.

56

'What can they be looking for?' Lalaga asked, more to herself than Peleiupu, who shrugged her shoulders. Lalaga left.

When her brother and sisters and the other young people in their aiga gathered eagerly around her Peleiupu retold her story, this time with extravagant embellishments, dramatic flourishes, hilariously accurate imitations of Barker's Samoan and deliberately misleading clues as to what the two men were up to. One: perhaps they were mapping the course of the Satoa River. Two: perhaps because both men were *scientific* — they were working out the types of sand, rocks, mud, and pebbles found in the valley. Three: perhaps they were excavating for the sites of ancient villages, hoping to find priceless artefacts. Four, perhaps — and this was the remotest possibility of all — they were acting out an adventure they had read in one of Barker's books.

Tired from the expedition, Peleiupu tumbled into a deep sleep soon after telling her tale. The other children lay awake late into the night, envying her and speculating among themselves, in whispers, about what Barker and Mautu were up to.

By the morning meal everyone in Satoa was talking about *the* expedition. At this point, with everyone hungrily awaiting the unravelling of the mystery, no one advanced the possibility that perhaps both men had gone mad or were chasing mirages as described in the Holy Book, the very thing that Peleiupu was protecting her father against by not mentioning gold.

For Peleiupu two impatient days had to be tolerated before their next 'expedition upriver' (a phrase she had read in a book). During that time Mautu spent the afternoons with Barker going over their sketch map and marking in large red Xs their next diggings. Then, out of the blue, Mautu told Peleiupu she was to stay home next time and help Lalaga. Hurt by this, she was a sullen, easily angered, resentful helper, and she had frequent quarrels with the other children, especially Arona who, as the only son, resented her being their father's favoured companion. Arduous upriver expeditions were for boys not girls, he complained to Lalaga who, when alone in bed with a silent Mautu that night, explained that it was time he took his only son with him and not Peleiupu. 'We shall see,' he said, and was immediately lost in his thoughts again.

'Your children, apart from Peleiupu, do not exist for you!' she complained.

'What did you say?'

She slapped the mats she was lying on and, trying to keep her voice down, said, 'Never mind!'

'You are angry with me?' he asked gently.

'No!' she snapped. Then quietly, she asked, 'What is happening to you? What are you searching for? You speculate, you dream, you pursue figments of Barker's imagination and what you read in those books!'

'I pursue God's mystery. His depths. His secrets. I want to understand Him.' It was stated simply, with total belief.

'It can lead you to heresy. Have you thought of that?'

'How can it be when I know that God is everything, including the wonders and dreams and fantasies and visions of the imagination and mind?' With that she was lost, she couldn't grasp his meaning.

'And this — this unreal search for gold?'

'Did Peleiupu tell you that?'

'No, your clever loyal daughter tried to put me off your track.'

'But what is so unreal about it? No one has tried to see if there is gold here, have they?'

Caught again by his logic, she felt like shouting. 'But everyone says there is no gold here!'

'But where is the actual proof?' When she didn't reply, he caressed her shoulder and said, 'I love you and our children more than my own life.'

'Soon you will be lost from my understanding,' she said. 'Please stop this search for gold before our people think you've gone . . .' She couldn't say it.

'Yes?' he asked. She said nothing.

While it was still dark on Friday morning, with a chilly wind weaving in from the sea, Mautu woke Peleiupu and Arona. They dressed without waking the others and, carrying a basket of food and their implements, went to Barker's house. The dew-covered grass prickled under their feet.

Barker and a yawning Moamoa and a half-asleep Tuvanu were waiting on the veranda. Without talking they were soon into the solemn shadows and breathing silence of the plantations.

That day the sun pursued them again. They covered about half a mile of river-bank, stopping, digging, sifting panfuls of sandy material, then shifting further inland. Barker and Mautu, oblivious to everything else, confined their talking to intermittent instructions to Moamoa and Tuvanu; the two children were like their shadows, always beside them, saying nothing, watching.

At mid-morning Peleiupu noticed that the still air immediately around them was tainted with Barker's flying-fox smell, which worsened as he sweated and as they moved into the humid dampness of the bush which, at the start of the foothills, groped right down to the water's edge.

They found nothing that day.

At the to'ona'i at his home on Sunday some of the elders questioned Mautu politely, obliquely, about his search. Light-heartedly, he told him they had found nothing yet. No one asked him what they were looking for; they had heard rumours, started by Moamoa and Tuvanu, that precious metals were being prospected for.

Lalaga refused to ask him about it, while Peleiupu, now the veteran explorer, let Arona explain to the other children what had happened so far. The slow Arona stuck, in his story, to the bare facts and details.

The following week they went out three times. Moamoa and Tuvanu, tired from the work and Barker's abuse, didn't appear the last time, a Friday, so the still-eager Peleiupu and Arona carried the implements and food.

After a heavy night's rain the ground under the bush at the river's edge was soft and stank of decay; their feet sank into it to the ankles. The undergrowth was denser, more tangled, and they had to cut a track through it. Around them the sad air was a blue sea of steam through which swam rapacious swarms of mosquitoes that Peleiupu and Arona fought off with small leafy branches. The riverbanks shot up sharply into rugged escarpments, hills, and ridges all smothered with virgin bush, which made them feel they were being watched.

As they worked, there was little conversation, only the rushing sound of the now swiftly flowing water and occasionally the lost cries of birds. Around them Peleiupu sensed the bush world growing, growing.

Late in the afternoon, wet and tired, the skins of their hands and faces wrinkled with the cold, they retreated from the bush and headed for home, locked in themselves, and Peleiupu wondered if her father and Barker were going to give up.

That weekend the Satoans, encouraged by Moamoa's and Tuvanu's enigmatic comments about the expedition, started joking about it behind Mautu's back. All the young people in Satoa, however, maintained their faith in the search.

On Monday morning, with the barely visible drizzle whirling around them as they tramped up the valley, Peleiupu sensed a more dogged determination in the two men. The bush still steamed with an inescapable dankness and, as they entered it, it closed around them. They worked in little light.

They went twice more that week. Still nothing. The drizzle continued. The terrain became more rugged, wilder, more difficult to penetrate. The mosquitoes fought for their blood.

Another week, then Arona's shovel stabbed, a few inches into the water-logged ground, and struck a solid but hollow object. He pressed down on the shovel with his large foot. The shovel refused to sink down any further. He scraped the mud off the object. Through the weeping scar in the mud, an opaque whiteness shone. He scraped off more mud.

'What is it?' Peleiupu asked.

'Don't know,' he replied.

Their father looked down. He took Arona's shovel and dug around the object. Suddenly he stopped.

'What is it?' asked Peleiupu. Mautu started covering the object with soil again but Barker reached over, grasped the shovel handle and stopped him.

With his boot Barker pushed the mud aside, reached down into the shallow hole with both hands, grasped the object and pulled it up. The children cringed. It was a human skull. In the blue light, it looked so nakedly white, veined with black mud.

With his hands Barker brushed all the dirt off it. 'Wonder how it got here?' he asked, poking his fingers into the skull's eye sockets.

'We go now!' Mautu said to him in English. The children gathered the implements quickly.

Barker, saying nothing, started digging up the ground around where the skull had lain. Peleiupu could feel her father's mounting anger as he stood watching. Bit by bit, as Barker dug, a broken human skeleton was revealed.

Panting heavily from the exertion, Barker asked, 'It's so far inland — how did it get here?'

Mautu had no answer. 'Let's go home,' he instructed his children.

'But it's early!' insisted Barker. 'And there's nothing to be afraid of.'

'The message, it is clear,' Mautu said in English. 'There is nothing here. Not now.'

'But the mystery, don't you sense the mystery? How come he is here? There may be others.'

'We leave it alone!' Mautu said. It was an order.

For a moment Barker hesitated, then, dismissing Mautu with a curt nod, started exploring the nearby ground with decisive stabs of the shovel.

Mautu wheeled and started for home. His children followed him.

Behind them, caught in the blue tangle of bush, they could hear Barker foraging like a hungry boar. Even when, miles later, they were free of the bush, they could see Barker in their minds, black with wet and sweat, his muscular body pulsating with inquisitive blood, his eyes focused hypnotically on the ground, his arms pounding the shovel into the softness, searching for the bones, the skeletons.

At home, they didn't tell anyone about their terrible find.

After their evening meal, during which he ate little, Mautu disappeared into the wet darkness.

'Barker won't find any more, will he?' Arona whispered to Peleiupu when they were trying to sleep.

'No,' she reassured him. Around them the dark was filled with aitu and other fearful phantoms.

'I'm — I'm scared!' he murmured.

'Mautu will make sure it's all right!' she said. He shifted closer to her. 'Go to sleep now,' she whispered.

They woke early but Mautu had left already. They ran to Barker's house. He was gone too.

It drizzled again all day. Everything smelled of mould and dampness. Even the sun refused to leave its bed of black cloud. While Peleiupu and Arona worked around their home and, in the afternoon, attended their mother's classes, they waited anxiously for Mautu to appear out of the rain.

Wet and grim-faced he came, bathed, conducted the lotu, ate quickly, and then disappeared into his side of the fale behind the curtain. Peleiupu went to ask if they were having an English lesson that night. She peeped through the gap in the curtain. He was sitting cross-legged, arms folded across his chest, eyes shut firmly, praying. In the gloom she saw a bright aura of sadness surrounding him like a second skin.

When the other children were in their mosquito nets, Lalaga called her and Arona.

'What happened yesterday?' she asked them.

'Nothing,' replied Peleiupu, gazing straight into her mother's face.

'Arona?' Lalaga demanded. Arona, who had been sitting with head bowed, glanced up at Peleiupu. 'Arona?' Lalaga repeated. He bowed his head again and picked at the edge of the mat. 'Your father is in pain. I must know why.'

'Perhaps it was something that happened today,' Peleiupu offered.

'I am waiting!' Lalaga said. 'Arona, do you love your father?' Arona nodded. 'Then you must tell me.'

Arona looked at Peleiupu, who nodded once, finally.

'A skull,' he said, without looking at Lalaga.

'We found a skull and his bones,' said Peleiupu.

'Where?'

'Way upriver. Arona found it with his shovel. Barker dug it up. Then the rest of the skeleton,' said Peleiupu.

'Mautu did not want Barker to dig it up,' Arona continued.

'Mautu was angry when Barker refused to stop, and he brought us back. Barker continued to dig for more bones.'

'You must not tell anyone else about it,' Lalaga instructed them. They nodded. She reached over and caressed Arona's shoulder. 'There is no need to be afraid.'

61

Later when Lalaga went to bed she knew that Mautu was only pretending to be asleep but she decided not to question him. She lay down beside him.

In her dreams she heard his desperate cry for help. Waking, she found him sitting beside her in the darkness. His muted weeping was an incessant low stirring into which she reached, found his face, and held it between her warm hands. His tears washed over the backs of her hands.

'They are here all around me,' he murmured. 'They filled my sleep with their cries, their awful dying!' He paused and, when she took her hands away, wiped his face with a corner of his sleeping sheet. 'We searched for gold and found *them*!'

'So there is more than one?' she asked.

'Yes. We spent all day yesterday clearing the ground and finding them clinging even to the roots of the trees as if they hadn't wanted to die.'

'An old burial place?'

'If only it was that, I would be less disturbed. They were all killed — slaughtered!'

'What are you going to do?' She was satisfied that his gruesome discovery had shocked him back to the realities she knew, and she hoped he would remain there.

'There are more to be dug up. Once we have done that, we will bring them down and give them a Christian burial.'

'We must tell our village and they will help you.'

'Not yet,' he said. 'When we have found all of them I will tell Satoa and we will all go up and bring them down and bury them beside the church.'

'How did they die?'

'Barker says it was a battle. Up at the top of the nearest hill under the vegetation we have found the remnants of an ancient village. Barker thinks the village was invaded, conquered, burnt to the ground, and most of its inhabitants killed and left there.'

'But is there a story of that in Satoa's history?'

'Not that I know of. It must have happened a long time ago and been quickly forgotten. Or that unfortunate village was destroyed even before the original Satoa village was founded.'

At dawn when Peleiupu and Arona got up to go with Mautu, Lalaga told them not to. They obeyed when they saw the weight of pain on their father.

Every day for a week Barker and Mautu went up into the hills. Mautu's hair was suddenly freckled with grey, his physical fragility became more pronounced, his conversations were no longer laced with that spark, he moved like a creature caught in a self-destructive dream. Conscious of the sadness they saw each day in their pastor, the Satoans stopped joking about the expeditions. Their pastor (misled by that insane papalagi) in his incredible search for gold had discovered a new pain, and they were waiting for him to reveal it to them.

The following week Barker and Mautu went up twice. The second time, on a Thursday, Mautu insisted that Peleiupu and Arona accompany him.

'But why?' Lalaga asked.

'Arona found the first person. Peleiupu was there too. Now they must come and see the rest of them before we bring them down.'

'I still don't understand!' she insisted. 'Our children are still too young to be near — near those things!'

'They must learn what death is; they must *see* the people. They will not frighten them.'

Again she couldn't comprehend him.

The area where they had found the first skeleton was now a fairly large clearing, basking in bright sunlight. All the undergrowth had been cleared away; some of the trees had been cut down, chopped into short pieces, and stacked by the water. In the clearing, among the boulders, was a scatter of shallow graves, about sixty in all. In them, lying in grotesque postures, were the skeletons. Many of them were badly broken, shattered, scattered; many skulls and bones were missing; some of the graves were occupied by more than one skeleton.

'Don't be frightened,' Mautu encouraged Peleiupu and Arona. 'After being with them for this length of time, I know they won't harm us.' He walked around the graves. 'Come and see them.'

Barker, who was standing back, called in Samoan, 'Go, they only harmless bones!' Peleiupu saw her father wince at Barker's remark. 'I not know why your father tell me help dig up all that useless bones!' Barker looked away when Mautu glared at him, sat down on a log, and started scraping the mud off his boots.

'Come on,' Mautu invited his children.

Arona moved protectively against Peleiupu as they walked into the midst of the people. 'It's all right!' she whispered, trying to control her own trembling. They both refused to look down at the skeletons, feeling as if they were at a great height and would tumble to their death if they looked down.

'Look, no harm!' Mautu called, holding up one of the skulls.

Gold, Peleiupu heard Barker repeat in her head. Gold. Gold. Gold. She gazed down and the heap of bones in the grave in front of her looked golden in the sunlight. All around a golden luminosity was bursting up from the mouths of the graves, and inside her the bones transformed themselves into huge pua blossoms, and she was floating through a garden of white magic flowers.

She broke from her delicious wandering when Arona said, 'Mautu is right. They will not harm us.'

'No, they are our friends,' she said.

After their inspection Mautu motioned to them to follow him. A narrow track, which Barker and Mautu had cut, led up the hill from the clearing and disappeared into the bush. The slope was steep and slippery and they had to hold on to nearby branches as they clambered up the hill. Disturbed by their noise, gnats, butterflies and other insects fluttered up from the undergrowth.

The top of the hill was covered by huge trees matted together at their heads by creepers and lianas, which allowed little light to penetrate to the ground.

'This is where they lived,' Mautu said, pointing at the creeper-covered mounds that lay under the trees and spread out ahead into the vegetation. 'Those were the paepae of their fale. That is all that is left. It was a fairly large village.'

'But why did they live up here?' asked Peleiupu.

'It was always safer to build your village in a well-protected place. Up here the people could see who was coming. They built a palisade around their village. The river was their source of water.'

'What was it called?' she asked.

'I don't know. Perhaps an old person in Satoa can tell us.' Their voices sounded unreal in the enclosed vegetation. 'Are you still frightened?' Mautu asked Arona, who shook his head and smiled. 'You will remember them and their village for the rest of your lives, carrying them as part of your dead, in your blood.'

Right then Barker broke noisily through the undergrowth and, confronting Mautu, his face red with exertion and sweat pouring off him, said in English, 'And what, my pastor friend, are you going to do with all our mountain of bones and skulls?'

'You never going to understand, eh?' Mautu said in English.

'No, he not understand!' Peleiupu heard herself say in English. Surprised, she glanced up at Mautu, then at Barker, who were both looking at her in amazement because it was the first time she had ever spoken English to them.

'Graveyards and dead villages produce wonderful surprises!' Barker laughed.

'Yes, the dead can open the minds of innocent children to wisdom,' Mautu said in Samoan, and with pride.

Later, as they made their way down, Arona asked Peleiupu what she had said in English. That Barker would never understand, she replied.

'Understand what?' he asked.

'What Mautu told us about the dead and how important they are.'

'I didn't understand Mautu either,' Arona sighed. 'I'm too young!'

'Someday you will understand,' she consoled him, but immediately experienced a twinge of guilt for deliberately implying that she herself had understood.

'I want . . . I want so much!' he exclaimed.

'So much what?'

'Everything! To know everything!'

'But no one can do that!'

'Someday I will!' At his determination she felt a more abundant love for him. 'I want to be grown-up, now!'

By the river, as they wandered once again among the graves, they experienced no fear, as though they had left it up on the hill in the village snared in the choking tentacles of the bush. Arona even stopped at one of the graves, sat at the edge and dangled his feet down until they were only a few inches above the skull. His feet looked like large fish-hooks seeking the mouth of the skull. Peleiupu sat down beside him and remembered how the graves, the bones, had burst with a golden light.

That Friday and Saturday the young men of Mautu's school dug a series of graves beside the church. Most of the men of Satoa, when they heard about it, joined the work. At the Sunday morning service Mautu described from the pulpit his expedition and what he and Barker had discovered. He asked that their village give 'the People' (his phrase) a Christian burial. The church buzzed with questions. During to'ona'i Mautu answered all the elders' questions. None of them knew anything about the village on the hill.

Sao, the ali'i of Satoa and Barker's father-in-law, called a meeting of the matai at his fale on Monday morning. After weighty discussion concerning the burying of so many strangers in their village, they organised a party to go up to the hills with Mautu on Tuesday and bring down 'the People'.

The large party was led by Mautu and Sao, who wore ties and their white Sunday suits. All the other elders and their wives were in their Sunday best too. The untitled men, who were to carry 'the People', wore only black ie lavalava. No children were allowed to go.

They reached the graves just before midday. Immediately Mautu conducted a service. A hymn was sung; he read from the Bible; then prayed. Standing at the perimeter of the clearing in their best clothes and caught in the bright stillness of the hills and mountains, they seemed incongruous, strangers visiting another village for the first time.

After Mautu's prayer the old men moved into the shade while the women worked in groups, oiling the bones with coconut oil and wrapping them in tapa cloth. No one spoke. No one was afraid.

When all 'the People' were clothed in tapa the young men picked them up and, carrying them on their shoulders, followed Mautu and the elders down towards Satoa. Beside them the river ripped and swerved and danced and fingered its way towards the sea.

Awaiting them around the graves beside the church were the rest of the Satoans.

Again no one spoke. A hush lay over the village.

The young men lined 'the People', eighty bundles, in a row below the church steps. Gradually, like a rising tide, the old women started the customary funeral wailing, and their sound was that of the morning sea. Many of the people wept. Peleiupu and Arona, who were standing beside Lalaga, cried too.

His white suit dazzling the noonday sun, Mautu stood on the church steps. 'Let us sing hymn 129: *God be with us now in our sorrow!*' The powerful singing broke up to the crystal-clear sky and sent the heat retreating into the shade.

'Lord, we gather here today to send to You people we never knew,' prayed Mautu. As he prayed, Peleiupu saw thin lines of tears trickling down his cheeks, and she wept some more.

Another hymn, then Mautu's sermon. 'The dignity of Satoa, from the youngest to the most noble, we are gathered here today to mourn the death of brothers and sisters who died before Christ's message reached our shores. We never knew them but up in the wilderness they have been waiting for us to come and find them with love, to rescue them from the Darkness in which they were dwelling, to save their wandering souls and send them peacefully to God . . .'

His words were a steady healing comfort in the heat. Once again he was their pastor with the spark, the fire, to make them believe. In his foolish but God-determined search for gold, he had lost the fire until he had discovered 'the People', who had brought him back to them. And many more of them wept.

'. . . In one of the kingdoms of South America there lives to this day a creature called the Webbed Light. It has no body and yet it can become anything it wants. It lives in the air above the highest peak of the Andes and watches over all the creatures in the kingdom. Every year before the season of death, usually associated with winter when ice and snow kill everything, this wonderful creature pierces its throat and, assuming the shape of the eagle, flies over the barren land crying the cry of a newborn lamb. Its rich blood gushes from the wound in its throat and on entering the soil makes it strong enough to endure the winter and, in spring, burst forth again with new life. This creature, people of Satoa, is like our God who, with His blood, saves us every year, every minute of our lives, so that we can save others for our God, the souls of our sisters and brothers who have endured a winter in the wilderness . . . They died a pagan death in the days of Darkness. Today we mourn their deaths and, at the same time, celebrate their waking to God's brilliant Light and Love . . .'

In groups the men took 'the People' and lowered them into their graves. Then Mautu said, 'Dust to dust, earth to earth,' and they scattered the rich grains of earth over 'the People'.

They sang hymns while the men filled the graves.

After everyone else had gone home, Peleiupu, Arona, Ruta and Naomi and a small group of friends lingered in the shade of the pua trees beside the graves.

'They were killed, weren't they?' Ruta asked Arona, who looked at Peleiupu, who nodded.

'In a war?' Naomi asked. Peleiupu nodded again. The mounds of earth were drying quickly in the heat.

'Their aitu will haunt our village!' Naomi remarked.

'No,' said Peleiupu. 'Because we have saved them, they will not harm us.'

'Are you sure?' Ruta asked.

'I am sure,' Peleiupu replied, turning to go.

As they followed Peleiupu, Arona said, 'Barker didn't come?'

'No, he didn't come,' Peleiupu said.

'Why not?' asked Naomi.

'You ask too many questions!' she said.

'Yes, she's always asking about this and that and this and that!' said Ruta.

'So are you!' Naomi accused her. An argument erupted. Peleiupu ran off, Arona followed her and their friends dispersed too, leaving Naomi and Ruta to the twitching heat and sun.

From their fale, at mid-morning the next day, they observed Barker and Poto and their whole aiga arriving at the graveyard, with shovels and picks and baskets of river stones and pebbles. They started piling the stones and pebbles neatly onto the graves. Mautu went out to them.

'So you believe in our bones, eh?' Mautu asked Barker in English.

'I never said that!' Barker replied. Mautu chuckled. 'I suppose being human beings like us they needed to be buried decently.' He paused, then, turning and focusing his smile on Mautu, said, 'And after all, we found them and are therefore equally responsible for them. You can say we are now their family!' They laughed together for a long while, and the others were puzzled by it. 'You can even say we struck gold!' And their laughter continued to echo around the graves and ripple through the church and dance across the malae and dive mischievously into every

Satoa home, bringing all the Satoans running, skipping, hobbling, scuttling to the graves and 'their People'.

While the old people and Mautu and Barker sat joking in the shade, everyone else built up the graves with the sleek black stones and pebbles that the young people had brought in baskets from the river.

Mautu's aiga and other nearby aiga made umu and cooked a delicious variety of food. When the work on the graves was finished, they invited everyone into Mautu's home and ate heartily and laughed at Barker's and Mautu's exaggerated stories about their futile, mad, ridiculous prospecting for gold up-river, up-valley.

It was the first time Barker had been in Mautu's home.

As the sun was setting, after Barker and the Satoans had left with their infectious laughter, Peleiupu cut some branches from the pua trees and started planting them between some of the graves. Arona observed her for a while, then dug up some shrubs and flowers from around their fale, took them and, without saying anything to Peleiupu, replanted them around the centre grave. Ruta and Naomi and a frisky gaggle of friends got more plants from the neighbouring area and planted them around some of the other graves. Yet more children came with more flowers, shrubs and plants.

And the same darkness that fell on the deserted village on the hill in the wilderness fell protectively over the noisy mushrooming garden of children.

Daughter of the Mango Season

'I'm fifty-five years old today,' Barker said to Mautu as they sat in cane chairs facing each other on the store veranda overlooking the malae. Poto, as usual, sat beside her husband's chair, on the floor. Peleiupu sat on the floor beside her father's chair. They were having a breakfast of strong tea and cabin bread, which some of the women had served. 'Fifty-five is old, isn't it?' Barker asked. Mautu nodded as he dunked his cabin bread in his mug of tea. 'Not many people here or in England live beyond forty,' Barker continued. 'I've been lucky. Haven't been seriously ill, ever . . .'

'Only once when you had the mumu,' Poto interrupted.

'I forgot about that,' Barker said. 'But it was not serious.'

'Aren't you going to eat?' Mautu asked him.

Shaking his head, Barker said, 'I'm not hungry.' He paused. 'How old are you?'

'Nearly forty-five,' replied Mautu.

'The oldest man I've ever known was a Chinaman we took aboard in Hong Kong. About eighty, he was. Small fist of a chap but very, very tough. Never said anything — not to me, anyway. Bloody pagan he was. So you see, Mautu, we don't need to be Christians to live a long life.' Mautu refused to take the bait. 'The next oldest was Hindu. As black as midnight, and at seventy-something years old, not a wrinkle on his face. Another heathen. In fact, the longest-living people I've met were not Christians!' Mautu refused to reply. 'If old age is proof of the gods' blessings, then the pagan gods are more powerful!' Pausing dramatically and staring at Mautu from under lowered bushy eyebrows, he said, 'Perhaps your God doesn't exist!'

'Going to be a good mango season,' Mautu said in English, gazing up at the mango trees to their right shading the store. The high sprawling trees were pink with blossoms and buds.

'Yes, this going to be a rich harvest of mangoes.' Poto said.

Peleiupu, noticing the quiet desperation on Barker's face, wanted her father to offer their friend some consolation, an answer to grasp at. Mautu pushed away his food tray, then, looking at Barker, asked, 'Why is God's existence important to you if you do not believe in Him?'

'It *isn't* important!'

'Then you don't need to chase your own questions.' Mautu glanced up at the mango trees again. 'Yes, the mangoes, they are going to be plentiful this season.'

'Why do you always talk in riddles?'

'It is you who deals in riddles!' Mautu replied. Barker looked away.

Peleiupu timed it perfectly: just before Barker could jab his frustration at Mautu she jumped up and picked up her father's tray.

'Thank you, Pele,' Poto said, pushing her foodmat forward. Peleiupu stood looking at Barker's tray.

'Yes, take mine too,' he said finally.

'But you have not eaten!' Mautu insisted.

'It's not the food of this world that I need.'

'Not even sweet mangoes,' joked Mautu.

For the first time that morning Barker relaxed and, looking up at the mango trees, said, 'Perhaps the sticky juice of the mango can hold my tattered fifty-five-year-old body together for a while longer.'

Poto laughed softly. 'You're still healthy!' Barker ignored her.

When Peleiupu returned from the kitchen fale a few minutes later Barker said, 'Pele looks more like Lalaga than you.'

'Yes, she really does,' Poto echoed.

'Then she is not beautiful!' chuckled Mautu. Embarrassed, Peleiupu avoided looking at them and sat down behind Mautu's chair.

'I wish my children were like Pele. The brats are total savages!' Barker said. Poto looked hurt.

'Like their father perhaps,' Mautu quipped.

'I'm not a savage!' Barker pretended to be hurt.

'You are a palagi savage!' Poto joked.

'You don't believe in the English God. Or English civilisation. You don't respect other papalagi, not even the missionary, so Poto is right: you are a palagi savage,' Mautu said.

'But I do believe in other things.'

'What?' Mautu trapped him. Once again Peleiupu sensed that Barker was a tight knot of pain. 'What?' Mautu whispered.

'Yes, in what, my savage palagi?' Poto asked.

'In many things!' Barker stood up suddenly and, turning his back to Mautu, recited: 'I believe in birth; I believe in death; I believe in thirst, hunger, pain, desire, joy — because I can experience all those. I believe in the earth, the sea, the sky. In birds too. And mangoes. Especially mangoes because I'll be tasting their delicious flesh in a few months' time.' Wheeling to face Mautu, he tried to smile. 'I have no need to believe in a supreme being, in a god: I don't need such a crutch!'

'But you continue to search . . .'

'Not for God!'

'. . . across all the Earth's seas and islands . . .'

'Not for God!'

'Why have you searched all these fifty-five years?'

'Not for God, I tell you!'

'Then for what, for whom?'

Peleiupu saw Barker's huge hands as helpless anchors dangling into the emptiness around him, and she wanted to reach out and hold up their immense weight of doubt. She glanced at Poto, who looked immensely sad as she contemplated her husband.

'As I have said already, the things I can feel and taste and experience, those are enough for me.'

'If that is enough, then you don't need to keep asking me . . . You don't need anybody, my friend,' Mautu insisted.

'That is right,' Poto said.

It was as though the mellow morning light had solidified around them into a healing hand, and, for a long moment, they said nothing.

'I don't know what answers you seek,' Mautu said. He reached out and touched the back of Barker's hand. Barker sat down again. Poto put a hand on his bare foot and started caressing it. 'All I know is you are an English lord who was shipwrecked on a desert island full of sun and sky and mangoes and need nothing else!'

'Yes, I am the civilised English lord shipwrecked in paradise and have no need of a Christian God, missionaries, other white-skinned lords, or crucifixes!' He laughed softly and clutched Mautu's shoulder. 'I am a pagan in the midst of so much plenty. I am fifty-five years old today and I seek nothing and need nothing!'

'Perhaps just mangoes?' Mautu quipped.

'Yes, perhaps mangoes!'

They laughed and their laughter lost itself in the thick foliage of the mango trees, as Poto and Peleiupu watched them.

'Our annual church fono is to be held in two weeks' time,' Mautu said to Barker. 'Will you take us again in your fautasi?'

'Yes, but on one condition.'

'And what is that?'

'That you take Pele and Arona with you.' Barker winked at Peleiupu.

'You should let her go — she'd love it!' Poto encouraged.

'Do you want to go?' Mautu asked Peleiupu. She nodded. 'You'd better ask your mother, then.' She wanted him to ask Lalaga but knew she would have to face her.

'We'll leave you and your party at Salua, and I'll take Pele and Arona into Apia.'

'I don't think so,' Mautu insisted.

'Don't you trust your palagi pagan friend to care properly for your children?'

'It's not that,' mumbled Mautu. 'I don't like Apia.'

'Apia, and the whole life that goes with it, is here to stay whether you like it or not. Your children will have to live with it.' He reached over and ruffled Peleiupu's hair. 'And Pele can cope with anything, including Apia! She watches and learns and understands quickly. Don't you, Pele?' Peleiupu blushed. 'She is fortunate.'

Poto smiled at Peleiupu. 'And you can come and get some money from me before you leave, to spend in all those rich shops in Apia,' she told her.

Later, as they walked away from Barker's store, Peleiupu glanced up at the mango trees: the dark green foliage, peppered pink and red with flowers, stirred like slow spring water. She shimmered with joy at the thought of visiting Apia.

'Do you like Barker?' Mautu asked. She nodded. 'Why?'

She pondered and said, 'He is a very sad man, eh?'

'Barker is right about you: you do watch and learn and understand.'

They walked in silence the rest of the way.

'Mautu,' she pleaded as they walked up the back paepae of their fale, 'I want to go with Barker to Apia.'

'All right,' he whispered. Lalaga was weaving a mat in the centre of their fale. 'But you had better ask your mother.' Before she could insist on him doing it, he hurried to his desk at the other end of the fale.

'How is the papalagi gentleman?' Lalaga asked her. She had taken to calling Barker that but there was no malice in it.

'He is well,' Peleiupu replied formally, thus undermining Lalaga's line of attack. 'Let me do it.' She sat down. Lalaga slid away and let her continue the weaving.

For a while they said nothing and, as Lalaga observed Peleiupu's deft hands and fingers weaving the mat, like quick spiders, she experienced an upwelling pride in her daughter: at fifteen Peleiupu was already an expert weaver of mats, and highly skilled in other female crafts. Everything came easily to her — too easily, Lalaga often thought. 'It is a gift from God,' Mautu had once allayed Lalaga's fears about Peleiupu. Even her English was now better than Mautu's. Yet Peleiupu always made herself appear less skilled than other people in order to make them feel more secure in her presence. For this, Lalaga loved her deeply, knowing that Peleiupu would not use her gift, her superior talents, to harm others.

'What did your father and the papalagi discuss this morning?' Lalaga asked, expecting Peleiupu, as usual, to see if anyone else was listening, before replying.

Peleiupu looked around the fale, then said, 'Mautu says it's going to be a good mango season this year.'

But Lalaga wasn't going to be deflected that easily. 'What did the papalagi gentleman and your father, the prophet, talk about?'

'The usual,' said Peleiupu. Her hands worked more quickly.

'And what is the usual?'

'The search for God.' Peleiupu's hands stopped their furious weaving. 'You believe in God, eh?' she asked, looking intently at Lalaga.

'Of course I do!' Lalaga protested.

'That's what I thought.'

'You thought so!' Lalaga was now angry and upset.

'Lalaga, some people don't believe in God.'

Lalaga was frightened by what she felt she had to ask. 'Are you one of those people?'

Peleiupu's hands continued their nimble weaving. Shaking her head and gazing down at what she was doing, she said, 'Barker doesn't believe and I think many other papalagi are the same.'

'I know that,' sighed Lalaga, but when she noticed the abrupt halt in Peleiupu's weaving she tensed again.

'Mautu believes, doesn't he?'

'How can you ask such a thing? Your . . . your father is a servant of God!'

Peleiupu reacted as if she hadn't noticed Lalaga's anger, and said, 'All I meant was that Mautu sometimes doubts.'

'Doubts what?' Lalaga insisted.

'God,' was all Peleiupu said.

'Peleiupu!' Mautu called to her.

'Yes?'

'Get me a drink of water.'

Peleiupu scrambled up and out of the fale, leaving Lalaga gasping for meaning, an answer, like a fish kicking at the end of a line.

Lalaga continued her weaving but Peleiupu's revelation about Mautu's doubts kept picking at her.

Peleiupu was soon back with a mug of water for Mautu. Raising the drink to his mouth, Mautu whispered, 'What are you and you mother arguing about?'

'Nothing,' she whispered back. 'I just told her that you sometimes doubt the existence of God.' Mautu choked and coughed the water out in a splutter. 'It's true, isn't it?' she asked. He wiped his mouth with the back of his hand and, trying to steady his trembling hands, drank the rest of the water slowly.

'Have you asked her about going to Apia?' He handed her the empty mug.

She shook her head. 'Why don't *you* ask her?'

'It's best that you ask,' he whispered, avoiding her eyes. Before she could plead he added, 'Go now. I've got a lot of work to do.' He picked up his pen.

She hesitated for a moment, turned swiftly and hurried out of the fale.

'We haven't finished talking!' Lalaga called her back.

Peleiupu went over and sat down beside her. She was confused by her mother's unexpected anger and her father's timidity. Everything was straightforward but adults, especially parents, made things complicated, stupidly unreasonable, she thought. She was only fifteen yet she had to be so patient with their lack of understanding, their slow decision-making, and the eternal complications they made of their lives and everyone else's. Most of them were so unwise — yes, that was her conclusion.

'Going to be a good mango season,' she remarked. She tried to erase her confusion with the thought of fat, succulent mangoes, but couldn't. Beside her, Lalaga's presence was a solid rock pillar. She wasn't going to offer to do any more weaving. 'Where are Arona and the other children?' she asked.

'I don't know,' Lalaga replied. She looked at Peleiupu's profile and realised that her daughter no longer referred to herself as a child. It wasn't out of any pretence or arrogance: Peleiupu simply did not think of herself as a child. And, physically, she was quickly blossoming into a woman, tall and supple, who wasn't going to acquire Mautu's bulk. She wasn't self-conscious about this physical transformation either. It was as if, anticipating well beforehand every change in her life, she adjusted to it before it took place.

'Very hot, eh?' Peleiupu observed, noticing the beads of sweat slithering down her mother's arms and face. 'Where's everybody gone?' All the neighbouring fale appeared empty of people.

'Working in their plantations or fishing, you know that!'

'Yes,' sighed Peleiupu, 'but where are Arona and Ruta and Naomi and the other children of our aiga?'

'Swimming, probably. Now stop your questions. Here, you weave.'

While Peleiupu worked, Lalaga watched her. When she looked out of the fale and saw that their mango trees beside the road were covered with blossoms she heard herself saying, 'Yes, it is going to be a rich mango harvest.'

'Mautu said that this morning.' Peleiupu paused in her work and, gazing at Lalaga, said, 'Funny how you can make an important observation the property of everyone by just pointing it out to someone else. Of course it has to be an observation that is important to those other people. Like the other morning, while Arona and I and the other children were in our plantation collecting coconuts, I suddenly heard the silence in all that growth . . .'

'Heard it?'

'Yes, I heard the silence — it was deep and still, a huge, kind presence around us and in us . . . And when I heard it I told Arona to stand still and listen to it. He did. I told him to shut his eyes. He did. Then I asked him if he was hearing it. He nodded. Then we asked the others in turn to listen. And when we had all had a turn, we closed our eyes together and listened as a group. And we all heard it and allowed it to become part of us.'

'What did you think that particular silence was?'

'It was the island itself,' Peleiupu explained. 'The silence of these islands. It must have been here when God created our country. And has always been here.'

'But why is it important?'

'I don't know yet how to explain it,' she said. 'Perhaps it is important because if we refuse to hear it, or let it be part of us, we will become other creatures . . . I don't know. Arona knows better. He doesn't let his thinking get in the way. He just knows. He lets things become what they are in himself. I can't explain it.' She continued weaving. 'It is bad to think too much, Barker keeps telling Mautu. He is right . . .'

'But he does nothing else but chase his thoughts round and round!' laughed Lalaga. 'That's why he can't believe in anything!'

'That's the palagi way, that's how palagi people are.'

'And your father?'

Aware that Lalaga had once again led her deftly to a discussion she wanted to avoid, Peleiupu said, 'May I go for a swim?' Before Lalaga could pin her down, Peleiupu turned and called, 'Mautu, may I go for a swim?'

'All right,' he replied.

And Peleiupu was out of the fale and running towards the pool.

Lalaga continued to weave her mat, refusing to ask Mautu about his doubts because he was, like Peleiupu, adept at dodging her questions.

It was almost midday and the sun was snared in a smother of thick cloud that seemed to have oozed out of the sky's belly. Only the soft quick squeaking and scratching of Lalaga's fingers against the pandanus strands cut at the silence. Occasionally she heard Mautu shift in his wooden chair. Mangoes, she thought inadvertently, and then cursed herself for having thought it. Why did her daughter understand more than she? She had no right to — she was only a child!

On their way home from the pool Peleiupu edged up to Arona and whispered, 'Do you want to visit Apia?' Arona looked straight ahead: a brother, at his age, should no longer be seen displaying affection for his sister. 'Barker and Mautu will take us if we want to go.'

'Who said?' Arona asked.

'Not too loud!' she whispered. Ruta, Naomi and the others were too busy talking among themselves to hear anyway. 'Mautu and Lalaga and the elders are attending the church fono at Salua. Do you want to go?' He nodded once. 'Lalaga hasn't said we can, though,' she added, hoping he would volunteer to persuade her. He said nothing. 'Did you hear?' He nodded once. 'Well?' she asked.

'Well what?'

'We won't be able to go if Lalaga says no!'

'You ask her, then,' was his curt reply. He looked so aloof in the noon sun, with the droplets of water glistening like fish scales in his hair and over his body, that she hesitated from persuading him any further.

'You're her favourite,' she ventured.

'I'll ask Lalaga,' Ruta volunteered.

'Ask her what?' Peleiupu snapped.

'Whatever you want me to!'

'It is not your concern,' Arona said firmly, just like their father when he wanted quiet. Ruta shrugged her shoulders and resumed her whispered conversation with her friends.

They noticed that some older girls and boys were gathering in the fale classrooms for their afternoon lessons. Lalaga was still weaving.

'I'll ask her,' Arona said finally, and then walked away.

As usual, after lotu and their evening meal Mautu conducted an English lesson with Lalaga, his children and the brightest Satoa children. (Two years earlier, Lalaga had persuaded him to include the latter in his English class.) During these lessons, whenever Mautu didn't know the meaning of words or their correct pronunciation, he called on Peleiupu. However, he always checked later with Barker. Sometimes when Mautu couldn't take the class Peleiupu took it, and, secretly, Lalaga and the others preferred her relaxed, democratic, patient style. Mautu also gave her the students' written assignments and exercises to mark.

After the lesson that night Peleiupu and the older girls strung up the mosquito nets, and soon all the children were in the nets and falling asleep. Instead of sitting up with her parents, Peleiupu got into the net where she slept with Ruta, Naomi and three other girls, pulled her sheet up to her chin and pretended to be sleeping. Intermittently, however, she would peer through her half-closed eyelids at her parents and Arona, who were playing cards beside the lamp a few paces away, awaiting, with a frantic tension, Lalaga's decision about their going to Apia.

As if someone had suddenly pulled back a curtain, she was awake. It was bright morning and the other children were outside picking up the fallen leaves. Peleiupu rolled out, untied the net, folded it with her sleeping sheet and placed it on the lowest rafter with the sleeping mats.

Arona and three of his friends were scraping coconuts behind the kitchen fale, to feed the chickens, but because there were no girls with them she couldn't go and ask him.

At the drums of rainwater under the breadfruit trees she filled a basin, washed her face and combed her hair, all the time keeping an eye on her brother.

As she helped the other girls to cook their morning meal in the kitchen fale, she tried not to think of Lalaga's decision. When she saw Arona strolling alone through the scatter of banana trees towards the beach she got up and pretended to be going to the lavatory, which was at the edge of the beach behind a thick stand of palm trees.

'What did she say?' she called to him. He was standing up to his thighs in the sea, his back to her, washing a coconut strainer he had brought with him. He continued as if he hadn't heard her. She moved up to the water's edge. The stench of decaying coral invaded her nostrils. 'What did Lalaga say?' she repeated. Raising the strainer with both hands, Arona squeezed it in one long drawn-out action, and the water dribbled through his hands like solid white smoke and splattered into the surface of the sea.

Without looking at her, he walked back towards the beach. 'She will decide tomorrow.'

'Tomorrow?' she cried, stamping her right foot into the thickly wet sand. He nodded and started walking past her. 'But why?'

He had never seen her so agitated before, and he felt an affinity to her, knowing she was capable of losing control of her emotions just like other people. 'Don't worry, she'll let us go,' he said.

'She had better!' Peleiupu snapped.

There was no one else in the main fale as she sat with Arona facing Lalaga, who, she sensed, was avoiding her eyes. In the pit of her belly a ferocious beast was inflating itself, threatening to fill every nook and cranny of her being. She could hardly breathe; sobs were breaking up from her chest like huge bubbles about to burst and she swallowed them down repeatedly.

'. . . Arona may come with us,' Lalaga was saying, 'but you'll have to stay and run our classes . . .'

'I won't. No!' The choking cry broke out of her mouth. She slapped at her knees and was sobbing.

'Don't you talk to me like that!' ordered Lalaga. 'No child talks to her mother like that!'

'I want to go!' Peleiupu cried. She sprang up, fists clenched at her sides, her huge tears dripping down to the mat. 'I'm going!'

'I won't allow any child of mine to talk to me like that! Hear me?' Lalaga rehitched her ie lavalava. 'If you don't watch out, I'll beat you!'

Peleiupu scuttled across the fale. At the threshold she wheeled, wiped her face fiercely with her hands, and called, 'I'm going and you can't stop me!'

'Get me the broom!' Lalaga ordered Arona.

Peleiupu jumped down onto the grass and started running across the malae.

'You wait!' Lalaga threatened. 'You wait until I get you tonight!'

They watched Peleiupu disappearing into a stand of bananas and into the plantations. 'Go and bring her back, now!' Lalaga ordered Arona, who rose slowly, glanced at her, and started ambling out of the fale. 'And hurry up!' she chased him.

For a while Lalaga stood on the front paepae gazing after her children, her whole body quivering with anger. Then, realising that the neighbours were watching her, she retreated to her weaving.

'I'll show her,' she kept repeating. 'She thinks she knows more than her own mother! Just wait. I've spent my life slaving for her. Just wait!'

A short while later, however, when she remembered how determined her daughter was, she visualised Peleiupu in a fragile canoe paddling suicidally across the hungry straits which would inevitably swallow her up. Then, more frightening still, she imagined Peleiupu up in a tree fixing a noose around her neck. She scrambled up and out into the classrooms and instructed the older students to help Arona search for Peleiupu.

The undergrowth was a dense green sea sucking her into its depths as she ran, her feet making plopping, sucking sounds in the muddy track. 'I'll show her! I'll show her!'

Peleiupu repeated. Ahead, the ifi tree was a massive mother, with arms outstretched to welcome her.

She jumped up, clung to the lowest branch, kicked up and then, branch by branch, climbed until she reached a platform of interlocking branches. She lay down there on her back and cried up into the maze of leaves and branches and thin rays of light.

This was 'her tree' — her refuge whenever she was troubled. When she had first discovered it five years previously it had intimidated her with its heavy brooding presence: it was like an octopus, she had thought. Its rich, fertile smell of mould had made her think of supernatural beasts. However, one morning after a nasty quarrel with Arona and Lalaga she had found herself up in the ifi's cool, protective shade and, as she had lain on the platform, the tree's breathing and aromatic odour had healed her hurt.

Soon after that she had heard Filivai, the Satoa taulasea, say that certain trees, in pre-Christian times, had been the homes of certain aitu and atua. After about fifty years of missionary preaching, aitu had become evil beings to be feared, and there was now only one atua. Her ifi tree had an aitu, she had come to believe after hours of relaxing in its dark green healing. And her tree was part of nature, a spiritual force she kept reading about in English books.

She often wondered which ancient aitu lived in her tree, and in her imagination tried to give it form. She tried her mother, then the taulasea Filivai, then various other women she admired. One day she pictured her tree's aitu as one of Snow White's dwarfs; she tried the supernatural beings she had read about in Barker's books — the Cyclops, the genii, the unicorn. None of them fitted. Then she tried all the animals she knew, and all the fish and other sea creatures. Her patient search led her deeper into the fabulous garden of her imagination. Years later, especially in moments of crisis, she would realise that in her search for her tree's aitu she had explored and groped her way towards the wisdom of her imagination, to a faith that lay beyond logic and belief.

One overcast afternoon, as she had sat cross-legged on the platform, hands on her knees, her back straight, gazing motionlessly into the green foliage, she had let her thoughts settle into a pool so still a whisper could shatter it. She waited. She thought she was dreaming: she saw herself sitting cross-legged on the platform. She waited. Gradually, almost as if a slow melting were radiating through her pores into all the corners of her being, she inhaled the tangy odour of the moss that covered the bark of her tree, like a cloak. She relaxed, with an ecstatic sigh, and the odour not only filled her but the sky and bush and all the creatures in it. Everything was drunk with it. And she knew that the presence of the moss's odour was the aitu of her tree, and now it was in her soul.

When she had surfaced from the spell, evening was starting to cover her tree like a silk black garment.

A few days later, when she had begun to doubt her faith in her aitu, she had wandered to Filivai's home and played a game of lape with Filivai's grandchildren. Halfway through the boisterous game she had pretended she had taken ill and had gone into Filivai's fale.

Filivai was using a stone pestle to pound a mixture of leaves and coconut oil. The pungent odour of the potion reminded Peleiupu of her tree's aitu, as she sat down opposite Filivai, a few paces away. Because she was thought of by the Satoans as Mautu's very gifted daughter, she was welcomed in all their homes at any time. However, like almost all Satoans she was wary of Filivai, because she was a healer not only of physical ailments but of ma'i aitu. Filivai's powers, she had heard Satoans whisper, came from the days of the Darkness: she was heir to an evil heritage that the missionaries and pastors had tried to exorcise. But unlike other taulasea Peleiupu had heard about, Filivai was an earnest Christian who only healed ma'i aitu if it was absolutely unavoidable. And before performing such healing she always asked Mautu, her pastor, for permission to do so. Her father, Peleiupu remembered, had never refused Filivai, and she wondered why. Later in her life Peleiupu would observe that her people's belief in the Christian atua, the Holy Spirit, was only the top third of a pyramid that included, in its three-dimensional body and belly, a feared assembly of savage aitu, sauali'i, sauai and the papalagi-introduced ghosts, vampires, Frankensteins, demons, devils and Satan. Linked to this observation would come the perception that all living creatures were part of a world inhabited by other beings that were visible and invisible, benevolent and destructive.

Now that they were Christians, the Satoans tried not to discuss those other beings within Mautu's hearing. From what Peleiupu had heard and observed, she knew that many Satoans, especially the elders, sometimes met and talked with some of the spirits of their ancestors, at times suffered the wrath of those spirits, and were sometimes possessed by them. Even her parents, who professed utter faith in reason and the Bible, were not free of the feared menagerie that inhabited the murky depths of the pyramid. To her death Lalaga would deny the existence of the menagerie but Peleiupu knew Lalaga feared its existence. On the other hand, her father, whose ancestors had been taulaaitu, as he read more would come to believe more profoundly and without fear in what he would call 'that other reality', in which dwelled the banished spirits of his taulaaitu ancestors and their Atua Fatutapu and all the other presences and spirits. Being a Christian pastor, Mautu would never reveal this to his congregation, but Peleiupu would know and love him more abundantly for it.

'How is your father?' Filivai had greeted her that day.

'He is well, thank you.

'And your mother?'

'She is well too, thank you.'

Filivai trickled more coconut oil into the potion and continued pounding it. Peleiupu watched her. Filivai was over sixty, one of the oldest Satoans, but she looked as young as Lalaga. Only the network of wrinkles on her forehead and cheeks and the looseness of her flesh betrayed her age. Her pendulous breasts, blue-veined around the almost black nipples, hung down to her belly and shook in rhythm to her pounding. She wore only a stained ie lavalava and a towel draped over her shoulders.

'It's going to be a good mango season,' Peleiupu heard herself saying and immediately regretted such a stupid remark.

'If it rains heavily while the mangoes are in flower, there won't be many mangoes.'

'Why not?'

'The rain will break many of the flowers,' Filivai said. Peleiupu wanted more details but wasn't going to be impolite. 'Is it true you read a lot of books?' Filivai asked.

'Not as many as my father or Barker,' she admitted. Then quickly perceiving the opening, added, 'Do you like Barker?'

'He's married to a woman of my aiga,' Filivai evaded her.

'He doesn't go to church or believe in God, eh?' Peleiupu sensed that Filivai wasn't surprised by that.

'You didn't come to talk about the papalagi, eh?' Filivai's unexpected parry surprised Peleiupu who, for a while, didn't know how to counter. 'I'll wipe my hands, then we'll talk.' Using her towel, Filivai started wiping her hands clean of the sticky bits of leaves and oil. 'How many years are you now?'

'Fifteen.'

'But your mind is much, much older.' Filivai smiled. Peleiupu wondered how Filivai had lost her two top middle teeth; there was a thin, white perpendicular scar on her upper lip also. 'Your brain is much older!'

Flattery always embarrassed Peleiupu, so she said, 'I must go!'

'Don't go,' Filivai ordered her gently. 'I am glad you came to talk with me.'

A short while later they were conversing easily.

'I have a tree,' Peleiupu said.

'What kind of tree?'

'An ifi. I remember you telling my parents that in the olden days some trees had aitu or atua.' Peleiupu paused. Filivai nodded. 'My tree has one.'

'Have you told your parents that?' Filivai asked, as if Peleiupu's revelation weren't unusual. Peleiupu shook her head. 'You shouldn't let them know: they are God's servants and may not understand.'

'That is why I came to you.' No reaction from Filivai. 'The atua in my tree reveals itself to me through the odour of the tree. Is that possible?' Filivai nodded. 'It is a kind atua; it heals my pains, always.'

'It comes easily, doesn't it?' Filivai asked. Peleiupu didn't comprehend. 'You know, you see without knowing how you do it. It is a great gift,' she said. 'From God,' she added hurriedly. 'Because of it most people will be frightened of you. Do your parents know about it?'

'If you mean I have intelligence then my parents know I have it, especially my mother.'

'Is she happy about it?'

Peleiupu pondered for a tense moment, and then admitted, 'Don't think so.'

'What about your father?'

'He knows but he is too busy with his books.'

'I knew a young girl once: she had the gift too,' Filivai said, more to herself than to Peleiupu.

'Were people wary of her?'

'Yes,' Filivai emphasised. 'Yes, very frightened when they discovered she could see into the world of atua and aitu and other presences. A world outlawed by the Church . . .'

'What happened to her?'

Filivai gazed at the mat in front of her for a moment. Peleiupu thought she could see tears in her eyes. 'She is alive. She is a simple healer.'

'And the gift?'

Filivai looked away. 'I must continue with my work.'

'I will go now,' Peleiupu said, rising reluctantly to her feet.

'You must learn to hide the gift,' Filivai said as Peleiupu turned to leave. Peleiupu glanced back at her. 'Don't ever try to destroy it. Or betray it. It is what you are.' Filivai refused to look at her.

'May I come and see you again — if I need to?'

Filivai nodded once. 'I don't have the courage and may not be able to help you.'

'Thank you. I'll go now.' Peleiupu made it easy for her.

'Don't expect too much from me!'

Peleiupu walked out onto the malae where the scramble of children were still playing lape.

'Pele's in our team!' one of her friends called.

Peleiupu took a long lingering look at Filivai. Peleiupu waved once. Filivai nodded. Peleiupu decided quickly what she had to do to survive, and skipped into the noisy game of lape, laughing and joking, a girl who appeared to be totally absorbed in the game.

The sun was setting. Two of the search groups had returned only to be instructed by Lalaga to continue the search. Mautu was due home from his fishing trip with Barker and Lalaga didn't want to face his wrath. Some of the old women came and consoled her as they sat on the paepae, gazing hopefully up at the bush and hills and mountain range that darkened, like a fierce tidal wave, as evening dropped. 'She's too smart; she thinks she knows everything!' Lalaga kept saying. 'She's rebellious, disobedient, difficult!' They nodded in sympathy but none believed Peleiupu was like that.

Then Lalaga saw Mautu at the kitchen fale, pulling his bushknife out of the thatching. She hurried towards him.

'I know already,' he called to her. She stopped. He marched past her.

She waited until he was at a safe distance, heading for Barker's home. 'That's why she's like that!' she called. 'You always side with her!'

For a while, as the cicadas cried around her, Lalaga wept. Then she wiped away her tears and returned to sit with the other women in the main fale, waiting for Mautu and Barker and the search parties to return.

'Mautu and Barker told us to come home,' Arona informed Lalaga and the elders. They had their lotu, the young people served the elders (nearly all the old men and women of Satoa who hadn't gone on the search) their evening meal, which they ate in silence, with everyone trying not to look at Lalaga, then the young people ate, bathed, got into their nets and fell asleep, exhausted from tracking through the plantations and bush.

Most of the elders tried to stay awake with Lalaga but fell asleep one by one as the night progressed. Beside the centre lamp Lalaga kept her vigil. At times she prayed for forgiveness, asking God to save her daughter, whom she had mistreated. Every time she dared look into the darkness outside, unwelcome images of a dead Peleiupu jumped into her mind and she would shut her eyes and pray more fervently.

The rooster's crowing unclenched in the centre of her head, it seemed, forcing her out of her sleep. She was still sitting beside the lamp; the elders, wrapped in their sleeping sheets, lay in rows around her; someone was snoring like a boiling kettle. Dawn was spilling out of the east and splashing across the sky. No Mautu. No Peleiupu. She held back the cry. She staggered up, gripped by the most overwhelming sense of helplessness she had ever experienced. Her daughter: how she loved her!

There were people washing themselves at the drums of rainwater beside the kitchen fale. In the half-light she saw Mautu and Barker. Her feet started running, dragging her with them, towards Mautu before she could stop them, and she watched their quick prints melt in the dew-covered ground.

Mautu turned his back slowly, surely, towards her. She stopped. She looked at the other men. They looked away.

Barker stepped in front of her. 'Peleiupu is all right,' he said in Samoan. 'She sleeping with her sisters . . .' Lalaga blocked her mouth with her hands, wheeled, and started hurrying back to the main fale. 'She came back on her own. We found her in the net when we returned this morning,' Barker called.

She was ripping up the side of the mosquito net and reaching down at Peleiupu. 'Don't you touch my daughter!' Mautu's command stopped her. No one moved. Not a sound. As though Mautu's order had stilled everything. She again tried to push her outstretched hands down towards the sleeping Peleiupu. 'Don't!' Mautu's threat was final. 'Let her sleep!'

Lalaga stumbled past him towards the beach.

Mautu got a towel and, with Barker and the other men, headed for the pool. Once they were out of sight, the elders and their children dispersed quietly to their homes, unwilling to face their pastor's anger.

Ruta, Naomi and the other children (who stayed, during the week, at the pastor's home) made little noise as they put away the mosquito nets and sleeping mats and then went to the kitchen fale, leaving the spacious main fale to Peleiupu. She was sleeping peacefully in the large net that was shivering, like a live white creature, in the breeze.

No one, not even Arona, would dare mention anything to Peleiupu about her rebellion. Not ever. They all sensed that Mautu wanted it that way.

They also assumed, without asking Mautu or Lalaga, that Peleiupu and Arona were accompanying the elders and Barker to the Salua fono and Apia.

But from that morning on, they noticed that whenever Peleiupu needed to be chastised or disciplined — a rare occurrence — Lalaga left it to Mautu. 'After all, she is his daughter!' Lalaga told the Satoans.

The Magician of Words

There were three fautasi: Barker's was the lead one and was carrying Sao, Vaomatua, the high-ranking elders, Mautu, Lalaga, Peleiupu and Arona; in the second one were the deacons and some of their wives; the third one carried their food provisions (ta'amu, taro, bananas, yams and pigs) for two weeks. Each fautasi had a crew of rowers, under the command of a tautai, a removable mast and canvas sail that were used when the winds were favourable, and a drummer who beat out the various rowing rhythms.

Barker, in his captain's cap and striped singlet, sat at the stern steering his fautasi; he had invited Peleiupu and Arona to sit on either side of him.

Once they were through the gap in the reef into the open sea, the drummers beat out a smooth, long rhythm and the crews settled into a steady pace. They tried not to think of the sun and the painful length of their journey. The oars dipped, turned, pulled. Dipped, turned, pulled. Peleiupu, afraid at first of the deep blueness of the depths and the waves that pushed up the fautasi and then released it to fall into the troughs that pulled her belly down with it, focused her attention on the drumbeat and the dip, turn and pull of the oars, and was soon distracted from her fear. Ahead, green-blue in the haze, were the islands of Manono and Apolima; behind them, stretching across the brilliantly white horizon, was Upolu, which reminded Peleiupu of a whale she had seen in one of Barker's books.

'Nothing to worry about,' Barker reassured her and Arona. 'It's just water!' Unfolding a hand-drawn map he had made of Samoa, Barker used it to explain that they were going first to the village on the northern tip of Manono — they would spend the afternoon and night there resting, and the next morning make the long haul to Upolu. 'If the wind and current allow us to use our sail, we'll be there by mid-afternoon. The winds between Manono and Salua are usually good, so it'll take us a shorter, easier time to get to Salua tomorrow.'

'Very hot, eh?' Peleiupu said. Barker handed her a sheet of canvas and she covered her head and shoulders with it. Their parents and the elders, who occupied the front of the fautasi, were already hiding under the shade of mats. Sweat was brimming freely from the rowers' bodies.

'Put up the sail!' Barker called to the rowers in the middle of the fautasi.

Soon they were shooting along swiftly, powered by the fully stretched sail. The rowers lay back in their seats; some scooped up seawater and dashed it against their faces.

'Here, you steer!' Barker said to Arona, who grinned and shook his head. 'It's easy. Just rest this under your armpit.' He pushed Arona against the handle of the steering rudder. 'Lean your weight on it . . . That's right. Now just hold it steady . . . Very good. Now, see that hill jutting up on this side of Manono?' Arona nodded. 'Just aim the brow of our boat for that and keep it there . . . Very good.' Barker patted him on the shoulder. 'You'll make an excellent sailor. And you'll be able to visit all those places and countries I've told you about. When I've built my next ship I'll take you with me. Would you like that?' Arona nodded, the rudder bucking like a playful dog under his arms, the fautasi cutting haughtily through the waves, the dizzy air swirling around him. Yes, someday he would go with Captain Barker and explore the world, Arona promised himself, and he experienced a boundless feeling of freedom as he surveyed the sea stretching beyond the limits of his imagination.

'Sailing in these islands reminds me of the Dutch East Indies and the trading I did there,' Barker began another chapter of his adventures. Peleiupu was alert at once. 'I haven't told you about the Indies before?' he asked Peleiupu, who shook her head. 'Good. I don't want to repeat myself. Well, one day while sailing between islands green and golden just like these, we were attacked by Moslem pirates. Do you know what Moslems are?' His listeners shook their heads. 'Keep your eyes on that hill,' he reminded Arona, who straightened up. 'Moslems are people who worship Allah and other heathen gods. Black and ferocious and merciless, they are. In the Indies they were feared by all ships, coastal towns and villages, for they knew no fear and attacked without warning. They didn't fear death either; they believed their souls went to Allah no matter how they died.' Turning to Peleiupu, he said, 'Remind me to give you the books I have about them.' She wished he would stop interrupting his own story. 'How is your English?' he asked Arona. (Hurry! Peleiupu was thinking.)

'Not very good,' Arona enunciated carefully.

'You should read many books, like your sister.' Arona nodded. 'Once your father was the only person I could talk to in English. I even taught him English. Now I have you two, your mother (who doesn't really like me), your other sisters and a few of your father's students. Someday all our people may be speaking English.'

'Why don't your children speak English?' Peleiupu interrupted him.

'Well, as I was saying, our ship was attacked by two pirate ships from both sides with cannons. A devastating barrage that tore into our ship's sides. Then, in the fire and smoke and screaming, they swarmed over our ship like hungry black crows, beaks glittering. We tried to fight them off but they were too many and utterly merciless. I killed one, two, three. But they kept coming at me . . .'

As Barker described the battle in chunks of vivid, powerful description, his body seemed to inflate, as though the stories were vital to its continued survival, recon-firming Peleiupu's observation that, without this endless stream of adventures, Barker wouldn't believe in his own existence.

'. . . Soon we were in chains, all of us who were still alive: some of the crew, some passengers — men and women and children. They refused to believe we had no gold aboard. Our captain, a coward, tried to lie to them. He was soon hanging upside down from the mast, screaming as they whipped him.' He paused, then came alive again. 'Then the pirate captain, a one-eyed snake of a heathen as black as midnight, pulled out his sabre and — zzzttt! disembowelled our luckless captain. His entrails tumbled out and down over his chest and face like long streams of curly hair. And his blood spewed out over the deck and splashed over my feet . . .'

The children were now snared in the weave of Barker's story as he described the elaborate torturing and killing of each crew member and passenger, one by one. Out of all this, Peleiupu would remember for the rest of her life, without horror or moral condemnation, how the youngest passenger, a three-year-old boy in immaculately white clothes, was speared by the pirate captain and, while the screaming child kicked and squirmed at the end of the spear, was held up into the burning air. The evil pirates laughed and laughed, their silver spittle spraying up into the sky, as the boy's blood snaked down the spear in a crimson red rivulet and over the pirate Captain's gold-ringed fingers and hands. Every time she crossed the straits she would see that child, kicking like a balloonfish, at the end of the spear.

She wouldn't remember how Barker had escaped that night while the pirates were drinking and killing and doing other ungodly things to the women: he had untied himself, had crawled down to the water and, floating on a plank, had reached a nearby island. So simple and familiar an escape, yet she wouldn't remember it.

When Peleiupu surfaced from the depths of Barker's adventure, she saw that nearly all the rowers and passengers were now asleep under their mat shades. And as Barker unleashed his second action-packed adventure in the Indies, Peleiupu found she too was getting more and more tired under the increasing weight of her eyelids. She tried pushing off that weight. The hissing, sucking sound of the fautasi gliding through the water slipped like an endless lullaby into her head. 'Manono! Manono! Manono!' whispered the sail of the fautasi.

She was fast asleep when their fautasi glided into the still, mirror-bright waters of Manono.

The next afternoon they arrived in Apia Harbour, after dropping off Mautu, Lalaga and the other elders at Salua for the fono.

She counted nine schooners and yachts in the harbour as their fautasi skimmed across the rocking water. Some of the sailors waved to Barker, who was describing the sights to Peleiupu and Arona.

'. . . Mulinu'u,' he pointed to the peninsula to their right, 'centre of government: bloody scheming Huns trying to take over the whole country!' He spat into the water. 'Apia is made up of three foreign spheres of influence: German, British and American. The foreign area is known as the Eleele-Sa.'

The heat was oppressive, but Peleiupu was oblivious to it because, around her, circling like an embrace, was Apia, the Sacred Zone. She was at the start of a new adventure. She already knew, from Barker's and Mautu's tales, much about the town — its buildings and businesses, geography and atmosphere. Now Apia was flashing in the light, set up against a shimmering backdrop of bush-clad foothills rising steeply to Mt Vaea and the range submerged in a thick bluish haze.

Two of their crew climbed up a ladder to the jetty. Barker tossed them a rope and they moored the fautasi to some pylons. The children followed Barker up to the jetty as the crew unloaded the cargo. 'Nothing to be afraid of,' Peleiupu whispered to Arona, who refused to look at anything but their fautasi. A small crowd had gathered. Barker instructed the crew to take their cargo to Apia village, where they were staying until Tuesday the following week, when they were returning to Salua to pick up the elders. He gave them some money. 'And make sure someone looks after our fautasi all the time. There are thieves in Apia. Understand?'

Peleiupu and Arona picked up their bags from the pile of cargo and, led by Barker, wove their way through the crowd. 'Don't worry, Apia is quite safe,' Barker reassured them. 'And we're going to stay with a good friend, an English gentleman and a famous writer, Leonard Roland Stenson. Have you read him?'

'No,' whispered Peleiupu, clutching her basket of clothes. Arona just shook his head and stared straight ahead.

'You must read him,' he said. 'He's the best!'

They stepped off the wooden jetty onto the soil of Apia. Arona stopped. Peleiupu bumped into him deliberately and forced him to follow the long-striding Barker towards a row of corrugated iron warehouses.

'I didn't want to come!' snapped Arona.

'But we can't go back now, eh?' she replied.

Once around the warehouses they confronted the main street, which, like a dry riverbed, meandered along the beachfront and was lined on both sides by wooden stores and buildings, a few palms and flame trees. Horse-drawn carriages and carts streamed along the street, kicking up a coughing screen of dust.

'Wonderful!' sighed Peleiupu. The books and stories were true. 'Very beautiful!' she said to Arona, who nodded once.

Barker made them wait on the veranda of a large store while he entered it. The air smelled of burning copra, heady and rich.

'Hungry?' Peleiupu asked Arona, who didn't reply as he watched a papalagi woman in white, weaving her bold way across the street, holding above her an orange parasol, the dust surging up and smothering her white shoes and the bottom third of her dress. Peleiupu noticed that the woman was not casting a shadow, and wondered why.

Barker emerged from behind the store on a small cart drawn by a grey horse.

The mango trees along the beach road were in flower, Peleiupu noted as they drove. Some had fruit on them already. Barker had to drive carefully because the road was rutted and alive with treacherous potholes. She observed that only a few Samoans were about, strangers in the Sacred Zone that was controlled by the papalagi. And the town gave out an air of impermanence, as if it were a dream that was here today but would vanish tomorrow; a fairytale town which, when she looked at it, appeared to have been nailed together, haphazardly, and was being allowed to age quickly. She had to possess Apia before it vanished again: she had to.

Turning inland they drove through the village of Apia: fale arranged around a malae and focusing on the largest fale-tele, home of the leading ali'i. Behind these fale was a ramshackle section of papalagi-styled shacks, hovels and houses: a wave of the foreign encircling the traditional centre.

Soon they were beyond the town's outskirts and swamp smell, on a rougher track, and the horse was struggling to pull them up the slope through the cool dampness of a dense rainforest. From out of the deep ravine to their left rose the incessant rumble of the Vaisigano River. The horse's snorting and hoofbeats, the creaking and clanking of their cart, sounded foreign in the solemn embrace of the dark blue bush. She realised Barker had stopped his chatter; she was aware again of his flying-fox smell. She glanced at Arona. He looked more at ease.

Around them the vegetation was streaked with rays of light that were cutting down from the gaps in the creeper-entwined heads of the trees. In the light swam swarms of insects. Occasionally she glimpsed a sparkling spider's web. Pigeons cooed overhead; their cries made her tingle. Caught in the bush's spell, she imagined she was being carried by a flying carpet through an enchanted forest to meet a spinner of tales, a magician of words, Barker's friend, the famous writer.

They broke into the clearing. She surfaced from the spell.

To their right the clearing opened out for about five hundred yards and then ran up against the steep eastern slopes of Mt Vaea. Barker pulled up the horse and, while the sweating animal pawed at the ground and its harness jingled, they surveyed the clearing and its centre, a white red-roofed house that made Peleiupu think of the sedate English country church she had seen in a book. Set in the level greenness studded with tree stumps and stacks of tree trunks under the immense skies and the surrounding hills and mountains, the house looked lost, a puny but valiant attempt by the magician to forge a sanctuary in the wilderness.

'He loves it here,' Barker said. 'He says he's found a home.' He slapped the reins on the horse's flanks and it moved along the track towards the house. 'He's very ill but never shows it publicly. Please don't mention anything about illness to him.' The children nodded. 'He's a brilliant man. But best of all, he is my dearest friend.' There was no sign of life in or around the house. 'You must read his works. I'm sure he'll give you copies, but if he doesn't, please don't ask him. All right?' They nodded again. 'Don't be shy. He likes talking to young people. And he's going to be surprised that you speak fluent English.' His eyes twinkled as he added, 'Yes, he's in for a big surprise at how good an English teacher I am. And how bright my pupils are!' He punched Arona's shoulder.

Barker stopped the cart in front of the veranda steps. The house was smaller but more solid than most Apia homes; it was of rough-hewn timber and had narrow windows and doors, a steeply sloping iron roof and, most surprising of all, a red brick chimney. The wide front veranda had thick wooden beams from which hung pots of orchids, ferns and creepers. So neat and tidy; the house didn't even look lived in. Yes, a magician's home, thought Peleiupu.

They followed Barker off the cart. 'You wait on the veranda,' he said. 'I'll take this to the stables.' He started leading off the horse.

As they walked cautiously onto the veranda, Peleiupu sensed that Arona had again withdrawn into his protective silence.

A circle of six cane chairs surrounded a white cane table on the veranda. At the far side was a canvas sun chair coloured like the rainbow. A large ava bowl leant against the house wall. They stood at the edge of the circle of chairs, facing the front door, which was black like river boulders.

When Barker returned and stood between them, the lonely emptiness of the veranda vanished, defeated by his familiar odour.

'Anybody home?' Barker called. 'I need a drink!' He moved up to the door and was just going to knock on it when someone pulled it in.

Into the doorway stepped the thinnest papalagi Peleiupu had ever seen. She thought that if you shone a bright light into his yellow paleness you would be able to see all of his bones and veins. The man's face was one radiant smile when he saw Barker. 'I need your expensive Scotch whisky!' Barker laughed. 'God knows, you're the only bugger this side of the Equator who can afford it.' The writer opened his arms and Barker stepped into his embrace.

'Welcome,' the writer said. 'Welcome, my lost adventurer who carries the White Man's burden!' Barker hugged him.

Over Barker's right shoulder the writer gazed down at Peleiupu and Arona, with the bluest eyes Peleiupu had ever looked into. The eggshell-white skin of his face was so tightly stretched over the bones, it appeared to be on the verge of tearing. His long, almost fleshless fingers, now pressed into Barker's back, were tinged with prominent pink veins and blond hair.

'And your beautiful friends?' the writer asked. He stepped around Barker and stood between the children who refused to look at him.

'Ask them — they speak excellent English!'

'Your children?'

'Christ, no!' Barker guffawed. 'Do they look ugly like me?'

'No, they are too noble, too beautiful, too well mannered, and too shy!' The writer wore starched white trousers and shirt, a blue cravat, a thick Texan leather belt with a gold buckle, and brown boots.

'This is their first visit to Apia and to the home of another papalagi,' Barker said, sitting down in one of the cane chairs. The writer held Peleiupu's chin gently and turned her face up towards him. She refused to look at him. He smelled of tobacco. 'We all smell vile to them,' Barker added. 'Like flying-foxes. Don't we, Pele?' Peleiupu didn't respond. 'They also consider us uncivilised, barbaric, terribly stupid, clumsy, cruel and very, very ungodly. Sinful atheists, in fact. Isn't that right, Arona?' Arona was trembling visibly, sweat trickling down his legs onto the floor.

'You're frightening them,' the writer cautioned.

'Frightened of us?' laughed Barker. 'My learned friend, the natives tolerate us as beings only one level removed from the state of the beast! I should know, Mr Leonard Roland Stenson. I live with them!'

Ignoring Barker, Stenson asked, 'And, young lady, what . . . is . . . your . . . name?'

'Ha, you . . . are . . . being . . . bloody . . . condescending!' Barker imitated him. 'Like . . . every . . . other . . . bloody . . . bearer . . . of . . . the mighty . . . British Flag . . . and . . . arrogant civilisation!'

'My name is Peleiupu Mautu, sir,' Peleiupu said.

'She even has your accent!' Stenson exclaimed.

'What did you expect? I'm her ingenious language teacher!'

'And you are . . . ?' Stenson asked Arona, who glanced at Peleiupu, who nodded.

'My name is Arona,' he enunciated carefully. 'And our father is Mautu.' Barker was now shaking with suppressed laughter.

'Our mother's name is Lalaga and our village is called Satoa,' Peleiupu recited. 'It is on the island of Savai'i. And I have read many books.' Then, remembering, added, 'All in English, your language.'

'Wonderful, unbelievable!' Stenson whispered. Putting an arm around the shoulders of each child, he said, 'Welcome to my humble home, my refuge. I am honoured having you here.'

Peleiupu looked at Barker, who nodded. 'Sir, thank you for welcoming us to your most gracious home,' she said, copying the dialogue of a heroine from a novel she had read. Barker clapped.

Stenson bowed to his young guests. 'Please go in,' he invited them.

Heads held high, the children walked into the house with Stenson. Barker's loud clapping snapped at their happy heels, echoed through the stillness of the house and then, like a flutter of pigeons, burst out of the back windows and up into a sky that was as intensely blue as Stenson's eyes.

'Sit, sit!' Stenson pointed at the velvet-covered sofa in front of the fireplace. 'You must be hungry.' He disappeared into the next room.

Cautiously Peleiupu and Arona sat down on the sofa. The velvet felt like dog's fur under their thighs and against the backs of their legs.

The room was lined with bookcases stacked neatly with books. A large mahogany desk and high-backed chair with furred back sat to the left of the fireplace.

'Plenty of books,' Arona whispered.

'It is because he is a writer.' She scrutinised the books.

Barker's smell preceded him into the room. 'He really likes you, so don't be afraid,' he said. 'I need a bath.' He left, flicking the sweat off his arms with his hands. They listened to his heavy boots thumping down the corridor into a back room, and the door shutting with a sharp click.

'Are you scared?' Peleiupu asked. Arona shook his head. 'I'm not either,' she said. They sat in silence for a while, listening for the writer to return. Eventually she couldn't resist it any more. She went over to the bookshelves.

'He'll be back soon,' Arona cautioned.

She read the titles and ran her forefinger along the books' spines. 'I haven't read any of these,' she said. She started pulling out a thick leather-bound volume.

'Don't!' Arona called.

Opening the cover, she read. 'It's by him,' she said. 'It's called *The Island of Treasures*.'

Footsteps were hurrying up the corridor. She snapped the book shut, pushed it back into the shelf, ran back and sat down.

'Sorry I took so long,' Stenson said, putting a tray with glasses and a jug of lemonade down on the table. His guests tried not to look at him as he poured three drinks, gave them one each, took one himself and, raising it, said, 'Here's to the most beautiful guests this unhappy home has ever been fortunate enough to have. Cheers!'

Arona glanced at Peleiupu, who raised her drink and, in imitation of their host, said, 'Thank you, sir!' Stenson started drinking; Peleiupu did the same. Arona followed suit. Stenson drank a third; the children copied him.

'Drink some more,' Stenson encouraged them. Peleiupu drained her glass. Arona did the same. 'Good, very good,' Stenson said.

He refilled their glasses. They drank. He refilled them again.

'It must have been a difficult journey?' Stenson asked. They didn't reply. 'One day I'll get Barker to bring me to your village.' Still no reply. 'Your lunch'll be ready soon. Mrs Pivot, my housekeeper, is preparing it now. I hope you're hungry. Mrs Pivot will be upset if you don't eat everything. Are you hungry?' Arona started shaking his head but, when he saw Peleiupu nodding, he did the same. 'Good!' Stenson said, sitting back in his chair, crossing his legs and clasping his bony hands around one knee.

He was determined to make them talk, Peleiupu thought. They had been raised never to talk freely to adults unless spoken to, and she wasn't initiating any impoliteness. According to her parents, papalagi children were spoilt and treated their parents as servants. 'I'm sorry but I can't pronounce your name properly. You must help me.'

'My name is Peleiupu,' she said. She glanced at Arona.

'My name is Arona.'

'They have a beautiful sound. You must spell them for me. Will you do that for me?' They nodded. He pulled a small notebook out of his shirt pocket. Peleiupu spelled her name while he wrote it down. Then he sounded each letter. 'Now spell it in Samoan.' Peleiupu did so. He tried to copy her pronunciation, aloud. 'Not very good, is it?' Smiling, she shook her head. 'You must say each letter for me again.' He copied her repeatedly and, every time he said it correctly and she nodded, he slapped his knee and chuckled.

'Arona is from the Bible, isn't it?' Stenson asked after he had spelled the name correctly in Samoan.

'Yes, Aaron was a prophet,' Arona replied.

'And a very great prophet!' said Stenson. 'Someday you too will be a prophet.' Arona straightened with pride. 'And what does Peleiupu mean?' Stenson asked.

From the doorway Barker said, 'Pele means beloved. I-upu means in words. So the name of this intelligent young lady is Beloved-in-words. How's that?' Barker skipped into the room and winked at Peleiupu.

'A melodious and apt name,' Stenson chorused.

Barker, whose hair was plastered in wet ringlets to his head and down his neck, danced up and, stopping in front of the two children, said, 'And you thought my Samoan wasn't very good, eh?' He smelled of soap. He collapsed into the chair beside Stenson, who started pouring him a lemon drink. 'No, not that!' Barker insisted. 'What I need is whisky. I haven't had a drop in over three thirsty months!' Drops of water sparkled in his beard.

'First, I'll take our friends to the kitchen to eat.' He beckoned to them to follow.

Barker stopped them and said, 'If I get drunk, make sure we get back to the fautasi and then to your parents, on Tuesday, like I promised them. All right?' They nodded and followed Stenson. 'And enjoy yourselves while you're here.'

They had never seen anyone getting drunk before, though they had been told about it by Mautu, Barker and other Satoans. Mautu condemned the taking of alcohol as a sin, and used people and incidents from the Bible to illustrate the evils of drink. As she followed Stenson down the passage she realised that she wanted to see Barker getting drunk and being drunk. (She couldn't imagine Stenson even liking whisky, let alone getting blindly drunk like Noah in the Bible.)

Peleiupu and Arona expected Mrs Pivot to be a papalagi. But when they saw her they weren't sure, for the short, slim woman had green eyes, a delicately narrow face and long nose, and ebony-coloured skin. Mr Stenson introduced them to her and she greeted them in Samoan and told them to sit down at the dining table.

'Yes, sit here,' Stenson told them. Mrs Pivot returned to the stove and continued stirring the pot on it. Peleiupu sat down in the chair Stenson pulled back for her. The food smelled delicious, she thought. The table was set with silver cutlery and plates. Arona sat down opposite Peleiupu when she nodded to him. They stared at their plates. 'Don't be shy: treat my home as your home.' He patted Arona's shoulder. 'And eat as much as you like. Mrs Pivot's cooking is excellent.'

When he left, Peleiupu observed Mrs Pivot from the corner of her eye. Everything about Mrs Pivot was papalagi, Peleiupu decided. Even her dress, yet she was Samoan.

'Is anything the matter?' Mrs Pivot asked when she turned and caught her examining her. Peleiupu shook her head and looked down at her plate.

Mrs Pivot scooped the contents of the pot into a casserole dish and brought it to the table. 'He wanted the meal served exactly as we would serve papalagi,' she said in Samoan without looking at the children. She brought some sliced bread. 'Go ahead and eat,' she said. She smelled of perfume. 'Are you from Savai'i?'

'Yes,' Peleiupu replied.

'Which village?' Mrs Pivot was now getting cups and saucers out of the cupboard.

'Satoa,' she replied.

'Where's that?' Mrs Pivot brought the crockery to the table. 'Don't you like the food?' she asked.

'It is good, thank you,' Peleiupu replied.

'Then eat it!' Mrs Pivot instructed. Peleiupu sensed that Mrs Pivot had placed herself beyond their reach. When she glanced at her brother, she knew he was also experiencing a frightened humiliation. For the first time since leaving Satoa, she wished they hadn't come.

'Is this the first time you've eaten at a table, with knives and forks?' asked Mrs Pivot. Peleiupu nodded. Mrs Pivot collected the knives and forks and placed dessert-spoons by their plates. 'Spoons should be more suitable for you then,' she said. 'Now, I have a lot of other work to do. Make sure you've finished eating by the time I return.' She left, but her threat lingered in the room.

Peleiupu glanced across at Arona. His face was streaked with sweat. 'Let's eat,' she said. They bowed and she said grace.

They wanted to avoid seeing their humiliation in each other, so they dug into the dish of hot, steaming stew and heaped large helpings onto their plates. Peleiupu filled their glasses with water, then, as if by prior agreement, they started devouring the food, stuffing large spoonfuls of stew and hunks of bread into their mouths.

'I don't like her,' Arona said, with bits of bread spitting out of his mouth.

'She thinks she's a palagi,' she said. Her hunger was suddenly a down-sucking vacuum she couldn't fill as she pushed stew, bread and water down into it.

'We shouldn't have come!' Arona gasped in between massive mouthfuls. Peleiupu kept eating as if she were devouring Mrs Pivot's flesh. He tried to keep up with her. They didn't taste the food or feel the hot stew burning the insides of their mouths.

The dish was soon empty. Peleiupu brought the pot and emptied the rest of the stew into their dish. She cut the rest of the loaf. Again they raced through the food, tears welling out of their eyes and mingling with their sweat and the food in their mouths.

They ate.

And ate.

Until there was no food left on the table or in the pot on the stove.

Onto the table they dropped their spoons, leaned their elbows, and lowered their panting heads over their empty plates. 'I still don't like her!' Arona said.

Peleiupu wiped the sweat off her face with the end of her ie lavalava. 'We have to stay with her until Tuesday.'

'I don't want to stay here!'

'We have to,' she said. 'Barker and the writer are good to us. We don't want to offend them.' She paused. 'All right?' He nodded and wiped his face.

Peleiupu started clearing the table.

'So you did like my cooking!' Mrs Pivot said when she noticed the empty pot. When she saw the neatly stacked plates, dishes and pots she added, 'Very good. You're learning quickly how to live in a palagi family.'

'Is there anything else we can do?' Peleiupu asked.

Mrs Pivot told Arona to sweep the room, and while Peleiupu washed the dishes, Mrs Pivot stood beside her telling her what to do. Afterwards she showed them how to polish the cutlery and silverware, and then let them do it at the table while she talked to them. She talked in a thin monotone, in an awkward mixture of Samoan and English. She assumed the children didn't know any English, and explained all the English terms she used.

'My husband, bless his soul, was the captain of a ship, *The Swift Hawk*. He was from Bristol, in England. Mr John Robert Pivot, his name was. A righteous and gentle soul who loved me deeply . . .' She paused. 'He was lost at sea between Tonga and New Zealand six years ago.' Mrs Pivot stopped and Peleiupu expected to see tears. 'We had no children, yet I'm from a large family of nine brothers and six sisters. We were to settle in England after he had made a lot of money in the copra trade, but he died at sea. I had hoped all my life to live in England, in London where my father, Captain James Rutherford Withers, was from.'

Then she described her parents and their thriving business and her childhood in

Apia. 'It was difficult growing up in this small town among the Samoans, so my father sent me to New Zealand to a boarding school for rich people's children. I loved it there among my own people . . .' As she described that phase in her life she became more intense, as though by lengthening and savouring every detail of it she could possess it forever. 'My parents meant for me and my brothers and sisters to return and live in England, our true country, but God hadn't wanted it that way.' There was a bitter pause. 'The dishonest Samoans who worked for my parents stole their money eventually. They even burnt our ship. I had to come back from boarding school to — to this place!' She turned her head away from Peleiupu. 'Now I'm just a paid servant.'

Mrs Pivot must have been beautiful once, like those heroines in the novels she'd read, Peleiupu thought. But fate, by denying her England, had killed that in her. An English lady who'd never been to England, her rightful home. Like Barker she lived in exile, but, unlike Barker, she had not chosen exile. All this Peleiupu would remember and re-examine years later, and, instead of disliking Mrs Pivot, learn to love her.

Late in the afternoon, when they had finished polishing the silver, Mrs Pivot led them through a small garden of shrubs and flowers over a concrete walkway to her one-room house. She showed them the end of the airy room where Peleiupu was to sleep. (Arona was to sleep by the front door, well away from Peleiupu.) She gave them some sleeping mats and a small mosquito net for Peleiupu. The inside walls were a brilliant white, and Mrs Pivot's massive bed occupied nearly the whole of the other end. Around the bed were dressers and cupboards overflowing with her clothes.

'You need to bathe,' she told them. 'You can't use the bathroom — that's for Mr Stenson.' She gave Peleiupu a fat piece of washing soap. Peleiupu got out of her basket the towel Lalaga had packed for them. 'The river isn't far.' Mrs Pivot opened the back door and pointed to the track that led across the clearing and into the bush and Mt Vaea. 'Don't be long!' she called as the children went down the steps.

'She's treating us like animals!' Arona said.

'Perhaps we can do something about her,' she suggested.

'What?'

'I don't know.'

He stopped. The track meandered ahead through the long grass and tree stumps and a thick stand of mango trees into the thick tangle of rainforest and the sound of rushing water. 'I'll think about it,' he said. His shadow, because the sun was now dropping behind Mt Vaea, was a swelling tide of blackness that flowed from his feet backwards over the track and clearing, and Peleiupu imagined it enveloping Mrs Pivot's house and the east, where the sun rose in the mornings.

As they entered the damp coolness of the rainforest she shivered, anticipating the cold of the mountain water in which she would soon be bathing. For an instant she was afraid for Mrs Pivot.

Evening was falling quickly; Mt Vaea's shadow covered the clearing and houses. Their presence, as they hurried back to the house through the grass, stirred the cicadas to life, and their shrill crying was soon a quivering chorus that shook the earth.

Mrs Pivot wasn't in the room. They put on their dry clothes, and Peleiupu hung their wet clothes on the outside line. Arona sat on the back steps and combed his hair. She came and sat on the veranda and, while they gazed up at the darkening mountain, listened to the cicadas and thought of Satoa and their parents at Salua.

They became aware of Barker's and Stenson's laughter and conversation coming from the main house.

'Let's go and help her,' she suggested.

No one was in the kitchen. No sign of a meal being prepared. They could hear Mrs Pivot in the sitting room with the two men. Her laughter was high-pitched. Quietly, Peleiupu and Arona went around the house and, sitting in the shadows on the veranda, watched what was going on in the sitting room, oblivious to the mosquitoes stinging their flesh.

Stenson and Barker sat at a small table in the middle of the room. On the table were two decanters of dark brown liquid. Both men, as they talked, drank from crystal glasses; their faces flushed red as though sunburnt. Behind Stenson, perched in a cane chair near the door into the passageway, was Mrs Pivot. She refilled the men's glasses every time they were empty, and joined in their conversation occasionally.

Peleiupu soon noted that as Stenson drank the whisky, his jade-white complexion became suffused with a healthy pink glow, his manner became more sure and definite, his voice assumed a freer, more melodious tone, and he laughed easily. The whisky wasn't awakening violent demons in Stenson as Mautu had predicted, Peleiupu observed. It wasn't transforming Barker into a violent beast either: he was sinking into a mellow sadness.

She concentrated on what they were saying. '. . . At times they're like precocious children — wilful, capricious, cruel, quick to violent anger. Like children they can also be forgiving, generous, totally without fear or reason. In fact, they live more through intuition and their senses than through reason,' Barker said.

'But isn't it true they have a highly complex social system?'

'Of course, but it evolved over centuries through trial and error — not primarily through thought. There is little innovation; they fear any innovation and change. There is too much respect for customs and traditions . . .'

Arona stirred beside her. 'It's getting cold,' he whispered.

'Get your shirt,' she told him. He disappeared into the darkness.

A few minutes later, he handed her her sleeping sheet and she wrapped it around herself.

'They're terribly arrogant,' Barker was saying. 'They consider themselves more civilised than any other race . . .'

'Including the enlightened, civilised English?' laughed Stenson.

'Yes, even us devils! Cheers!' They drained their glasses. Mrs Pivot refilled them.

'And like human beings everywhere else, they are extremely racist . . .'

'But racism is based on colour.'

'So it is, my friend. Their name for Negro is Meauli, Black-thing, an object — not human. They even make fun of their kin who are darker-skinned . . .'

'So it is based on colour!'

Nodding slowly, Barker raised his glass and said, 'But who doesn't treat others as their inferiors? Here's to my natives and their tolerance and hospitality — and they are kind to me!' They clinked glasses and drank.

'Is that why you've chosen to live among them?'

'I suppose so,' sighed Barker. 'At first, I had to — I was shipwrecked there physically and spiritually. I had nowhere else to go. Nowhere. And I've lost the courage to begin the circle, the search, all over again.' He stopped and, for a few heavy minutes, Stenson waited for him to continue. After drinking another glass, Barker said, 'I was definitely not returning to England and Europe, to the spiritual poverty, the meanness, the sick anxiety of an industrialised society drowning in its own self-love and poisonous vapour, in its ideal of Progress . . . But don't misunderstand me: I didn't choose to stay here because I'd discovered the South Seas paradise, the El Dorado, the Noble Savage that Europe has been searching for since the Fall. No. I came to trade, to try and make a killing — and the "noble savages" will cheat you like anyone else. I was shipwrecked and, for a hellish while, thought I was going mad in all that lushness and kindness. I lived with a chief's daughter for protection and so I could continue trading, and, to my surprise, found I couldn't leave. Today I often think of escaping. But to what? To where?' He emptied his glass and thumped it on the table. 'I think I have become an integral part of Satoa, our village: I am their European trader, a useful pet, and, being a pagan, I'm their living proof of the Europeans' sinfulness and inferiority!' He motioned to Mrs Pivot and she refilled his glass. 'I did find a friend, though — a remarkable man who accepts me for who I am, who sees past my being Satoa's pet European. He is the father of the two exceptional children I brought today.' Remembering the children, he asked Mrs Pivot where they were.

'They've been fed and are now asleep. No need to worry about them,' she said.

Barker described to Stenson how he had taught Mautu English and how he, in turn, had taught his wife and children and a few others in Satoa. 'Now I have people in Satoa I can talk to, especially Mautu and his children, who have an insatiable hunger to learn about the world. He is already far ahead of me in his knowledge of theology and the sciences.' He shut his eyes as if he were in pain, lay back in his chair and said, 'Why do we always end up discussing why we are here in this godforsaken group of islands? Why?'

'Because it is where we are. And you do belong here now!'

'Yes,' murmured Barker, wiping his forehead with his shirt sleeve. 'But what is the meaning of it all? To be stranded on these islands on this exiled planet suspended in the ocean of God's loneliness?' Peleiupu saw the glitter of tears in his eyes. He sat up. 'And why should I worry about it always? Why?' He jumped to his feet. 'You are the author, the thinker — you should know why we're here. After all, you have told me countless times that you sailed here to die.'

'I propose a toast to Her Majesty, Queen Victoria!' Stenson said, rising to his unsteady feet. 'May she continue to produce more expensive heirs!'

'And to the Royal Stud, Prince Albert. May he continue to find the energy!'

The whisky sloshed in their glasses when they clinked them together, hard. They gulped down their drinks and slumped back into their chairs. Mrs Pivot replenished their glasses and took the decanter back to her seat. Peleiupu and Arona watched her pour herself a drink and then, unnoticed by the men, drink it quickly.

From then on, Mrs Pivot drank with the men without their knowledge. She drank one to their every three, then one to their two. Her movements became more restricted; every drink made her sit more still like stone. What was she afraid of? Peleiupu wondered.

'Every time we talk, my friend, we end up wallowing in our maudlin self-pity,' Stenson was saying. His speech was slow now, and Peleiupu had to concentrate to understand him. 'We were reared on God, Queen, country, empire, and our divine right as Englishmen to rule the world. But look where you and I are.' His delicate hands swept the room. 'Cut off from God, Queen and country, in exile in the freedom we searched for, but we feel so alone, derelicts abandoned — yes, abandoned — in what you so poetically identified as "God's ocean of loneliness".' He sank deeper into his chair. 'But it is spiritually good,' he said. 'Sir, it is where I want to be.'

'Enough of this picking at our own boils!' exclaimed Barker. He jumped to his feet, straightened the sleeves and lapels of his imaginary dinner jacket, extended his arms as if he were holding a dancing partner, then, humming a Viennese waltz, started waltzing around the room in time to the music. 'Madam, may I have the pleasure of this dance?' He bowed to Mrs Pivot, who raised her head, stood up, back ramrod straight, and moved into his arms, her face fixed in a radiant smile. To the tune of Barker's humming and Stenson's clapping, they danced round and round the room. 'Bravo! Bravo!' called Stenson.

To Peleiupu, Mrs Pivot appeared as light as a dry leaf caught in the strong arms of the breeze. Soon she was Mrs Pivot on tiptoes whirling and whirling, her senses dizzy with the delight of the waltz.

'They dance funny, don't they?' Arona remarked. Peleiupu tried to ignore him, though she was irritated by his reaction.

Holding an imaginary partner, Stenson stepped onto the floor and danced after his friends. In the white lamplight his sweating eggshell whiteness looked ominously breakable. 'Beautiful, beautiful!' he kept saying. And Peleiupu danced with him. Round and round . . .

Then unexpectedly Stenson seemed to ram into an invisible wall. For a moment he maintained his dance posture, as though he was hooked up by the light, then his knees buckled and he was clutching at his chest as he collapsed to the floor, where he squirmed and coughed, head flung back, face rippling with pain. Mrs Pivot rushed over and, kneeling beside him, pushed back his shoulders, held up his head and said, 'Breathe, breathe, more deeply!' He sucked in air through his mouth in one long gulp and out again. 'Again!' she instructed him. His coughing eased as he sucked in air and exhaled it. Sucked. Exhaled.

Peleiupu, who'd rushed to the window when Stenson had fallen, clutched her sheet around her body. 'I've told him to stop drinking!' Mrs Pivot said to Barker, who was kneeling beside her, wiping Stenson's forehead. 'But he won't listen!'

'Does it happen often?' Barker asked.

'Yes, and getting worse. And you can't do much about it.' She loosened his cravat and unbuttoned his shirt. 'He's very ill but he acts as if he's well.' Stenson was breathing normally again, Peleiupu observed. 'He has little time left.'

'Perhaps that is the way he wants it to be,' Barker said.

'But why? He has so much to live for. He must return to England: this country is bad for him!'

'He doesn't like England; he wants it to end here. Samoa is a beautiful place for that purpose, he keeps telling me . . .'

'He must live!' she insisted.

'Why?'

'For his family . . .'

'He has no family, you know that!' When she didn't reply, he said, 'Get his bed ready and I'll bring him.' She refused to rise. 'You get his bed ready, now! He won't be going to England — and neither will you.'

Peleiupu saw tears on Mrs Pivot's face as she sprang up and hurried out of the room.

'Is this really what you want to be?' Barker said to the sleeping Stenson, thrusting one arm under his shoulders and the other under his knees. 'It's so far away from home, isn't it?' He lifted him up.

Peleiupu and Arona crept across the veranda to the windows of the front bedroom. Mrs Pivot was straightening the pillows and sheets and mosquito net.

Barker came in and placed Stenson on the bed. Mrs Pivoy started taking off his shirt, remembered Barker was present and looked at him. Barker backed out of the bedroom.

As she watched Mrs Pivot stripping off Stenson's clothes, Peleiupu concluded that Mrs Pivot was obviously used to doing it. Her hands lingered as she massaged blood back into Stenson's arms, then his chest and belly.

'What's she doing?' Arona asked.

'Healing him,' Peleiupu replied. She gasped audibly when Mrs Pivot bent down and kissed Stenson's sleeping mouth. Peleiupu glanced at Arona, whose eyes were wide with fascination.

Mrs Pivot pulled away from Stenson, drew the sheet up to his neck, tucked in the mosquito net, dimmed the lamp, then, before leaving, whispered, 'Don't leave me, please!'

In the soft glow of the bedside lamp, Stenson, in the white net, looked as if he were incubating in a luminous cocoon: Sleeping Beauty, shrouded in silk, caught in her enchanted sleep; the Magician of Words would wake only to the kiss of a true princess who wasn't Mrs Pivot, thought Peleiupu.

'I'm going to sleep,' whispered Arona.

They hurried to Mrs Pivot's quarters.

'A lot of mosquitoes,' Peleiupu complained.

'You use the net she gave us.'

She spread his mat by the door, then returned to her net at the other side of the room. He turned down the lamp.

'She'll be angry!' she cautioned as he untied Mrs Pivot's net. He ignored her. He even got Mrs Pivot's pillows. She watched as he tied the net above his own mat and got into it.

Aloud she said a short prayer and lay back.

'You are not to go there again tonight!'

'To where?' she pretended not to understand.

'It is not for your eyes!' It was final. She was gripped by a sudden shame, remembering her curiosity as she had watched the two men and Mrs Pivot, and, most shameful of all, her own brother had witnessed her enjoyment of it.

A while later, as the dull roar of the river was brought to her by the breeze, she heard Arona slip out of the room. In her mind, she watched his feet leaving wet footprints in the grass and on the boards of the veranda.

For a long time she couldn't sleep as she tried exorcising from her thoughts what she imagined Arona was watching.

The sharp thudding cut into her dreams. She woke. Bright morning. Arona had put away his net and mat; Mrs Pivot's bed hadn't been slept in. Peleiupu crawled quickly to the open door.

Arona was chopping firewood behind the stables. She sprang up to go and ask him; knelt down again when she remembered that the discussion of such matters between brother and sister was forbidden.

When she saw Arona going up into the kitchen with an armful of firewood she dressed and hurried to the kitchen. There was a large black kettle on the woodstove that Arona was stoking with firewood. He just glanced at her, then back at the fire. She got cups and saucers and a teapot, the tablecloth and started setting the table. 'Where is everyone?' she asked.

'Still asleep.'

'They drank too much.' No reply. She got a loaf out of the bread bin and started slicing it.

'The kettle is boiling now,' he said. She put some tea leaves into the teapot and he poured the boiling water over them. The steam stung her cheeks momentarily.

'Shall we wait for them?' she asked.

'I'm hungry,' he said, sitting down at the table. She tossed him a rag and told him to wipe off his sweat.

'She mightn't like us eating first,' she insisted. He glanced at her. She sat down, sugared the whole teapot, and filled their cups. She said grace.

She sensed a new confidence in him. She buttered a pile of bread that he ate ravenously, with four cups of tea. She refused to watch him, but when she remembered Mrs Pivot, she didn't resent him his new-found independence.

While she washed the dishes, Arona sat at the table, picking at his teeth with his fingers.

Barker's bedroom door opened and, before it closed again, they heard his sharp snoring. Footsteps approached the kitchen. Peleiupu glanced at Arona.

The doorknob turned. The door was pulled back. Mrs Pivot's sweaty musky odour wafted in. The night had transformed the neat, flawlessly dressed Mrs Pivot into a dishevelled stranger. When she yawned, her mouth seemed to fill the doorway. She hadn't seen them. She stood in the doorway, picking the sleep out of her eyes, then, noticing the fire, she saw them.

'We have eaten,' Arona said.

Yawning again, she slumped into a chair at the table, rested her chin on her hands and closed her eyes. 'Get me some water,' she said. Peleiupu brought her a glass. Eyes still closed, Mrs Pivot emptied the glass in one long motion. 'Have you made any tea?'

'It's in front of you,' Arona replied.

'Pour me a cup,' she instructed. He just sat there. 'A cup of tea!' she repeated. Peleiupu moved towards the table but, when Arona looked at her, she stopped. Mrs Pivot opened her eyes. 'Pour me a cup of tea!'

'The pot is in front of you!' Arona challenged.

'What did you say?'

'Pour your own tea!' Arona emphasised each word.

For an instant Peleiupu thought Mrs Pivot was going to slap him. 'You're very cheeky,' she chastised him. She fumbled with the teapot handle. 'Very cheeky!' She looked away from him. He continued staring at her. Her hands trembled as she poured and some tea splashed onto the tablecloth. Grasping her cup with both hands, she drank. 'It's too sweet! You shouldn't sugar it in the teapot!' She looked at Peleiupu. 'Who did it?'

'Me,' Peleiupu replied.

'Very stupid!' she said in English. 'But what do you expect from Samoans from the back?!' Peleiupu knew that Mrs Pivot believed they couldn't speak English.

'I saw you last night,' Arona said in English. The air seemed to solidify around Mrs Pivot. She couldn't speak. She couldn't move. 'I saw you and Mr Barker.'

'You . . . you are children, you don't understand!' She cried. Only her mouth moved, her eyes seemed trapped in her face. Crrrackkk! Her desperate hand slapped at his defiant face. His head didn't move with the blow; he continued defeating her with his unrelenting eyes. 'You — you *Samoan!*' She pushed back her chair; it crashed back onto the floor. 'Just wait!' She wheeled, her billowing dress pushing her heavy sweaty smell up into their faces.

She fled through the back door.

A short while later, while they were resetting the table for Barker and Stenson, they heard Mrs Pivot's sobbing coming from her quarters across the garden of ginger flower, hibiscus, hydrangeas and gardenia.

'We shouldn't have . . .' Peleiupu began.

'No!' Arona stopped her. The irrevocable finality of his judgement frightened her: she was never going to allow herself to be judged by him. Never.

He squatted and started cleaning the stove.

Peleiupu went and sat on the back steps. The flowers and shrubs were stirring in the soft wind that was sweeping down from the mountains; she concentrated on the movement and the brilliant colours of the flowers, and her mind soon settled into a submerged, silent reef.

For a startled moment she thought everything around her was beating like a gigantic heart. The persistent beat continued. She recognised the booming of a church lali and remembered it was Sunday and time for morning service. She thought of her parents at Salua and her sisters and friends in Satoa, and, realising again that Arona had put himself outside her reach, she looked at the mountains and sky, feeling as though the universe was indifferent to her existence.

She found herself moving silently down the passageway and into the sitting room.

The stale smell of whiskey and sweat rushed at her as she picked her way through the overturned furniture to the bookcases. She pulled out *The Island of Treasures*, and hurried out and sat in a cane chair on the veranda.

She devoured the story: the hunt for treasures through a pirate-infested world.

'She's all right,' Arona told her when he came to get her for lunch.

A neat, self-assured Mrs Pivot was washing dishes at the sink. 'Mr Barker and Mr Stenson won't be having lunch,' she said.

The table was once again set with the best silverware, glasses and crockery. In the centre was a roast chicken decorated with vegetables. And roast potatoes, peas and gravy. Peleiupu trembled as she sat opposite Arona while Mrs Pivot carved the chicken and put large helpings on their plates. 'Is there anything else you want?' They shook their heads. 'I'll be in my quarters if you need me.' She left, still refusing to look at them.

For a while they tried eating with the knives and forks, then Arona gave up and used his fingers. Peleiupu persisted a little longer, but, seeing that Arona was also eating her share of the food, switched.

'Wish there was some taro,' he said.

'And some luau and fish.'

'Palagi food is too light. You get hungry again, too fast.'

After lunch Peleiupu went to sleep in Mrs Pivot's room, while Arona got a mat and pillow and slept under a breadfruit tree near the stables.

Peleiupu dreamt of black-eyed, diamond-ringed, turbaned Moslem pirates with sparkling teeth and evil smiles as sharp as swords, and dolphins leaping through crimson seas, their childlike chatter propping up a sky of laughing children. Just before she woke in the late afternoon she was on an island, digging for treasure with a horde of one-eyed pirates with orange headscarves. Up from the black depths of earth sprang the rusty treasure chest. The lid fell open, like the mouth of a whale, and a slab of white light whipped up into their faces, blinding them. Her arms and hands plunged down into the light and shattered it into a million exploding pieces. She sobbed as she tried to catch the pieces.

'Is there any work I can do?' she asked Mrs Pivot, who was kneading dough at the bench.

'Take Mr Stenson his dinner. It's on the table.' A bowl of soup and one buttered slice of bread, on a silver tray. 'He wants you to bring it,' Mrs Pivot added.

She trembled as she pushed open the bedroom door and stepped into the room.

'Bring it here,' he invited her. With bowed head she went, placed the tray on the table beside his bed, and turned to leave. 'Don't go,' he said. Her body burned as she watched him propping himself up with pillows; he sounded as if he were breathing through thick water. 'Sit here and talk to me,' he said. She placed the tray on the pillow in his lap and sat down, afraid to look at him.

She heard the spoon scrapping through the soup, then his soft sipping. She glanced up. His hair was slicked down over his head, his egg-white skin glowed, his lips were bluish and red-veined. He was trying to control his shaking hands.

'Shall I help you?' she asked in English. He lowered his spoon and she started feeding him the soup. As he ate, his shivering and laboured breathing eased away.

'Are you and Arona enjoying your stay?' he asked. She nodded and lifted the tray off his lap. 'Don't go!' She sat down again. 'Is it bad manners in your culture to look directly at someone?'

She nodded. 'At someone older.'

'Are you missing your parents and village?'

She hesitated. 'I'm not missing them,' she lied.

'That's good. I have a family. Over there.' On the far wall was a row of black-framed photographs. 'If you get them, I'll tell you who they are.'

She unhooked the photographs and brought them to him.

'My wife and I when we got married,' he showed her. 'She was sixteen and I was twenty.' In the photograph was a young woman in a long white wedding dress, and a young man in an immaculate black suit. Unsmiling and stiff. The woman had a delicately thin face freckled with dots like full stops on a page. Her hair was almost silver-white, and her left hand clenched around a bouquet of flowers as if it were a weapon. The youth was paler, his face fuller than now; his fragility seemed trapped in the blackness of his suit. 'That was a long time ago,' he sighed. 'Rebecca was her name. She was music and love . . .' He withdrew into his memories, then said, 'Sorry.'

'My children,' he introduced the next photograph. His wife was plumper now, with a baby in her arms, two teenage sons standing behind her, and a daughter, about Peleiupu's height, sitting beside her. All very formal, unsmiling, posed in front of a large castle — their home. The front of the building was covered with a creeper. 'John, my eldest son, is a lawyer in London, with ambitions of being a Member of Parliament. A soul loved and worshipped by the Almighty and an over-ambitious wife and two very spoilt children. He should've been an artist, a painter, but he fell in love with the daughter of a poverty-stricken lord. I shouldn't be too harsh on her: now I know he wanted to be converted to the pursuit of status and wealth. After all, we all find it difficult to resist the temptations of material comfort . . . I thought Matthew, our second son, would become the scientist I wanted him to be. But after two miserable and expensive years at Cambridge, doing extremely well at his studies, he left without my permission. Now he's an actor in a mediocre troupe performing mediocre plays. Thank God he's happy.' Stenson chuckled. 'He had the courage to be what he wanted to be.'

He paused and asked Peleiupu, 'In Samoa, do young people always have to obey their elders?' She nodded. 'Well, Katherine, our oldest daughter, is obeying her parents. Her mother wanted her to be the wife of an Anglican vicar, preferably one with wealth. Poor obedient Katherine is still looking.' He was turning the photograph over, when Peleiupu asked:

'And your little daughter?'

'She died in an accident,' he said. He showed her the other three photographs of his family at various stages of their life together. 'I had everything,' he said. 'Wealth, fame, a beautiful wife and loving children. I believed I needed nothing else.' He stacked the photographs and she put them on the side-table. She started to leave. 'Stay!' he called. 'I sense you want to know how my daughter died, don't you?' Surprised, she sat down again. 'If you look at me once directly, I will tell you.' She did, quickly, and then away. 'Very good,' he said.

'Marianne was about twelve when she died. She loved horses. When she returned from boarding school during the holidays there was a horse, a birthday present, waiting for her. She was already an expert rider — and a fearless one. It was so quick. One morning while she was out riding on her own, the horse stumbled and she fell off it. When she was found, she was dead.' No sorrow or regret in his voice. 'No one was to blame. It was an accident, pure and simple. But guilt has a strange, cruel, unforgiving way of hunting us out. Within a week of Marianne's burial her mother was speaking less and less to me. At first I interpreted her silences as sorrow, but when I started catching glimpses of intense dislike in her manner, I knew. Unexpectedly, just after dinner one evening, she gazed at me and said simply but with a burning hatred, "You killed her!" Yes, it was as simple as that. She cried, I consoled her, she apologised, and for a few weeks our relationship seemed normal. Then the silences returned, more sullen, more accusing; they got longer and more unforgiving. Soon our home was a house under siege: we avoided each other; talked only when we had to. Fortunately our children were at boarding school . . . One evening, and I can't recall the exact moment of my discovery, I realised *she* had caused Marianne's death — she had persuaded me to buy the horse. Yes, she was responsible . . .

'At dinner that night we sat at the table, locked in our self-righteous hatred of each other. "You killed her!" she whispered. "You let her persuade you to get her that horse for her birthday!" Deliberately, I continued eating as if I hadn't heard her. "Murderer!" she cried, jumping to her feet. I lowered my knife and fork and, gazing at her, said, "You are going insane. Now sit down!" "I won't sit down!" she cried, tears streaming down her face. "Not with a murderer!" I got up slowly and left the table, leaving her to her anger and hatred.

'Eventually we found ourselves sleeping in separate rooms, and whenever the servants weren't there had our meals separately. We were utterly convinced of each other's guilt. Do you understand?' he asked. Peleiupu nodded, even though she didn't. 'I've spent years analysing what happened; there was no logical, sane explanation for our blaming each other, but we did — and that was the important fact. And the more we refused to discuss it, the more it festered inside us. I nursed it and refused, deliberately, to react the way she wanted me to.

'Our friends visited us less and less. We stopped going out. It was as if we loved our silent, destructive war — our destruction of each other. One morning I woke to find she had collected all our children's pictures and locked them in her bedroom. I retaliated: I locked all their toys in my bedroom. That night while she stormed around the house collecting everything else that belonged to our children, I broke into her bedroom and retrieved our children's pictures. On her bed I left a note that read: YOU MURDERED HER. Later, when her anguished cries and curses burst through the house, I experienced a gleeful elation, a joy, and fell asleep with her crying: "I'll fix you! I'll fix you!" . . . And she did,' he sighed.

Remembering who he was confessing to, he spared her the details of her retaliation, her self-destruction. 'She disappeared for a week. The police found her body in a cheap hotel . . . And here I am. To this day, I've tried to persuade myself that I should feel guilty about her death. But I don't — that is the awful, pitiless truth of it all.

Somewhere during our war I lost the love I had for her. And I did love her!' He was again talking to himself. 'The terrible beauty of that love haunts me even now. Not the death of my daughter or the destruction of my wife but the beauty of the love we had for each other.'

Peleiupu waited for him to continue, and when he didn't she asked, 'May I go now?' She noticed that evening was entering the room, and he was falling asleep.

'What's the matter?' Barker asked her at breakfast. She shook her head. 'I'm taking you two into town. Mr Stenson has given me money to buy you whatever you want, as long as it isn't too expensive.' She tried to smile. 'That's the girl. He's well again and in his study, writing. Every day he rises at 5.30 am and writes until breakfast, which Mrs Pivot takes to him. After breakfast he works until midday. He spends the afternoons on his correspondence and things concerning his land and house. Many chiefs from this district come to him for advice, as well . . . You're not listening, Pele!'

'She's all right,' Arona said.

That morning Barker took them from store to store, and, in his flamboyant, loquacious way, showed them the 'treasures' of what he described as the 'world beyond the reefs'. Arona joined in the adventure of discovery, noticing with pride that Barker didn't care whether the papalagi owners and their employees were unhappy with Samoans being treated as papalagi. To humiliate the owners further, Barker insisted on his wards speaking their very correct English, aloud.

Peleiupu tried but couldn't enter wholeheartedly into the adventure. It was as if after learning Mrs Pivot's fragile secrets and, even more devastating, the dark key to Mr Stenson's fate, the treasure house that was Apia was no longer infused with wonder: to her, Apia was now a shabby scatter of buildings and businesses through which the dust moved incessantly.

At lunchtime Barker tied their horse and cart under an almond tree in the centre of the town. He opened a tin of corned beef and a packet of cabin bread. 'Here, eat,' he told them. 'I'll be back soon.' He headed for the bar across the road.

Thirsty and hungry from a morning of walking, Peleiupu and Arona sat on the back of the cart and ate their food. As the shops closed for lunch, they saw many papalagi going into the bar.

An hour passed. The shops opened again. Still no sign of Barker. Arona lay down on the grass under the tree and went to sleep. Peleiupu ripped open the bag of sweets Barker had bought them. For another hour she watched the bar and ate her sweets. The bar grew noisier as the afternoon aged; singing started and she could hear Barker's raucous baritone above the others. She thought of Satoa.

As the shops started closing she nudged Arona's shoulder. He woke up. 'Barker is still in there,' she told him. 'What shall we do?'

'I don't know,' he replied, annoyed at being woken up.

'You should go in there and get him,' she suggested. He shook his head. 'I can't go in there,' she insisted. 'The bar is for men only.'

'So let's just wait.' He knew she knew he was afraid to go into the bar and, knowing that, he was angry with her; she was equally angry with him for being scared. She sat on the edge of the cart's tray, kicking her feet.

The main street emptied of people and traffic; the dust settled; the bar was now full of customers and their singing could be heard all over town.

'I'll go,' she said finally, springing down from the cart.

'We'll wait.'

'What if something has happened to him?'

'We will wait!'

She started across the road. 'I'll get him myself!'

'You're trying to be smart again,' he called. When she didn't stop, he ran up and blocked her way. She stepped to one side and hurried past him.

'Don't!' he pleaded as she stood facing the bar door.

She pushed open the door. The stream of noise and the dizzy stench of beer and smoke hit them. She stepped into the torrent. He slipped in behind her. In front of them was a frightening gallery of papalagi men laughing, talking, drinking, in command. They couldn't see Barker anywhere.

'Let's leave,' Arona whispered. She stood her ground. A tall Samoan waiter was hurrying over to them. Arona tugged at her sleeve. She pulled her arm away.

'You're not allowed in here,' the waiter ordered. When she refused to move, he held her left shoulder.

'Please,' she said in Samoan, 'we came to look for Mr Barker.'

'Wait outside.' The waiter pushed open the door behind them. Arona started to leave. A few papalagi beside the door were now looking at them. Gently, she jabbed her forefinger into the waiter's arm. He looked down at her.

'We're Mr Barker's children, and we are not going to wait outside for him,' she said in her most forceful and perfect English. The waiter hesitated. 'Please find our father for us,' she said. 'Tell him we're here to take him home.' She looked up at him. 'Do you understand me?' He bowed slightly, wheeled and hurried off. Peleiupu's trembling stopped. She had won by discovering intuitively one of the secrets of how power operated in Apia.

Peleiupu turned her back to the bar so she wouldn't have to see the intimidating

tangle of papalagi; she also tried not to smell the cloying flying-fox stench; the ciga-
rette smoke stung her eyes. Arona stood looking at the floor.

Clatter of laughter. Cries of derision. She looked over her shoulder. The crowd
at the bar parted and through it came the waiter, trying to hold up Barker. 'The Savai'i
savage is once again drunk to his eyeballs!' someone called. Laughter tore through the
bar. Everyone applauded. Barker, head rolling loosely, waved and waved.

'How are you going to take him home?' the waiter whispered to Peleiupu, in Samoan.

'In our cart,' she replied.

'I can carry him,' Arona offered.

The waiter wound Barker's limp right arm around Arona's shoulders. Arona
squatted to his knees and the waiter shifted Barker's body across Arona's broad back.
Then, as everyone cheered and clapped, Arona stood up slowly, lifting Barker's huge
drunken weight.

Peleiupu pushed open the door. Arona shuffled out into the street.

'Sorry! Sorry!' Barker kept mumbling, as Arona spread him out on the tray of the
cart. 'Had only one wee, wee drink!' Kicking up his legs, he laughed. His legs landed
limply on the wooden tray. He lay still, then started snoring.

'I'll look after him,' Arona said, sitting down beside Barker.

'But who's going to drive?' she asked. Arona shrugged his shoulders. Inwardly, she
cursed him: now that he needed her, he was quite willing to let her be the older sister
who had to make all the decisions.

She untied the horse, got onto the seat, grabbed the reins and held them tightly
for a tense while, in an attempt to control her fear of the horse and cart. In her mind
she rehearsed every action she'd seen Barker carry out while driving the cart.

Straightening up, she tugged on the reins, the horse's head rose; she pulled on the
right-hand rein, the horse started towards the street; she slapped the reins down
on the horse's back and it broke into a steady walking pace. Her sweat turned cold,
cooling her. As they went through Apia she imagined everyone was watching her and
admiring her ability to drive. She started enjoying it when they reached the turn-off,
and they turned and headed up towards Vaiuta. The mountains were blue and streaked
with the light of the setting sun.

Mr Stenson and Mrs Pivot rushed out of the house when Peleiupu stopped in
front of the veranda.

'Are you all right?' asked Mr Stenson.

'Mr Barker is drunk, that is all,' Arona said, sternly.

'I had to drive all the way,' Peleiupu said.

'Clever girl,' said Mr Stenson. 'Mrs Pivot, you'd better help Arona.'

'Barker's not worth helping, 'she insisted. 'Drunk all the time he comes to stay here!' She helped Barker onto Arona's shoulders.

That evening, after bathing in their first hot baths, which Mrs Pivot prepared, Peleiupu and Arona joined Mr Stenson for a sumptuous dinner of roast pork, vegetables, thick gravy and, most welcome of all, baked taro and palusami.

After saying grace Mr Stenson said, 'Eat, eat. You must be starving after all that walking and having to take care of that overgrown child!'

'May we eat with our fingers?' Peleiupu asked, and, for the first time, found she could look directly at him and not feel frightened.

'By all means!' he laughed.

Then he sat back and enjoyed observing his guests enjoying their meal. Every time he thought they were going to stop, he heaped more food onto their plates.

Afterwards he took them into the sitting room, and for a long time showed them his library. Whenever they showed interest in a particular book, he talked about the book. Science. Philosophy. Biography. History. Travel. Fantasy. Fiction. Drama. Peleiupu was almost overpowered with the yearning to read them all, and all at once. Arona grew bored, and with boredom came sleepiness.

'And those?' Peleiupu pointed at the glass-cased bookcase behind Stenson's desk. So far he had avoided those.

'Just my own books,' he said. 'Would you like to read some of them?' She nodded. Strange that he was embarrassed showing him what he'd written, she thought.

He opened the glass doors of the bookcase, sorted through the books, picked out six of them and, turning shyly to her, said, 'These three are for you, and these are for Arona.' She looked around for Arona: he was sitting in an armchair, nodding off to sleep. She moved to wake him but Stenson told her not to.

She watched Stenson go to his desk and write in the title pages of the six books. In the lamplight's glow he seemed more spirit than flesh, a golden presence.

'Next time you visit me, you must tell me what you think of them,' he said, handing her the books, which she cradled against her body.

'Thank you very much,' she said.

'You and Arona must go to bed now,' he murmured, looking away from her. 'You have to leave early tomorrow.' Slowly, as though carrying a heavy load, he walked to the window and gazed out at the darkness.

Peleiupu shook Arona and he followed her to the door. 'Thank you!' she called, this time in English.

He was motionless; his body seemed to be drinking in the darkness. 'Come back and visit me again soon!' he called.

She followed Arona down the passage and then into the night, which was alive with the cries of cicadas, clutching to her chest his precious gift. Above her the stars — an endless field of them — were like tears that had solidified into sapphires.

Three days later, while they were with their parents at the church fono at Salua, she worked up enough courage to open her three books and read what Stenson had written on the title pages.

His handwriting was meticulous, as unique as her father's. In the first novel, entitled, *The Earl of Bellingtroy*, he had written:

> For my friend Peleiupu, Beloved-in-Words, for her kindness in bringing
> to the heart of an exile the radiant joy of youth, the gift of God.
> Truly yours, L. R. Stenson.

The second novel, *The Island of Treasures*, had in it:

> Peleiupu, may your gift of seeing lead you to see only what is good and
> godly.

And in *The Tide at Falelima*:

> There is little at the end of our journey. Perhaps just the courage to face
> the Night and our Maker. Just a brief glimpse of the fierce light in
> Peleiupu's eyes.

She sat on the rocks in front of the fale by the sea and let the tired waves wash through her grief, until evening wound around her like a warm cloak.

Ten days later they returned to Satoa and she waited. A month passed, then another and another.

'My father has just returned from Apia and he would like to see you,' Tavita, Barker's oldest son, said to Peleiupu and Arona, who were in the kitchen fale cleaning up after their aiga's morning meal.

Without looking at Arona or slowing down, as they hurried to Barker's house, Peleiupu said, 'He's dead. Mr Stenson is dead.' No sorrow or regret: just like Stenson's description of his daughter's death. Stenson would have been proud of her.

As they entered, Poto motioned to Peleiupu to sit in the chair beside her. She held Peleiupu's arm. 'He left this letter for you,' Barker said, holding the large white envelope out to Peleiupu. She placed it in her lap and continued, with Arona, to gaze at Barker, who was avoiding their scrutiny as he sat in his chair. 'Oh, and in his will he left you all his books. That is, all the books you may want from his library.' He paused. 'Good, eh?' They refused to look away. He fidgeted; he sweated. Poto continued caressing her arm. 'Next time I go to Apia I'll bring back the books you choose. Is that all right?' Peleiupu nodded once. 'That's all,' he said, half standing up and then flopping back into his chair. They made no move to leave.

'Paka, that is not all,' Poto reminded him.

'Yes, and, ah, Mrs Pivot is well provided for. Yes, ah, he left her the house and everything in it. And ten acres — lucky woman. She doesn't really deserve his generosity. The rest of his property he's left to relatives.' Barker stopped again and, for the first time, looked beseechingly at them. 'What are you waiting for, eh?' No reply. 'He's dead! That's all! You know he came to Samoa to die! What else do you want me to tell you, eh?' He was in flames, he couldn't hide. 'Damn you, what do you want from me? You want to see me cry? Well, I won't. He's dead. Finished. Buried. Maggot-meat! Now go.' They got up.

Poto put an arm around Peleiupu's shoulders. 'The children are in pain,' she said.

'No, sit down. Who told you to leave?' Barker demanded. They sat down again. 'Bloody hell, you're only children. Why should I treat you like equals? Eh, why? And why he ever bloody well discovered a deep affection for you during one short visit I'll never fathom. Why do you think? Answer me!'

'Because we speak fluent English,' Peleiupu replied.

'God, the bloody cheek!' he exclaimed. 'The bloody brazen cheek!' He slapped at his knees and laughed. Poto started laughing too. 'The wonderful cheek!' he cried. 'No wonder he liked you. You weren't scared of him one iota, were you? And you saw right into his skeleton, didn't you? When he got to know you, he saw the meaning very quickly: he was just a sick, dying European in exile; a poor benighted consumptive who believed in nothing.' With quick hands he wiped the tears from his face. 'And to think that I took you to show you off to him!' He paused. 'Without knowing it, you made him see so very clearly, starkly, the futility of it all.' Quiet now, composed, he gazed at them for a long while. Poto smoothed down Peleiupu's hair. 'You knew he was dying then?' he asked. Peleiupu looked at the floor. 'Was he a good man?' She nodded. 'Even if he didn't believe in God?' She nodded. 'Because that isn't impor-tant?' She nodded. He sighed as if a great guilt were lifting from him.

'. . . I *loved* him,' he admitted, finally. 'We Englishmen avoid using that word. We are raised to consider it womanish, weak, something sick, especially in relationships between men. But I did love him. Who would have ever dreamt that I, an uncouth buffoon, would, in the wilderness, find a real friend? A true, loving friend who was utterly honest about our condition and our end. I was fortunate to meet your father and Stenson. So *tragically* fortunate. Why tragically? Because they opened my heart to who and what I really am and what I am on this planet and in the universe. To the beautiful futility of it all. And to love — yes, and especially that!' He stopped weeping.

Poto threw him a cloth, with which he wiped his face. 'Someday, Pele and Arona, you will grow to understand what I'm trying to say. Someday. But today, Stenson is dead and we are here. That is all. I must, as a true Britisher, continue to live the best way I know how. According to the flag. According to the standards of a true English gentleman!'

Barker then described how Stenson had died. For the rest of her life Peleiupu would cherish every detail of it as a vital story in the mythology of her life.

The night before his death, Stenson had invited Basil Huggett, the British Commissioner of Lands, to dine with him and Barker. A cheerful meal, with the fine claret wine that Stenson loved, delicious food, and invigorating conversation that brought the world beyond the reef and all its richness into his house again. As usual he went to bed early, rose at six o'clock and wrote until lunchtime when he ate soup (as usual) with Barker, and told Barker with pride that his new novel, *Weir at Lammington,* was going well. Afterwards, while Barker supervised the workers who were cleaning out the stables, Stenson lay on the veranda, reading.

At about five o'clock Mrs Pivot called Barker to the house. Nothing was wrong, thought Barker as he walked in and found a frightened Mrs Pivot chafing Stenson's hands while he was slumped in his chair, unconscious and breathing heavily. Barker touched Stenson's forehead: it was fiercely cold and slippery with sweat.

'He's dying!' she cried.

Barker rushed back to the stables, saddled the swiftest horse and galloped down for the doctor.

The doctor could do nothing when they reached Vaiuta.

Barker arranged Stenson's funeral and burial and was surprised to find that he was loved by so many people. The matai, who were his friends, arrived in ceremonial groups with ie toga and sat around his body and coffin that night. Church choirs from nearby villages sang all night in his house.

When Reverend Ashley of the Anglican Church arrived, Barker explained that Stenson had wanted a simple service: a prayer that Stenson had written was to be read at his graveside. That was all. Reluctantly, Reverend Ashley accepted.

In discussions with the matai, Barker informed them that Stenson had wanted to be buried under the splendid stand of ironwood trees by the river. Quickly they cleared the spot and dug the grave.

As Stenson had wished, they buried him at three o'clock in the afternoon.

After Mrs Pivot's grief had eased a little, she described to Barker how Stenson had collapsed. After fetching a bottle of wine from the cellar, Stenson had helped her make mayonnaise. With a steady hand he dripped the oil into the mixture, drop by drop.

'What's that? What a pain!' he had cried suddenly, clasping his hands to his head. 'Do I look strange?' he asked her. He collapsed to his knees, body shaking painfully. Clasping him around the waist, she half lifted, half dragged him into the sitting room.

Within minutes he was unconscious.

'Stenson died at ten minutes past eight that evening, at the age of forty-four,' Barker ended his story. 'Eleven years younger than me. Because he had been ill with tuberculosis for a long time, everyone had expected him to die of that. But his cerebral haemorrhage came swiftly and suddenly.'

Peleiupu looked up at Poto. 'God will make everything right again,' Poto whispered.

On their way home, Peleiupu read Stenson's letter and then gave it to Arona. That night when everyone else was asleep she read it aloud to her parents, with a fierce pride.

The next morning she remembered Stenson had bequeathed his library to her, so she told her father that on his next visit with Barker to Apia they should bring back as many books as their fautasi could carry.

The week before Christmas, while Satoa was harvesting its richest mango crop ever — everyone got fed up with eating mangoes and much of the fruit fell and rotted, the stench of decay gripping the village — Mautu and Barker, to the astonishment and awe of every Satoan, brought home the biggest library of books in Savai'i and, some said, in the whole country. A grand total of 3999 books.

Barker and every Satoan elder who knew something about carpentry helped Mautu construct twelve double-shelved bookcases. While this was happening, every Satoan found an excuse to visit Mautu's home and inspect the work and, if lucky, be allowed to help Peleiupu and Lalaga wipe the dust off the books.

Only Barker and Poto were absent the night Mautu, Lalaga and Peleiupu stacked the books, one by one, into the bookshelves. The Satoans witnessed the public storing of all the thoughts and ideas and wisdom in the world, in their pastor's house in their humble village. They would treasure that memory for the rest of their lives, and tell those they met that the treasure of wisdom had been a gift to the beautiful Peleiupu from the most famous writer in Barker's country, England.

About a month after what came to be known as 'The Storing of Wisdom', the mango trees in Satoa were bare of fruit.

Rain in the Box

It was a light, persistent rain, which first swirled in from the sea in pursuit of a flock of matu'u, and stopped to wash the children who rushed out of their homes and splashed and laughed and danced in its silver coolness. When the children lost interest, it stayed over Satoa and extended up to the top of the inland range, making everything smell of fresh seaweed and coral. As mould mushroomed in the fale — in the damp places, in the rubbish heaps, and even under the Satoans' toenails — the rain acquired, over a month of persistence, the inescapable odour of decay.

During its life, most Satoans forgot what sunlight was like. The grey blanket of cloud blocked out the sun and affected their sense of colour: the world became a swimming, shadowy place of greys, dark blues, dull wet greens and browns, with flashing shades of running water. A dank dampness and fermenting mould everywhere. In the humid heat seeds germinated and grew lushly. Some people believed that their hair was lengthening at a phenomenal rate.

The rain wasn't heavy enough to disrupt the usual pattern of life: the children went to school, the men tended their plantations and fished, the women did their usual chores. However, the rain's incessant, relentless drone, its hypnotic, throbbing rhythm, surreptitiously became the heartbeat of Satoa. The beat muffled other sounds. People talked less, listened more, and withdrew more often into their thoughts and dreams.

During its first week of occupation, the rain washed the dust and dirt off everything, gathered it on the ground in rivulets and eager, snaking streams and drove it with other rubbish down the slopes into the pool and the river and the sea. It was a cleansing of the whole village as though in preparation for an important visitor or event.

In the time of the rain, Mautu and Barker didn't visit each other. Rumour had it that Barker was confining himself to the back room of his store where, in the light of candles, he was writing a manuscript that grew fatter with every rainy day. It was as if he had been seized by a demon that was not going to free him until he had finished writing down whatever terrible confession it wanted him to make. With every unwashed day his flying-fox smell germinated and fermented and expanded, like a drowned corpse, in the room. Even Poto and their children couldn't bear the stench, not that they dared disturb him. And, as his confession fattened, Barker himself thinned, became gaunt and hollow-eyed.

Without explanation, just before church service on Sunday morning, the rain stopped and left the air to the usual acrid smoke of umu, and a booming silence.

Barker, so Poto would later describe, shuffled out of his room, his dirt-caked clothes around him like a ragged second skin, his stench weaving out into the bright light, and stood on the store veranda, manuscript under his right arm. As he surveyed the village, he laughed softly. Then for a long, long time he gazed up into the deep sky, as if he were searching for an end to infinity. 'He's old, old!' Poto would tell others. 'His month-long fight with that demon has left him very old, empty of his usual fury.'

'It's very beautiful!' Peleiupu said when her father handed her the small wooden box.

'Yes. It was sent by Barker,' he said. Afternoon classes were over and they were alone in their fale.

Carved into the wooden lid were Chinese mandarins holding umbrellas and standing before a gathering of students. 'Is it very old?' she asked.

He nodded. 'Barker must have got it from China on one of his trips.'

'What's in it?' The small bronze lock was open.

'Papers that Barker has written. It is not to be opened and read until after he has . . . until after he has passed away.' On Mautu's desk was a letter. He picked it up. 'And when the box is opened I am the only one allowed to read what is in it.' He gave her the letter. 'And after I die, the box and its valuable contents are to be yours. No one else is to read it.'

'Not even Lalaga?' she asked.

'Not even your mother.'

'And after me?'

'His letter doesn't say. Perhaps it's meant for the eldest child of every generation in our aiga.'

He watched her as she read Barker's letter.

'What are you going to tell Lalaga and our aiga?' she asked as she returned the letter to him.

'She will be dissatisfied that the box and Barker's papers are meant for us only. But she will respect his wishes. So will your brother and sisters.'

For a while she was thoughtful. Then she asked, 'What do you think he has written?'

'I don't know,' he murmured. 'But it must be important. Perhaps it is all the knowledge he acquired on his voyages.'

'And stories about all those creatures he has seen!'

Later as she returned to the kitchen fale, the concluding sentences of Barker's letter wound around her and she couldn't escape their pain:

> I do not need to remind you, my friend, that curiosity killed the cat. If
> out of curiosity you open the box before the prescribed time, I will be
> the cat and become maggot-meat before I am ready for it . . . By the
> way, when I die please bury my carcass up in the hills in the village of
> the People. I will find peace with them. There is to be no church service
> for me.

That night, after their English lesson, when everyone else had gone to bed, Mautu told Lalaga and his children about the box, its contents and Barker's wishes.

'No one, absolutely no one, is to touch or open the box!' he emphasised. 'It will be locked in my trunk until it is time. And if anything happens to me before then, only Pele may open it and read its contents. That is Barker's wish.'

'But why should it only be her?' insisted Naomi. He looked at her. She fell silent.

They watched as he wrapped the box in a piece of new calico and placed it under his clothes in his trunk, and locked the trunk.

Barker's book was perhaps the magic key to unlock their past and future: the prophecies that would give meaning to the generations of her aiga, Peleiupu thought.

After the children went to their mosquito nets, Mautu turned down the lamps.

'Is he dying?' Lalaga asked.

'I don't think so.'

'Then why has he made his will?'

'I want to sleep.' He lay down. She spread his sleeping sheet over him.

'Why?' she whispered.

'It is a papalagi custom to make your will well ahead of your death.'

They lay in silence for a while. The night pressed down on them. 'I'm afraid,' she said.

'Of what?'

'Of the box and its contents.'

'You've never liked him, have you?'

'I never said that!'

'But it's true?'

'Yes,' she admitted. 'He doesn't believe in God, and he has no respect for God's Church.'

'What has that got to do with his written legacy?'

'I am just afraid,' she tried to explain. 'Afraid for you and Peleiupu.'

'Because we will be the only people to know what he has written?'

'Yes,' she whispered.

'I'm afraid too,' he admitted. 'Fascinated by what I may find, but afraid of it as well.'

He remembered that it wasn't raining any more. In Barker's ancient Chinese box was locked the source of the rain, Mautu speculated.

A Tatau for an April Fool

1 April 1896 was a day Mautu and Peleiupu would always remember, because at midnight the night before, a manuali'i had flown over their fale, screeching piercingly in the limpid quietness and waking them. They believed that someone in their aiga was going to die, but instead of the morning bringing death, it brought the rumour that Barker was having a tatau done.

Peleiupu sensed that Mautu was upset by it. After their morning meal he insisted that she accompany him to Barker's home. Mysteriously, Barker had been absent from his home for over a week, and now they knew why.

'Where is he?' Mautu asked Poto, who was in the back fale, breastfeeding her latest baby. He stood with Peleiupu on the paepae.

She avoided looking at him, and took her time. 'And how is your family, sir?'

'Well, thank you,' he hurried. 'Is it true what I have heard? Where is he?' Poto pretended she was having problems feeding her baby. 'Is it true?' he repeated.

'Sir, what is it you have heard?' She looked straight back at him.

'That he is having a tatau done.'

'Sir, I don't know if that is true,' she replied. 'But if it is, then I support his decision.'

Mautu wheeled. Peleiupu had to run to keep pace with her father as they hurried through the plantations. Slow down, she wanted to tell him. She remembered that their church didn't allow any man with a tatau to be a deacon: that's why her father was angry.

Peleiupu glanced up into the tall, bushy mango tree that marked the entrance into Barker's plantation. The shadows in the tree looked like rows of people facing each other. She hurried after her father into Barker's plantation.

Through the lines of banana trees they glimpsed a small fale with a raised wooden floor; they couldn't see into it because the blinds were drawn. A lean sow with her piglets scampered away from under the fale as they approached. Mautu told her to wait outside, then he disappeared around the fale and she heard him raising a row of blinds and going inside. The air smelled of decaying coconut.

'No one, absolutely no one was to come here!' she heard Barker say in English. 'I told my family that.'

'Please leave us alone for a while,' Mautu instructed the others inside the fale.

'You, you no go anywhere!' Barker ordered them in Samoan. People started rising and shuffling out. 'You no go outside!' Barker insisted.

Peleiupu peered around the fale. Paepaeali'i, the leading tufuga ta-tatau in Satoa, and three of his apprentices were coming out and heading towards the small kitchen fale, which was half-hidden by clumps of hibiscus and ginger. The crimson ginger flowers reminded her of long bleeding tongues.

'They're scared of you, aren't they?' Barker was saying in English.

'Perhaps it is respect, not fear,' Mautu replied.

'Respect? Respect! They're all afraid of the Church!'

'You are trying to distract me.'

'From what?'

'From your tatau.'

'Oh, that. It's half-finished. And, as you can see, its covered with sores and blood . . .'

Peleiupu peered through a hole in the nearest blind. Barker, wearing only an ie lavalava, was seated on the floor, his legs covered with a mat. He was nearly all skin stretched tightly over bulky bones; his flesh hung from his arms, and she could count his ribs. Above his ie lavalava his back up to his midriff was covered with a black tatau, which was barely visible under the lines of sores and scabs caused by the serrated edge of the chisel puncturing the skin.

'Are you well?' Mautu asked in Samoan. Barker nodded and closed his eyes. 'How long has it been?'

'How long?' Barker sighed. 'About two weeks. But it has seemed like forever. The pain, that is.'

'How much more?'

Shaking his head, Barker said, 'Got half my arse and thighs down to my knees to go yet!' He leaned back on his hands and stretched his body. 'Now I understand what physical pain can be.' He paused. 'And what a youth has to endure to become a man!'

'You should take longer to have it done.'

'I can't afford the time,' Barker said. 'And I do have the courage to have it finished in record time.'

'It usually takes about fives weeks. You can die from loss of blood if you have it done too quickly.'

'I don't have the time,' Barker murmured. 'What day is it?'

'Tuesday.'

'The date?'

Mautu thought for a moment. 'First of April,' he said.

Barker sat up immediately, his body inflating with laughter that burst, in large spasms, out of his mouth and echoed around the fale and out into the plantation. As she watched him, Peleiupu imagined that his loud happiness was the bird motifs on his yet unfinished tatau detaching themselves from his skin and scattering, in a humming clatter, through the vegetation up to the mountains and across the seas to England and Barker's castle, where they would tell his family that their lord was converting himself into a tattooed pagan and enjoying the magnificent pain of it.

Mautu let him laugh it all out.

'Do you know what the first of April is in my country?' Barker asked. Mautu shook his head. 'It is called April Fool's Day. It is the day during which you're free to play practical jokes on anyone, including our short Queen!' Smiling, he added, 'This year, the joke is on me!'

'Why did you decide to do it?' Mautu asked. They were back into their usual pattern, with Mautu speaking mainly in Samoan and Barker in English.

'Of all people, you should know why. Your father and his father both had tatau.'

'But that was before we Samoans knew better.'

'You mean before the missionaries banned the tatau as being pagan and evil.' Barker waited for Mautu to reply; he didn't. 'Do you believe it is evil?' Barker pursued him.

'It is something from the time before the Light,' Mautu countered.

'But do you believe it is evil?'

Mautu looked away. 'That is what the Church has ruled.'

'Yes, but do *you* believe?'

Peleiupu wished Barker would stop his attack. She waited. Mautu lowered his gaze.

'It's all right, my friend,' Barker saved him. 'There are times when we do what we have to do.' He smiled. 'History is irony: I am now the pagan and you are the Christian missionary. Or, let's say, because my tatau is only half-finished I'm just half a pagan!' Mautu laughed with him.

'Where's Pele?' Barker asked. Mautu told him and he called her into the fale where, as was the custom, she sat down at the back posts. 'Don't be afraid,' Barker said. 'I'm not a complete skeleton yet. And when it's over, I'll fatten up again quickly.'

'When it is healed, the black tatau will look striking on your white skin,' Mautu said. He then explained that the worst disgrace was a pe'amutu, an unfinished tatau; once the first black line was tattooed across your back you had to have the tatau finished. 'The disgrace of a pe'amutu won't die after you die — it will live as the shame of your children and aiga.'

'I'm not going to disgrace my children. Or you, eh!' Barker chuckled.

'I'll come and be with you every day,' Mautu said.

'What about what your Church and the others will say?'

'I'll tell you humorous stories to distract you from your pain,' Mautu replied, ignoring his question. 'We certainly don't want you to be a pe'amutu!'

On their way home that afternoon Mautu instructed Peleiupu not to tell anyone about Barker's tatau. 'It is not for your eyes either,' he said.

She remembered Barker's remarks about April Fool's Day and his being his own April Fool, and was puzzled by them for a long time.

During to'ona'i that Sunday some of the matai informed Mautu that Barker was being tattooed. 'It is almost unbelievable that a papalagi is having a tatau!' someone added. The others laughed, believing that papalagi were not courageous enough to withstand the pain.

'He'll be our first pe'amutu!' someone else said. Their laughter continued.

'Why is he having it done?'

'Because he is the only pagan left in Samoa!' someone improvised.

'Yes, a Pe'a Pa'epa'e that'll fly back to Great Britain!'

'Without wings!'

'Or a tail!'

Throughout it all, Mautu pretended he was enjoying it; he avoided Lalaga's accusing gaze.

That night, after their children were asleep, Lalaga asked, 'Are you helping him through his tatau?' He refused to answer. 'Our Church does not allow tatau any more,' she reminded him.

'He is a palagi,' he excused himself.

'But I thought you considered him one of us?' She stalked him.

'Yes, he is my brother! And don't dare remind me that, being a pastor, I have to enforce our Church's laws. Understand?' When she maintained her accusing silence, he threatened, 'And don't remind me about what our people are going to say once they find out I'm helping Barker through his trial!'

'Why do you call it "his trial"?'

'You know why.' Roughly, he pulled up his side of their mosquito net and rolled out. The pebble floor cracked and crunched under his feet as he rushed out of the fale.

Once again, Lalaga cursed Barker for being the perpetually questioning darkness in the life of her aiga. Barker was a pagan, a white demon, from the pagan past of England, and now — and she didn't want to accept it — an aitu out of the time of Darkness before the Light, clothed in the most pagan of clothes, the tatau. Why did Mautu refuse to see him for what he was?

She fell asleep waiting for Mautu so she could apologise to him and he could reassure her that they were safe from Barker.

Out of the shimmering pools of infinite starlit space Barker emerged like a fabulous sea creature, his naked body aglitter with droplets of water. Defiantly he stood above the down-sucking waves, which were as blue-green as his eyes. His tatau was the sleek sheen of shark skin. Suddenly she saw Mautu floating spreadeagled on the water; he looked so naked and helpless, she wanted to reach out and embrace him. She wept in gratitude as Barker clasped Mautu's right hand, pulled him up to his feet and around Mautu's waist and thighs wound his tatau, clothing him, covering his nakedness.

Barker turned slowly and faced her. Reaching out, she cupped Barker's genitals in her hands and caressed them until they grew warm and strong. Around her the light sang of her gratitude for the marvellous gift Barker had given her husband.

It was early dawn when she woke to the wind shuffling noisily through the fale blinds, bringing with it the musky tang of low tide. With a breathless shame she remembered the sexual nature of her dream and tried immediately to obliterate the memory and the thought that she had betrayed Mautu with Barker, but Barker's penis grew insistently larger and stronger in her thoughts.

She caressed Mautu's chest and, after a while, the easy rhythm of his breathing reassured her once again that he knew what he was doing with Barker.

In his sleep Mautu turned to face her. She moved up against him and his warmth burnt into her breasts and belly.

That afternoon she started cooking special dishes and sending them with her children to Mautu and Barker in the plantation; she also refrained from discussing Barker's tatau with Mautu.

'This is the last day,' Mautu told her one clear morning. 'He's too weak, so we'll have to bring him home on a dais . . .'

'Like a victorious warrior . . .'

'More like a badly wounded one!' he said. She smiled. 'Thank you,' he added.

'I am not afraid of him any more,' she confessed.

'Perhaps God sent him to our aiga and village for some special purpose,' he said.

Standing on the paepae, she watched him walking away through the bright air and into the plantations. Her love for him was a vibrant song that held everything together. How she loved him!

'Are they bringing Barker back this afternoon?' The voice shattered the spell. It was Peleiupu. 'Mautu said they were.'

Lalaga pressed against her daughter and realised that Peleiupu was now as tall as her. 'Yes, they're bringing him this afternoon,' she replied.

'I love him,' Peleiupu admitted to her for the first time.

'Who?' Lalaga asked.

'My father!' she said. Lalaga wound her arm around her daughter's waist and held her tightly. For the first time she didn't care if anyone was watching. 'Barker too,' Peleiupu whispered.

A crowd of mainly children gathered around Barker's fale when Mautu and the tufuga brought Barker home on a dais of branches that they had tied together. Poto had prepared the fale because Barker had insisted on occupying the fale instead of his bedroom.

They lay him down on a thick layer of mats behind drawn curtains, and Poto covered him with a sleeping sheet. 'Enough!' she instructed her youngest children, in Samoan, when they started crying. 'Enough! Your father isn't dead yet, even though he looks it.' Their weeping grew louder. 'Sir, you tell them, please.'

'Your father is all right!' Mautu ordered. 'Go and cook something for him to eat.' Obediently, the children scrambled up and rushed out to the kitchen fale.

'Mautu, they listen to you. They not listen to me, never,' Barker said in Samoan. 'We should've stayed in my plantation; it's quiet without those people,' he added in English.

'Ia, that's enough!' Poto called to the crowd. 'Go home now!' They dispersed. 'You rest. Just eat, sleep, rest. Let your tatau heal,' she said to her husband.

'Thank you; you helped pull me through,' Barker said to Mautu.

'What is a friend for? Now sleep. I come and see you tomorrow.'

'Thank you for all your help,' Poto said to Mautu.

A few paces away from Barker's fale the image jabbed at the core of Mautu's head.

Barker was almost a skeleton: a ragged, dehydrated bundle of flesh and skin wrapped around a brittle frame of sticks. Frightened, he glanced back at his friend.

Mautu and Peleiupu visited Barker at mid-morning every day except Sunday, and stayed until mid-afternoon. While Mautu and Peleiupu were there Barker allowed only Poto into the fale. Soon a routine was established. On arrival Mautu said a prayer in Samoan: Barker, the supposed pagan, insisted on this. After that, the two men discussed anything and everything; when that proved boring, Peleiupu read aloud from the books she had brought. Barker wanted her to read from Stenson's library, progressing systematically from A to Z. She was not allowed to omit even the reference books. 'What about the dictionary?' she asked. 'That too!' Barker replied. 'Especially that — it's good for taming the soul.'

At midday, when the sea was warm enough for Barker to bathe in, Mautu helped him to his feet and, propping him up, steered him down the paepae, through the breadfruit trees and bananas to the beach and into the water.

When the salt water stung Barker's healing sores and scabs he yelped with pain, bobbed up and down and wheeled round and round, slapping at the water, while Mautu sat on a boulder laughing and telling him that was not the way of the courageous warrior.

'It feels like a million knives!' Barker cried.

'Salt heals your wounds!' Mautu called.

Afterwards, Barker emerged unsteadily out of the water, and Mautu and Poto helped him across the soft sand. Barker would stand in the shade of the breadfruit trees, with the water weaving like brilliant worms down his wrinkled body, while Poto dried him carefully so as not to hurt the sores. Every time Barker winced, Poto said, 'E, you're a coward!'

When they reached the paepae Peleiupu handed Barker a dry ie lavalava and returned to the back of the fale while he stripped off and put it on. Poto then drew the curtain across the fale. Behind it, Barker lay down and his wife dabbed coconut oil into his healing tatau, soothing the stinging pain.

'You need haircut and shave,' Mautu suggested at the end of the second week.

'That's what I've been telling him,' Poto said. 'He's looking like a real savage.'

Barker pulled the two long plaits that were his beard, then the thick ponytail that was his hair, grinning. 'You cut it then,' he said to Mautu.

'I don't know how to,' said Mautu. Peleiupu wondered why her father had lied, then remembered Barker was a papalagi and a person's head was sacred.

'Then I won't have it cut!'

'Poto can do it.'

'I'll go and get the scissors and comb,' Poto said, and hurried off.

The scissors gleamed in Barker's right hand as he reached back with his left hand, gripped his ponytail and pulled it around his neck. Quickly, heavily, he cut through it. 'Don't! Your hair's going to look terrible!' Poto cried.

Dangling it like a dead sea eel in front of Mautu's face, Barker said, 'See, it is very easy.' He twirled the ponytail around once and then spun it out of the fale. It floated slowly and lay on the paepae. Handle first, he extended the scissors to Mautu, who edged away. Barker gripped the bottom ends of his beard, opened the scissors and pushed the V-shaped mouth across the plaits just under his chin.

Before he could cut it, Mautu said, 'Don't!' Barker smiled as he handed Mautu the scissors. Poto gave him the large yellow comb. They all went to the back of the fale and Barker sat down on a chair. 'Short — I want it short,' he told Mautu.

Peleiupu noticed that Mautu was sweating as he unplaited Barker's hair and combed it with long careful strokes. The first snips of the scissors were hesitant, afraid. 'Not enough — be braver!' Barker egged him on. The scissors snipped and snapped and made long cuts that sounded like paper being ripped. Soon Mautu was humming to the scissors' rhythm, and the hair tumbled.

'Getting old,' Barker said, picking up a handful of hair and rubbing it between his fingers. 'Nearly all grey.' He flung the hair at Poto and Peleiupu, who laughed. 'Shorter!' he said to Mautu.

'Are you sure?'

'Yes. I want to look younger, a new man.'

The mat under them was growing thick, furry hair as Mautu snipped away. Soon it was a blanket of gold flecked with sparkling grey: a throne appropriate for the young prince Barker was being transformed into as his enormous camouflage of hair shrank.

'How do I look?' Barker asked Peleiupu and Poto.

'Beautiful!' Peleiupu replied in Samoan.

'Hear that, Mautu? Your princess thinks I'm beautiful!'

'She does not know ugliness when she sees it!' Poto joked.

'You're envious, that's all!' Barker countered. They all laughed.

As Mautu set to work on Barker's beard Peleiupu watched more intensely, eager to see what Barker looked like without it.

'Don't come any closer!' Barker said. Peleiupu looked around. The whole blond, cats'-eyed tribe of Barker's children was gazing at their father. 'If you're going to watch, then remain silent,' he instructed them.

'Yes, don't make a sound,' Poto cautioned.

The children sat down at the back posts. Barker shut his eyes and withdrew into his thoughts. The scissors continued to free his face.

'Beautiful!' Peleiupu murmured a while later as Mautu dropped his arms to his sides and stepped back to admire his work.

'Yes, he looks less savage and pagan now,' Poto said, holding her husband's shoulders. Barker's eyes blinked open; their piercing greenness was no longer lost in his now youthful face.

'Yes, you're handsome!' Mautu chuckled. 'I cut twenty years off your age!'

'I feel naked,' said Barker, running his fingers over his face and through his hair. 'Naked! The air feels cold on my scalp.'

'My pagan friend, you are young again!' laughed Mautu, sitting down. 'Isn't he, Poto?'

Poto slapped Barker's shoulders playfully. 'Yes, you look good again.'

Picking up handfuls of hair from the mat, Barker laughed and said, 'Gold. Gold. Gold!' The hair scattered round the fale as he tossed it up into the air. Then he asked, 'Do I look bald? Do I?' Mautu shook his head. 'You're lying!' he shouted.

'Ask your children,' Mautu suggested.

Barker cupped his hands to his head and called, 'Children, come closer!' They did. 'Do I look bald — and ugly?' he asked. Mautu, Poto and Peleiupu looked at the children. 'Do I?' Barker repeated.

Tavita, the eldest son, shook his head. The others copied him. The younger ones giggled. 'Come!' Barker called, stretching his arms out to them. 'Come to your handsome father!' Except for Tavita, the others scuttled across the fale into his arms. In a moment he was scooping up handfuls of cut hair and sprinkling it over them as though he was baptising them. They laughed and hugged him. Peleiupu looked up at Poto. She was trembling, almost crying.

Peleiupu glanced at her father. His eyes were brimming with tears. This was the first time they had seen Barker showing any real affection, in public, for his children. She walked out of the fale.

'See that? You like it?' she heard Barker saying to his children. She saw him lifting up the side of his ie lavalava and displaying his tatau. 'Your father is brave, eh?' They ohhhed and nodded.

Barker quickly gained weight and grew stronger. His tatau healed, and every time it was oiled it shone brightly against his pale skin and was envied by the young men of Satoa. He didn't wear papalagi clothes any more, he lived in the fale instead of the store, he went everywhere barefoot and spoke Samoan most of the time. Because they were with him almost every day, Mautu and Peleiupu did not consider this transformation unusual, but it provided the basis for hilarious, often cruel commentary among other Satoans.

For instance among the matai: 'Barker, our papalagi, doesn't want to be a papalagi any more!' one said.

'No, his lordship is now a tattooed savage who isn't a palagi or Samoan or aristocrat!' another wit remarked.

'. . . But his tatau is exceptional!' a just matai objected.

'It is the beautiful work of Satan, you mean!' A deacon cut the just matai's justice from under his bare feet. The just matai, who always paid his debts at Barker's store promptly, did not want to commit heresy so he remained silent and promised himself the pleasure of telling Barker what the deacon, who had a large debt with Barker, had said.

'Pity our palagi no longer wears trousers!'

'And boots . . .'

'And his lovely blond beard . . .'

'And his strong gun!' The married women, who were inclined towards bawdiness, improvised during one of their group mat-weaving sessions, without Poto.

'Pity he's now so thin . . .'

'And small . . .'

'And without his large pink tongue . . .'

'Which he was so expert at using . . .'

'For what?' an innocent interjected.

'Why, for speaking English!' an experienced matron replied. The fale shook with an earthquake of laughter.

Among the taulele'a, who admired Barker's tatau but refused to admit it to one another, the gossip was more serious and therefore nasty: 'The illegitimate lord thinks he's brave!' the puny son of one matai said.

'Yes, he thinks he's got liver like us Samoans!'

'No liver, that is!'

'Bet you he used some magic palagi potion to kill the pain!'

'Yes, bet you that weak palagi did that!'

'Let's go and pull off his ie lavalava and see his ugly tatau!' the puny son of a matai suggested. Silence.

'Yes, let's!' a few others replied.

'Yes, let's go tonight, whip off his ie lavalava and see his ugly tatau!' the puny one encouraged them.

But, alas, no one wanted to be encouraged any further: they knew how expert Barker was with his guns and fists.

Among the unmarried women and girls there was agreement (not voiced for their male folk to hear) that Barker, once a weak papalagi, wasn't weak any more: he was carrying a tatau, uniform of courage; he was now also quite handsome without his beard and ugly hairiness.

Nearly all the children of Satoa were afraid of Barker: he was a papalagi, part aitu and part devil; that's why he was so pale and hairy and spoke devil-like Samoan.

Parents and elders used him to frighten their children into obedience. 'You want the palagi to come and eat you?' they frightened disobedient children to sleep.

'You want the palagi to come and steal you?' The terrified child either screamed louder, frail heart threatening to burst with hysteria, or swallowed his tears and nearly drowned in his own fright.

Or in some particularly imaginative aiga, when a child was imaginative enough to ask his parents where he had come from, they told him, 'We bought you at Barker's store.' If the child started whimpering, the parent consoled him, 'Don't worry, we had to pay a lot of money for you — that shows we love you very much!'

In those homes ruled by extraordinarily imaginative sadists, after whipping an errant child into uncontrollable screaming and then whipping him some more to try to stop his screaming, the sadist pulled the hysterical child towards Barker's store, all the while threatening, 'If you don't stop crying I'll sell you to the palagi!' If the child didn't stop — and it didn't matter if he was no longer able to — the sadist shouted, 'I'm going to ask the palagi to eat you if you don't stop now!' If the child didn't stop, the sadist dragged him nearer to Barker's store, and only desisted when the child sobbed for mercy.

Now that he was slimmer, without his shock of hair and with a brave tatau, and he spoke better, less angry Samoan, Barker wasn't so scary a devil — but he was still a devil to watch out for. No matter how fiercely, adamantly, persuasively, and sometimes angrily Peleiupu and Arona defended Barker to other people, they were nearly always left with the infuriating feeling that their listeners had not believed anything they had explained. Not a word of it.

'How do I make our people believe that Barker is not a foreigner and a papalagi to be frightened of?' Peleiupu asked Mautu not long after Barker got his tatau.

'Do they treat him like that?' Mautu asked, surprised.

'They don't accept him — they see him only as a papalagi.'

'I never knew that,' sighed Mautu. 'He's my friend. I don't see him as a papalagi.'

'What about when you first met him?'

'Yes, I suppose I did see his colour then.'

'Our people have never gone beyond that. Not even now that he has a tatau.'

'Do you think that's why he got it?'

'I don't know,' she retreated.

The next morning she noticed that Mautu was specially caring for Barker.

'We have a request to make,' Barker said in Samoan. Mautu nodded. 'We want . . . we want our children to attend your school.'

'Haven't you been teaching them yourself?' Mautu asked.

'No, he's taught them little. They're little savages. They can't read or write,' Poto said.

'Not even Tavita?' Mautu asked Barker.

Barker shook his head. 'I wanted my children to be free of European "civilisation" . . .'

'Even its learning?'

'Especially that. But I now know that savages, in particular "noble savages", are becoming obsolete. It would be criminal for me to make savages of my children in a world that is Christian and quickly converting to papalagi ways and diseases.' He paused. 'Yes, it would be criminal to leave them to the mercy of the literate, civilised savages from Europe.' He patted Poto's shoulder. She pressed against him.

'I don't understand.' Mautu replied.

'Mautu, even in our remote village we are not safe any more from so-called civilisation. I want my children to be armed with the weapons of reading, writing, arithmetic, science, arrogance, money and guns.'

'I want my children to be educated,' Poto insisted.

'Don't worry, Poto, I'm sure Mautu and Pele and Lalaga will turn them into well-groomed, highly literate savages!' Barker laughed.

On Monday afternoon, just before classes began, eight of Barker's children arrived at Mautu's school. The group reminded Peleiupu of a scared brood of piglets. Lalaga got Peleiupu to record their names and ages in the thick exercise book that was the school roll. By the time she had extracted the names and recorded them, the other students had arrived and were gathered around the Barker children, trying not to be too obvious in their surprised scrutiny of them. The Barker children were unique with their tattered ie lavalava and clothes, their uncut blond tresses that flowed down their backs, and their golden tans and cats' eyes. As odd as their father, they thought.

'Do you speak English?' Lalaga asked the Barker children who looked at Tavita, the eldest. Tavita shook his head. The others followed suit. 'It doesn't matter; we use Samoan in our classes.'

No one present that day would forget the unusual names of the Barker children.

For weeks they would mimic Peleiupu's pronunciation of the names, stringing them out as if they were reciting a nursery rhyme: 'David Dennis, Anna Arabel, Elizabeth Elinor, James Jason, Frances Florence, Michael Mason, Ronald Reginald, and Genevieve Gwen.' Some would sing the names and laugh.

'For our school your names will be: Tavita, Ana, Elisapeta, Semisi, Faranisisi, Mikaele, Roni and Siniva,' Lalaga told the Barker children. 'You will all be in my class. Don't worry — I didn't start my learning until I was fifteen. Mautu started even later. Work hard and you'll catch up to the others.' As she looked at them she remembered Barker's story about the Inca king who was covered with gold. She was surprised they were so shy and quiet: she had heard they were rude, disrespectful and without shame — replicas of their father.

'They're not afraid of the other children; they always fight together and they don't give in!' Peleiupu told Lalaga that evening.

Most Satoans would refer to that surprising day as 'The Morning the Tattooed British Lord's Heirs Started to Learn the Alphabet'.

The Alia

'He's — he's caught our Disease,' Arona said. They were alone in the school fale; their students were cleaning the grounds.

'Who?' asked Peleiupu, continuing to write on the blackboard. For almost a year Arona had been teaching a junior class. He was about fifteen.

'Barker.' The name slipped like a startled fish into Peleiupu's hearing and, for a moment, she didn't want to know it was there. She glanced at him; he was refusing to look at her. 'He's got the Disease of Satoa!' he whispered.

'How do you know?' She was breathing in the sweet scent of frangipani. She noticed the sun was caught in the embrace of luminous clouds.

'Tavita and I have been with him most afternoons. He's been teaching us about ships.' He waited for her.

'Does Mautu know?' she asked. The smell was insinuating itself, like the roots of weeds, down her throat.

'No, Barker has told no one else.'

'What about Tavita, does he know?'

'No. I've told no one but you.'

'Mautu will know what to do,' she offered.

'I promised Barker I would not tell anyone. He's taught me many wonderful things,' he said. She didn't want to hear him. 'Many things about the sea and the stars and ships.'

'They're returning to class,' she said.

He got up. 'He's been very good to us, Pele.' He walked off.

The students were entering the fale. 'Be quiet!' she ordered.

They stopped talking at once.

That evening after lotu, while they were having their meal, Lalaga asked Mautu why he hadn't been seeing Barker lately. Mautu told everyone that Barker was too busy designing a large alia he was going to build.

'Arona's been helping him,' Lalaga said.

'Is he teaching you how to design ships?' Mautu asked Arona, who was sitting with the other young people at the back posts. Arona nodded.

'Tell us what Barker has been teaching you,' Mautu asked Arona.

So while the elders ate, Arona detailed, in his ponderous, thorough manner, how he and Tavita were learning how to use a compass, a sextant and the stars to steer by. He gave the English and Samoan names of the stars. His eyes glowed as he described Barker's alia, giving the exact measurements, the revolutionary changes Barker was introducing to the traditional design, the timber to be used, and the other qualities needed for the alia to come alive. Not once did he lose his way, or the attention of his audience. Peleiupu found herself flowing with his tale, and forgetting that Barker was dying.

'And when the alia is built has Barker asked you to sail with him?' Lalaga asked. Peleiupu felt Arona looking at her. She daren't look at him.

'Has he?' Mautu asked. 'Just think, you could sail around the world!'

'Yes, he has asked me,' Arona replied.

'Good, good!' exclaimed Mautu. 'If only I was younger.' Peleiupu caught Lalaga gazing at Arona and knew that Lalaga wasn't going to allow Arona to sail away from being the pastor she wanted him to be.

That Sunday after to'ona'i, while everyone rested in the fale, Mautu reminded Peleiupu about reading aloud to him. He got her to bring his favourite collection of stories, *The Jungle Book* by Rudyard Kipling.

So while he lay, covered with his sleeping sheet, his eyes shut, his head resting on his bamboo ali, she read to him.

'Are you not well?' he asked.

'I'm all right.'

'Then concentrate and read properly! You're ruining a very exciting story!'

She tried. She had read it many times to him, but he was like a child: he wanted his favourite stories repeated over and over again. She was fed up with Babu and his jungle friends and their ridiculous adventures, but she didn't dare tell her father, so she persevered.

Straight after the second story she said, 'Arona told me to tell you that Barker wants to see you tomorrow.' The lie was so easy.

'Remind me tomorrow morning,' he murmured. 'I want to see his designs for the alia.'

'He should have asked you earlier,' she tested him.

'Yes' he said. And she knew then that he was hurt that Barker had left him out of his alia project. She pretended to be looking through the book for another story to read, then, pausing dramatically, asked, 'Since you became pastor here, how many people have died from the Disease?'

'What disease?' He sounded as if he were falling asleep.

'The Disease of Satoa.'

'Can't remember.'

'What causes it?'

'Why do you want to know?'

'Some of my students asked me about it. I have got to give them an answer tomorrow.' Again it wasn't difficult to lie.

'I've tried to find the answer in the papalagi medical books but I haven't been able to: my English isn't good enough, and my understanding of the sciences is very inadequate.' He paused. 'Perhaps you should read the books yourself, your English is now better than mine. Or, why don't you ask Barker. He's seen people dying from the Disease. Come with me tomorrow and ask him.' Her lies had led her back to Barker. 'Now let me sleep,' he sighed.

Next morning Mautu didn't need to be reminded about going to see Barker. He hurried through his morning meal and told Lalaga where he was going. That afternoon, before Lalaga could ask her to do something else, Peleiupu dismissed her classes, told Ruta and Naomi that Mautu wanted to see her at Barker's, and left. She hadn't seen Barker for a few weeks so she dreaded what she might find.

Poto and another woman were weaving mats at the far side of Barker's fale. Seated at the desk at the centre of the fale, Barker and Mautu were discussing the drawings of the alia, which were spread out over the desk. It was clear to Peleiupu, as she approached, that the two women were pretending not to be listening to what the men were saying, and she remembered, regretfully, that because she was now a young woman it was not proper for her to be a confidante of her father and Barker. People accepted that Mautu and Barker treated her as a son and, at times, as an equal, but that was no comfort because she knew — and Lalaga reminded her often — that now she had to keep her distance. Only papalagi daughters treated their fathers in that over-familiar way, discussing everything with them openly, publicly.

Arona and Tavita were in the new shelter, which extended from the right side of the fale, sawing through a hefty log. When they saw her, Tavita smiled. It was so restrictive, she thought. She could not now even talk freely with her brother or any of the boys she had grown up with.

'Come and see these,' Barker called as soon as he saw her. She nodded but veered off to the back of the fale. 'No, come through the front!' Barker instructed. She wished he wouldn't treat her so equally, not in front of other people. She insisted on doing the proper thing, entering the fale through the back. 'Here, come to the table,' Barker said. But she sat down beside Poto.

'It's all right here,' she said. 'I came to see Poto.'

'It going to be a magnificent alia,' Mautu said.

Soon the two men were again immersed in their discussion.

Peleiupu asked Poto where her children were. Next door, she told her. Peleiupu had never felt close to Poto. She had tried to but Poto just didn't interest her: what she talked about, what she did bored Peleiupu. That was how she felt about most of the women. Their being women, in Satoan terms, was too narrow, and she didn't want to be like that, but she had to disguise her dissatisfaction. For instance, right then, while she pretended she was interested in what Poto was saying, her attention was on Barker and Mautu and the alia. She wanted to be part of the alia, the building of it, but the way of Satoa denied her that: she was a young woman, a child still, who had to stay away from what was male and adult. It was so unfair. Barker and Mautu had taken her out into the boundless adventure that was the world, but the Satoan way wasn't allowing her the full dimensions and richness of that adventure.

Once, when she'd explained how she felt to Lalaga, her mother had told her to be satisfied she was a very intelligent girl who would one day marry a man of God and help spread God's message in the pagan Pacific.

'. . . And how are my children doing at school?' Poto broke into her thoughts.

'Doing well,' Peleiupu replied.

'I hope they're not too naughty!'

'No, they're well behaved.'

Poto continued talking about her children while Peleiupu observed Barker surreptitiously. Only the sun-bleached tips of his hair and his blue-green eyes showed he wasn't Samoan. And you had to listen carefully to his Samoan to know he had an accent. He had succeeded in 'going native', he was fond of telling visitors; and Mautu kept telling him he now belonged to Satoa.

There was no new blemish on his skin, no change in his mannerisms and speech; in fact he appeared healthier, happier, and openly enthusiastic about what he was describing to Mautu as 'our new project: a ship to outspeed any thing, even death'.

'You know what an alia is?' Mautu saved her. She nodded. 'We're going to build a modern one: lighter, faster and stronger than any built before.' In his voice Peleiupu once again detected that limitless delight which, years before, had driven their search for gold.

Peleiupu couldn't sleep that night. It started raining at midnight, and the incessant drone strengthened the grip of the darkness around her. Over and over, she examined Barker at his desk with Mautu, looking for the sign he had the Disease. But where? Where?

At dawn, in a dream, she was in a warm, slow-circling current. The alia, white as bone, black mast veined with fissures, and winged with a white sail fat with the wind pushing the craft forward, sailed into the centre of her head and circled and circled with the current that was now her completely. No one on board, just the silent circling vessel tracing the veins in the water, in her, lifting her up, up, up, the sail shimmering and shivering in the invisible breeze. And she was the sail, her body stretched out in one taut skin with the wind singing through her pores.

Suddenly (and she didn't want to see it) she was kneeling on the deck that joined the two hulls, beside a corpse that was covered up to its neck with ie toga. She leaned forward but a blinding light burst up out of the mound of mats, and, as her mouth started swallowing the light, it turned into a solid, choking liquid that tasted like blood . . .

The memory of the dream gripped her all day while she taught her classes.

When she remembered that Hawaiians buried their chiefs at sea by placing them on canoes and sailing them out into the horizon, she hurried out of her classroom and, hiding among the bookshelves in the main fale, she prayed.

When she got up to return to her class she glanced back at where she'd been sitting. On the mat were three large drops of blood. She clamped her hands over her mouth. She looked down at her dress. A thin red stain extended from below her belly to the hem.

She waited under the breadfruit tree until Filivai was alone in her fale, then she entered. Since their meeting years before, when Filivai had warned her about her special gift, Peleiupu had not visited her. They met often around the village but never referred to that meeting.

Filivai greeted her formally and then said, 'It's been a long time, eh?' Pele nodded. 'Are your parents well?' Pele nodded again and waited for Filivai to continue talking, but she didn't, so she looked up at her. 'Are you well?' Filivai asked. Peleiupu looked at the mat. 'Something is wrong?'

'Is there a cure for our Disease?' Peleiupu couldn't stop the question.

'I don't understand your question,' Filivai replied. 'Are you referring to your gift?'

Peleiupu shook her head. 'I'm asking about the Satoan Disease.'

'I know of no cure for that. Why do you ask?'

'Have you — or anyone else — tried to find a cure?'

'I haven't, but some others have tried.'

'Why haven't you?'

Filivai used the end of her ie lavalava to wipe the dried sleep out of the corners of her eyes. 'Because there is no cure. During my life I've seen thirteen people die from it, and I've made certain observations about it.'

When she didn't continue, Peleiupu asked, 'Will you tell me?'

'First, you must tell me why you want to find a cure. Is someone you know ill with it?'

Peleiupu nodded. 'It is not my parents.'

'You see clearly, always. So I won't lie to you. Let's go for a walk,' Filivai instructed her. 'And pick the leaves I need for my medicines.'

Peleiupu helped her up to her unsteady feet and handed her her siapo tiputa, which she put on. 'Come, I need you to lean on. My old body weighs on me like a sick animal.' She wound her left arm over Peleiupu's shoulders and, putting some of her weight on Pele, asked, 'I'm not too heavy, eh?' Peleiupu smiled.

As they picked a path through the shrubs and undergrowth Filivai described to her the various medical concoctions she made and the ailments they cured. She stopped periodically and asked Peleiupu to pick the leaves of one plant or another. Whenever they disturbed some insects and birds and the creatures escaped into the greenery, Filivai identified each one for Peleiupu.

'Are you feeling better now?' Filivai asked. Peleiupu nodded. Filivai then told her what she'd observed about their Disease.

Of the thirteen victims she had seen, two had been young children, five had been in their twenties, and the rest had been old. Eight, she recalled, had been male. 'So you see, it can claim anyone of any age or sex.' She pondered for a moment and then said, 'Yes, not all of them were direct descendants of our people either. Three, I remember, came here from somewhere else. However, they lived here for over fifteen years. You could say that all thirteen belonged to Satoa, or had decided Satoa was their home, the place in which they wanted to die. No stranger ever contracts our Disease.'

The walking was tiring the old woman so she got Peleiupu to sit her down on a boulder in the shade of some cacao trees. She gathered her breath and continued. 'Of the four I knew well and helped nurse through their dreadful ordeal, all wanted to die.'

Peleiupu looked at her. 'Yes, Pele, they wanted to die. One of them admitted it to me: the other three didn't know they suffered the wish to die . . .'

'But how did you know?'

Filivai gazed up at her. 'How do you know?' Peleiupu looked away. 'Yes, Pele, all the victims of our Disease want to die and be buried here in Satoa.' Peleiupu refused to believe it of Barker and was going to say so, but Filivai said, 'I don't want to know who it is, Pele. Not yet.' Reaching up, she grasped Peleiupu's arms and pulled herself to her feet. 'I'm old, Pele, and it's not easy carrying the pain of my own carcass, let alone sharing someone else's pain. You understand?' Peleiupu nodded. 'Let's continue to pick leaves to cure simpler maladies!' she chuckled. They moved deeper into the cool vegetation.

'When I was convinced all the victims wanted to die, I thought I'd discovered the cure: restore the person's will to live and the Disease would leave his body . . .'

'And?' Peleiupu urged.

'I tried it with the first two victims. With their loved ones, I tried to make them see their death-wish, to see it clearly and want to live. But it didn't work. Don't ask me why. We thought we'd succeeded but . . .' She scrutinised Peleiupu's face and said, 'You're telling yourself: where Filivai failed, I'm going to succeed, I'm going to get the victim to believe she doesn't belong to Satoa and that she is suffering from the wish to die. Am I correct, eh?' Peleiupu nodded. 'And once that is done, our Disease will leave her alone?' Peleiupu nodded again. 'But there is another question which, if you haven't arrived at it already, you'll eventually face after suffering hours, days, months watching the victim dying. It's this: Perhaps our Disease is a blessing, a reward for a life of virtue and goodness? Remember, God is a god of love not cruelty.'

'I don't understand,' said Peleiupu.

'Think of this, Pele: if God is a god of love, would He inflict our Disease on someone as punishment or as a reward?' She paused and added, 'All thirteen victims I knew led exemplary Christian lives.' Before Peleiupu could say it, Filivai held up her hand and said, 'No, don't tell me who it is or that she has not led a virtuous life. I don't want to know just yet.'

After they stored the leaves in a basket under the bed in the fale, Filivai said, 'Pele, I try to cure what is within my power to cure. Many years ago I learned, after much suffering caused by too much hope, to accept the limitations of my ability, my gift, call it what you like. I learned, with great bitterness but with wisdom, that I couldn't heal the world or be greater, more powerful, than I was or am.' She reached over and brushed back Peleiupu's hair, then added, 'Your gift is much greater than mine but it also has limitations. You continue to hope. You believe you can heal the world. For your sake — and the sake of anyone you love or will love — learn quickly your limitations, then hope within them. Do you understand?'

'Yes,' murmured Peleiupu, but she was convinced she could save Barker.

'You're going to try, eh?' Filivai laughed. 'Go now. God may help you win!'

For nearly a month Peleiupu struggled with the science and medical books in their library. She realised, not long after she started, that she didn't have the basic scientific knowledge to understand the books, but she persevered, using dictionaries and encyclopaedias to decipher unfamiliar terms and formulae. The less she understood the more tenacious she became. Even when she was doing other chores, her mind battled with the maze of terminology. She could recall, word by word, sentence by sentence, formula by formula, whole areas of what she had read but she understood little of it. She decided she needed a teacher. When she told her father she was trying to teach their students some science and needed someone to explain the books to her, he suggested Barker. All her attempts to save Barker seemed always to return to him.

Next morning, with an armful of books, she accompanied Mautu to Barker's home.

'Now, what is it you want to know?' Barker asked. 'I hope you don't expect me to read all those books!'

Peleiupu shook her head and said, 'I need to know about diseases, so I can teach our students better hygiene and health.'

'All right, fire ahead. I probably won't be able to answer most of them.'

'What causes human illness?' she began.

'Many things. But germs cause most of them.'

'And germs?'

He explained in detail what they were and how they could be destroyed. She knew this already but she wanted him to lead her, step by step, from what she knew into the jungle she needed to see, tree by tree, vine by vine, and far away from any awareness of why she wanted that information.

She got him, later, to discuss epidemic diseases, such as measles, smallpox, influenza and mumps, which, Barker pointed out, the papalagi had introduced into the Pacific and which were killing hundreds of islanders who were not immune to them. She asked him about immunity, and he explained.

'Most medicines merely help strengthen the body's natural defences,' he said.

'But why are there diseases we can't cure?' she couldn't help herself.

'Because we haven't discovered what causes them. Or what those diseases are . . .'

'I need help,' Mautu called to him. Mautu was working on the drawings.

'Coming,' Barker replied. 'Let's continue later,' he told Peleiupu. He stood up. 'By the way, young lady, not all diseases have physical causes. And I'm not referring to aitu. Sometimes your spirit, your soul is ill. This shows itself in the body. And your books won't tell you much about those illnesses.'

While she waited for him to return she skimmed through the books, and sometimes observed the craftsmen working on the alia in the alia shelter. Arona and Tavita were among them. Tavita smiled at her every time she looked over.

An hour or so later, when she knew Barker was too absorbed in the alia, she headed home. As she went past the shelter Tavita waved to her. She smiled back.

Their meals were now tuned to Mautu's excited narratives about the alia: its history, the various types and their uses. He concentrated on describing how fleets of alia were used in warfare and how certain warrior matai in the past had conquered Samoa by using swifter alia fleets and better naval tactics than their enemies. He went on to describe many of the great British naval victories he had read about. From there he descended into the mythology of the Odyssey and, later, Sinbad's adventures. Whenever he taught his classes, which was rarely now since he spent most of his day building the alia, he took his students adventuring with Christopher Columbus, Captain Cook, Abel Tasman, Vasco da Gama, and their heroic Polynesian ancestors who, using mighty alia, had discovered and settled the Pacific Islands scattered over millions of square miles of ocean.

Into the pulpit on Sundays he took these tales, this mythology, and wove them, sometimes for two hours, around the hearts of his spellbound congregation. He even transformed Noah's Ark into an epic tale of exploration, combating evil and saving humankind.

At home, after Sunday to'ona'i, he insisted that his children read him books about ships. Peleiupu was conveniently absent whenever he was choosing a reader, and the burden fell mainly on Ruta or Naomi.

One Sunday, while Naomi was struggling to read to him a manual about British naval ships, and doing a tortuous job of it, he called, 'Pele, you come and read to me.'

So for what seemed to Peleiupu like an eternity she read to him, in naval fashion, about the various British warships. She almost slammed the book shut when she finished one chapter, indicating she didn't want to read any more. 'Mautu, can someone have our Disease and not know he has it?' She knew that whenever she showed she was annoyed with him, he became defensively obliging. She didn't exploit this often, though.

'He may not know at first, but he'll soon know when it starts erupting from his body.'

'Is it true all the victims get the Disease because they wish to die?'

'Who told you that?'

'I heard it somewhere. I also heard that if you can make the person realise that's why he's got the Disease, and make him want to live, the Disease will go away.'

'That's not true.'

'If it is true, though, then there is a cure for our Disease.' She watched him. He pondered, his eyes shut. 'Think of all the victims you knew,' she encouraged him. He sat up and, pushing his sleeping sheet down to his waist, gazed out into the village burning with sun.

'It's not true!' Lalaga shattered the limits Peleiupu had trapped her father in. 'It's just superstitious talk. I knew many of the victims — they certainly didn't want to die.'

'But Pele may have a point,' Mautu interjected. 'A point I've never considered before.'

'Barker told me that some diseases do not have natural causes,' Peleiupu encouraged him.

'Are you talking about ma'i aitu?' Lalaga cautioned her. Peleiupu glanced at her father. 'There are no such diseases!'

'Pele is not referring to ma'i aitu, which I don't believe in. I too have read in scientific books of maladies caused by not having the will to continue living,' Mautu countered Lalaga.

'God punishes sinners by sometimes inflicting illnesses on them,' Lalaga reminded him.

'God works through love, not hate,' he said.

'But he punishes also!'

'Then you believe our Disease is God-inflicted?' he pursued. Peleiupu avoided looking at her mother.

'Perhaps it is,' Lalaga replied.

'You've seen the terrible way it destroys people? You still believe it is sent by God?'

'Perhaps . . .' Peleiupu tried to rescue Lalaga.

'I want your mother to answer.' Though he said it quietly, it was like a blade.

'Why are you angry?' Lalaga countered.

'Answer my question.'

Gazing at the floor, Lalaga admitted, 'Our God is not a cruel god.'

Peleiupu wanted to get out of the way so she got up.

'Why did you bring up our Disease?' Mautu demanded.

Peleiupu shrugged her shoulders and started walking away.

'Sit down. Your father wants an answer to his question!' Lalaga insisted.

Peleiupu sat down again. 'As you know, Barker's been helping me understand those medical books so I can teach better hygiene to our students.'

'What's that got to do with our Disease?' Lalaga continued her attack.

'You know what she's like,' Mautu said. 'She's curious about everything, and she has to teach our children better health.' Peleiupu didn't look at Lalaga.

'Go and sleep. It's nearly time for church,' Lalaga ordered her. 'I'm going to sleep too.' And, before Mautu could say anything else, Lalaga turned onto her side and pulled up her sleeping sheet.

When Peleiupu heard that Barker was taking Arona to Apia to buy materials they needed for the alia, she instructed Arona to see two of the missionary doctors Mautu knew, and give them a list of questions she had drawn up about the Disease.

They were away for just over a week. In that time Peleiupu distracted herself by helping Mautu draw the last designs for the alia, and at night by studying the medical books. Whenever she hunted for Barker's reasons for not wanting to live, Stenson entered her thoughts. Stenson had searched for a place to die, and had found Samoa. Perhaps Barker had chosen Satoa, and by belonging to Satoa now qualified for their Disease. But as long as Arona was in Apia consulting those doctors, her hope was boundless.

'The doctor I saw couldn't offer any cures: he has to examine Barker,' Arona informed her. 'From your list and your descriptions of the Disease he said it may be a form of leprosy. But he couldn't be sure.'

She turned away from him. 'I'll get Mautu and Lalaga and Poto to *persuade* him to live.'

That night she asked Mautu if their aiga should help feed the craftsmen, and in the morning Mautu told Lalaga to provide food for them every Friday. In turn, Lalaga asked Peleiupu to organise it. When the other aiga heard their pastor was feeding the craftsmen, they too took a day each, and also sent their skilled craftsmen to help. By Saturday, fifty men were helping Barker and Mautu, and all the old men were coming to watch, offer advice, and plait sinnet for the alia. Whenever the boys were free of their family chores, they came to learn and help too. At first the skilled alia and fautasi builders were sceptical of Barker's innovations and designs, but, as he deciphered the drawings for them and showed them how to fashion the various parts, they came to respect him.

During Sunday to'ona'i Mautu and the matai talked enthusiastically of their alia. Had he and Barker decided on a name for it yet? someone asked Mautu. When he told them no, they made various suggestions. Peleiupu listened to their discussion, and was convinced the elders now accepted Barker as one of them. Some of them still referred to him as 'our palagi', but it was in jestful admiration. How were they going to react to his contracting their Disease? Would they see it as proof of his sinfulness? Or as a reward from God? She had to tell her parents, and they, in turn, would prepare Satoa for Barker's illness. But she dreaded telling them — Mautu particularly.

'Aren't you feeling well?' Lalaga asked her as they prepared for classes. Peleiupu shook her head. It was going to be a still day, muggy with heat. They started walking to the classrooms. 'What's the matter?' Lalaga asked again.

Still looking away from Lalaga, Peleiupu said, and she had to say it all at once, 'Barker is ill, he is ill with our Disease.'

'Are you sure?'

'Yes. And Mautu doesn't know yet,' Peleiupu anticipated her. 'Arona's the only other person who knows: Barker told him.'

'What are we going to do?' Lalaga murmured, more to herself than to Peleiupu. 'So that's why you've been asking all those questions about the Disease?' Peleiupu nodded. 'We'll ask our Heavenly Father to save him, that's the only way. We'll all pray; we'll get everyone in Satoa to pray for him: he's one of us now.'

'God didn't save the others,' Peleiupu reminded her.

'God always makes exceptions. First we'll tell Mautu.' She paused. 'Yes, we have to tell him.' Peleiupu reached over and clasped Lalaga's trembling hands. 'Our aiga, all of us, will help him. Should we tell your father?'

Peleiupu nodded.

The night was cool and a slow inquisitive wind was exploring the village. Mautu was reading beside the lamp while Lalaga and Peleiupu were playing cards. Everyone else was asleep.

'How is the work on the alia coming along?' Lalaga asked.

'Very well,' he replied.

Peleiupu watched Lalaga's fingers picking bits off the ragged corner of the mat she was sitting on. 'We have something important to tell you,' she heard her mother saying.

'Well, tell me quickly, I'm falling asleep waiting!' he joked.

Lalaga looked across at Peleiupu, who nodded. 'Barker . . .' Lalaga began.

'Yes?' Mautu encouraged her.

'Barker-has-our-Disease!' Lalaga blurted out. Lalaga looked to Peleiupu for help again, but Peleiupu was looking away from her.

'Say it slowly,' Mautu said.

'Barker has our Disease,' she said, gazing up into his face.

'He looks perfectly healthy to me,' he said. They continued to look at him. 'You must be wrong.' They maintained their silent gaze. 'How do you know?' He looked from Lalaga to Peleiupu. 'It can't be true!'

'It is true,' Peleiupu said.

Mautu shook his head slowly. Then, as they watched him, his body seemed to be filling, starting from his feet, with a dark vapour. As the vapour rose higher, he started stretching his body upwards as if he didn't want the vapour to reach his throat. Before they could stop him, his protesting head had pulled his body up to a standing position, and was dragging it backwards out of the fale into the night, on running feet. Away.

Peleiupu woke when Mautu's footsteps crackled across the pebbles of the paepae. It was dawn; a faint glow was emanating from everything outside. She sat up and, with Lalaga, watched him get a dry ie lavalava out of the trunk. Stripping off the dew-wet one he wore, he put the dry one on. He sat down, a few paces away, with his back to them, and gazed out through the dark palms at the sea, at the horizon that was now streaked with the dawn light. They waited. They could hear the cries of roosters and pigs. The breeze was huddled in their fale, listening.

'I have decided,' Mautu spoke out at the dawn and the waking world, 'that what I'm going to say will be the last word I will say about this . . . this matter. Who else knows?'

'Arona, only Arona,' replied Lalaga.

'You, Pele and Arona will not tell anyone else. We will all continue to live as if he were well. Only if he chooses to tell us will we then work out another way of dealing with it . . .'

'But shouldn't we try to help him?' Lalaga asked.

'No! It is clear he has decided to live — yes, live — through and with the Disease, alone. We must respect that. We must not even ask God to save him.'

'You will let him die?' Peleiupu was surprised at how calm she was.

'Yes, if that is what he wants. You will respect my decision. Tell Arona. All we will pray for is that he admits to us that he has our Disease.'

'He is your friend,' Lalaga tried again.

'Yes, he is my dearest friend. I don't want him to die. But I respect him too well to interfere with his decision.' She tried to speak again but he raised his hand. 'Don't you realise? He may be welcoming the Disease as proof that he belongs to us, to Satoa, to this little bit of earth. Don't you see?'

'But why did he tell Arona?' Peleiupu asked.

'In a moment of fear. The thought of being attacked by our Disease can frighten anyone, even someone as brave as Barker.'

'And when it appears on his body and people see it?' Lalaga asked.

'They must continue not to see it,' he said. 'Only if he admits it to us will we then see it!' The wind had uncurled and was weaving lazily around the figures sleeping in the fale. The dawn light was now burning fiercely on Mautu's face and shoulders. 'We will build the alia,' he added. Peleiupu sprang up. 'You will obey me.' Mautu looked back at her for the first time that morning. 'It is not easy for me either!' he pleaded with her.

Quickly, Peleiupu walked out of the fale. 'Pele!' Lalaga tried to stop her.

'Leave her,' Mautu said. They watched the tangled mass of banana trees behind the fale, swallowing up their daughter.

'Next year she'll be going to Vaiuta School,' Lalaga said. 'The papalagi missionaries will teach her discipline.'

Everything was armoured with dew, and the rising sun was caught in the droplets of water. As far as Peleiupu could see, the vegetation was aglitter. She didn't notice her blouse and sleeping sheet getting soaked as she waded through the undergrowth. The cold air licked at her wetness.

Her tree. She gazed up at it, at the fluttering body of leaves and branches humming in the breeze, opening their arms to her. She hadn't visited it for two years. It looked smaller but harder to climb. She gripped the lowest branch and tried to swing up. She was bigger, heavier, and now too grown-up to be climbing trees. She tried again and got up to stand on the branch. Hitching up her wet sleeping sheet, she started climbing.

She was wet through when she reached the platform. Water was even streaming out of her hair. She squatted, peeled off her blouse, squeezed most of the water out of it, then spread it out on the platform. After squeezing her sleeping sheet, she dried herself with it, then squeezed it again and spread it out to dry.

She wrapped her arms around her torso and sat back against the trunk, her skin already goose-pimpled with the cold. She shut her eyes.

As the wetness dried on her, the cold of it fingered through her body. She concentrated on welcoming the cold, and the discomfort of it distracted her from Barker and the world, which was threatening to disintegrate.

Soon she was floating in the heady aromatic odour of damp moss and the slow rocking of her tree. She opened to the current and became part of it.

It was Friday morning and they were cooking food for the craftsmen. The smoke of the umu was surging up into the dome of the kitchen fale. Caught there, it started finding holes in the thatching and escaping through them like white eels.

Arona and the boys who'd helped him light the umu were at the valusaga scraping the skins off the taro, while Peleiupu was supervising the girls in the shade of a breadfruit tree beside the kitchen fale. 'Peel the bananas,' Peleiupu instructed Ruta and Naomi, who'd just plucked and gutted the chickens. Peleiupu continued wrapping the small reef fish in breadfruit leaves.

'You do it!' Ruta objected.

'Why don't you stop ordering us around?' demanded Naomi.

Peleiupu couldn't believe it: they'd never challenged her before. 'Watch out, eh, or some little girls'll get slapped!' she warned them, in the style of their mother.

'Go ahead!' Ruta challenged, standing up. The others were now watching.

'Hey!' Arona called. 'You just do what Pele tells you!'

Peleiupu picked up the fofo'e and started peeling the green bananas. The others resumed their work.

Ruta stamped her foot and, squatting, muttered, 'He always sides with you!' She grabbed a banana and started peeling it.

'So do Mautu and Lalaga!' Naomi said.

'The only thing you do well is complain!' Peleiupu said, but she was regretting Arona's interference — she would've regained control without his help.

For the rest of the morning, while they cooked the food, Peleiupu observed her sisters and concluded that Mautu and Barker, by pulling her into their adult and male world, against usual practice, had taken her away from her sisters. Her closest friends were adults — and elderly adults at that. When she noticed the boys vying — but trying to disguise it — for Ruta's and Naomi's attention, she envied her sisters' beauty. She was lauded as the exemplary model of how a daughter should be, but no boy was interested in her the way they were captivated by her sisters.

When the umu was cooked, they took the baskets and pots of food to Barker's fale, entered through the back and started serving the food onto the foodmats. Poto and the women of her aiga helped. 'Remember to thank your mother for all this food,' Poto whispered to her.

After Mautu said grace, the craftsmen ate hungrily, with the loquacious Barker praising the quality of the cooking. When the flies became annoyingly numerous the girls got fans and, sitting down in front of each elder, fanned the flies away.

'How's your English?' Barker asked Ruta.

'Good, thank you,' Ruta replied in English.

'Why do you want our children to learn your barbaric language?' one of the old men joked.

'So I'll have people to talk to!' laughed Barker.

'But you speak our language well!' someone remarked.

'Only just well!' Mautu laughed.

As their lighthearted banter continued, Peleiupu noticed nothing unusual in Barker's appearance. There was nothing unusual in Mautu's behaviour either.

After they had eaten and washed their hands and mouths, the craftsmen lay down and rested. The young people cleared away the food and served Poto and the other women in the back fale.

Soon Barker was snoring.

'Our palagi can really snore!' someone said. The others laughed.

'Just like a real Samoan!' someone else quipped.

Peleiupu and the other girls picked up the baskets of food and headed for home. They reached the alia shelter, put down their loads and went in and inspected the craft. Laid out on large logs the hulls were higher than their heads and looked like white sharks that had turned into white stone.

'Big, eh?' sighed Naomi.

'It'll be able to sail anywhere,' said Ruta.

'Even to Barker's home in England?' someone asked.

'Yes, even to England,' Peleiupu replied. The wooden hulls, as she ran her fingers over them, felt like oiled paepae stone, like an imagery of light caught and crushed into unbreakable rock and then oiled to preserve it.

She realised, as she walked out of the shelter, that her feet were crunching over a thick layer of wood shavings, chips and sawdust. She glanced down: the floor was a white sea being ruffled by a strong wind. She looked back at the alia propped up by an intricate network of scaffolding. It appeared to be rocking in the white sea of wood waste. Rocking, moving almost imperceptibly.

In her dreams that night the mastless alia glowed bone-white as it rose, dipped and slid through an icy sea towards a lava-black castle whose battlements and towers were choked with mist. (She knew it was England without being told.) On the central tower stood a man dressed in glistening white robes that shimmered silkily like diaphanous membranes. The man beckoned to the alia with his long sinewy arm. Then Peleiupu was suddenly gazing into Stenson's face: into those deep blue eyes. Stenson was trying to tell her something but no sound was coming out of his mouth. She moved closer to him. All around, the air hummed with the beating of wings, and she was struggling against the singing emptiness, which was pulling her down towards the alia and the swirling sea. Nothing to hold on to! Nothing! She was choking, no air to save her. Barker! she heard herself calling.

It took another two months to complete the alia, which, during the elders' to'ona'i one Sunday at Mautu's, was named, at elder Sao's suggestion, *Le Sa-o-le-Sauali'i-Pa'epa'e*, the Ship of the White Phantom. Within a week every Satoan was referring to it affectionately by that name, as they prepared for its launching.

Because Mautu and Arona were busy with the alia, and Lalaga had to organise their contribution of fine mats, money and food to the launching, Peleiupu had to run the school. Ruta and Naomi helped her, and sensed that Peleiupu was deeply worried about something to do with the alia, Arona, their father and perhaps Barker: Peleiupu kept reading books about ships and sailing and exploration and tropical diseases. In her lucid lessons, she conveyed the information to her students and, for puzzling reasons, related it to the alia's construction. Peleiupu even described, to them, one night before they went to sleep, her frightening dream of the alia sailing to England, to Stenson and his dark castle, like a death canoe, and asked them to interpret those omens. They told her dreams were just dreams, not omens or prophecies, but Peleiupu insisted that in pre-papalagi times dreams were believed to be part of what was real — the future — and that the atua spoke to humans through their dreams. During the dreaming, she said, the dreamer sometimes left her body and travelled into other people's dreaming. When Ruta asked her if she believed that, Peleiupu half shook her head and said, 'Christians shouldn't believe that.' Then she considered further and added, 'Strange that our aiga were once the taulaaitu of the Atua Fatutapu; now we're priests for the Christian atua. And in our ancient religion, dreams were a vital script to guide us in our living . . .'

'Who told you that?' Naomi asked.

'Mautu,' she replied.

'It's bad to learn more about our Atua Fatutapu, but Mautu should tell us more about it,' Naomi sighed.

'It was in the Days of Darkness,' Ruta cautioned, but she too was interested in learning more.

Peleiupu pushed up the side of the mosquito net and sat up. It was not yet time to wake the others. She started combing her hair, untangling the knots. The mango trees behind the kitchen fale drew her attention, up to the highest one. A shadow? No, a dried branch, broken and hanging down. She continued combing; the comb snagged in a knot and she had to undo the comb carefully. The mango trees again. The highest one. No — not a broken branch, just a shadow. She hummed as the comb swept through her long hair and she remembered that the alia, now floating behind Barker's home, was to be launched the next day. The alia sang as it sailed swiftly in her imagination when she recalled Barker's confession that he'd been wrong in thinking he'd contracted the Disease. No sign of it, he'd admitted, two days before. Her heart was the sail of the alia, fully stretched with the wind's song of freedom. Perhaps Barker would teach her how to sail too, she thought. But girls couldn't be sailors.

The shadow again, in the mango tree. It was darker now, in the shape of a sack bloated with fruit, dangling from a short rope. Strange that there were no other shadows in the trees. Well, none as distinct.

Then it gripped her: her breath was a hand around her throat and pulling her up to her unsteady feet. She stepped out of the fale onto the paepae. Sucked in air. Her gullet unclogged but somehow a small ball, which felt like a green mango, remained. She swallowed again. The ball expanded and started pulling her across the paepae, as if it were attached to a line someone was pulling. Towards the mango trees. Cold dew on the grass under her feet. Breathe!

The shadow, the presence, wasn't in the mango trees. The ball tugged, pulled, and she moved with it. The shadow was now in the breadfruit trees down by the beach. The ball hurried her. It was not a sack — just mere outline cut out of black paper or black vapour, taunting her, pulling on the invisible line attached to the ball in her throat.

Bare earth under the breadfruit. She stumbled and her right knee stumped into the ground, the pain jabbing up into her thigh. No time to rub the hurt away or examine the cut on her knee — the line was pulling her head up. No shadow up there. It had retreated towards the sea, into the kapok tree, chuckling, pulling on the line. Fish caught. Her, the fish. The air whimpered in her head; her throat was being dragged out of her, so she moved with the line towards the kapok. Stumbled again. No time to clean the bleeding on her knees. Up, the line pulled her head. Nothing in the kapok, just dawn light as sharp as a bushknife blade.

The shadow, the presence, the creature of vapour was scurrying along the shore from tree to tree, dragging her behind it, along the beach, the sky, the world reeling in her head and eyes.

No one in sight. No one to save her. The sharp coral, rocks and shells cutting into her feet. The ball unforgiving in its insistence for her to follow. Fish hooked.

She didn't want to know. Forced her body to stop, dead still, hands clasped to her eyes, refusing to look at the shadow. She couldn't breathe. Falling forward, the sand rushing up to hit her. Rolling over. Gagging, and away again into the shallow water. The line was pulling her through the shallows, towards the shadow sitting in the green coolness, still taunting her — a mocking creature, the shape, feel, sound, the movement of a creature she'd always feared but had never put a name or identity to. Fear itself?

Satan? The Devil? Evil? She looked up into the belly of the air, the blind morning.

'God, forgive me!' she cried. 'Please, I don't want to see!' But God wasn't there, and the water was deepening, sucking at her. She shut her eyes but the line tugged up her head again. In the water, under her unwilling eyes, was the clear reflection of the alia, as if it had always been waiting for her to discover it. She raised her gaze up to the ball of fire breaking over the horizon, and the morning air, tanged by sea, rushed down through her gullet and she was breathing freely again. She spat out the bile and pain and fear into the reflection of the alia. She looked up at the craft.

Abruptly she shoved her head back into the water, wanting to drown her eyes, her mind, which could never leave her alone. She wanted to be protected from the truth, to see only the pleasant surface of things, this tide's skin but not what held it up, powered it, gave it shape, truth, intelligence.

But the water pushed up her face, expelled her, wanted her to see.

She shut her eyes again. Against the tears. Against the creature in the branchless tree above the alia, floating as the sun rose and illuminated all that was — is — as it must be, together in the wisdom of the unity in Peleiupu's sight.

She heard the tide lapping against the hulls of the alia, as the earth rocked around, waiting for her to open her sight to another dimension of knowledge into which, she sensed, only grief could take her.

And she opened her eyes to the vision of the tree, the central mast of the alia, to the taut rope arm of the creature that was fastened to the top crosspiece, to the creature hanging down, heavy, still, no longer black vapour without name; shadow become flesh become man.

Barker.

The sun continued rising to the silence of *Le Sa-o-le-Sauali'i-Pa'epa'e*.

Rising.

The Price of the Healing

'Lalaga! Lalaga!' Arona's urgent cry thrust into Lalaga's dreaming and wrenched her up out of it. In front of her, in their mosquito net, knelt Arona, with Peleiupu stretched across his arms, limp, soaked to the skin. Lalaga scrambled to them on her knees. Arona rolled Peleiupu into her arms. 'Barker's dead. Pele found him!' Arona said. Peleiupu was a shivering weight in her embrace.

'Mautu!' Lalaga cried. 'Mautu!'

Mautu, who was asleep, rolled over and sat up.

'Barker is dead!' Arona told him.

'And look!' cried Lalaga, holding Peleiupu up to Mautu.

He slid over on his haunches and felt Peleiupu's head. 'Get a towel!' he called into the fale. The others were waking and rushing over to them. 'She'll be all right,' he tried to calm Lalaga. 'Dry her and change her clothes.' Right then, Ruta and Naomi hitched up the mosquito net and, kneeling down, gave Lalaga a towel and dry clothes for Peleiupu. 'I'll go and see how Barker is.' He rehitched his ie lavalava as he stood up.

'He's on the alia,' Arona told him. They rushed out of the fale, followed by most of the older students.

'Pele, Pele, Pele,' Lalaga crooned to her daughter as she dried her. Ruta helped to change her and wrap her up in a blanket. Then Lalaga hugged her against her body to warm her, while Naomi and Ruta massaged her limbs. 'Pele, what's happened?' Lalaga asked.

Outside, the Satoans were hurrying to the beach and the alia. Eventually Peleiupu fell asleep with her arms around Lalaga's waist, but when Lalaga started stretching her out on the sleeping mats she wouldn't let go of her, so Lalaga continued hugging her.

When Peleiupu's grip relaxed around her, Lalaga stretched her out, with pillows under her head, combed her hair and, holding her hand and fanning the flies away, waited for Mautu. She refused to look in the direction of Barker's home, where she knew most Satoans were now gathered; refused to hear what students were telling Ruta and Naomi about Barker; refused admission to memories of Barker and the alia and how committed Mautu and Peleiupu and Arona were to Barker, the pagan foreigner who'd become so much one of them their Disease had even preferred him to anyone else; and in her determined refusal tried to swallow back the fear that she wouldn't be able to save her husband and children from their grief.

Naomi brought Peleiupu some koko and fa'alifu talo but she didn't touch it.

When Mautu's footsteps crunched over the paepae towards her Lalaga was too frightened to look around.

He sat down beside her; she was relieved she didn't have to look into his face. He poured himself a mug of koko and started sipping it. She waited. His arm stretched past her and he was smoothing down Peleiupu's hair. 'I don't understand,' he murmured.

'Understand what?'

'Why he did it.' His hand was suddenly a trembling fish stranded on the reef of her knee. She gripped it.

'Did what?'

'He didn't die of the Disease.' He withdrew his hand. 'He ended his own life.' She looked at him. He looked away. 'He hanged himself on the alia.'

'Pele must've seen him there.'

'Why? Why did he end it all when he was well again, and so happy building our alia?' She handed him the towel. He wiped his face.

'What are we going to do?' he asked.

'Be brave. God will help us through it.'

'What's going to happen to Pele?'

'She'll be all right again soon; I'll take care of her. You concentrate on organising Barker's funeral and service.'

'Remember, he willed there was to be no church service or Christian burial,' he said. 'And he wants to be laid at rest where he and I discovered "the People". How are we going to carry that out?'

'We *must* give him a Christian burial,' she said.

'Why?'

'Because he was a human being and our friend.'

'No. I am not going to betray him in death.'

'What if Poto and her aiga insist on a proper burial?'

He shook his head once and Lalaga knew he was not going to change his mind, ever. 'What else are we going to do?' he asked.

'Take one thing at a time,' she said calmly. He looked puzzled. 'Pele is not well,' she reminded him. 'And Arona loved him too; we'll have to help him too.'

'He was a good person, eh?' he interrupted. 'He had so much to live for.'

'I loved him too,' she tried to hold on to him. Peleiupu stirred, the blanket slipped off her shoulder, Lalaga pulled it up again.

Soon afterwards, Mautu went to his desk and books and, huddled in his chair, tried burying his sorrow in reading the Bible.

Later that day, as dusk was slipping into Satoa, Sao and Poto entered Mautu's fale. Mautu was alone apart from Peleiupu who was asleep behind the far curtain. He knew why they'd come. He hurried over and embraced Poto, who wept into his shoulder. 'It's all right,' he murmured. Over the years he'd grown very fond of her, recognising her to be Barker's strongest protection from his loneliness and sense of abandonment.

'It's so unfair, Mautu!' she cried.

'He has gone to God,' he said, and felt stupid at having done so.

After the formal greetings Sao said, 'I'll come to the point, sir, as time is short. I've come with my daughter to ask that Barker, the father of my daughter's children and the continuation of our line, be given a full Christian service and burial — if that is all right with you. It is Poto's wish. Despite the circumstances and manner of his death, he deserves a Christian service. At least that's what we believe, sir.'

Mautu considered Sao a just and compassionate leader, who usually placed the welfare of others before his self-interest, but that was also his flaw — which others, including relatives, used to their advantage. Mautu sensed that Sao was carrying out what Poto and the elders of his aiga wanted. 'It would be easy on everyone if we gave Barker, your son, the funeral that you want,' Mautu said. 'But he didn't want that. He wrote a mavaega and sent it to me. I have it here, sir. Would you like to see it?'

Poto was now weeping mutely into the corner of her ie lavalava. 'My children and I want him buried decently, as a human being!'

'In his mavaega he asks that he be laid to rest where we found "the People" up in the mountains. And without a Christian service,' Mautu said.

'But what about my children and me?' Poto cried. 'You know, sir, he was a

Christian even though he didn't attend church.'

'Poto, as I've said, a Christian burial would suit us all, but it was not his wish,' Mautu insisted. 'A mavaega is a sacred thing and should not be broken or ignored. To do so is dangerous, unchristian, and against our way of life.' He paused. 'Barker was a non-believer, though he was a better Christian than most of us. And, Poto, that's why you loved him. He lived by what he believed in. And if we didn't carry out his wishes, we would be betraying him.' She lowered her gaze. 'He came from far away and you, Poto, gave him a home in your heart.'

'You helped him too,' she said. 'You were his brother and you and Pele loved him.' She started crying again.

'I am satisfied,' Sao declared. 'At dawn tomorrow I'll send men up to the mountains to prepare his grave.' He started to get up.

'I'll send Arona to show them the way,' Mautu said. 'And thank you for understanding, sir.'

'I too learned to respect him,' Sao said, picking up his walking stick. 'He was a strange man.'

Poto started to get up. 'I think I understand,' she murmured. Then she followed her father out into the evening and the mournful crying of the cicadas that was an ocean around Barker's wake, leaving Mautu to live with the unalterable picture of Barker dressed in his starched white suit, tie and black shoes, thick hair slicked back with coconut oil, beard shaven off to reveal the yellow pallor of death, eyelids weighted down with two silver coins, as he lay in the fale in the open coffin, out of which he would never escape.

Mautu's memories of how he and Barker had prospected the river valley for gold and found the miracle of 'the People' returned vividly as he walked beside Sao behind the men who were slashing a path through the undergrowth. Since they'd buried 'the People' beside the church years before, they'd not returned to the foothills. Now they were, but Barker was dead. Was it a just swap? Barker's body for theirs? Yet it felt right, Barker's choice to be buried in 'the People's' deserted village.

Behind Mautu and Sao came the rest of Satoa, the strong men taking turns as pall-bearers, the others singing hymns to distract their attention from the load, the distance, the rising heat. They stopped often while the path was being cut — welcome rest periods. Some people cut large ta'amu leaves and passed them around to be used as umbrellas. Soon most of them were drenched in dew and sweat.

The coffin, which was covered with ie toga, was being carried on a wooden dais. Whenever it was lowered to the ground, Poto and her older daughters straightened the mats and wiped off the blobs of water that had fallen onto it from the canopy above.

As they veered away from the river's roar and deeper into the listening silence of the bush, they each withdrew into their own silence. Mautu's suit was wet skin around him but he was oblivious to it: he was locked into their discovery of 'the People's' graves, their careful uncovering of them, how Peleiupu and Arona had come to accept them as part of their dead, and how Barker, after professing cynicism, had finally revealed his respect for 'the People' by bringing his aiga to help construct the graves. The bush and hills and the silence and heat around were just as they had been that day they'd taken 'the People' down to their village, he thought.

A short while later, as they climbed the hill, he imagined that Barker would have been happy in his death. God understood too.

'. . . We have come here today to bring home to where he wanted to rest, our brother and friend, Ralph William Virgil Barker. He came to us as a stranger from England . . .' Mautu continued outlining Barker's life. The coffin lay above the open grave across wooden supports. Around it were the mourners, with Poto and her children and Lalaga and Peleiupu weeping softly. '. . . Some of us didn't accept our brother but he became one of us and he is now to be part of our earth. Our wise God must've sent him to us for a purpose.' He stopped. Gazed up into the sun's glare. 'He brought us much of the papalagi world, yet that world denied him — he didn't feel part of it, and for a while he lived in exile among us . . .' He sensed 'the People' around them, welcoming Barker home: after all, Barker had discovered them.

After his sermon Mautu moved over and stood beside Poto and her children, and they watched as the men, using ropes, lowered Barker into the earth. Then Sao started a hymn, which they all sang. And the sky, sun, trees, birds, hills, mountains, valleys and ravines became one with them and 'the People'.

On their way home Peleiupu held Poto's hand, while Arona walked beside his father. 'He must've been happy,' Arona said. Mautu was surprised by his son's remark. 'He must've been, otherwise why choose such a death, at a time when you are most satisfied with your life?'

'Yes, it was deliberate. But suicide is against God's way, against our way,' Mautu said, and then felt stupid.

'I must learn the ways that allow such choice and freedom,' Arona said.

No, Mautu wanted to caution him, but didn't. He envied his son and decided not to discourage him from following Barker into the ways of freedom. But what if it took him away from God and Christianity, into Darkness, the void, death in exile, and the terror of it all?

Two days later, when the flotilla was well beyond the reef pointing north and their island had become a featureless grey outline in the haze behind them, To'alemu, Satoa's tautai, who was on the Sa-o-le-Sauali'i Paepae, signalled them to stop.

The fautasi and the canoes gathered around the alia. It was a warm morning, with the sun hidden behind clouds, the sea breathing lightly. The crew pulled down the alia's sail. To'alemu and a crewman reached down and pulled Mautu out of the fautasi onto the alia's deck. As Mautu stood under the mast, with the Bible open in his hands, the crew helped the other elders onto the alia, where they sat down and faced their pastor.

Mautu started the hymn; the others joined in. The ocean around listened. So did the hushed sky. Twice during the previous two days Mautu had attended the fono of matai, at Sao's faletele, and tried to save the alia. At their first meeting, he'd argued that though Barker had sinned against God by taking his own life, the alia was free of that. He thought he'd convinced the fono but, that night, friends had informed him that most of the matai favoured 'burying' the alia at sea, well away from Satoa, because it was cursed. There'd been no discussion of Barker's suicide, the whys and wherefores of it: they simply condemned it as an unnatural and sinful act, against sane and civilised behaviour.

Next morning at the fono, Mautu had again pleaded for the alia's life: they'd spent months building it, learning to love it as the most magnificent craft they'd ever designed; what was the sense of destroying it now? Couldn't Barker's sinful act not be interpreted to have given birth to a great blessing, the alia? He spoke directly to Sao, who could sway the fono. The old man listened but said nothing. 'It would also be a decent memorial to him,' Mautu added, when the matai maintained their silence.

Just as he was getting ready to leave, Sao said, 'Thank you for your views. The papalagi did become one of us, and, unlike other foreigners, he didn't try to change us and our way of life. He brought us many helpful inventions and skills. And he was my daughter's husband, father of my grandchildren. We also know he was your dearest friend . . .' As Sao spoke, Mautu realised — and he resented it — that Sao was killing (that was the word) the alia to get back at him for not having agreed to a Christian burial for Barker. Sometimes Sao's justice was revenge, but always done with grace, the aristocratic way. '. . . We can't risk people's lives when they use such a craft, which has been cursed by the Almighty. Though we are willing to listen to any further views you may want to express, sir.'

Mautu had thanked them and had gone to consult Poto. He was surprised by her reaction. 'He loved that boat, so it is best that it be buried with him. If we keep it alive it will always remind me of him. I won't be able to bear that,' she had said.

After the hymn, Mautu read from the Bible. His prayer, after the reading, was brief and they would remember it: 'Dear God, please forgive us for the act we are about to commit. Accept into the depths of your forgiveness and love, the victim of our fears. Amen.'

He didn't look at any of them as he climbed back down into the fautasi and, sitting down at the helm, turned his back to the alia. 'Let's go,' he ordered his crew.

The other fautasi and canoes moved away, leaving only To'alemu and five other men with axes on board the alia.

'Don't stop!' Mautu instructed his crew when they stopped rowing so they could see the sinking of the alia. 'Row!' They obeyed immediately, for they'd not seen such anger in their pastor before. 'Faster!' he called.

The sharp relentless thudding of the axes biting into the hulls of the alia echoed across the water, and each blow cut into Mautu's head. Kluttt! Klutt! Klutt! 'Faster, I told you to go faster!' He called, standing up.

He couldn't look back. But the Ship of the White Phantom drowned slowly in his head, the sea bubbling up into its body through the gashes in its hulls. With his hands he tried blocking the holes, pushing the flood back out, but the pressure thrust his hands back and the sea shot up into his face, choking him.

He would remember that drowning every time he thought of Barker, and drown a little bit more with each remembering.

At first, during what the Satoans came to call her illness, Peleiupu would sleep for long periods, wake and, sleeping sheet wrapped tightly around her as if she were frightened her body was disintegrating, sit and gaze out through the palm trees at the bay. Someone was always with her when she was awake because Lalaga feared her wandering off into the sea or bush or — and she dreaded this most of all — into an irretrievable inner darkness where aitu would imprison her forever. Though Peleiupu didn't seem to hear anything they said to her, they talked to her as if nothing were wrong.

At the morning and evening lotu most of the aiga prayed for her recovery; her students did so fervently because they were suffering Lalaga's harsh discipline and Mautu's sad indifference, and they wanted Peleiupu to save them from both.

One by one the taulasea of Satoa, except Filivai whom Lalaga avoided, tried to heal her. They all failed, and recommended taulasea from nearby villages. Lalaga got those but refused to get Lefatu, Mautu's sister, who, like Filivai, was a healer of ma'i aitu. They failed too.

By then Peleiupu was sleeping normal hours and, during the day, participating in their everyday life but as a mute observer. The taulasea agreed that it was as if her agaga were outside her body observing what her body was doing. Did her agaga want to return to the body? one taulasea asked.

'What are we going to do now?' Lalaga demanded of Mautu one afternoon as they watched Peleiupu plaiting a mat.

'We have to accept how she is now.'

'You accept it; I won't! You haven't been much help.' He got up to leave. 'That's your usual way now, eh? You walk away from our problems. You escape into those useless books. But I won't give up on my daughter!' He didn't leave; he went to his desk and fiddled with his papers. 'Your sorrow won't bring Barker and Pele back,' she continued. Since the drowning of the alia he'd withdrawn from his aiga and village affairs. True, he took Peleiupu's classes, he preached and hosted the elders' to'ona'i on Sundays, and conducted weddings and funerals, but there was no spark, spirit, commitment or joy. Gone was the rich daring that Barker had drawn out of him — the fertile, free-floating imagination, the firing of souls to believe in their limitless possibilities. To save him, Sao admitted he'd erred in destroying the alia, and asked for his forgiveness, but Mautu said it had been for the best.

'Perhaps I should resign as pastor,' he said to Lalaga. 'There's no depth of belief in me any more.'

'I've had enough — enough of your self-pity,' she said. 'If you've lost your belief, say so, admit it to God. I've got Pele, our aiga and everything else to look after.' She paused. 'Mautu, do whatever you like.' She turned away.

She heard him getting up and hurrying out of the fale. A short while later she looked around and saw him marching across the malae. She went and sat beside Peleiupu, who glanced at her and then continued staring out into the bay as her fingers plaited the mat, faultlessly.

Two hours later Lalaga left Ruta with Peleiupu and, with Naomi, started their classes. As Lalaga was writing on the blackboard Mautu returned, acknowledged her with a curt nod, and hurried to his classroom.

Once she glanced over at the main fale, and saw a woman, her back towards her, sitting with Ruta and Peleiupu. She thought nothing of it because Peleiupu often had visitors. It was only after the students had gone home and she sat down to rest that she looked again. She recognised the woman and sprang up.

'Wait,' Mautu asked, as he entered her classroom. 'Leave them alone.'

'No!' she protested. 'She's not . . .'

'Not what?'

'She's not Christian; her cures are not of God!'

'But you've tried everything else.'

'Why are you doing this to me?' she countered. He wheeled and hurried to the fale where he sat opposite Peleiupu and Filivai, the taulasea, who was massaging Peleiupu's forehead with oiled ti leaves.

'Shit!' Lalaga caught herself exclaiming for the first time since her childhood. 'Shit!' But didn't feel guilty about it. She sat at her desk, refusing to go to the fale.

She refused to talk to Mautu until they were in bed that night. 'Why are you doing this to me?' she demanded.

'It isn't for you. You're not the one who's sick. It's for my daughter, and I'll do anything to make her well again.'

'Even sell your soul to Satan?' She had him.

'Yes!' was his undeniable heresy. 'Yes, if it'd heal Pele.'

'You're talking like — yes, like Barker,' she accused. He didn't answer. 'His paganism is in you now!'

'Your trouble is you've been conditioned by our papalagi missionaries to condemn our pre-Christian past, our religion and cures; to dismiss them as superstition, as works of the Devil. I was once like you . . .'

'But Barker saved you.'

'Yes. He helped show me we should be proud of who and what we were and are. I still admire the missionaries but much of what they preach and teach is arrogant, narrow; not Christian ways but English ways and prejudices. They've made many of us ashamed of being Samoan.'

'I'm not as clever as you and I've never had the luxury or time to question what I was brought up to believe . . .'

'This morning you accused me of withdrawing from our problems and leaving them to you. You were correct. Now I'm trying to help.' He stopped. 'Do you want me to help?' he added.

'Yes!' she snapped, caught again.

'Then don't stop Filivai from trying to cure our daughter.'

Helped by her granddaughter, Filivai came every afternoon, except Sunday. Lalaga was never there, but Ruta helped Filivai. First Filivai massaged Peleiupu's body and got her to drink a thick green concoction, and then, while Peleiupu lay gazing up into the dome of the fale, Filivai played cards with Ruta and talked to Peleiupu, who didn't seem to hear her.

One evening Ruta told Lalaga that Peleiupu was starting to respond to Filivai's treatment. How? By crying softly, and Filivai would hold her and hush her to sleep. 'Don't tell your father yet,' Lalaga said.

Next day Filivai brought a bundle of young ifi leaves. After the usual treatment she opened the bundle. 'Here, smell these.' She raised the leaves to Peleiupu's face. 'They're from your tree, the ifi.' Peleiupu buried her face in them, raised her head and smiled at Filivai. 'Here, you help me oil them.' Peleiupu helped Filivai oil each leaf, then sew them into two ula. 'Beautiful!' Filivai congratulated her. When she put one around Peleiupu's neck, Peleiupu chortled like a child, held it up and rubbed the leaves into her face until her face glistened with the coconut oil from the leaves. 'Here, put on this one.' Filivai said to Ruta.

As Ruta leaned forward, Peleiupu lowered the ula around her neck, hugged her, withdrew and chortled some more. 'Good, you're getting better. You see, it was good you told me about your tree and its spirit, a long time ago. I never forgot, Pele.'

'I was wrong,' Lalaga apologised to Mautu as they lay in their net that night. 'Pele looked so happy tonight. She's even sleeping with her ula on.' When he touched her breast she moved up against him.

They made love for the first time in many weeks, and enjoyed it.

Filivai arrived unexpectedly during their morning meal. Naomi put a foodmat in front of her. Mautu thanked her for the improvement in Peleiupu. Filivai talked all through the meal, but not about Peleiupu.

After she'd washed her hands and dried her mouth using a basin of water and teatowel Naomi brought her, she thanked them for the meal and then said, almost offhandedly, 'I'm still afraid for her. I've done all that I can for her.'

'But you're our last hope,' Lalaga was quick to say. The old woman looked at her. 'We've tried every other taulasea.'

Filivai looked at Mautu. 'Are you sure?' she asked.

'Yes,' Lalaga replied.

'Mautu knows,' Filivai said. 'Eh?'

'Yes,' Mautu admitted. 'There is my sister.'

'Yes, there is his sister,' Filivai said to Lalaga. 'If anyone can cure Pele, she can.'

'But how do you know? You've not met her,' Lalaga objected.

'I've not met her, true, but she is the most gifted of us all. Ask those in your congregation who've been healed by her.' She stopped, laughed. 'Oh, I forgot: you being their pastor, they wouldn't dare reveal to you that they still consult the so-called forces of Darkness and Satan. Once upon a time, I was too scared to tell you too. But your congregation tell me about your sister's mana. And you know, Mautu, eh?' Mautu nodded. 'I'm glad you consulted me first. At least your sister will see — and know — I have the gift, modest though it may be.' She stopped. 'Now I must carry this old body home before the sun gets too hot.' Ruta helped her to her feet. 'Mautu knows of course that she may ask a price for her healing.' Lalaga glanced at Mautu. He indicated nothing. 'You have another beautiful daughter here,' Filivai said of Ruta.

The tulula had a crew of six rowers, and carried Mautu, Lalaga, Peleiupu and Ruta, their luggage and some foodstuffs for Mautu's aiga. It would take about two hours to reach Fagaloto, Mautu's village. Lalaga held an umbrella above Peleiupu and tried not to think of what lay ahead. Ruta hummed now and then, dragged her arm alongside the tulula in the water, told Peleiupu about how she was looking forward to seeing their Aunt Lefatu, who, she claimed, was the wisest person in the world, and how she wanted Lefatu to teach them to read dreams.

'That's not possible,' Lalaga said. 'Dreams are dreams, not prophecies. Lefatu is a wise person but she's had no education. She can't even read and write.' When she realised Ruta wasn't listening she was hurt but didn't show it.

When the tulula touched the sand the crew and Mautu helped them ashore, unloaded and then pulled the tulula up into the shade of the palm trees and covered it with mats. Lalaga sensed that Mautu wanted her to take the girls and go on ahead; she wasn't having any of that — no, let Mautu meet his own arrogant, sinister sister first and tell her why they hadn't been to visit her for three years and why they'd consulted every other taulasea and not her. She fussed with Peleiupu's clothes.

'Let's go,' Mautu said finally. He marched past her up the narrow track.

They reached the clearing of the compound. Relatives rushed out of the fale to greet them. Mautu had never exorcised Lefatu and that other side of his aiga from himself, Lalaga observed. No, in fact Barker had encouraged him to respect and love them. She moved among their relatives, embracing and kissing them. She glimpsed Lefatu in the main fale, pounding some mixture in a small wooden pestle. She lingered with the others.

'Come to the faletele,' Tuifolau, Mautu's cousin, invited them.

'Lalaga, you go ahead with Tuifolau,' Mautu tried to get out of it.

'We'll wait for you,' she said. Mautu and the crew took their things to the fale where they were to sleep.

'Lefatu's been expecting you,' Tuifolau told her. 'She's been having bad dreams about sickness in your children. Other taulasea have been to tell her about Pele, so she's been waiting.'

'Let's go in,' Mautu whispered. He headed for Lefatu. Lalaga steered Peleiupu with her arm. The elders and Ruta followed them.

Lefatu did not greet them or even look up from her work. Mautu and the others sat down at the posts opposite her. Tuifolau sat a few paces to her right. She maintained her silence. She was younger than Mautu, and a spinster, as was the tradition for any woman who became their taulaaitu and taulasea, but she looked older than her brother: her long hair was almost totally grey and glistened with coconut oil. She dripped more oil into the mixture.

'Mautu and Lalaga have come,' Tuifolau said to her.

'I'm not blind,' she said quietly, as she continued pounding the mixture. 'Why didn't you bring the girl earlier?' She looked across at Peleiupu. 'Come!' she coaxed her. She stretched out her arms. Peleiupu gazed into her face. 'Don't be afraid, Pele. Come. Bring her to me,' Lefatu instructed Lalaga, who hesitated. 'Bring the girl!' An order.

'Take the girl to Lefatu,' Mautu urged. Whenever Lefatu and Mautu were together they tended to treat the rest of their aiga as servants, Lalaga had concluded previously. Mautu treated no other woman as Lefatu's equal.

Lalaga put her arms around Peleiupu and coaxed her to Lefatu, who smiled up at her and, patting the mat in front of her, said, 'Sit here, Pele.' Peleiupu sat down and continued staring into Lefatu's face. 'You're really grown up, eh!' Lefatu told her. She ran her hands over Peleiupu's face and down her shoulders and arms. Pulling an ali from behind her, she told Peleiupu to lie down with her head on the ali. Peleiupu obeyed. Lefatu dripped oil onto her forehead and started massaging it. 'Why didn't you bring her to me when she fell ill?'

'We didn't think she was that sick,' Mautu lied.

'It is because your wife does not trust me and your aiga,' Lefatu said. Lalaga lowered her head. 'She has never trusted me; she is afraid of us.'

'That is not true!' Mautu objected. He was the only one who dared argue with her. 'You are being unfair and impolite to my wife.'

'I speak only the truth, and without anger or rudeness. You know that.' She glanced at Mautu and added, 'I need to be alone with Pele. To heal her — if I can.' Lalaga caught the threat and looked up. Lefatu was smiling as if saying, your daughter's fate is in my hands. Lalaga got up to leave. The others followed her. 'Ruta, you stay and help me,' Lefatu said. 'Come and mix the medicine for me.' Ruta did so eagerly.

They were served a meal in the back fale where they were to stay. The others left to carry out their daily chores. 'Why is she always arrogant?' Lalaga demanded of Mautu.

'She is honest, not arrogant. She never pretends. She always speaks the truth — even if it wounds. And she is my sister, and therefore our feagaiga, so we must treat her with respect. You know that.' He left for the kitchen fale where the men were making an umu.

Without her established routines, her busy schedule, Lalaga usually experienced a painful sense of aloneness. Existence was to work and work, serving others and teaching them the virtues of hard work. Now she was caught in the midst of an aiga led by a woman who had no work, time or love for her; who was healing her daughter and in that healing would take her daughter's love away from her; who was cultivating in her children a love and respect for the mana, superstitions and cruelty of their pre-Light past.

She got out her Bible and tried reading it. But throughout the afternoon she couldn't stop observing Lefatu, Ruta and the two women helpers in the main fale. Sometimes they laughed, and Lalaga thought they were laughing about her.

That evening Lefatu, Ruta and the two women didn't attend the family lotu and meal. Food was taken to them by the oldest women. Lalaga wanted to go and see Peleiupu but Mautu stopped her. 'When Lefatu is healing someone she has to be left alone. She will ask for us eventually. It has always been that way.'

'What if Pele asks for me — for us?'

'Lefatu will decide.'

'Why is she keeping Ruta there?'

'Because she wants her to learn.'

Lalaga was too frightened to ask about the knowledge Ruta was being taught.

That night she kept waking and looking at the one row of raised blinds in Lefatu's fale, out of which the weak flickering light of the lamp was being sucked by the thick darkness. Why was the one raised row facing the west? And she remembered Mautu saying, years before, 'It is for the atua to enter through.' She knew which atua he meant.

At dawn, with the cold breeze shuffling through the fale blinds, Lalaga and Mautu woke to Lefatu sitting outside their net, smoking a cheroot of home-grown tobacco wrapped in dried banana leaf.

'Is anything the matter?' Mautu asked her.

She shook her head and spat out onto the paepae. 'She's asleep,' she said. Lalaga sat up. 'Lalaga, Peleiupu almost died because you refused to trust me. We are Christian. We are also Tuifolau. There is no contradiction.' She paused and sucked on her cheroot. 'There's no need for you two to stay. When Pele is well, we will bring her back. I want Ruta to stay with Pele.' She left before they could say anything.

'We're not leaving without my children,' Lalaga said to Mautu.

'Why, because you still don't trust my sister and my aiga?' No reply. 'She is testing you. She wants to know if you're willing to trust Pele's life to her. You show you don't trust her now, and she'll never talk to you again.'

'What about Ruta?'

'It'll be good for Pele to have her around.'

'You know that's not what I mean,' Lalaga pursued him. Mautu refused to reply. 'Is Ruta the price Filivai referred to?'

'What do you mean?' he tried evading her.

'Is Lefatu asking Ruta to stay for good, to learn those . . . ?' She couldn't say it.

'I don't know,' he said. 'Anyway, what is wrong with Ruta inheriting the knowledge?'

'Because it is — it is not right!'

'But you're willing for Pele to be healed by it?'

She had no answer for that.

Before they left at mid-morning they went to see Ruta and Peleiupu. Lefatu wasn't around. Peleiupu was asleep, and appeared safe and content. Lalaga caressed the side of her face. 'Lefatu is very good to us,' Ruta said. 'She loves Pele very much. She says Pele will get well.'

'Do you want to stay here with Pele and Lefatu?' Mautu asked.

'Yes, very much. She's taught me a lot already. And I'll come home with Pele.' She remembered her mother and looked at her. 'Is that all right?'

Lalaga said, 'It is what Lefatu wants.' She bent forward and kissed Peleiupu's forehead. 'You look after your sister,' she said to Ruta.

She locked herself away from the brilliant spread of coast and sea and sun, the swaying of the water under their tulula, and the rise and dip of the oars, refusing to talk to anyone, refusing the umbrella Mautu offered her. Her daughters' absence was an extravagant pain. She'd abandoned her daughters to a past and a way that Misi Peta had considered cruel and uncivilised, but was the last chance of saving Peleiupu.

Letting Go

Lalaga feigned a headache so she could stay in the fale and finish sewing Peleiupu's dress. Mautu, Naomi and Arona were taking the classes. She dripped sweat as she worked. In the slow breeze from the sea she smelled the musky odour of coral. One more seam and the dress would be finished. She'd already sewn dresses for Lefatu, Ruta, and Tuifolau's wife: gifts she was to take next morning on a secret visit to Fagaloto.

Almost three months had passed since they'd left Peleiupu and Ruta in Fagaloto. They'd heard no news of them for the first month. But when she demanded that they go and visit their children, Mautu reminded her that such a move would be interpreted, by Lefatu and his aiga, as a lack of faith in the way they were caring for Peleiupu. Lalaga struggled for another week, and then demanded that they send someone else then. She wept when Mautu refused, and accused him of not loving her children, so Mautu asked some Satoans who were visiting Fagaloto to ask after the girls, discreetly. After four days they returned and Lalaga squeezed every drop of information from them: Peleiupu was improving, she was talking again even if it was only to Lefatu, and Ruta was loved by everyone. Lalaga lived off that news for a month, and then pleaded again that they visit. This time Mautu admitted he missed them too, but still refused her request. 'I'll go on my own!' Lalaga threatened. Mautu didn't try to stop her. She didn't go.

The atule season started the following week, with large schools of the fish running along the coast from east to west. Even Mautu joined the fishing. The large catches were shared among the aiga. Being pastor, with a large household to support, Mautu got the most, so every week he sent Arona and Tavita, Barker's eldest son who now slept at their home, with atule to Fagaloto, on the tulula. Lalaga survived on the news they brought back about Peleiupu and Ruta. After their first visit Arona asked if he could stay with their aiga at Fagaloto. 'No!' was Lalaga's abrupt reply. 'But why?' Mautu asked, after Arona had stamped off. 'No!' she whispered, and hurried off to her class.

In October the palolo rose: a harvest so rich they distributed it to other villages. Lalaga sent Arona, Tavita and their crew to Fagaloto with baskets of palolo. They didn't return for two days, and Lalaga got Mautu to organise another tulula to go after them.

Arona arrived as the other crew were preparing to leave. In front of everyone Lalaga berated him: 'Have you no love for us, eh? For two days we've been worried about you. We thought you'd drowned!' Arona stood, head bowed, in silence. When she stopped he turned abruptly to leave. 'Aren't you going to say anything about your sisters?'

'They're all right!' he snapped. He rushed off, with Tavita and his friends trailing him.

When they were alone Mautu said to her, 'There was no need for that.'

'Your sister is even trying to take my son away from me,' she replied. He walked away. 'She is!' she called. 'You just don't want to see the truth!'

Lalaga turned the handle of the sewing machine. The needle began jabbing down into the fabric. Tutt-tutt-tutt-tutt. She stopped, held her breath, looked at the track down to the beach. No one. She turned the handle. Tutt-tutt-tutt-tutt. A clatter. Of what? Once again. Of oars? Voices. She looked again and was up onto her feet, hurrying, repinning her bun. Towards the beach.

The narrow track was brittle dry under her feet. She glimpsed a figure approaching through the trees on the bend. A figure running. She started running too. Around the bend.

Pele! Pele! She opened her arms, and into her embrace rushed her daughter, smelling of fresh oil and the sea and the promise of joy without end, as she held her. Held her. Pele.

'Lalaga, I'm well again,' Peleiupu said.

'Good, good,' murmured Lalaga, hiding her tears. Then she saw Ruta, who was standing a few paces away. 'Come!' she called. Ruta slid into her encircling arm and into her side, and she held her too. 'I've got new dresses for you,' she whispered.

'Lefatu came with us,' Ruta said. Lalaga stepped away from her daughters, wiping her eyes with the hem of her dress.

When she looked up Lefatu stepped towards her. They hesitated. One step forward each. Lalaga stopped. Lefatu leaned forward and kissed her on the cheek. 'Thank you for Pele,' Lalaga said. 'Thank you.'

'God has been kind,' Lefatu said. 'The mana is His.' And Lalaga wanted to believe her.

By then Mautu and most of their aiga and school were around them. 'I thought I'd bring them back so I can see your home and enjoy the comfortable life of a pastor's family!' Lefatu said to Mautu, who laughed softly.

They started moving up the track, Ruta and Peleiupu chatting noisily with their large tribe of friends. Lalaga noticed that Naomi was being left out, so she moved over and held her arm.

When they were seated in the main fale the matai of Satoa, led by Sao, arrived to welcome them. Though Satoa's tulafale never referred directly to Lefatu, and her tulafale spoke as if they were the leaders of their party, everyone knew Lefatu was the centre of the Aiga Sa-Tuifolau and the village of Fagaloto, and respected her more because she was le tama'ita'i o valoaga, the woman of prophecies, daughter of the Tuifolau, taulaaitu of the atua, with a mana and powers they feared and needed. Throughout the formalities she rolled a cheroot and smoked it, and tried to appear as if she weren't the centre of the ceremony. Even when the ava cup was taken to her, she insisted it be given to Mautu.

That evening Lefatu asked, 'Who was Barker, who Pele talks a lot about?' Mautu told her. During her stay Lalaga, Arona, Naomi and other Satoans would add their chapters to Barker's saga. Not that many Satoans visited. Lalaga attributed it to their fear — and awe — of Lefatu.

Lefatu was up at the first rooster's call and, gazing out at the eastern mountains, smoked a cheroot. Then as the sun hurdled the range she started singing the hymn for their morning lotu. They woke and joined her, but she left the biblical recital and prayer to Mautu. She then washed and lit the fire and, despite Lalaga's insistence that she not do the cooking, did so, helped by the girls.

Later, most mornings, the girls took her through their collection of books. 'I'm uneducated, I can't read or write,' she confessed as she flicked through the books. But Lalaga sensed that Lefatu wasn't ashamed of it. While they took their classes Lefatu wove sinnet — a man's occupation — or ironed, or cleaned the fale. After classes Peleiupu, Ruta and Naomi took her up the river valley. Lalaga thought they were collecting herbs and medicines, but they usually brought back nothing.

Other days, if the tide was right, she went fishing for sea-slugs, sea-eggs and loli. Women who went with her told Lalaga she was an expert fisher and had great knowledge of the sea's creatures.

Soon after Lefatu arrived, Lalaga had hints, then direct requests, from Satoans seeking for Lefatu to heal their ailments. She refused to ask Lefatu who, throughout her stay, did not encourage patients, including those from Fagaloto, to come to her.

'I'm having a really good rest,' she remarked at their morning meal a week after she came. 'No responsibilities, good food, good companions, the comforts of being a pastor's sister!' She laughed. 'And daughters and sons who serve me as if I were a queen. Good to see that Pele is herself again, but not as talkative as before.' Peleiupu blushed and wished Lefatu wouldn't talk about her. 'And Arona is not as fat as before!' Arona managed a smile. 'And Ruta and Naomi don't squabble as often as they used to!'

'Not my fault!' Naomi interjected, then clapped her hand over her mouth.

'Still as bold as ever, eh!' Lefatu guffawed. The elders laughed with her. 'The women of this aiga were never known for meekness.' She glanced at Lalaga.

'That's true,' Lalaga said.

'And we men have had to suffer that,' Mautu said.

Lalaga sensed that Lefatu was ready to return to Fagaloto and, when alone or in bed at night, she wept silently, dreading what was going to happen. For two days she managed not to be alone with Lefatu. Then, after school, while she was resting at her desk, fanning herself and gazing out at the bay, she heard someone entering and standing behind her. 'Sit down here,' she said, pointing at the chair to her right.

Lefatu slid into the chair, and they watched the sea sparkle, darken, ripple under the noonday light.

'Our aiga has always had a taulasea. I am that now, and I've tried to find a child within our aiga to continue after me,' Lefatu spoke quietly, as if to the sea. 'Within our aiga at Fagaloto there is no one.' Lalaga heard the buzzing of a fly; wondered why she was listening to it. 'You guessed early why I came back with Pele?' Lalaga nodded once. The fly was gone; the silence ticked like her pulse. 'Your children are our most gifted. And Pele most gifted of all.' Lalaga looked at Lefatu. 'But I won't ask for her. She is destined for other things for our aiga. I mustn't alter that.' Lalaga sighed. 'I'm asking that Ruta become my child, the heir to our healing.' She paused. 'I'm asking that of you.'

'It was gracious of you to visit us, to stay,' Lalaga began, holding her arms across the desk to control their shaking. 'To bring our daughters back to us, with Pele healed. You could've kept Ruta, without coming to ask me. I wouldn't have been able to object. Thank you for coming and asking.' She had to stop. 'You are our feagaiga and the heart of our aiga. I can't deny you anything. That is the way it must be. That doesn't mean I don't feel any pain, even resentment, about the matter. Ruta is my flesh and blood. I love her deeply.' She wiped away her tears. 'What is to be her future, though? Even in the healing, the new medicine will take over.'

'I must not be the last in our aiga,' Lefatu said. 'It is not just for the healing.'

'What then?'

'It is for all of us — our history, traditions, way of life and ways of seeing.'

'And?' Lalaga insisted. 'I want you to admit it to me for the first time. Even your brother won't admit it!'

'All right,' Lefatu replied, turning to look at her. Her eyes were darkly clear. 'And for the Atua, our Atua.'

Lalaga suddenly felt light: for the first time she felt safe in the Aiga Sa-Tuifolau. Part of it. Valued by it. In letting go of Ruta she was becoming all that was Lefatu, heart of the Aiga Sa-Tuifolau. Besides, after Lefatu, Ruta, her daughter, was to be the atua's keeper.

On Saturday afternoon while everyone else was busy preparing the Sunday umu, Lalaga called her children together.

'On Monday Ruta will go with Lefatu when she returns to Fagaloto,' she told them.

'What about me? I want to go too,' Naomi insisted.

Ignoring her, Lalaga said, 'Ruta is going to stay with Lefatu. She has no children of her own.'

'That's not fair!' Naomi objected.

'Don't talk like that again!' Arona threatened. Naomi slapped the mat.

'Do you want to go?' Lalaga asked Ruta.

Ruta nodded and said, 'Lefatu is very kind to me. She needs me, and I want to learn from her.'

'It'll mean your not going to modern school to learn science, English, numbers and things like that,' Lalaga explained.

'That doesn't matter. Pele and Naomi can do that,' Ruta replied.

'Ruta is fortunate,' Peleiupu said. 'With Lefatu things will last, they'll be what they are.' They waited for her to explain. She didn't.

'And you'll be going to Vaiuta to study next year,' Lalaga revealed to her. There was no visible reaction from Peleiupu. 'Is that all right with you?'

'Many years ago you told me I was going,' Peleiupu replied. 'So it has to be.'

'And me?' Naomi asked.

'You can go to Vaiuta too, year after next.'

"I don't want to study to be a pastor yet,' Arona anticipated her. When Lalaga looked at him, he lowered his gaze. 'I'm not ready for the ministry yet.'

She had to accept his excuse, though she sensed he didn't want to go at all, ever. 'We'll wait, then,' she countered him. She had time to persuade him.

'Everything is but changes,' Peleiupu said, more to herself than to the others. That was Lefatu talking, Lalaga thought. Puzzles, riddles, beyond her comprehension. 'This is probably the last time we'll be together as we've always been. We are starting to go our own ways.'

'Don't worry, there'll be many more meetings like this,' Lalaga declared. 'We're aiga, and the love between us is unbreakable.'

'Yes!' chorused Ruta and Naomi. Arona and Peleiupu glanced at each other.

Lalaga wanted to hold them all in her arms.

Goodbyes

'For about three months I kept my fears to myself, hoping the Disease would treat me kindly and go away,' Barker had said. 'But I got so scared I had to tell someone. And I did — in a moment of terror, I told Arona.' It was a Sunday afternoon; Barker had sent Arona to fetch Peleiupu. 'He wasn't supposed to tell anyone. He told me two days ago he'd told you.' Barker had stopped planing the board on his work bench and glanced at her. 'Have you told anyone?' Peleiupu shook her head. 'Good,' he said. His plane slid across the board; a long shaving curled out of it and fluttered to the floor. 'Well, as you can see, I'm as fit as a fiddle!' She looked at him. 'Yes, I was wrong about having the Disease.' Peleiupu had thought the shavings, strewn across the floor, looked like white sea eels someone had dried and curled and twisted. 'See?' He stood up and pointed at his bare torso. 'Not a sign of it!' She picked up a shaving and wound and unwound it around her fingers. 'I'm healthier now than I've ever been. In building the alia, I seemed to have rebuilt myself.' She broke the shaving into pieces and let the pieces drift to the floor. 'Are you sure you never told anyone?' he asked. She shook her head again, and hoped Arona hadn't told him about their parents knowing. 'Good,' Barker had repeated.

Through the large back windows of the shed, Peleiupu had noticed that everything was ablaze with noon sun, and she thought of snow on mountains in the books she'd read, of the Eskimos and polar bears Barker had told them about years before. Her hands tingled with the burning feel of snow, the way Barker had described it. Tingled, burned, to the bone. He wasn't going to die; God had released her from her burden of trying to save him. The miraculous burning was radiating out from her hands to all her limits. Beautiful!

'Is there anything else?' she had asked. He was gazing out at the alia which was moored to a pole in the water a short distance from the beach. It turned slowly around the pole until its stern was pointing at them.

'She's a beauty, eh?' he had said. Yes, she sighed inside, a beauty: it could take them to England and those wonderful places Barker had built into their lives and possibilities.

'Is there anything else?' she asked.

'No,' he replied. 'We launch her in two days' time: a new beginning for me.'

That was how she described, to Mautu, her final meeting with Barker. They were returning from the beach after seeing off Lefatu and Ruta and their party, and she was compelled to tell him. As she did so, she couldn't unclog her memory of Ruta sitting at the tulula's stern, gazing back and waving, then the tulula was around Totoume Peninsula. Lalaga and Naomi hurried on ahead as a light drizzle started sweeping across the trees. Mautu said nothing. Her story seemed caught in the white net of rain, and was to be the basis of all the future versions of that meeting she was to tell her children and their children and their children's children; and with each telling came the questions: Had their Disease chosen Barker? Had he lied about getting it, and then lied about not having It? And what did that have to do with his suicide?

Once inside their main fale Mautu tossed her a towel. She dried herself. She heard him open the metal trunk in which he kept his valuables. She waited, picturing him lifting out the small ornate box, which was wrapped in calico.

He came back through the curtain, sat down on the mat and untied the calico. She sat down opposite him. 'Remember this?' he asked. The box glistened. The mandarins and students carved across the lid seemed to be dancing a slow dirge, in unison. 'He wrote that only I was to read this, remember?' he murmured. She got up. 'No, stay, this may explain why he decided to end his life, and end it the way — the way it ended.' She sat down again. 'His death caused you to be ill,' he said. 'Knowing why he died that way may help you.' His hands hesitated over the lid. He glanced at her. She refused to help him decide. 'Yes, I'm not going to obey his wish that I see this alone.' When she maintained her silence he added, 'The will is to come to you anyway, after I die, that was his wish.'

He turned the key in the small brass lock. A barely audible click. The lid went up and over. He didn't hesitate, his hands dipping into the box and around the sheaf of papers. Up and out. Around the papers was a red ribbon. He untied the knot and pulled away the ribbon. He glanced at her, then back to the first page. Then at her again. It was nothing to do with her, she thought.

Mautu started reading to himself. She waited. He turned over the first page. She watched, and was embarrassed watching herself watching him reading that private testament, which might contain answers to the puzzle of Barker's death. When she sensed he was absorbed in Barker's confession, she crept out of the fale.

She looked back at him from the paepae. Suffering had sucked in his bulk, leaving him to that vulnerable gauntness she had recognised in Barker on her second visit to him during a childhood that was now like a useless skin she'd shed. Around Mautu was that same luminosity that exposed in minute detail every scar, wrinkle, evidence of age. She hurried away from it. She didn't want to know what was in Barker's last testament: Lefatu had explained that her illness had been a forgetting, a dreamless sleep, and Peleiupu feared that Barker's confession might return her to that drowning.

Mautu would mention nothing about it to her, ever, as if he had not inherited Barker's testament, or read it.

Momentarily, she didn't realise that the shadows that had spilled across her table from behind were those of two people. 'I need help with these,' Arona said, placing a page of sums in front of her. 'I have to teach them tomorrow.' She looked up. Tavita grinned at her.

Since Barker's death Arona and Tavita were inseparable, and the young people referred to them affectionately as Crusoe (Arona) and Friday (Tavita), deliberately reversing the roles of the main characters in an exciting story Lalaga had told them (and which Peleiupu knew as *Robinson Crusoe*, a boy's adventure tale that she detested.)

She took out a slate and started explaining the problems. Their shadows kept nodding. 'Sit down,' she said. Tavita's very papalagi hand was suddenly pointing at what she was writing on the slate. Golden hair covered his arm.

'I can't ever work that out,' he said past her left ear, which started burning inexplicably. She edged away from him.

'No one's as bright as Pele!' Arona joked. She imagined they were laughing at her and wished they'd leave.

'I don't know how to do these ones,' she lied. 'Get Lalaga to show you.'

Their scrutinising presence lingered after they'd left and she couldn't stop the burning inside, and her memory detailing how tall, blond and cat-eyed Tavita was, and wished he'd stop being Arona's best friend and not come to sleep at their home and stop looking at her (though he pretended he wasn't) — boys shouldn't do that to the sisters of their friends.

In November Arona, Tavita and a group of friends gathered coconuts from the plantations, husked them, scooped out the copra and spread it out daily to dry in the sun. (The money from the copra was to pay for Peleiupu's uniforms, bedding and fees at Vaiuta School.) The youths worked outside the kitchen fale. Peleiupu kept out of their view, with her books and helping Lalaga.

When the copra was dry, Mautu and the youths loaded the sacks onto a fautasi and took the copra to Apia. Arona captained the fautasi and surprised Mautu with his navigational skills. They brought back material for Peleiupu's uniforms, and food and presents for the aiga of the youths who'd helped.

In the evenings Peleiupu and everyone else who slept in the main fale had to listen to Arona and his friends talking about Apia and its wonders. Arona was their key narrator: he turned every feature, discovery and incident into a rich tale. For instance, ice-cream was a miracle of sweetness — 'long and smooth and exquisitely cold on the tongue', he said. And papalagi were 'sunless creatures, spotted brown like dying frangipani flowers, who wore false teeth and could therefore chew only baby food'. Peleiupu was surprised that Arona was so talkative. Tavita was Arona's main chorus: he reaffirmed the wondrous truths of Arona's tales with melodious yesses, and 'that's true, yes, true, the real truth'. Their exaggerations were obvious to her but she was a captive and attentive listener, trying to figure out who Arona's storytelling style reminded her of. For a week she couldn't, then, on Saturday night, when Arona's tale broke into English, she recognised Barker even in his gestures. So much of Barker. 'Someday we have to sail beyond Apia, to the world,' Arona ended that night. Immediately Peleiupu feared for his safety, for his declaration was Barker's fearless commitment to exploring the Seven Seas. 'Yes,' echoed Tavita, and she feared for his safety too.

During the next few days she helped Lalaga sew her uniforms. At lotu and meal-times she caught Arona looking apprehensively at their parents, and sensed that he was close to a decision. She was missing him already but she wasn't going to stop him. And she longed for Ruta and Lefatu to confide in.

As soon as she opened her eyes that morning she caught the wary, listening stillness of a creature crouched, watching. She couldn't see Arona anywhere. At their morning meal she avoided the space where Arona usually sat. She kept observing her parents, wanting to shield them from what was coming. After the meal she retreated to her space behind the bookcases. She trembled as she waited. Cautious footsteps across the pebble floor, like the sound of brittle bone crunching underfoot. She shut her book, bowed her head.

'Pele?' he whispered. 'Pele?' She kept still. He sat down behind her. 'Pele,' he said, 'I've decided to go away.'

'Why?'

'I have to find out.'

'About what?'

'Everything. I must learn about those other places and peoples.'

'But what if the world isn't what Barker filled our lives with?'

He waited. She heard the silence humming. 'Barker wouldn't lie. No. And I'll be back.'

'Don't go! It may be dangerous out there.'

'If I stay I'll always regret not having gone, not having had the courage to go. Besides, many palagi have come to our country, I'll be one of the few Samoans ever to go out there. If you were male, wouldn't you want to try?'

He had her. So she whispered, 'I suppose so. But what about our parents?'

'If I ask them, they'll refuse. Besides, I don't have the courage to ask them.' He stopped. 'I want you to tell them — after I've left. Would you, Pele?'

'Is Tavita going with you?'

'No. He doesn't know. I can't ask him — there's only him to look after his mother and brothers and sisters.'

'Aren't you scared of going alone? You know so little about what's out there.'

'I'm scared all right, but I have to find out. Remember, Barker was scared too when he ran away from home as a boy, but he mastered his fear and enjoyed those wonderful places. Our God will protect me.'

'I'll tell Mautu and Lalaga,' she managed to say.

'I'll be back,' he said. She heard him getting up. She forced herself not to look around at him. 'Bye, Pele. Look after our parents.' His footsteps took him away quickly.

At lotu that evening Lalaga asked after Arona. Someone said he was at Tavita's.

Next morning before school, Lalaga asked again. Probably still at Tavita's, Naomi replied, but when Tavita arrived and told them Arona hadn't been with him, Lalaga rushed to Mautu, who sent out students to look for him in the village. Peleiupu retreated to her class and started teaching.

During the morning she watched searchers returning, only to be sent out again with more searchers. Mautu joined them eventually. Soon all Satoa would be involved in the search: she had to stop that.

'Arona was playing cards at Mitimiti's home last night,' Lalaga told her when she entered the main fale that afternoon. 'He's never done this before!' Then she remembered and added, 'Except his absence at Fagaloto, but it was Lefatu who'd kept him back.' Peleiupu put her books and slates away in the bookcases. Lalaga rambled on, talking more to herself than to Peleiupu.

'Arona has gone,' she heard her voice say, clearly. Lalaga glanced over at her. Peleiupu sat down. 'Arona has gone,' she heard herself repeating.

'Where to?'

'Apia.'

'How do you know?'

'He told me yesterday.'

'Why didn't you tell us then?' Lalaga's anger was not her concern.

'He didn't want me to.'

'Who's he gone with?'

'I don't know.'

'When's he coming back?'

'He didn't say.'

'He didn't say!' Lalaga's wrath was now aimed at her. 'You didn't ask him? You didn't try to stop him? Why's he gone to Apia?'

'I wanted to stop him but it was his choice, his life.'

'Children have no choice but to obey their parents. Didn't you stop to think about us? What if he dies of an accident on his way to Apia? He is only sixteen!' Lalaga was glaring at her but she didn't look away. 'Didn't you consider that?' Lalaga demanded. Peleiupu refused to answer, so Lalaga called Naomi and sent her to fetch Mautu. 'Wait till your father comes!'

While they waited, Peleiupu watched herself watching her mother, who was muttering to herself.

'See what your daughter has done!' Lalaga was at Mautu as soon as he came in. 'Arona told her yesterday he was going to Apia, and she didn't tell us — deliberately!'

He sat down beside Peleiupu. 'Is that true?' he asked. Peleiupu nodded. 'How did he go?'

'She doesn't know!' Lalaga snapped. 'For all she cares, her brother could have drowned by now!'

'Arona is going to Apia first, then he's going overseas,' Peleiupu told Mautu. She watched him, and ignored the weeping sound of Lalaga's grief when it erupted; she watched him and loved him more as he struggled to believe and then accept. 'He said he has to find out what the world is like.'

'On his own, alone? My son, my poor son, aue!' Lalaga's cries beat at the edges of Peleiupu's attention.

'He didn't have the courage to tell you and Lalaga,' she added. Mautu nodded.

'You must find him and bring him back before it's too late!' Lalaga demanded. 'Go with some men to Apia and bring my son back!'

Peleiupu would never forget what her father did then: he bowed his head, hiding his face from her, and, clasping his hands in his lap, withdrew into a silence as durable as Barker's stillness on the mast. 'I ask for your forgiveness for not telling you earlier,' she whispered to him.

'Why do our children hurt us? Why?' Lalaga continued. 'We should never have allowed Barker into our lives. He filled Arona's head with foolish dreams!'

'That is enough!' Mautu whispered, without looking up.

'He's going to die out there!' she cried.

Peleiupu left quietly.

Late that afternoon Mautu, Tavita and a crew sailed for Apia. When Peleiupu told Naomi about their brother, she wept.

They waited for almost a week. Peleiupu stayed away from Lalaga, who maintained a sorrowful vigil in the fale with some of the elders. With Naomi she took the classes. None of the students mentioned Arona to them. At night when she heard Lalaga's muffled weeping she stopped herself from going over and consoling her.

Mautu emerged out of the cool night breeze just as one of the elders was finishing the prayer of their evening lotu. He sat down beside Lalaga, who kept her eyes shut as if she hadn't seen him enter. Peleiupu identified the weight of sorrow in him, an anchor that could not be pulled up.

The elders greeted him. He replied formally. The young people left to bring the meal. Peleiupu held Naomi back.

'And how was your trip?' an elder began.

'It went well. People were helpful,' he replied. They waited. 'We found out that he signed on a British ship bound for New Zealand, then England. I even talked to the company manager. He was very helpful. He promised he'd get in touch with their company in New Zealand, and get them to put the boy on their next ship back . . .'

'How long will that be?' Lalaga interjected. The elders ignored her rudeness.

'. . . I told him Arona was only a boy . . .'

'How long is he going to be away?' Lalaga insisted.

'About six months,' Mautu said, without looking at her. 'And the manager, a palagi, told me he was impressed with Arona's education, especially his English. I told him Arona had been taught English by a high Englishman . . .' Lalaga scrambled to her feet and rushed through the curtains into the bookcases. The elders pretended nothing unusual had happened.

Peleiupu and Naomi pretended they were leaving to help prepare the meal, but once out of the fale they circled back to see Lalaga. They sat with Lalaga between them, in the darkness, and held her arms as she wept almost soundlessly into her cupped hands. 'Arona'll be back soon,' Naomi whispered to her. 'He'll be back in six months.'

'He's broken my promise to God that he'll be a pastor,' Lalaga declared. 'He doesn't love his mother.'

'He does,' Naomi insisted.

'Why has he left me then? Why has he broken his vow to God?'

'He'll return and be a servant of God one day,' Peleiupu said. Lalaga pulled her arm out of Peleiupu's grip.

'You always think you're cleverer than all of us, eh! If anyone could've talked Arona out of leaving, you could've. So why didn't you?'

Recalling Lefatu's plain and honest integrity Peleiupu said, 'Because my brother had to make that choice.'

'Had to?' Lalaga attacked.

'Yes, and I envy him.'

'I'm astounded by your cleverness! What if your brother dies out there, eh?'

'It would be out of his own choice. He must've considered that.'

Lalaga slapped the mat. 'You really act like a palagi, don't you?'

'If I was a boy, I would've gone with my brother.' She jumped up and ran out of the fale into the darkness.

In the next six months, while they waited for the shipping company to bring Arona back, Lalaga would descend into what everyone came to refer to as 'mourning', though she tried to fill it with endless work. Sometimes at night after everyone else was asleep she'd sit gazing seawards into the darkness. At lotu she or Mautu would always include in their prayers a plea to God for Arona's safe return. (Over the years that would become a family tradition.) Most of Satoa and the rest of their family, especially Peleiupu whose dreaded guilt threatened to overwhelm her every time she heard Arona's name, would avoid any mention of him within Lalaga's and Mautu's hearing. Among Tavita and his friends' stories would begin to circulate about Arona's possible whereabouts and 'adventures'. Aotearoa, they whispered, England, Ireland, America — and that would open up Barker's stories that they'd inherited to further embellishment, with Arona now featuring in some of them. This process would continue for the rest of their lives.

One Saturday, six months later, they would wake to find Mautu gone into Apia. The papalagi shipping manager with the kindly eyes would avoid looking at

Mautu across the counter; would find, momentarily, that he was whispering his reply to Mautu's inquiry about his son.

'Would you repeat that, sir?' he'd hear Mautu demand.

'I'm sorry . . . sorry, sir, but the boy disappeared when the ship got to London . . .'

'But you promised to return him to us!'

'We tried, sir, really tried,' the manager insisted. 'The captain instructed him not to leave the ship. We even searched for him — for him and his two friends who left with him.' The manager wanted to reach across and console Mautu, whose eyes were now full of tears. 'I'm sorry, very sorry, and I promise we'll keep looking for him . . .' Mautu would turn slowly to leave. 'We'll keep you informed!' the manager would call after him.

Two days later when Mautu entered their fale and, collapsing beside Lalaga with deep sobs, gave her the news, she would swallow all the sound of the world as she rose to her shaking feet, swooped down with a long swinging sweep of her right arm, and slapped him across the face. The vicious but forgiving sound of that slap would cut through everything and everyone in Satoa. It would be the first and last time their children and the Satoans would ever see her strike him in public. For Peleiupu it would jab through her every pore.

A week or so later Tavita and Poto, his mother, would return from Apia with the news from the shipping manager that Arona and a Fijian and Samoan friend had signed on a ship bound for the Americas.

And so would begin what would become known in Satoan history as *The Tales of Arona the Sailor*.

Lalaga had instructed the school to clean the grounds around the church for Christmas. The boys were cutting the grass, working in a long line, swinging their bushknives to the beat of a tin drum. While the girls weeded the stone graves of 'the People', Naomi told them the story of how her father and Barker had discovered 'the People' and brought them down to their village. Peleiupu worked silently beside Naomi. Occasionally she sensed Tavita looking her way and wished he wouldn't.

Peleiupu shifted into the shade of a kapok tree and weeded there. She found herself thinking of Lefatu and Ruta and imagined them in the cool of Lefatu's fale, joking as they mixed potions; and she envied Ruta for having chosen her future and enjoying it already. She envied Arona, too, for that: the Seven Seas might be unsafe but he had chosen the direction of his life. For a moment she felt as if she were suffocating. She sucked in air through her mouth, as Lefatu had taught her, held it in for a while and then exhaled.

'We've finished!' Naomi called to her. She emerged and found them setting fire to the mounds of weeds, cut grass and other rubbish they'd swept together. The flames swept up, crackling and spitting bits of ash into the air. Peleiupu tipped her basket of weeds onto the nearest heap and withdrew swiftly.

'Swim!' someone called. The boys rushed down to the lower pool, which was reserved for males, and hurled themselves into it. She noticed that Tavita was sitting on a boulder in the shade of a frangipani tree. The girls were getting into the water.

'Want to swim?' Naomi asked her. She shook her head. Naomi wandered over and sat near Tavita. Peleiupu went and sat beside her. Tavita occupied the corner of her view as she watched the bathers.

'Do you think Arona is all right?' he asked.

'He can look after himself,' Naomi replied.

'I hope so. He should've told me. I would've gone with him.' Tavita didn't look at them. Peleiupu had always admired Naomi's ease with boys. She made them feel relaxed, and she teased and joked with them, and the elders didn't consider her behaviour too forward or improper.

'. . . Are you able to care for your family?' Naomi was asking.

'Yes: Poto's running our store; I'm helping her run the business. That's why I keep coming to school even though my brothers have stopped. I wish I was as bright as you and Pele and Arona. I should've started school earlier.'

'It wasn't your fault,' Naomi said.

'My father didn't want us to; then when it was almost too late he changed his mind. And look: I'm the oldest person in my class.'

The boys were playing tuli in the pool, but were careful not to make too much noise. Peleiupu felt hotter as she watched them.

'Arona was my best teacher. He taught me a lot about adding and selling things, and reading, and money. He was teaching me navigation too: my father taught him that. My father really liked Arona . . .'

'And Pele,' added Naomi.

'Yes. I was jealous of that for a while. But when Arona became my best friend, he was my brother. So I didn't mind my father favouring him . . .'

'And Pele,' Naomi echoed. Tavita laughed. Peleiupu didn't know how to react. 'Well, Barker and Poto treated you as their favourite,' Naomi said to her.

'I suppose so,' Peleiupu said.

'Why do you think my father did what he did?' Tavita asked. Peleiupu hesitated. In the pool, churned white by the swimmers, she saw the alia's dark reflection again.

'Anything wrong?' Naomi asked.

Shaking her head she said, 'I don't know why.'

'I think about it a lot,' he said, 'and always conclude that he did it because he was happy. Stupid of me, eh? But that's how I feel. He was an unusual person.'

At once Peleiupu felt a huge sadness emanating from him. She looked at him. Her embarrassment had vanished, just like that. In the bright light Tavita shone like yellow flame. A beauty transcending the impermanence of the day, beyond grief and the reasons why his father had taken his own life. And there was no longer any guilt in her admiring him.

A week or so later Peleiupu heard that Filivai was very ill, and she felt guilty about not having visited her since she'd returned from Fagaloto.

On Saturday morning, when a neighbour brought them some parrotfish, she scaled the biggest one, cut it up and made a sua i'a. She also cooked a fa'alifu fa'i, Filivai's favourite. She bathed, dressed, told Mautu where she was going, and using a yoke, lifted the baskets of food onto her shoulder.

The village seemed longer, more crowded, as she carried her load through it. People kept inviting her in to eat; some youths offered to carry her load; she declined politely. Everything felt distant and she didn't want to feel that way, not when she was going to see someone she loved.

Just as she was turning into Filivai's aiga she remembered she hadn't visited her tree, the ifi, for years, and regretted that too. The memory made her nostrils tingle again with the smell and touch of the oiled ifi leaves with which Filivai had bathed her face when she'd been ill.

The fale blinds were drawn around the left-hand side of Filivai's fale. There was a mosquito net in which someone was sitting, fanning Filivai, who lay propped up by pillows. Peleiupu went around to the back, put her load on the paepae, crept into the fale and sat down. The fale smelled of crushed leaves.

'Come closer!' Filivai's daughter called. Peleiupu slid over to the net. The woman raised up the side of the net. 'Come in,' she said. Peleiupu did so on her haunches. 'It's Pele!' the woman told Filivai, whose eyes were closed. No response. Peleiupu hardly recognised her: emaciated to skin and bone, lips a bloodless purple, hair a wispy white. 'It's Pele!' the woman repeated. Peleiupu could barely hear Filivai's breathing. 'She doesn't recognise anyone,' the woman said. A large vein in the side of Filivai's neck pulsed to the beating of her heart.

'I've brought some fish and fa'alifu for her,' Peleiupu said.

'Thank you,' said the woman. 'You look after her for a while. She's always liked you. I want to go to the back.'

The woman heaved herself out of the net, staggered over to the food, lifted it and took it to the back fale, where Peleiupu knew she was going to have a hefty feed. She'd never liked Filivai's daughter, who'd been away for years and returned only when she'd wanted something from Filivai and her aiga. 'My fat, selfish daughter,' Filivai had once described her to Peleiupu. Choke on a bone! Peleiupu wished her as she visualised the woman gorging on the food she'd carefully prepared for Filivai.

Moving up, Peleiupu held Filivai's hand. It felt smooth and dry, like stone that had been heated by the sun. 'Fili?' she whispered. 'Fili?' Again no response. She combed the old woman's hair with her fingers. Brittle, dry, ready to break. 'You saved me many times, Fili,' she said, 'but I can't save you.'

The white net around them was a fragile membrane that would break apart with one gust of wind but, while it remained intact, it listened to Peleiupu's whispering, to the song that Lefatu had taught her while she was surfacing from her drowning, an incantation from the pit of her moa:

All things live in the Va,
which links them together
in harmony, in unity.
We must nurture the relationships,
the Va, for that's what makes us
who and what we are . . .

Filivai died three days later. Two days before Christmas. Peleiupu didn't go to the funeral service and burial that her father conducted, the next day.

The Christmas and New Year celebrations came and went; she avoided most of them. Now she was leaving for Upolu in a day's time. Her clothes, bedding, mats, broom and other requirements for Vaiuta were packed, neatly. (Lalaga had seen to that.) The previous night, the elders and their wives had participated in their special lotu to farewell her. Sao had spoken on behalf of Satoa, blessing her and wishing her well. Mautu had replied to Sao's speech and had asked her to pledge her life to God's work. After the lotu the students had served up a feast of roast pork, chicken, fish, palusami and curried beef, a new dish that Lalaga had cooked. Peleiupu got Poto to sit beside her.

'You are Tavita's friend?' Poto asked. 'That's good, because I know he likes you.' Peleiupu heaped more food onto Poto's foodmat. 'I'm going to miss you, Pele.' Peleiupu reached over and held Poto's arm. Everyone fed hugely, and there was enough food left over for each aiga to take a basketful home.

She was awake before anyone else and tugging at Naomi's sheet. 'You want to come?' she asked. 'I want to show you something.' Naomi sat up, re-hitched her ie lavalava, and followed her out, mumbling that she hadn't had enough sleep.

'We'll get wet and dirty!' Naomi objected as Peleiupu started clambering over the rock fence into the plantations. The stench of the pigpens was strong, and Naomi spat repeatedly.

'Go back, then!' Peleiupu said. When she heard Naomi clambering after her, she smiled to herself.

The vegetation was dripping with dew; the track was slush and they slid and slipped often, and Naomi complained every time she did so. 'How far?' she kept asking. Peleiupu hurried on, occasionally flicking the wetness off her arms with her hands.

'There!' she declared, nodding at the ifi.

'What? Where?' Naomi demanded.

'The tree,' Pele murmured. It was larger, a darker green, with heavier beards of moss and fungus on its trunk and branches. She moved into its cold darkness, stopped, and touched its bark.

'Its only an ifi, and it's dripping on me!' Naomi complained, and she rushed back out from under it.

Peleiupu was soon dripping wet from the large drops of water falling from the tree, and the cold burned down and set her bones alight with a tingling warmth. 'Are you stupid?' Naomi called. 'You'll get sick from the wet!' Peleiupu continued gazing up into the branches, the water running off her face. 'I don't know why we had to come all this way for that!' Naomi called.

Peleiupu stretched up, clasped the lowest branch with both hands. It was slimy wet. She gripped harder, steadied and pulled herself up. Her wet ie lavalava started slipping so she dropped back to the ground, and retied it over her breasts. When she grasped the branch again, Naomi called, 'You're not going to climb up, are you?' Peleiupu pulled, raising her body off the ground, and kicked her legs up. Not high enough. She swung back. Feet on the ground. Wiped her hands on her ie lavalava. 'Are you crazy?' Naomi called. Peleiupu tried again but her feet missed hugging the branch and, as her weight swung back, her hands slipped from around the branch and she landed in the mud on her back and slid towards Naomi. 'Are you all right?' Naomi asked, kneeling beside her. 'I told you!' Peleiupu sat up and tried to look as if she weren't in pain. Naomi started wiping the mud off her shoulders and back. Peleiupu stood up. 'You're not going to try again?' Naomi asked. 'You won't be able to get up there.'

'I've done it many times before.' Peleiupu flexed her arms, jumped up and gripped the branch again.

As she started swinging her legs up Naomi said, 'You're not the child you were. You're too heavy now!'

Ah, success: her legs wrapped securely around the branch, then the rest of her body. The branch felt slippery and cold but she wasn't giving up. 'Careful!' called Naomi. Peleiupu steadied for the final swivel to turn her body up to lie on top of the branch. Go! Heave! Too many smaller branches in the way. She started revolving backwards, her legs coming away first. Her arms held. She hung. 'Told you!' Naomi said. She couldn't hold: her arms were slipping, her ie lavalava falling off. She didn't care. Her fingers stripped through the waterlogged bark as she fell away. Crunch, on her feet, falling backwards. Pain jabbing up her backside, then up her spine.

'Your ie's come off!' exclaimed Naomi, kneeling down and picking it up.

'Arse!' Peleiupu said. When she caught Naomi's shocked look, she repeated, 'Yes, arse to everything!' and started laughing. Naomi tossed over her ie lavalava; it flopped beside her. Peleiupu lay in the mud, laughing and rocking from side to side while Naomi clapped and chanted: 'A-R-S-E! A-R-S-E! I-F-I, IFI, I-F-I, PELE'S TREE!'

The tree stirred above them.

After Naomi had helped her wring most of the wetness out of her ie lavalava, Peleiupu picked a basketful of young leaves from the lower branches. 'What are you going to do with those?' Naomi asked.

'You'll know tonight,' replied Peleiupu.

When they got home, Naomi helped her sew a wreath from the leaves. After oiling it, Peleiupu hid it in the rafters of the school fale.

That night when everyone was asleep Peleiupu gripped Naomi's hand as they crept through the dark and got the wreath. However, when Peleiupu started leading her into the village Naomi protested. 'I'm scared!'

'It's all right,' Peleiupu whispered. 'If you don't want to come, I'll go alone.' She moved off.

'Wait for me!' Naomi pleaded.

Only a few aiga were still up. Their lamps provided just enough light for them to see the track through the village. When dogs barked or they saw people moving about, they stopped. 'I'm scared,' Naomi repeated.

'Lefatu and Filivai taught me to live with the dark,' Peleiupu said. 'To feel good in it.' She led Naomi on. 'Smell it?' she whispered.

'What?'

'The frangipani.'

'Yes.' The darkness floated on the wave of scent. 'But we're among graves!' Naomi cried.

'Yes, but it's nothing to be afraid of,' Peleiupu tried to calm her.

'We'll get sick!' Naomi was almost in tears.

'Filivai won't harm us. She's been waiting for us to come.' Around them, like a solid sea of black, were the stone mounds, the graves of Filivai's aiga. She tugged at Naomi's hand. Naomi refused to move. Peleiupu moved on.

'Don't leave me!' Naomi scrambled after her. Peleiupu clutched her trembling hand and led her further into the graveyard. She stumbled over some rocks. Naomi held her up. The scent of frangipani was sharp, sweet.

'She's here,' Peleiupu whispered, feeling around in the dark with her hands. 'Yes, right here.' She took Naomi's hands and pressed then down on the large flat stone that marked the head of Filivai's grave.

'I want to go home!' Naomi begged. Peleiupu sat down on Filivai's grave. Again she pulled Naomi's hand. Naomi sat down reluctantly. The stones felt warm under their buttocks.

The sky was a sea of stars that focused and unfocused when Peleiupu tried catching them in her eyes. 'Let's go home!' Naomi pleaded.

'Fili, I've come to say goodbye,' Peleiupu said to the stone. 'Tomorrow I have to go to Upolu and Vaiuta School and a new life. I don't really want to go, but I have to find out if that life is for me. Thank you, Fili, for your alofa and understanding. I won't betray you, your faith in me.' Taking the wreath from Naomi, she placed it on the stone. 'I will carry the scent, the spirit, of my tree, with me always. You healed me with it; you put it back into me when I was drowning.' She stood up and Naomi moved against her. Peleiupu put an arm around her sister. 'Fili, look after Naomi too. I'll come back, someday.'

Vaiuta

She switched the suitcase to her right hand. Lalaga and Mautu, carrying bundles of mats, were a few paces ahead. Further up were the three men who were carrying the rest of her luggage on yokes. At least the high canopy of trees was shielding them from the morning sun. Not far past Vaiutu School was Stenson's house, and she recalled in detail her trip with Barker and Arona up this same track to stay with Stenson, the Magician of Words; and as she grew sad remembering his death, she vowed she would soon visit his house, which was now the German Governor's residence.

They'd arrived in Apia the previous afternoon, unloaded their fautasi, beached it in front of the London Missionary Society church and had gone to the pastor's house. Laupega, the pastor (a friend of Mautu's from theological college) and his aiga had given them a meal; they'd then showered and slept, exhausted and sunburnt from two days of sailing.

Peleiupu noticed a quickening in her mother's walk, an eagerness to rediscover Vaiuta, her old school. Since Arona's disappearance they'd not talked much. While they'd got her things ready Lalaga's wishes had been conveyed mainly through sign language, abrupt hand gestures and the odd verbal command. Peleiupu had emerged from her illness unafraid of Lalaga, but she pretended she still was. She also knew that Lalaga tried not to upset her in case she withdrew back into her illness.

As she watched the soles of her mother's feet turning up and down as she walked, she wished Lalaga was slower to anger (like Mautu), thought things out properly before acting (like Lefatu), was less protective of and ambitious for her, was more tolerant of Mautu's dreaming and search, more adventurous and willing to experience new things, and would stop working so hard and just enjoy being idle now and then. You could set a clock by Lalaga's daily work schedule.

Peleiupu surfaced from her wishing and found they were passing through Tanugamanono, a spacious malae surrounded by fale and a wooden church; a few youths were cutting the grass around the church; from among them rushed a dog: fur bristling, fangs bared. Mautu stamped his foot on the ground. The animal stopped, barked a few times and retreated. Peleiupu wished her sunburn would stop stinging from the salt of her sweat.

Up the steep Vaiuta hill her suitcase became a worsening weight. She dropped it down at the gate under some mango trees and sat on it, sighing, wiping her face with her sleeve. The sleeve stung as it slid across her sunburnt forehead.

'It hasn't changed much,' Lalaga said. Peleiupu realised they were high up. Through the trees she saw the hills sloping down to Apia and the coastline and the sea that stretched away into haze. She tried not to think of Satoa and how far away it was. 'No, it hasn't changed much,' Lalaga repeated.

Mautu came and picked up Peleiupu's suitcase. 'No, leave it to me,' she said, but he walked up the drive with it. The drive was lined with stands of flowering ginger, hibiscus, mango, hydrangeas and tall flame trees. 'I helped plant these,' Lalaga said. 'You'll have to learn to be a good gardener while you're here.' Behind the gardens, stretching out to paddocks in which cows were grazing, were fields of taro, lined by rows of bananas. A group of girls were pulling up some taro. One of them waved. 'Food crops,' Lalaga pointed out. 'Have to feed yourselves. Have to learn how to use the 'oso even. No men here to do it.' Strange but Lalaga was speaking English, Peleiupu realised, the language she hadn't mastered while at Vaiuta but had been taught her by Mautu and Barker. Lalaga obviously wanted to impress the Vaiutu staff they were soon going to meet.

The drive crossed through spacious lawns to a large double-storeyed building with wide verandas and two wings that branched back to a row of single-storeyed houses. Red roofs, cream-coloured walls, neat flower beds. Straight out of a book she'd read about the British in India.

The men put her luggage on the front veranda and retreated to the shade of a pulu tree on the lawn. Lalaga straightened her clothes, looked at Peleiupu, brushed back Peleiupu's hair and dusted her blouse. 'Misi Ioana, the new principal, won't like you looking untidy.' Peleiupu glanced at Mautu. He looked awkward.

'Tolu!' Lalaga greeted the squat woman who came out the front door. 'Are you still teaching here?' A large smile as the woman embraced Lalaga. 'It's been a long time.'

'Yes, about twenty years,' Tolu said.

'The length of time for me to have this daughter and watch her grow,' Lalaga said.

'She's a big girl,' Tolu said, kissing Peleiupu's cheek. Peleiupu smelled talcum powder on her.

'Tolu and I were here together,' Lalaga said to Mautu, who shuffled forward and shook Tolu's hand.

'Come in. Misi Ioana has been waiting for you. Most of the girls have checked in already. Pele is one of fifteen new entrants.' Tolu opened the door. Lalaga went in. Peleiupu edged up against Mautu and nudged him into the front office.

'Hasn't changed, eh?' Lalaga exclaimed.

Peleiupu found herself watching herself surveying the large room. High windows. Far wall lined with bookshelves but with few books; two office tables stacked with papers, slates, and other odds and ends. A couple of teachers and students, who tried not to look at them, were dusting the furniture. She wasn't really there, a part of it. She stood feeling sorry for her father, who looked lost. The teacher and students left quietly.

And then there was Misi Ioana marching through the door, all in white, black shoes, short-cropped hair, sharply chiselled face, firm steps: a soldier for Christ, thought Peleiupu. None of her books or Lalaga's memories of Misi Peta had prepared her for Misi Ioana.

'Lalaga!' she said. 'Tolu has told me a lot about you.' Her Samoan was that of a recent learner, intelligible but heavily (funnily) accented. Mautu shook her hand. They sat down around a low table in the middle of the room.

Tolu welcomed them formally in Samoan. Mautu's reply was barely audible. Peleiupu wished he was less smiling, less willing to please Misi Ioana.

'And is this Peeleeoopoo,' Misi Ioana mispronounced her name. Peleiupu smiled. Misi Ioana turned back to Lalaga and Mautu and tried to speak in Samoan, then gave up and reverted to English, which Tolu interpreted (badly, thought Peleiupu, wishing her parents would reveal to their hosts that they spoke fluent English).

In the papalagi missionary's presence her parents were behaving like obedient, grateful children. So she sat watching herself watching the others talking, with Misi Ioana asking the questions through Tolu's stilted and often inadequate translations, and her parents replying politely.

Two senior students brought in trays of tea and small cakes. Misi Ioana said grace and invited Lalaga and Mautu to eat. She instructed the students to take Peleiupu and her luggage to her dormitory.

Peleiupu followed them down the corridor, around the veranda and into the nearest wing. 'Where are you from?' asked the student with the bulbous black mole on her chin.

Peleiupu swallowed and replied, 'Satoa.'

'Where's that?' the other one, with the abundant breasts, asked.

'Savai'i,' replied Peleiupu.

'Savai'i, eh!' black mole said. Her friend giggled. 'A long way away, isn't it?' Peleiupu nodded.

The dormitory was a long rectangle, with latticed windows that let in the striped light onto the lines of mattresses under raised single mosquito nets. Beside the pillows at the head of each bed were the students' suitcases — some were huge wooden trunks. At the foot of the beds were ola in which the students kept their books and school implements. The polished wooden floor gleamed like ice Peleiupu had seen in a book. A world of beds afloat on ice, she observed.

'Your bed,' black mole said, taking her to the third space from the end, facing the east.

They helped her spread out her sleeping mats, put the mattress on them, cover it with a sheet, and then tie up her mosquito net.

'Your first visit to Apia?' black mole asked as they brought her back to the office.

Peleiupu didn't hesitate. 'Yes,' she lied. To survive without fuss in Vaiuta, she'd decided to hide what she knew, including her fluency in English and knowledge of books. Best to pretend she was from faraway Savai'i: ignorant, with little education. 'Yes,' she repeated. 'I'm afraid of being here.'

'Don't worry,' they said. 'We'll help you.' They meant it. Peleiupu didn't feel guilty about lying.

Soon after she got back, Misi Ioana and Tolu said goodbye to Lalaga and Mautu, and left. Peleiupu sat down in the chair opposite Lalaga. Mautu was looking out the window. Peleiupu bowed her head. She noticed a slight tear on her ie lavalava. She would mend it that night.

'Be good. Work hard,' Lalaga said in Misi Peta's voice and style. 'God will help you.' Peleiupu glanced up. Lalaga looked away.

The three of them didn't know what to say for a while. Peleiupu heard the surf of Satoa echoing in her ears: it sounded far away.

'I'm sorry about Arona,' Peleiupu said.

And Lalaga was immediately herself again. 'Don't worry,' she said. 'He'll be all right. He'll come back. Just do well here.' Peleiupu leaned towards her. Lalaga clutched her shoulders and looked into her face. 'We're very proud of you, Pele. We want the best for you. Don't waste your talents.' Lalaga's hands shook, so she withdrew them and clasped them in her lap. 'You know we love you?' Peleiupu nodded. 'When I'm angry with you, it's out of love and concern.' She turned her head aside. 'Lefatu is right. Pele, you're the most gifted of our aiga. Of Satoa. So gifted you frighten us at times.' She sniffed. 'You understand me?' Peleiupu nodded again. 'Remember you are a girl also. Being exceptional *and* a girl means you face severe limitations. As women we have prescribed roles. We have to act and behave as women. At times that's very unjust and unfair to ourselves, but we have to do it. We have to be good Christian women. Understand?'

'Yes,' whispered Peleiupu. Lalaga's arms were around her and she was into Lalaga's love and out again, with Lalaga on her feet and hurrying to the door. 'Fa, Pele!' Lalaga called over her shoulder.

Mautu continued gazing out the window. Peleiupu looked at her hands. The silence breathed; they listened to it.

'Perhaps we shouldn't have allowed Barker into our lives,' he said. 'He changed us. Made us want to search for more, to be more.' She wondered what he'd done with Barker's testament. 'It was my fault. I brought him into your life.' She looked at him. How vulnerable he looked. Tied to the tired earth again, visions and dreams gone. As lost as Barker had been. He'd rescued Barker from that condition, but who was going to save him? 'I feel tired,' he murmured. 'Arona shouldn't have left.' He sighed. 'But I'm happy for him. He's searching.'

'He'll return,' she said. She got up and stepped towards him. He rose slowly, glanced at her. How she wanted to embrace him, tell him everything was all right, no need to worry, but that wasn't the way between grown-up daughters and their fathers — not in public, anyway.

He bent forward, kissed her cheek quickly, turned and was out the door.

She listened to his footsteps thudding hollowly across the wooden veranda.

Later that afternoon, while she was alone in the dormitory unpacking her suitcase, she felt a hard object among her sheets in the case. It was the box, wrapped up the way Barker had bequeathed it to Mautu.

She pushed aside the contents of the suitcase, shoved the box to the bottom of her suitcase, buried it with the sheets and clothes, and knelt inhaling and exhaling through her mouth to control her fear of drowning. Barker was now an atua in the heart of the mythology of her aiga. She vowed never to open the box, not even after Mautu's death, as Barker had willed. She remembered the books she'd brought, especially the ones Stenson had autographed, got them out of her ola and buried them beside the box.

Tavita had stood, arms folded, with two friends on a fallen coconut tree trunk behind the crowd that had gathered on the beach at Satoa to farewell her. As she waved to everyone she kept looking at him. The oars dug in. The fautasi began sliding away from the shore. Wave, Tavita! she had willed him. Wave! The fautasi gathered speed and she nearly toppled, but hung on.

His left arm rose; her heart lifted with it. He waved once, twice, three times. Behind him, she saw Poto waving furiously.

Her first night at Vaiuta, unable to sleep, she lay savouring every detail of that farewell — a hope that would keep her happy, a future to return to.

She sat at church the next morning, feeling itchy and hot in her starched uniform. Misi Ioana read her sermon, in Samoan. Peleiupu kept thinking of Satoa and didn't listen until she sensed that Misi Ioana was upset about something. Then in English Misi Ioana departed from her written text and declared: 'Today is a sad day, a tragic day for us and our God and our work in this still pagan land. It is my sad duty, girls, to inform you that your country has been declared a colony of Germany, that barbaric empire ruled by the Kaiser.' She stopped and dabbed the corners of her eyes with her lace handkerchief. 'This year, as you know, is 1900. It is the end of a century in which Great Britain brought progress and civilisation to the known world. A glorious century for our God and Queen. But 1900 is also the start of another century, and we and your God-fearing people are to be under the Kaiser's rule. I'm sure God and Great Britain won't forget us. They will save us from the evil disciples of the Devil. And I promise you we won't be studying the Kaiser's language in our school!'

January 1900. She was almost twenty. A new century. An end and a new beginning.

Surveillance

Only Misi Ioana (Miss Joan Brakestaff), two staff members and a few senior students stayed behind during the long Christmas holidays and looked after the school, so each year when Vaiuta reopened, its large grounds and plantation were overgrown with weeds, and new vegetables and crops had to be planted.

'Tomorrow we will attack the weeds, the rubbish and the disorder which, like Satan's power, are threatening to smother our beautiful Christian settlement,' Misi Ioana explained during Peleiupu's first Sunday evening at Vaiuta. She was standing at the front table in the dining room, between two lamps. As a junior and new student Peleiupu was sitting on the floor in the front row, feeling homesick as the sad chorus of cicadas surged through the room.

'. . . Year after year, month after month, we have to be vigilant in our fight against such forces . . .' She was dressed in white, and with the flickering lamplight dancing over her and setting alight her red hair she looked like a luminous reflection shimmering in dark water. '. . . I know some of you are not used to plantation work, but in our school it is through such honest labour that we learn the true Christian virtues of hard work, frugality, dedication, determination. Such work strengthens our willpower, improves our Christian character and, by doing so, prepares us better to fight the forces of Darkness . . .'

Peleiupu wasn't afraid of such work — she'd done a lot of it at Satoa — but, as she observed Misi Ioana's unreal presence, her feelings of unreality at being away from home worsened. '. . . Here, there will be no separation between man's work and woman's work,' she was saying, smiling. 'We have no men here . . .' Peleiupu glanced around the room, at the other students, and, realising she was indeed in a community of segregated females, felt uncomfortably strange, as if part of the air she was used to had been taken away. She would grow accustomed to their segregation but the acute absence of males would remain with her to the day she left Vaiuta.

'. . . Weeds are like the ever-threatening temptations that the Devil confronts us with, but we must fight against them . . .' Misi Ioana reminded Peleiupu of Miss Milly Tilsley, the heroine in Stenson's *Daughter of the Mill*: long-suffering courageous Milly, who'd sacrificed her love for Captain Arthur Fludd to work in an Edinburgh orphanage. '. . . We know that most of you are missing your families and loved ones, but we will, in time, make you feel that this is your home away from home. I, too, have been five years away from my beautiful country, home and family but God's work in this pagan land has to be done . . .' In her self-sacrificing Christian work with the orphans Milly Tilsley had contracted consumption and had died, a year later, in Captain Fludd's arms. '. . . Don't hesitate to come and see me if you ever need help and advice, young ladies,' Miss Ioana ended her talk. Peleiupu straightened up and, with the back of her hand, wiped away her tears. Clothes still luminous with lamp-light, Misi Ioana floated out of the room.

Tolu, their senior Samoan teacher, got up and started explaining the school rules and regulations. Peleiupu had learnt them from Lalaga over the years, so at first she didn't listen to Tolu, but tried to forget her homesickness (and Milly's and Captain Fludd's tragic love) by observing the other new students. Some of them were in silent tears and were avoiding looking at one another. '. . . Some of the new girls are not listening to me!' Tolu jerked them out of their sadness. 'Peleiupu, what are two of the rules I've just explained?' Peleiupu wanted to disappear; it was difficult to breathe; why pick on her? 'Peleiupu?' Tolu demanded. Peleiupu glanced up at her. 'Your mother always knew our rules,' she added, smiling.

'No eating in the dormitories, no talking after lights out, no talking in church, no talking while we eat, no rings, no necklaces . . .' Peleiupu recited.

'Good, Peleiupu!' Tolu interrupted. Peleiupu sagged, relieved. 'Would you like to repeat them in English?'

Peleiupu shook her head. 'My English is no good!' she lied. Tolu ignored her then and continued. This time Peleiupu listened; she really listened.

Tolu, Peleiupu would find out quickly, was their most lucid teacher: she explained everything according to their levels of understanding, and she was patient. They'd had rules and routines in Satoa and Lalaga had enforced them vigilantly, but Peleiupu had never felt she was not to be trusted. However, as Tolu talked with her patient

195

clarity, Peleiupu sensed that an all-seeing system of surveillance was being stitched into the fabric of who they were: as juniors they were the most vulnerable, in their youthful innocence, to Satan's ploys and wiles. To survive Peleiupu decided she had to pretend she was the ideal student that system demanded. She hated it. She would hate it the whole time she was at Vaiuta but would tell no one, not even her parents.

That first week they were up at 5.30 each morning. They washed their faces, got into their working clothes, had morning lotu and were off into the dew-drenched plantation that sloped down into the ravine and river, slashing creepers from the palms and banana trees, clearing the tangled undergrowth, weeding the crops and planting more taro, bananas and vegetables. At mid-morning the girls on kitchen duty brought them their meal of boiled bananas and miti, and, though they were ravenous, they had to eat sedately (like well-brought up young ladies in England, Tolu said). Then it was back to work until the midday sun was too hot, into the shower and back into their dormitories to tidy up, then out again to weed the flower gardens and shrubbery around the buildings. When the sun dropped behind Mt Vaea and the range they showered again, had lotu, ate their evening meal and went to bed. Peleiupu revelled in that demanding schedule, though her muscles and bones ached and her hands were bruised and cut, because it left her no time or energy to be homesick. Each night she plunged into an exhausted sleep.

Tolu and their other three Samoan teachers supervised them while they worked, and they worked just as hard as their students. While they rested and had their meals, Misi Ioana inspected their work, returned to them and said, 'Malo lava, malo le galulue. Keep up the good work, ladies!' Once she stood above Peleiupu as she congratulated them, and before she returned to the office, she reached down and, patting Peleiupu's head, said in Samoan, 'Peeleeoopoo, are you learning to fight the forces of disorder?' Peleiupu nodded. 'Good, good!' she said. Misi Ioana never learned to pronounce Peleiupu's name — and the names of most of the other students — correctly, but they didn't mind.

As Misi Ioana walked away through the heat and mosquitoes and piles of rubbish there wasn't a spot of dirt on her, Peleiupu noted. She was Milly Tilsley, bringing to them enlightenment and Christian strength, yet not of their world.

By Friday afternoon they'd cleared right down to the river, which skipped and danced through their aching limbs and eyes as they rested on the bank and watched it; its weaving, fluttering, spitting, swishing sound was that of their breathing as the lush vegetation on the other side snared it and pulled it up to the summit of the range and the breathless immensity of the noonday sky.

And again she thought of Barker and Arona and the journey they'd made to visit the Magician of Words. Peleiupu decided she'd visit Stenson's house, and clean and weed his grave. She wondered what had happened to Mrs Pivot, whether she'd gone to England.

The subjects they studied in the first year were those Peleiupu had taught at Satoa: arithmetic, reading, writing, spelling, Bible studies, and what later came to be called home economics and art and craft. They were also taught at the level Peleiupu had taught them. So within three days of classes she was bored but tense because she had to act as if she hadn't mastered the material. She was worried also, knowing the mischief she got up to whenever she was bored. She regretted her decision to hide her real ability and fluency in English. From the second-year students' books and talk she learned that what they were studying was easier than the class two material she'd taught at Satoa. Only the senior syllabus contained some material she hadn't done already — but that was two years away!

To escape, she retreated into Stenson's novels, secretly. Sometimes she sneaked into the smelly latrines and reread them there. Milly Tilsley, Captain Fludd, the talkative Millicent Fanshawe, the Duchess of Branock who ate daisies compulsively, the villainous March Crafted and the other memorable characters of Stenson's world kept her company; they were more real than Vaiuta.

She also started reading the books in the main office, even the boring religious tracts. If other people were about, she pretended she was finding the English difficult. When alone, she feasted on the fiction and the missionaries' autobiographies and journals. One afternoon Misi Ioana noticed she was having difficulty reading a simple children's book. 'Persevere, Peelee, persevere!' she whispered. 'One day you'll master our beautiful language.' As Misi Ioana moved away she left behind her odour of peach-scented soap and the rustling of her starched skirt.

When they worked by the river Peleiupu sometimes sneaked off on her own and, with her feet dangling into the cold swirling current, talked in English to the birds, the bush, the air, the water.

Sometimes Arona walked out from the shadows of the bush on the opposite bank, and she talked and adventured with him in his tales about the great oceans and his search for the world. Not once did she allow herself to imagine that he was dead; not once, though her dreams were sometimes crowded with phantoms that wore Barker's face in death and whispered in Arona's voice.

Once, her father appeared on the opposite bank. He sat in the shade on a boulder and they talked, in English and Samoan, across the tongue of river: they talked of his youth and his parents, for the first time. (Why?) When Barker emerged out of the thick bush behind him, still dressed in the white tropical suit in which he had been buried, Mautu ordered him to return to his hole in the hills of Satoa. Barker laughed and vanished.

Mautu and Peleiupu were to talk many times across that river while she was at Vaiuta. Sometimes he allowed Barker to sit behind him and listen.

Proverbs

Mautu said that his father, Tuifolau Molimau, had twenty-six children. (Rumour had it there were other children scattered throughout the country, wherever he'd gone to heal patients.) Mautu and Lefatu were his youngest. Only eleven brothers and sisters were alive when Mautu was born: the others had died, over the years, in epidemics of influenza, whooping cough, smallpox and measles which the papalagi had brought. Mautu's father never forgave the papalagi for this though he continued as a Christian. He kept away even from the missionaries of his church. Whenever he couldn't avoid them, he acted as if they were invisible.

His father's father, Mautu continued, was Tuifolau Lei'a, the last pre-Christian taulaaitu of Fatutapu; he had converted to Christianity because he'd wanted Jehovah's superior technology and mana, and had publicly killed the frigate bird, their atua's physical manifestation, to show the finality of his choice. He'd raised Molimau, his youngest son, to be the pastor in their aiga. Molimau had gone to Salua and had suffered his training to be a pastor until his father had collapsed and died of a heart attack. He'd returned home to develop, over the years, what Mautu described as 'a life with two sides'. One side — the one that most people saw — was that of the staunch, quiet Christian whose main 'weakness' was for women, but this was a formidable flaw because it had been the weakness of every Tuifolau before him. The other side — the one that everyone knew was there but was afraid to discuss — was that of Fatutapu's taulaaitu, with the powers of what the missionaries condemned as Darkness. Their aiga's life had these two sides. And though the people of Fagaloto accorded their other ali'i and pastor the highest respect, Tuifolau and his aiga only needed to indicate what they wanted and the people obeyed, for Tuifolau was still the atua's taulaaitu, banned or otherwise. No one believed him when, on Sundays, as a lay preacher, he declared from the pulpit that he was just an ordinary man who was weak and sinful and mortal. Their Christian pastor was their anchor to Jehovah, their new god, but Tuifolau was still their anchor to their past and the atua of that side which, the missionaries argued, could turn upon them and destroy them.

As children, Mautu and Lefatu were soon conscious of this other side of their father and aiga, and, like everyone else, learned early not to refer to it publicly or directly. It existed: you observed it, learned from it to respect it, to be afraid of offending and mishandling it, and to be proud that your aiga possessed such power and knowledge. You accepted the missionary outlawing of it, but you also accepted it was in your moa, your centre.

Why had he chosen to be a pastor, then? Peleiupu asked Mautu. Even in the glare of the river's surface and across that distance she caught an expression of painful regret on his face. His father had chosen for him, Mautu admitted. He was chosen to continue the new and acceptable side of their aiga's heritage, to be a taulaaitu for Jehovah, while Lefatu was to be the keeper of the other side. And for a long sullen time he'd hated his father for it: he'd wanted to be Fatutapu's keeper. But he'd never once expressed his disappointment to his parents. Why hadn't he? Peleiupu asked. He refused to look at her.

He was sixteen and Lefatu fifteen when the choice was made. Sixteen years during which their parents had immersed them equally in the knowledge and ways of the 'two sides', without ever indicating he wasn't to be Fatutapu's anchor. By not choosing him, his parents were saying he didn't possess the sight and the ability to be a taulaaitu. He couldn't accept that rejection — the pain of it cut deeply and remained with him for many years. But he was a taulaaitu for Jehovah, Peleiupu consoled him. Besides, why had he wanted to be something of the past?

He leapt out of his sorrow. The concept of a time before the now and a time ahead of the now, of time moving in a one-dimensional way, was papalagi, he said. For them, time was everywhere, holding the Unity-that-is-All together; to change any part of it altered the whole; everything, including our dead, was in the ever-moving present, existing now. They knew already what the ideal life and society were; the aim was to maintain and balance that unity that their ancestors had created. Papalagi 'progress' was a belief that everything improved, got better, as you went forward. So Tuifolau as time-past wasn't true? Peleiupu asked. He nodded. But why had he wanted to be a taulaaitu? she pursued him. The mana, the mysteries of the mana, the depths of it he could explore and master, that was one attraction, he explained. Was it also the very special way (and awe) in which everyone treated whoever was Tuifolau? she suggested. He supposed that was true. But the main attraction had been who, what, and how his father had been: the totality of him. He was the embodiment of the ancient history of their atua and aiga — the toto, the ivi, the agaga, the loto, finagalo, masalo and atamai of all that. He was the atua's anchor among the people and the world, the moa through which the atua communicated and was; the web that held together their aiga, their village, their land and everything that was in the unity. But it was his father's individual behaviour, knowledge and ways that bound Mautu even more tightly to Fatutapu and that side of their aiga.

Tuifolau was in his seventies and Paia, their mother, was twenty or so when Mautu was born. Tuifolau had brought her back from Falefa, where he'd gone to heal the son of the ali'i. (He'd been a widower for three years after his previous wife had died of smallpox, a disease he had no cures for.) His aiga and Fagaloto thought he'd gone senile marrying someone so young, but, as usual, dared not say so.

Paia was the daughter of a low-ranking matai. She'd been at the ali'i's fale, helping feed Tuifolau and his party, but no member of that party saw how he persuaded her to be his wife. So they were surprised when, as they were leaving Falefa, she boarded his fautasi, with a basket of her clothes, and he instructed the rowers to let her sit with the other women. As soon as he told his aiga she was his wife, they accorded her the respect due to the wife of a Tuifolau.

Tuifolau spoke little but at any one time they knew what he wanted. His silent ways of communicating became theirs too, and their aiga became known as 'The Aiga That Didn't Talk'. Despite his all-encompassing presence, though, he was himself, separated from them by his mamalu, his mana, that aura that belonged to the keeper of Fatutapu, and into which they couldn't trespass. Even the children sensed this without being told. In pre-Christian times the Tuifolau's person was tapu: he ate separately and his leftovers, his excrement and anything he used, had to be collected by special matai who served him and buried, so no enemy taulaaitu could use them to harm him and his village. Since Tuifolau Lei'a's public 'killing' of Fatutapu, however, the Tuifolau's mamalu was less sacred: you could accidentally break into the aura of his mana and not be harmed.

With Paia, Tuifolau behaved as if he were a youth again. Some of his aiga's elders and his friends were alarmed by it. He went everywhere with her; he insisted on her sharing his foodmat, something no Tuifolau had allowed before; he consulted her openly in front of the elders about important aiga matters, another break from tradition. And when Paia gave birth to Mautu, Tuifolau started ignoring other conventions concerning a Tuifolau's behaviour towards women and children: he insisted on helping Paia bathe, feed, dress and sing Mautu to sleep, again breaking the separation between men's and women's work. He'd not done this with his previous wives and children. And for the Tuifolau to act in this unmatai, un Tuifolau manner was scandalous; it was an attack on the institution of marriage, the proper relationships between men and women, matai and non-matai, elders and the young. What was the world coming to? the elders complained. He was definitely senile, Folofa'i, his eldest sister remarked. And because tradition permitted sisters to advise and even reprimand their brothers, she was given the unenviable job of telling Tuifolau what he was doing wrong. It took her a week of sustained encouragement from the elders (and tears and fear) to persuade herself to do so.

Alone in their faletele, after their morning meal, she let him have it — poetically, and then in the direct manner sisters were permitted to use. He took it in silence, with his head bowed, as was expected of a loving, respectful brother. Then in his usual manner of using language sparsely, he apologised for not behaving as a Tuifolau and an old man should, staggered to his feet and, going to their sleeping fale, collected Mautu and the other children and took them swimming in the Vai-o-le-tetea, their village pool. His head is mad! Folofa'i exclaimed. He doesn't know he's trampling on everything we deem sacred! But they left him alone after that.

Tuifolau and Paia were excellent teachers, Mautu said. For instance when he was about nine, Tuifolau started teaching him, Lefatu and the other children the star-map that Tuifolau Afi had perfected centuries before. After their morning chores he gathered them in the shade of the breadfruit trees beside the faletele and, using a stick to draw on the sand, located and named the stars and their various formations during different times and seasons. They played it as a game of who could locate and name each star the fastest. If the evening sky was clear after lotu and their meal they lay on their backs on mats in front of the faletele and, observing the heavens, played the same game. Before the papalagi came and things changed, we navigated by the stars, he told them. We steered the oceans to other islands, and we fished and lived out our lives by them. Eventually Mautu asked if any tautai still used their map. A few, he replied. So of what use was the map, now? someone else asked. Of what use was any knowledge? was his reply. Besides, we lived in God's intelligence and wisdom, which was every-thing, including the stars and the heavens. The stars were God's tears, he remarked once. Why was God crying? Lefatu asked. For us, he whispered.

While their pastor taught them the biblical Genesis and genealogy of the world, Tuifolau, with a silent Paia beside him, taught them the Samoan Genesis: how

Tagaloaalagi, the supreme atua, created Samoa and the other countries of the Pacific as His stepping-stones across the water; how out of the seeds of the Fue Tagata, the Sacred Peopling Vine, He created the first human beings, put loto, finagalo, atamai, masalo and agaga into them and got them to populate Samoa and the Pacific.

Tuifolau got them to memorise the lengthy chant explaining that creation. As they sat by the Vaiuta River Mautu started chanting it. He stopped when Peleiupu told him Lefatu had taught it to her when she'd stayed with her. Had Lefatu taught her the genealogy of the Tuifolau title? he asked. Some of it, Peleiupu lied, so he wouldn't resent Lefatu some more. (She'd taught Peleiupu the whole genealogy.) There were things he knew that Lefatu didn't! he said. So that afternoon he recited the genealogy, pausing periodically to detail interesting features of the lives of some of the Tuifolau.

Leo'o, son of Vaimalu of Fagaloto, took as his wife Sinatava'etele, daughter of Tauilopepe of the Aiga Sapepe, and begat Ta'ape, (son), Sinalemoe, (daughter), and I'asami, (son), Mautu began. It was that Ta'ape who took as his wife Fafaolea, daughter of the Aiga Sa-Suluafi of their village, and begat Afi, (son), and two daughters, Popao and Tilisaua.

One stormy day the Tuitoga, while on a voyage from Tonga to Upolu, was ship-wrecked on Fagaloto reef. Ta'ape and his son Afi rescued the Tuitoga and his crew. Their fountainhead, the Aiga Vaimalu, housed and fed them. Ta'ape and Afi built, equipped and provisioned a new alia for the Tuitoga and his men. Before the Tuitoga departed for Upolu he conferred the title Tuifolau, Master Voyager, on Afi. So it was he who became the first Tuifolau. He became a master voyager and navigator as the Tuitoga had prophesied. He could sail vast distances and not lose his way; he read tides and seasons and stars, expertly, and evolved a new star-map for the Fagaloto people to live by. When he was so old he could barely see or walk, he asked I'asami, his brother, to take him out to sea one more time. I'asami and his crew returned a week later without him. No one needed to ask what had happened to him. I'asami took the Tuifolau title, but he was killed in a war against A'ana a year later and Afi's son, Ma'afana, became the Tuifolau.

Ma'afana was remembered mainly for the solos he composed, none of which have survived.

Five or so Tuifolaus after Ma'afana there was Tuifolau Tamatetea, one of the most famous. Tamatetea was born while his father was away in Uea. He was an albino. Ashamed and shocked by that, his mother, with the consent of Tuifolau's mother, hid him in the cave at the head of the village pool, the pool they now knew as Vai-o-le-Tetea, the Pool of the Albino. She went and fed him every day. When her husband returned a year later and asked after their child, she told him it had been born dead.

A few days after, while bathing in the pool, Tuifolau heard the crying of a child coming from the cave. He swam into it and found the albino, who he accepted as a gift from the atua to replace his dead child.

Tuifolau tried his best to protect his son against the people's superstitions and fears about albinos. Discriminated against, ridiculed, and considered mentally deficient and dangerous, Tamatetea developed his intelligence and cunning quickly. When he began to outfight, outswim, outwork, outthink and outmanoeuvre much older children, to his parents' loud acclaim, many of the people of Fagaloto accepted him begrudgingly, attributing his prowess to supernatural and dangerous powers that only albinos and other weird creatures possessed. When he began to outsail, outnavigate and outfish even some of the ablest tautai, they started respecting him, and the Aiga Tuifolau accepted him completely and with pride. When, in the annual sports tournaments at Moamoa, he represented Fagaloto for the first time and won in the use of clubs, their respect turned to applause. When in the following year he won in the clubs, spears and ti'a, they hailed him as their champion. No one who knew who he was dared discriminate against him then. He was truly a gift from the atua.

He took as his wife Lupetasi, daughter of the Aiga Malaetoto of Malaelua, and begat Sinalalelei, a daughter, and three sons: Vae, Fala and Ume. In time his father choked on a fishbone and died, and the title was conferred on Tamatetea.

While Tamatetea was out fishing one day a large frigate bird with a damaged wing alighted on the prow of his canoe. The bird wasn't afraid of people and behaved, as the crew gathered around it, as if it were a pet. Tuifolau Tamatetea wondered whose bird it was.

He brought it home and his daughter Sinalalelei, a gifted healer whose beauty was known far and wide, healed its wing and built a perch for it on the back paepae of their sleeping fale. Sina and her brothers cared for it, catching fish and bringing it to the bird daily. Every time Sina sang one of her love songs to it, the bird swooned and swayed to her tune.

Sina perched it on the back of her arm and, telling it to fly, raised her arm and released it into the air. It spiralled up and up until it was a circling speck, and then plummeted towards her, skimming over the roof of their fale, screeching out in joy as it spiralled up again.

Soon after that first testing of its damaged wing, it started fishing at sea daily, returning with its catches and disgorging them into a tanoa Sina placed before it. It also began sharing her foodmat at their evening meals. It eats like us, Tuifolau told everyone. To which it nodded its head. (Incidentally, everyone came to refer to it as 'Sina's bird'.) But human though its behaviour appeared to be, it started revealing its true frigate bird nature. Frigates are tenacious and persistent thieves — the worst thieves in the bird world; they even steal other birds' catches and the material from other birds' nests; they steal whatever takes their fancy. Sina and her brothers started finding baskets, clothes, ornaments and other items hanging from the frigate's perch. The village began complaining about the thefts. In a meeting of the matai Tuifolau admitted that the culprit was Sina's bird, and said the victims should collect their stolen property from his aiga.

Every time Sina found items on the perch she scolded her bird. It just looked at her with sad, soulful eyes, as if to say it couldn't help its true nature. She forgave it and, caressing its head, would sing to it.

One morning they woke and found it was gone. It didn't return that evening. Sina waited and watched the sky and horizon for three days, refusing to eat or drink, and at night Tuifolau heard her crying. 'It is only a bird!' he tried consoling her. 'It was a silly, thieving bird!' said Ume, who didn't like the bird. 'I'll never speak to you again!' she cried.

Next morning they found it was back. In its beak was a magnificent whale tooth necklace which it dropped into Sina's hands. She wept with joy at the bird's return but Tuifolau was full of concern: only atua could have made such a necklace. And when over a week passed and no one claimed it, he grew afraid.

Soon after, the bird disappeared again. It returned a few days later with a tiputa made of the finest siapo they'd ever seen — another gift for Sina, because no one came to claim it.

Tuifolau and the elders of their aiga decided it was time for Sina to take a husband. They allowed parties of suitors to visit. The handsomest manaia, from many villages, accompanied by their tulafale, courted her. But she turned them all down. Sometimes she was too busy with her bird to sit with the elders and be courted. Tuifolau reprimanded her for her discourtesy. 'That bird is not as important as your future!' he told her.

Unbeknown to her, her brothers had become suspicious of the bird, and during the night they took turns watching it. It was Ume, the youngest and the most volatile, who first saw the bird, while everyone was asleep, fly down from its perch into the fale and stand beside Sina. As the night deepened, the bird shed its bird form and became a handsome man. All night the stranger knelt beside Sina. At dawn he became bird again and flew onto its perch.

His brothers didn't believe Ume when he told them. The following night they watched together. And when the bird became man, Vae and Fala at first were angry but then grew afraid because the stranger was obviously a powerful taulaaitu or an atua or aitu.

Ume, the reckless, disagreed with their decision not to touch the bird — not yet, not until they consulted Tuifolau. He disappeared into the bush the next day and returned with a net woven out of strong sinnet. That night, just before the stranger became bird again, Ume netted him. As the man struggled to break free, Ume woke his brothers and Tuifolau. And together, to Sina's weeping protests, they trussed him up and tied him to the centre post of their faletele for the people of Fagaloto to see and condemn as an evil intruder who'd attempted to be, as it were, with Sinalalelei, their taupou.

Sina and the other women and children were banished to the back fale while Tuifolau and the matai interrogated their captive. He had the bearing, speech and manner of an ali'i's son, they concluded. He professed that his intentions were honourable: he wanted Sina to be his wife and had come to court her according to the customs of his people. His people? Tuifolau demanded. The Aiga Tava'eali'i of Manu'a, he said. But if his intentions were honourable why had he come in the guise of the frigate? The frigate was their atua, he replied, and it was their way of courting. Only aitu or atua or taulaaitu had the power to be other creatures, Tuifolau accused him. True, he said. His father, the taulaaitu Tava'eali'i, had transformed him into a frigate. The necklace and tiputa, which he'd brought as gifts to Sina, were his mother's.

For two days the matai council debated his case. The younger matai, encouraged by Ume, argued that the stranger was an evil taulaaitu who had to be destroyed. Tuifolau and the older matai, supported by Vae and Fala, cautioned against such action. Questioned by her mother and two aunts, Sina declared that she'd not known the bird was a man, and the man hadn't touched her as a man. He might be an aitu or atua, they told her. She loved him! she cried. When her mother told Tuifolau this, he was torn between his daughter's choice and the now majority view of the council that the stranger be killed.

Sina decided for them. When Ume and the warriors guarding the stranger fell asleep, she slipped into the fale and untied him.

They fled to the beach where he took his bird form and carried her up into the Ninth Heaven. There he revealed to her that he was Tagaloasavali, Tagaloaalagi's messenger. On one of his trips through Samoa he'd seen her and had fallen in love with her — a love he couldn't rid himself of. Against Tagaloa's advice he'd returned to Earth as a frigate so he could be near her.

When their first child was born, Tagaloaalagi called him Fatutapu, the sacred seed planted in the Aiga Tuifolau, mortals, by an atua.

Being half-tagata, Fatutapu as he grew up became increasingly curious about his human aiga. His curiosity was encouraged by his mother, who longed for her home.

Fatutapu eventually asked his father for permission to visit his aiga at Fagaloto. His father refused, telling him that as long as Ume, his mother's brother, was alive, Sina's children weren't safe.

A year passed, and another. One evening they saw a large frigate bird flying across the sunset. 'He's going!' Tagaloaalagi said to Sina. 'I'll stop him!' 'No!' she begged him. 'I want to know what has happened to my parents and aiga.' He relented.

It was as if Ume had been waiting for the bird's children ever since his sister had fled. Before Fatutapu could settle properly on the perch on the paepae, Ume's spear pierced him through his human side and dragged him down to the bleeding stones.

As he lay dying in Tuifolau's arms, he told them who he was. Tuifolau was sick with grief, but he hid his sorrow from his people as he buried Fatutapu in the site now known as Fanuatapu. He hid his sorrow and waited while Vae, Fala and their warriors hunted Ume, who'd fled over the mountains. He hid his sorrow as he instructed the matai council to banish Ume to Tutuila forever. In front of all Fagaloto he declared that Ume was no longer his son.

That night Tuifolau Tamatetea sailed out of Fagaloto, opening his grief to Pouliuli as he navigated his death by the star map.

'My aiga have mistreated our son,' Sina said to Tagaloasavali after Fatutapu didn't return. Tagaloasavali flew down to look for him. When he found his son's grave, he wept. Out of where his tears fell grew the sacred palm grove, Niuafei.

When he told Sina that their son was dead, she got up calmly and he watched her go out and gather their other five children. She stopped him from joining them. In the blazing sun they sat, heads bowed, as she talked to them.

That evening they saw a large frigate bird flying across the sunset. 'He is leaving,' Sina said. 'Who?' he asked. 'Taputoa,' she whispered. Taputoa was their second son. And Tagaloasavali knew and was glad.

They were near a peninsula in Tutuila when the frigate bird swooped down out of the clouds and, clutching Ume's long hair, dragged him out of the alia and into the air before they could stop it with spears or javelins. As it soared up and over to the peninsula it cried loudly in triumph.

It circled, hovered, and as Ume screamed and struggled it released him. He plunged to his death on the rocks of the peninsula, which became known as Totoume after that incident.

Her children carried Sina down to Fagaloto where they stayed in Niuafei, the Sacred Palm Grove, beside Fatutapu's grave, while she decided who was to replace their father as the Tuifolau.

She declared that Niuafei was to be the temple of their new atua, Fatutapu. Vae was to be the atua's taulaaitu and the new Tuifolau. Fala was to take the title Tonumailagi and be the Fatutapu's warrior leader and protector. Taputoa, her son, was to remain in Niuafei as the frigate bird, live manifestation of the atua. When he died he would be replaced by one of her other children, from generation to generation.

While Peleiupu was having a very papalagi education at Vaiuta, Mautu was giving her a thorough grounding in things Samoan, for the first time in her life. After telling her about the frigate bird, he detailed many of the sayings and proverbs that were derived from that story and the history of the Tuifolau and Fatutapu.

For instance:

E gafa umi le Tuifolau: Literally, the Tuifolau has a long genealogy. Used to describe an ali'i who has many well-connected children and descendants. (Mautu conveniently didn't mention the more well-known saying: Tuifolau-ma-le-Gaau, Tuifolau-with-the-Intestine.)

Alofa le tautala pei of Paia: Compassion/love without voice, like that of Paia.

Fasia fa'atuifolau: Killed or destroyed in the way Tuifolau Vaomatua killed the frigate bird in renunciation of his Atua Fatutapu. Used to describe an important act of renunciation.

Le Itu Fa'afatutapu: The side that is Fatutapu. To describe people who have supernatural powers or extrasensory perception.

Tautua fa'atuifolau: To serve like Tuifolau. To describe loyal and dedicated service to your aiga, district, church and country.

O togafiti a Lefatu: Lefatu's tricks and cures, which heal and rescue. The expression can be used to describe cures that depend on the healer's magical/supernatural mystical powers.

Aua ne'i fa'atuifolauina tu ma aganu'u: Don't treat our customs and traditions the way Tuifolau Molimau did when his children were born.

Le Ana-o-le-Tetea: The Cave of the Albino. A place of refuge or sanctuary, or an institution or person that provides that.

Le ioe a Folofa'i: Folofa'i's yes: Her agreement to hide the albino. To describe devious decisions to hide what you are ashamed of.

Ia e ola su'efetu i le Lagi Tuifolau: May you live searching for the stars in Tuifolau's star-map, or live according to Tuifolau's star-map.

Ua fetutagi atua: The gods are weeping stars. Used to describe the gods' sorrow caused by our pitiful condition as human beings.

Na lavea'i e Ta'ape le Tuitoga: Ta'ape saved the Tuitoga. To describe great acts of rescue or help.

Tautua pei o Ta'ape: To serve people the way Ta'ape did: in a generous, unstinting way.

O le Va'a a le Tuitoga na maua ai le Tuifolau: It was the canoe of the Tuitoga that brought the title Tuifolau. Used to describe a generous act of reciprocity.

Na o le Tuifolau e tautaia vasa loloa: It is only the Tuifolau, expert navigators and voyagers, who can navigate the great oceans. (Life's problems and troubles can be met and overcome by those who learn from experience and the Star Map.)

Vai-o-le-Tetea: Pool of the Albino: To describe sources of generous gifts and surprises.

E loto mama Tamatetea: Tamatetea is honest and clean-hearted. To describe such people or actions.

Ua maimoa Moamoa ia Tamatetea: The spectators at Moamoa have witnessed Tamatetea's victories and courage. To praise feats of courage and skill.

Tao ma ti'a ia Tamatetea: Literally, be a spear and javelin like Tamatetea. Arm yourself with Tamatetea's courage, cunning and skills.

Laoa fa'atuifolau: Choke on a fishbone, like Tuifolau Ma'afana did. A caution against gluttony, or trusting too much what others offer.

Le Manu-a-Sinalalelei: Sina's bird. To describe people who pretend to be something else or people who are part-human and part-atua, or people who, out of love, are willing to sacrifice themselves as Sina's bird did.

Pei o le apaau a le Manu-a-Sina: Like the broken wing of Sina's bird. To describe acts that falsely attract sympathy and compassion.

Mata o le Manu-a-Sina: The eyes of Sina's bird. To describe someone who is in love.

O Ume na vaai i le Manu: It was Ume who saw the bird. To describe the uncovering of a secret, or someone who is caught becoming his true self.

Le Upega a Ume: Ume's net. Referring to the ability to uncover and catch secrets — hypocrites and spies. Can also be used to describe a trap, an unforgiving trap or action.

Ua tino manu Tagaloa: Tagaloasavali has assumed the body of a bird. Describing the lengths to which genuine love will go.

Le Manu na velo e Ume: The bird that Ume speared. To describe the innocent victim of a callous and violent act, or something beautiful that is destroyed in an act of vengeance.

Fo'i i Lagi le Manu: Sina's bird has returned to the Ninth Heaven (with Sina). An escape from evil and harm, also describing when lovers unite finally against all opposition.

Le usuga a Tagaloasavali: Tagaloasavali's marriage to Sinalalelei, or his courtship of Sinalalelei. To describe a union that produces exceptional children, or a courtship that overcomes all odds.

Afio mai lagi le Fatutapu: Fatutapu came from the heavens. To welcome someone important, or to describe the birth of an important person.

Le feagaiga a Sina ma Ume: The covenant between Sina and Ume. To describe a covenant between a brother and sister that is betrayed by the brother, a falling out of the matrilineal and patrilineal branches of an aiga.

Ua to'otama'i le Tama'ita'i: The Lady (Sina) is angry. To describe acts of revenge against spiteful actions by brothers/men. Generally, to describe just acts of revenge and anger.

Ume-pau-mai-Lagi: Ume who fell from the heavens. To describe someone who earns the just wrath of his aiga or society, and who is punished justly, or those who, through evil acts, earn the wrath of the gods/god.

Le Tolotolo-o-Totoume: The peninsula where Ume spilled his blood. To describe a place of execution, or where an act of revenge is carried out.

Ua nofo le Fatutapu i Niuafei: The Fatutapu dwells in Niuafei. To describe places where the gods reside, or when a religion is established, or to describe a blessing on your aiga or village.

Le Mavaega a Sinalalelei: Sina's last will and testament before she returned with her children to the Ninth Heaven. To describe contracts/arrangements that bring peace and harmony to an aiga and society. To describe a structure that harmonises the human world and that of the atua: the balance between humans and the atua.

Mautu emphasised that the history of their aiga and district, since the establishment of Fatutapu as an atua, also produced other sayings, the poetic distillation of wisdom out of living and suffering.

Into the Box

Wrapped in soft calico, the Chinese box felt like a live bird between her hands. Warm, trembling. The river swished and coughed and roared and threw up a fine spray in which the bright noonday sunshine formed three rainbows, which arched over the river and disappeared into the bush on the other side. Peleiupu picked her way over the wet creepers and boulders to the shade of a tamanu that was choking under vines, and, sitting down on one of its massive roots, cradled the box to her breasts. Her mouth was dry, her heart thudding against the back of her throat, and the sight and roar of the swift river washed through her eyes and head. Mosquitoes started milling around her; she broke off a small branch and fanned them away. Because she was bored with school and inexplicably homesick, she could no longer deny the need to read Barker's last testament. She'd really tried . . .

Hands trembling, she inserted the brass key into the small lock; turned it. Click. Heart beating louder than the river. Right forefinger under the clasp, she flipped back the lid. Immediately she glanced away from the box, expecting some malevolent aitu to brim, like vapour, out of it. Nothing. She gazed inside.

The manuscript was tied up with a red ribbon. Swallowing again, Peleiupu was oblivious to the mosquitoes now stinging at her. She glanced up at the rainbow bridges, then dipped her hands into the box and untied the ribbon. Her eyes followed the rainbow bridges up, up, up into the dense heads of the tree, while her fingers worked their way around the edges of the manuscript. Delicately, she started lifting Barker's last will and testament out of the container, as if she were taking a vital organ out of her body. She shut her eyes tightly, counted ONE-TWO-THREE. Then gazed down again.

Neat, tight black handwriting, without decoration or extravagant flourishes, on paper that had turned light brown over the years.

She steadied her trembling and started reading . . .

> My dear friend Mautu,
>
> As you well know, I've never been one for offering or listening sympathetically to true confessions, but because of the alofa and respect I have for you, I feel — now that I'm well dead and therefore unable to see and suffer your reaction — I owe you the truth and nothing but the truth (so help me, Satan!) about my pelagic and untragic life. I know that my confessions will cause you much anger and pain but I also know that, because you're a true tamaali'i and Christian — the only one I know — you will forgive me, eventually . . .

There was a sharp stinging on the left side of her neck. Slap! She turned her palm up: a splatter of blood. She wiped it off with the corner of her ie lavalava. She tried not to read on, knowing now that Barker's confession was going to come at her as hard and unstoppable as the river, erasing almost all the history and mythology with which he'd nourished their imaginations, trust and alofa . . .

> We create ourselves. Without God we are left to invent ourselves and our paths into the darkness and out of it. At the end of my search I have found the consoling and healing Satoan view of that Darkness, Pouliuli. I've also found you and your Aiga, and a home — or one I can call home — for the first time in my life. I may not have shown it while I was alive, my friend, but Satoa became my home, my aiga . . .

As she read, Barker's revelations drew her in closely, cutting her off from the river and bush and the stinging mosquitoes . . .

> I was not born into a wealthy and noble family . . . No, I made up most of that history about my father being an earl. Forgive me for that, for I know that as you read this, you'll understand my reasons . . . I was born in London, of unknown parents. Found abandoned in an alleyway off Pall Mall, I was put into the Sir John Moore Orphanage and christened

Moses Mall, by Reverend and Mrs Trent Mears, who ran the institution along strict Methodist lines of not sparing the rod or being indulgent. I was adequately fed and clothed and, as long as I behaved like a good obedient Christian boy, I escaped Reverend Mears's wrath. I loved Latin, Greek, Shakespeare, and Miss Elizabeth Thrombone, who taught those. Miss Thrombone had been brought up in the orphanage, had trained as a Sunday school teacher and returned to teach at the orphanage. Reverend and Mrs Mears were the only parents I knew. But at fifteen, still hopelessly infatuated with Miss Thrombone, I discovered Reverend Mears in the act of knowing Miss Thrombone, so to speak biblically, and I fled from the orphanage.

I signed on as cabin boy on the ship *Lady Isabella*, captained by Earl Spenser Barker. Our ship traded between London and New Zealand, and for five often dangerous but enjoyable years Captain Barker and the other officers and members of the crew taught me to be a highly skilled sailor.

You see, being without parents I was free to assume any ancestry and heritage I preferred. And, possessing a good imagination, I found the possibilities were limitless, at any stage in my life, anywhere . . . In true confessions, the confessor is supposed to be utterly truthful. Captain Barker, in truth, became my father, more loving and caring than anyone I'd known before. In the years I was fortunate to spend with him, he taught me much of the wisdom and arts and skills of the world: he was a very cultured and literate man who was gentle towards me but very tough towards others. To survive the demands of the life onboard and at sea you had to be strong, and at times ruthless, he told me.

So in a sense I wasn't lying to you when I said my father was Earl Spenser Barker: he was an earl in my love for him. I loved him with a passion that would have made me give up my life for him. And I almost did.

In Russell, in the Bay of Islands, in the Seamen's Arms — a favourite pub for sailors — Captain Barker and some of the crew and I were celebrating my eighteenth birthday when a drunken captain from a rival firm broke into our group and, winding an arm around Captain Barker, said, 'Giv'us a kiss, Captain! Go on, giv'us . . .' Captain Barker pushed him away. 'Now don' tell us yah don't like it, Captain!' He embraced Captain Barker again; there was a struggle, with Captain Barker lifting the man up and hurling him against the wall. As the man staggered to his feet, some of his crew attacked Captain Barker. An upraised arm, a flashing dagger. I hurled myself between Captain Barker and the downward-plunging dagger, my right hand jabbing up and grabbing the attacker's wrist, but the force of the stabbing continued. I can't remember screaming as the blade exploded into my chest and the pain broke in waves throughout my body and erupted out of the top of my head.

When I regained consciousness our ship was two days out of Russell. I knew from the look in the first mate's eyes when he came into the cabin to tell me. I knew. God, I knew. And I felt and heard my whole body and self and life surge up in protest, in rage, in pain. No. No! The first mate held me; they tied me to the bunk. It was then that I knew, for the first time, the pain of loss — the pain of living death, the loneliness and endlessness of it, and having to live with it without him. I understood so well what you were going through, Mautu, when your son died. Yes, I knew, and knew also that no matter what I did to try to heal my pain, I would continue to suffer it, bear it, for the rest of my life . . .

Later they would tell me that Captain Barker had been stabbed by two other attackers, and had died instantly. They'd buried him at sea, the day after we'd left Russell.

What an eighteenth birthday present: the death of one of the first people I'd ever loved unconditionally. You could say that perhaps I've spent my life since then searching for the healing of that loss, that love. Even fabricating selves and other identities and lives to try to do it. Courting even danger and death — and thriving on the thrill of that — to try to end it.

Literally, I've searched the Seven Seas and the whole world over. I've found other loves, grown through them, broken away from them. Watched some of them die. They all added to that first loss and grief and my understanding of it — which is no consolation at all. As you know, my friend, even God is not enough to heal such a loss, to console us. You have said to me that we all exist in God's pain and His knowledge of it. What if God is dead, my friend? What then?

Not that I didn't get over my grief, as it were. Like everyone else, I learned to live with it. To control it. To bear it whenever the wound reopened. We can, Mautu, define ourselves by what we've lost. But I learned from you and your beautiful wife and children that we can also define ourselves by what we've gained, especially through alofa . . .

Barker signed off the *Lady Isabella* when they reached London.

Peleiupu stopped reading, and looked into the watching bush and sky and rainbows, and felt protected from the guilt of having opened Barker's testament and started reading it, thereby intruding into his secrets. Barker may have fabricated much of the life he'd transferred to them, but she now understood some of his reasons for doing so. Barker had lived without God — God was dead — and to sustain such a courageous stand he had created, invented, developed — call it what you like — a self and a way to do so.

One day she too would find a love as profound as Barker's. When? When would she experience it? And would she be able to bear the exhilarating pain of it and, later, the inevitable killing loss of it?

For almost five years Barker lived off his wits by selling his body, in London, with his mentor sitting in his centre of grief. Alcohol, opium, the flesh. It was as if he were watching someone who resembled him caught in a fog, trying to find his panic-stricken way through the beasts and preying creatures that inhabited that trap.

> Human beings are such sick and monstrous creatures! Powerless, penniless, they fed off me, and, I suppose, I fed off them. Behind the benevolent face of Queen Victoria was madness and sickness. (Sin and abomination, you call it, Mautu.) Even in the most respected houses of England.
>
> At one banquet, held by one of England's great lords, I was literally served up on a platter. They dressed me up as a sucking pig, even with an apple in my mouth, and carried me to the massive dining table on a golden platter. The civilised lords and ladies took their turns eating me. It was Sodom and Gomorrah, Mautu. And they loved it. There was some consolation: they paid me well.
>
> After each violation, each humiliation, each selling, I buried my sight in cheap gin and an unintelligible unconsciousness.
>
> One day I broke from that sleep and I was in the orphanage of my childhood, with Elizabeth Thrombone, now Mrs Smiles, nursing me. I must have gone to the orphanage during one of my drunken bouts because they found me unconscious inside the front gate. Fate, or some force like God, must have led me there to save myself. Reverend and Mrs Mears had passed away the year before, and Elizabeth was now running the orphanage, with a husband who could have come out of Dickens. In the ten years I'd been away from the orphanage, she'd changed into a

buxom matter-of-fact administrator who'd lost her fervour for Greek, Latin and Shakespeare, with five children of her own. When she found out who I was she was kind and nursed me back to health.

The orphanage now had about a hundred and fifty orphans, with a staff of twelve, and was very prosperous compared with when Barker had lived there.

Right from the start Barker sensed that Roger Smiles, a little man with hunched shoulders, long-fingered hands that seemed to be always searching for things to price, and an almost hairless head that peaked and reminded Barker of a stoat, didn't like him, but hid it behind his long smiles and grins and bowing. 'Yes, Mr Barker, we love our wards here at Sir John Moore's Orphanage, we do, we do,' he'd say. 'And we love having back one of our former students, who's been so successful in the world of shipping!'

When he was well enough to get out of bed, Elizabeth got Barker to talk to her classes about his travels and life as a sailor. He discovered, to his growing self-confidence, that he was able to hold the children's attention, and they asked for more of his stories. In the afternoons he helped out in the kitchen, using the skills as a cook that he'd acquired on the *Lady Isabella*. At mealtimes he refused to sit with Mr and Mrs Smiles at the head table; he ate with the students. It was there that he began to sense that most of the orphans were afraid of Mr Smiles — some were terrified. He tried to ask but none of them divulged why. Around the orphanage Mr Smiles appeared to be an efficient and pleasant teacher; he wasn't cruel and when he was cross he didn't even raise his voice with the children.

Elizabeth invited Barker to join the staff. He would consider it, he told her, and she invited him to join the weekly staff meetings in her office and learn more about the orphanage. He noticed that, even though Roger Smiles did not say much at the meetings, everyone — except Elizabeth who seemed oblivious to her husband's power — watched him surreptitiously, not only to see which way they had to vote, but in case he was going to strike at them. As with the children, Mr Smiles controlled the staff through the use of fear, and the staff tried to hide this fear from one another.

'We have a governing committee,' Elizabeth explained to Barker at one meeting. 'The chairman of it is Lord Sollful,' she added.

'He is one of our beloved Queen's main advisers!' her husband echoed. As she announced the names of the other committee members her husband echoed flattering remarks about their wealth and position. With growing trepidation, Barker recognised them — Lord Sollful and three others — as some of the men he knew exploited young children, sexually. He'd been used and abused in their houses himself. 'Without them we wouldn't be able to survive,' Elizabeth concluded.

216

'They are all extremely generous Christian gentlemen,' Roger Smiles chanted. 'They also organise the other lords and ladies of our beloved England to donate to our humble institution. Don't they, ladies?' The other staff members smiled widely when Smiles looked at them.

'We are very proud of the fact that nearly all our staff were formerly our wards,' Elizabeth mentioned later.

As a sailor Barker had learned to live with some privacy in very crowded conditions, to observe others without showing that he was doing it. He put that to good use as he tracked Smiles. He noticed that Smiles went into the city every Wednesday afternoon, with one of the female staff members — the women took turns — to buy supplies for the orphanage. They usually returned just before evening prayers and dinner.

The first time Barker followed them, Smiles stopped the carriage in front of a wealthy home fifteen minutes out from the orphanage. His vivacious young companion, Phoebe Polter, got out and went into the house and Smiles drove away. Barker decided not to follow Smiles but to observe the house from across the street in the warmth of the small pub. He inquired there about the house and was told by the publican that it belonged to a Mr Flit Wildchest, who'd made his fortune in the colonies. About an hour later Smiles was back. He went into the house and out with Phoebe and back into the carriage, which Barber followed to another house, two blocks away. There Phoebe spent another hour, and was again collected by Smiles, who then took her to the markets where they shopped for supplies. Barker knew what was happening but refused to admit it to himself.

Individual staff members sat at the heads of each table of wards. During dinner that evening Barker deliberately sat at Phoebe Polter's table and, as he talked with the students, watched her and drew her into the conversation. Not once did she look directly at him. For the next few days he made sure he was around her, gaining her confidence. One evening, as he rounded the corridor to his room, she stepped out of the shadows and, gazing up into his face, stuck her hand against his chest and asked, 'Why are you following me around?' He insisted he wasn't, but, pushing her fist deeper into his chest, her eyes burning, she said, 'You're lying! I've been watching you.' She paused. 'You know, don't ya? You know!' He shook his head. She turned and fled down the corridor.

It felt as if a gigantic hand were clamped tightly around his mouth and pulling him out of the liquid darkness of sleep. 'It's me!' Phoebe whispered into his ear when he struggled to free his mouth. She slid into bed beside him and, turning to face him, put her arms around him. 'You can do what you like,' she whispered, 'but you mustn't tell anyone what you know! Please!' When she started sobbing mutely into his neck he put his arms around her. 'I hate him, I *hate* him!' she sobbed.

'It's all right, it's all right!' he kept consoling her. Then she told him about Smiles and what he'd done to her and most of the other staff as they'd grown up in the orphanage; he was repeating it with many of the wards.

The next night when Smiles left with three boys and three girls, Barker followed the carriage. He was right: the carriage headed straight for Lord Sollful's mansion. Smiles led the children in and stayed with them.

For three days he gathered more information from Phoebe and two of her friends, and followed Smiles whenever he took children or staff to visit clients, knowing what it was all about yet compelled to keep reconfirming it. The terrible information fuelled his anger — and his fear. He stayed close to Elizabeth but decided, finally, not to confront her with what he knew.

I was afraid, terribly afraid, of Smiles. His kind of evil was capable of any horror. Why? Because Smiles was incapable of seeing that he was evil. He believed, honestly, that what he was doing was to the benefit of the wards and staff. No longer did they have to worry about money to live on, and live well. They could pay the staff and still have money left over for extras: birthday parties, Christmas parties, outings to the zoo and parks, a new set of clothes for each ward annually . . .

I even considered running away from it, but Smiles changed that.

'You've got to start earning your living with us,' Smiles said one evening after dinner. 'How?' I'd asked. Smiling and chortling, hand cupped over his mouth, Smiles winked and said, 'By giving of yourself, like all of us!' I tried not to move away when Smiles reached over and touched — more a caress than a touch — my shoulder.

The next evening he invited me to his quarters, which were upstairs in the middle of the complex of buildings. I was surprised, and was afraid, when I discovered that Elizabeth wasn't there. Smiles told me that his wife and children were visiting relatives. When Smiles offered me gin, I was even more afraid, because no alcohol was allowed in the orphanage. When Smiles let in two boys, from the orphanage, soon after I arrived, I was not surprised. I was now mortified, knowing what Smiles intended.

It was obvious to Barker that the boys were familiar with Smiles' quarters and were trying to appear relaxed and unafraid, but he sensed they weren't. Smiles drank steadily as he moved around the boys, touching them, at first lightly, then lingeringly, all the while talking to Barker: 'Elizabeth and I have devoted our lives to God and to saving His beautiful lost children — like these.' He looked at Barker. 'You too were saved by this institution, weren't you?' A wink. 'Yes, God's beautiful children must be saved . . .' Barker noticed that one of the boys had tears in his eyes but was trying his best to hide his fear. '. . . but they must also help us save them, mustn't they?'

Barker refused to answer.

'We are one big happy Christian family, and each member of our loving family must play his part in helping our family, mustn't he?' The older of the two boys refilled Smiles' glass. Smiles ran his fingers over the boy's cheek, then, cupping the boy's chin in his hand, turned up the boy's face and said to Barker, 'This is what God's face must look like, eh.' Then slowly he asked the boy, 'You believe in helping your family, don't you, Matthew?'

The boy straightened up and, upper lip trembling visibly, said, 'Yes, sir!'

'And you've been doing it ever since you were brought here, haven't you, my beautiful Matthew?'

'Yes, sir!'

Suddenly Smiles wheeled around to the other boy, who was hugging the arm of the sofa, and demanded, 'And what have you been doing to help your family, Evers?' The boy was too upset to reply immediately, so Smiles advanced on him. 'What are you afraid of, Evers? Haven't we treated you with great love and kindness?' As he reached down, the boy thrust his head into his hands and started sobbing mutely. Smiles clutched the boy's hair and, pulling it up, turned the boy's face towards Barker. 'This boy is ungrateful, isn't he? We have treated him with great love and brought him up to respect and love God . . .' Barker stepped forward '. . . and he doesn't want to help us, do you, Evers?' The boy's face was drenched with tears. 'Do you, Evers?' Smiles' hand clutched harder at the boy's hair, and reminded Barker of a spider. 'Now stop your whimpering, boy, and show us how you help your family!' He waited. 'Yes, you reciprocate the love and care we've poured upon your ungrateful head since your unloving parents left you at our doorstep. Hear me, boy! Show us!'

Smiles straightened up and they watched him as he emptied his glass in one long, lingering swallow. A piercing sliver of light shot out of his glass and, for an instant, blinded Barker. When Matthew, the older of the boys, started to move, Barker knew he was going to try to save his friend from Smiles' wrath . . .

The story of what happened next is not fit for any one's reading, Barker wrote.

Suffice to say, it was a story of the type of abuse I was used to — the total humiliation of the innocent and powerless— and I did nothing to stop it that night. Nothing. Smiles derived pleasure from watching me watching him exercise his violent power over those children, knowing that I couldn't stop him, and, more evil still, that I was deriving some pleasure from watching . . .

Barker realised the next morning at the staff meeting, when Smiles kept smiling and gazing at him, that Smiles now had a hold over him: he was now part of the guilty secret of the orphanage, of the power and terror that held it together. As he was leaving the meeting Smiles sidled up to Barker and, running his fingers up Barker's arm, whispered, 'God's little children know how to love those people who love them, eh?' Wink. 'You know how to love too, don't you?' Wink. 'You're one of us.' He chortled as he moved off down the corridor.

Barker fled from the orphanage that evening, and spent two days wandering the pubs, getting drunk, telling himself it wasn't his concern. He even concluded that without the terrible patronage that Smiles was procuring through the female staff and students, the orphanage would collapse. But he couldn't get past Smiles' evil abuse of the children for his own pleasure. That was not patronage. As he drank, the sliver of light out of Smiles' glass, which had pierced his sight, kept cutting into his conscience. It's got nothing to do with me, nothing! he kept replying to it.

On his third day out of the orphanage, a Wednesday, Barker waited outside and then followed Smiles and the two female staff he had in the carriage. The morning cold cut into his hands and ears and his breath was like heavy smoke but, as he jogged after the carriage, he realised that for the first time in years he was at peace with his grief concerning Captain Barker, and happy — yes, happy — with himself.

After Smiles dropped the women off, at two different houses, Barker caught up with the carriage and jumped in beside Smiles who, surprised, pretended he wasn't and said, 'Our long-lost orphan has decided to return!'

'I couldn't stay away from my kind, could I, sir!' Barker replied, mirroring Smiles' large smile as he placed his hand on Smiles' thigh. 'Yes, we are a kind,' he continued. 'You showed me that the other night, eh?' Wink, wink. Smiles reached down and caressed the top of Barker's hand. 'I knew it all along,' he whispered.

Shortly after, Barker found himself in a small but exclusive hotel, which Smiles obviously patronised regularly and generously because the staff were attentive to the point of obsequiousness, in a spacious room and in a silk-sheeted bed. Barker did not go into detail about what happened next:

Suffice to say, I put to effective use all the things I'd learned about men's sexual desires and secrets, and discovered more of Smiles' secrets . . .

Afterwards, Barker told Smiles he wanted to stay on at the hotel for a few days because he wanted to spend more time with him and him alone. No problem, Smiles declared — and he too wanted more time with Barker. Before he left, Smiles fixed it with the hotel that he would pay Barker's bill — anything he wanted was to be charged.

Next day, Barker sent a note to Phoebe. They met and it didn't take long for him to outline his plan and get her unconditional support. She would also need to recruit another staff member. 'No shortage of those', she told Barker. 'Apart from his wife, they all hate him.'

I'm very reluctant to describe in detail what happened next, but I'm also compelled, in a strange and exhilarating way, to let you know the details of my triumph. I want to detail it forever for whoever of your descendants will read this. I do so knowing that you will be repulsed/reviled by it, my friend . . .

When Smiles was tied, with silk straps, by his hands and ankles, to the four corners of the bed, his mouth gagged with another silk strap, Barker told him he had many surprises for him that night. Smiles' eyes bulged with anticipation. As instructed by Smiles, Barker was wearing immaculate black and white gloves, and before Smiles was gagged he kept referring to Barker as his 'strict but loving undertaker'.

'Surprise, surprise!' Barker announced. Phoebe and Clarise, dressed in black like Barker, slipped into the room and into Smiles' now fervent view. 'Two of your slaves, sir!' The women bowed. 'Willing to obey your every command! Of course it was your wish that tonight we do anything to you that we wish . . .' Smiles nodded eagerly. '. . . that we punish you for all the foul deeds you have inflicted on us and your loving orphans, sir!'

For a while he didn't realise we weren't acting, and he squirmed and shuddered with enjoyment. Poking at him with the handles of their whips, the women chanted, 'Ya shrivelled-up, small vile thing!' Every time they chanted and poked, Smiles grew larger, more erect. Poking turned to long loving strokes of the whips. 'Yes, yes, yes!' he cried. Swish, smack, swish, smack, long red whip marks on his porcelain white skin . . .

Her pulse beating rapidly, her ears and head ringing, Peleiupu forced herself to stop reading. There! But she was alive with it. She flipped over the page and continued reading, quickly . . .

When Smiles realised that the lashes were real pain, his eyes burned with a panic that intensified as he tried breaking his bonds but couldn't, as he heaved, pulled, struggled and appealed to Barker for help, and the lacerations opened and poured blood — his blood — into the sheets, as the women, faces contorted with triumphant rage, danced around him, and Barker, the only person he'd allowed himself to love, just kept smiling down at him . . .

Peleiupu hugged the manuscript to her chest. She was glad, glad, glad: Smiles was getting his just punishment, but she was also afraid of the way she was feeling.

> . . . I hadn't anticipated the knives, but when the women pulled them out, extended them towards Smiles and looked at me, I nodded once, twice, and cried, 'Yes, yes!' And as the knives slit and slit across Smiles' chest and moved downwards, the bed was suddenly a sea of blood on which Smiles was lost and afloat, his eyes silently screaming and screaming. A knife seemed to have grown out of my right hand and was wielding me as its weapon. My left hand was around Smiles' manhood, twisting and twisting, and the knife dug in and around, cutting swiftly, and I was looking up at my upstretched arm and hand, holding aloft Smiles' manhood, which dripped blood until my whole arm and shoulder were covered with it. When I looked again, Phoebe's knife flashed across Smiles' taut, protesting throat, and his eyes were turning inwards to his disbelief that he was going to die. His body jerked once, hugely, and I pushed down on his chest to try to still him, but it jerked again, and again, as if it were shedding his evil, his life — shedding it forever, like a skin it had outgrown . . .

Peleiupu held it and held it — the whole pleasure of Barker's revenge — then it surged outwards from her centre in waves and up through her forehead and out of her mouth in a long, jerking series of cries, as if she were herself being released from a huge pain. Her triumphant cries joined the roar of the river, whirled around the heads of the trees and crossed to the other side over the rainbow bridges . . .

> We wrapped him up securely in sheets and canvas, placed him in the large box I'd had constructed for the purpose, addressed the box to a

non-existent Mr Peter Saddly, at a non-existent address in Wales, cleaned up the room, and then got the hotel porters to have the box delivered by rail.

In a moment of passion during our first encounter Smiles had divulged where, over the years, he'd banked much of the money his wards and staff had procured. The day after we mailed him to Wales, so to speak, I drew the money from those accounts. It was a handsome sum which I shared with the orphanage, Phoebe and Clarice, and used to falsify my identity papers and pay my way to Australia, bribing anyone along the way who threatened my way. I had enough left over to buy a small schooner, which I used to trade along the Australian coast . . .

I was free, at last. Free of Smiles, of any guilt to do with his dramatic demise, free of my grief and free of that sick country, Great Britain. Free to explore the world, for six wonderful years . . .

And look where that got me to, eventually, Mautu! To Poto, my beloved wife, and my savage children and your family and Satoa. And my death . . .

Barker confessed that he had not felt an ounce of guilt at killing Smiles. Not an ounce. Because of that he believed he was insane; after all, people guilty of murder had consciences, and should be haunted by guilt. For six years as he travelled the planet he kept expecting to be disturbed, haunted, plagued by guilt eventually. But it never happened. In fact, he was going to carry to his grave the exquisite joy of having erased Smiles.

Peleiupu put the manuscript back into the box, and for a long while sat gazing into the bush, as if every particle of her had been transformed into the white light of the rainbows that now suffused the whole bush and river, a light that held her past and future in the ever-moving present.

Later as she crossed back over the river, with the box tucked under her arm, she again wondered why Barker had ultimately taken his own life, but this time the puzzle didn't disturb her. It didn't matter, she concluded. Barker had committed suicide, that was all: there didn't have to be reasons for it, or a meaning to it. All that mattered was the truth that Barker was a vital part of her mythology and her future.

As the shadows grew across her path from the canopy and the bases of the trees, she thought of Arona and wondered where he was and what he was doing.

The Choice

Peleiupu marched briskly down the corridor, swinging her hips and deliberately exaggerating the squeaking of her bare feet on the polished floor. SSQQQQUU-UEEEEEK! SSSQUUEEEK! Misi Ioana had sent for her.

'Malo, Pele!' friends called, as she squeaked past. She waved and dug and swivelled her feet in the floor, SSSSSSQQQQQQUUUEEEEKKK! 'Malo, Pele!' they called and laughed.

She halted in military fashion in front of the door, pulled in her stomach, raised her shoulders, rapped Rat-tat-tat-tat-tat! and stood at attention.

'Enter!' Misi Ioana's voice sopranoed through the door. 'Please come in!'

Gripping the door knob securely, Peleiupu turned it, pulled back the door, slid over the threshold, and stood at attention, gaze fixed squarely on the small Misi Ioana, who was in her high-backed chair behind her large desk, glasses almost on the tip of her long sharp nose, a stack of school reports in front of her.

With her right hand Misi Ioana motioned Peleiupu forward to the white cane chair in front of the desk. Peleiupu straightened her uniform and sat down, her back ramrod straight and her head held high, the way Misi Ioana had trained them.

Misi Ioana finished signing the report and looked up. 'You graduate next Friday,' she said in what Peleiupu had described to her friends as Misi Ioana's quaint missionary Samoan. 'It is obvious you decided to work hard this year — and to behave properly for a change — and you've done well.' This time it was in a mixture of English and Samoan. 'In fact, to my surprise, you have done *exceptionally* well!'

Misi Ioana held up her report. 'You are top of arithmetic, Bible knowledge, hand-writing, English . . .' She looked down. 'Almost 100 per cent for English, Samoan — ninety-five per cent for that. You have come top of every subject.' Peleiupu continued gazing at Misi Ioana. 'Like me, all your teachers were surprised. Two of them came and discussed it with me: they couldn't believe you'd done so well . . .'

'Do you mean, Misi Ioana, they thought I'd cheated?' Peleiupu articulated perfectly in English.

A glint of fire in Misi Ioana's eyes. 'No, that is *not* what I meant! I meant your teachers wanted to make sure they had marked your exams correctly.'

'And had they, Misi Ioana?' This time Peleiupu used Barker's immaculate accent.

'Your marks are correct!' snapped Misi Ioana.

'I decided at the end of last year, after you and my mother chastised me for being "lazy, irresponsible and at times rebellious", to show you what I was really capable of,' Peleiupu pushed her attack. 'I knew how to speak and write English before I came to Vaiuta.'

'Well, why didn't you show it?' Misi Ioana's eyes were razor-sharp slits.

'Because I didn't want to earn the envy of my teachers and fellow students.'

'Have you always been this arrogant?' Misi Ioana thrust her face forward.

Peleiupu refused to retreat. 'I did what I did so I could live here without being singled out, being envied or admired.'

'Did your parents know you were hiding your *great* talents and skills from us, your ignorant teachers?'

'My mother knew but didn't say anything about it to me,' Peleiupu said in Samoan, deliberately undermining Misi Ioana's attack.

'Speak English, girl!' Misi Ioana was on her feet and shaking visibly.

'What is wrong with my language?' Peleiupu thrust straight into Misi Ioana's razor-sharp eyes, which opened wider.

Misi Ioana's arms rose up like wings, hands like threatening talons. But every time she tried to speak, her mouth trembled out of control. Peleiupu continued staring at her. 'You — you you you you *Samoan!*' Misi Ioana screeched, then slumped back into her chair, trying to control her shaking, her face ashen white. 'I will be speaking to your parents about this! I will!' Peleiupu refused to look away. 'In all my life no one has ever dared speak to me the way you have. Get out of my office!'

'Thank you for all your help, Misi Ioana,' Peleiupu added in Samoan. 'I have learned much at Vaiuta. And I have enjoyed most of my time here.'

She was surprised when, at the graduation ceremony the following week, she was presented with all six prizes. She was not surprised, though, that for the rest of her time at Vaiuta Misi Ioana refused, absolutely, to acknowledge in any other way that she existed.

A week later she was back in Satoa, helping her mother run their now even larger household and school, but she knew it was only temporary, for her parents and the elders of her aiga at Fagaloto were already arranging her marriage to a pastor. During her life at Vaiuta, despite moments of profound doubt, she had persuaded herself that was her proper future. What else was there for a pastor's daughter with a good Christian education? It would destroy her parents if she married an 'uneducated villager'. She imagined that Barker and Stenson would be disappointed too. This reminded her that the library that Stenson had bequeathed her hadn't been dusted and checked for a long time. They had shifted the books and shelves into one of the smaller classrooms, two years before. So after school she took some students and they dusted the books and shelves, putting the books back in alphabetical order. Many were missing; others were tattered and brown with age.

At school assembly the following morning she announced that she wanted them to check their homes and return any books they found. No one would be punished for having taken the books.

'Here are four books I found in our home,' a familiar voice said over her shoulder as she was working later in the library. Believing it was a student, she didn't bother to turn around. She just pointed at her desk. The hands holding the books came into view as they put the books down. When the person didn't move away she glanced around. 'My brothers and sisters forgot to bring them back,' Tavita said, grinning. She felt silly and watched herself blushing as she tried to suppress her trembling. 'Are you well?' Tavita greeted her.

'Yes, thank you,' she mumbled.

'And your family?'

'They are well too.' She hadn't seen him for a year. He looked so different — much taller than her now, with delicate features like his mother's. Apart from his voice, cats' eyes and light blond hair there was nothing else of Barker about him.

'I hear you topped your class at Vaiuta,' he said. 'Topped everything. You were always the cleverest of us.' Smiling.

She looked at the ground. 'How is your mother?' She felt stupid when she heard herself asking.

'She is well. Our business is doing well because of her. She's far better at business than my father was. She asked after you the other day. It was the anniversary of our father's death, and she remembered how he'd treated you and Arona as if you were his children.'

'It's been four years?'

'Yes. Last week we went up to his grave and cleared it. We cleared the site of "the People" as well. It was hard work because much of the bush has grown back.' He paused. 'Poto says that you and Arona found "the People" with your father and mine? Barker was a strange man, wasn't he?'

'It was Barker who dug up the first skull.' She couldn't continue.

'Have you heard from Arona?' he asked.

'No, no one has. Lalaga is still very worried about him.'

'I should've gone with him,' he said, more a question than a statement. She didn't reply. 'Your students have come, I'd better go.'

'Thank you for bringing the books,' she said. Grinning, he turned and started walking away. She was glad, so glad, he hadn't gone with Arona, she realised as she watched him gliding through the mellow morning light. Why was she breathless?

On Friday evening, Tavita appeared with some of his sisters and brothers for choir practice. It was his first time and he surprised everyone. He sat in the bass section and, as Peleiupu tried not to look at him, her breathlessness returned. The choirmaster read out the hymns for that Sunday, then got Lalaga to sing the first line of the first hymn. The choirmaster repeated it. The rest of the choir joined in. Peleiupu tried, but she couldn't concentrate.

After Barker had died, Poto and her children, except Tavita, had continued partic-ipating regularly in church and its activities. So devout and generous as a church member was Poto that Mautu, with Sao's agreement, made her a deacon. As such she nagged and threatened Tavita with God's unforgiving wrath for not attending. But Tavita stayed away. Lalaga used his brothers and sisters to try to make him return, but Tavita simply smiled that Barker smile, which charmed almost everyone, and said, 'Someday, someday, when I'm ready.'

'Just like his pagan palagi father,' many of the Satoans declared. 'What do you expect from the intestines of a papalagi?'

During the choir practice Peleiupu sensed that Tavita was avoiding looking at her. She also noticed that most of the choir were according him the respect usually reserved for elders and matai. It had a lot to do with his being Sao's favourite grandson, and she remembered that because of his store most Satoan aiga now owed him and Poto money, which they tried to pay through the copra they sold them. He and Poto were generous in extending credit and helping anyone financially, and Sao, through Poto, was now the biggest contributor to village and church affairs.

As she followed Lalaga and Naomi out of the church into the cold wind blowing in from the sea, Peleiupu glanced back. Tavita was smiling at her above the heads of the other people. She looked away quickly.

The way she was feeling and behaving was ridiculous, she kept telling herself. But late on Saturday afternoon she found herself on the veranda of Barker's store, gazing into the gaping doorway, out of which was wafting the smell of copra and flour, and feeling exposed to the scrutiny of Tavita's fa'afafine brother, Semisi, who was leaning on the veranda railing, watching Tavita and a group of youths playing cricket on the malae.

Semisi, who insisted on being called by his English name, James, called, in Samoan, 'Look, it's Pele!' He scurried over. 'Pele, what a surprise! What you doing in our neck of the woods?' he asked in English. Semisi had left pastors' school two years before, and was now the main shopkeeper at the store. Before Pele could answer, Semisi touched her shoulder in a sweeping gesture. 'Gosh, don't you look beautiful!' he exclaimed in English.

'I came to buy some things,' Peleiupu said.

'Come in then, Pele.' Semisi held her elbow and guided her into the store. 'By the way,' he added in English, 'I need to practise my English to you, Pele. After all, you the best English teacher I've had.'

'I want to buy . . . ' Peleiupu started.

'You not in a hurry, is you, Pele?' Semisi interrupted. 'We need to talk, find out what you been up to over the last few years, eh? Sit, sit!' Semisi instructed, brushing the top of the wooden chair in front of the counter. Peleiupu took the chair and Semisi jumped up and sat on the counter. Semisi opened a large jar of sweets and tossed her some hardboiled lollies. 'Come all the way from England, my father Barker's country,' he said. 'One day, my mother and I going to visit England.'

For the next hour or so, prompted by Semisi's uninhibited questioning, Peleiupu gave him a carefully edited history of her life at Vaiuta. 'Gosh, gosh, I envy to you, Pele!' Semisi kept encouraging her. At the end Semisi said, 'I would've loved Vaiuta. Loved it. Loved to be taught by Miss Brakes, your beautiful English principal.' For a moment Peleiupu forgot he was referring to Misi Ioana.

A short while later, while Semisi was filling her small order, Tavita and his brothers Mikaele and Roni and their friends entered, bringing in a strong smell of sun and sweat. 'Look who's here!' Semisi declared. Peleiupu wanted to hide, but Semisi held her elbow and turned her round to face them. 'Surprise, surprise, eh, fellows? Pele, our great teacher!' Semisi switched to Samoan. ('They useless in English so I got for to speak to them in Hamo,' he said in an aside to Peleiupu.) The youths kept to their end of the counter. 'This is Pele, don't you remember Pele?' Semisi chastised them. Tavita smiled; the others just nodded and refused to look at Peleiupu. 'Don't worry, Pele, they're just shy!'

'That's enough,' Tavita stopped Semisi's whooping laughter. 'Have you given Pele the things she came for?' He sounded so much like his father, Peleiupu thought. Uncannily so.

'She clutch them to her dainty breast!' Semisi said in English.

'Is there anything else you need?' Tavita asked her. She shook her head and started for the door.

'Pele, you must come again soon!' Semisi called.

She sucked in air through her mouth once she was on the edge of the veranda and the sea breeze curled around her. In, in, filling her breathless lungs.

She sensed him watching her as she crossed the malae and, for the first time, she did not feel oppressively self-conscious about it. Her skin and nerves hummed. She turned just before she disappeared from his sight and waved.

After the next choir practice, as Peleiupu and Naomi left the church, Naomi whispered, 'He can't stop looking at you!' Peleiupu ignored her. Naomi jabbed her elbow into Peleiupu's side and whispered, 'Look, he's still trying not to look at you!' Peleiupu couldn't help it: she looked and caught Tavita staring at her from the doorway. 'See, I told you!' Naomi said. 'He's keen on you, Pele!'

'Don't be stupid!' Peleiupu snapped. She started hurrying. Behind her, all the way home, she heard Naomi and her friends whispering among themselves.

She and Naomi shared the same mosquito net, so when Naomi came to bed, Peleiupu told her, 'I don't want you to discuss Tavita and me with others, because none of it is true.'

The next day when they needed salt and flour, Naomi went to the store. 'He was out fishing and I spent the time talking to Poto, who said she wanted to see you,' Naomi said when she returned.

'Did she say why?'

'Maybe she wants to arrange something between you and you-know-who!' No reaction. 'Only kidding. She just wants to talk — she said she hasn't seen you for a long time.'

Peleiupu entered the store the following afternoon, just as a light shower began to fall, and found Poto and Semisi behind the counter. Everyone in Satoa knew Semisi was Poto's favourite child. He accompanied her everywhere she went, even sat with her among the women in church, wove mats and made siapo with her at the women's mat-weaving fale, made sure she got anything she wanted, accompanied her to Apia to sell the copra and buy goods, and anyone who dared slight her or his father's memory he lashed with his uninhibited tongue.

'It is Pele, Mother,' Semisi said in English. 'It is Pele, the Beautiful!'

Poto opened her arms and reached forward. Peleiupu moved into her embrace. 'You *are* beautiful! So grown-up. You look just like your father. Doesn't she, James?'

'She sure do. I told you, Mum!' Pushing his mother aside, gently, he said, 'Lo'u turn, Mum!' His rich perfume enveloped Peleiupu as he embraced her. 'Before you go, I give you some of my English perfume,' he declared. 'Mum use it too. Don't popole about the stupid rule about pastors' daughters not being allowed to use perfume . . .'

'James, that's enough!' Poto interrupted. 'Go and get Pele and me something to drink.' He rolled his eyes, waved and disappeared around the shelves of goods. 'Auoi, he can really talk, eh, Pele?'

Peleiupu relaxed as they talked, and once more summarised her life at Vaiuta.

'Barker and your father were like brothers, eh,' Poto was saying. 'It was you and your father who made my husband feel welcome in Satoa. Samoans can be so cruel to palagi and other foreigners. They think they're more civilised than anyone else, yet they're so ignorant! They thought I didn't know about their cruel jokes about my husband, but I did, Pele. I did. My children, they call afakasi. But we'll survive it, we'll survive their ignorance.' There was a long pause. 'Without your father I don't think Barker would have survived that long in Satoa.' She looked away. 'Do you think, he . . . he ended his life because of Satoa's treatment of him?'

Be careful, Peleiupu warned herself. Poto must not find out you've read Barker's last testament. 'I've thought about it a lot, Poto. He couldn't have been that lonely and homesick for England because he loved you and your children . . .'

'Strange but every time I think of that alia that he and your father built, I feel that the name they gave the alia was also a very apt description of who he was.' Her eyes were bright with a forgiving understanding. 'Do you remember the name, Pele?' Peleiupu decided to lie and shook her head. '*Le Sa-o-le-Sauali'i-Pa'epa'e,*' Poto whispered. 'What is that in English, Pele?'

'The Ship of the White Phantom.'

'Now, do you see what I mean, Pele?' Poto declared. Peleiupu shook her head. 'He wasn't quite real — a sauali'i, a phantom — and a white one at that, made of dew. A phantom not real to itself or to others; one who keeps sailing, belonging nowhere but always searching for a home.'

'Which in his death he found with God.'

'I hope so, Pele. I really hope so, because he needs to rest. All his lonely life on Earth he kept sailing, searching. It's been four years since he left and I miss him so badly still.'

'We miss him too.' Peleiupu looked at the window. The light steaming rain was drifting noiselessly across the breadfruit trees and fale.

230

'Rain, rain, rain!' Semisi complained as he poured them lemon drinks out of a large jug. He placed a plate of cabin bread with jam on the counter and watched his mother taste her drink. 'How is it, Mother?' He asked. 'Too sour, too sweet, eh? How is it?'

'Beautiful,' Poto said. 'Just right.'

'Yes, just right,' Peleiupu joined in their game.

Beaming with pride, Semisi produced from behind his back three red hibiscus flowers. 'For the two most beautiful women in Satoa and Samoa!' He leaned forward and placed one over Poto's left ear. Peleiupu followed suit. Poto took the third flower from him and placed it over his left ear. He stepped back and, examining them, corrected the angles of their sei, whispering, 'Auoi, you going to steal all the hearts of the men in this lalolagi!' Poto and Peleiupu started laughing.

Just then Tavita came round the shelves, dressed only in a stained working ie lavalava, his body streaked with dirt. 'Auoi, auoi!' Semisi exclaimed, holding his nose. 'Go and bathe before you enter our sacred company!'

'Pele is here,' Poto said to Tavita, ignoring Semisi. 'We've been talking about your father.' Peleiupu found she no longer felt self-conscious in Tavita's presence. 'Your brother is right, you need to bathe,' said Poto.

'I'll been working at the plantation,' Tavita said. He poured himself a drink while they watched him, picked up a cabin bread and bit into it with a loud crunch. 'A beautiful sei,' he told his mother.

'What about Pele's?' Semisi asked, raising his eyebrows.

Gazing boldly at Peleiupu he said, 'Very beautiful too.' Semisi laughed. Peleiupu was upset by the brothers' behaviour: it was not the proper thing for young men to publicly show their affection for women. It was their palagi side, she would excuse them to herself later. 'We brought some taro and yams for Pele to take home for their to'ona'i,' Tavita said to Poto.

'You always think of the right thing to do, eh, David,' Semisi said. 'Did God tell you Pele was here?'

'That's enough!' Poto instructed. 'Tavita, you go and bathe.' When Tavita hesitated she said, 'Quickly!' He bowed curtly to Peleiupu and, munching on the cabin bread, wheeled around and disappeared around the shelves. 'And you,' Poto turned to Semisi, 'you go and get someone to take the taro and yams home for the pastor.' Semisi squirmed in protest. 'Go now!' She waved him off with her hand. Semisi winked at Peleiupu and dragged his feet as he left.

'There is something important your father wants to discuss with you, Pele,' Lalaga said one Saturday afternoon while the rest of their household were playing cricket with the other Satoan youth on the malae. Lalaga pointed to the post near Mautu, who was watching the match. Peleiupu sat down and watched too.

The batting team sat in a large group in the shade of the breadfruit trees by the store, singing to Semisi's hilarious conducting. Spread out over the malae and between the surrounding fale, the fielders danced to the beat of a pate every time a wicket fell. 'Mautu, your daughter has come,' Lalaga urged. Mautu continued watching as if he hadn't heard her. Peleiupu waited.

'As you know, I was in Fagaloto last week,' Mautu began. The batter hit a huge six over the fale onto the beach. The batting team, led by Semisi, cheered loudly. 'I talked with Tuifolau and the other matai of our aiga.' Another wild swing. Missed. The wickets cartwheeled backwards as the ball hit them. The fielders danced tauntingly to the beat of the pate. 'It has been arranged,' Mautu started again.

Lalaga couldn't wait any longer. 'Yes, our tulafale have visited the Aiga Sa-Tutete'e and talked with their ali'i and tulafale. And it is very acceptable to them,' she recited. 'And so it should be!' They waited for Peleiupu but she wasn't going to make it easier for them. 'You know what we're talking about?' Lalaga had to ask.

Peleiupu nodded and, looking at her father's back, said, 'Marriage, my marriage,' and stopped.

'Good batting!' Mautu exclaimed. More loud applause as the ball curved onto the beach again, with two fielders chasing it. Semisi danced in exaggerated mincing foot-steps, waving his arms triumphantly.

'They like the match very much,' Mautu began.

'Your father is not talking about the cricket,' Lalaga interjected.

'They like the young man's aiga and their aristocratic connections. His father is the ali'i of Sagata,' Mautu explained. 'He graduated from Salua the year before last and has been invited by Malie village to be their pastor.'

When Peleiupu looked out at the malae, Semisi was performing the tamure and his team were whooping and beating out the rhythm. She started cheering, then remembering where she was, stopped and bowed her head.

'What do you think?' her father asked.

'If that is your wish, then I will obey,' she replied.

'Thank you, Pele,' Lalaga said. 'You are a good daughter of our church and aiga. Both aiga have agreed the wedding should be in January, during the New Year holiday period. There is much to be prepared before then.'

'His father and their tulafale are coming here next week to meet us,' Mautu added. Peleiupu nodded as she surveyed the malae. She couldn't see Tavita anywhere. 'Lefatu and our elders from Fagaloto are coming also.'

Everyone in Satoa knew about her intended marriage, Naomi told Peleiupu that night as they lay in their mosquito net. It had been the talk of the cricket match. When Peleiupu refused to react, Naomi asked directly, and Peleiupu told her she'd agreed to it. But how was she feeling about it? Naomi asked. There was nothing to feel about it, Peleiupu replied. Naomi held her sister's arm and asked, 'What about you-know-who?'

Peleiupu didn't want to pretend any longer. 'Yes, what about Tavita?' More a question to herself than to Naomi.

'He wasn't at the cricket,' Naomi said. 'He's gone to Apia to get some things for the store.' Naomi gripped her sister's trembling arm. 'I think he knows about it,' Naomi added.

The malaga, which was made up of the young pastor and his parents and a group of matai, arrived late on Tuesday morning. Lefatu, Ruta and matai of their Aiga Sa-Tuifolau arrived soon after. As was the practice, Sao and the Satoa matai and aumaga gathered and welcomed them with an ava ceremony.

Ruta, whom they hadn't seen for over three years, joined Peleiupu and Naomi and they helped prepare the meal for their visitors. The women teased Peleiupu as they worked.

'The young pastor is *very* handsome!'

'Yes, like his palagi missionary teacher with the shiny head!'

'No, he needs more hair oil.'

'Any girl from the back would be proud to be his second house . . .'

'I wonder if he can speak English?' Ruta asked.

'They say English is the best language for romance . . . ' Naomi taunted her.

'And love!' another joined in.

'He looks as if he's fluent in the romance language of the albinos!' Ruta said.

'To me, he looks more fluent in German, the language of war! So you'd better watch out, Pele!' an old matron said. By now laughter was bubbling up all around.

'I'm pretty good at defending myself!' Peleiupu finally joined in.

'Do you use the German method or the American or the British?' the matron asked.

Peleiupu pondered and replied, 'What's the British method of defence?'

'Oh, you just talk your way out of war!'

'That's not an effective way,' someone else interjected. 'The best is the Satoan way.'

'And what is that?' Ruta asked.

Chortling wildly the someone said, 'The kick. The backward kick between the posts, or pulling off the attacker's ie lavalava . . .' The whole group broke into laughter.

Afterwards, as they prepared to serve the food to their visitors and elders, Peleiupu was painfully aware that everyone was observing her and her future husband, who was sitting beside his father at the far side of the faletele, and to whom she felt no connection. Like her, he remained silent while the elders talked of everything else but their marriage. She started shaking when she was handed the foodmat for her future in-laws, shook some more as she took the mat and placed it in front of them, shook almost out of control as she took another foodmat to the young pastor, and almost crumpled to her knees when Sao declared, just as she placed the mat on the floor: 'Pele, it is good that you and your intended have now met.' The other Satoa matai echoed his congratulations. 'He is quite good-looking, eh?' Sao added. She burned with embarrassment as the elders, Lefatu being the loudest, laughed. She scurried back to her place in the safety of her sisters.

There were no other references to the matter during the rest of the meal, after which the Satoans dispersed to their homes, and the malaga and their Fagaloto relatives bathed in the pool and then slept at the front and far side of the faletele.

Instructed by Lalaga, Peleiupu organised a group of men to make the umu for their evening meal, and then hurried to join her sisters in the fale by the beach.

Peleiupu asked Naomi, 'Is he back from Apia?'

'No. Semisi told me Tavita stayed in Apia after he heard about your marriage,' Naomi replied.

'Naomi has told me about Tavita,' Ruta said.

Ignoring her, Peleiupu said, 'Semisi always exaggerates. He lies, also.' Naomi remained silent. 'Tavita has no deep feelings for me.'

'How do you know?' Ruta asked. 'Have you talked with him about it?'

'You know that is not done!' Peleiupu insisted.

'Semisi and his brothers and sisters say he is — he is *keen* on you,' Naomi said.

'They're so afakasi in their forwardness, their lack of shame and reserve about their thoughts and feelings!' Peleiupu protested. 'Just like their palagi side, they believe in following their heart's dictates, not their parents' and aiga's wishes.'

'So you *do* have feelings for him?' Ruta pursued.

'I didn't say that!'

'Times have changed, Pele. Women can now choose,' Naomi said.

'I am meant to be a pastor's wife. It is God's decision,' said Peleiupu.

'And your parents' and aiga's, and especially our mother's wish,' Ruta added.

'It is also my wish,' Peleiupu heard herself saying. 'There: it is *my* wish!'

Naomi gazed into her face and Peleiupu had to look away. 'You're lying, Pele,' Naomi accused. Ruta nodded. Peleiupu turned her back on them.

'You feel trapped, don't you, Pele?' Ruta said, putting her comforting hand on Peleiupu's shoulder. Peleiupu bowed her head. 'You don't really know what to do, eh?' Peleiupu did not reply.

'You should talk to Lefatu,' Naomi suggested. 'She has always made her own choices.'

'Lefatu will understand and sympathise with you, Pele, but she will not encourage you to follow your true feelings,' Ruta said. 'She too will not go against our aiga's decision. She can't.' Ruta hesitated and, while caressing her sister's shoulder, added, 'And I don't know if she'll want our aiga's genealogy to include papalagi.'

'That is — that's not fair!' Peleiupu protested. 'Tavita is not papalagi!' Ruta and Naomi kept looking at her. 'What is wrong with having papalagi blood in our aiga, anyway?'

'Nothing as far as I'm concerned,' replied Naomi. She and Peleiupu glared at Ruta, who shrugged her shoulders, but Naomi wasn't going to let her escape. 'Yes, Ruta, what *is* wrong with having palagi blood?'

'I live in a world so different from yours,' Ruta explained. 'It is still Samoan. Yours is changing into a palagi world. We are also the Aiga Sa-Tuifolau. That is very, very important . . .'

'It may be important to you,' Naomi interrupted, 'but it has little meaning for us.'

'Listen to Ruta, Naomi,' Peleiupu advised.

'Naomi, if you don't understand why the Aiga Sa-Tuifolau *is* important, then you're already in that other world the papalagi and his atua will dominate and change . . .'

'The Tuifolau world is already past, or passing,' Naomi insisted.

'It is not, my clever sister!' Ruta challenged. 'Lefatu and I are still here!'

'But everything and everyone else is leaving you behind,' Naomi argued.

'Are they?' Ruta asked. 'Perhaps spiritually we are already where you and your palagi world want to be eventually. Or put in Lefatu's words: "We have always been here, we will always be here." And what does "being left behind" mean, my clever sister?' Her voice shook with suppressed anger. 'Don't you know that the future is already past and guiding us?'

'Now you are too clever for me,' Naomi attacked.

'Pele, you tell this — this sister of ours what I mean,' Ruta said.

'I am not stupid!' Naomi snapped.

'But you are arrogant: you look down on our aiga and our being Samoan . . .'

'I do not!' Naomi insisted.

'That's enough, both of you!' Peleiupu ordered. 'We haven't been together for over three years, and you're arguing again.' Playfully she slapped her sisters on their shoulders and started laughing. The others joined her. 'It is good to be together again, eh, even though you still argue?' They continued laughing. 'How we got into this heavy discussion, when you two were only offering me free advice about my heart, I'll never know!' said Peleiupu. 'And what's wrong with being totolua, eh? After all, the Aiga Sa-Tuifolau is already of two bloods: that of the thieving bird and that of the philandering atua. Adding papalagi blood to it may calm it down!' Tears filled their eyes as they laughed.

As they joked and laughed they moved closer and closer until their foreheads were pressing together and they breathed in one another's laughter. And Peleiupu decided to heed Ruta's advice and not consult Lefatu.

The next day after their morning meal, during which Lefatu insisted that Peleiupu share her foodmat, everyone else apart from Peleiupu left the main fale to the elders of both aiga.

The leading tulafale of the Aiga Sa-Tutete'e made the formal proposal of marriage and Tuifolau accepted it. Then they discussed the wedding arrangements. During it all, Peleiupu kept gazing at the floor, cauled in an inexplicable but comforting serenity, with Lefatu holding her hand and whispering, 'Be brave, be brave.' It all seemed unreal; it had nothing to do with her — her thoughts were on Tavita.

It was mid-afternoon. Naomi and Ruta stayed on the store veranda while Peleiupu went inside. For a moment she thought there was no one there but her eyes quickly grew accustomed to the gloom. 'My brother, his mind is valea on you,' Semisi's voice bubbled out of the corner of the room. He yawned as he flopped into the seat behind the counter. 'He's gone to Apia to try and forget.'

'That is not true,' Peleiupu said defensively.

'I told him he was stupid going valea over you, because you can't marry him even if you wanted to! You have to marry the young pastor.'

Peleiupu sat down opposite him. 'I don't know what to do,' she admitted.

'No, there is no choice,' Poto's voice intruded. She was standing at the back door. 'James, you go and get us something to drink.' Semisi grunted in protest but shuffled off. Poto took his seat and couldn't look at Peleiupu. 'I've never been very observant, Pele. I didn't see it happening.'

'I need your advice, Poto.'

'Semisi is usually silly when it comes to people, but what he said to you just as I entered is true, Pele.'

'But we can exercise individual choice.'

'What choice, Pele? If you were an ordinary girl, daughter of a minor matai or untitled person and not a pastor's daughter who graduated from Vaiuta, you would have some choice: you could simply defy your aiga's and village's wishes by eloping with the choice of your heart. Your parents and aiga would proclaim their shame and pain loudly and publicly but they wouldn't be shattered by it. In your case, Pele, such defiance could kill your parents, if not physically and emotionally then in reputation and standing. As pastor your father represents tradition, order, public morality and God. His children are expected, by society, to live up to those very demanding standards of morality. Of course what I've said you know already, Pele.'

'So you believe in duty and doing what is right and proper?'

'No. I defied my parents. As you know, my father, being our ali'i, represents right and proper behaviour. My aiga arranged for me to marry the son of the Ali'i of Safune. But my heart *demanded* that I elope with the youth I was in love with. A month before my marriage we eloped to his mother's village. The public disgrace was terrible for my father and aiga. We were too afraid to return to Satoa.' She paused. 'But he wasn't good to me, Pele. Neither were his relatives. They treated me like a slave. My father did not free me from it — I was getting what I deserved. As it was, my husband ran off with another woman four years later. I returned childless and poor to the silent wrath of my aiga who, in their treatment of me, ranked me last of all my sisters and brothers, even though I am the eldest.' She pondered sadly for a while. 'To escape from that, I eloped with a man who was part of a government malaga. To his village, Safata. It was a good and kind aiga but he fell ill and died a year later.' She bowed her head. 'When I returned to Satoa my mother and other elders forgave me. My father just said, "God has punished you." When Barker decided to remain in Satoa and build a store, Sao married me off to him so our aiga could acquire the palagi's wealth.'

She stopped and wiped her eyes with the corner of her blouse. 'You see, Pele, the defiant choice exacts a terrible price. They were marrying me to Barker, a strange foreign creature everyone looked down on, because I was now the lowest of the low, though Barker believed he was getting the ali'i's eldest and most valued daughter!' She started chortling. 'Mine was an arranged marriage that I didn't want. But I grew to respect and love that strange, haunted palagi. Who knows, like me, you may come to love your chosen husband. Don't worry too much about Tavita: he's young, he'll learn from the pain and suffering and be a better husband for another woman . . .'

When Peleiupu emerged from the store she stood between her sisters at the railing and let the strong sea breeze ripple through her clothes, hair and pores until her whole being was taut and humming with anticipation.

'Did you and Poto have a good talk?' Ruta asked.

'Yes. I now know what I have to do,' Peleiupu said. She started walking down the front steps before her sisters could question her further.

For two weeks the aumaga cut and dried a substantial amount of copra, sold it to Poto, and Sao presented the money to Mautu to help with Peleiupu's wedding. Sao also organised two fautasi and crews to take Mautu and his family to Apia to shop for the wedding.

As usual, they stayed at the pastor Leupega's house where, tired from their long trip, they showered and slept the morning away. Lalaga dragged them up in the early afternoon, instructed Mautu and the men about what to buy for the wedding, and then rushed her daughters to a dressmaker recommended by the pastor's wife. Ruta and Naomi were measured for their bridesmaids' outfits and Peleiupu for her wedding dress.

Ruta and Naomi had not been to Apia for almost four years so they were keen to explore the shops, with Peleiupu as their outwardly enthusiastic guide. But Lalaga kept telling them, 'We didn't come all this way to enjoy ourselves. We have limited time, limited money, limited energy!' For the rest of their stay Naomi and Ruta would parody their mother behind her back.

At lunchtime, on their second day of heavy humidity and dust, they found themselves in front of the market. Emphatically, Peleiupu told Lalaga, 'We are stopping here for something to eat and drink.' She put her hand out to her mother.

Lalaga hesitated, then fished in her bag and handed her five shillings. 'Are you sure you'll be safe here?' Lalaga asked. Because of the oppressive noonday heat, most people were sitting under the verandas, having lunch. The only noise came from the direction of the saloon at the far end of the market complex.

'Of course we'll be safe,' Peleiupu replied. 'You've always advised us to trust Germans and English people and other palagi!'

Lalaga had no answer for that. 'I have to hurry ahead and see if your father has bought the right things,' she said.

'That's right, Lalaga,' Ruta encouraged her.

'You know what he's like — he's probably spent money on the wrong things,' Naomi echoed.

Before Lalaga could change her mind, Peleiupu took her sisters' arms and pushed them towards the nearest food stall.

'Are you sure they'll accept us here?' Ruta whispered. Most of the stall owners and customers were papalagi. Those serving were mainly Samoan.

'This is *our* country!' Peleiupu declared.

'This is also the Eleele Sa, the zone ruled by papalagi,' Naomi reminded her.

'That doesn't mean Samoans can't shop here.' Peleiupu tried to be brave. 'We used to come here from Vaiuta,' she lied.

They took a vacant table under the shade of a spacious veranda. 'There, you two look just like rich palagi!' Ruta said.

'What would you like?' Peleiupu asked. After they told her, she wove her way through the other tables, all occupied by papalagi. Though feeling painfully self-conscious, she pretended she was used to being there.

At the counter she waited for the middle-aged papalagi woman with greying hair to serve her. The woman glanced up and continued what she was doing. A bushy-bearded man came and stood beside Peleiupu. The woman smiled at the man and asked, 'What can I do for you, sir?'

No, she was not going to retreat, Peleiupu determined. The woman took the man's order and turned and gave the order in broken Samoan to her Samoan assistants.

'Am I invisible?' Peleiupu asked. The woman paused; then her head swivelled around and her eyes focused on Peleiupu for the first time. 'Am I invisible?' Peleiupu repeated in immaculate English. The woman's lips started trembling. 'I want three orange drinks and three of those cakes,' Peleiupu ordered. She put her money on the counter. 'How much is my order?'

The woman hesitated, looked away, and replied, 'Ten pence.' Her assistants started filling the order.

'Please bring my order and change to our table.' Her back burned as she strode back, knowing the woman was watching her.

They ate in silence: Ruta and Naomi were too preoccupied with observing the other customers. Peleiupu ate quickly, then pushed back her chair and said, 'I'll be back shortly; I've got to find a toilet.' Her sisters looked distressed so she said, 'Don't worry. Just act like the aristocratic daughters of Tuifolau that you are. Any palagi savage who tries to mistreat you, tell them in your perfect arrogant English to go back to wherever they escaped from!'

Once out of sight of her sisters, Peleiupu edged towards the saloon that Semisi had told her was one of Tavita's favourite places.

A thin man in a dirt-stained singlet and ie lavalava was sweeping the front veranda. He glanced up at her and said, 'Women are not allowed in there.' His top front teeth were missing. 'Not women like you, anyway.'

'I need to get a message to someone who's in there,' she said.

'A palagi?'

Peleiupu pondered quickly. 'Yes, his name is Mr David Barker.' The name sounded so unfamiliar when she said it; it had very little to do with the Tavita she knew. 'Yes, Mr David Barker.'

The man thought for a moment, then his eyes lit up. 'From Satoa in Savai'i?' Peleiupu nodded. 'You mean Tavita?' Peleiupu nodded some more. 'He's my friend. He brings me food when he comes from Savai'i, and gives me money when he leaves.'

'Is he here?'

'He's been staying there for nearly a month.' He shook his head sadly. 'Drinking heavily most of the time. And committing other sins. He's not causing trouble though. The others leave him alone — they're afraid of him 'cause they know he's not afraid of anyone. He's the first Samoan to be allowed open entry to this saloon. Must be because he spends lots of his money here.'

Peleiupu pulled the letter she'd written out of her pocket. 'Will you give him this, please?' The man nodded. 'Will you make sure he gets it?' He nodded vigorously when she extended a sixpence to him.

'I'll make sure the very generous Mr Tavita receives this important epistle, Madam!' he said, the money already safe in his left hand behind his back. 'I promise on my unworthy, poverty-stricken honour that he will receive it and read it, Madam.'

Sweat was already drenching her clothes. She wrapped her sleeping sheet around her pillow, listened until she was sure everyone was asleep, then slid out of the mosquito net. She tried to control her shaking as she tiptoed around and over the bodies of the other sleepers, and out of the fale.

The lights of the few anchored ships dotted the harbour. Behind those rose the black shape of Mulinu'u Peninsula, which was propping up the insucking depths of the night sky sprinkled with stars. Still and humid. She wrapped her spare ie lavalava around her body, darted over the empty street and felt her way carefully through the darkness over the massive roots of the talie on the sea wall in front of the LMS church, snuggled down between two roots that were as high as her shoulders, leaned up against the trunk, and started wiping her sweat with her ie lavalava as she waited. The tide was crawling in like a slow fat animal.

She peered over the edge of the roots. A thin dark shadow was moving towards her from the direction of the market, over the path along the sea wall. As she watched she was again gripped by that inexplicable serenity. When the shadow reached the talie it stopped and turned towards her.

'Pele, Pele?' Tavita whispered. She stood up and beckoned him towards her. He slid his way over the roots and dropped down into her narrow sheltered hollow. He smelt of soap and shaving cream; his knee pressed against her leg. She moved her leg away.

For an awkward while they didn't know what to say. 'I think I have some news about Arona,' he began hesitantly. ' Picked it up from that shipping company and at the saloon. Maybe just rumours but . . .'

'Yes, go on,' she urged.

'That someone who could be him is now on an American ship that goes from Los Angeles to some of the ports in South America. They say it's someone from Samoa who's fluent in English and is being trained to be an officer.'

'We keep waiting for him to return — and my mother deep down still blames me for Arona's departure — but he keeps returning only in story and more stories.' She paused. 'One time I think your father said: "Stories, that's all we are and continue to be after we die."'

'I suppose so,' he said, hesitantly. 'Arona's not dead, is he?'

'No!' was her emphatic reply. 'No.'

'He — the man at the saloon — gave me your note,' he tried to turn her away from the pain of Arona's absence. 'He said it was from a very beautiful lady.' The tide lapped at and rubbed its body against the sea wall.

'I'm glad you came, Tavita. I have something important to tell you.'

'I know already.' Silence again. 'The tide is coming in,' he added. 'We are being foolish meeting like this.'

'I wanted to talk about it with you.'

'Why?'

She decided he was again reacting in that open palagi way, so she followed his lead. 'Because — because I have deep feelings for you.' Stupid, clumsy. Try again.

'I have deep feelings for you too, Pele.'

'I have alofa for you,' she admitted at last, believing he would continue in his palagi way, but he didn't.

'It is foolish, Pele. Nothing good will come of our admitting and expressing our true feelings for each other. You must obey your parents and aiga and what you've been raised and trained to do.'

'That is what your mother told me to do!' She was surprised she was angry about it.

'I have not stopped thinking about it since you returned from Vaiuta and I knew I had deep feelings for you, Pele. It has pursued me constantly. But you must marry him, Pele. That is the only choice that will protect you and me and your parents and aiga and our community.' His odour and warmth had curled around her and she felt utterly safe in it.

'But it is not what your feelings tell you, is it, Tavita?'

'We can't give in to the wild dictates of our passions,' he said, reminding her of his father.

'Is that what you've been doing in that saloon over the past few weeks?' He refused to answer. 'Giving in to the wild dictates of your passions?'

'I'm beginning to behave just like my palagi father,' he said, surprising her.

'No, you're not. Your father rarely gave in to his passions.' She knelt and, leaning forward, put her arms around his shoulders. He tried to push her away but she was determined. She pressed her cheek down on his head and tightened her embrace.

'Don't,' he said. But his arms came around her back and he pressed his face into her neck.

Then with lucid clarity she told him what she wanted to do. At first he kept saying no, no, no, but as she shushed him and explained her reasons, he withdrew into what she interpreted as acceptance. She kissed him quickly on the mouth, withdrew, rolled over the tree root behind her and started crawling over the maze of roots through the darkness.

Just before she fell asleep, she knew Arona would support her decision.

The Consequences

Wings fully outstretched, the frigate bird hovered high above the heart of Fagaloto Bay, the midday light gleaming on its body as his breath stretched and stretched out towards it. A woman's voice breaking from the depths of her moa in that seemingly endless wailing for the dead surged into his sleep, noosed his throat, tightened and pulled him out into the cool, dew-drenched morning. Of Apia. The pastor's house. Preparations for Peleiupu's wedding. And Lalaga beside him, with a letter crunched up in her strangling hands, bent forward. 'What has happened?' Mautu whispered. 'What is it?'

She started beating at her face with the letter and her hands. He grasped her hands, stilled them. 'That's enough!' he ordered. She flung the letter at Mautu and away from herself as if it were a poisonous creature. 'It's all right,' he whispered. But when he recognised the handwriting in the letter as Peleiupu's, panic surged up from the pit of his moa. If someone had warned him previously that one day one of his children would threaten to destroy his family, he would have dismissed it as unthinkable. If that someone had identified the threat as Peleiupu, he would have laughed. But now as he panicked and struggled to control it, afraid to straighten out the letter and read it, he *knew*. 'Lalaga, I promise God will make everything right, eventually.' He flattened out the letter on the floor, shut his eyes momentarily, and then read. Lalaga twitched, her body contorting wildly, then sagging in his embrace. Right then Ruta and Naomi pulled up the side of the net and knelt down beside them.

'What's happened?' Ruta asked, sitting down beside her mother. Mautu released

Lalaga into her arms. 'Get me some water and a towel,' Ruta instructed Naomi. 'She's unconscious.' By then pastor Leupega and his wife and other people were around the net. 'She'll be all right,' Ruta reassured them. 'She's just fainted from the heat.'

When Naomi returned, Ruta wet the towel and started washing her mother's face with it. Mautu hid the letter under his leg. 'We have a friend who is a doctor,' the pastor said. Before Mautu could stop him, Leupega instructed his wife to send someone to fetch the doctor. 'He lives just next door.'

Ruta placed two pillows under Lalaga's head, and Naomi covered her with a sleeping sheet. Ruta started massaging Lalaga's forehead with coconut oil. The other women took the net down and stretched a curtain across that section of the fale, giving Lalaga privacy. Lost for something to do, Mautu massaged Lalaga's arms. 'She's been too busy and worried about the wedding,' he offered. His hosts agreed, adding that the high humidity and heat didn't help.

Mautu and his daughters looked at one another when they saw the spindly papalagi man, with a handlebar moustache and dressed in a white singlet and ie lavalava and sandals, entering the fale, carrying a small leather bag. Head bowed, he hurried to them and sat down cross-legged beside Lalaga.

'Welcome, sir,' the pastor greeted him in Samoan.

'Thank you, Mr Pastor and your sacred family,' the man replied in Samoan with an American accent. 'What has happened?'

'My wife has fallen ill suddenly, sir,' Mautu replied in English.

The man held Lalaga's right wrist and started taking her pulse. He asked if Lalaga had been unconscious for long then using his stethoscope, he listened to her heart and breathing. He opened a vial and held it under her nostrils. Lalaga's head jerked away and she opened her eyes, struggling to speak. The doctor held her shoulders and, gazing down into her eyes, said, 'You'll be all right; you're with your family.'

Mautu bent forward so Lalaga could look up into his face. 'You just fainted,' he whispered. She continued struggling to speak.

'Has she suffered any serious illness before?' the doctor asked Mautu, who shook his head. 'I think she's suffered a minor stroke,' the doctor said. 'Has she been under a lot of strain recently?'

'Yes, we're getting ready for our daughter's wedding,' Mautu mumbled in English. 'We've come all the way from Satoa. I'm the pastor there.'

'And which daughter is getting married?' the doctor asked, smiling at Ruta and Naomi.

'Not us,' Naomi replied in English.

'Our other sister who's not here at the moment,' Ruta added in Samoan.

'We'll have to get your mother well for the wedding, eh!' The doctor fished a bottle of pills out of his bag, handed it to Ruta and told her the dosage. 'She may recover quickly, or it may take a while. She can't be shifted for now.' He got up. 'I'll come and see her again this evening. If she gets worse, come and get me immediately.' Mautu thanked him; Leupega invited him to stay for the morning meal but he declined.

As the doctor left through the back of the fale Leupega told Mautu he was Professor Mardrek Freemeade from Harvard University, America, an anthropologist who was also a medical doctor.

They sang a hymn and Leupega prayed for the restoration of Lalaga's health, then he and his household went to prepare the morning meal.

'She is conscious but she can't speak,' Ruta said to Mautu. They looked down into her eyes, which were alive with panic as she tried to say something but couldn't.

'It's all right, Lalaga,' Mautu consoled. 'You try and rest.'

'Have you noticed?' Naomi asked. 'The left side of her mouth is partly paralysed.'

'It is your selfish sister who has done this!' Mautu declared softly, so only his daughters heard. 'She has decided . . .' He couldn't say it. He bowed his head, then holding up the letter, he muttered, 'I will never forgive her if anything happens to your mother! She has betrayed your mother, me, us, our aiga!' Ruta took the letter and read it. 'No one else must know the contents of that letter,' he instructed them. 'No one. We must try and minimise the effects of this on everyone, especially on your mother.'

That afternoon he met the Satoan elders and the leaders of the two fautasi crews and instructed one crew to return to Satoa and inform Sao and the matai council of Lalaga's serious illness and the indefinite postponement of the wedding. They would return to Satoa when Lalaga was able to travel; meanwhile Sao and the other deacons were to carry out his pastoral duties. The other crew was sent to Fagaloto to instruct his aiga to meet the Aiga Sa-Tutete'e and ask that the wedding be postponed.

Without him telling them, the crews knew they were not to mention what an elder described, out of Mautu's hearing, as 'that pagan afakasi's evil, unforgivable, disgraceful actions eloping with our beloved pastor's innocent daughter'. Yes, what do you expect from the 'intestine of a papalagi trader'? his wife echoed. Someone reminded them that Tavita was also their ali'i's grandson, so their ali'i had to take some responsibility for disgracing and shaming their pastor; and because Sao was their ali'i they, as a village, were to blame too. All Samoa was going to hear of their guilt, their moral laxity in allowing such a sin to occur. And what a sin — the grandson of their ali'i running off with their pastor's daughter. This had not happened in any other God-fearing Christian village!

Just before evening lotu Professor Freemeade came to see Lalaga and told them she was improving. He got Lalaga to indicate she understood everything he said by raising her right hand. Ruta asked if the paralysis would disappear eventually. The possibilities were very good, he said. Before he left he asked Mautu if he could come and study their way of life in Satoa. It would be an honour, Mautu replied.

After the evening meal, during which everyone avoided reference to Peleiupu's absence, Mautu retreated with his daughters to Lalaga behind the curtain. Using herbs and techniques she'd learned from Lefatu, Ruta massaged her mother carefully until Lalaga fell into a deep sleep. Ruta was to do this every morning and night after the doctor's visits, without his knowledge. While she worked, Mautu would pray fervently for Lalaga's recovery. He agreed to Naomi's suggestion that if the papalagi doctor couldn't heal Lalaga fully, they should take her to Lefatu when they returned to Satoa.

Most nights since Lalaga's collapse Mautu couldn't sleep. His mind refused to tire as it analysed, lucidly and endlessly, the events that had resulted in Lalaga's stroke, and his role in those. Lalaga had total and unquestioning faith in God and the value of their work, but he'd doubted, had lost faith countless times, and had allowed the Devil to tempt him into educating his children in the world's worthless and arrogant knowledge represented by Barker, that tortured atheist. And look how his children had turned out: Arona had fled his promise to be a pastor in order to be a sailor who didn't bother to communicate with his family; and most evil of all, he'd indulged his eldest daughter into pursuing her selfish desires and thereby trampling on his dignity and that of aiga, church and community. He was to blame for it all, he confessed to Lalaga whenever they were alone. She would press his hands and shake her head. 'What a shame, what a disgrace!' he'd cry.

On Saturday morning Professor Freemeade arrived earlier than usual and, after treating Lalaga, asked Mautu if he'd like to walk with him.

An overcast sky that wouldn't rain, a refreshing breeze licking his face, the sea wall empty of people, the smell of acrid woodsmoke. 'My Samoan is still not very good,' Professor Freemeade began, in English. 'When I come to study your village, will you teach me Samoan, sir?' he asked in Samoan.

'Yes, but I'm not a very good teacher of language,' Mautu replied. Even the papalagi knew about his guilt and shame and was trying to be kind, he believed.

A few ships lay in the harbour. None of the dew-covered shops that glittered in the morning light was open yet. Ahead, four fishermen were pulling their canoes out of the water into the shelter of the gigantic pulu trees in front of the Godeffroy Company headquarters. Mautu jumped down to the beach; the American followed.

A thick flickering tangle of live atule filled the bottoms of the canoes. Mautu greeted the fishermen who were starting to string their fish. They returned his greeting; their skins were goose-pimpled and shrivelled from the cold. 'A rich catch,' he remarked. The oldest fisherman, with hair bleached blond by the sun, explained that the atule were running at Fagali'i Bay; they were lucky to have reached it before other fishermen had arrived.

'How much, sir?' the American asked in Samoan.

'Fifty pence a string,' the fishermen replied. 'Your friend speaks beautiful Samoan,' he said to Mautu. His companions nodded.

'It is not very good,' the American said. The fishermen grinned. He handed them a shilling and said he wanted two strings.

Handing him three strings, the fisherman said, 'The extra one is for being able to speak our language well!' The fishermen and Mautu laughed.

Mautu moved to carry the strings of fish but the American refused. He turned and thanked the fishermen.

'They are delicious cooked on coconut shell charcoal,' Mautu remarked as they resumed their walk.

'You think your wife will like them?'

'She'll love them: her appetite is returning. She'll love them even more because I'll cook them myself.'

Wavelets pancaked around their feet as they walked on. 'Please stop me if you think I'm intruding,' the American began. 'I know what has occurred, and I want to offer you any help that I can.' Mautu continued walking.

'My wife and I and our aiga will suffer the consequences of our daughter's foolish actions forever,' Mautu heard himself declaring. 'Our honour has been trampled on, and our disgrace is national and inescapable.' The American had to walk faster to keep up with him. 'Right now, I don't think I have the strength to survive the pain of that disgrace. We can't hide anywhere.'

'I'm sorry, very sorry,' the American said.

In the kitchen fale Mautu ignored the people who were cooking, started a charcoal fire, and, refusing help from the others, he gutted and washed the atule, spread them out over the hot charcoal and watched as they cooked. He couldn't remember the last time he'd done any cooking. The enticing smell of the cooking fish made him feel hungry for the first time since Lalaga had fallen ill.

When the fish was cooked he told Ruta and Naomi he would feed Lalaga. His daughters joined the rest of the household.

The keen alertness was back in her eyes, he noted. That sharp awareness that missed little that happened around her. And she was again able to mask her true feelings with a smile. She observed his every move as he laid out the meal: fish, fa'alifu talo, bread and butter, and koko. 'I cooked the atule,' he boasted. She dug her fingers into the side of a fish, pinched a lump of it, put it in her mouth and, as she chewed it, nodded and smiled. 'As you know, I used to be a *good* cook!' he said. She shook her head, her whole body trembling with laughter. 'I was not a *bad* cook?' he asked. She nodded furiously. He laughed with her. 'The American professor bought it for you.'

She handed him a piece of taro and, pointing at the fish, indicated that he should eat too. He did and, as he chewed the taro and then his first piece of fish, he smiled and nodded and said, 'Wonderful, wonderful!'

Together they ate, ravenously, knowing that their love was stronger than before. Unexpectedly, he thought of Arona, and for the first time since their son had left and they'd scrupulously avoided talking about him, he wanted to discuss him. 'Arona's safe,' he said. The light in her eyes brightened. 'I heard from some sailors who'd been away for a few years that they'd met another Samoan sailor in San Francisco, America. I asked them if his name was Arona; they didn't know. Only that he was the son of a pastor. I asked them to describe him, and my heart sang when I recognised him in their descriptions.' Her tearful eyes were alight with happiness. 'One day, Lalaga, our son will grow tired of his search and return. One day.'

From that meal on she insisted on doing everything unaided. She learned to disguise her slight limp by walking more slowly, more upright, and control her facial movements better so as not to show that half her mouth was paralysed. Under Ruta's expert massaging, the paralysis would disappear over the next few weeks.

'I . . . I . . . I can . . . cannot forgive her, ever.' For an unbelievable moment they just stared at her. 'Yes, I . . . I haven't . . . lost my tongue,' Lalaga said.

'She's speaking again!' Naomi exclaimed. Ruta embraced her mother.

'God has been kind!' Mautu murmured.

That morning Professor Freemeade stayed for the meal, and he and Leupega and his wife talked freely with Mautu and Lalaga. The pastor's wife kept referring to Lalaga's recovery of speech as a miracle.

'We're a burden to Leupega and his congregation,' Lalaga whispered to Mautu a few days later when they were alone behind the curtain. 'It is time we returned to Satoa.'

'I don't really want to go back, but we have to, don't we?' Mautu replied. Lalaga looked away.

Shaking her sleeping father's shoulder, Ruta said, 'Mautu, Mautu, Sao and his aiga have come!'

He sat up quickly. The fale was still in darkness but the morning light was poking its fingers through the blinds. 'Who's come?' he asked. Ruta told him again. They'd arrived back at Satoa the previous afternoon and had been welcomed back by the Women's Committee.

'The village must be coming to welcome us,' Lalaga said. She scrambled up and, in a hushed voice, instructed their household to put away the nets and mats, clean the fale and prepare a meal for the matai. 'Quickly!' she ordered.

Mautu brushed back his hair, rehitched his ie lavalava, put on a shirt and went over to sit at the front, peering down at the malae. The white light from the east was spreading like a slow wave across Satoa, illuminating everything as it spread. Once it hit the malae, it uncovered the shapes of men seated in rows on the wet ground with heads bowed. In front of them, facing Mautu's fale, were two figures lying face down on mats.

'Lalaga, come!' he called urgently. Lalaga, Ruta and Naomi knelt down beside him and looked. 'It is an ifoga,' he said. 'What are we going to do?'

'If it is an ifoga, it can't be to us,' Lalaga insisted. 'Sao's aiga has done us no wrong.'

'It *is* an ifoga,' Ruta said. 'They consider that Tavita has done you a great wrong and dishonoured their aiga and village.' They looked again at the group on the malae and recognised the two elders of the Aiga Sa-Sao who were at that moment using fine mats to cover the prostrate figures on the ground. Around the malae the rest of Satoa were waking and sitting up and watching.

'What are we going to do?' Mautu asked. 'We are the guilty ones, not them.'

'Ruta is right. Tavita has dishonoured Sao and his aiga,' Lalaga said.

Mautu started rising. 'I'll go now and invite them to come inside.'

Lalaga held his shirt and pulled him down. 'We must act as if they are not there. It is expected that they suffer publicly for a while before we forgive them.' And before Mautu could stop her, she walked around helping the others prepare the fale.

Mautu turned his back to the malae and, opening the Bible, started reading it. Soon he was the only one left in the fale. He listened and was disturbed not to hear the usual sounds of the neighbours waking and going about their usual morning chores. He looked at the surrounding fale. All the people were moving about silently, respectfully. He glanced at the ifoga. The bright morning light seemed to be setting the figures on fire. He observed the neighbours again, Semisi and some of the Barker children were on the store veranda, looking over at him. Mautu gazed up into the heavens. A solemn silence now filled the world like a voiceless sea in which he was alone and adrift. Lalaga had told him that Poto was so ashamed of Tavita's actions, she was hiding in her fale. He started praying, asking God for the courage and ability to cope with Sao's ifoga and the pain and rage that were again invading him.

Lalaga came and sat down beside him. 'Be brave. God will give us the courage and strength to survive all this,' she whispered.

'How much longer shall we let them suffer the hot sun?' he asked. She glanced down at the malae. 'For the Ali'i of Satoa and his whole aiga to ask for our forgiveness, publicly, is the most severe punishment and humiliation anyone can suffer,' he reminded her.

'I don't want to admit it but knowing *your* daughter and how stubborn and selfish she is, I'm sure she, and not Tavita, is responsible for what they've done.'

'So we cannot allow Sao and his aiga to suffer this humiliation for too long.'

'I can never forgive her.' Lalaga jumped to her feet. 'When the food and drink are ready, welcome them to our home,' she said. She hurried off to the kitchen fale.

Mautu continued reading the Bible. Occasionally he would glance down at the ifoga. None of the men moved; sweat glistened on their bodies. A slight breeze wove around them. An old man behind Sao collapsed sideways, fainting from the oppressive heat. None of the ifoga moved to help the old man. Mautu sprang up to go and help. Stopped. Neighbours hurried out and carried the old man into their fale.

Shortly after, Lalaga and their household were seated along the back of their fale, with fresh coconuts and other food for the ifoga. 'We're ready,' Lalaga called to him.

He sucked air in through his mouth, deeply, exhaled, rose slowly to his feet and walked out onto the front paepae, into the gaze and scrutiny of all Satoa.

He couldn't sleep; his body ached. He slid out of the mosquito net and sat looking out at the sleeping village. The sea shifted and murmured in the heart of the darkness. When mosquitoes started zinging around his ears he covered his head and body with his sleeping sheet. He was grateful the public reconciliation with the Aiga Sa-Sao was over. Now that Sao's ifoga had been accepted, the rest of Satoa had to behave as if everything were back to normal. He knew though that many would continue to ridicule him behind his back. How could he continue as their pastor when they all knew about his daughter?

He felt Lalaga beside him. Together they gazed into the darkness for a long silent while. 'I shall resign as pastor,' he murmured.

'No!' she said. 'No!'

'I can't bear the shame.'

'We must go on with our Christian work. God is already helping us.'

He admitted he was afraid of giving his sermon — the first since their return — that Sunday. He said if he found the courage to do so, he would ask their congregation for their forgiveness. Lalaga was adamant he shouldn't mention what had happened.

He sighed deeply. 'It is getting too difficult to bear!'

'We have to do it, Mautu,' she whispered. She slid behind him. 'Don't be afraid. We're not going to let the irresponsible, inconsiderate actions of our children destroy our work for God.'

The first liquid drop pinged on the back of his neck. His loins jumped. He smelled coconut oil. More drops pinged-pinged-pinged, jolting alive his sexual desire. And when her hands started kneading the back of his neck he clenched his teeth trying to suppress his jagged breathing. She parted her legs and, stretching them along-side his buttocks, moved up against his back, her strong hands massaging his shoulders. He was amazed at how overwhelming his desire was. When he started shivering, as the tantalising memories of their first sexual night returned, she wrapped her arms around him from behind, pressing her face into the top of his back and whispering, 'Be still, be still, it'll be all right.' He shut his eyes tightly, wound his arms around hers and pushed back against her breasts. She lifted her legs and buttocks, and he turned around and under her. Burying her face in his neck to muffle her breathing, and wrapping her legs around his waist, she pressed down. As he entered and she encom-passed him entirely in her clutching heat, it was the most beautiful feeling he'd ever experienced. He wanted it to go on forever.

While he preached that Sunday he focused on Lalaga, who was sitting with the children in front of the pulpit, and was able to forget the congregation's gaze. He wasn't aware of his tears until large drops of them stained the third page of his sermon, and he looked up and noticed the concern on Lalaga's face. Quickly he bowed his head and ended his sermon. During the last hymn he knelt in the pulpit, out of sight, and wiped his eyes and face with a corner of his shirt.

Because it was their pastor's first Sunday home, all the matai and their wives came to the to'ona'i, bringing sumptuous food in large quantities. Briefly they discussed Lalaga's illness in Apia; they congratulated God (and her) for her miraculous recovery, and then, for the rest of the to'ona'i they avoided any mention of Peleiupu's and Tavita's 'crime' and Sao's ifoga the previous day.

On Monday Lalaga, Ruta and Naomi reopened the school. Within a few days it was as if it had never closed. Mautu, however, decided to take only classes in Bible study and on Wednesday mornings only; the rest of the week he'd visit the families. (Lalaga had suggested that such visits would allow him not only to minister to the Satoans' spiritual needs but also to restore their faith and trust in him.)

As they underwent and survived each step in the process of public atonement and reconciliation, Mautu discovered, with wonderful insatiable gratitude, that his sexual life with Lalaga was becoming more daring and exquisite and intense and, though they didn't discuss it, they wanted it to go on and on. Unashamedly.

'I don't want *that* name mentioned ever again in this house!' Mautu heard Lalaga chastising Ruta when Ruta inadvertently referred to Peleiupu at their evening meal. 'Never again!' Lalaga repeated. He dug into his food, trying to suffocate the unexpected realisation and pain that he missed Peleiupu. Missed her.

That morning, after Lalaga had left for school, he couldn't stop himself. 'Have you heard anything about what she is doing?' he asked Ruta and Naomi. They pretended they didn't understand. 'What are the stories about them?' His daughters looked at each other.

'They were married secretly in the Pago Pago LMS church, by one of Sao's relatives,' Naomi said finally.

'And they're living with Sao's relatives in Fagatogo,' Ruta added.

'And he's working for a trading firm there,' said Naomi.

'And?' he demanded.

'She is well — and happy, I think,' Naomi replied and looked away.

'They're also very sorry about what they've done,' Ruta added, quickly.

'How did you get this information?' he asked.

'From Tavita's sisters and brothers,' Naomi said.

When they saw Lalaga hurrying back from the school they stopped talking about Peleiupu.

'The papalagi professor has arrived,' Lalaga informed them. 'They're unloading his things at the beach. I've sent some students to carry them here.' Naomi asked if he was going to stay with them. 'If he wants to,' Lalaga replied.

'I think we'd better consult Sao,' Mautu suggested. 'The professor is here to study our way of life.'

The women and some students cleaned the far side of the fale where Professor Freemeade was to sleep. They covered the paepae with mats and strung up a siapo curtain.

Professor Freemeade and the students carrying his luggage and equipment came up over the edge of the beach and made their way past Barker's store. More and more people, particularly children, joined the crowd that followed them at a safe distance. At the middle of the malae Professor Freemeade stopped unexpectedly and swivelled around. The crowd stopped. Freemeade laughed and took one large exaggerated step towards them. They backed off. 'Palagi! Palagi!' some of the children chanted.

'What rude arrogance and ignorance,' Naomi told her parents.

'The children are going to pester him all the time,' Ruta remarked.

'I'll order them at school not to,' Lalaga ruled.

'And I'll tell Sao to declare to the whole village that Professor Freemeade is to be respected and left alone,' Mautu added.

Mautu met Professor Freemeade on the front paepae. They shook hands. 'Come in, come in,' Mautu invited, in English. Some of the crowd murmured.

Once inside the fale Professor Freemeade sat down at the front; the students took his possessions and put them behind the curtain. Mautu greeted him formally in Samoan. Professor Freemeade returned his welcome, haltingly but correctly, in Samoan. The crowd sighed in admiring disbelief.

'Go to your homes now!' Lalaga ordered them. The older ones dispersed quickly, but the children retreated and hung around the back paepae.

'Are you well now?' Professor Freemeade asked Lalaga. She said she was; God had been merciful. 'And you two?' he asked Ruta and Naomi, who lowered their eyes.

'We are well,' Naomi said softly.

Lalaga noticed that the uncovered part of the American's body was sunburnt. She asked Ruta to apply coconut oil to the sunburn. Reluctantly, and embarrassed by the crowd's comments, Ruta slid over to him. 'Go on!' Lalaga called. 'Rub some oil on it.'

'Thank you,' Professor Freemeade said. When he took off his shirt the crowd ohhed, teasingly, and he chuckled.

'The palagi has a *beautiful* body!' someone remarked. The others laughed.

'It's red like the comb of a rooster!' someone else remarked.

'That's enough!' Lalaga ordered. 'Go to your homes now!' When only a few started moving off, she hurried out and waved the others away. 'Go, now!' They dispersed reluctantly. 'They don't know any better,' she apologised to the American in English.

'I don't mind,' he replied.

While Ruta rubbed the oil over his sunburn he talked freely in English with Mautu and Lalaga. He said his skin was stinging so Mautu told him to leave his shirt off. Ruta and Naomi disappeared and returned a short while later with fresh banana leaves, which they spread out over his sleeping mats behind the curtain. The leaves would cool his skin and stop it from sticking to the mats, Lalaga explained. Mautu urged him to rest.

As soon as Freemeade was asleep, Mautu visited Sao and, while they were having their morning meal with Sao's wife Vaomatua and Poto, Mautu told Sao of Professor

Freemeade and why he was in Satoa. 'Strange what these palagi are interested in,' Sao said. 'Why would a highly educated man be interested in us and the way we live?' Mautu told him that Professor Freemeade taught at a famous university and on his return from Samoa would teach the Americans about Samoans.

'We might be able to show Americans how to live and behave like civilised human beings who love God,' Vaomatua commented.

'He might also teach them mistaken and false observations about us,' Sao said. 'He might claim we are savages and godless and witless!' He chortled and slapped his knee.

'Well, aren't we?' Vaomatua joked. They laughed about that.

Mautu told them Professor Freemeade would be very useful because he was a skilled physician who was offering to heal their sick; in that way he would reciprocate their hospitality and generosity. Mautu suggested that Professor Freemeade should stay with him while the aumaga renovated the fale on the beach for his use. 'Papalagi like solitude and being alone,' he added.

'We must protect him from the ill-mannered and ignorant,' Poto urged.

'I'll declare him and his home off-limits to everyone except Mautu and me,' Sao pronounced.

'My family and I will look after him,' Mautu offered.

'Professor Freemeade is our second palagi,' Sao declared. Mautu glanced at Poto, who looked upset. 'I hope this one is not an atheist and a renegade from his culture.'

'He isn't,' Mautu reassured him.

The next morning Sao, the matai and aumaga visited Mautu's home and, in an ava ceremony, welcomed Professor Freemeade to Satoa. Mautu was not surprised that the American knew Samoan protocol well: he acted as his own tulafale, replying in formal oratory and then presenting Sao and the matai with lafo and foodstuffs to be divided among the aiga. Everyone was impressed with his performance. During the meal that followed, some of the elders remarked to Mautu that the papalagi was 'very intelligent and civilised' and 'a good palagi who respects our culture and language, and wants to learn more about us'.

They laughed when Sao declared, 'Mr Professor, your Samoan is better than that of our first palagi!' Mautu was relieved that Poto and her children weren't present.

That evening Professor Freemeade asked him about Barker. He found himself describing Barker and his life in Satoa with love, care and admiration. 'You sound as if you miss him,' Freemeade observed.

'Yes, I've missed him more deeply since the crisis in my family,' Mautu admitted. And perhaps Pele had chosen Tavita because she too was missing Barker, he thought.

The renovations to the fale on the beach were completed by the end of the week and Freemeade moved. He would continue to have his meals with Mautu and his family. In the next few days Mautu noted that the people were obeying Sao's instructions about not pestering the professor. When curiosity and fascination got the better of some children and they followed him, calling, 'Palagi, palagi!', their parents beat them severely. Though the Satoans tried to appear they were not scrutinising him, they noted his every move and exchanged information about it.

When Mautu announced at church that Professor Freemeade was treating patients from mid-morning to midday every weekday, they flocked to his fale. Mautu had to help Professor Freemeade restrict the numbers he treated daily. Many weren't sick; they just wanted to observe their 'marvellous papalagi' up close. When word of his healing powers and skills spread, people from neighbouring villages started coming. Professor Freemeade asked if Naomi could help him. Lalaga instructed Naomi to do so two mornings a week; Ruta had decided to rejoin Lefatu at Fagaloto.

'It is a blessing having him here,' Lalaga remarked one morning as she prepared for school. 'A blessing in more ways than one.' Mautu asked her to elaborate. 'The attention of our people is now focused on him.'

'And away from us?' Mautu asked. She nodded. He looked down and saw that a few patients were already waiting under the breadfruit trees beside Freemeade's fale. He didn't recognise any of them. 'We never mention her now, do we?'

Picking up a stack of slates she said, 'It's almost time for school,' and started leaving.

'Satoa's attention may be distracted from — from Pele, but ours isn't, eh?' he called, defiantly glad he had uttered Peleiupu's name.

When Ruta told him that Sunday evening she was returning to Fagaloto, he tried to dissuade her because he dreaded another empty space in his life. The worst times were during meals and lotu. Sometimes when he felt Peleiupu was present he looked but she wasn't there. Ruta's absence would intensify that. Ruta explained that for five nights Lefatu had entered her dreams, beckoning her back to Fagaloto. Automatically he dismissed her reason as superstition but, remembering who Lefatu was, he agreed to Ruta's request. After she left, on the Fulula the next day, he retreated to his desk and, pretending he was reading the Bible, wept silently.

Mautu began to spend longer and longer periods with Freemeade, after their evening meals. Lalaga left them alone. Freemeade questioned him about Satoan life and concepts basic to that life; sometimes he got Mautu to describe customs, traditions, rituals, crafts, tattooing and more; sometimes he detailed what he'd observed and Mautu would assess how accurate those observations were. Mautu kept looking for Barker in Freemeade but had to conclude there was little of his friend there. Barker had tried to *live* the Satoan way to escape his loneliness; Freemeade was merely studying that way, using what he described as 'the objective, scientific method'. Barker had been open to people, embracing them for what they were; Freemeade stood apart, watching and not allowing anyone too close.

In their conversations Freemeade did not mention a wife or children. Once he talked of his parents, who were lawyers, and a brother and sister in a city called Boston. But every time Mautu led the discussion to Freemeade's immediate family the American diverted it. So Mautu decided he'd never divulge any information about his Aiga Sa-Tuifolau to Freemeade. He sensed that that was really what Freemeade was interested in.

Only a month to Christmas. Naomi gave Mautu the latest news about Peleiupu and Tavita: they were now acting as import-export agents for German Samoan merchants who wanted goods from American Samoa. Even Poto was ordering goods through them. 'How could she do that after swearing she never wanted to see her son again?' Naomi declared. But Mautu was glad of the news.

Before Naomi left, she gazed at him for a moment and then said hesitantly, 'Some men are spreading the story that Arona was recently seen in a port called Singapore, on an American ship; he was in charge of cargo or something like that.'

'What men told you?' Mautu asked urgently.

'Men who've just returned from Apia. They were told of it by some black sailors.'

'What else did they tell you?'

'That it must have been Arona because he was Samoan and had boasted that he was from Savai'i.'

That night in their mosquito net when he told Lalaga about Arona she cried silently while he held her. 'God will continue to care for him,' he whispered, but the fear picked at the centre of his moa.

The piercing beat of the tin drum. Mautu and Sao sat in Mautu's fale, watching the line of men that was stretched across the malae, cutting the grass with bushknives, to the drumming. As the blades rose and swung down and across in unison, Sao and Mautu kept expecting a severe slashing of someone's body, but it never happened. As long as the cutters kept to the same rhythm no one would be wounded.

'I came to seek your advice, Reverend,' Sao said, formally.

'Yes, speak, sir,' Mautu replied. The bushknives rose into the sparkling air and curved down.

'I do not know what to do, who to believe — whether I should believe what I've been told, sir.' Sao paused, cleared his throat, and then spat the phlegm out onto the paepae. 'I will speak frankly. I have been told . . .' He stopped again. Mautu waited. 'As you know, the professor has been questioning our people about our lives. He has been doing that even with some of our children.' He swallowed. 'I don't know how to put this.' Screwed up his face. 'He has been questioning our children about things grown-ups should *not* discuss with children.' He sighed, relieved he had said it. 'I know palagi ways are very different from ours. They spoil their children by treating them as equals and discussing everything with them, but he is *not* in his country.' The line of cutters was advancing towards Mautu's home, swing after swing. 'As yet, only one person has told me about it. It may not be true at all.'

'Leave it to me, sir. I will speak with the professor about it.'

'Someone is going to get cut if they're not careful!' Sao remarked as they watched the cutters. Mautu knew that Sao would not refer to the matter again: his pastor was to clear it all up.

Mautu worried about it all that night. Near midday the following day, when he noticed that Freemeade was alone, writing at his desk, he strolled to the American's fale through the piles of ash, remnants of the grass the cutters had burnt the previous day. He decided to use English with Freemeade: English would allow him to discuss topics that were tapu in Samoan.

Freemeade was wearing only an ie lavalava. After five months in Satoa he was quite tanned. Mautu encouraged him to talk while he tried to find the courage. 'Apart from Lalaga and I, who else have you been discussing the fa'a-Samoa with?' Mautu started, trying to sound casual.

'Sao and most of the matai and many other people,' Freemeade replied.

Mautu asked if they'd been helpful.

'Yes, in the Satoan way of telling me what I want to hear, or what they *feel* I want to know,' Freemeade said. They laughed about that. Mautu asked if the young people had been informative. 'Yes, very. But it is not right and proper to discuss some subjects with them, sir.' Freemeade was unexpectedly formal, using that to keep him out.

Mautu struggled to counter and said, 'Sometimes, because you are papalagi and they believe mistakenly that you can be drawn into discussing subjects considered tapu in Satoa, they will question you about those, professor.'

'I learned that early in Satoa,' Freemeade replied, smiling. 'I have not allowed them to question me about those subjects, Reverend.'

'I am relieved to hear that our young people are behaving properly and respectfully towards you,' Mautu said.

Later, as he left the fale, he hoped Freemeade had understood his warning.

Early the next morning, while on his way to his plantation, Sao paused in front of Mautu's fale. They greeted each other. Mautu invited him in but Sao declined, saying he wanted to get to work before the sun got too hot.

'I have discussed that matter with the professor,' Mautu called.

'That is good,' Sao replied and continued on his way. Their understanding now was that Mautu would guarantee Freemeade's correct behaviour within Satoa.

Preparations for Christmas and the New Year intensified: they cleaned and tidied the whole village; shut down the school for the holidays after the prizegiving in which two of Poto's children won the main prizes; decorated the church and the deacons took turns leading evening lotu. Mautu persuaded Freemeade to talk about Christmases in Boston and America during one of the services, and most of the Satoans prayed for that marvellous element snow to fall for the first time in Satoa. The fono inspected the aumaga's plantations of taro and yam to ensure there was enough food for the holiday period; the aumaga organised the annual kilikiti tournament; the leaders of the aualuma inspected their members' homes for cleanliness and adequate kitchen utensils; Sao and Poto organised fautasi to take people into Apia to shop, paying their fares with copra.

Caught up in all that activity, Mautu couldn't continue observing what Freemeade was doing. Immediately after their evening meals Freemeade returned to his fale, saying he had a lot of writing to do. Mautu felt relieved: he was too tired to talk, and he had to prepare his Christmas and New Year sermons.

From Christmas Day to New Year, Mautu overate hungrily, despite having promised himself he wasn't going to. He couldn't ignore the feasting and the scrumptious umu the aiga delivered to his household daily. One afternoon as he flopped into the pool he realised, with shock, that his breasts jiggled and his belly was a series of large rolls. 'I'm getting fat,' he murmured as he dressed when he got home. Lalaga told him he certainly was. He felt hurt by that. That evening he took a few mouthfuls and pushed his foodmat away.

After their meal on New Year's Eve, Freemeade invited him to his fale, where, to Mautu's shocked disbelief, he offered him a drink of whisky to toast the New Year. Mautu declined politely. Freemeade poured a large one, raised his glass towards Mautu and said, 'May we enjoy a prosperous New Year!' Freemeade drank steadily as they talked, and Mautu's discomfort mounted.

'You may not know it, but the fono does not allow alcohol in Satoa,' he told the American, in English. Freemeade drained his glass, mumbled an apology, and wished him goodnight. Mautu noticed that Freemeade's fiery red eyes were filled with defiance, so he left quickly.

Before he reached his home he looked back. Freemeade's fale was in darkness but he knew the American was sitting in the dark, drinking.

Heat waves brimmed and shimmered out of everything and made the world look as if it were dissolving. Most people were asleep in their fale or in the shade of trees by the sea, satiated and bloated by the heavy New Year's Day meal. Shirtless, Mautu lay on his back on his ali, gazing up into the dome of his fale and drifting. Lalaga was sewing a new dress for Naomi; now and then she talked to Mautu.

He suddenly sensed that the silence was changing, and glanced over at Lalaga. She was clutching the unfinished dress to her breasts, her face thrust forward as she gazed wide-eyed at the people who were entering through the back of the fale. For a moment he didn't recognise them. He sat up quickly. Poto, Peleiupu, Sao and Tavita.

'No, aue! No!' Lalaga cried, burying her face in the dress.

A weeping Peleiupu threw herself forward, prostrating herself behind her mother. 'Please forgive me! Please forgive me!' she cried. Tavita crawled forward and prostrated himself beside Peleiupu.

'No, go away. I don't want to see you!' Lalaga wailed. Peleiupu clutched at Lalaga's arm but she pushed her away. 'You are not my daughter!'

Sao and Poto sat with bowed heads. At first, Mautu was ecstatic at seeing his daughter, but as the reality of what she'd done rushed back he exclaimed, 'Your mother does not want you, and I don't want you!' His anger increased when he realised that Sao and Poto had planned this move, expecting that they would not be able to withhold their forgiveness. 'You have disgraced our family before God and Samoa, disgraced us beyond repair!' Peleiupu continued weeping into the mat. Poto echoed her. 'You almost killed your mother!'

For a long tense while they wept. No one dared come near the fale. Then, as was expected, Sao made the next move. 'Pele and Tavita, you have disgraced all of us, even our village. We now have to bear that shame for the rest of our lives. Yet you dare return to ask for Mautu's and Lalaga's forgiveness? Who do you think you are?' He continued in this loud, oratorical manner until everyone had stopped weeping. Then, as was expected, he spoke to Mautu and Lalaga, telling them they had every right to be angry and unforgiving. 'The wound inflicted upon you by these selfish, headstrong children will bleed and bleed forever.' He paused. 'In fact I wanted to kill them but the Almighty God stilled my hand . . .'

When he ended, Poto took her turn to chastise the whimpering culprits. She emphasised her son's evil role in the affair. 'Tavita enticed our innocent Peleiupu to commit this unforgivable sin!' she whipped him. 'Now, Tavita, you must pay dearly for your crime. Understand?' Tavita nodded through his huge flow of tears. 'I wanted to die when I was told about your sin. I was so ashamed!' She ended by pleading with Lalaga and Mautu to forgive her disgraceful son and their misled daughter.

Then, as was expected, Sao resumed. This time he wept silent tears as he begged Lalaga and Mautu to forgive him and Poto because they'd raised such a sinful, inconsiderate son. And if they could find it in their God-inspired generosity, would they forgive their undeserving children. He instructed Peleiupu and Tavita to sit up and face their parents' wrath. 'Pele, it is time now for you to admit your guilt and ask your loving, generous parents for their love.'

During all this, Mautu found he was relenting, so he kept observing Lalaga's reactions. She looked old and tired in her heavy, mournful silence.

Then in shocked disbelief they all watched Lalaga fold up the dress, brush back her hair with her hands and tie it in a bun, rise swiftly to her feet and, without a word, straighten her shoulders and march out of the fale, head held high. Peleiupu sprang up to follow her, but Mautu ordered her not to. He and Lalaga were the wronged party, so he was not going to apologise to Sao for Lalaga's behaviour. 'Please leave it to me, sir,' he said to Sao. 'I will speak with Lalaga . . .'

'Sir, it was all my fault,' Tavita started saying.

'. . . I am sure she will learn to forgive,' Mautu continued addressing Sao.

'Let us leave it there, sir,' Sao declared. 'May God continue to heal the grievous wound *our* children have inflicted on the mother of our aiga. Perhaps some day soon your generous and loving wife will forgive our ungrateful children.' He staggered up. Poto followed.

When Peleiupu lingered, looking beseechingly at Mautu, Poto told her they had to leave. Mautu refused to look at his daughter as she scrambled after the others. For a long while, he sat trying to deny her to his heart. When he remembered Ruta was absent, too, he rushed out into the shelter of trees on the beach.

By evening lotu all the Satoans were talking animatedly about the meeting and how Lalaga had rejected their ali'i's plea to forgive her own daughter and his wayward grandson. Many sided with Lalaga, arguing that such a crime and sin could not be forgiven; others described Lalaga's rejection as further proof of her unChristian arrogance, unpastorlike behaviour and hard-heartedness; others blamed Mautu, saying he should have intervened and made his wife behave like a good pastor's wife should; and a few maintained that such selfish children should be returned to exile in Pago Pago and never forgiven.

Just as the dawn light spread, like a tender skin, over the bay, Lalaga shook Mautu awake and asked that he accompany her to get some pandanus. He hitched on his stained working ie lavalava, got his bushknife, and followed her over the rock fence and into the plantations.

Soon they were wet with dew, and the hems of their ie lavalava slapped against their legs. They'd not been together in the plantations for a long time and, as they walked and stopped and she cut the pandanus leaves and he tied them in bundles, he experienced a profound sense of security and partnership. Once when she sensed him staring at her, she looked up and smiled. Vividly, the memory of the first smile which she'd given him, in her Vaiuta principal's office, eased into his mind.

As they worked, they touched each other more and more: accidental bumps, his hands gliding over hers as he took the leaves from her, her shoulder brushing against his side, his thigh pressed into hers . . .

When they'd cut five large bundles, she strapped three onto his back, and he strapped the rest onto hers. Because of their heavy loads they took short quick steps as they headed back, with her leading the way. He tried stepping into every footprint she made in the muddy track. When she realised what he was doing she laughed softly and varied her steps, trying to fool him. Every time he mis-stepped he laughed and she slapped his thigh.

'Your daughter has grown into a very beautiful woman,' she remarked as they dumped their loads outside the kitchen fale. Momentarily he couldn't believe he'd heard her correctly.

They hurried to the pool between fale in which people were still asleep, and found to their relief they were no other bathers. The water was a slow dark swirl in which a few leaves floated. She took the highest bank and, rising to her toes, dived into the water. Dismissing his worry that people might be witnessing Lalaga's very unpastorlike behaviour, Mautu scrambled up to the same rock and dived after her. Their laughter, when he surfaced, reverberated around the rock banks. 'Yes, your daughter is a beautiful woman, but I'm not going to forgive her!' she called, as she trod water, her long hair plastered to her head and shoulders. She arched up, dived into the depths and swam swiftly towards him. The water burst up in front of him as she surfaced, gasping for air, her arms outstretched to the sky, which was now alive with light. 'No, I want your daughter and the son of your best friend to experience some of the terrible pain they've put us through.' Unexpectedly — but he loved it — she jumped onto him and, holding his shoulders, pushed him down into the water. He didn't care if anyone was watching. No, not one iota. She'd infected him with her cheeky, challenging happiness. 'And don't ask me what I've got planned.' Pressing her forefinger into the left side of her top lip, she added, 'They owe me for this paralysis, my loss of beauty and health and innocence and our good name.'

That Sunday to everyone's wonderful surprise, Peleiupu and Tavita accompanied Sao and Poto to the morning service. Peleiupu sat with Poto behind Lalaga, and

Tavita, who looked extremely uncomfortable in his white suit and tie and being in church, sat beside his grandfather in the front side pew reserved specially for the Ali'i of Satoa. Sao beamed with pride because he knew his people were happy that the atheist son of the atheist palagi had decided to rejoin God's flock. Mautu beamed with pride because his daughter looked so beautiful and radiant with repentance. To everyone, Lalaga appeared totally indifferent to Tavita's conversion and Peleiupu's public display of humility and repentance.

After the service two deacons stood in front of the pulpit and read out the names of the aiga. Aiga representatives took their donations to the deacons, who read out the amounts. After everyone else, Peleiupu, with bowed head, went up and handed the senior deacon an envelope.

'Two hundred pounds from Tavita and Peleiupu to commemorate their return to us!' the impressed, widely grinning deacon declared. The elders called out their gratitude; the others murmured with grateful amazement — no one could remember anyone giving that amount before.

On Monday morning Mautu noticed that Lalaga couldn't stop smiling as she prepared and left for school. She continued to do so when Peleiupu arrived at school and Lalaga announced to Mautu, Naomi and the other two teachers: 'Mautu's favourite daughter is replacing me as the head of our school. She is also taking over half my classes because I want time to do other work. Besides, I deserve a rest.'

Before that day was over, Mautu's elation at Peleiupu's readmission into the school turned to angry regret when it became clear to him that part of the bargain was for Peleiupu to stay away from him. Every time he tried talking to her she edged away. Just before school ended she almost burst into tears when she had to walk away from him. Wounded and angry though he was, he decided not to confront Lalaga.

At school the next day he made it easier for Peleiupu by staying away from her.

On Friday morning as they were preparing for school Tavita and his brothers, Mikaele and Roni, and three men of their aiga arrived with spades and bushknives, and waited by the kitchen fale. Lalaga hurried out to them. Mautu noticed that an uncomfortable Tavita kept looking at the ground while Lalaga talked to him. Mautu's curiosity deepened when he saw Lalaga leading the group to a bare area of land a short distance from the kitchen fale. Lalaga's sweeping gestures indicated that she was setting boundaries of some sort. Roni and Mikaele, who, like Tavita, wore trousers and singlets, paced out those boundaries soon after. Then Tavita went up, stood beside Lalaga, stabbed his spade into the ground, kicked down on it with his boot, and, pressing back on the spade handle, turned up the first spadeful of soil. The other men formed a line alongside him and started digging up the ground.

It was obvious that Lalaga was not going to tell him what was going on when she returned to the fale, with that intolerable smile. She washed and dressed, humming loudly. Mautu couldn't resist any longer. 'What is going on?' He tried to sound casual.

'Your daughter's husband, in his next trip to Apia, will bring me some books on gardening, and your supremely intelligent and knowledgeable daughter will help me teach gardening,' she said. He looked out again. The upturned soil was already drying in the hot sun and the men dripped rivulets of sweat. 'Your daughter's husband has also offered to provide the materials and implements for our garden and teaching.' She paused and added, 'Your daughter's husband is very generous, isn't he?'

After she left for school, Mautu instructed his household to take their morning meal to the professor's fale. Freemeade insisted that they use his small table and canvas chairs. When flies started attacking their food, a woman fanned the insects away. 'So you've forgiven Tavita?' Freemeade asked, gesturing with his head at Tavita and his helpers.

'Not yet — well, not until Lalaga tells me so,' he said. They laughed. Freemeade admitted that he was fascinated with Poto and her children because even though the children looked papalagi they were Samoan in the way they lived and behaved. He said he'd read some interesting studies about beachcombers like Barker and their descendants, and wanted to add to that by studying the Barker family. 'Beachcomber?' Mautu asked.

'That's the term given to Europeans who desert their ships or renounce their ways of life to live with the natives,' Freemeade explained. 'Men who comb the beaches for useful flotsam — and whatever else has ended up there — to use.' When Freemeade chuckled, Mautu discovered he was getting angry, and when Freemeade went on to describe beachcombers as 'the rejects and dregs of European civilisation' Mautu had to look away to hide his anger. 'All around the world, in the colonies, a whole race — or is it, non-race? — of people are being produced by that union of beachcomber and native; they're called half-castes.'

'So Barker's and Poto's children are half-castes?' Mautu asked.

'Yes, afakasi,' Freemeade replied. 'Beings lost between two cultures, and who belong nowhere. Not Caucasian, not Polynesian, but lost — even more rejected than their beachcombing fathers.' Looking over at Tavita and his brothers he said, 'Pity, because they are so often beautiful, physically.' Mautu noticed that Freemeade was caressing the arms of his chair with his long thin fingers. When Freemeade asked if it was true that Barker had taken his own life, Mautu nodded. Soon after, he left.

Tavita and his men, who were now drenched with sweat and caked with dirt, moved into the shade of the kitchen fale. Naomi and another girl brought them a bucket of water and food.

Afakasi: what a hurtful, stupid name! Mautu cursed Freemeade. If Barker were alive he'd castrate Freemeade, thereby turning him into a non-producing pure Caucasian without a superior future!

Two days later Naomi came home after helping at Freemeade's clinic, and informed her parents that she'd told the professor she was not continuing at the clinic because she had more teaching to do. 'Besides, our professor now has Semisi and two of Semisi's kind to help him,' Naomi added, and then rushed off.

'What's the matter with her?' Mautu asked Lalaga.

'Is the honourable professor studying fa'afafine too?' Lalaga replied. That wasn't a just accusation, Mautu insisted. 'Accusation?' she retorted. 'I'm only posing a scientific and objective question,' she imitated Freemeade. Before Mautu could counter, she hurried to the vegetable garden.

Early the next morning when he saw Semisi, dressed in white and with a red hibiscus sei, arriving with two of 'his kind' at Freemeade's clinic, Mautu was immediately gripped by anger, but as he considered the implications of Freemeade's move, his anger turned to alarm and trepidation. He wanted to rush over and confront Freemeade but he hesitated and his courage dissipated. He excused his timidity by telling himself that Sao and the people would treat Freemeade's hiring of fa'afafine as a joke, and eventually accept it as another strange thing that strange papalagi did. You also never knew what extremely intelligent and educated papalagi might find through their clever research. He decided to keep away from Freemeade's fale while Semisi and his friends were there.

He also kept away from Lalaga's hectic and popular gardening project. At church that Sunday morning Lalaga and Peleiupu explained the project to Satoa. Sao insisted that the men should get the training first; after all, they were the agriculturists. Politely but firmly Lalaga reminded him that gardening was 'women's work'.

On Monday morning, when a large number turned up, she divided them into single-sex classes that would come on alternate days. Tavita had already provided the implements and seeds, and books for Lalaga to learn from. Within a day, the news spread that Lalaga was an expert teacher of gardening, papalagi-style. Tavita helped her with the men's classes, and Peleiupu helped with the women's. Within three weeks most aiga had dug up garden plots and were waiting for seedlings from Lalaga's garden to plant; and the aualuma had set up a roster of garden inspections.

At the end of the month, as Mautu made his weekly round of spiritual counselling, he learned that Sao and Tavita were establishing a large coconut plantation, using the aumaga to clear the bush and plant the palms, just like papalagi planters were doing in many parts of the country. Tavita was extremely generous in feeding the aumaga while they worked and, at the end of each week, he distributed more food to their families.

When Freemeade, during their evening meal, asked Mautu what he thought of Tavita's actions, Mautu said it was good for Satoa to learn new agricultural methods and other ways of making a living; besides, the production of more copra meant more wealth for Satoa. But money and these foreign economic ways would radically change the beautiful fa'a-Samoa, Freemeade argued. Though annoyed by Freemeade's claim, Mautu said he'd never thought of that. He supposed that the professor, being a very learned man, knew far more about such things than he did. In his pedantic, didactic mode Freemeade went on to say that research — his own and others — showed that in the process of cultural contact, the culture with the superior technology and knowledge survived while the weaker, frailer one — and the fa'a-Samoa was in that category — would be destroyed. Survival of the fittest! he claimed. Was it therefore inevitable that weaker cultures would die out everywhere? Mautu asked, warily. Freemeade said that was why he and other social scientists were desperately researching and recording the lives of native peoples before they disappeared forever. 'As I've told you, sir,' Freemeade continued, 'not only is the rapacious, corrupt, technologically superior European changing your way of life, he is also changing your heirs genetically. Look at the Barker family.' (And my future grandchildren! Mautu thought, shocked.)

Mautu kept away from Peleiupu, but Naomi, Freemeade and the news network in Satoa kept him informed in detail about what his daughter was doing. And the more he learned, the more his pride in and love for her increased. Without complaint, she and Tavita were fulfilling their bargain with Lalaga, and more. She and Tavita now ran the choir; Peleiupu helped Vaomatua and Poto run the aualuma and other village projects; and with the leading tulafale, Tavita was the driving force in the aumaga. Apart from teaching at and running the school, Peleiupu now supervised the whole Aiga Sa-Sao. According to Freemeade, Peleiupu, with Sao's and Poto's consent and Tavita's firm support, was restructuring their aiga, the largest in Satoa.

Poto and Semisi continued running the store but Peleiupu was expanding it into a business that imported goods from Apia and American Samoa and sold them to stores around Savai'i. Mikaele and Roni were being trained to run the plantation and copra drying unit; Elisapeta and Ana were in charge of their main home and taking care of the children; the youngest, Faranisisi and Siniva, were still at school.

Outwardly Tavita appeared to be in charge of the whole operation, Freemeade continued parodying what he called 'the language of capitalism', but acknowledged that Peleiupu was 'the brains, business acumen and imagination behind it'.

'My daughter was always exceptionally bright and determined,' Mautu remarked.

'But wasn't she raised by you to view profit-making as usury, sir?' Freemeade argued, smiling.

'I'm sure she's not doing it for personal gain,' Mautu replied, 'but for the whole community.' He turned and left before Freemeade could say anything else.

The elders now talked enthusiastically of how the once wayward pastor's daughter — and their favourite daughter — and their ali'i's once pagan and uncivilised grandson were now making up, generously, for the enormous sin they'd committed against their aiga and community. This was genuine repentance and atonement! And Peleiupu was once again the example they wanted their children to emulate. Whenever they needed financial help or more credit at the store, they went to Peleiupu instead of that 'mean Poto and that loudmouth Semisi'. Peleiupu was more generous and understanding.

They were also benefiting from Sao's and Poto's contributions to church and village affairs: since Peleiupu's and Tavita's return, those had increased threefold.

'Pele is like our mother,' Naomi said to Mautu. 'Work, work and more work!'

'And planning and brain power!' added Mautu.

'And no complaining! I'm glad she's come home.'

'So am I,' whispered Mautu. 'So am I.'

'Have you heard the latest story about Arona?' Naomi added. 'That he's now first mate on an American whaler called *The Prodigal*, the first darkie and native to reach that rank . . .'

'And he's hunting those great beasts.' He stopped himself from laughing aloud.

'Even my mother is learning to live with that!' she said.

'Have you news of Ruta?' he found himself asking. 'I worry about her too.'

'Some people came back from Fagaloto yesterday,' Naomi informed him, 'and said she's well and everyone is starting to respect her healing powers.'

'Do you miss arguing with her?' he joked.

'I'm sure my sister is missing argiung with me!' she laughed.

BOOK TWO
The Epidemic

The Anthropology of Gardening

Mautu wandered out onto the paepae, allowing the breeze to cool his body. Even from that distance, he recognised Freemeade approaching from the beach, waving to him. Was there something different about the professor? Yes: the thick beard covering the lower half of his face. For about a month Freemeade had been away in the neighbouring villages 'collecting data from informants', as he had described it. In that time he and Lalaga and most of their household were happy to be free of Freemeade's inescapable voice, which analysed and then burdened them with irrefutable opinions and views about 'the Samoans and their fascinating way of life'.

Mautu wheeled to retreat, but Freemeade waved more furiously. Reluctantly, Mautu waited on the paepae for Freemeade to arrive and then invited him in.

'It looks very healthy,' Mautu said, once they were seated.

'This?' Freemeade said, pulling at his beard and grinning.

Mautu nodded and said, 'We envy you papalagi. Samoans can't grow much hair.'

'So I've noticed,' Freemeade said, and before Mautu knew it, the professor was off into a detailed scientific explanation of body hair and how it varied from race to race. 'I got tired of shaving while I was away and decided to let it grow,' he ended. 'What I really want to do is discuss some of the things I observed in the other villages. Is that all right?'

'I want to learn too,' Mautu lied politely and cursed himself for not being honest.

'Did you know, sir, that Satoa is now the only village that still clings to one church?' Freemeade began.

'Is that so?' Mautu continued to be polite.

'Most villages now have two or three different denominations. One has four — the LMS, the Catholics, Methodists, and, recently, the Mormons. But it's in keeping with what you had in pre-Christian times, isn't it?' Mautu nodded appropriately. 'Samoans had many religions with their own atua and priests. And the survival of each one depended on how able and strong their priests were. Atua came and went. So there's nothing new in Samoans selecting and promoting many Christian sects. When an atua got too tyrannical, people converted to rival atua . . .' Where was the polite, academic researcher, who wanted to *learn*? Mautu asked himself as he tried to look interested. '. . . By the way, Mautu, our village is the only one in Savai'i that has only one store.'

'Are you trying to tell me something?' Mautu heard his irritation find voice.

Freemeade smiled and shook his head. 'But doesn't it make sense that if you're going to have stores, you should have more than one?' Mautu's irritation grew when he realised he didn't know what the professor was referring to. 'Free enterprise — getting the stores to compete — keeps prices down and the quality of goods and services up, sir.' He waited for Mautu to catch up. 'Look at my country: it's the home of capitalism, of open business competition,' he continued.

'But up to now, you've been against capitalism,' Mautu pointed out.

The professor was nimble all right. 'I was only playing the Devil's advocate in our previous discussions. I believe firmly in capitalism as the cure for our world's economic ills, sir. Capitalism, developed properly, will create heaven on Earth for all mankind.' Looking sadly at Mautu, he continued, 'Because Samoan society is communal and the group is put before the individual it's never going to be wealthy or develop the individual talent and initiative so vital to progress.'

'But why be concerned about that?' Mautu was sure he now had the professor. 'You've told me in the past that weak, primitive societies like Samoa are going to die out.'

'But Samoa doesn't have to be weak and primitive!'

'If we adopt the American Way: capitalism?' Mautu intervened. Freemeade nodded. 'So why are you wearing a beard?' Mautu continued, remembering the time Freemeade had attacked the philosopher of communism, a German called Karl Marx, jeering even at the man's wild hair and beard. Freemeade looked nonplussed. 'Better watch out: if your beard gets any longer, people will call you Karl Marx.' He laughed and Freemeade had to laugh with him.

Shortly after, when Freemeade resumed talking about what he'd observed in the other villages, Mautu said, politely but firmly, 'You must be very tired from all your research — go and have a rest and join us later for lotu and food.'

That evening Freemeade appeared for lotu, without his beard. 'Marx is gone, my friend?' Mautu remarked.

Freemeade smiled. 'Yes, he didn't last long.'

While they ate, with Freemeade in his usual forceful manner describing his recent findings in great detail, Mautu noticed that Lalaga and most of their household, though trying to look engrossed in what Freemeade was saying, had lost interest. Lalaga ate quickly and then disappeared behind the curtains, supposedly to prepare her lessons.

A few nights later, as they lay in their net being lullabied to sleep by the soft rhythmic thudding of rain on the thatching, with Mautu snug against her back, Lalaga asked, 'Have you noticed that your professor doesn't stay long after our evening meals?'

'What do you mean?' Mautu asked.

'I've heard stories from other villages.'

'What stories?' Mautu was sitting up, dreading the panic that was firing his belly. 'What stories? Months ago, Sao told me about Freemeade questioning our children in an inappropriate way, and I warned him about it. Is that it?' He could feel it: his panic re-igniting the 'worry diarrhoea' he'd started to suffer as soon as the professor had returned from his latest research trip.

'About his being with other men.'

'Why, why did you have to tell me that?' he demanded.

'Because you're responsible for him. And at least it's not our village saying that . . .'

'But why tell me? You know my stomach's been playing up!'

'You brought him here and got Satoa to be the "object of his research".'

He was hurt by her lack of sympathy; the familiar jabs and twitches in his stomach worsened. 'Why did I ever agree to let him come here?'

'Because he healed me . . .'

'And we had to reciprocate . . .'

'You didn't *have* to. Samoa and the fa'a-Samoa were already reciprocating by letting him do his research. He claims he's doing it for our benefit, putting us on the scientific map of the world, and adding to the world's pool of knowledge . . .'

'We personally owe him a debt — your health, Lalaga . . .'

'He invited himself here — you couldn't refuse him. And how were we to know that he is . . . is . . .'

'An arrogant collector of cultures? He may know and understand much about us but, unlike our friend Barker, he'd never dream of living permanently with us.' Mautu clung on to Lalaga, wanting to melt totally into her and not have to get up in the morning and deal with Professor Fiapoto and the vengeful return of his worry diarrhoea.

The rain was gone; everything outside dripped and glistened. Dawn could barely penetrate the dark clouds that clogged the sky. A lone rooster crowed from the other end of the village. Surprised by his pulsing hardness, Mautu debated against Lalaga's warm body, decided against it, and slid out of the net.

It snagged for an incredible instant in the corners of his eyes, and he shut his eyes firmly against it. But it pierced right through the centre of his sight down into his fears: Semisi sneaking out of the side of Freemeade's fale into the stand of bananas. No, couldn't be! He then cursed the Devil for putting it there. He looked again, and gasped audibly, his stomach now a twisting bundle of pain. Another youth — one of Semisi's friends — was raising a row of blinds and creeping out.

Mautu staggered up and, clutching his belly, tried not to trip over the sleepers as he stumbled towards the latrines.

That morning he rushed to the latrine five times, feeling as if he were turning into painful, liquidy excrement and stench. Each time he grunted and dribbled and blasted, his end threatened to split apart, and his resolve to confront Freedmeade dribbled away. Until Lalaga returned from school at midday and found him pale and shivering and lying foetus-like in their net, and asked him why he hadn't sent someone to get medicine from his doctor friend. 'I don't want to ever see that man again!' he muttered. She got some anti-diarrhoea medicine from Semisi at Freemeade's clinic, and plugged him up with that.

Why was the Almighty plaguing him with such demanding problems? Why were other people causing problems that had little to do with him personally, but that he had to deal with because he was their pastor? The shadowy, flickering imagery of Semisi and his friend and the frightening implications of their furtive presence in Freemeade's fale in the evil dead of night kept tidal-waving through his self-pity. He just wanted to stay in bed and be sick forever. And for two days he did, wallowing lushly in his household's sensitive and indulgent care. Fearing a visit from Freemeade, he put the word out that he was too sick to receive visitors.

In the almost midnight dark, Mautu squatted in the banana stand outside Freemeade's fale, relieved there weren't many mosquitoes about. The space smelled of damp and mould, and occasionally he felt ants crawling over his feet.

Two rows of blinds at the back of the fale were still up, and the turned-down lamp on Freemeade's desk spilled a weak, watery light onto the paepae. He couldn't see Freemeade. He waited.

A blur of movement? The blinds fell down in an almost audible chat-chat-chat and a figure wrapped in a sleeping sheet was slipping into the fale. Puffttt! And the lamp was out. Darkness. Muffled conversation. Freemeade and Semisi. The stones of the paepae clicked and clacked as someone walked over them. A row of blinds was pushed aside noiselessly and another person entered the fale. More whispering. Semisi's suppressed, high-pitched laughter. Freemeade shushing him. Silence. Shuffling over mats. Pillows falling onto the floor.

Expecting another panic attack, Mautu steadied himself. Nothing. Not a twitch. He wasn't even angry or shocked any more. He was in control, sure of what God wanted him to do.

Once back in their net he slid up against Lalaga, who was on her back and snoring softly through her mouth. He caressed the tops of her thighs and, slowly lifting her left leg, scissored his left leg across hers. Sometimes she loved pretending she was asleep while he was making love to her. He loved it too. Gently, so as not to wake her, he caressed her until she was moist and he was hard, and he slid in. His whole body sighed Ahh, Ahh! as he pushed in. He moved slowly, her snoring stopped, and he knew she was only pretending sleep, and that intensified his desire. Pictures of what he imagined was occurring in Freemeade's fale also added to his strength and pleasure. No arrogant, sick professor was going to interfere with him and his people and get away with it! he told himself in American English. He moved harder and faster. She tightened and pushed back . . .

For three days, when Freemeade came for their lotu and meals, Mautu behaved as if nothing were wrong. Soon after every meal, Freemeade would say he was tired and return to his fale. And Mautu delayed acting.

'It is a very delicate subject,' Sao said as soon as Mautu was seated. (Sao had sent for him.) 'A subject Christian and civilised people shouldn't discuss, but people are starting to talk not only here but in other villages. To be blunt, sir, Freemeade, *your* palagi, is behaving like the sinners of Sodom and Gomorrah. Do you get my meaning, sir?' Mautu nodded. Right then Tavita entered and sat down at the back. 'I've sent for Tavita because he was the one with the courage to bring the matter to my attention.'

'I was asked by Poto and Vaomatua to do so, sir,' Tavita said.

'See how serious it is, Reverend?' Sao emphasised. 'Tavita, you tell the Reverend about the other villages.'

'Reverend, there are stories about him . . . about him *being* with other men.'

'Like in Sodom and Gomorrah,' Sao interrupted. 'Behaviour unbecoming of civilised humans.' Clearing his throat, he added, 'As you know, Reverend, Semisi and his kind have a place in our society. We tolerate and love them because they are our flesh and blood, and they are excellent aiga members: they are loyal, hard-working, and they serve us, their elders, with enormous love and generosity. So I don't mind your professor being one of Semisi's kind. No one minds. Papalagi may also allow such behaviour in their society. However, he is a famous, highly educated seeker of knowledge who we have admitted to study us. In return we have accorded him the respect we reserve for ali'i and servants of God like yourself, sir. And we expected him to behave like an ali'i. He hasn't. He has shamed his aristocratic family, and betrayed the trust and friendship you and our village have put in him.'

'People in the other villages are joking about him,' Tavita prompted his grand-father.

'Soon your palagi will be the brunt of ridicule and contempt even in our village. We don't want that to happen, do we, Reverend?'

'I will see to it, sir,' Mautu promised, and asked if he could borrow Tavita for a while.

'I don't want to know what you're going to do or how you're going to do it,' Sao ended their conversation.

Once out of Sao's hearing, Mautu ordered Tavita to have a fautasi and crew ready for a dawn departure, and a group of trusted people to help the professor pack that night. No one else was to be told about this. No one.

To stop Freemeade from coming for their usual evening meal Mautu arranged for his meal to be delivered to him. While their household prepared for bed, Tavita signalled to Mautu from the edge of the light, and with Roni, Mikaele and two other men, they hurried to Freemeade's fale.

The blinds were drawn already. Mautu told the others to wait outside. He would conduct their conversation in English, he decided. That way he could discuss the tapu topic more freely.

Dressed only in an ie lavalava, Freemeade was at his desk, writing. Mautu felt as if he were encased in a birthsac of utterly calm fluid, ready to exercise God's and his village's will and justice. Freemeade glanced up at him over the rims of his glasses. 'Have you come, sir?' he greeted Mautu in Samoan.

Mautu sat down in the canvas chair. 'Violence may erupt in Satoa if we don't do something about it, Professor.' He was pleased at Freemeade's puzzled expression. 'I need your help to stop it.' Freemeade nodded. 'You have to leave Satoa immediately, sir.' Total puzzlement in Freemeade's eyes. 'You have to.'

'But . . . but why and for how long?' Freemeade asked, his hands clutching the arms of his chair.

'For good, my friend.' Freemeade's eyes threatened to burst, his mouth widened in disbelief. 'Yes, for good, Professor.'

'But . . . but . . . but . . . ' Freemeade stuttered.

'You know why, Professor. You know *why*!' Freemeade struggled out of his chair, fists clenched. 'You have no defence, sir,' Mautu continued his attack. 'And we do not need to discuss your offences.'

'Have you Sao's and the fono's authority to do this?'

'Yes, it was Sao who instructed me to come and tell you. I am your host and friend so I am responsible for what you do in Satoa, sir.'

Freemeade smashed his fists down on the desk. Papers and bottles scattered. 'You are bloated with your own self-importance, Mautu: fat and corrupted by power! And these people follow you blindly.'

'We don't want all of Satoa to hear us, do we, sir? We don't want your crimes and sins to be known to everyone, do we? Let's do it the civilised way, the educated way. You've studied us long enough, Professor, to know what that way is.' Freemeade slumped into his chair, hands to his mouth. 'After you leave, no one in Satoa or else-where will know the real reason for your unexpected departure. We'll tell them you had to return to your father's funeral.'

'What about what I've done for you and Lalaga?'

'Look what we've done for *you*, Professor. On your return to your capitalist Heaven-on-Earth, America, and your illustrious university, you will write up your research, lecture on it, and publish it in books that will astound and change the papalagi world. You'll be more famous and richer than you are now, sir. Isn't that enough, Professor?'

'I'll not be talked to like that and ordered out by some . . . by some . . . '

'. . . By some ignorant savage?' Tavita's threat in Samoan came over Freemeade's head. Freemeade turned. Tavita took three measured steps towards him. 'I, the savage, I now tell you to get out before we . . . '

'That's enough!' Mautu ordered Tavita. ' Tavita and his men will help you pack tonight,' Mautu said to Freemeade. 'A fautasi will take you to Apia. Even the neigh-bouring villages aren't safe for you any more.' He reached over to console his friend. Freemeade jerked his arm away. 'I am sorry it had to end this way.' Mautu turned and strode out of the fale into the darkness.

At morning lotu, his voice rich with sadness, Mautu informed his surprised household that the professor, their dear friend, had left during the night to return to America and his father's funeral at Boston. By midday every Satoan knew about it.

Sao and Tavita ordered Semisi not to ever mention 'Freemeade's secret activities'. 'Control your mouth or I'll control it for you!' Sao threatened his loquacious grand-son, who controlled his mouth for a desperate two days and then unleashed it, secretly, to all the customers who shopped at his store, who in turn unleashed it to whoever was willing to be surprised and horrified and entertained . . .

Led and managed by Peleiupu and Tavita, Lalaga's gardening project flourished: every aiga now had a vegetable garden and enjoyed a healthier diet, though it took a while for most Satoans to acquire a taste for the new vegetables — beans, Chinese cabbage, tomatoes, carrots, eggplant, spring onions, pumpkins and squash. In one of his sermons Mautu prescribed these vegetables as 'miracle food for the muscles, eyes, heart, intestines and soul'. Sao went one better: he stated in a sermon that 'Our Lord tuned His sacred spirit on the miraculous vegetables that we now enjoy.' Only their relatives knew that during the week Mautu and Sao ate only beans, and then the beans had to be fried with expensive corned beef 'to make it taste', Mautu instructed.

At to'ona'i Mautu demonstrated that he enjoyed all God's vegetables by eating them enthusiastically in large quantities in full view of the other reluctant elders. Only Lalaga knew that her husband suffered wild flatulence after each of his Sunday vegetable binges.

From behind his store counter Semisi recommended eggplant — especially the large, bulbous, round, purple-black variety — to all his customers, claiming sensuously it was *the* remedy for flaccidity and lack of stamina. 'One beautiful, strong eggplant and you can last all day and night!'

Throughout Savai'i, Satoa became known as Le Nu'u o le Au Aivao, the Village of Grass-eaters. Some Satoans were ashamed and hurt by that until Mautu proclaimed from the pulpit that 'only the ignorant and uneducated from the back' would think that about God's vegetables, whose health properties and scientific value for the humble human body had been explained to them by the most educated person ever to visit Samoa, Professor Freemeade of Harvard University. 'Let the uneducated wallow in their bad health and ignorance, while we, who know and understand the latest findings in science, continue to enjoy good physical and spiritual health, consuming God's vegetables,' he concluded.

In early January Mautu and Lalaga, in a fautasi tautaied by Tavita, took Naomi to Upolu and Vaiuta School. In their farewell in the principal's office they all wept together, but Naomi was glad she was going to be away from Satoa and her parents and the arduous workload thrust upon her, particularly by her mother. She would continue to miss Peleiupu and Ruta, though.

Mautu was scraping coconuts into a tanoa and feeding the chickens with it when he saw Lalaga approaching. Every time he scattered a handful of scraped coconut among the large flock, the chickens squawked and fought for it. He tried to ignore the strong smell of drying mud, coconut and the latrines.

Lalaga's shadow netted him. 'Your most-loving daughter Ruta is now becoming known as a healer,' she said. 'A visitor from your pagan village is here — he told me Ruta's going to have powers greater even than your pagan sister!' She paused, he remained silent. 'Your selfish wealthy daughter Pele is with child.' He dropped the empty coconut shell into the basket. 'She told me this afternoon before she left school.' Peleiupu was twenty-six. Tears blurred his vision when he looked up at Lalaga. 'It's been almost four years since they married and people, as you know, were starting to talk,' she continued. His tears dripped down his face and he didn't try to hide them from her. 'What's the matter?' she asked. Noisily he sucked back the phlegm and tears in his throat. 'You're not a child!' she tried to joke. She could be so insensitive, he decided. He sucked back his tears, caught them in one ball at the back of his throat and then SSSHHHRRRAAATTT, he spat the ball at the chickens, scattering them. 'A'e, that's not hygienic!' she berated him.

'I don't care,' he whispered and, for no reason, he started laughing softly. 'I don't care!' He paused, laughing still. 'It's going to be a girl, a girl, a beautiful girl!' he chanted.

'Have all the chickens come in?' she asked. When he didn't reply, she called, 'Ku, ku, ku, ku!' A speckled hen, trailed by her brood of chicks, rushed from the undergrowth; a few others surged in from other directions. She scooped up handfuls of coconut and scattered it among the newcomers.

'Has Pele fulfilled your demands?' he asked. She looked away. 'Has she? I want to talk to my daughter again, now!' She started walking away. 'Why did you force her to stop seeing me?'

She stopped and, with her back to him, said, 'Because you were the one who spoilt her. If she'd been raised like our other daughters, she wouldn't have betrayed us.'

'Hasn't she paid enough for that?'

She shook her head and said defiantly, 'Not yet! No, not yet!' He let her go.

He continued scraping the coconuts and feeding the chickens, which swirled and regrouped according to where the coconut landed. In his imagination he saw a little girl, who looked just like Peleiupu when she'd been that age, trying not to fall over as she wandered through the chickens. Eyes as huge as a morning sky, smile as wide and winning as a morning tide. Chortling, cooing. Ah, his beautiful, wondrous granddaughter!

He bathed and changed into a clean ie lavalava and the colourful floral shirt Peleiupu had given him for Christmas, leaving the shirt unbuttoned because it was hot. 'Where are you going?' Lalaga asked. 'It'll be lotu soon.'

'Visiting,' he replied, and then strode out of their fale and down to the malae.

The breeze was dragging the evening shorewards from the horizon, and being butted by the palms and trees along the beach. Some children were playing outside the church; they paused and smiled at him. He told them to go home: it was time for lotu. Smoke billowed from the kitchen fale as aiga prepared their evening meal, and was swallowed up quickly by the falling darkness. The chorus of cicadas started. Some of the elders invited him into their homes; he declined.

The strong smell of kerosene invaded his nostrils as he entered the store. Poto was at the counter, reading the Bible. At the far side Semisi was weighing bags of sugar on the small scales, and whistling. As Mautu had expected, Peleiupu was immersed in recording accounts in a large ledger. No Tavita.

He stood, saying nothing. Poto glanced up and said, 'Sir, have you come?' He nodded.

'Get Mautu a chair, Semisi.' Semisi pushed Mautu the chair he'd been sitting on. Peleiupu shut the ledger and got up. Poto saved him from having to plead with his daughter. 'Pele, don't go. I think your father has come to talk to you.'

'And Tavita if he is around?' he asked.

Poto started leaving. 'Semisi, you come too.' They left quickly.

Awkwardly he stood gazing out through the front door at the darkness that was gliding in over the beach, and trying to find the words to say to her, knowing she found it difficult making small talk. When he glanced at her, she too was looking out the door. She looked drawn and tired, the mellow soft contours of youth were gone from her face.

'It's the anniversary of Barker's death next week, isn't it?' he heard himself asking.

'Yes, I think so,' she replied. 'Tavita and Poto are organising for us to visit him.'

'Your mother has told me you are with child.' He was surprised at the spluttering sound of his voice. She nodded once, her hands clasped together on the counter. 'I am very happy,' he murmured. She gazed directly at him for the first time. 'So is your mother. It will be our first grandchild.' There was a long pause as she struggled to reply. 'You have been punished enough, Pele,' he said.

'I had no other choice, Papa,' she began. 'I chose to follow my heart, knowing it would bring shame and pain to you and Lalaga. For that I am very sorry.'

'But you do not regret it?'

'No, I do not regret marrying Tavita.' He'd always admired and loved her determination and honesty.

'Your mother and I and our community have made you pay dearly for it . . .'

'They certainly have . . .'

'. . . and your mother continues to exact her payment.'

'Yes, she certainly does, but I knew Tavita and I would have to pay for a lifetime, for our choice.'

'I am satisfied. That is what I came to tell you. From here on, I'm ignoring Lalaga's demands on you and Tavita. So promise me you'll not keep away from me?'

She nodded. 'My mother is like me, Papa. She finds it difficult forgiving anyone who has hurt her and her aiga. So when she finds out what you've done, how's she going to react?'

'The usual way, but I'll do my usual back — I'll just ignore her.'

Just then Tavita entered and, seeing Mautu, looked at Peleiupu. 'It's all right, Tavita, I'm no longer keeping Lalaga's contract with you,' Mautu told him, smiling. 'And I want to come with you when you visit your father's grave next week.' Tavita nodded and asked if he would conduct the memorial service. Mautu agreed. Silence. 'It's going to be a girl, eh?' Mautu asked. They looked puzzled. 'Your first child?' Tavita grinned; Peleiupu shrugged her shoulders. 'May I name her?' he requested. 'I'll consult Sao, of course.'

'Sir, it would be an honour for us,' Tavita said.

'Sao and I will come up with a relevant and poetic name.' Mautu tingled with joy.

As the dark settled into Satoa, the chorus of cicadas and the evening hymns embraced it. 'Shouldn't you hurry home for lotu, Papa?' Peleiupu asked.

'You can have lotu with us,' Tavita invited him.

'I don't feel like being in a lotu tonight,' Mautu said. 'Let's just stay here and talk.' He wanted to know about their life since they married in American Samoa.

'It might bring back painful memories,' Peleiupu cautioned.

'Leave out the bits that might,' he joked.

So while the sound of lotu and cicadas and mosquitoes measured the edge of their hearing, Peleiupu and Tavita did what he wanted. By the end of it they could barely see one another in the darkness. Tavita lit a lamp.

'I hope my granddaughter doesn't look like your father!' Mautu joked with Tavita.

Peleiupu laughed softly. 'Papa's right — your father wasn't handsome!'

'No, he wasn't handsome like you, Tavita!' Mautu emphasised. They laughed about that.

'Anyway, how do you know it's going to be a girl?' Tavita asked.

'Because God whispered it to me on my way here.' They laughed about that too.

Tavita went to the shelves and started getting goods for Mautu to take home.

'No, I don't need that,' Mautu insisted. 'All I need is your alofa and forgiveness. We've made you pay far more than you needed to. I'm proud of your service to our church, our school and our village.' He turned to leave. Peleiupu stopped him and straightened his collar and buttoned his shirt. 'By the way, are you keeping an eye on Ruta?' he remembered.

'Yes, every time the *Lady Poto* calls in a Fagaloto, I send her and Lefatu some supplies,' she replied. 'Everyone there loves her.'

It had rained all night and, as he picked his way over the soggy ground to the school, mud oozed up between his toes, so he had to wipe his feet on the sacking in the doorway into the classroom. Lalaga, Peleiupu and the other teachers were there already.

'We need to continue our classes in gardening,' Lalaga was telling the others.

Mautu sat down beside Peleiupu, who smiled at him and didn't move away. 'Do we need to do that?' he asked Lalaga. 'All our families have gardens now and can't eat all the vegetables they produce.'

'Yes, our family is feeding the surplus to the pigs,' one of the others said.

'I support Mautu's view,' said Peleiupu. The other avoided looking at Lalaga. 'Those who've been trained can teach the rest of their families,' she added. The tension intensified as Lalaga struggled to reply. 'And Tavita and I can't continue teaching gardening — we have a lot of other work.'

'I'll do it on my own then!' Lalaga snapped. 'Do we need to discuss anything else?' No one responded. 'So, let's start our day.' She jumped up, glared at Mautu and hurried out. Her limp seemed more pronounced.

'I thought you were in charge of this school!' Mautu quipped as Peleiupu got up.

'So did I, so did I!' Peleiupu said.

At interval Mautu kept well away from Lalaga and Peleiupu. From the playground he saw them through the windows, arguing heatedly. He couldn't hear what they were saying. Lalaga waved her arms and pointed repeatedly at Peleiupu, who just stood there motionless. Periodically Lalaga would turn her back to her daughter and clutch her face. Their soundless argument, their mime, looked funny and melodramatic.

Lalaga didn't even wait until the servers had cleared away the remnants of their evening meal. 'So you and your daughter have reconciled, eh?' she started.

'Yes, she and Tavita have atoned for their bad actions as far as I'm concerned. And you have no right banning her from seeing me.'

'What about our bargain with them?' she demanded. The embarrassed servers packed quickly and left.

'You made the bargain, Lalaga, remember? You even told me you weren't going to tell me the conditions of it.'

280

Furiously she shook her head and said, 'Once again you've given in to her, allowed her to get away with it.'

'I have not given in to Pele,' Mautu stressed. 'There is nothing to give in to. Pele has paid the price and far more.'

'You and your spoilt daughter are again siding against me!' She started weeping. 'She almost killed me. Your daughter almost killed me!'

'That's enough!' he interrupted. 'I want our family to be as it was. Pele has paid enough.' Lalaga buried her face in her hands and continued weeping. 'The work and responsibilities you and Tavita's aiga and others have imposed on her would break anyone else.' He paused, breathing deeply, and then added, 'Besides she is now with child, remember?'

She slapped at her sides and rolled away through the curtain to where they slept.

Later, she slept well away from him, and, throughout the night, tossed and turned and sighed. She was at school before he was awake, and refused to speak to him when he got there. Throughout the day, she set work for her classes and then just sat at her desk gazing out to sea.

'She's very cross with me,' Mautu told Peleiupu, 'but I'm not giving in to her.'

'Neither am I,' she said. She went in and, while Lalaga glared at her, informed her she couldn't run the school any more because of other demands. 'Tavita and I are setting up a bakery.' She left before her mother could say anything.

When Lalaga reached Mautu at their home she loomed above him. 'I'm going to have another stroke! Is that what you and your ungrateful daughter want, eh?' He wrapped his arms around her. She struggled and fought against him. 'Your daughter wants to see me dead. That's what!'

'That is not true, Lalaga. Pele loves you.'

As he held her, her shaking eased away. 'You have always loved our children more than me,' she accused him. 'And Pele the most.'

'That's not true, Lalaga.'

That night and all that week she slept away from him, and refused to talk directly to him or Peleiupu. During the week she visited all the wives of the matai, supposedly to discuss their gardens. Mautu knew something was up and warned Peleiupu who hesitated and then said, 'I don't want to speak ill of my own mother, but I have to, Papa. She is gathering information about what's happening in Satoa, and in particular what's happening to Tavita and me.' She pondered again and added, 'She's trying to get their support.'

'For what?'

Peleiupu smiled. 'Papa, I am so like her, I can read her easily. She wants them to help her put me back into "my proper place". My own mother!'

'Your mother is not like that, Pele. She is not a devious and calculating person.'

'You've always been a hopeless judge of people, Papa, especially of those close to you!' Peleiupu laughed.

Hurt by her remark, for he'd always believed he was an astute judge of people, he said, 'I suppose so.'

With a slow, wicked smile she said, 'The wives will pledge their support to her, but will not act against me, Papa.'

'I don't understand.'

'You will, Papa, you will soon.'

Two days later, on his counselling round, some of the wives asked him, respectfully, if Lalaga was *well*; others asked, respectfully, if Peleiupu was *well*; still others asked, respectfully, if Lalaga and Peleiupu were *well* together; one, the bravest of them, asked, plainly, if Lalaga and Peleiupu were quarrelling. To her, Mautu told the truth; to the others he pretended surprise that they should even think his wife and daughter were not well, singly, and not well, together.

All the wives started their conversations with him by declaring their love and respect for Lalaga and her 'remarkable and generous daughter'. Then they left Lalaga out, and heaped praise on his 'remarkable and generous daughter', whose great intelligence, judgement, planning, unbelievable capacity for work, money and husband were transforming the whole of Satoa into the most prosperous and progressive community in Samoa.

'I think I understand now,' Mautu said to Peleiupu the next day at school. She didn't know what he was referring to. 'You know, remember?' She smiled. 'Your poor mother doesn't know, does she?' She shook her head and smiled again. 'She hasn't got a chance, eh?' Her smile widened, her teeth gleamed. She turned and headed home briskly.

The congregation grew quiet, waiting for the service to start. Mautu knelt in the pulpit and prayed, then sat up and gazed down at the front entrance. Sao, who looked frail and weak, entered with Peleiupu and Tavita supporting him on either side. Their white clothes gleamed in the morning light.

Theirs was a slow procession up the aisle as Sao shuffled and surveyed the congregation, smiling and nodding at the other elders. The congregation exuded an enormous feeling of pride as they observed the procession. Tavita walked with an easy confidence, no longer the shy, self-conscious youth Mautu had known. As for Mautu's daughter, well, she was playing the role of daughter-in-law perfectly, with the proper degree of shyness, humility and respect, the appropriate lowering of her eyes, and the devoted attention to her ali'i. Unexpectedly, she glanced up at Mautu. He saw a mischievous sparkle in her eyes, the faint trace of a wry smile before she looked away again. At that moment, Mautu understood and was breathless. In the proud possessive way Sao was holding on to Tavita's and Peleiupu's arms and displaying them in front of his whole community, his message was clear: these were his heirs. And the congregation was applauding.

Tears threatened again when Mautu remembered Barker and how proud he would have been of his son and Peleiupu, and even prouder that his children were now part of Satoa. When Freemeade's lecture on afakasi started intruding, he rose to his feet, held on to the front-piece of the pulpit and declared 'Today is a beautiful day to praise our Lord. Let us begin this service . . .'

On 3 December 1908, his first grandchild, a girl, was born. Sao and his wife and Lalaga agreed to his choice that their granddaughter be called Lefatu.

It was as if he and his family were back on that first evening when he had brought home the English Bible that Barker had given him, in the expectant hush and stillness of evening with Lalaga and their children circling him and the large parcel in his hands, waiting for him to open it; with the same tightness in his belly as the trembling rippled up from the book and up through his arms into his eyes.

They were waiting for him to open the hefty parcel with the black waterproof canvas wrapping that Poto had brought from Apia, saying she'd been given it by the German firm she traded with. The parcel had been handed to the firm by a black sailor — a Fijian? — from an American ship docked in Apia Harbour. The firm knew Poto was from Satoa, the village to which the parcel was addressed.

Dirt-caked, scratched, hand-written address on white paper stained wet brown, the thin rope around it frayed, the parcel looked as if it had travelled a long way over a long time, and passed from person to person, ship to ship. Now it was with the people who owned it and who desperately wanted to open it but were afraid to do so. Finally Mautu pushed it towards Lalaga, who shook her head once, then reached down and started unknotting the rope. As she untied the rope she rolled it neatly around her right hand and then laid it on the floor, and looked at him.

He watched his hands as they gripped the opening between the central edges of the black canvas wrapping and pulled it open slowly. He looked at Lalaga as she pulled up the lid of the paper box, and looked away from the contents.

'It's from *him*, isn't it?' he dared.

'Don't know!' When she glanced at him his arms were in the box almost up to his elbows. A rich satiny smell rose up from the box.

'Here, you take out the things,' he said.

Out of the box came three rolls of calico and silk, five long-sleeved shirts, three silk ties, four white hats for church, four dresses . . .

'No letter?' he ventured.

From the depths of the box she took a white envelope and, with a trembling, fearful hand, handed it to him. Slitting it open with his forefinger, he showed her what was in it. Money, notes: a thick wad of money.

'No letter?' she asked quietly.

He shook his head. 'Just money.'

'I'll look again,' she offered. He watched and waited as she searched methodically through the contents, unfolding even the material, emptying everything onto the floor and running her hand along the bottom of the box. He sensed she was trying not to cry.

'Are we sure it is from him?' he asked.

Nodding her head furiously, and clutching one of the dresses to her face, she murmured, 'Yes, yes, it is from Arona, our son, our son!'

And so began another strand in *The Tales of Arona the Sailor* — of large black parcels, with exotic gifts and money, arriving when the Mautu family least expected them; parcels that came without letters from Arona.

In the House of Sorrow

Every Friday, an hour before the cicadas erupted in chorus and the sun started slotting into the darkness, Peleiupu and Tavita retreated into what Satoans referred to as 'Pele's office' and shut the door on Satoa, and no one dared intrude. For that hour, she told them, she and Tavita belonged to themselves, and were not to be fed upon by others.

She would relax in her prince's chair, which Tavita had given her for her thirtieth birthday eight years earlier, while Tavita smoked (and drank a glass or two of whisky that no one was supposed to know about). Most Satoans believed that wanting privacy, cutting yourself off from family, was a strange thing to do: privacy encouraged conspiracy, plotting, furtive consumption of food and other things you should be sharing with your community. Sao claimed it was a very papalagi characteristic, and said it was really Peleiupu who insisted on it, not his grandson, who was a *true* Satoan who loved being with others, always. As for her insisting that she and Tavita speak only English during that hour, that was really peculiar! (It was strange enough that she spoke mainly English to her children.) Her office was cluttered with books that she actually read, Sao reported. All those books and all that reading was one of the reasons she was so different from normal people.

Peleiupu fanned herself with quick pecking movements as she observed the village and sea. From her parents' house eased the chorus of children reciting their times tables: 'Two ones are two, two twos are four, two threes are six . . . !' She visualised Maualuga, eyes shut tightly, trying to fish the correct answers out of her memory, and

I'amafana, Sao's namesake and as over-confident as his namesake, trying to outrace the other children.

Two canoes were crossing the bay, struggling against the receding tide. She paddled with the fishermen as they dug their paddles into the water and pushed back, dug and pushed, dug and pushed . . . Ahh, it was good for easing the tightness and pain in your neck and shoulders! Tavita usually massaged the pain away before she settled into her chair, but he was in Upolu with Mikaele and Faranisisi checking the viability of four trading stores they might buy from German owners who were leaving the country.

Jutting out from Totoume Point was the jetty that, with the help of the whole village, they had built a few years before when they'd bought their first motor vessel and renamed it the *Lady Poto*. Roni, Tavita's fourth brother, who'd spent four years on foreign ships, captained the vessel, which they used to supply their other stores and transport passengers and goods to and from Apia.

Before the Great War they'd worked closely with the German company, selling it all their copra and buying nearly all their goods from it. So when New Zealand took control of the country at the start of the war, and the company was forced to sell its trading stations, it gave them first option in Savai'i, and they'd bought six of the stores cheaply. Against Tavita's wishes Peleiupu had put Semisi in charge of the chain of stores, telling Semisi that 'your oldest brother thinks you're going to make a mess of it'.

'Does he, does he, now?' Semisi had exclaimed in English. 'Well, I going to show that . . . that Afakasi son-a-bitch, who don't even speak proper English, that I the best bloody businessman in this afakasi family!' So far, Semisi was proving just that.

Since the start of the war, they'd bought three adjoining German businesses in the centre of Apia. At the moment people were renting them, but she planned at the end of the war to demolish them and build a large business complex that would be the headquarters of their company.

With pride Peleiupu gazed up at their new steepled church with the fifty front steps, amazing stained-glass windows and bright red roof. To the right of that was the pastor's new house, a spacious rectangular building with red corrugated-iron roof, an abundant communal room and bedrooms. To the left of the church was the new school made up of two long buildings divided into classrooms.

A year after Lefatu's birth Sao and Mautu, through the fono, had declared that God wanted to be praised by Satoans in a new church reflecting His importance and value. (Other nobody villages, orated Sao, are building churches that make our church look like a nobody church!) So she and Tavita had had to work behind Mautu and the fono, to ensure that the church was built properly, efficiently.

For the building fund the fono had levied monthly contributions on all aiga, and had all the copra cut and sold through Peleiupu's store. When she discovered that Sao and the other trustees were misusing the building funds, Peleiupu got Tavita to 'persuade' Sao to appoint Poto as a trustee. Poto ensured that none of the trustees misused the funds any more. The others knew little accounting, so Peleiupu had to keep all the books, and an incensed Sao complained to Tavita that 'your cheeky wife is getting too cheeky treating me like a dishonest child'. (She'd stopped all Sao's and his friends' unauthorised spending on tobacco, chewing gum, corned beef and other 'essentials'.) And when Tavita had cautioned her about 'mistreating' his grandfather she'd handed him the books and told him to keep them, and pay for his own grandfather's 'expensive habits'. It didn't take long for Tavita to realise that his interest did not lie in satisfying his grandfather's insatiable appetites but in getting the church built as quickly and honestly as possible. She also persuaded him — and through him, Sao — to have the school and pastor's house built. It would be cheaper that way and he'd also earn the love and respect of all Satoans.

The lavish official opening of the new buildings, attended by 'nearly all of Samoa' — Sao's description — brought in enough money to cover all their costs and make a profit, which Peleiupu had to get Tavita to persuade Sao (who wanted to keep the bulk of the money) to divide evenly among all the aiga. She laughed about it now but the whole building project had often threatened the unity of her own family, and of Satoa, with some aiga threatening to convert to other churches and Sao and Mautu threatening to ostracise them from Satoa (and the 'true Christian heaven') forever.

A few months after the church opening, Sao had summoned a meeting of their aiga and, with tears in his rheumy eyes, had declared, 'My favourite palagi grandson, David, otherwise known to you as Tavita, in his dynamic, selfless service to me and Satoa in building our church, pastor's house and school, has proven he is a *true* Samoan, a *true* Satoan, and a *true* and most loyal member of our aiga. He has through his service raised this difficult, sometimes factious aiga to the level of being number one in this jealous village, in this envious district, in this faction-ridden country.' Pausing dramatically and blowing his nose on the corner of his ie lavalava, he'd then ruled, 'Toanamua, the second-highest title in our obedient aiga, is to be conferred on my grandson.' With his regal right hand he'd motioned to Tavita to come forward and patted the mat next to him. A shy, suitably humble Tavita took that place. Then Sao had looked at all the leading matai of each branch of his aiga and asked them for their views — objections — to his God-inspired choice.

Each elder had spoken solemnly, expressing support, and Sao had congratulated them on agreeing with his 'suggestion'. Happiness had filled every part of Peleiupu:

Tavita deserved the title. She'd been happier still knowing that the matai of their aiga were pledging their support to Tavita not because of Sao but because they recognised that their self-interest would now be best served by Tavita (and 'the unusual but gifted pastor's daughter'). They would continue to pander to the old man's vanity but Tavita was their new Sao.

A month later the title Toanamua was formally conferred on Tavita in the 'largest, most generous, most aristocratic saofa'i ever witnessed in Samoa: thousands of pounds, hundreds of pigs and ie toga, and enough food to sink every glutton in the world!' Sao would boast for the rest of his life. Peleiupu hadn't minded the extravagance in this instance: the patronage had further strengthened their position in Satoa and the district and had declared to the country that a new leader had emerged in Savai'i. It was all good for business.

Though everyone now addressed him as Toanamua, Peleiupu would never want to call him that — he would always be Tavita, the reticent, sometimes clumsy young man who'd obeyed her decision to go to Pago Pago and get married there. That reckless courage had changed the course of her life, making her part of what that infuriatingly racist American Freemeade had described as 'a beachcomber's half-caste family, neither Samoan nor British, but lost between those cultural and genetic poles'. Freemeade, look where that in-limbo half-caste family is now! Peleiupu wanted to shout.

She wandered up to the windows and, letting the soft breeze cool her body, surveyed their compound. Barker's old store was gone; in its place they'd built this large complex of store, warehouse, offices, bakery, copra-drying unit and shed. Her aiga's faletele, with the highest paepae in Satoa, remained in front on the edge of the malae. And Sao and Vaomatua now had a new house just like the pastor's.

Behind Sao's house, nestled under sprawling monkeypod and mango trees, was her double-storeyed house with four bedrooms, a large sitting room, dining room and kitchen, designed after Jeanne Somerset Maun's home in one of her favourite novels, *The Sun and Shilling*, by Graham Creme.

She'd almost died giving birth to Maualuga, the youngest, who was almost seven. She tried to suppress the memories of the pain: it felt as if she were being turned inside out. Everyone had sympathised with her, saying how sorry they were that Maualuga's difficult birth had ended her chances of having any more children. But she was glad she would not have to go through that terrible experience again. Having children had been a matter of duty. She'd never had what Freemeade had described as 'the maternal instinct', but had never told anyone because they would have considered that unnatural. She loved her children more than anyone else, of that she was sure. Lefatu, at ten, had her Aunt Lefatu's facial features, Lalaga's small and tight body, Tavita's stocky legs and

Mautu's large feet. Her green eyes and blonde-tipped hair were straight from Barker. Iakopo, nine, and named after Peleiupu's brother who'd died of the Satoan Disease, had Lalaga's prominent forehead, Sao's bulbous and alert eyes, Vaomatua's squatness, Poto's slim legs — and Mautu's large feet. I'amafana, eight, was Sao's favourite, and Sao claimed that 'the son of my daughter's son looks just like me when I was his age'. There was no resemblance at all, but no one was foolish enough to tell Sao that. Mautu was partially brave and had told Sao that I'amafana's large feet were his. Feet being lowly parts of a person, Sao had agreed with the pastor. Once, when I'amafana was talking excitedly, Vaomatua had commented to Sao, 'Aren't his blue eyes beautiful?' Sao had accused her of being colour-blind. 'Can't you see his eyes are brown like mine?' he'd ordered. Maualuga, Tavita's favourite, was as beautiful as Ruta and Naomi were at her age, except she had cats' eyes and golden brown hair. It was strange but no one in their aiga had ever said that any of Peleiupu's children resembled her. Not even Tavita.

The large fireball was sinking into the western horizon, setting the sea and sky ablaze with a molten-lava red. As the crimson red flowed in from the west and over the beach and malae and up towards the range, Peleiupu followed its progress. Their plantation was spreading up over the foothills.

This was what they had achieved since their return from American Samoa, about fourteen years before. No one in Satoa had ever achieved so much in so short a time. Mautu told everyone that Peleiupu had 'the Midas Touch'. Sao and the children wanted to hear that story, and Peleiupu had to tell it.

She'd never intended the success, but she was proud of her achievements.

She shielded her eyes and gazed into the sunset.

She woke at 5.30 am, as usual, kissed Maualuga, who was asleep in her father's place, washed, dressed and hurried through the rich aroma of fresh bread to the bakery. She was free of all household chores. Poto and other relatives took care of those — and the children.

The two bakers, whom she'd sent to Apia to learn the skill, were taking the bread out of the oven. The room was a sea of heat, and the bakers and their two helpers were drenched with sweat. Another hot day in Paradise, Tavita would've remarked. The horses and cart were ready outside. She checked the orders, and the helpers loaded the baskets onto the cart for distribution to stores in the neighbouring villages. She thanked the bakers, wished them well for the day and hurried to the store.

She glanced up. The sun was squatting on the rim of the range. As usual a non-stop-talking Semisi and his assistant, Feleti (but known to everyone as 'Frederiko') were serving the customers. She discussed with Semisi what needed to be done that day. 'Gosh, you still look young!' Semisi made her day.

As usual Sili, Mikaele's plantation foreman and his uncle, was waiting for her in the tool shed, where he and his six workers were having their morning meal of tea and bread. She greeted them formally. He told her what needed to be done. She approved it. As she started to leave, Sili said, 'Isn't that the *Lady Poto*?' She turned to the bay.

Tavita was standing on the prow, arms folded, as the boat nosed through the slight swell. She waved; he didn't see her.

She tried not to run as she made her way to the jetty.

The cheerful crowd, many still wrapped in their sleeping sheets, parted and let her through to the boat. Roni, Mikaele, Faranisisi and the crew were greeting their families, but she couldn't see Tavita or any passengers. She embraced Roni, then Faranisisi, and felt puny in Mikaele's huge arms. Of all the Barker children, Mikaele most resembled their father in size and appearance.

'An epidemic has started in Apia and is spreading to other parts of the country,' Mikaele told her.

'It's sweeping through the whole world, killing more people than the World War that's just ended,' Roni added.

'We left Apia before we got sick,' Faranisisi said. 'We didn't want to bring it to Satoa.'

'That's why we didn't bring passengers,' Roni said.

'Don't worry, we've had epidemics before!' Tavita declared so the crowd could hear him. He stepped over the boat railing. 'We've had smallpox, the fever, measles, mumps — and we're still here!' Some people laughed.

Peleiupu moved to him and he enveloped her in his arms and kissed her deeply. Embarrassed by this 'very papalagi behaviour', the others tried not to look. Breaking breathless from their kiss, Tavita said, 'We'll defeat the epidemic with kisses!' Most of the crowd laughed again.

Later, as they moved through the crowd, Peleiupu heard them whispering about the epidemic 'killing hundreds in Apia — killing them like flies'.

Tavita hurried her away from the others. 'It's very bad,' he whispered. 'I've instructed Roni and the others who were on the boat that if they start feeling sick they have to report to the clinic.'

They found Fa'amapu, the government nurse, bandaging a boy's knee. She'd been in Satoa for about three years, with her husband and child, and was respected. Tavita told her about the epidemic. She would prepare the clinic in case people got sick, she said. She didn't have enough medicine but would do her best. Peleiupu promised she would help her.

Most people greeted Tavita as they hurried through the village. Tavita waved and called but she sensed he was as focused on her as she was on him. The familiar burning sensation was cruising through her belly and down. A quick touch on his arm and shoulder. A long caress of his fingers over her hip, side, flank. 'Accidental' bumping of hips and thighs . . .

By the time they were on the veranda and Tavita was mobbed by their children, she was trembling almost visibly with desire. They had to be patient while the children had their breakfast — they weren't allowed to talk, but Maualuga kept breaking that rule. Peleiupu sat on her hands to still her shaking — while Galu, Poto's sister, fussed over the children and Siniva checked their clothes and combed their hair, and then took them to school. They had to be patient while Tavita answered Galu's questions about the epidemic. Then finally, pretending he was tired, Tavita got up and headed for the bedroom. Pretending she had to hurry to her office, Peleiupu left too.

At the corner of the veranda Peleiupu checked, then slid around the corner of the house and around to the back. The door to their bedroom was ajar. She pulled it back quietly and slid into the room. Every pore and nerve of her was alive — more alive than ever before.

Wearing only an ie lavalava, Tavita lay on his back on their bed, eyes shut, but she knew — and was aroused knowing — that he was only pretending to be asleep. She cherished making love to him, though she rarely came. That only happened, they had discovered, when she was aroused in her head. Usually she would take her time, savouring the sight of him caressing her body, then she would watch him arousing himself. They could be bold and take their time now they had their own bedroom. For years, she'd not enjoyed it because they'd slept and lived in communal quarters. Always confined to making love at night and noiselessly so as not to wake the others. More recently when it had become a bit routine, she found she loved describing to him how she was feeling as he made love to her. He loved it too — the frank language of sexual desire.

Now, because they'd been apart for twelve days, she needed none of that. She lifted her ie lavalava, pulled off her wet panties and, trying to suppress her throat-deep groaning, she straddled him, knees on either side of his hips. He felt full and hot in her left hand as she raised her buttocks and then lowered herself down and around him, slowly. He started moaning and moving his hips. 'Don't, don't!' she stopped him. She clutched him and moved. 'I've missed you so much, so much . . . ' She pulled off her blouse, bent forward and, holding her full breasts, she rubbed her nipples over his quivering mouth and tongue.

He pumped his hips up hard, once. She gasped. He thrust up again, then again.

'Ahh! Ahhh!' she cried each time. When he thrust up again, she remained suspended, her whole body ready to burst. Then, gasping loudly, her body broke out in long shuddering waves as she came, burying her face in the pillows, clutching his thighs between hers.

As usual they waited until her sensitivity eased, then he started moving again.

A short while later she was in her office. Relaxed, feeling utterly safe now that Tavita was back home.

Running footsteps approached; she recognised them as Poto's. 'I was at the clinic helping Fa'amapu, and they've just brought in Samani. He was in Apia with Tavita!' Poto said. 'Fa'amapu ordered me out so I wouldn't get infected. It's definitely not our Satoan Disease. He's delirious and vomiting and with the hottest fever I've ever felt. He feels as if he's going to burn to ashes!'

On their way to the clinic they tried to walk normally so as not to alarm the others. 'I've seen other epidemics, Pele,' Poto said. 'This is terrible.'

A worried group of Samani's relatives sat on the veranda, kept out there by Fa'amapu who, with Samani's mother, was covering the shivering patient with blankets and swabbing his face with a wet cloth. 'We'll sweat out his fever,' Fa'amapu told them.

As Samani complained of an overwhelming headache and then continued coughing and vomiting loudly, his mother started weeping. Poto held her shoulders and steered her to her relatives outside. 'He'll be all right. God will heal him,' she told her.

They agreed that all the people who'd been on the *Lady Poto* should be quarantined. Peleiupu instructed one of Samani's brothers to fetch Mikaele. (Tavita would still be asleep.) 'Hurry!' she urged the boy.

'You're overreacting,' Mikaele insisted when Poto told him the disease was the epidemic. She pushed him towards Samani. Peleiupu and Fa'amapu pulled the sweat-drenched blankets aside. The sight of a delirious Samani was enough. Mikaele rushed off to gather the others.

'You'll have to wake Tavita,' Peleiupu called after him.

Shortly after, Mikaele had them in the clinic, with their sleeping sheets and mats. Tavita examined Samani and confirmed that it was the epidemic he'd seen in Apia.

For a long while they sat in silence around a patient who was lapsing into a coma and looked as if he were going to disintegrate and with it shatter their lives and the prosperity and happiness they'd achieved. Outside, the people gathered.

'We must declare the clinic and the immediate area around it a quarantine zone,' Peleiupu said. 'Frightened people will not respect invisible boundaries so we must put up a fence.'

'I'll get Sao to call a meeting of the fono to issue regulations the people must follow,' Tavita suggested.

'It's too late,' Poto said. 'Best to gather all the people in the church and tell them.'

So Tavita, Mikaele and the crew hurried to the warehouse, got supplies of timber and barbed wire and started erecting a fence twenty paces from and around the clinic. Many people offered to help but Tavita sent them home to check on their families. Peleiupu wrote a notice forbidding entry into the quarantine zone, and Tavita nailed it up on the entrance.

Whenever fears of inadequacy threatened to overwhelm her, Peleiupu sought her mother's counsel. She slipped away from the clinic and hurried to the school.

The classes were still on, but Lalaga came out to see her. She told Lalaga what was happening. 'Where's Naomi?' Lalaga asked Peleiupu. 'Did Tavita stop at Manono to see how she and her children are?' Peleiupu sensed her mother was trying to hide her fears for Naomi's safety.

'No, I don't think they did, but I'm sure the epidemic hasn't reached Manono.' She tried to calm her. After graduating, Naomi had been hired as a teacher at Vaiuta and, for a few years, had refused to marry any of the young pastors Mautu and their family elders had recommended. Eventually with Lalaga's relentless encouragement, Naomi had married Pate Mufale, a widower, and they had shifted to be the pastors at Manono.

'My daughter! What's going to happen to her?' Lalaga continued. 'And what about Ruta?'

'I'll remind Tavita and Roni to visit Naomi and Pate the next time they go to Apia,' Pele replied, putting her arm around her mother as they headed for the clinic.

'We rarely see them,' Lalaga said. 'Only once a year at the Salua annual fono.' Peleiupu recalled that the rebellious Naomi had demanded that Mautu marry them in a simple ceremony at Vaiuta without the fa'a Samoa — the extravagant exchange of gifts between the two aiga. They were all surprised when Lalaga had supported her demands. Naomi and Pate now had five children, two from Pate's previous marriage.

'God will protect us but you're quite correct, Pele, we have to protect ourselves.' Lalaga whispered. 'And don't forget Ruta, send the boat to see how she is, please!'

Sao, Mautu, Vaomatua and other elders were already at the fence, challenging Tavita about his decision to declare the quarantine. Other people were milling around them. Some of Samani's relatives were complaining about not being allowed to see him. 'This is only another palagi epidemic: we've survived all the previous ones,' Sao was saying.

'What Tavita and Fa'amapu have done is absolutely right,' Lalaga told Mautu, ignoring Sao.

'Do you want this evil disease to spread?' Mautu started to challenge her.

'Do you want to die?' she attacked. That shut him up. Lalaga was franker and less diplomatic about her views. Those who didn't like her described that as being crude, cruel, brutal and arrogant. 'Tell Fa'amapu to come!' she called to Mikaele, who was sitting with the crew on the clinic veranda. Mikaele disappeared inside.

The message of the long, high-pitched wailing that erupted from the heart of the clinic was clear. Tavita ran back inside. Even before he was back, the crew members were at the fence, telling people that Samani had died.

'He must have a proper Christian burial,' Mautu insisted. Sao supported him.

'Are you stupid? If you go in there you'll rejoin us as carriers of that evil disease!' Lalaga insisted. 'You can conduct the service from here. Samani's body can be brought closer to us.'

Samani's uncle demanded that his nephew be buried on family land. Sao agreed. Peleiupu looked at Tavita, who hesitated and then said, 'Sir, we have to bury him here, away from infecting you and your family.'

'That would be burying him like an animal without a family!' the man protested.

'If I die, I too will be buried inside this fence,' Tavita consoled them. 'So will my brothers and sister. We're doing this so the epidemic doesn't kill our loved ones.'

At Lalaga's suggestion — more an order — Sao sent messengers to gather the people in the church. By this time most Satoans were in the shade around the fence. They followed Sao and Mautu to the church, oblivious to the fierce heat. Peleiupu lingered behind, too frightened to leave Tavita. 'Be brave!' Tavita called to her.

Peleiupu chose to sit at the back of the church by the main entrance. The church was packed, and smelled heavily of sweat. After Sao greeted the people, and Fa'amapu started talking about the symptoms of the epidemic, Peleiupu slipped out and hurried to the school. She looked down at the clinic. Mikaele and the remaining four crewmen were extending the barbed-wire fence along the road to the jetty, while Tavita and Roni were digging Samani's grave under the breadfruit tree to the right.

She had to get her children home and away from all sources of contamination. She had to. So she gathered them as they left their classrooms, herded them protesting to the house, instructed Tavita's sister Siniva and Galu to keep them inside and rushed back down to the clinic.

Tavita came up to the fence, dressed in a clean ie lavalava and singlet, after cleaning off the sweat and dirt from digging the grave. How she wanted to reach over and hold him! He told her Samani's body was being prepared for burial. What about a coffin? she reminded him. No time for that, he replied. They'll wrap him up in mats, like they used to in pre-Christian times.

'His skin has turned blue,' Tavita said. 'Strange. Fa'amapu says he may have contracted pneumonia, too.'

Roni, Mikaele and Faranisisi joined them. Faranisisi, who usually radiated energy and invulnerable confidence, looked pale and frightened. She was Peleiupu's favourite sister-in-law, the most intelligent of the Barkers' children, quick at reading what was happening, adept and clever at negotiating — marrying different people's and groups' interests no matter how divergent. She was still single, though Poto, Vaomatua and Semisi had tried matchmaking her with a string of men. Whenever she turned down a suitor, Poto criticised her loudly, but Sao always said, 'Leave my granddaughter alone. He's ugly anyway, and a nobody!'

Poto came and stood across from Faranisisi. 'You feeling well?' she asked the ones who were on the boat. They nodded; Faranisisi looked away. 'The Almighty will be kind to us,' Poto said. 'He will withhold His wrath.' The others looked at the ground.

Roni coughed and Peleiupu caught him gazing at her. He looked away; he could never look anyone in the face. Some Satoans called him 'Roni Soso' behind his back. With his hunched shoulders and thin frame, he moved and spoke slowly, reinforcing the impression that he was not very intelligent. But Peleiupu knew that Roni was quick-witted, cunning and fearless. During crises he was cool, didn't panic, and formulated solutions carefully. He was also loved for his guitar playing. And loved most of all by Semisi, who would defend him to the death.

When he was twenty, with rumours circulating about two pregnancies, Roni had told Poto he was going abroad, and left before the Barker clan could discuss his request. (The Barkers always discussed such matters as a group.) They were so confident in his ability to survive, they didn't worry about him too much. Then four years later, on Christmas morning just before lotu, he returned, sliding smoothly into their midst and occupying his usual post, as if he'd never been away. He brought with him an American accent, an even slower manner of speech, traces of grey hair, gifts for everyone, a weakness for whisky and his black guitar, and an almost total silence about where he'd been and what he'd done. Once, when drunk, he boasted he'd been to the Tsar's palace in Moscow, the King's palace in London and the White House in Washington, and had tasted ice and snow.

Because he loved Peleiupu he took her aside not long after his return and told her the stories he'd gathered about Arona or people who could've been Arona. How in San Francisco he'd happened to mention Arona and a Spaniard at the bar had said he'd spent three trips on a British ship, with a Polynesian called Aaron Midas as first mate, who'd treated him kindly and talked incessantly about one day returning home to his ageing parents. How on another ship, a Portuguese one, Roni had been told of a

Polynesian sailor who'd bragged he was the 'last pagan on Earth', who would eat any Christian who tried to convert him; everyone had been afraid of him. How sailors across the seas were talking about a group of South Sea Islanders, led by a man called Aaron Knife, who controlled any ship they signed on. Yes, the stories were so real — but where was he? Peleiupu wondered.

Most amazing of all was Roni's ability on the guitar and the songs he sang in Russian, English, French, German and Maori, the language of the Tangata Maori of New Zealand. Whenever he played and sang, the Satoans, especially the young ones, flocked to him.

Poto told everyone that Roni was too soso to catch a woman. But within a few months of his captaining the *Lady Poto* his notoriety for drinking and 'catching' women spread rapidly. Poto threatened that God was going to have him swallowed by a whale. A few times when Roni returned drunk, Sao beat him with his beautiful ebony walking stick with the pearl-shell inlays, which Roni had given him on his return.

When the rumour spread that he had the 'fire illness', his brothers jokingly told him the fire would 'burn off his naughty, unruly firestick'.

Then he brought home Pa'ugata, a no-nonsense, well-organised woman who mothered him, controlled his drinking, and produced three children he adored. With Pa'ugata around they expected him to stop 'catching' other women but he didn't — he claimed it wasn't his fault: the women were catching him! Pa'ugata ignored those rumours: to her, her handsome husband was an excellent father and a scrupulously faithful husband. When Semisi's mouth got out of hand (again) and he praised Roni for 'hooking many wild catches and fattening them with his delicious roe', Pa'ugata lost her cool, and Mikaele and Tavita had to restrain her from bushknifing off Semisi's own catching instrument.

How Roni got the alcohol they would never know, but they all knew he'd been drinking when, as he was leaning against the quarantine fence, he started singing softly:

> The sadness is coming.
> We will live in the House of Sorrow.
> So we must prepare for that
> and face the Terror . . .

'Don't say that!' Poto ordered him.

'Mother, I am not talking, I am singing!' Roni retorted. 'You know the song.'

Before Poto could stop him, he continued:

> We cannot turn the Terror away,
> We cannot stay God's wrathful hand . . .

And when Mikaele's booming voice provided the bass, and Faranisisi the soprano, Poto turned impatiently to Tavita who looked away and joined the singing.

> So we must be brave,
> we must try and understand God's design . . .

Peleiupu and the others joined in too.

As the power of their hymn of praise and courage allayed their fears of the epidemic, Poto finally joined in.

Samani's uncle and relatives carried out Samani's mat-wrapped body and laid it on mats at the quarantine entrance. They continued singing as they waited for Mautu and Lalaga to come and conduct the funeral service.

That evening at lotu, Sao and Poto suggested they shift their meal to the clinic. When they got there, other aiga were outside the fence, eating with the quarantined people. Two large fires illuminated the area and kept away most of the mosquitoes. Peleiupu and her children sat by the fence opposite Tavita and shared their food with him. The children monopolised him; their rapid-fire conversation distracted Peleiupu from her fear. When she gazed up into the heavens, the black depths of space sucked up her breath and made her feel puny and abandoned to the mercy of the epidemic.

When Mikaele slid up and sat beside Tavita, the children demanded that he tell them a story. Peleiupu thought of Mikaele as Tavita's shadow — following, supporting and enforcing Tavita's decisions. Most men were afraid of him for once he decided to enforce a family or fono decision, he tolerated no opposition. He maintained long periods of silence but when he spoke it was in amazing, intense, poetic language. 'He's inherited my gift for storytelling,' Sao boasted to everyone. 'No, he hasn't!' Mautu contradicted Sao behind Sao's boastful back. 'He's inherited it from his father, Barker!'

Mikaele rose and started pacing around the fire. The flames threw his gigantic shadow over the clinic and his audience, who pressed in closer. Maualuga snuggled into Peleiupu's lap, curled up and started sucking her thumb.

'I begin our story . . . ' Mikaele started, voice low and inviting. 'I begin our story with a couple: their names were Eleele and Lagi. They lived and lived and a girl was born. They called her Olatasi. They lived and lived and another child was born, another girl, Olalua. Then Olatolu, Olafa, Olalima, Olaono and, most beautiful of all, Olafitu.' He beckoned the children closer. Lowering his voice, he continued, 'As they grew, their parents observed that each one was immune to certain diseases. For instance, Olatasi was immune to all diseases except one, the common cold. Olalua was immune to all except ringworm and filiariasis. Olatolu was susceptible to three: yaws, tinea and arthritis; Olafa to four: diarrhoea, stomach ulcers, headaches and fever . . .'

Peleiupu realised that the diseases were all pre-papalagi ones.

'. . . So you can say that their youngest and favourite daughter, Olafitu, was the most vulnerable to disease. And so forth. But they weren't so concerned about their children's health because Lagi was a gifted healer who could cure all the illnesses . . .'

As Peleiupu was snared by the story, she realised Mikaele was deliberately conjuring up a tale to tie it in with the threat of the epidemic.

'. . . As they blossomed into beautiful women, tales of their beauty and special immunities spread throughout Samoa, and suitors came to court them. Nearly all of them chose Olatasi because not only was she as beautiful as the others but she was also vulnerable to only one disease. The least desirable was Olafitu, of course. The parents married Olatasi to the most aristocratic suitor, the son of the Tui-Manu'a; Olalua to the second most aristocratic, the son of the Tui-A'ana; Olatolu to the next one, and so on until only Olafitu was left.' He paused. 'Poor Olafitu, poor Olafitu!' he sighed. 'No one wanted to marry her because she was the one most open to death.' Then, looking slyly at his audience, he said, 'The stories that are our lives have strange ways of unfolding, eh?' Straightening up suddenly, arms akimbo as if he were going to encompass them all, he continued. 'Yes, every year Olafitu, spurned by suitors, struggled to survive her seven maladies, with her mother's healing powers. She struggled with the pain, and through that learned about the ways of curing herself. She learned, yes, she learned . . .'

Mikaele went on to tell about the successful and blessed lives of the other sisters, while Olafitu was left to care for their ageing parents. Until one morning they found a strange castaway unconscious on their beach. 'A slender, hairless man with eyes as luminous blue as a morning sky, ears like those of a pig, a sharp nose that pointed at you like a small knifeblade, and who wore a double skin and things like shoes . . .'

'Like a papalagi?' I'amafana offered.

'Yes, like a papalagi but there were no papalagi in those days,' Mikaele replied. 'And he wasn't a Samoan either. So he must've come from a place outside the then-known world.'

'Aotearoa?' Sao offered.

'Perhaps where he was from is not important to our story,' Mikaele said. 'What is important is that he was from a world not then known to our ancestors.' The audience murmured their agreement. 'Olafitu suggested that they take him to Lagi to be healed. They did. Lagi checked him, and found there was nothing visibly wrong with the stranger. But she couldn't revive him.' Mikaele paused and looked slowly around the audience. 'Because Olafitu had learned from her illnesses not to trust surface wellness, Olafitu wanted to isolate the stranger from the village, just in case, but even her mother dismissed her caution. "He looks harmless," she laughed. "Like a baby!" So as the story about the stranger, 'the sleeping baby', spread, crowds gathered to see him. Even Olafitu's sisters and their families came to see. The elders allowed them to touch his body, breathe his breath, joke about his appearance: after all, they were immune to most diseases. Only Olafitu kept well away from him.'

'Olaono and her three children were the first to die, three days later; then Olalima and her three children three days after that; then Olafa and her children three days later, and so on. With them died many others until there were only the 'sleeping baby', Olafitu and her parents, and twelve others who'd not visited the stranger. For about a week Olafitu tried to save her parents but they died too. The disease was like an inevitable sleep you drifted into and didn't want to wake from, with no physical symptoms. This was truly a malady from outside their world — that was why even her sisters were not immune to it. But why was Olafitu not infected by it, especially when, of her whole family, she was the most vulnerable to disease? Helped by the few survivors, she took the 'baby' out beyond the reef, tied anchors to it, and dropped it into the depths out of which it had come. They burned all the remaining corpses and buried their ashes.' He stopped and Peleiupu knew he wasn't going to continue.

'What happened after that?' Sao demanded. The audience chorused.

'Well, Olafitu and the other twelve survivors rebuilt our whole civilisation out of that great tragedy and sorrow.'

'Yes, but what can we learn from that story?' Mautu demanded.

Peleiupu waited eagerly for Mikaele's reply.

He shrugged his shoulders, smiled sadly and said, 'Olafitu never married!' Disappointed, they waited.

'So she never married — what's that got to do with the meaning of the story?' Mautu demanded.

'It's up to you what Olafitu's story means,' Mikaele replied. The audience was very dissatisfied. 'Do stories have to have moral lessons? Meaning?' Mikaele asked. 'Do they have to be about our condition? Can't they just be spellbinding stories that fire our imaginations, make us feel more than we are, make us want to conjure up more stories? Can't they just be about other stories?'

Many of the children were asleep. They were picked up and piggy-backed home. It was colder and Peleiupu wrapped her sleeping sheet around her body. The elders left. She joined Pa'ugata, Roni, Tavita, Mikaele and Faranisisi around the fire, which had collapsed into red embers and ash. The chorus of cicadas had subsided but Peleiupu could still hear it in her memory. As it grew darker, the features of her loved ones around the fire disappeared, but she sensed Tavita's intense and concerned scrutiny. That morning, when they'd made love, her senses had been extravagantly alive, more so than ever before. Now, though her senses remained heightened and lucid, it was not to the joys of life but to the fear of death claiming those she loved. She knew it was only a matter of time before the epidemic — the hairless, blue-eyed, sleeping baby — would strike at her family. Her hand reached through the fence to Tavita who withdrew and reminded her of possible contamination. 'What are we going to do?' she whispered. 'Pray and hope God protects us,' he replied, his voice devoid of conviction.

A cold, wet hand touched her forehead. The numerous presences that had been crowding around her vanished. It was not yet half-past five but she washed and dressed quickly in the dark, groped her way into their children's rooms and, after checking that they were still breathing, hurried out into the dawn that was starting to lick the dew-covered malae.

The people on the clinic veranda were still asleep. She hurried around the fence until she was looking into the ward. Fa'amapu, Mikaele and Tavita were working on two blanket-wrapped patients who were shivering uncontrollably. Her heart danced knowing that Tavita was well, but when she saw his tears, she *knew*. She could not see Faranisisi anywhere. Tavita was rising and stumbling through the ward, over the fence and into her arms. 'The quarantine is not working. Some people who didn't come with us to Apia are sick too,' he said. He tried to hold her back but she pushed him away and rushed into the ward.

Mikaele glanced up at her. Peleiupu fell to her knees and embraced Faranisisi, who was on fire and melting away in Peleiupu's grasp. 'Aue, aue, Faranisisi, don't go!'

Suddenly Poto was wrenching Faranisisi away and, cradling her to her body, wailing and wailing as if the essence of all grief were the piercing lone sound of her voice. 'My daughter, my daughter!' she cried. 'My beloved!'

'Poto, Poto,' Faranisisi cried, clutching her belly, 'help me, they're taking out the lining of my insides! The pain!'

Tavita held Peleiupu and half-carried her away from Poto and Faranisisi. Mikaele and Roni followed them. 'Pele, you're better than any of us at organising. What are we going to do?' Tavita pleaded. 'Look at me, Pele. We need you to plan what we have to do.'

Through the tears and sobbing, they discussed and agreed on a plan. The clinic needed medical supplies and a doctor — Roni and a crew would go on the *Lady Poto* to Apia and get those; the people would need food — Mikaele was to organise the men to ensure that food supplies were adequate, inspect every family daily, bring the sick to the clinic, and bury the dead; all gatherings were to be banned — the school would be shut indefinitely; Peleiupu would organise the women to help Fa'amapu nurse the sick, and enforce high standards of hygiene and sanitation in the village. 'Be brave!' Tavita called before they dispersed to carry out their various duties.

Peleiupu re-entered the clinic reluctantly. Another crewman had died. The ward was crowded with mourners. Sao, Vaomatua, Semisi and other relatives were with Poto and Faranisisi, who was cauled in that luminous aura Peleiupu had first seen around Barker when she was a child. The aura was illuminating every detail of Faranisisi as she struggled to breathe. 'My beloved, don't go!' Poto kept crooning, but Faranisisi seemed at home in her birthsac. Peleiupu watched Faranisisi's body and breath relax slowly in acceptance, in Poto's arms.

She turned and left. There was much to do, and her methodical and defiant mother would help her. On her way out she instructed Mikaele to dig Faranisisi's grave among those of their ancestors by the faletele, and then to help the other aiga dig graves for their dead.

Lalaga was in the church, preparing it for the funeral services. Peleiupu told her about Faranisisi and the other dead. The bodies must be buried as soon as possible, Lalaga agreed and said she would notify the aiga that there would be one funeral service at midday. 'We will survive; we will defeat the epidemic. God will help us,' Lalaga whispered, 'Have you heard from Ruta?'

Peleiupu shook her head. 'But I'm sure God's protecting her and Lefatu.'

At her house Peleiupu sent Galu to gather the senior women, and while she waited she tried to console her children and Siniva about Faranisisi's death. 'Why did God take her away?' Lefatu asked. Holding Siniva, she told her it was her responsibility now to help Poto and Semisi run the stores. 'Forget your grief; you have a very important job to do. As the people become less capable of caring for themselves, you will have to use our stores and plantation to feed them.' She sent her to fetch Sili, Tavita's uncle who managed their plantation.

After she had explained to Sili that their plantation was to supply food for the whole village as the epidemic worsened, she told him to take his family and some of their relatives to help in that work. 'Keep away from the village and contamination,' she instructed him.

'Shall I take your children to live with us?' he suggested. Of all Sao's children, he was the most loyal and hardworking, ashamed if he had to live off others.

With Siniva's help, Peleiupu packed a bag of clothes for Maualuga and Lefatu. The boys refused to go. Lefatu sobbed into Peleiupu's shoulder. 'Look after your sister,' Peleiupu whispered.

Sili gathered up Maualuga, and Peleiupu turned her back as they left. Be safe, please be safe!

'This way, some of our children may live,' Peleiupu justified her decision to Tavita later. 'And I trust Sili with my life.'

At the midday funeral service Peleiupu again sat at the back. Many of the people wheezed and coughed. 'My beloved sister was not killed by God,' Tavita ended his eulogy for Faranisisi. 'God does not kill good people. She was killed by arrogant papalagi administrators who allowed a ship, the SS *Talune*, to dock in Apia, despite warnings it had the epidemic on board. American authorities did not allow that cursed ship into American Samoa; consequently the epidemic has not struck them.' Wiping his eyes, he vowed, 'We must never forgive them for killing our loved ones!'

After Mautu's sermon consoling the mourners, Sao shuffled up to the front. Fiercely he stabbed his walking stick into the air and declared, 'Our whole village now supports the movement for self-government. We must drive these foreigners from our land. For too long we have suffered their arrogance! As a boy I watched my father and many relatives die in a mumps epidemic, my aunts and friends die in a smallpox epidemic, a sister and brother and half our village in a measles epidemic. All introduced by the papalagi. Now they have killed my granddaughter and your children!' He started sobbing. Vaomatua and Poto helped him back to his seat.

Angry and defiant as they carried the dead out to the graves, the Satoans were still with hope that the epidemic would not be too severe or, if it was, that they would have the will and strength to overcome it. But Peleiupu could not afford such hope: she had to prepare for the worst.

Third day of the epidemic. The room was languid and smelt of dried sweat as Peleiupu moved through it. Galu was snoring softly. Beside her was Siniva. She went to her sons across the room, shut her eyes, reached down and placed her fingers against the side of I'amafana's neck. His pulse was strong; his temperature was normal. She sighed, relieved. Caressed his cheek and moved to Iakopo who was curled into a ball. He was well too, she concluded.

With Mautu, Lalaga and two other matai they started their inspection of the village. Mikaele and a group of young men followed her. Everything was clearly defined in the bright morning light. All around them was the sound of coughing and vomiting and exclamations of pain.

In the nearest fale, the family were still asleep. No sickness, the mother told Peleiupu. The next fale had a sick mother and baby. They checked the rest of the family and instructed them to take their sick to the clinic. The husband protested; the others started weeping. Mautu consoled them, and told them why the sick must be shifted.

Five people were sick in the next four families. From the small fale by the beach came muted weeping for the dead. They hurried to it and found that their matai had just died. Peleiupu and Lalaga helped his wife bathe and dress the body, which was now darkish blue.

The rest of their inspection found three more dead and fifteen at various stages of the illness. Mikaele and his men helped shift the sick to the clinic, and complained of the stench of diarrhoea that now tainted the sick.

When they returned to the clinic, they found three more had died. Peleiupu felt as if she were trapped in an endless buzzing sound. Real yet unreal. There was a smell in the air that nagged at her to identify. Nagged at her. Nagged.

Mikaele and his men dug graves wherever the mourners wanted them. He told Peleiupu it was getting too difficult to dig individual graves — many of his helpers were sick or falling sick. She consulted Tavita, Sao and Mautu. The first mass grave — a long trench — would be dug by the clinic alongside the road to the jetty.

After the women had helped the families wrap the bodies in mats, the men carried them to the church. Seven in all. They were laid on mats in front of the pulpit. Only about half the congregation attended the service. Many were sick, most were nursing the sick, many were afraid of being infected.

The service was short. In the pulpit Mautu looked emaciated, pale, tired, lost in grief. He spoke of hope and faith in God's ultimate compassion and forgiveness. Peleiupu sensed that most of the people were too deep in grief to hear.

All day Peleiupu helped Fa'amapu and the other women at the clinic. The medical supplies ran out and they tried indigenous medicines and cures. But by evening lotu, two more had died and some of their helpers had fallen sick.

Two more would die in the clinic during the night.

At home, without meaning to, Peleiupu fell asleep waiting for Tavita, who was helping dig the mass grave. He woke her. He started falling asleep on his feet as she washed him down with buckets of water, dried him and led him to bed. She asked him if he was hungry. He murmured that he was too tired even to grieve. He curled up and slept.

Even though it was stifling hot, she wrapped herself around Tavita from the back. For a moment he struggled to be free, then relaxed and started snoring. They burned and sweated into each other and, as sleep eased into her eyes, the persistent, tenacious sound of coughing picked at the edge of her hearing, replacing the healing, lulling sound of the sea that she had heard all her life.

Fifth day. Frantically Siniva woke Peleiupu. Galu was delirious and vomiting, complaining of pain in her limbs. Vaomatua and Poto were with her already. Peleiupu got Siniva to take the children out of the room. She made Galu drink the liquid cough medicine but she vomited it up in explosive gasps. 'What are we going to do?' Poto asked. Peleiupu refused to admit that Galu could not be saved, that the epidemic was an all-powerful creature that was laughing at her.

There had been two childless marriages in Galu's life, so she'd devoted her boundless affection to Poto's children, her nieces and nephews, and now to Peleiupu's children. She had demanded little for herself and hated asking for help, but Peleiupu always ensured she was treated as well as Poto. And all her wards indulged her. Before her nephews grew into fearsome men, many suitors had courted her, and she had allowed a few furtive affairs to happen. However, a slick-talking government interpreter, who came with the Governor, had secretly wooed and won her. He promised to return and marry her, but didn't, and Tavita and Mikaele and Roni had fautasied into Apia, traced the culprit to his office and pulverised not only him but those who came to his aid. After that the number of suitors — even the confident ones — had decreased drastically. However, when her nephews matured and understood her loneliness, they encouraged her to accept suitors — even arranged them without her knowledge. But Galu turned them all down, including the famous widowed, retired, ex-New Guinea missionary whom Sao had ordered her to marry.

When Peleiupu saw the luminous aura begin cauling Galu, she left the room and lay down beside Tavita, too afraid to tell him.

At dawn Vaomatua's piercing wailing hooked Peleiupu and sent her scrambling to Galu.

Only half their inspection team turned up later that morning. Most of them were too tired and overwhelmed with grief. Mikaele arrived with only a few of his helpers. Despite Galu's death, Sao insisted on accompanying the team. He shuffled along as if the air were the weight of the whole universe, and wept whenever they found the dying.

Their inspection yielded nine sick and three dead. In the last fale they found Pili, a one-year-old, playing in his excrement beside his dead parents. Lalaga cleaned him up and took him home to look after. 'Another son,' she said.

Peleiupu stopped as the others headed for the clinic. From the sea wafted the smell of coral and salt and fertile life, and that other smell she still couldn't identify. All the dew-drenched fale with their lowered blinds looked as if they were under the total siege of the epidemic. No one dared move about.

At the midday burial service, the church was only half full. The twelve dead were buried side by side in the mass grave. Mikaele insisted on carrying Galu, who had raised him, down into the trench. He kissed the head of the bundle and scrambled back up, whimpering as he stumbled from the grave. 'You're an arsehole, an arsehole!' he screamed at the sky.

Along the grave's edge stood all the people Galu had raised. Wheezing, coughing, shivering. Head lowered, hands on his walking stick, which he had stabbed into the edge, Sao gazed down at his dead daughter. Most of the mourners had their heads covered with ie lavalava as if they were offering themselves to the epidemic's unforgiving axe. Yes, arsehole, arsehole! Peleiupu wanted to shout at the epidemic.

Eighth day. Peleiupu was suddenly aware that she was trapped in the heavy liquid-like tiredness of her body. She tried to pull herself out of that body, desperately afraid it was going to die with her in its grip. She watched herself, an elastic creature, hands and feet digging into the chest and belly of her body, pushing down, pulling up, long gum-like strings detaching from her body as she did so. Pull, pull! The strings snapped in loud twangs, but new strings appeared and pulled her down. She heard her throat making frantic gulping sounds as she tried to breathe. Her arms and legs started jerking intermittently. Leg. Arm. Leg. Arm . . . The jerking became wild flailing as she struggled to stay out of the drowning, out of the thick liquid that was pouring into her mouth. Help! Help! Help! And she was awake and almost crying with relief, knowing it had only been a dream.

She lay gazing up at the early morning light swimming in waves across the ceiling. Wiped the sweat off her face and dried her armpits with a towel. It was so good to be alive. So good. But when she looked at Tavita, who was in a foetal position wrapped tightly in his sleeping sheet, she remembered the unforgiving, rapacious creature out there, and her joy at being alive turned again to fear and the desire to sleep.

Body, rise! Yes, roll off this bed. Feet, stand firmly on the floor and hold me up! Good. Left foot forward. Now right foot. Good, good. Peleiupu followed her feet step by step to her children's room.

Siniva was purring softly. Across the room Iakopo lay on his side, his chest rising and falling. When she saw I'amafana, her panic stirred like a trapped bird. She took one step at a time — five steps to reach him. She still could not see any movement. Forced her left hand down towards his throat. Stopped. Pushed again. Her fingers discerned a faint pulse in the side of his neck. She pressed harder. The beat seemed regular, but she knew he had a high temperature. He stirred. His eyes opened suddenly and she was gazing down into their depths. 'Mama, I'm not feeling well,' he said. 'My back, my stomach — the pain!'

Peleiupu felt his forehead, held his right wrist and took his pulse. One step at a time. Slow down. Pour a glass of water and make him drink the medicine. She undressed him, wiped his body with cold water until he was feeling cool, then she bundled him up in a clean sheet and blanket. He complained he was hot — very hot. 'We have to reduce your fever,' she told him.

Siniva sat down beside her. Iakopo woke and joined them. 'Shall I tell Tavita?' he offered.

'No!' Peleiupu ordered. 'What are we going to do?' She asked Siniva, who wound her arm around her shoulders and reminded her that Roni and the *Lady Poto* were due back soon with new medical supplies and, perhaps, with a skilled government physician who knew how to cure this new papalagi fever. There it was: hope, again. Hope for her son. Siniva also advised that Tavita, at least, should be told about I'amafana.

Tavita was still asleep on his back, arms outstretched over the pillows. 'He . . . he is . . . he is sick!' Peleiupu lengthened the sentence as she moved to the bed. 'He . . . he is . . . he is sick!' Like a chant that, if repeated correctly would effect the healing. Like a prayer that, if intoned correctly, would persuade God to grant her her desperate wish. 'I'a . . . I'ama . . . I'amafana. I'amafana . . . I'amafana is . . . I'amafana is sick, Tavita!' Tavita stirred and turned his head towards her. 'Tavita, Tavita, our . . . our son is . . .' She was locked in his eyes. He sat up and shook his head. 'Yes, Tavita, our son is ill!' He continued shaking his head. Before she could catch him he was escaping from the room and out of reach of her prayer.

Poto, Vaomatua, Sao and Mautu circled I'amafana's bed while Lalaga nursed him. Silent, beaten, riven with grief, they were the elders of a community who no longer knew how to save that community. Peleiupu stepped into that equation. No sign of Iakopo, Siniva or Tavita. She rushed to Lalaga, who engulfed her in her arms the way she used to when she was a child searching for comfort and consolation. And for the first time since the epidemic invaded Satoa, Peleiupu released all her fears, pain and anguish. Her high-pitched, breathless screaming settled into an endless cry that circled the room, thrust out over the malae and through the church and clinic and all the fale of Satoa, searching and searching for God's mercy.

Poto sent people to look for Tavita. She was told Tavita had taken Iakopo into the bush. 'I'amafana is sick; why isn't he here?' Poto chastised him.

God was not merciful: I'amafana's condition worsened. And as Lalaga and Poto fought for his life, Peleiupu withdrew into a fearful silence. Mautu held her and took her to her bedroom, where he fanned her as she lay on the bed, clutching I'amafana's shirt. 'Our forgiving Father will save him!' Mautu told her.

'Don't, don't say that to me!' she attacked. 'God doesn't care about us. He is killing even our children!'

'God did not bring this epidemic — the papalagi did. You heard what Tavita said in church.'

'But God is doing nothing to stop it! He is a worthless, cruel God!' When her father started to counter her, she said, 'Only real people and real things and our efforts can save us, Papa. Roni and the medicines and doctor I hope he is bringing today.'

But the *Lady Poto* did not arrive that day. And Tavita did not come to be with Peleiupu when I'amafana died near midnight.

Peleiupu sent everyone away. She bathed him, oiled him with coconut oil until the whole room was reflected in his skin, dressed him in his favourite shirt and ie lavalava, selected their finest sleeping mats and siapo from under their bed, wrapped him in those, and tied it with sinnet Sao had plaited.

She sensed Tavita even before he opened the door and entered. 'This is your son,' she said, pointing at the mat-wrapped body on their bed. 'Pick him up!' He hesitated. 'Pick him up!' He stooped down and, in one sweeping motion, swept up the body.

Following Tavita and I'amafana, she picked up the two lamps and marched out and up the corridor and through the sitting room where the elders were waiting, and into the night. Lalaga and the others tried to follow. 'No, no, no!' she called.

When they returned at dawn, only Sao dared ask her where his great-grandson was buried. 'Not even the epidemic will ever know,' she promised.

Ninth day. Peleiupu and Tavita sat in their bedroom, gazing out at the bay. Peleiupu said, 'The epidemic has dealt us the blow we dreaded most. The worst. But we're still standing. I'm not afraid of it any more.' The early morning light seemed to be emanating from the heart of the bay, and spreading out across the still water. In the wind was that smell.

'The *Lady Poto* is coming,' Tavita said. 'Look!' They watched it as it crossed the golden water and docked at the jetty.

'I want Iakopo to be with me wherever I go,' Peleiupu said.

They collected their remaining son as they headed for the jetty.

On the jetty was a small crowd, mainly their relatives. Pa'ugata and her children milled around Roni, who looked more gaunt and drawn. Iakopo ran to his cousins. Behind Roni stood a short, bespectacled man with a large balding head, chunky body and legs, and wearing khaki shorts and a white shirt. He was holding a small suitcase. 'The authorities wouldn't release any doctors to us,' Roni said. 'This is Malie. He's been working at the hospital with the German doctors for a long time,' Roni introduced the stranger. They shook hands. 'We've also brought medical supplies we were able to buy, borrow or steal. Apia is short of them, for reasons I don't need to tell you.'

'I hope I can help,' Malie said.

'We also had to pay exorbitant prices for the supplies and the goods,' Roni added.

'Did you see Naomi?' Peleiupu remebered.

'Yes, we called into Manono, but she refused to come with us: they have to stay and help their people,' Roni replied.

'You tell Lalaga that,' Peleiupu instructed him. 'Did you see Ruta?'

'We didn't have time to go to Fagaloto,' Roni replied.

'You tell Lalaga that too.'

Peleiupu led Malie to the clinic, explaining to him what they'd been doing.

'I've never seen any epidemic like this before,' Malie said. 'No one, not even the scientists in Europe, know what is causing it.'

'Are you saying there is no cure?' Peleiupu asked, reluctantly.

He shook his head, saying, 'But we shouldn't let the others know, should we? To have hope is a cure, isn't it?' He paused. 'Many also develop pneumonia — that causes their skin to go dark blueish — it's not the Black Plague.'

While they unloaded the boat Roni said that he and his crew had been forced to break into some stores and the hospital pharmacy at night, to get the supplies they needed. Because many of the police and store owners were dead or sick, security in Apia was lax.

Tavita and Mikaele arranged quickly for the boat's cargo to be shared, daily, among all the families. 'For free?' Semisi asked.

'What the hell do you think?' snapped Mikaele. 'Do you want us to profit from others' misery?'

'That's enough!' Tavita intervened.

They then arranged for the well members of the aumaga to take care of all the plantations and distribute the produce to those who needed it. Others were to go fishing daily.

That morning's inspection produced ten sick, three dead; they buried nine that day, including one of Roni's crew.

Mautu and Sao decided to shorten the service and hold it by the grave. Iakopo and other boys had to help Mikaele and his diminishing group of men carry the bodies to the grave and bury them. Many relatives were too sick to attend the funeral for their dead.

At the clinic they were impressed with Malie's manner and skills. While he worked he also trained Fa'amapu, Peleiupu and his other helpers. Even Peleiupu was inspired, though she knew there was no cure.

That evening Peleiupu, Lalaga and Poto stayed on at the clinic. They ate with the patients and their relatives, and then continued helping Malie, in shifts, through the night.

Four died — no loud weeping, just a silent resignation and farewell prayers. After the four bodies were prepared for burial their relatives left quietly for home. Peleiupu told Malie that the four victims had survived longer than previous ones. That was a good sign, he said. They were entering the second phase of the epidemic. In Apia, where the epidemic had struck first, more and more people were surviving longer. He didn't know why.

At dawn a baby girl died in Malie's arms. He handed her to her grief-stricken mother and rushed out of the clinic. They heard his sobbing above the roaring of the surf on the reef. They were to learn later that Malie had lost his wife and four children to the epidemic.

The stench of death, as it worsened, seemed to produce with it larger and larger swarms of flies.

Fourteenth day. It seemed as if she'd been asleep for only a few minutes when Iakopo woke her and, handing her the clothes she'd asked him to bring, said he had to rush back home and help Tavita and Uncle Mikaele and his cousins make the largest umu ever made in Satoa because they had to cook enough food for everyone. Couldn't he talk to her for a while? He shook his head and said that after making the umu, Mama Poto wanted him and his cousins to sweep out the church, and after that Papa Mautu wanted him to beat the lali for church, and after that, while the morning service was on, Uncle Mikaele wanted him and his cousins to help collect the sick and the dead. Wasn't he afraid of being infected? she asked. 'If I get it, I get it,' he said. What about the dead? she pursued him. 'What about them?' he replied. Wasn't he afraid of them? Shaking his head curtly, he said, 'I know all of them well and they know me well, so they won't harm me. We're all aiga, remember?'

Yes, the wisdom of the innocent was amazing, she thought as he watched him running across the malae. The living, the sick, the dead, the future were indeed all aiga — family — sharing everything.

There was an acrid smell of fire and ash. Only a few columns of smoke rose from the kitchen fale; most people were too sick to cook their usual Sunday umu. The grieving for I'amafana began to swamp her again; she got up and continued working with the patients.

Even before the lali sounded for the morning service, eight more patients and two dead were brought to the clinic. The few who struggled to carry them were exhausted and sick, and most of them returned home immediately after. The ward and verandas of the clinic were now crowded with the sick and dying. Though they were meticulous in cleaning and disinfecting everything, the smell of vomit, blood, urine and excrement lingered. Through that, the unidentifiable smell kept taunting Peleiupu.

When she saw Mautu and Sao leading the small congregation and realised they were shifting the morning service to the clinic, she slipped out the back way, jumped down onto the beach and headed for the jetty. She had to shield her eyes from the painful glare of the sun on the white sand and the water.

The jetty and *Lady Poto* were deserted. Needing shade, she boarded the boat and, sitting down on the deck area, gazed out to sea. The boat rocked gently under her, and, as she melted into that rhythm, and the detailed memories of her son filled the blank whiteness of the horizon, she lay back and wept . . .

She awoke to the rich odour of octopus cooked in coconut cream, and hot palusami and taro, and sat up. 'Our food is ready,' Iakopo said. Tavita was standing beside him. The food was on two foodmats beside her.

'It didn't take us long to find you, Pele,' Tavita said. 'Did you have a good sleep?'

'Yes, free of the epidemic for a while.'

'Iakopo, you say our grace,' he told their son, who closed his eyes and raced through the memorised family grace, and then shifted over to share his mother's foodmat.

She looked at their food. Iakopo waited for her and then said, to encourage her, 'I helped Sao make the palusami.'

At once she broke off a piece of taro and dug it into a palusami. As she chewed, Iakopo watched her. 'Tastes very good,' she congratulated him. 'You're a great palusami maker!'

'He helped me make the octopus dish too,' Tavita said.

As she watched her son digging hungrily into the food, her appetite returned and she joined him. When she looked over, Tavita was also eating.

'What's the matter, Pele?' Iakopo interrupted her, a while later.

'Your brother should be here, eating with us,' Tavita saved her. 'He's not here

— but he is here, and will always be with us.'

Every Sunday after to'ona'i everyone slept, or tried to sleep. So apart from the coughing, the crowded clinic was quiet as they passed it. However, when they reached the edge of the malae it hit them. Everything in Satoa had a story, a memory, of their dead son. So their walk through the village in the heat was one of navigating that pain, which intensified with every memory. There, by the pandanus, I'amafana had fallen and grazed his right knee; there on the malae he'd played his first game of kilikiti — a duck; there in front of their faletele he'd been told off by Sao for pissing; there and there and there; that smell, that sound, that . . . In his death, he'd become the whole world of Satoa. Iakopo sensed his parents' pain, so he reached out and held their hands.

Alone in their bedroom, Peleiupu and Tavita held on to each other and the enormous absence of their son, which they knew they had to live with for the rest of their lives.

'I want to die, I want to die!' Tavita whispered.

Fifteenth day. They were surprised when Semisi and Feleti brought them their morning meal. On two large trays covered with embroidered hand towels were papaya, mango, fresh bread and jam, and koko. In the middle of each tray, in small vases, were small branches of gardenia blossom. 'A real palagi breakfast for real Samoans!' Semisi declared, placing a tray on Peleiupu's belly. 'Don't get out of bed.' He sat down by Peleiupu's legs while Feleti, a large figure with rolls of fat, sat down beside Tavita's. 'You need cheering up — this bloody Fa'ama'i is a hungry bitch!' And before they knew it, Semisi started bawling into his hands. 'It's not fair; God's not fair!' he cried. Feleti started crying too. Tavita put his arms around both of them and drew them in to his sides.

'It's not bloody fair — Roni and Taimane and Ma'a are sick now!' Semisi said.

Peleiupu got out of bed carefully so as not to upset the trays and, standing by the bed, hugged Semisi's head to her belly. 'The bitch won't get all of us. It won't,' she crooned.

Semisi told them Poto wanted them to visit Roni and his sick daughters. Roni, Pa'ugata and their children lived with Mikaele and other relatives in the afolau behind Sao's.

The sky was overcast. Semisi hoped it would rain. Peleiupu stopped in front of the bakery and looked down at the malae. Everything was overgrown — the grass, the patches of taro and ta'amu, the stands of bananas and sugar cane. Rubbish, fallen leaves, branches and coconuts were left lying about. Because they weren't being fed regularly, the pigs had broken over the rock fences and were foraging through the village, digging up the malae and gardens. The chickens were doing the same. More emaciated and hungrier, the dogs roamed the night, fighting over the little food they could find. She refused to believe the rumour that the dogs were also devouring untended bodies. The white horse that belonged to a neighbour who'd died three days before was still tied to the palm tree behind the church; it had eaten all the grass within the length of its rope, down to the bare ground, and was now standing utterly still on three legs, its ribs and backbone almost protruding through its hide. Peleiupu sent Iakopo to untie it.

Even from that distance she could hear Roni wheezing and sucking back the mucus and phlegm, then spitting it out in explosive squawks.

Roni lay in the only bed in the fale. His sick daughters, Taimane and Ma'a, were curled up in their sleeping sheets on the floor, with Pa'ugata and Poto sitting with them. Semisi sat down in the chair beside the bed. Tavita and Mikaele lay near Poto, who, when everyone was seated, prayed to God to protect all their people, especially their children, Elisapeta and Ana and their families, who were living elsewhere.

'Have a whisky, Pele,' Roni greeted Peleiupu. 'It'll cure your grief!' He laughed and drained his glass. Pa'ugata took the bottle away. 'Compared to this bloody disease what harm can that whisky do?' he complained.

'Don't be silly, ese lou fia tough!' Semisi admonished him, tapping his head. Throughout their lives, Roni had always been Semisi's 'special young brother', the one he indulged, giving him everything he wanted; the one he protected fiercely even against Poto; 'the best guitarist on the planet I love singing duets with'; and the one who reciprocated Semisi's love and devotion 'one hundred and ten per cent.'

'So because you think I'm dying, you've come to visit me, eh? All the Albino-white children of the drunken palagi trader, Lord Almighty Barker!'

'Ronald, now you *are* being stupid!' Semisi retorted in English. 'Our father was a brave and magnificent lord.'

'See, Mama? My handsome brother can speak beautiful English, my father's guttural language. No thanks to our neglectful father. It was Pele and Lalaga who taught Semisi. It was our precious father who taught Mautu and Pele. Why didn't he teach us, Mama?' Roni waited but Poto refused to reply. Smiling impishly, Roni said, 'Being an afakasi I should be able to speak half-English and half-Samoan, but I can't. I speak all-Samoan, so I'm Samoan. I eat Samoan. I shit Samoan. I sleep Samoan, and I . . .' He hesitated.

'Don't say it!' Pa'ugata stopped him.

'I sing Samoan, I pray Samoan and I'll die Samoan!' Then, looking at Poto, he asked, 'Mama, why do I have this palagi appearance and body when I am Samoan, eh? Every time we go to Apia or those arrogant Albinos visit us, they treat us as afakasi, illegitimate dregs of their civilisation, lost, unwanted, definitely inferior to them. Well, they're all arseholes: lily-white albino arseholes!'

'That's enough, Ronald!' Semisi demanded.

'This is the Lord's day, even if you don't go to church any more,' Poto attacked him. 'And don't swear like that in front of the children.'

'You used to swear at Papa in front of us!' Semisi turned on their mother.

'That was the only English our Mama knew!' laughed Roni.

'Very colourful English too!' joked Mikaele.

'At least I know *some* English,' Poto countered. 'At least your self-centred father taught me *some* English.'

Tavita, who'd been drowsing, sat up and called, 'Semisi, give your foul-mouthed brother the guitar!'

'Yeah, get me my weapon!' Roni said.

'You're too sick,' Pa'ugata insisted.

'And it's Sunday,' Poto reminded them. But she didn't object when Semisi handed Roni his guitar, a large scratched, written-upon, battered instrument that Semisi boasted Roni had stolen off a Spanish ship in a Russian port called St Petersburg.

Semisi puffed up Roni's pillows, sat him up and placed the pillows behind his back. Quickly Roni tuned his guitar and then started plucking it in the distinctive style Satoans had come to associate with him: a lilting, mournful, lucid style called 'the Satoan slack key'. As he played, the music flowed over and through them like a soothing balm, a prayer that made them forget the epidemic and the suffering. His sick daughters stopped coughing and fell asleep. Then Semisi started singing:

> O le sipi o le gata,
> e u ono e o ona,
> aua lava e te fefe
> i le oti uigaese . . .

Roni sang with him. Peleiupu looked around. Poto and Pa'ugata were singing too. The Barker brood were again singing the world into their shape and balance in defiance of the albinos and the death they'd brought to Satoa.

> . . . Inu vave, inu loa,
> inu i le pia ina ia ona . . .

Roni died a few nights later, refusing to be taken to the clinic. His daughter Taimane died the day after. Ma'a was shifted to the clinic where, under Malie's care, she survived for seven days, the longest anyone had lasted.

It was almost midday; a sea of heat covered Satoa and worsened the condition of the sick. From the ward, where she'd just finished bathing a patient, Peleiupu saw her parents and Sao standing in the shade of the breadfruit tree in front of the clinic. She sent out Iakopo with mats for them to sit on. Every now and then she paused in her work and observed them. They sat with a heavy stillness, gazing out to sea, so alone and lost. She excused herself to Malie and went out to them.

They smiled up at her, and continued their silent vigil. She sat down beside her mother. Through the palms along the shore she watched the breeze turning up the surface of the green sea as it headed towards them, her body tingling with anticipation of it. The palms bent and the foliage hummed as the breeze scurried through them. Then it was around them, weaving like a pet cat. She glanced at her elders: their eyes were shut and they were obviously enjoying the coolness.

Iakopo and two of his cousins arrived with foodmats. Breadfruit, miti and tinned fish. Politely, they put the food in front of their elders and retreated. 'We are sorry there is no corned beef or salmon,' Iakopo apologised for not bringing Sao's and Mautu's favourite food. 'Semisi says we must be frugal.'

'This is more than enough,' Lalaga said. 'Come and eat with us.' But Iakopo declined, saying they had to rush back to Semisi, who wanted them to deliver food to other people.

Sao and her parents had always looked younger than their age, Peleiupu had observed. Yet within weeks of the epidemic and the devastating loss of loved ones, they now seemed old. Especially Sao and Mautu: prematurely white hair, their faces a geography of wrinkles, their eyes lost in deeply sunken sockets. They walked with a slow shuffle, their speech had slowed noticeably and they often withdrew into themselves for long periods.

Mautu's large hands broke the food and delivered it to his mouth. He chewed slowly.

'When will it end?' Sao asked. Mautu continued eating as if he hadn't heard. Peleiupu glanced at her mother and sensed she wasn't going to answer either.

'When it runs its natural course,' Peleiupu replied. Sao looked at her. 'Yes: all infectious diseases have cycles.' Mautu nodded and continued eating. 'This new type of influenza is much stronger than previous ones. It's killing palagi too, even though they've built up immunity to influenza.' She was going to tell them there was no cure but stopped herself.

'When this curse is over, I'll go with other matai and confront the Governor,' Sao declared. 'We must win back control of our country from these . . . these stinking, arrogant, uncivilised pigs!' He almost choked as he swallowed back his tears.

Mautu reached over and laid his hand on Sao's shoulder. 'Be satisfied, sir. It is just the way things are.' He started weeping too.

'I'll never be satisfied, Mautu. Never!' Sao declared. 'Pele is right: this could've been prevented. The foreign animals who rule us do not care about our lives!' He pushed his foodmat away. So did Mautu, as they fought to control their sobbing.

'They're tired,' Lalaga whispered to Peleiupu. Her hair was white too, her face more lined. 'We're all tired.' Peleiupu held her hand. 'Naomi, Ruta and Arona will be spared,' Lalaga murmured.

'I'm sure they are safe,' Peleiupu consoled her.

Peleiupu collected their foodmats. As she walked away, she looked back. In the dark shade of the breadfruit tree, sitting in a triangle, her elders looked like fragile figures made of grey wood ash that could blow away with the breeze.

Her shadow pulled her forward. No one else was about. Because of the heat, even the pigs and dogs were resting in the shade.

The next morning Vaomatua, who'd been sick for a few days, woke and found Sao dead, staring up at the fale dome with a bemused smile. They got Malie to examine his body. He'd died in his sleep of a heart attack, Malie diagnosed. But the story that the Satoans believed and would spread was that their generous ali'i had died of a broken heart, and was smiling because he'd escaped the clutches of the epidemic.

When Vaomatua died two days later they said that she had died of a doubly broken heart: witnessing the death of her village and her loved ones, especially Sao, 'the love of her life despite his having been a dictatorial and domineering husband'.

A few days after Sao and then Vaomatua were buried among their aiga dead beside their faletele, Mikaele reported to Tavita and Peleiupu that because they could no longer carry out daily inspections, people were dying in their homes without anyone knowing about it for days. That morning he and his helpers, now mainly boys such as Iakopo, had heard dogs scrapping viciously in a fale with drawn blinds. Before they got to the fale the stench of blood and rotting flesh struck them. He'd gone into the fale alone. Dogs were fighting over the bodies of the couple who owned the fale, who had been dead for a few days. He got his party to promise they'd tell no one about it, and they'd buried the remains behind the fale. In future they would have to burn those homes.

315

He and his overworked helpers were also struggling to harvest the plantations every third day, and cook and distribute the food to the people, most of whom were now too sick to look after themselves. He started weeping. 'We're trying our best but the arsehole epidemic is too strong!' he cried.

Peleiupu sent Iakopo and his cousins to summon all the well people to Sao's faletele. They had to regroup against the epidemic.

The few matai present insisted that Tavita occupy Sao's post in the faletele. As Tavita spoke, Peleiupu counted eighteen men over the age of thirty, and twenty-seven under that; twenty-eight women over thirty, and thirty-seven under. All looked exhausted, dispirited. Tavita exhorted them to keep caring for their sick ones. 'God has not forsaken us; God is merely testing our faith and courage.' But Peleiupu noticed it was having little effect on them.

At the end of the meeting Lalaga said, 'There is hope — signs of hope. Many are surviving longer. And Malie believes some of the children will recover fully.'

'What hope?' one of the deacons asked. 'Jehovah will continue to test our faith until we are all dead!'

After the others left, Peleiupu walked out onto the paepae and looked across the village. Satoa was now populated more by the haunting presences of their recent dead than the living, she thought, and nobody complained any more about that clinging, sickly sweet smell of the epidemic. They were used to it, as if the epidemic were now a natural part of their existence.

'Have you heard from Sili about Lefatu and Maualuga?' Lalaga asked her when she got to the school that afternoon to help prepare it to house those sick families who had no one to care for them. 'I miss them very much. So does Mautu.' Peleiupu told her that she'd agreed with Sili that a visit might infect them with the illness.

As they worked, Lalaga said, 'I'm beginning to feel guilty about surviving, about God giving me and Mautu preferential treatment. Not a twinge of the epidemic: not a sniff or a cough.'

'Why do you think it is not touching us?' Peleiupu asked.

'Perhaps God has other things for us, other deaths. I hope he is also saving Naomi and Arona.'

Shortly after, Peleiupu sneaked out of the school, found Iakopo, pretended she was taking her son to help at the school and, after getting Tavita's bushknife, yoke and two baskets, told Iakopo they were going into their plantation to get fruit for the patients.

The river looked cool and inviting as Iakopo led her up the track through the plantations. She remembered how she and Arona had accompanied Barker and Mautu in their mad search for gold along the river, and they'd found the dead on the foothills.

It felt so long ago, and sadness and grief started hugging her again. She remembered also how she'd read Barker's testament beside that other river, the Vaisigano, at Vaiuta School. The roar of the river saved her from drifting deeper into her grief. Pigeons cooed from deep within the vegetation. Now and then a branch snapped in the wind. She noticed that the plantations were choking in weeds and mile-a-minute creeper, now that the people were unable to care for them.

The land started sloping up to the foothills and, as they veered away from the river, the long sad silence of the land and bush buzzed in their ears. She'd always been afraid of that silence, which her Aunt Lefatu had once described as 'the eternal, observing silence of the atua and the land'. Peleiupu noticed that Iakopo was keeping close to her. 'The silence out of which we came and into which we will return,' Lefatu had repeated.

'We're there,' Iakopo said. The crops were free of weeds. Ahead, above the heads of the bananas, protruded the roof of Sili's fale and a thin column of smoke. 'I'm not a fool, Mama!' Iakopo surprised her. 'I knew we were coming to see my sisters.' He laughed. 'Fruit? Who eats fruit?'

'Malie reckons fruit speeds up the healing,' she countered. He started to run towards the fale. She held him back. 'We must not contact them. We may be carrying the illness.' He understood. 'We'll hide and watch and see how they are. All right?'

Carefully they picked their way through the bananas, yams, papaya, taro and cassava that surrounded the fale. Through the vegetation seeped the pungent smell of burning wood and husk. A child — was it Lefatu? — was singing a well-known lullaby, someone was scraping coconuts, a dog growled and snapped and then whelped in pain as someone struck it.

They squatted behind some ta'amu and watched.

Lefatu and Sili's daughters were in the kitchen fale, drying banana leaves on the burning umu. They joked and recited rhymes. In front of the kitchen fale Sili's wife sat on a tuai, scraping coconuts into a tanoa. Behind her sat Maualuga munching a hunk of coconut. Behind them, Sili and his oldest son were preparing the taro leaves for the palusami. From the fale came the voices of people. An idyllic aiga scene: Satoa as it was before the epidemic imposed its imagery of death and hopelessness.

She kept looking and looking at her daughters as if through sight alone she could possess them forever. Lefatu and the other girls brought the leaves to Sili, who thanked them. Maualuga jumped up from the tuai and joined the older girls as they sat peeling green bananas into a tanoa of water. Sili's wife started showing her how to do it. As Maualuga concentrated, screwing up her face, Peleiupu concentrated too and imitated her daughter's every move . . .

Iakopo tugged at her ie lavalava. She surfaced and discovered tears blurring her vision. She wiped them away. When she looked again, the girls were around Sili and his son, who was pouring the coconut cream into the taro leaves cupped in his father's hands. Her daughters looked so well, so beautiful, and appeared as if they weren't missing her and Tavita, at all.

On their way back they picked ripe papaya and a bunch of bananas and packed them into the baskets. She put the yoke through the baskets but, when she tried, she couldn't lift the load. Iakopo pushed the baskets to the middle of the yoke, took one end of the yoke and told her to lift the other. 'Lift!' he called, and they lifted it to their shoulders. Together, with him leading — she marvelled at his determination — they carried it through the plantations, which were being invaded by the bush, beside a river that skipped and danced like her happiness as she'd observed her daughters, following a sun that was setting.

She found Tavita in the warehouse helping Semisi divide up the supplies, and signalled to him that she wanted to see him. He followed her into their bedroom.

'Guess what?' she enticed him. He started chuckling. 'Well, go on, guess what?'

'You've been to see Maualuga and Lefatu!' he surprised her.

'Iakopo told you, eh?' He shook his head and laughed. 'He did. Wait till I get him! He promised!'

'Guess what?'

'No!' she cried. 'No — you didn't?'

He nodded and said, 'Yes, I did. I've visited them twice already!'

Shrieking with laughter, she pummelled his shoulders. He hugged her tightly. 'I'm so glad they're well!'

That evening as she hurried through the surging chorus of cicadas to the clinic for lotu and her night shift, she heard what she refused to believe was laughter. She concentrated. Another short burst. She looked at the clinic veranda. Fa'amapu was talking animatedly to a group of patients and their carers who, as she listened, laughed periodically. She started running, with the cicadas' cries pecking at her heels.

Fa'amapu met her at the top of the steps. 'Two, Pele. Two of the children have recovered!'

Two patients died that night, three fewer than the previous night.

The next day's inspection brought in two dead and three sick, half the number of the inspection two days before — and Mikaele and his team had to burn down three of the fale. Peleiupu noted, with increasing hope, that many people were again complaining about the cloying smell of the epidemic.

Boats, fautasi and other vessels had stopped calling into Satoa as soon as the epidemic had set in. So it was a surprise early on Monday morning, as Peleiupu and Iakopo crossed the malae after her night shift at the clinic, to hear a woman calling, 'A boat, a boat is coming!'

'It's the government boat!' someone else added.

She rushed up to their house. Poto, Tavita and other relatives were already on the store veranda, gazing down at the bay. The boat trailed a thin column of smoke as it nosed through the placid sea. 'Bloody bastards!' Semisi growled in English. 'They got the fiakagaka to come here after what they done!'

'They are probably going around Savai'i, *helping*!' Mikaele sniggered. Only a few people were heading for the jetty.

'They bloody uncivilised kekea from New Zealand!' Semisi said.

'Yeah, as usual they'll be expecting us backward villagers to welcome them properly as our enlightened rulers!' Mikaele said.

'What are we going to do?' Peleiupu asked Tavita.

'You're Sao now. If you want the matai to welcome them, you'll have to call them — the few who're left — immediately,' Poto advised him.

'There will be no welcome,' Tavita decided. He sent Mikaele and other relatives to instruct the people to stay away from the jetty and the government officials.

Peleiupu went to bed, the others had their morning meal. She couldn't sleep so she sat at the bedroom windows, reading and watching the boat docking beside the *Lady Poto* and an empty jetty.

A couple of crew members jumped onto the jetty and tied up the boat. Then three Samoan policemen in grey uniforms disembarked and stood at attention while two papalagi officials in khaki safari jackets, shorts and long white socks disembarked. After them followed two Samoan interpreters in white.

The papalagi officials surveyed the empty jetty and talked with their interpreters, who pointed at the clinic. Then the older interpreter, with the grey, almost bald head, bowed to the officials and talked with his colleague, who scurried to the clinic while the others waited.

She watched as Malie and Fa'amapu met the interpreter on the clinic veranda. While talking to the interpreter, Fa'amapu pointed at Sao's faletele. The squat interpreter, who from that distance reminded Peleiupu of a crab, scurried back to his employers, who gestured towards Sao's faletele. Most families kept their blinds lowered. Peleiupu returned to her family on the veranda.

'Look at them: they're servants of the New Zealand gang!' Poto was saying. They laughed as they watched the interpreters heading towards them. Poto ordered

Iakopo to go and tell their family to vacate their faletele.

The younger interpreter was setting a pace his older companion was huffing and puffing to keep up with. Semisi sprang to his feet and, with exaggerated gestures, imitated the older interpreter. 'Auoi, auoi, my heart is going to die!' he sing-songed. The others laughed. Clutching his genitals through his ie lavalava, he cried, 'Auoi, auoi, the palagi boss is going to cut me off if I not do what he want!' More laughter.

The interpreters stopped and looked up at them. Semisi clicked to attention, saluted and bowed. Their rich laughter puzzled their visitors. The older one called, 'Please, where is his lordship Sao I'amafana's maota?'

'Please, your lordship, Sao I'amafana's is over there!' Semisi replied, pointing weak-wristedly at their faletele.

They tried not to laugh as the interpreters clambered up the high front paepae and into an empty faletele. After some discussion the younger one came onto the paepae and called to Semisi, 'Please, your Lordship, there is no one here!'

'Tell him!' Poto ordered Semisi, who glanced at Tavita who nodded.

'Please, your lordship, his lordship Sao I'amafana was killed by *your* epidemic,' Semisi replied. Tavita and Peleiupu moved to either side of Poto, who was sitting in her favourite chair. Semisi sat down behind them.

The interpreters reached the top of the steps. Hesitated. Smiled. Tavita recognised the older one: Peliia Lelua, well-known aide to the Governor, and son of a famous pastor. The interpreters looked around. No one invited them to sit down.

When no one bothered to welcome them, Peliia asked, 'Please, who am I speaking to?' He was supremely confident because he was backed by the government and in his own right a high-ranking tulafale. No one replied. 'Ah, we have come to inform you that important representatives of your government are visiting your village to help you.' He waited. Still no reply. 'Mr Mallard, secretary to the Governor, and Sergeant Mackintosh, his aide, are here to find out how you have fared during the epidemic. They want to help you. *We* want to help you.' Again no reply. 'Is there a problem, sir?' he asked Tavita.

'Before you enter territory you will not be able to defend, I must tell you that we *do* have a problem,' Poto interjected. The interpreters looked disdainfully at her and nodded. 'The problem is, you are only messengers of the important papalagi officials. That *is* the problem.' The insult wounded, deeply, and Peleiupu knew that Peliia couldn't believe Poto had the gall to ignore his rank, his title, his power. The younger one, son of an ali'i, was also wounded; he shut his eyes and pretended he hadn't heard Poto. 'So if you want to speak with the Ali'i of Satoa, go and fetch your papalagi masters, sir!'

'Oi, auoi, kafefe, such insulting behaviour!' Peliia exclaimed. 'No one speaks to Peliia in such a manner. No one!'

'Don't you realise you are speaking to le Tofa a Peliia Lelua?' the younger one intervened.

'Go and fetch your masters!' Tavita said. 'Don't forget, sirs, we are the government here.'

'Get the hell outta here!' Semisi's voice erupted in English from inside the store, where he'd retreated with the other relatives who laughed.

The tension broke. The interpreters scrambled to their feet and backed off the veranda, with Peliia muttering threats, and Semisi's and his friends' crackling laughter chasing them.

Poto asked Tavita if he was going to welcome them in the faletele. Tavita asked her what she thought.

'No,' Peleiupu heard her anger speaking. 'No, Mama. They have killed almost all our people.' She started weeping. Poto hugged her.

Tavita summoned Mikaele and the other well men of their aiga. Other Satoan men arrived also. They sat on the veranda floor alongside Tavita and Poto, and waited for the government party. No mats were to be put out for their visitors; no speeches of welcome or ava either, Tavita ruled. A total denial of proper practice and hospitality. Some of the matai were uncomfortable about it. 'They are murderers,' he told them. 'They have murdered our loved ones.'

When the three policemen came up the front steps, no one said anything. The policemen examined the group and withdrew to stand beside the steps. The interpreters entered, saw no mats, and sat to the side. Holding their helmets and wiping their faces with large white handkerchiefs, the papalagi smiled and, seeing no mats or chairs anywhere, looked at their interpreters, who refused to look up at them. When the papalagi met Poto's unwavering stare they sat down and tried their awkward, painful best to sit cross-legged.

It was customary for the hosts to speak first, so the officials and their interpreters waited, and waited, and waited. The papalagi kept glancing at their interpreters, who refused to stop gazing at the floor. Eventually the chunky Mr Mallard, with the massive thighs and legs and chunky hairy arms, asked his chief interpreter, in English, 'What's happening, Joe?'

'Mr Mallard, sir, this village has very different ways from the rest of Samoa,' Joe, or Peliia, replied in English. 'It is for us, the guests, to speak first.' An outright lie. Peleiupu glanced at Tavita and Poto; like her, they were trying not to reveal that they understood English.

'If that is the case, should I speak first, or should you open our discussions with a speech in Samoan?' Mr Mallard asked.

'Sir, I beg you to speak first. This village is of simple people who are very impressed you have come,' the younger interpreter suggested, sure that 'the simple people' didn't understand a word of English.

'What do you think, Sergeant Mackintosh?' Mr Mallard asked his companion, who was trying not to drown in the heat.

'Quite frankly, sir, I'm getting impatient with all these ceremonies and speeches. Jesus, they take up hell of a lot of our valuable time. It's all right for them — they've got nothing else to do all day but sit round and orate!' Mackintosh replied.

'That is enough, Sergeant. I know you have better things to do, but it is our duty to help these people. Like us they've lost loved ones in this awful epidemic. They're suffering still.'

Joe straightened up and announced, 'Your lordship Sao and the aiga of Satoa, Mr Mallard, the second most important person in your government, is going to speak to you!'

Mr Mallard licked his thin lips and, deepening his voice, said, 'The dignitaries and chiefs of Saytoarr, I come to see how you have fared in the hands of this cruel epidemic . . . ' He stopped. Joe translated into Samoan what he'd said. '. . . I bring with me the greetings of your Governor, who is in great sorrow because he knows of the enormous suffering you, his people, have been through . . . ' Joe translated that. From inside the store erupted a high-pitched fart that trailed off into a long sweet note. They pretended they hadn't heard it. '. . . Our Almighty Father, I am sure, has been with you as He has been with us, comforting us in our grief and pain . . .'

Peleiupu noticed that Joe's translation was deviating from what Mr Mallard was saying. '. . . Our Governor, who loves you, is also very angry with the disrespectful way you have welcomed his representatives this beautiful morning,' Joe translated. Mr Mallard continued: 'We are very happy to be with you; we want to help in any way we can. We want to prove to you that your government has as much love for you . . .'

Joe's translation: 'We feel insulted, we feel trampled on. This is not the way *true*, full-blooded Samoan aristocrats treat guests. True Samoans are full of generosity and hospitality . . .'

'Mr Mallard, I think you should stop your arrogant servant from insulting us further!' Tavita interjected in English. Joe blinked repeatedly and kept swallowing. 'Yes, Peliia, I can speak English, even though I am an ignorant afakasi from the back!'

'Joe, what's happening?' Mr Mallard asked.

'Yeah, Joe, what have you been saying in Samoan to these people?' Mackintosh choroused.

Joe was obviously used to wielding power and manipulating the relationship between the English-speaking government and their Samoan-speaking wards. He controlled the process because, as go-between, he controlled the two languages. He recovered his composure quickly. 'Sir, we try our best for to protect you and our Governor from these half-castes' insulting welcome to you,' Joe explained in English. 'In all other villages, sir, you have been received properly, the true Samoan way.'

'That's correct, Joe,' Mackintosh said, turning to Tavita. 'Sir, whatever your title is, you and your people have been very disrespectful to your Governor and your government. It may be because you are *not* true Samoans . . .'

'That is enough!' Tavita interjected, in English. 'Sao I'amafana was my grand-father. Your epidemic killed him and my grandmother and hundreds of our people.'

'*Our* epidemic?' Mr Mallard exclaimed. '*Our* epidemic, sir? Please explain yourself.'

'This is all I'm going to say, then we want you to leave our village.' The sergeant, the interpreters and the police closed in on him but Tavita continued. 'The *S.S. Talune*, which brought the epidemic to Apia, should've been stopped. The Governor knew that ship had the sickness on board.'

'That is the most dangerous lie I've ever heard!' Mackintosh snapped. The inter-preters glared at Tavita. 'Where did you get that information from, sir?'

'Our discussion is over,' Tavita declared. The police stood threateningly behind the interpreters. 'You must leave now.'

'This is insulting half-caste behaviour!' Joe tried to incense his masters. 'No true Samoan ever treats you and the Governor this way, sir!'

'No, sir, no full-blooded Samoan treats the government this way,' his companion echoed.

'That's enough!' Mr Mallard said. 'Sir, I know you and your people have suffered greatly,' he said to Tavita. 'We too have lost loved ones.' There was genuine sorrow in his voice. 'I am very sorry if our . . . our *officials* have insulted you . . .'

'Sir, that is not the way. We must be firm with them,' Mackintosh interrupted.

Mr Mallard glanced at his aide. 'Sergeant, you may be used to speaking to your underlings that way, but you will *not* speak to me or these people that way. Understand?' Mackintosh looked away. 'Sir, may I have your name, please?' Mallard asked Tavita.

'Toanamua Tavita, that is my title.'

'His real name, it is David Barker, sir!' Joe intervened once again.

Dead silence as Mr Mallard swung to his interpreter. 'Sir, you have insulted the people of Saytoarr enough! Get up now and return to the boat. Go on, up!' The policemen stepped back and their presence hurried Joe to his old feet. 'You too, Sergeant.' Mackintosh staggered up. 'Wait for me at the jetty.'

They all watched as Mackintosh and the others retreated from the veranda. 'May I ask, sir, how many of your people passed away in the epidemic?'

Tavita looked at Peleiupu. 'About half of our population,' Peleiupu said.

'I am very sorry. That is more than in other villages. Nothing I can say will ever heal your pain and anger, so I won't try. Perhaps one day I will be able to help you. Please let me know if you ever need help.' He struggled up. 'By the way, the epidemic is almost finished in Apia. It is also receding from the other villages we have visited. God has been merciful.'

The haze that covered the bay was glowing with the morning light as it shimmered up into mountains of cloud that filled the sky. Peleiupu opened her bedroom windows and let the breeze wash over her face. More and more people were recovering, though there was still the occasional death, and fewer people were getting sick. Peleiupu made the mistake of looking out at the bay again. For an instant her heart stopped: the haze was the shape of I'amafana's smiling face. She sucked in air, gasping. Lefatu and Maualuga, were they still safe? She stumbled, breathless, to her bed and, lying down on her back, cupped her hands over her mouth and nose. Panic attacks, hyperventilation Malie had diagnosed when she had suffered her first attack in the clinic. Breathe! Breathe! You must live for your other children. Her guilt at being alive threatened again but she knew now there was a purpose to that: the reconstruction of Satoa and her aiga and business.

She hadn't been in her office for weeks. She opened the windows, the breeze rushed in and foraged among her books. She browsed, touching and turning the pages and reading random paragraphs, enough to take her into that other world of the imagination that the epidemic had kept her away from . . .

Iakopo and Semisi brought in her breakfast: fa'alifu fa'i, koko and papaya. 'It's good, Pele, that you're on a diet because that's all we have to offer you!' Semisi joked.

'That's all we can afford, eh?' she joked back.

'Yeah, nothing left in the warehouse, little left in the store,' he said. 'By your instruction, we've shared everything with the people in need — which is everybody.'

'Not the way to do business, eh? Giving away your goods,' she quipped.

Semisi was suddenly sobbing. 'I miss him, miss him!' he cried. His friend Feleti had died the week before. 'He was such a beautiful person, Pele!'

She held him. 'Yes, Semisi, he was. But we have to keep on going.' She felt stupid saying that. 'We've all lost people we love dearly.' She started crying too. 'We have to be brave. We have to rebuild our lives.' She straightened him up and wiped away his tears. 'I need you to help me and Tavita get our business and family back on our feet. We can't help Satoa if we don't do that.' He nodded his large head.

While they waited for Tavita, Poto and the other elders of their family to gather, Peleiupu got Semisi to give her an inventory of their business. They had no goods to sell — but there were no customers either; their bakery was shut — no flour, no bakers; they had no copra; their plantation was feeding Satoa for free; they had only £803 in cash. 'Nothin' comin' in, Pele,' Semisi concluded. They didn't know what had happened to their other stores; they had a boat that was not earning anything; most of their key people had died in the epidemic; and most of the population, because of the epidemic, would take a while to recover as customers and producers of copra, Peleiupu added.

Later while they ate with the others, that was the inventory Semisi conveyed to them. Peleiupu kept two things from them: her plan to relocate their business head-quarters to Apia — she didn't want to upset Poto yet; and her large secret savings accounts in Apia, which she would use to refinance their company.

'What are we going to do?' Semisi asked.

Poto, as usual, spoke first. 'First, I'm more concerned about your sisters and their families than making money.' Peleiupu did not flinch at that deliberate hurt. 'We have to find out what's happened to them. They're *your* sisters, Tavita!'

'We're going to do that,' Tavita replied. 'But we may not have enough money to pay for fuel for the boat so we can visit *my* sisters.'

'Pele's right, Mama,' Semisi defended Peleiupu. 'And we're all exhausted and grieving, so let's not get bitchy with one another!'

'Who told you to speak like that to me?' Poto threatened.

'That is enough, Mama!' Mikaele said. Poto looked away from Peleiupu, nose in the air.

Siniva, who usually said little at their family discussions, cleared her throat. Peleiupu glanced at her. 'Mama, Tavita and Pele are right. We have to rebuild the business, or what you and Papa Barker built may be lost. And we won't be able to help our village.'

'I apologise if I am *again* the problem in this family.' Peleiupu heard herself hitting out at Poto. 'I know I am *married* into this family so I'm not entitled to the same rights as all of you. So I'll keep quiet.'

'See what I've told you, Tavita?' Poto countered. 'See? Your wife thinks she rules *our* family!'

'Mama, that is enough!' Tavita ordered.

'No, I want to hear what else your mother has to say!' Peleiupu demanded.

'That's enough,' Mikaele intervened. 'The whole village is listening.'

'I don't care if they're listening — let them listen,' Poto said. 'Better teach your spoilt wife to respect me, your mother!' she ordered Tavita.

Relatives were outside the windows, trying to appear as if they were not watching them. Peleiupu didn't care — all she wanted to do was hurt Poto, and it was wildly exciting, exhilarating. 'Tavita, you teach *your* mother to respect me!'

Tavita smashed his fist down on the arm of his chair. 'A'e, I've had enough of these creatures called women!' he exclaimed.

'What did you say?' Poto demanded.

'Yes, why are you criticising women?' Peleiupu echoed Poto. Tavita sprang up.

'If it wasn't for a woman you wouldn't have been born!' Poto shouted.

Before Peleiupu could continue slashing him, he wheeled around and started storming out. 'These creatures called women should all be cast into the sea!' he shouted.

'And why are *you* looking at us like that?' Poto turned on Mikaele.

'He's another man, that's why!' Peleiupu slashed him too.

Mikaele rose slowly, and Peleiupu was suddenly aware of his bulk filling the room. 'You bloody women are valea!' he said. 'Bloody crazy!' He lumbered out of the room. Once outside he shouted at their relatives, 'Get away from here. You all owe your miserable lives to Poto and Pele.' Peleiupu started laughing, Poto started laughing, Semisi started laughing and, as they laughed together, Peleiupu became aware of her son gazing into her face, puzzled but grinning with happiness.

It was so good to be alive and laughing in the face of the epidemic: ready to go on living and rebuilding.

Afterwards Poto sent Iakopo to bring back Tavita and Mikaele, and in front of their family she acknowledged Peleiupu's leadership by asking her for her plans for saving and developing their business.

They needed a source of quick revenue, Peleiupu explained. During the epidemic people couldn't harvest their copra, so throughout the country there was an enormous crop of fallen coconuts that they had to harvest before the other companies did so. Quickly she outlined how they were to do that. To get money to run their boat so the harvesting could be done throughout Savai'i and their other stores could be restored, she suggested they harvest their crops in Satoa and sell them at the Apia market where, because of the epidemic, there were large shortages of food. 'We have to do it now before our competitors can start,' she urged them. 'Five large cargoes of foodstuffs should return enough money to reprovision our Satoa store and pay for the boat to visit our other stores.'

'Don't forget to stop at Manono and see how Naomi and Pate and their children are,' Lalaga reminded Peleiupu when she heard about this. 'And go to Fagaloto, too, see how Ruta and Lefatu are.' Her plea was laden with fear.

The Recovery

'No, I don't want to go ashore!' Peleiupu changed her mind when Tavita reached out to help her into the punt. The *Lady Poto* was anchored off Manono and they were ready to go and see how Naomi and her family were.

'But you have to go!' Lefatu, Peleiupu's daughter, insisted. Peleiupu refused to look at Tavita. 'I'm too afraid.' Peleiupu pleaded. So Tavita and the two crew members pushed off. 'Don't stay too long,' she called.

Lefatu and Maualuga pressed against their mother as they watched the punt, which was laden with baskets of foodstuffs, heading in to the loud, fearful clarity of the moving sea and sky and the beach on which people were now gathering.

They watched as the punt reached the shallows and a few men waded out and pulled it on to the beach. They watched as a woman — was it Naomi? — rushed up to Tavita and held him. Naomi? Yes it was her! As the woman waved and waved and they waved and waved back, Peleiupu's joy filled the clarity of the sky. 'It's her, my sister, my sister!' she cried, hugging her children.

While the punt was being unloaded, Naomi stood with Tavita. She'd wave to them periodically. When Tavita and his crew got back into the punt and the Manono people started carrying the baskets of food back to their village that stretched along the shore, Naomi remained alone on the beach. She and Peleiupu locked in their gaze that the punt traced from the shore to the *Lady Poto*.

Everyone gathered around Tavita as he reboarded. 'God has been kind, Tavita said. 'Naomi has recovered.' He stopped, unable to look at Peleiupu. 'Pate is recovering.'

'And the children?' Siniva asked.

'Their lives . . . their lives have been taken by the epidemic,' Tavita replied.

Peleiupu looked back at the shore. Naomi was gone. The beach was empty.

The *Lady Poto* docked in Apia in the late afternoon. Tavita and the crew unloaded the large cargo of foodstuffs and, hiring two carts, transported the food to the Tauese market. Even before they unloaded, the crowd was demanding to buy the crops, so they sold from the carts at double the prices they'd decided on in Satoa. Peleiupu's bag was soon fat with money. Within minutes the carts were empty and heading back to the boat for more.

Her daughters, Maualuga and Lefatu, refused to let her and Siniva hold their hands as they walked along the main street of Apia. Only two ships lay in the harbour. Late morning, dusty, only a few people about, their heads down, eyes dazed with grief. After the epidemic the buildings and dwellings looked drab and shabby, piles of rubbish lay everywhere and, in the heat, gave off a putrid stench that the inhabitants seemed unaware of. Animals foraged through the rubbish. It was her daughters' first visit to Apia and they were observing everything in hungry silence. A horse-drawn carriage clattered by, the driver gazing ahead while his papalagi passengers — a bearded man and a woman — talked.

She and Tavita hadn't been able to resist getting their daughters back from Sili as soon as they had gone into their plantation to harvest the crops for Apia. She hadn't bothered to consult Malie about whether it was now safe for her daughters — after all, the epidemic was virtually over, she believed. When in the afternoon her daughters had broken away from Tavita and into her office, she'd wept as she'd embraced them. Wept with happiness; wept some more when memories of I'amafana had burst upon her. From then on she'd not wanted them out of her sight, insisting even that they sleep in her bedroom. Hurt by this, Iakopo had retreated to stay with his grand-parents. She had decided her first gift to her daughters on their safe return would be to show them Apia, for the first time.

The shops they went into had little to sell; new shipments were due soon, they were told. The shop assistants were gaunt-eyed and morose, but because it was their first visit, her daughters nevertheless viewed Apia as a wondrous storehouse of goods and papalagi.

Near the middle of the main street they stopped in front of a small bungalow under huge sprawling mango trees. She told them she was going in to see her lawyer, gave Siniva some money and told them to have lunch somewhere. She watched them until they disappeared around the bend.

Years before, when they'd returned from Pago Pago and she and Tavita had wanted to establish their company legally, someone had recommended that they see a New Zealand lawyer called Jim Mackson. For two days they'd tried persuading themselves to go: they considered themselves simple villagers intruding into the complex and forbidden world of the papalagi. Also, they'd not consulted a lawyer before — let alone a papalagi one. They had agreed finally, but at Mackson's door, Tavita had fled.

Peleiupu had found herself in the office, with a squat woman typing at her desk. The woman had taken one look at her bare feet and dress and continued typing. 'May I see Mr Mackson?' she'd heard her arrogant, stubborn side asking in English. The woman had stopped typing. 'May I see him?' Peleiupu had repeated.

'And you are?' the woman had asked, in Samoan.

'Mrs Peleiupu Barker,' she'd replied, firmly, in English.

'Are you here on business or what?' the woman had asked, in English.

'I am not here for work as a servant, if that is what you think.'

The woman had smiled and said, 'I'm Mr Mackson's secretary. My name's Mrs Louisa Frech. Mr Mackson is a very busy man. What can he do for you?'

'My husband and I would like to set up our company properly, legally.'

'What kind of business is it?'

'I would really like to see Mr Mackson and tell him.'

While Peleiupu had waited, she'd looked around the office. On the walls were photographs of different sports teams and she'd figured out quickly who Mr Mackson was in the photographs.

'He'll see you now,' Mrs Frech had said, refusing to look at her.

Somewhere in the jowly, extra-large man who glanced up at her was the fit, muscular, blond youth from the photographs. Mr Mackson lumbered to his feet. He was bigger than Mikaele, and breathing heavily. 'I don't have much time,' he'd wheezed, sweat pouring down his face and soaking his shirt collar.

'We have a business in Savai'i, and we want to set it up properly,' Peleiupu had explained. 'It's registered but we want a new ownership structure for it.' She had his attention and curiosity at last. 'By the way, my husband's name is David Barker' — the name had felt foreign in her mouth as she'd said it — 'my name is Pele, and we own a store and plantation in Satoa. You've probably never heard of Satoa or us.'

'You are correct there, Mrs Barker.'

'It's a small business but we sell a lot of copra each month to the stores here. That is increasing. We also sell goods to most of the trading stations and stores around Savai'i.'

'You really must have your husband here to discuss this,' he'd said.

'Why?' she'd confronted him. 'He is busy and I'm quite capable of understanding what has to be done, Mr Mackson.' He'd looked offended.

'Very, very few women conduct business, Mrs Barker.'

'What has my being a woman got to do with making money, sir?'

His eyes had lit up, his face rounding into a cheeky smile. 'Yes, indeed, what has that got to do with making a healthy profit?' His booming laughter had shaken the small room.

'It'll be profitable for you and us, sir,' she'd guaranteed.

As they'd discussed the type of business she wanted established, he'd chortled intermittently, impressed by her intelligence and business savvy. When she'd risen to leave, he'd congratulated her on her English. 'I learned it from books and my father, who'd learned it from a renegade beachcomber.' She'd shaken his hand. 'I'll bring David tomorrow afternoon to sign the papers.' She paused. 'And pay your fee, sir.'

As their dealings with Mr Mackson had grown, they had come to enjoy devising new business deals and ventures with him. He was a breathing encyclopaedia of business information and gossip, and kept them informed about business opportunities. Early in their relationship they'd also asked Mackson to use his overseas connections to search for Arona, and over the years he'd provided some information, again mainly in the form of stories and rumours that added to the mythology of Arona the Sailor. Because they didn't want to raise Lalaga's and Mautu's hopes, Peleiupu kept most of these from them.

They kept inviting Mackson to Satoa but he declined politely, and never invited them to his home. Rumours had it that Mrs Mackson was a strange woman who drank secretly and hardly ventured out of her home. His enemies whispered that, when inebriated, Mrs Mackson wandered the night, 'talking to herself'.

Peleiupu pushed open the front door. Mrs Frech rushed over and embraced her. 'I'm glad to see you, Pele. How's your family?'

'Almost half of our village died in the epidemic,' she replied, and was again caught firmly in her sorrow.

Mrs Frech started crying. 'My mother, two uncles, an aunt and four other relatives died . . . And Mr Mackson, poor man, lost his wife, Sandra, and two of his children. He took ill but thanks to our heavenly Father he has recovered. I don't know how this town is going to recover from this. Very little money, very little food.'

'Is Jim in?' Peleiupu wanted to get away from Mrs Frech's grief.

'He's in but he's still depressed and sick. Very depressed . . . '

'We've only got one day left in Apia so I need to see him now.'

When she saw the bespectacled man behind the large teak desk, she wanted to leave again. The white-haired figure was a skeletal caricature of the huge, boisterous, confident Jim Mackson she'd known before the epidemic. 'Come in, Pele,' the squeezy, thin voice invited her. She hurried in and sat down. His face had collapsed into rolls of skin that hung down from his jaw and neck. 'It is wonderful to see you, Pele, and that you are well. Is David here too?' She shook her head. 'It's been terrible. Terrible. So much death that death became normal, eh?'

'Jim, I am very sorry about your wife and children.'

'I wasn't a religious person. I'm more religious now that I've survived the fire of grief. But I'm convinced there is no God. Well, not one that I can conceive of or believe in.' There was a long heavy pause. 'My wife never wanted to shift to Samoa from our comfortable middle-class existence in Auckland. But she now has to stay here permanently!' Again, thin wheezing laughter. 'I didn't die, Pele, and that is the crux of the matter. I was spared!'

'That assumes that something or someone spared you.'

'The epidemic did, Pele.'

'But the epidemic is merely an illness, without a will or consciousness or sense of justice that sentences some to die and some to live.'

'We are getting too philosophical, aren't we? Let's be real, let's stick to what we know, to things and people we can touch and maybe love . . .'

'Or hate?'

'That too. Pele, of all my clients, you see most lucidly the real world as it is, and deal with it as it is.'

'I negotiate, I make deals!' she parodied herself. 'I too lost a son to the epidemic, and other loved ones. I couldn't negotiate with the sickness . . .'

'We are all equal in our loss,' he sighed. 'And perhaps we'll find hope again.'

'In business, in deals, in money, in the present that keeps moving until we too die.'

'Pele, you're too much!' he laughed. 'Just too much. So what can the thin Jim Mackson do for you this time?'

She told him quickly, while he took notes. 'The new company is to be called Ralph William Barker Company,' she concluded. 'As you know, we valued four village stores that were up for sale before the epidemic; we want to buy them now.'

'Great move. They'll be cheaper now. Some of the owners have died, others are leaving indefinitely.' He paused and then added, 'Why don't I make a list of all the other businesses that may be up for sale? The sickness has killed other businesses. The war, of course, and the New Zealand take-over have killed the German companies and plantations. They have to either sell or put them in British ownership.'

'So when we return in a few weeks' time you'll have that list?'

He nodded. 'As long as you have the money.'

'We do,' was all she was going to tell him. 'And within six months we'll have enough to buy more.'

'Pele, as the daughter of a pastor — one of the most respected in Samoa — I thought you condemned usury and profiteering?'

'That is *not* fair, sir!' she laughed. 'And my usury and profit-making have been good for you too, Jim.'

'Of course, Pele!' He laughed and wheezed.

She got up. 'David and I will sign the new company papers — later today?' They shook hands. He felt so fragile and vulnerable.

The next day she and Siniva and her daughters bought gifts for their relatives and elders and the other surviving Satoans: for Mautu an extra-large floral shirt that shone like a multi-coloured afternoon sun; for Lalaga and Poto identical feathered white hats for church; for Semisi white sandals from Italy; for Sili and his wife and children some clothes; an ie solosolo for Malie; a dress for Fa'amapu; and, for the other survivors, rolls of calico, cartons of cabin bread and tinned corned beef and fish and biscuits, bags of flour and sugar, sweets, jam', liquorice all-sorts and barrels of salted beef. 'This is going to be our first celebration as a village since the sickness,' Tavita declared.

The jetty was alive with their people as they entered Satoa Bay. Nearly all the survivors, Peleiupu figured. Hobbling, being piggy-backed, dancing and waving as the *Lady Poto* docked. Singing and dancing as they disembarked, singing and dancing as they followed them to Sao's faletele and prepared and ate a huge feast of the papalagi food they'd brought and which they'd missed during the epidemic. During their celebration, many broke out of their laughter and joy into loud tears and sobbing as they remembered their loved ones who'd died.

The next morning they loaded another cargo of foodstuffs, and Tavita returned to Apia, taking Iakopo, Poto and Lalaga (Mautu refused to go), and those who had recovered fully, for a holiday.

In the following two weeks they took four more loads of cargo, which they sold quickly and at higher prices each time. By this time the largest harvest of copra ever produced in Satoa was drying in the sun, and more copra was being cut.

As they approached her parents' house after midday, Peleiupu's daughters ran on ahead and up the front steps. She could see her father asleep in the canvas chair she'd given him years before. White hair gleaming, his body lost in the large embrace of the chair. Of all the survivors he was one of the few who didn't seem to be breaking out of his sorrow and depression. He now spent long periods in stillness, gazing into himself, and Lalaga insisted that he be left alone to contemplate his future life with God. The Satoans simply forgave him his grief and melancholy: he had earned it, and would be their spiritual guide and pastor until he died.

He still taught Bible studies at the school, but he rambled and bored his students. The effervescent enthusiasm he'd possessed before the epidemic had gone. Tavita was the first to point out to Peleiupu that her father now hardly mentioned God in his sermons. She listened carefully to his next sermon and had to agree with Tavita.

Worried about him, she tried to visit him once a day. Sometimes he appeared at her office, sat in her prince's chair and browsed through her books, or slept. He tried but couldn't get into the novels, especially the romances. Too unreal, he told Peleiupu. In the late afternoon, after biscuits and orange drink, his grandchildren took him home.

When Peleiupu reached them, Maualuga and Lefatu had woken him and he was questioning them. 'Did you know your mother was the cleverest child in our school?' he was asking.

'You've told us that lots of times, Papa!' Lefatu replied.

'Yes, lots and *lots* of times!' Maualuga chorused.

'And is she still the cleverest person in the whole world?' he asked.

The girls screwed up their faces, pretending they were thinking about it deeply, then chorused, 'Yes, she is, she *really* is!'

'Ah, and here she is,' Mautu greeted her.

'Where's Mama?' Maualuga asked.

'Where else but in her vegetable garden?' he replied. So the girls rushed towards the back of the house. Lalaga's garden was the largest in Satoa, stretching from the house to the rock fence behind the village. As people had recovered from the epidemic she'd revived her gardening project, and each aiga was now weeding and replanting the gardens they'd neglected for all those months. She and her students helped those aiga that had only a few members left.

'And how are you, Papa?' Peleiupu asked, sitting down on the mat opposite him.

'Where's Iakopo?' Mautu avoided her question. (Iakopo was his favourite grand-child, though he tried to hide it.) She told him he was with Tavita cutting copra. 'You work Iakopo too hard, Pele,' he complained. 'He's only a boy.'

'He chooses to do it.'

'Yes, he's going to be like Lalaga — work, work, work.'

For a pleasant stretch, Peleiupu answered all his questions about the business, then, unexpectedly, he asked after Arona. 'He's probably still in New Zealand,' she replied.

'Why have we never heard from him?' he repeated the twenty-year-old question that lay at the heart of their aiga. 'I didn't hurt him, Pele. Lalaga didn't hurt him. We loved him, we were good to him.' She looked away. 'Yet for two decades he has punished us with guilt. What's the use of sending us gifts and money, of collecting all the news and stories about him? Most of them are lies anyway. All we want is a word, just a word from him — a word about how he is, where he is, would free your mother and me, Pele.' He dabbed at his eyes.

She hesitated and then lied. 'I'll ask Mr Mackson, our lawyer, to continue looking for him in New Zealand.'

His face lit up. 'When, when, Pele?'

She'd do it the next time she was in Apia.

'And your mother is very upset that you haven't kept your promise to see how Ruta and Lefatu are!' He chastised her.

She promised she'd do that when they visited their stores around Savaii. 'Would you like to go with me?' she asked.

'Yes, I want to weed my parents' graves, which must be overgrown with weeds after all these years,' he replied. She tried to ignore the sad sense of finality in his remark. 'I'm sure your mother will want to come too,' he added. She told him they'd drop them off at Fagaloto and pick them up on their way back from inspecting the stores.

She was used to his sudden shifts into contemplative silence. She liked just sitting beside him letting her thoughts drift. They enjoyed it for a long time.

'I wonder about him often,' he mused. 'He fills my dreams too.'

'Arona?'

Shaking his head slowly, he said, 'Fatutapu. It's a beautiful name, eh, Pele?' She nodded. 'Fatutapu,' he rolled the name lovingly over his tongue. 'Fatutapu.' A smooth round pebble which, as it dropped down the well of her imagination, brought to life again the ancient atua of her aiga.

While the heat ticked at the edge of their attention, he reminisced again about his childhood — these were stories she knew well and loved. When they gave way to stories of their early years in Satoa, and focused on Arona and Ruta and Naomi, sadness gripped her again.

Every Satoan wanted to go on the *Lady Poto* to Fagaloto and the six stores around Savai'i, but Tavita, through Poto who didn't mince words when she wanted to be obeyed, announced that only she, the four crewmen, Semisi, Mikaele, Lalaga, Mautu, Iakopo (because Mautu needed someone to carry his bag; the other upset grand-children were bribed with the promise of a trip to Apia), Peleiupu, Tavita, and Malie and Fa'amapu, who needed a holiday from the clinic, were going.

At first light even the disappointed Satoans turned up to farewell them. As the boat left the jetty two youths jumped onto the bow but dived off again when Mikaele advanced towards them. Everyone laughed and cheered.

High tide. Just a slight swell within the reef as the boat headed for Fagaloto. Clouds blocked out the sun so they felt cool. They hugged the coast and could see in detail the landscape, vegetation and villages. A few started feeling seasick; they lay down on the deck and tried to sleep. 'See, you've all become sea-less creatures after years of being denied sea travel!' Mikaele joked loudly. 'You've become navigators who can't read the sea and the stars!'

Almost an hour later they were taking the passage into Fagaloto Bay, a v-shaped indent in the high, rugged volcanic coastline. Black water, black rock, black sand, the village nestled around a white church at the head of the v, under palms and breadfruit. Immediately behind it, the bush-clad volcanic shelves tiered up to the high mountain range.

People gathered on the shore. Some waved. They dropped anchor. They couldn't see Ruta or Lefatu in the crowd.

'Papa, are you sure you're well?' Peleiupu asked, straightening his collar.

'Don't worry, Iakopo and Lalaga will look after me.' He paused and, gazing at the village, said, 'I am so happy to be home.' She kissed him on the cheek. Iakopo edged away as she moved to do the same to him.

'I'm afraid, Pele,' Lalaga whispered. 'I hope Ruta and Lefatu did not . . .' She couldn't say it.

'I'm sure God protected them from the sickness.' Peleiupu tried to console her but she too was riven with fear.

Mikaele and the crew loaded the two punts with their luggage and sacks and cartons of food. Tavita helped Mautu and Lalaga into one of the punts. Iakopo jumped in after them.

As the punt headed ashore, Peleiupu kept waving to Iakopo, who was standing on the bow; her son refused to wave back.

Three hours later light rain fell as they anchored off Falealupo. Peleiupu remembered what her father had told them about Falealupo: how in pre-Christian times the Atua Nafanua had established her religion in Falealupo and through her priests had dominated the country for three hundred years until the coming of Christianity; how Falealupo was where the sun set each evening, and how their pre-Christian ancestors had believed that the spirits of the dead departed from the Fafa, at the western edge of Falealupo beach, for Pulotu, the spirit world.

At the centre of the long line of fale that stretched along the beach was the large Roman Catholic church, which rose high above the vegetation. Not far from it was their store. They could see a few people gathering on the beach as the haze of rain swept across it. They dreaded having to go ashore to see if Ana, Tavita's sister, and her husband, Atamai, were still alive.

The goods and supplies were loaded into the punts. Poto insisted on going ashore with them on the first punt. 'I'm so afraid,' she whispered to Peleiupu.

In silence they rowed ashore, and were soon soaked to the skin.

Most of the people on the beach were emaciated and hollow-eyed and struggling to stand up. Some of them waded in and pulled the punt in. No sign of Ana or Atamai. While Tavita, Mikaele and the crew unloaded the punts, Peleiupu and Semisi pulled Poto away and up over the beach to the edge of the malae.

'Where *are* they?' Poto demanded.

The village was overgrown with weeds, rubbish lay everywhere, many of the fale looked deserted, and some were burnt-down ruins. From that distance the store looked deserted too: its shutters were down. The gardens Poto had helped Ana plant around the store were smothered with creepers. They hurried. The rain intensified.

Someone had nailed boards across the shutters and the front door. They hurried to the fale behind it, to where Ana and Atamai had lived. Through the screen of rain they could see a woman, a youth and two young girls in the fale. Poto started whimpering. Semisi put his arm around her shoulders. 'It's all right, Mama,' he kept telling her.

The youth and girls, who wore ragged, dirty clothes, came out to them. 'Where is Atamai?' Peleiupu asked.

'He's in there,' the youth pointed into the fale. 'We have been looking after him.' Poto and Semisi rushed past them into the fale.

'And Ana, where is she?' Peleiupu asked. The girls looked at the youth, who gestured towards the church. Peleiupu started scrambling towards the building. 'No!' the youth called. 'She died a few weeks ago.' Peleiupu kept running to the mound, her wet clothes flapping and squishing around her.

A mass grave? She stopped at the edge of it, her feet buried in the rich mud that the rain was washing off the mound. Dropping to her knees, she thrust her hands into the mud.

Over the clatter and thudding of the rain she caught Poto's and Semisi's shrill wailing rushing towards her. She turned and her sight was filled with Poto stumbling towards her through the haze of rain, which made her appear as if she were evaporating. 'Ana, Ana, Ana, my beloved!' Poto's plea clogged the world.

That was where Tavita and Mikaele found them, and Mikaele swept Poto up in his arms and carried her back to the fale.

Behind a curtain, Peleiupu forced Poto to change into dry clothes, and she and Semisi sat holding her. Peleiupu could hear Tavita talking to Atamai. A while later they stretched Poto out on a soft layer of mats and wrapped her in a sleeping sheet. Peleiupu dried herself, changed and joined the others.

Mikaele and Semisi went off to supervise the cleaning and re-provisioning of the store. Though he was thin and hollow-eyed, Atamai was recovering well. He'd been sick for over two weeks after Ana died. In his grief, the epidemic had attacked him, he said. While he was delirious, people had raided the store and taken almost every thing. Because of the epidemic, the matai fono had not yet done anything to find and punish the culprits. As he talked, Peleiupu began to sense the presence of a woman hovering in the background. Fanua was her name. Atamai explained that Fanua had been their closest friend since they'd settled in Falealupo. Three of Fanua's children had died early in the epidemic, and when he fell ill, she and her remaining children took care of him. Fanua's presence felt protective, Peleiupu sensed, as she tried to identify the person Fanua reminded her of.

Later as she and Fanua went to the store to get food, she identified her Aunt Lefatu as that person. Fanua had the same ageless physical features and sense of perma- nence and wisdom.

Some villagers were helping Semisi and Mikaele and the crew clean the store. Others were weeding the gardens. 'Please forgive our people for taking your property,' Fanua said. 'Some of these people took part in the theft.'

'And most of them owed money?'

'Yes, all of them, including me,' Fanua confessed.

Peleiupu filled a basket with tinned food, rice, flour, sugar, salt and lard. Fanua took the other side of the heavy basket and they carried it to Atamai's kitchen fale.

'At first we thought Ana was strange,' Fanua said, as they cooked. 'You know — the golden hair, the cats' eyes and freckles. And even more weird when we found out she was a compulsive and expert fisher. She outfished our best — and our men didn't like that. I think all our men fell in love with her, but she was unaware of it!' Soft laughter. 'Yes, oblivious to the effects her spectacular strangeness was having on our males. Of course we jealous women were waiting (and hoping) for the Lady to grow jealous too — jealous of Ana's long golden hair and beauty. But we waited and waited and the Lady didn't punish her at all, thereby telling us that Ana had her blessing and protection. Ana was the first long and golden-haired female in our district who didn't have to cover her hair or wear it up.'

338

'Excuse my ignorance, but "the Lady"?' Peleiupu asked.

'Nafanua,' she replied casually. 'I shouldn't really be discussing her so openly but who cares? She can't punish us worse than the papalagi epidemic has done.' Sensing Peleiupu's discomfort, Fanua added, 'She's harmless most of the time. Plus, we're Christians now and don't believe in the power of our pagan atua any more!'

'You mean, you *shouldn't* believe in her any more?' Peleiupu asked.

'If you want to put it that way.' That impish wisdom again. 'She was certainly useless in defending us against the epidemic.'

The smell of their cooking attracted Fanua's and the neighbours' children to the kitchen fale. So, as they cooked, Peleiupu filled plates for them. They ate ravenously.

'Don't you think She may have been punishing you for deserting her for palagi ways?' Peleiupu asked Fanua.

'That's what my father and the elders believed. So when the sickness struck them, they just gave into it as just punishment from the Lady. I believe the Lady had nothing to do with the sickness. The papalagi brought it. It is their fault. She didn't have the knowledge and, therefore, the mana to repel it, cure it.'

'Why do you think you were not touched by it?'

'Luck, pure luck.'

'You don't think she protected you?'

'Do you believe the Christian God protected you from the sickness?'

Peleiupu nodded, but felt strangely uncomfortable as Fanua gazed at her. 'Well, I suppose you could call God, luck!'

They packed the food, and the children helped carry it to the fale where they found a group of matai talking with Atamai and Tavita. When they entered and sat down at the back of the fale, ready to serve the food, one of the matai, a small man with a leg swollen with elephantiasis, welcomed Peleiupu formally. Peleiupu was surprised when Fanua interrupted him. 'Well, are you hungry again? Is that why you've come?' she asked. The matai grinned; the others gazed at the floor. 'Why didn't you come before to see how Atamai was?'

'There you go again, Fanua!' their leader tried to joke. 'You forget we were all ill . . .' His companions nodded.

'You should've died too!' she said. 'The good people died and you lived. When the epidemic is all over, our village will meet to resolve the crisis of leadership — your very poor and selfish leadership since my father died.'

'Please be satisfied, your ladyship,' the youngest matai started apologising.

'That is enough!' Fanua ordered. 'You will be given this food to fill your selfish bellies!' Fanua and Peleiupu filled the foodmats and the children delivered them to everyone. 'And when you finish gutsing, we'll return and pack up your scraps,' she insulted them further. 'Toanamua, I am sorry I've had to be very honest with our leaders in front of you,' she apologised to Tavita.

They filled a foodmat for Poto and took it to her behind the curtain. Poto refused to eat. She started shivering, so Fanua stretched her out and, oiling her hands, started massaging Poto's forehead, neck and shoulders. As Peleiupu watched Fanua's strong, long-fingered hands slipping, pressing, slipping, pressing and sliding over Poto's forehead, she, like Poto, started feeling calm and relaxed. Poto drifted into sleep. 'The death of our children is what we parents dread the most, eh, Pele?' Fanua asked. The rain continued thudding on the thatched roof and sliding down in a screen from the eaves onto the stone paepae in a loud clatter. 'I almost went insane when my children died.'

Tavita, Semisi and Mikaele were in the store when Peleiupu and Fanua went in. 'Why aren't you stacking the goods in the shelves?' Peleiupu asked.

'Who's going to run the store? Atamai isn't well enough yet,' Semisi pointed out.

'We may have to close it,' Tavita added.

Without hesitation, Peleiupu asked Fanua, 'Will you run it for us?'

'Me? I've had no palagi education.'

'I'm sure Atamai will teach you what to do,' Peleiupu said. 'And when he's well enough, he'll do it.'

Fanua continued shaking her head. 'There's no money in Falealupo to buy these goods anyway.'

'But there are a lot of coconuts, eh?' Peleiupu countered. 'The people can pay with coconuts. While we're here we can work out with you how many coconuts you should charge for each item.'

In the late afternoon, while Poto slept in the lulling beat of the rain, they met with Atamai and Fanua and worked a currency out. Fanua also agreed to organise gangs of workers to cut all the copra in Falealupo. Throughout their discussions Tavita maintained a suspicious stance, and when Fanua left with her children to visit patients, he attacked Peleiupu for offering Fanua the job without knowing much about her. Semisi agreed with him.

'I know enough!' Peleiupu insisted.

'Pele's choice is very sound,' Atamai intervened.

'Why?' Tavita demanded.

Atamai looked around to see if anyone else was about. 'Don't you realise who she is?' Atamai asked Tavita.

'What are we supposed to know?' Semisi asked.

'She is the daughter of the tuua of Falealupo.'

'What's that got to do with knowing how to run a store — how to add and subtract?' Tavita said impatiently.

'She is also the guardian of the Lady,' Peleiupu offered.

'After her father, who died early in the epidemic, she is the most powerful — or, is it most feared? — person in this district,' Atamai added. 'Did you see the way she handled those matai earlier on?'

'She'll have no problems organising the men to cut copra,' Peleiupu said.

'And no one will dare steal from or raid our store. No one!' Atamai said.

Before lotu that evening, while she helped Fanua and her son cook the evening meal, Peleiupu learned from Fanua that whenever their village suffered a crisis, their fono met late at night in her father's faletele, in darkness, with all the blinds drawn except for one row facing the west. When Peleiupu asked why, Fanua hesitated, then, gazing full into her face, said, 'For the Lady to enter the fono and be consulted about the crisis. During the sickness not once did she participate in the fono. For her own reasons, she seems to have abandoned us to the mercy of the epidemic.'

The chorus of cicadas thundered in their ears as the rain eased away.

In the next two weeks they visited the rest of their stores, and set up new people to run them and schemes to cut all the copra that was on the ground.

Poto refused to go ashore at Salelologa, where Elisapeta, her daughter, and her husband Heinrich ran their business. Since discovering Ana's death at Falelupo she'd remained on board, playing patience or fishing from the boat. But before they could go ashore, Elisapeta and her surviving son were rowed to the *Lady Poto*, where she collapsed into Poto's arms and told them her husband and other children had died two weeks before.

Tavita, Semisi and Peleiupu went ashore. (Peleiupu was relieved to be away from Elisapeta's grief.) Before the epidemic, this had been their second most profitable store. Heinrich had been an excellent manager, adding a bakery, a plantation and a fautasi transport wing, and producing more copra than even their Satoa store. Since Heinrich's death, his sister and her husband had managed the business, and were doing well.

When they were on their own Peleiupu told Tavita she didn't want to return to the boat until they were ready to leave because she couldn't face Elisapeta's suffering. She was also dreading what they'd find at Fagaloto when they stopped to pick up her parents and Iakopo.

That night they slept in Elisapeta's fale by the sea.

She woke to him caressing her back and flanks, deliciously, and she moved so he

341

could remove her lavalava. For a long while he ran his fingers over her buttocks and between her legs from the back, until she was wet and trembling with anticipation. Lying on her side, she lifted her knees and thrust back her buttocks against him. His hand slid down between her buttocks and caressed her. She jerked, gasped, as he slid in. Reaching back, she held his buttocks still. Held him in there.

Later he moved slowly to the rhythm of the slow tide lapping at the rocks a short distance away. Slowly. For a long, long time they escaped the present and their grief . . .

Next morning, after breakfast with Heinrich's family, Tavita told Peleiupu there was something important he wanted to discuss with her. She sensed he'd been thinking about it for a long time. They went back to the fale.

'Please don't misinterpret what I'm going to say.' He paused and looked away. 'I know you're brighter than any of us, Pele, and that you've been brought up by your father to be honest and frank about your views . . .' The more surprised she became, the more shocked she was. '. . . You are a very different and exceptional person, Pele. That is one of the reasons why I love you. But . . .' He couldn't continue, and she wasn't going to help him. 'But it is also the reason why I get annoyed with you.' Looking directly at her, he said, 'Pele, you must try not to keep making me look and feel inadequate and unintelligent in front of others.'

'I don't do that!'

'See what I mean?' he pleaded. 'You're angry even before you consider seriously what I've just said.' He turned to leave. She held his arm.

'Tavita, I'm sorry,' she said in English.

'See, every time you want to control our conversation you use English because you're much better at it than me. Every time you use English when we're with others you show how inadequate my English is.'

It was incredible that he held these views about her and their relationship and had not told her before. 'Tavita, I don't do that — I don't do it deliberately. It's just the way you're choosing to see it.'

'Is there any other way for me to see it?' he attacked. 'That is the way most people, including many of my aiga, see it, Pele. Look at this trip. In all our negotiations and deals you've made Semisi and me look like idiots, in public. The ideas and plans have been yours — and you've said so in front of everyone. Pele, I resent your making me look less of a man in public. I resent the way you think I don't know when you're manipulating me to do what *you* want.'

'So what do I do, Tavita? If I try to convey my ideas and views to you privately so you won't look unmanly in public, you accuse me of being manipulative. When I voice my views publicly I'm again accused of that!' He refused to answer. 'So what do we do, Tavita? What do you want me to do?'

'Shit!' he shouted in English. 'Shit!'

'Tavita, you're the one who leads and runs our life and business. I may have the ideas but you have the qualities others respect and love. You trust people, you believe in them despite their awful failings and meanness, you're not interested in making money for its own sake, you put the welfare and interests of our aiga and community before your own, and most precious of all . . .' she started chortling. '. . . you're insightful enough to realise that you love me and without me your life would be a misery!' He swung around and started laughing. 'Yeah, David, you not speak English better than me!' she imitated his English. For once she didn't care if people were watching as she grabbed him around the waist, hugged him and kissed him full on the mouth.

She felt as if she were moving back into the skin she wore as the girl who'd fallen ill on Barker's death and had been brought to Fagaloto for Lefatu to heal, as she jumped off the punt onto the beach and watched her feet imprinting themselves in the soggy sand.

It was mid-morning and cool because the sun was hidden in cloud.

She dawdled behind as the others hurried up the track. The pandanus leaves reflected the mellow morning light. There it was: the heady scent of ripe guava and pandanus fruit.

She emerged from the vegetation and saw, up ahead through the rows of palms, their aiga's fale. Tavita and the others were already seated around the main fale being served food. Lefatu's husky laughter fondled Peleiupu's hearing, and she tingled with happiness knowing that her aunt was alive and well. Lefatu was sitting with Iakopo sharing her foodmat. Opposite her were Lalaga and Mautu. No other elders. Ruta? Peleiupu searched again. She couldn't see Ruta anywhere. Her feet refused to go forward. In the faleo'o were two people sitting beside someone lying in a stained mosquito net. The earth released her feet, Peleiupu started rushing to that net.

'Ruta, Ruta!' Peleiupu called, pulling up the side of the net.

'I'm here, Pele!' Ruta's voice snatched at Peleiupu, who turned. There she was, right there outside the net. Thinner — older, much older — but beautiful, so beautiful in being alive. Her sister.

Hugging each other, they cried and laughed and cried.

'Have you two gone crazy?' Semisi called from the faletele. 'You *sound* crazy!' The rest of their aiga laughed.

'Bring us some food!' Ruta called.

A few minutes later as they ate, they talked and talked and talked as if they were conversing themselves into existence, into versions of themselves they'd missed over the past few years. Soon Lefatu and Lalaga joined them, and when they had finished serving the meal all the other women and girls joined them too. That night Tavita would ask her about what they, the women, had talked so animatedly, and she wouldn't be able to recollect any details of it, but she'd never forget the intimate, blood-warm, renewing, reaffirming sound and feel of it all.

Later that day Ruta took her through the village, telling her that twenty-six aiga members had died in the epidemic, and only about two-fifths of Fagaloto's population had survived.

Fagaloto looked and felt more alive than the other villages they had visited, with people repairing their homes, weeding their gardens, penning their pigs, cutting and burning the grass on the malae, and cleaning their church and communal pool. People smiled and greeted them as they walked through. Ruta attributed Fagaloto's rapid recovery to Lefatu's persistent, indomitable leadership after the leading matai had died.

The only store, owned by a German firm, had closed down. Most of the family who ran it were dead, Ruta informed Peleiupu, who knew it wouldn't reopen because all German businesses had been closed down by the New Zealand administration. Ruta agreed with Peleiupu to persuade Lefatu to let her build a store.

On their return they found Mautu and Iakopo weeding around the faletele. Peleiupu cautioned their father about the heat, but he grinned and told them he was fitter than ever. 'Here, I'm at peace,' he added.

'May we go to the pool later?' Iakopo asked.

'Yes, but only after we've weeded right around the fale. And if your mother and her sister help us, we'll get it done quickly.'

'Come on then, Mama and Ruta!' Iakopo ordered.

'What do we get out of it?' Ruta asked. Iakopo glanced at his grandfather.

'A visit to a secret and sacred place,' Mautu replied. 'I'm not saying any more until you two help us.'

Within a silent, quick half hour they'd done the weeding and Iakopo was complaining about having to pile the weeds into his baskets and empty them into the sea.

Because of the heat most people had retreated into their fale. Iakopo fetched Mautu's bright red umbrella and sheltering him with it they went to the pool. A few young people were standing in the water, talking. They acknowledged them. Mautu washed his hands, face and head and retreated into the small poolside fale.

Iakopo followed his mother up the bank and laughed as he pushed her into the water, and then dived in after her. Ruta lowered herself into the water. 'Since we've been here, I've taken Iakopo to see all the important places of my childhood,' Mautu said. 'Lefatu has probably told Ruta about them already . . .' As he talked Peleiupu floated, letting the cool grip of the water relax her. 'Every place is made up of many layers of maps: physical maps imposed by different periods of settlement; historical maps of those people and periods; story maps; music and song maps; maps of suffering and joy and inspiration. My father knew most of the maps that are Fagaloto, and he told us about them . . .' Peleiupu drifted into herself. '. . . Fagaloto is a small and unimportant place. But if you know its maps, it becomes a profound and complex place, a home in the present that contains all that was before. It is everything that was, is and will move with us until we die and we take different forms that will continue moving with the present . . .'

Peleiupu told Iakopo it was time to leave the pool. He rushed up to the bank, did another dive and skimmed past her. 'Nobody's been listening to me!' Mautu complained.

'You know that's not true, Papa!' Ruta replied. She came out of the water, put up his umbrella and handed it to him. 'Let's go home and you can rest.'

'Then you can take us to that place, Papa,' Iakopo reminded him.

'Don't you ever forget anything?' Mautu joked, tossing his grandson the towel.

As they strolled home, with Mautu in the middle under his red umbrella, they took turns drying themselves with the one towel. 'So you see,' Mautu continued from where he'd left off at the pool, 'this walk is a walk over, through and with all that was and still is.'

'That's too complicated an explanation of reality for me, Papa,' Peleiupu teased him. 'I run away from history and all those other maps.'

'Yes, you confine yourself to the present, trading with it!' Ruta parodied. Peleiupu was hurt by the truth of it. Since living in Fagaloto, Ruta had stripped away all but the essential about herself and her life. Whenever Peleiupu heaped gifts and material possessions on her she gave them away. An attentive listener who talked only when she had to, Ruta moved unelaborately, without embellishments or unnecessary gestures. 'Papa, reality is one humorous story, isn't it? A story about the Va-nimonimo giving birth to the Rocks and the Rocks mating with the Sea and begetting the . . . ' Ruta continued.

'I'm hungry,' Iakopo complained.

Mautu started guffawing. 'Yes, nothing as real as the hungry belly!' Peleiupu and Ruta laughed. Iakopo looked puzzled.

'Or death, which nearly swallowed up all of us,' Ruta whispered to Peleiupu.

Before they entered the fale Lalaga chastised Mautu for keeping Iakopo out in the heat. She handed Iakopo a clean ie lavalava and told him to hurry up out of the sun. 'What about me?' Mautu complained. 'He can take the sun, he's young. My carcass can't!'

'You have a hide as thick as a buffalo's!' she replied.

'What do you know about buffaloes?' he quipped. She tossed him a dry ie lavalava and singlet.

'When are we going?' Iakopo asked him.

'Going where?' Lalaga asked.

'Just to get some pineapples from Ruta's plantation,' Iakopo lied. Mautu had sworn them to secrecy.

'You can come too, Lalaga,' Mautu invited her. Peleiupu was surprised by that, but was glad her mother was to be included in what she anticipated was going to be a complex revelation.

Peleiupu and Ruta went to the other end of the fale and changed. 'What do you think he's talking about?' Peleiupu asked Ruta.

'I don't know. I know most of the maps he's talking about. Lefatu has taught them to me. So I'm really curious, too.'

Peleiupu was surprised when, instead of heading into the plantations and the rugged interior, Mautu started across the malae towards the eastern end of the village. The sun was still hidden behind the range, which was casting its shadow over the village. The track felt wet and gritty under her bare feet. Only a few chickens and pigs were about. Most fale were hunched in sleep, still. Past the church, Mautu turned to the track that led along the seashore, his right hand on Iakopo's shoulder.

Ruta and Peleiupu walked on either side of their mother. Peleiupu could tell from the spring in her mother's step that she was excited too. It was getting hot already, so she was relieved they were not going into the bush. The slight breeze wafting in from the sea smelt faintly of decaying coral and fresh salt, and she could tell from the feeling in her bones that the tide was coming in.

At the last fale, deserted since the epidemic and now collapsing around its centre post, Mautu turned left and took the track over lava into thick vegetation and Totoume Peninsula. Ruta and Lalaga hesitated. Peleiupu wanted to ask but didn't. She couldn't remember much about that time Lefatu had taken her and her sisters into the peninsula: most strongly she recalled the feeling of solemnity laced with fear, and Lefatu walking as if she hadn't wanted to damage the ground she was walking on.

346

The peninsula, made up of massive lava outcrops, was now covered with thick bush and tangled undergrowth. No one had ever been allowed to cut any of it. 'Why is he taking us there?' Lalaga asked.

Ruta, who obviously knew the track well, entered it and the bush and, as she led, pushed aside the branches and shrubs, making it easier for their parents. It was dank and dark and thick with the smell of decaying leaves and vegetation. Soon they were wet from the dew, and Peleiupu's ie lavalava felt like a second skin. Around them sounded the cooing of pigeons and the cries of manutagi, miti and segasegamo'u. Peleiupu peered up into the tangled canopy and glimpsed some of the birds.

The track got steeper, more broken and strewn with boulders and rocks. Peleiupu started panting audibly, and envied Ruta and her mother who were fit, unflustered, unbothered by the steepness and difficulty of navigating boulders, rocks and gigantic tree roots. As they climbed, Peleiupu looked back, glimpsing the sea and the edge of the seashore. The tide was well in.

At the top of the rise she leaned against the side of the trunk of a gigantic tamanu tree and sucked in air. 'You all right?' Ruta asked. Peleiupu nodded and noticed that Mautu and Iakopo had disappeared down the other side, which was free of trees and undergrowth. Palm trees had replaced the other vegetation.

Peleiupu followed Ruta and Lalaga down the slope, holding on to shrubs and rocks to stop her from slipping.

The palms thickened into a large grove where the air was dark and cool and hurt their lungs as they breathed it in. Then they were in the centre of the grove, a circular clearing with seven flat boulders spaced around its circumference. The floor of the clearing was covered with shredded white coral, black river pebbles and broken shells. Ahead on the centre boulder was seated Mautu, on the next boulder to his right, Iakopo. Niuafei, centre of the Atua Fatutapu, Peleiupu remembered. And she was suddenly tense, heart beating faster. She glanced at her mother who was obviously feeling the same.

Ruta walked into the clearing, her feet clicking over the loose covering. She stopped at the centre, turned and beckoned them to enter. Because Ruta looked so secure and safe, Peleiupu accepted her invitation and went to her. Lalaga followed. Walled in by palm trees, Peleiupu felt as if she were in the calm eye of a whirlpool.

'You've looked after it well,' Mautu congratulated Ruta who sat down on the boulder to his left.

'It is easy to do because most of our people dare not come here,' Ruta explained. Lalaga sat down beside Iakopo. Mautu patted the place beside him on his boulder. Peleiupu took that.

'Ruta knows everything — well, *almost* everything — about Niuafei,' Mautu said. 'And I've spent this week telling Iakopo about it.' He paused. 'But there's an important part of it that I've never revealed to any of you. Lefatu and I were sworn to secrecy by our mother and our father's sister.' He rose awkwardly to his feet. Pointing his walking stick at the lava outcrops under the towering trees at the eastern edge of the clearing, he moved off towards them.

The rays of the morning sun penetrated the vegetation and armoured him with a white luminosity. 'Come on!' he called. Ruta followed him. As Peleiupu followed, she found her son almost hugging her side. Lalaga stayed close to him.

At the clearing's edge Mautu pushed his walking stick into the thick undergrowth and pushed some of it aside. Ruta wrenched the branches off, revealing a narrow coral-covered path up to and through the outcrops. As Peleiupu entered, the cloying smell of decaying vegetation and damp earth clogged her nostrils. Moths and gnats scattered into the air as they moved deeper into shadow and the long, sad, watching silence.

The path ended twenty paces in. Mautu stopped and pointed up into the gap between the lava outcrops. Ruta clambered up over the rocks and tangled tree roots, and stood between the outcrops. 'Move forward four more paces,' Mautu instructed her. She did so and was in the middle of the outcrops. She stretched out her arms and touched both sides. 'What are you standing on?'

She squatted down and, with both hands, dug up the loose surface. 'Soil and loose pebbles and coral,' she replied.

'Dig further down,' he called. Iakopo broke from Peleiupu's side and, scrambling up to Ruta, dug with her. Ruta and Iakopo held up handfuls of shattered coral. 'That *is* the place!' he declared.

Peleiupu joined Ruta and Iakopo and examined the floor between the outcrops. Just under the rich layer of decaying leaves and soil was a thick layer of coral turned bone-white by the rain leaching down through it. Lalaga joined them and helped clear off the covering until the whole coral layer was exposed to the brightening light.

When Peleiupu looked down at her father, he was gazing up at them, with tears streaming down his face. 'That is where he is buried,' he announced. Peleiupu didn't understand. 'My father, Tuifolau Molimau, is buried there. Has Lefatu ever told you that, Ruta?' She shook her head. Peleiupu stepped off her grandfather's grave.

'But what about the grave with the other aiga graves by the faletele?' Lalaga asked.

'My mother's grave there is genuine, but my father is buried here. He made my mother and his sister Folofa'i promise to bury him here overlooking the centre of Niuafei.'

They came down and sat around him. Ruta wiped away his tears. 'They buried a coffin packed with sacks of sand beside the fale,' he confessed. 'My mother and Folofa'i took out his body at night when everyone was asleep, and hid it away until after his coffin was mourned and buried. Then, at night, they brought him here. They kept it a secret even from me — until the night before I went away to Salua to study for the ministry. Because I was ashamed of our pagan heritage, I didn't tell anyone about it until now. I was also afraid of what would happen to me if I broke my promise to my mother.' Lalaga edged closer to him. 'I'm glad they buried him here, in the heart of our aiga of master navigators and Fatutapu. I'm glad.'

'You've come home at last, Papa,' Ruta consoled him.

Lalaga held his arm. 'We've all come home,' she said. 'I've been so condemning, Mautu, of the so-called pagan past of our people.'

'Ruta, in the short time left before we return to Satoa, I want you to school Iakopo in our ways and maps, which our Tuifolau ancestors devised to live our lives by,' he instructed. 'One day he will need those maps to guide him and his mother back to Niuafei.' Suddenly Peleiupu was aware that even the birds were silent. Their dead were with them and they felt safe and complete. 'Lalaga, I want you to promise . . .'

'No, no!' Lalaga denied him. 'I know what you're going to ask!'

'Then you'd better leave us, so I can discuss it with my daughters,' he said. She rose, stopped, and sat down again. 'Lalaga, my beloved, you have been my star-map all our life together. I want you to help me return to the start of that map, to here.' He pointed to his father's grave. 'I want you to promise that I will be buried here beside my father.' Silence, long and demanding. 'Ruta and Pele, you will devise a way to get me back here, secretly. Bury only my work and my life in Satoa, but bring my bones back to Niuafei and my aiga.'

'Papa, I'll help Mama do it!' Iakopo promised.

'I also want you to promise that when you find Arona, you must persuade him to return home . . . ' He stopped, unable to finish.

'If he is dead, promise you will bring him home still,' Lalaga finished his wish.

'And bury him here, beside me,' Mautu added.

Lalaga's Song

Monday 27 October 1919, three months after their return from Fagaloto. From the school, through the fierce noonday heat and light, wafted the sound of singing:

> Amuia lava o peau o le sami
> E aga i sisifo, e aga i sasa'e,
> Ae le iloa mai lo'u tino a mate . . .

Mautu's eyes were heavy with drowsiness. It was time for his afternoon nap. He staggered up from his desk, rehitched his ie lavalava — his body was covered with a thin film of sweat — and shuffled out to the veranda.

Just before he took his canvas chair he looked down and across the village and bay — a methodical loving sweep of a world in which everything and every creature knew its proper place and role, a world he'd helped to build in the wisdom of God's Light. When he gazed up into the sky the light stung his eyes and, for a burning instant, he was blind. He reached back, found the chair and slid back into it, into the familiar smell of his own sweat impregnated into the canvas; wriggled his frame left, then right, then left again, until the pliant chair fitted him snugly, like Lalaga's embrace; leaned his head back on the wooden support, turned it a little to the left to correct the touch of dizziness, sighed and relaxed. Just before he shut his eyes he caught sight of Lalaga framed in the centre classroom window, frizzy white hair gleaming, face suffused with pleasure as she conducted the children's singing:

. . . ma lo'u fatu e ua momomo, le ula,

i au amio e fe'olo,

Anei a malepe si a ta soa,

Ma si a ta soa . . .

For a while as he sang with them, he caressed Lalaga's image in his mind. Caressed it . . .

'Is this all you're entitled to, Mautu, after your long dedicated service to God and community?' the question came over his left shoulder. That voice? . . . Mautu turned and was surprised he could move so swiftly and painlessly at his age. But there was no one there — just the watching, lush bush and that familiar flying-fox smell. 'Is a comfortable nap your only reward, my friend?'

'Barker?' he asked the surrounding bush, but his friend refused to step out of the green. 'Where are you?' He felt the bush and sky shaking with Barker's ironic laughter. Mautu glanced at his arms, his legs, his torso. Incredible! He was again the young pastor who'd first come to Satoa. 'Is that all you're good at, eh?' Mautu taunted. Still the invisible Barker laughed on. 'Yes, you're a callous, know-it-all cynic!' Dead silence. Mautu knew he'd gone too far, and wanted his friend to forgive him. He heard footsteps running away decisively through the dry, brittle undergrowth. 'No, please, Barker!' he heard himself pleading, but the sound of Barker's unforgiving escape continued.

'And you're a bloody liar, too!' Mautu shouted as he started crashing through the undergrowth, which scratched and tore at his skin. 'A bloody con-man!' When he realised he was young and fit again he ran faster, his feet tracing Barker's hobnailed-boot prints in the thick carpet of dead leaves print by print and gaining on him. 'You're a bloody con-man!' he shouted, his blood pumping wildly with the exhilaration of the chase.

He broke into a narrow clearing that was covered with shattered lava rock. The clammy air was heavy with Barker's exhausted panting and smell. 'You can't run any more, eh? I've got you!' Mautu called.

For a long fascinated while he watched as the shattered lava moved and, like a jigsaw puzzle, connected piece by piece to form the Barker with whom he'd explored the Satoa Valley for gold: the pith helmet, red bushy beard and hair, sunburnt nose and forehead and all.

'So you've got me!' laughed Barker. 'What are you going to do with me, la'u uo?'

'More correctly, I've got one version of you!'

'So I'm a cynic and a con-man, eh?' Barker confronted him.

Mautu didn't want to offend his friend further, but he heard himself saying, 'Yes, you see no good in people, and you lied to me and my children about your life . . .'

'Lied?' Barker raised his voice. 'Lied?' He jumped to his feet.

'Yes, the confessions you *bequeathed* to me and Pele are — are *incredible!*'

Barker settled back. 'No, my friend. I was an orphan and queer . . .'

'. . . But . . . but!' spluttered Mautu.

'But what, Mautu? What?'

'When you came to Satoa you married a woman!' Mautu felt ridiculous saying that.

'And had children and in no way showed I was of Sodom?' Mautu nodded. 'Perhaps God answered my prayers and *cured* me of my disease,' Barker added. 'You *do* believe your God can do that, Mautu?' Mautu had to agree. 'Yes, God cured me of my evil,' Barker repeated, a cynical smile on his lips.

'How do I know you're telling the truth now?' Mautu couldn't stop his doubts.

'You just have to trust me.'

Mautu found the whole world empty of sound. He tried speaking but the emptiness swallowed up his words, while Barker just stood there smiling. Mautu grasped at the silence, and felt as if he were trying to swim through thick oily liquid. As he shouted to be heard, the silence started clogging his mouth. Smiling still, Barker plunged his right hand down into Mautu's throat and in one swift motion pulled out the silence. Mautu gagged and spluttered and the sounds of the world rushed into his ears again. 'Are you all right?' Barker asked.

'You took our son away!' Mautu finally had the courage to say. 'You filled Arona's head with your stories of the world beyond the reefs; filled it with your lies, your exaggerated, fanciful adventures, so much so he had to go away and find out . . .'

'No, Mautu, you can't hang that seduction on my head,' Barker interrupted.

'My son had to find out!' Mautu wept. When Barker reached over and touched his arm, Mautu jumped away. 'Don't touch me!'

'I love you!' Barker whispered.

'You're dead, and that's that!' Mautu countered.

Inexplicably, Barker started peeling off his human appearance and, as the rubber-like layer snapped and ripped away, feathers, sleek wings, bird body and then the head and beak of a frigate bird appeared. Mautu's heart lifted in wonderful admiration and love as the bird preened and strutted. 'Do you believe me now, Mautu?' Barker whispered. Mautu nodded and nodded. 'Do ya wanna fly with me, lover?' the frigate winked.

'Yes, please, please, please!' Mautu pleaded.

He was on the frigate's back, his arms and legs wrapped around its neck and body, the feathered body lush and silky and warm against his bare chest and torso. As the Frigate lifted, wings outstretched across the heavens and the whole expanse of the world, Mautu felt profoundly secure and safe for he knew — and his happiness was complete — he was going home . . .

The heat was lifting, and the house was cooler now that it was covered by the shadows of the mango trees. Relieved her teaching was over, Lalaga placed the stack of slates on Mautu's desk and, as usual, hurried out to the veranda to see him.

She stopped a few paces away, surprised that he was still asleep. He looked weightless, free, suspended yet utterly at home in the embrace of the chair. The white of the canvas and his wispy hair and stubble made him appear as if he were turning into light. And there, right there at the centre of the light, was the smile of a child who'd discovered what the light was all about and wasn't going to reveal it.

She knelt down beside him and, as the shadows lengthened and the breeze grew stronger, she caressed his face, caressed his shoulders and arms, caressed his hands . . . 'Thank you, beloved. Thank you for the good life you provided for me, for us and our children . . .' She placed her head on his thigh and said, 'We have only one wish that God has not granted, Mautu: our son has not returned.' And she wept, silently.

Iakopo found them and rushed off to get Peleiupu. Their household and other Satoans gathered quickly, but Lalaga refused to let them touch Mautu's body. With Peleiupu's help she carried him to his bed, drew the curtains and shut out Satoa. She instructed Peleiupu to prepare the house. 'Don't cry,' she ordered her daughter. 'Make sure no one else — absolutely no one — comes in here.'

She fetched water, washed and oiled his body, dressed him in his favourite suit. The chorus of cicadas was pulling in the evening from the horizon.

When Lalaga emerged from behind the curtain Tavita and all the matai were seated around the house. 'He is ready,' she told them. Toanamua's tulafale started to speak, but she said, 'No, no speeches will be made.' Turning to Peleiupu, she asked, 'Is his bed ready?' Peleiupu gestured to the thick bed of mats and ie toga near the middle of the room.

Aided by Tavita and Peleiupu, she brought his body and, after laying it on the mats, covered it up to the neck with ie toga. She sat down beside his head.

Poto and other leading members of the aualuma gathered beside her. The ritual wailing began. 'Stop, that is enough!' Lalaga ordered. 'Mautu lived a long and happy life: there is no need to mourn.'

Peleiupu dispatched the *Lady Poto* to fetch Lefatu, Ruta and the other elders of their Aiga Sa-Tuifolau. On its way back, it called in to Manono and collected Naomi and Pate. Peleiupu, Ruta and Naomi, with Tavita's support, would organise and control the whole funeral.

The Satoans expected Lefatu, their pastor's supposedly pagan sister and curer of ma'i aitu, to behave in bizarre pagan ways. She didn't. She came into the house quietly, with head bowed, sat down by her brother's head, opposite Lalaga, leaned forward and kissed him on the forehead. 'Mautu, I have come,' she said to him. She would say little else for the whole period of mourning, but the large numbers of mourners who came to pay their last respects knew who she was and why she had come.

'Our pastor must be buried here with us,' the matai instructed Tavita. 'That is the practice. We cannot let Lefatu and her aiga take him back. What would Samoa think of us?'

So they were surprised and relieved when Lefatu made no such demand. On the fifth day of mourning, in the late afternoon, with Lalaga's agreement, Lefatu declared politely to everyone in the house that, because the heat and length of time were treating her brother's body 'unforgivingly', they had to close his coffin that evening.

Iakopo was the last mourner to kiss his grandfather goodbye. Copying his grandmother, he didn't cry.

The Satoans expected Lalaga and her daughters, at least, to weep and wail and try to stop Tavita and Mikaele from nailing down the lid. They didn't. In fact, Peleiupu handed Tavita the nails. 'Such unfeeling afakasi behaviour!' many of them said, but not within Tavita's hearing.

The next morning Pate, Naomi's husband, aided by two LMS pastors from neighbouring villages, conducted Mautu's funeral service. The Satoans expected it to last at least three hours, befitting their beloved pastor's status. It lasted one hour. Again they blamed it on Peleiupu's and Tavita's afakasi behaviour. They were mistaken. Lalaga had ordered Pate to have a short service.

Mautu was buried in a large grave beside his beloved church. It was the first concrete grave to be built in Satoa; it was also going to have a gravestone, designed by Mikaele, and ordered from New Zealand.

That evening, when the matai gathered at the pastor's house for lotu and to continue comforting Lalaga and her family, they were told by Lalaga, through Tavita, that she had to return the following day with Lefatu and her aiga to Fagaloto to have a funeral service there for Mautu; she told them it was a practice unique to the Aiga Sa-Tuifolau. She asked the elders to continue welcoming the late mourners, on her behalf. She knew the elders were worried about having to feed the mourners, so she assured them Tavita and their aiga would continue 'treating the mourners in the aristocratic manner they are used to'.

Peleiupu told Tavita to use the opportunity to send Semisi and some carpenters to build their store at Fagaloto. 'We're supposed to be mourning!' he insisted. 'One day's mourning at Fagaloto will suffice,' Lefatu told him. So Semisi and Mikaele chose two carpenters, and loaded the boat with building supplies. They didn't pay any attention to the long crate that came on with the supplies, and they would not notice it disappearing when the cargo was unloaded in Fagaloto.

Of the grandchildren, only Iakopo was allowed to accompany Lalaga, Lefatu, Ruta, Peleiupu, Naomi and the elders of the Aiga Sa-Tuifolau.

After their first night in Fagaloto, fearful stories erupted in Fagaloto of mysterious lights carried by floating female figures and a boy, in a funeral procession, moving through the outskirts of the village and disappearing into the wild darkness of Totoume Peninsula. When the elders gathered at the Aiga Sa-Tuifolau's faletele for Mautu's commemoration service, Lefatu calmed their fears by interpreting the mysterious funeral procession as the spirits of Mautu's ancestors returning to welcome him home.

When the crew of the *Lady Poto* spread the stories in Satoa on their return, the Satoans scoffed at Fagaloto's pagan backwardness, and congratulated themselves on their enlightened Christian ways: they had Mautu's Christian body buried in their Christian soil, and his Christian soul was now with their Christian God.

It was the practice, when a pastor died while still serving, for the village to return his wife to her aiga. So while Lalaga and her daughters packed her things and the house, Tavita and the matai organised for the journey. Elders of her aiga had attended Mautu's funeral and were now back in their village organising to receive Lalaga and the elders of Satoa.

Ruta, Naomi and Peleiupu assumed that was what their mother wanted. And for the first few days, while they packed, she didn't indicate otherwise. She set her usual quick pace, kept at her chores methodically, and they found it difficult to keep up with her. Then she surprised them, she started laughing, joking and then humming. The hesitant, broken humming gained confidence and turned into a tune, a melody, about Mautu and Arona, which started infecting them all. This was another wonderful surprise because their mother had never composed a song before.

The lyrics emerged as Lalaga worked around the house, and they picked it up bit by bit:

> Ali'i o le Galuega, ua e sola i Niuafei
> Lua te fa'atasi ai ma le atua lalelei.
> Ua e sola i Niuafei
> O lagomau ai gafa paia o le Tuifolau.
> Loa tausaga o le ta mafutaga

I galuega na tofia ai taua e le atua.

Ae paga ua motusia le ula o le alofa

Ae le'i fo'i mai Arona i ana tafaoga.

Po'o fea o i ai le ta tama

Na sola i le vasa o folauga?

Fea o i ai Arona le i'omata?

Paga, Mautu, ua e alu ae le'i sau le tama . . .

Iakopo taught it to his sisters and friends, who taught it to theirs, until many Satoans were singing it.

Tavita suggested to Moegamalu, Satoa's songmaker and leader of their choir, Ali'i ma Faipule o Satoa, that they should learn and sing it at the annual church fono at Salua to honour their pastor, who'd been a Faifeau Toeaina in their national church.

Moegamalu would do that and, after the Salua fono, the delegates would take the song home with them and teach it to others.

Pese A Lalaga would become a national hit.

But before that happened, Lalaga sat alone with her daughters and asked, 'Pele, why haven't you invited me to stay here with you in Satoa?' There was a huge surprised silence. 'I've been waiting, Pele. I can't invite myself to stay.'

'Mama, we'd love you to stay!' Peleiupu crawled over on her knees and hugged her mother. 'We never thought you'd want to.'

'This is my home. I've spent most of my life here. I've taught just about everyone in Satoa.' For the first time since Mautu died, she started weeping, openly.

Her daughters engulfed her in their embrace.

Lalaga refused to live in Pele's and Tavita's house, so a large fale was built for her behind it. There she lived with Pili, her adopted son from the terror of the epidemic, her grandchildren, and the women Peleiupu chose to care for her.

Lalaga sensed rain on the dark morning horizon as she sat up and wrapped her sleeping sheet around her body and gazed out at the village and sea. The pain in her joints and the smell of the air told her that. Six months, three weeks and eleven days since Mautu died. Pili stirred beside her; she put her hand over his shoulder. Each day as the boy and her grandchildren grew, she hoped they'd fill the enormous, ever-present emptiness left by the death of Mautu, which made her feel unreal and divorced from the life around her. She tried to persuade herself that the children were a reason for continuing her life. Mautu had been the largest presence in her reality, and even now her dreams were full of him. At times and to her shame — pastor's wives shouldn't — she craved him sexually . . .

. . . This day were are reborn with the morning
We are given the Light to live by . . .

She started singing to ward off the memories and pain. Some of her grandchildren and helpers woke, and, sitting up reluctantly, joined her singing. Pili curled up against her flanks; she picked him up and, putting him in her lap, wrapped her arms round him. He continued sleeping as she sang:

Bless us, Oh Lord, with physical strength
To work another day . . .

Just before the end of the hymn she observed that the mango trees to the right were flowering, and recalled that mangoes were Mautu's and Barker's favourite fruit. Wasn't it Barker who'd once remarked that Satoans were children of the mango season? What had he meant by that? From over the sea the rain was advancing towards Satoa, like a transparent green curtain. She wondered what revelation was hidden behind it.

She closed her eyes and started praying aloud. The rain hit the palms, banana trees and fale on the seashore with a loud clatter, and then it was upon their paepae, sounding like the frantic flapping and gyrations of the chicken whose head she'd chopped off with her father's bushknife, on her father's instructions, when she was a child. How she missed Mautu! How she missed Arona! Pili snuggled back against her breasts. The rain passed over their fale quickly.

Iakopo, her favourite and the most Mautu-like of her grandchildren, brought her usual morning mug of koko from the house, and took Pili away with him. How Iakopo reminded her of Arona, she thought as she took her first mouthful of hot koko, and didn't understand why it tasted acidic and slightly rancid. She took another: the same taste. Now she was feeling cold, feverish. She usually drove away such ailments with hard work so she slipped on her working tiputa and, sitting on her tattered work mat, started weeding under the mango trees.

When she saw Lefatu and Maualuga moving about in the fale she called, 'Come out here and pick up the rubbish!' She ignored their muffled grizzling as they dragged their feet out to her and started picking up the fallen mango leaves. Mango blossoms fluttered down over them as they worked.

Peleiupu emerged from her office and called Lalaga in to breakfast, which she and Tavita usually had with her, but Lalaga told her daughter to go ahead without her. The fever got worse so she got a towel and some soap and hurried to the deserted pool, where she immersed herself up to her neck in the cold water until she believed her temperature was back to normal.

By midday, however, she was shivering almost uncontrollably as she tried to continue weaving the ie toga she'd been working on for almost ten years. She wrapped Mautu's blanket around herself — his smell comforted her, lay down with her head on her bamboo ali, and tried to sweat out her fever, but the burning and pain in her bones and behind her eyes worsened. Soon she drifted off to sleep.

Her conscience told her that a pastor's wife should not be having such a shocking and sinful dream. She tried switching it off but it became more deliciously vivid and deliriously real.

The mangoes hanging down from every branch and almost touching her head were enormous: fat and ripe for her picking. She plucked one. Pluck! Plucked two. Pluck! Ahh, she sighed as she weighed their apt solidity in her hands, rolled them across her lips, licked them with her hungry tongue. From the depths of her throat, tremors of desire shimmered down into her heart and belly. She visualised her teeth sinking into the succulent mango flesh, the thick juice bursting out and dribbling down her lips as she tried to suck it all in, in one gulping *suwiittcchh*! Aware she was wet, so wet, she opened her eyes. Stop! her conscience demanded. Get out of this Satan-inspired dream! But she knew she'd kill to stay in it: all her senses and pores demanded that. Lick and suck, lick and suck! The slick, smooth feel of the mango skin turned to the soft, hot touch of skin and hair. She dared to look. There, right there in the centre of her vision, her hands cupped around them, were the testicles and quivering erect penis she'd enjoyed for about forty years. Her head and body sang . . .

'I'm not sick!' Lalaga told Peleiupu. Lefatu had told her Lalaga was ill. Peleiupu could feel the heat emanating from her mother's body. It was almost time for evening lotu.

'Have you taken any tablets?'

'You know I don't take any of *that* medicine.' Lalaga tried to sit up. Peleiupu helped her and found that the blanket was soaked through with sweat. 'It's just a slight fever,' Lalaga insisted.

Lefatu and Maualuga brought a towel and dry clothes for their grandmother. Peleiupu dried Lalaga and put the clothes on her. 'You're not well,' Peleiupu said. 'You will shift into the house so we can take better care of you.'

'I was born in a fale; I'll die in one!' Lalaga protested.

Many of their aiga had arrived for the lotu; they tried to look as if they didn't notice the tension between Lalaga and Peleiupu. Since Mautu's death the tension and heated silences had worsened.

'You won't have to stay in the house forever,' Peleiupu argued.

'I . . . I miss your father,' Lalaga said. 'I just dreamt about him — and my parents.'

'I miss him too, Mama.'

'So you should — after all, his love for you was greater than for any of his other children.' A deliberate wounding but Peleiupu excused her mother because, as Poto had told her, 'Lalaga is now grumpy and forgetful.' 'Well, don't you think that was so?' Lalaga pursued her.

Peleiupu couldn't stop herself. 'Yes, Mama, and because you want me to admit it: yes, he loved me even more than you.' She didn't care that the tension level in the fale rose alarmingly with that remark. 'But you loved and still love Arona — or should I say, all the beautiful stories you and others have made up about him — more than me and my sisters.' Before she could wound further, Pili scuttled into the fale and, rushing over, slid into Lalaga's arms.

'Mama, you're very hot,' the boy said.

'Ask Pele why!' Lalaga snapped.

That night Peleiupu couldn't sleep. She feared for her mother: during lotu she'd seen that luminous aura of light that she saw every time someone was about to die. Eventually she got out of bed and, using a torch, picked her silent way into Lalaga's fale, over the other sleepers, into her net, where she snuggled down into her mother's familiar smell and presence.

The next morning when Tavita asked her why she wanted Mikaele to take the *Lady Poto* to fetch Lefatu and Ruta she told him, 'Only they may be able to heal my mother. And Naomi needs to be here too, in case . . . '

'But we now have palagi medicine,' he insisted. 'We can even afford for the *Lady Poto* to go to Apia and bring back a palagi doctor.'

'That won't heal her!'

'Healers who use pagan cures certainly won't!'

She slammed her frustrated fist down on the table and shouted, 'My mother is dying: she has *your* Disease!'

'What do you mean? Are you mad?'

'She has your Satoan Disease!' She hugged herself. He put his arms around her.

'It can't be. No one's been sick with it for years.'

Over the next few days, while they waited for Mikaele to bring the others, Lalaga's condition deteriorated rapidly. The nurse tried all the appropriate medicines in her clinic — none worked. Lalaga burned and vomited up everything she ate or drank, and she winced with pain whenever anyone touched her. She didn't complain, though.

As soon as Ruta arrived with Lefatu she started treating Lalaga. 'Ruta will ease your pain,' Lefatu told Lalaga. 'She's now a much better healer than I am.'

Ruta mixed a nonu paste in a glass of warm water. 'What a horrible smell!' Lalaga complained as she drank it.

'It'll relax you, help reduce the pain,' Ruta said.

'You've taught her well,' Lalaga congratulated Lefatu.

Later, while Ruta bathed her, Lalaga said, 'Soon I'll only be bones and weigh what I did at birth!' Lefatu laughed with her. 'I'm disappearing!'

Naomi dried her gently, and then Ruta started rubbing a herbal potion all over her body. Slow soothing strokes. 'It feels good, good!' Lalaga whispered. 'The pain is going away.'

She feel asleep quickly. They lowered her mosquito net. 'It is time to tell our family,' Lefatu advised Peleiupu, who sent Iakopo, carrying Pili on his hip, to fetch Tavita.

Tavita came and sat with them around Lalaga's net. Peleiupu sent everyone else away. They waited in silence until Peleiupu realised they were expecting her, the eldest, to speak first. She kept looking at Ruta.

'All right,' Ruta complied. 'Our mother has been chosen by the Satoan Disease.'

'It is pagan to believe such . . . such superstition,' Naomi pronounced.

'The Disease has considered her worthy of its ultimate blessing.' Ruta chose to ignore her sister's remark.

'How can such a terrible pain and suffering be considered a blessing?' Naomi attacked.

The others looked at Peleiupu. 'Are you speaking as a pastor's wife or as our sister who grew up in Satoa and knows that Ruta's diagnosis is correct?' she asked Naomi.

'Our Christian mother, the wife of our Christian father and pastor, would reject such a diagnosis!' Naomi retorted.

'Are you sure?' Lefatu intervened, knowing a nasty argument was erupting. 'Are you sure your mother wouldn't agree with Ruta?' Naomi withdrew into a soft whimpering, hands clutched over her face. Peleiupu wound her arm around Naomi's shoulders. 'The name of her illness is unimportant. What is important is that she has chosen to go to Mautu — and to God. Your mother has lived a long and wonderful life. I envy her,' Lefatu said.

'What are we going to tell the rest of our aiga and Satoa?' Peleiupu asked them.

For lotu that evening their new pastor, Taleni Sola, and his wife and many of the elders and Lalaga's friends gathered in Lalaga's fale. Halfway through the hymn Lalaga sat up, pushed the net aside and slid out to join the singing. Lefatu slid over and sat with her. They looked so old, yet content and happy to be old, Peleiupu thought. Pili ran over and Lalaga gathered him into her arms and lap.

After the meal, when she was alone with her daughters and Tavita, Lalaga made them promise there would be no fa'a-Samoa at her funeral. 'I'm not an ali'i, so there's to be no lagi, no extravagant, wasteful exchange of ie toga and money and goods. The fa'a-Samoa is being used by greedy and unscrupulous people to benefit themselves; it is a killing burden on all of us.' She made Tavita promise he wasn't going to let the greedy matai of Satoa persuade him otherwise. 'I also hope that my funeral will begin a new tradition of freeing our people of the burdens of the fa'a-Samoa.' Naomi and Tavita agreed with her. Then, looking directly at Peleiupu, Lalaga said, 'And don't forget you promised your father that you'd find your only brother and bring him home.' Peleiupu reached over and held her trembling hands.

'And if we find his life has ended,' Naomi declared, 'we will bring home his body.'

'And bury it at Niuafei beside Mautu,' Ruta ended.

'Thank you,' Lalaga whispered. 'Thank you.'

Tavita summoned the fono to his faletele the next morning. Peleiupu insisted on being there, even though she knew she shouldn't be. All the matai came, knowing a very lucrative funeral was about to happen.

'I want to dispense with all formalities,' Tavita welcomed them. 'You know that our mother in Christ and the wife of our illustrious father is very ill. We believe she has our Disease.' Peleiupu noted the appropriate look of shock on the matais' faces. 'Yes, our Disease has chosen her because she has led an exemplary Christian life.' They nodded enthusiastically. 'It is also God's will.' He paused and coughed. 'I've called this meeting to organise her funeral and farewell.'

Tutusa, Tavita's leading tulafale, expressed the 'great sorrow of our living and our dead at our mother in Christ's illness'. His speech became more verbose, more ornate, more dramatic as he continued. Tavita coughed once more and his tulafale got the message and ended with, 'We must, as a caring, loyal, grateful village, accord our mother a funeral worthy of her true aristocratic lineage and her great aristocratic aiga.'

Tavita countered immediately. 'Lalaga has instructed me that she does not — and I repeat — she does *not* want any fa'a-Samoa at her funeral. There is to be no exchange of ie toga. I respect her wishes and will carry them out.'

Peleiupu noted that most of the matai revealed no signs of dismay, shock or protest. But she knew better.

'Our mother is of the highest royalty in this sinful country,' Tutusa opened. 'We are very fortunate to have the daughter of the Aiga Sa-Malietoa as our mother and our connection to God and our salvation.' There were tears in his clear eyes. The others nodded; some echoed their leader's praises of Lalaga. Here it comes, Peleiupu thought. 'Toanamua, our ali'i, the great son of Satoa, heir to the sacred Aiga Sa-Satoa and Sa-Tuala: this most unworthy person, because he is your most loyal and obedient servant, feels he must remind your lordship, that you and our most loving mother belong to the most noble aiga of Samoa.' Tutusa stopped and swept his solemn gaze over the others. 'How are those aiga . . . how is the whole of Samoa going to view you and our most sacred village if we do not farewell our mother in the true aristocratic manner worthy of her and her sacred connections and you, your lordship?'

'That is enough!' Tavita stopped him dead. Peleiupu couldn't believe it: Tavita had never before demanded obedience from his tulafale in public, and so rudely. She believed it, though, when he added, 'This matter is closed. I have just told you what we're going to do. Hold all ie toga — you know what that means. Tell everyone!'

'What happens if mourners insist on presenting ie toga?' she heard herself asking. No untitled person, let alone a woman, had ever spoken in their fono. The other matai looked to Tavita to chastise his presumptuous wife.

'The ie toga will be politely but firmly returned to them, with a sua,' Tavita disappointed them. 'Furthermore, from here on all funerals in our district and village will follow that principle. And when we attend other villages' funerals, we will not take ie toga. We must teach other people to get rid of the wasteful features of the fa'a-Samoa.' Most of the matai were now truly shocked.

'What happens, sir, if Lagaga's most noble aiga arrives and demands that they take her back with them?' Tutusa was trying another ploy.

'My mother will not be taken back,' Peleiupu blocked him. 'She has said she wants to be buried beside Mautu and in the village she loves.'

Again they expected their ali'i to push her back into her proper female place, but Tavita said to them, 'You've heard what Pele has said. And you all know that what Pele wants, Pele gets, eh!' Some of the minor matai, who supported her because she always extended them credit, laughed with Tavita.

Straight after their meeting and the generous aristocratic meal Peleiupu and her aiga provided them — they even got a fat basket of food each to take home — Tutusa and his supporters, who owed Peleiupu large debts, spread the story throughout the district that their 'poor and loving mother, Lalaga, is to be accorded a very miserly, very un-Samoan, un-Christian, papalagi funeral by her very un-Samoan, afakasi, miserly children. And, most shameful and destructive of all, our ali'i, the son of a poverty-stricken beachcomber, has ordered that no ie toga will be allowed at any Satoa funerals from now on, Amen. Alas, what is the *true* fa'a-Samoa and alofa coming to?'

Lalaga's relatives from around the country started arriving to farewell her. Ruta's remedies had stopped her vomiting, so she was able to talk freely. 'Why do I, a non-Satoan, deserve this rare and final Illness?' she joked with her visitors. 'Why doesn't it bless someone else with its rare, aristocratic and exquisite pain? I don't deserve this honour!'

When some of the visitors commented on how beautiful, gracious and generous her daughters were, she said, 'They are really lucky to have me as their mother: they're beautiful because I'm beautiful: they're generous and gracious because I'm all that!' They laughed with her. 'They're certainly not like that because of their father. He was a hopeless dreamer who'd chased after the guttural English language and fantastic creatures such as sea-horses, mermaids, the Roc and the Unicorn . . .'

A few days later, while the others were having their morning meal in the house and faletele, and Peleiupu and Lalaga were on their own, Peleiupu said, 'Please forgive me, Mama. I've always been headstrong and disobedient . . .'

'And very spoilt by your father — and me! Why? Because you've always been our most gifted and, therefore, most vulnerable.' They remained silent for a long time, with the surf swishing at the edge of their hearing. 'You must find your brother,' Lalaga broke the spell. 'The pain of his birth continues. And not to know what has become of him . . .' She started crying. 'Now it's too late — I'll never see him!'

'Tavita and I will go to New Zealand and look for him,' Peleiupu promised.

'Arona's absence remains the one great emptiness in my life.' Again they let the sound of the sea wash through their sorrow. 'You and Tavita will take Pili as your own son,' Lalaga said. 'Promise me that. He has no one else.'

'He has Iakopo.'

'Yes, Iakopo looks after him, takes good care of him, loves him.'

'I'll make him Iakopo's younger brother and my youngest child.'

'God gave him to us in return for I'amafana.' Once again the full pain of the epidemic was upon them, and they embraced and wept.

On Saturday afternoon, as the shadows lengthened across Satoa and high tide peaked, Tavita picked up Lalaga and, sheltering under a large black umbrella held up by Peleiupu, carried her down to the church and her grave, which Mikaele and the aumaga had dug and lined with concrete, beside Mautu's grave. Her daughters and grandchildren, with Iakopo carrying Pili, and some of her friends accompanied them. The grave was lined with siapo. Tavita carried her slowly around the grave's edge, while she inspected it.

'I am satisfied,' she declared. 'It is more than adequate for the purpose.'

At dawn on Sunday, with her three daughters around her gently massaging her limbs, Lalaga died in her sleep.

That afternoon her funeral service was conducted by their pastor according to Lalaga's strict instructions: the service was to last only an hour at the most; they were to sing her three favourite hymns — she listed those; Iakopo was to read her two favourite biblical texts; and if they considered her life worthy of eulogising, Peleiupu, her oldest child, was to give one that was no longer than three minutes.

'Our mother was of that first generation of women who were blessed, by our beloved Christian missionaries, with an enlightened Christian education in all the good things of the papalagi way of life . . .' Peleiupu continued reading the wording she and her sisters had agreed to — a eulogy which, as she observed the congregation and heard the doubt in her own voice, started feeling 'untruthful', very distant from the mother she'd known. She wanted to depart from the text and talk from the heart about Lalaga, even joke about her, but the congregation looked so 'inspired' by her eulogy, she decided that they wanted (and needed) exemplary Christian models to emulate. '. . . She was the humble daughter of an uneducated village couple who wanted to gift her to God and the Christian conversion of this sinful country . . .'

Peleiupu stood between Tavita and Lefatu at the head of the open grave as the pastor recited the Prayer for the Dead and the setting sun cast a blood-red light over the mourners, the church and the village, and turned the blossoms of the mango trees a brighter flame-red. Naomi and Ruta and many of Lalaga's friends wept mutely. The air was saturated with the smell of sun and drying frangipani and earth. Someone touched her right hand. She turned. It was Iakopo, carrying Pili. 'Where's Mama?' Pili asked her. In silence she took the boy from her son and, holding him against her chest, gestured down at the coffin at the bottom of the grave.

'Mama has gone to God and Papa,' Iakopo said to Pili.

And for the first time that day, Peleiupu wept openly. Tightly she held on to Pili. Iakopo and Lefatu pressed against her.

Tina o le Galuega, ua e sola i Niuafei
Lua te fa'atasi ai ma lou Au lalelei,
Ua e sola i Niuafei
O lo'o lagomau ai Mautu,
Le Manaia o le Aiga nei . . .

Lefatu and Ruta sang, as the men started filling Lalaga's grave. Immediately everyone joined in the singing, and Lalaga's Song flowed away over the mango trees and the sea into the sunset and up into the welcoming currents of sky . . .

BOOK THREE
The Way of the Frigate

On Board

Paddling, paddling, paddling furiously, his feet flap-flap-flapping against and through the dark green water, churning it up into millions of sparkling bubbles, his hands clutching at the air and finding a grip, and he was inexplicably on land, in the familiar landscape of Satoa by the river at night and hemmed in by hordes of people he couldn't see in the darkness — people who whispered, their whispers like quick slithering eels, and groaned and complained about him, though he couldn't hear what they were saying — people who suddenly stank of putrefying flesh, and he was again in the epidemic, his arms wrapped tightly around the mat-wrapped body of his son I'amafana, his throat clogged with desperate pleas to be rescued, to be saved, to die . . .

He was awake and in the dark on the sofa in his office, his clothes drenched with sweat, and he remembered he'd been drinking after Peleiupu and Siniva and the other workers had gone home. Since settling in Apia two years before in 1920, when New Zealand was awarded the mandate by the League of Nations to govern Western Samoa, he'd not been able to rid himself of the recurring nightmares about the epidemic; nightmares that began the first night they slept in Apia.

He lit a lamp and took it to the bathroom, where he washed his face and neck, gargled the stale smell and taste of whisky out of his mouth and noted, in the mirror, that his hair was heavily flecked with grey. How much more anxiety could he take? Two years of feeling insecure in himself, two years of feeling inadequate dealing with Apia, their rapidly expanding business, his complex aiga, and all the endless trivia that had to be attended to in order to survive. Outwardly, publicly, he was *the* fearless head of an aiga rising to wealth and power, unafraid of the Governor or jealous business rivals and the racist quagmire of Apia European society.

The more successful he and Peleiupu became, the more complex and anxiety-ridden his life. He was a simple Satoan: Tavita, the villager, who'd been forced into being David Barker, a papalagi who had to be successful in the papalagi world. Peleiupu was thriving in that world, dealing fearlessly with it and overcoming the discrimination against them as 'half-castes'. At times he resented her for that, and the more he did, the more he resented himself for blaming her for his inadequacies. It was unfair that he looked like a papalagi and everyone expected him to *be* a papalagi in every way, while she looked Samoan and everyone expected her to behave like one, yet she was superb as a papalagi. He was a better Samoan than her, about that he was sure — and pleased.

After locking his office, he groped his way down the dark corridor and up the stairs. He envied their aiga at Satoa: they were in the world he knew and loved.

He paused at the top of the stairs and looked out at the buildings, which stretched back over the swamps and up to the foothills in the falling dark. They'd built a new business headquarters (a large store, offices, a spacious apartment upstairs and a ware-house); they'd bought, cheaply, from companies and people leaving Samoa fourteen trading stations around the country (now they owned twenty); they'd acquired two more vessels (the *Lady Vaomatua* and the *Le Satoa);* they owned a car and two trucks (some of the first in the country), fifteen hectares at Lotolua just outside Apia, and almost three hectares at the town centre along the Apia waterfront; and they'd estab-lished their own copra trading and exporting business. All this had been financed by the huge profits they'd made (and were still making) from the copra harvesting scheme they'd initiated immediately after the epidemic, and money Peleiupu had saved without his knowledge.

Now their children were preparing to attend boarding schools in New Zealand, and that frightened him because he'd never been abroad. He was afraid for his children but, once again, Peleiupu had persuaded him they needed to have a better education than was available in Samoa. They could afford it. She also wanted to use their trip to find Arona.

Jim Mackson, their lawyer, had arranged for Lefatu and Maualuga to attend Mrs Mackson's old school, and Iakopo his old school, in Auckland.

The enticing smell of cooking sapasui, fa'alifu talo and fish immediately held him by the nose and pulled him into the large kitchen when he opened the back door.

Peleiupu was supervising the two women who were doing the cooking at the large wood stove, while Siniva was sitting at the kitchen table munching peanuts and drinking lemonade. 'Want a beer?' Peleiupu asked. Did she need to drive it home?

'Have we got a permit to buy any?' he asked.

'You are Mr David Barker, classified as a "European" by the New Zealand author-ities, so you are entitled to points to buy alcohol!' she mimicked the official she'd seen the previous year to get a liquor permit.

'Yes, I will have a beer,' he said, bowing.

'Don't forget, we're going to the Winsomes' tonight for dinner. 'The Governor will be there.'

'But there's better food and company here.'

'We'll leave you some of *our* food!' Siniva said.

Tavita took his mug of frothing beer into the sitting room.

Lefatu and Maualuga were playing with Pili. Iakopo was drawing at the coffee table. The children fell silent when they saw him. 'Have you done your homework?' he asked.

'We don't have any,' Maualuga replied.

Pili rushed over, and Tavita swung him up and sat with him on the sofa. 'Are we going to speak English tonight?' Pili asked in Samoan.

'Not if you don't want to,' Tavita replied.

'Good — my English is not good,' Pili said.

Lefatu took her father's satchel into the bedroom, returned, took off his tie and coat and took those into the bedroom.

Maualuga unlaced her father's shoes and took them off. 'Papa, we don't want to go to New Zealand,' she announced.

'Why not?' he asked.

'It's a country of papalagi,' Lefatu replied.

'You're a palagi,' he insisted. 'Your grandfather was an Englishman, a full-blooded European.'

'She doesn't *look* papalagi,' Pili reasoned.

'Your surname is English, you are European: you will fit into New Zealand,' he tried to reason.

'But our school here is for Europeans and the teachers and the other kids don't treat us like Europeans,' Iakopo said. 'We look too Samoan!'

'It'll be different in New Zealand,' Peleiupu said from the doorway. 'The Europeans there are far more civilised and well mannered than the ones here. And our money will be just as good as theirs.' She paused and then added, 'Your dinner's ready now,' stopping the difficult discussion.

The children hurried to the dining room. Tavita was puzzled and disturbed by Peleiupu's last remarks but didn't pursue it.

'Why do you think the Governor has been invited to the Winsomes'?' she asked, sitting down beside him.

'The opposition against him and New Zealand rule is getting worse, more organised,' he replied. 'He needs support from some of us *European* merchants.'

'What are we going to do?'

'Play along with him for a while,' he said, trying to sound casual.

'We shouldn't jeopardise our business, should we?'

The wealthy merchants who were opposing the New Zealand administration were trying to recruit him. 'Our son and many of our loved ones died in the epidemic,' he reminded her in Samoan. Always when he wanted to feel comfortable in a discussion with her he used Samoan. 'We must never forget that.'

As the SS *Matai* cut through the calm water towards the harbour entrance into the deepening night they stood on the upper deck, looking back over the stern at the waving crowd on the wharf, at the thin spread of lights that blinked along the waterfront, at the darkening hills and mountain range looming above the town. Above them, the moon was a fingernail, pale grey and transparent. Lefatu and Maualuga stood on either side of him. 'I can still see Mama!' Maualuga said, waving at Poto on the wharf. Peleiupu was holding on to Iakopo's arm. His son looked miserable, Tavita noted. Of their three children, Iakopo was the least enthusiastic about going to New Zealand.

'I'm going to miss Pili,' Lefatu said.

'So am I,' Tavita said.

'We all are,' Peleiupu said.

'And Poto — I'm going to miss Mama most of all!' said Iakopo.

It was strange; out of his whole aiga Tavita missed Pili most of all, yet Pili was adopted. He was going to miss the little fellow slipping into their bed in the mornings and waking them with his cuddles. Sometimes he had to change his urine-soaked clothes before letting him into their bed. Peleiupu refused to do it, saying Pili was *his* responsibility.

In Apia, ships had to anchor outside the reef and have their passengers and cargoes loaded and unloaded by lighters. Earlier that evening the other passengers had taken the lighters to the *Matai*. Mikaele had insisted on using the *Lady Poto* to take them and the other elders to the ship. There'd been very loud, tearful farewells on the wharf and on board the *Lady Poto*.

Tavita noticed they were breaking through the harbour entrance into the open sea. The ship started rising and falling on the incoming waves and tide. Peleiupu shifted up against him, her arm touching his. 'We'll have a good holiday,' she murmured. 'We've earned it. We must also find Arona.' The children wanted to go into the ship's lounge directly behind them; she let them.

The cold wind flicked at their faces as they continued watching Upolu receding into the darkness. Peleiupu told him she was feeling cold, so he led her into the ship's lounge.

Because the *Matai* was mainly a cargo vessel, it carried only about a hundred passengers. At a quick glance Tavita estimated that most of those were in the lounge. Mainly male and all papalagi. Some of the men were at the bar; a few families occupied some of the tables.

'Over here!' Maualuga called. Their children were at the far table, talking politely with Father Tomasi, a middle-aged American priest whom Tavita knew well from Mulivai Cathedral. Tavita felt exposed, imagining the papalagi watching them as they hurried across the lounge. They shook hands with Father Tomasi, and sat down.

'Would you like a drink, Father?' Tavita asked.

'My friends and I have ordered already, Mr Barker,' the priest replied in fluent Samoan, in his very American accent. Father Tomasi was respected throughout the country as an authority on the Samoan language. 'I understand from my friends here that the children are going to school in New Zealand?'

'Yes, they're lucky, aren't they, Father?' Tavita replied.

Father Tomasi nodded. 'Yes, you must be the first Samoans to do that,' he said to the children. 'You *are* lucky!' It was obvious to Tavita that Peleiupu and their children were fascinated by Father Tomasi's very blond, very un-priestly appearance — neatly trimmed goatee beard, silky shoulder-length hair, black soutane and leather sandals — so he encouraged him to talk.

They learned that Father Tomasi had been in Samoa for almost thirty years, starting as a parish priest in Olosega, Manu'a, once the centre of the ancient Samoan religion. 'We Catholics learned early in our colonisation of the world that in order to win pagans for our Christian God we had to study their religions and then move into the centres of those, and either destroy them physically or convert their priesthoods to our God. That's why we established our first missions in Samoa in Falealupo, the centre of the Nafanua religion, and in Manu'a, seat of the Tui-Manu'a, the most sacred of Samoa's paramount chiefs and priests,' Father Tomasi explained, his eyes twinkling mischievously. After six years in Olosega studying the ancient religion and trying not to be erased by the LMS Church, which dominated the island, he was shifted to Falealupo, Savai'i, where Catholicism reigned supreme, and he had to save the LMS and

Methodist churches from being banished by the Falealupo fono. 'Competition is healthy, isn't it, Mrs Barker?' he laughed. 'Monopolies and dictatorships destroy adventure, search, inquisitiveness, invention. That's why I helped my Christian brothers in Falealupo. I also respected the Lady, Nafanua.' He stopped and enjoyed his listeners' shocked silence. 'Yes, Mr and Mrs Barker, I respect all religions, especially those we've tried to erase cruelly, inconsiderately.' He paused. 'Mind you, the Bishop almost had me erased as a Catholic priest. He accused me of loving pagan Gods and practices!'

The waiter interrupted Father Tomasi when he arrived with the drinks the priest had ordered. 'What would your friends like, Father?' the waiter asked, in his very New Zealand accent. Father Tomasi looked embarrassed.

'I'll have a whisky and my wife will have . . . ,' Tavita rescued him.

'A beer, please,' Peleiupu said, in English. Still the waiter stood looking at Father Tomasi.

'You heard what Mr and Mrs Barker said?' Father Tomasi asked him.

'I'm sorry, Father, but we can't serve . . . We can't serve alcohol to these people.'

'Then tell *us*, sir!' Tavita ordered. 'It has nothing to with Father Tomasi.'

Emphasising each word, the waiter said, 'I am sorry, Mr Barker, but we cannot serve alcohol to non-Europeans.'

Before Tavita could reply, Peleiupu said, 'Sir, I think you had better get your superior and get him now.'

The waiter scurried off, and they could see him talking animatedly to the bald-headed pink waiter behind the bar, who dropped his hand-towel and marched over, with everyone now watching what was happening.

'Father, I'd like you to explain to your friends . . . ' the stout, bald-headed, pink waiter started saying.

'Stop right there, sir,' Father Tomasi interrupted him. 'Mr and Mrs Barker speak better English than you and I. You tell *them*, and you'd better be prepared to take the consequences of your rude and arrogant ignorance.'

The waiter hesitated, then, eyes lowered, said, 'We cannot serve natives alcohol, sir. It is not our fault. We just carry out orders.'

'Then get us the person who gives those orders,' Tavita said. The waiter shuffled off and out of the lounge, which was now tense with silence.

'I'll take the children away,' Father Tomasi offered.

'No, I want our children to witness this because we now know what they'll have to deal with in New Zealand,' Tavita said. Iakopo pushed his soft drink over the table to him. Tavita drank it quickly, the ice tinkling in time to his swallowing. Peleiupu pressed her leg against his.

The purser was a huge, red-haired man, with his belly, neck and arms threatening to burst through his white uniform. He swaggered across the lounge, stopped and gazed down at them. Tavita refused to look away. 'I am sorry, sir, but the law is quite clear: we cannot serve your wife,' he pronounced.

'Why not?' Tavita asked.

'Because she is non-European,' the purser replied.

'How do you know she is non-European?'

The purser shook his head impatiently. 'Because she does not look European, sir.'

'And because I *look* European, you are assuming I am one?' Tavita pursued him.

They waited while the purser struggled to understand the implications of Tavita's question. 'You must be European!' the purser said finally. 'You look more European than I do!' He guffawed but stopped when he noticed that Tavita and Father Tomasi weren't laughing at his joke.

'I may look European but I am Samoan,' Tavita continued. 'I was born in a small village you've never heard of. I was raised a Samoan. My name — and I am a chief — is Toanamua Tavita.' Visibly, the large purser was deflating. 'I am also European because that is how your New Zealand administration has classified me and my wife and our children.'

'So you see, appearance is *not* a legal way of defining people's official status,' Father Tomasi continued the attack.

'And it can get you into trouble with your law, sir,' Peleiupu said.

'And your European name, sir?' the purser asked, his stance and voice no longer laced with arrogance.

'David Barker,' Tavita replied, watching his name sinking into the startled depths of the purser's blue eyes. The lounge buzzed with conversation.

'We . . . we . . . we are very sorry, Mr Barker,' the purser stuttered. 'Our waiters did not know who you are, sir.' He beckoned the waiter over. 'All the drinks are on us, Mr Barker.' Turning to Peleiupu, he bowed and said, 'Mrs Barker, please accept my deepest apologies.'

'Money and power override even the law and appearances, eh?' Father Tomasi laughed.

'No, Father. Mr and Mrs Barker *are* Europeans,' the purser replied.

'Yes, Father, it does help if you have money,' Tavita added. 'Over half the copra on this ship is my company's.'

'Please accept our apologies, Mr Barker.' The purser ignored his remark. 'For the rest of your trip, you and your beautiful family will have no further problems with our staff. If you do, please let me know promptly.' He wiped his forehead. 'By the way,

Captain Howard Trease invites you and your good lady to dine at his table every night.'

'Please thank Captain Trease for his generous invitation,' Tavita replied. Peleiupu pressed her foot down on his toes.

Three quick whiskies later, he was floating and talking animatedly. 'The children are tired,' Peleiupu told him in Samoan. 'I'll take them to bed.'

'It it time I was in bed too,' Father Tomasi said. Tavita was disappointed that his drinking companion was leaving. He got up with Peleiupu and the children. 'Thank you for the pleasant evening, Tavita and Pele,' the priest said in Samoan. 'I'm sorry about what happened earlier, but that's the way some ignorant people are.'

Maualuga started leading Tavita to the door. He beckoned to the waiter, who hurried over. Opening his wallet, he stuffed some notes into the eager waiter's coat pocket. 'For our drinks and for such good service.' Peleiupu started moving off with their children. He followed them.

After they had seen the children into their cabins, they went through the connecting door into their quarters: a spacious bedroom-sitting room with a large double bed and separate toilet and shower.

'I was so angry,' he whispered as he undressed. 'It was bloody humiliating!'

'But we got our own back, Tavita,' she said. He sat down on his bed and tried to still his shaking. She rushed over and held him.

'I hope it isn't going to be like this all the time in New Zealand.'

'It won't be,' she consoled him.

'What are our children going to find in those schools?'

She helped him finish undressing; he put on an ie lavalava, ignoring the expensive pyjamas she'd put out for him, and slid into bed. He watched as she undressed. 'You Samoans certainly look far healthier and sexier than us pink Europeans!' he quipped. She dived on top of him and enveloped his head in her arms. He opened the sheet and she rolled into his embrace. She caressed his back.

The ship groaned, rolled, rose and fell more noticeably. As he fell asleep, he felt as if he were retreating into the fertile depths of the Satoan bush. Snug and safe.

The nightmare of the epidemic swamped him up to his drowning mouth, and he was awake and weeping. Peleiupu held him. 'It's all right, it's all right,' she kept whispering. Wrapping his arms around her torso, he buried his face between her breasts, in the familiar smell of her body and perfume, and held on. Held on.

He felt nauseous and, as his head spun, he clutched on to the sides of his bed to stop himself from toppling off it. He clenched his eyes. When he opened them again, morning was the white shafts of daylight cutting across the cabin from the open portholes and the long swishing of the ship cutting through the water. He rolled out of bed, planted his feet firmly on the floor, re-hitched his ie lavalava, pulled on a clean shirt and, refusing to give into the nausea, hurried out into and up the narrow corridor, trying not to inhale the sickly smell of diesel that filled it, and into the crisp morning air of the upper deck.

For a long time he held on to the railing as the salt spray splattered over his face and shoulders, sucking in huge gulps of fresh air, which kicked open his lungs and kicked out the nausea. All around, the dark blue sea rose and fell and rolled eastwards, while the sun hid behind a screen of cloud.

He relaxed and wiped the water off his face and head with the end of his ie lavalava. Iakopo joined him. 'I never get seasick, never. Pele's with Maualuga and Lefatu; they're vomiting.'

He hurried down and helped his daughters vomit into the washbasins, wiped their faces with wet facecloths and put them back into their bunks. 'We don't get seasick, do we?' Maualuga remarked.

'You are now!' Peleiupu said. 'But you'll get over it by the end of today.'

Once seated in the dining room, they ordered some orange juice and papaya for their daughters, and told the waiter to take the food to their cabin. Tavita ordered fruit juice and papaya, and while he ate he turned away from Peleiupu and Iakopo, who were digging hungrily into fried eggs, bacon, sausages, tomatoes and toast. When he imagined himself tasting the fried fat, nausea gripped at him again, and he sprang up and rushed out into the fresh air.

At mid-morning, while the sun refused to come out from behind the screen, they took the girls up to the deck and lay on deckchairs while Peleiupu read to them from a desert romance called *A Fatal Touch of Love,* by Michael Onthejay. Iakopo lost interest by the fifth page and wandered off to explore the ship; Tavita pretended he was falling asleep but was absorbed in the story; Lefatu kept sighing and saying how she was loving it; Maualuga imagined she was lost in the Sahara, dying of thirst and yearning to be rescued by the Bedouin Prince, Ahmed . . .

Father Tomasi joined them for lunch. Peleiupu insisted that they order ham and lots of vegetables so the children could get used to healthy New Zealand food; they got Father Tomasi to vouch for the superior nutritional value of vegetables. 'It's great brain and muscle food!' he told them.

'Look, all those palagi are eating heaps of cooked vegetables!' Peleiupu said, pointing to the other tables.

Maualuga took a healthy mouthful of cabbage, chewed vigorously at first, then slowed down and said, 'It tastes like grass!'

'Swallow it — it's good for you!' Peleiupu threatened. 'And don't forget to use your knives and forks properly, like papalagi.'

Tavita glanced at Father Tomasi, shrugged his shoulders, and they both attacked their vegetables.

Iakopo, who ate almost anything and in healthy quantities, copied them. 'It'll give you big muscles, eh, Papa?' he joked.

Lefatu pretended she was feeling seasick again, and disappeared to their cabin.

For the rest of the afternoon they explored the ship and tried out all the deck games. Occasionally some of the other passengers joined them.

For the remaining six days of their trip they would not feel seasick again.

Tavita had learned from Sao, his arrogant grandfather, that 'real ali'i' always arrived late, so, although they were nervous and had finished dressing well before dinner, in front of their admiring children in their new clothes tailored specially for their trip, he insisted on leaving their quarters at 7 pm, when dinner was to start, arriving shortly after Captain Howard Trease and his other guests were seated.

Peleiupu put her arm through his as they entered the dining room. All the tables were occupied; many diners turned to look at them. He straightened and, in the sedate, aristocratic pace of his grandfather, they wove their way through the other tables, acutely conscious — but not showing it — that they were being watched by everyone.

Captain Trease and his other male guests stood up. 'Good evening!' the captain greeted them. They shook hands firmly. Then Captain Trease introduced them to the others. Father Tomasi bowed slightly and greeted them in Samoan. The immaculately uniformed waiters seated Peleiupu on the captain's right, and Tavita opposite him, between two women whose perfume enveloped him immediately.

Tavita mapped the Captain's table swiftly as the waiter took their orders for drinks. He always did that when he was anxious and insecure. To his left was Mrs Bileen Griff, wife of Bernie 'Faithful' Griff, who was seated further down. He knew them quite well from business dealings and the protestant church where Bernie was a deacon and Bileen taught senior Sunday school. Bernie was the manager of the Apia branch of Burt Phills, a large Australian trading company that had branches throughout the Pacific Islands. Whenever Tavita was close to Bileen, he was extra careful not to touch her. Her deliberate slowness, her slow sidelong glances and slow full-lipped smile, her full slow body always 'stirred' him. Now she was right there beside him.

The other merchants called Bernie 'Faithful' because whenever he preached in church he emphasised the virtues of being 'faithful to your God, your family, your country, your customers and friends, and even your pets'. But Tavita knew from his dealings with him that beneath that facade he was vindictive and ruthless.

On his right was Mrs Wendy Pike, a thin, porcelain-pale New Zealander who was refusing to make eye contact with anyone as she fidgeted with her wedding ring. He assumed her husband was the squat, bull-necked, sun-tanned man who looked hot and uncomfortable in his tight dinner suit, seated opposite Bernie. (Sheep farmers holidaying in the South Seas, he'd find out in the course of the evening.)

To the captain's left was Mrs Melanie Melt, the petite, talkative, quick-eyed wife of Mark 'Melodious' Melt, manager of the Apia branch of Morric Heedstead's, another Australian company and Burt Phills' main competitor. (Appropriately, Mark was seated opposite Bernie.) Mark was known as 'Melodious' because whenever he believed he had the upper hand in a deal, he hummed *God Save the King*, out of tune, without realising he was doing it.

Seated on either side of Father Tomasi were Reverend Nigel Putelle and his wife Alicia, British missionaries who'd been inspecting the work of the London Missionary Society in Samoa. Their faces were peeling with sunburn.

Next to Mrs Putelle was Mr Peter Fry, a senior civil servant in the New Zealand Administration, who was returning home for six months' leave. Tavita thought of him as a barely visible presence; he didn't seem to want the position he was in but couldn't reject it.

As Tavita sipped his first whisky and silently observed the conversation, Peleiupu kept glancing over at him and smiling. She too was unfazed by silences and enjoyed observing the 'conversers and their conversations'. He knew, though, that if she was drawn into the conversation and was in a generous mood she was expert at maintaining it, making it feel meaningful for everyone. Once she had explained to him that all she needed to do was to assume the role of a favourite character from a favourite novel and she was away. But right then, the papalagi, apart from Father Tomasi, assumed she couldn't speak English. In her mischievous moments when she didn't want to talk she would pretend she didn't understand English and they'd leave her alone. Other times, when she wanted to humble them, she out-Englished them with her fluency and broad general knowledge. Tonight he couldn't guess what she was going to do.

'. . . My crew and I are very honoured to have such distinguished company,' Captain Trease was saying in his clipped, precise way. 'The whole ship's cargo belongs to three of you.'

'I understand Mr Barker's company has the most,' Bernie Griff said.

'Yes, sixty per cent, while you and Mr Melt have twenty per cent each,' Captain

Trease detailed. He was a compact man with a thin moustache, short-cropped hair, small alert eyes, and quick, neat movements.

'We're stopping in Suva, aren't we, Captain?' Melanie Melt asked.

The captain nodded. 'For two days, to load more copra, and for you to do some sightseeing and shopping.'

'. . . In the islands of the cannibals!' Mark Melt joked.

'Father, what did the natives consider the tastiest bit of the human anatomy?' Bernie Griff continued the joke.

Tavita keenly awaited Father Tomasi's reply. He caught an impish smile, a cheeky glitter in Father Tomasi's eyes. 'It depended on what aspect of your victim you wanted to *absorb* unto yourself, sir!' Father Tomasi replied.

'Absorb? I love that!' said Bernie Griff. 'Don't you, dear?' And Bileen started laughing too.

'If you wanted his courage you absorbed his liver; if you wanted his mana, his heart, if you wanted . . .'

'Enough, enough, Father!' Bileen interjected. 'You're being naughty!' Except for Peleiupu and the Putelles, the others laughed sedately.

'What about sheep, Mr Pike?' Mark Melt asked the New Zealand sheep farmer, who looked non-plussed and squirmed shyly under their scrutiny.

'Well, you wouldn't absorb its brains if you wanted to be brainier,' Wendy Pike chortled. 'A sheep hasn't got any!' They laughed some more. Tavita was fascinated by Mrs Pike's unusual accent: thin, twangy, nasal.

'And it's got only tiny, wee kidneys!' Mr Pike improved the merriment. 'So if you want courage and that other kinda strength, a sheep wouldn't be much use!' Strange that Peleiupu wasn't enjoying the ribaldry, Tavita observed. She was fiddling with the stem of her glass, her right forefinger drawing the figure eight, repeatedly: a sure sign her subtle brain was creating some brilliant scheme.

The waiter poured Tavita's third whisky. The captain invited them to order their food.

While they waited for their entrées, Bernie Griff, who grew redder as he drank, asked, 'Mr Barker, is it true Samoans were "absorbers"?'

Looking at Peleiupu and Father Tomasi, Tavita asked, 'You mean, man-eaters, sir?'

'That's good, mate!' Mark Melt chuckled. 'That's *really* good!' Except for Mrs Putelle, the other papalagi women laughed.

'Yes, we absorbed a few, especially when protein was in short supply,' Tavita replied. He stopped laughing with the others when he noticed that Peleiupu was not appreciating his humour. Beside him, Bileen was thrilling his left ear with her naughty, sensuous laughter; her strong perfume was also caressing his left nostril.

The soup arrived. Thick French onion and croutons. Captain Trease asked Father Tomasi to say grace.

Tavita ate slowly. Bileen and Wendy started talking to each other across him; their presence enveloped him. Tavita sneaked his fourth whisky, and was aware he was imagining all sorts of sexual happenings with the two women. He tried choking them off by concentrating on the other guests.

The fish course came and went quickly and without taste for Tavita as he had another whisky and battled with the guilt of committing adultery in his out-of-control imagination. The women were drinking more wine too.

The main course arrived: roast lamb, mint sauce, roast potatoes and pumpkin, parsnip, green peas and thick gravy. Everyone fell silent, admiring the food.

'If I may, Captain, I'd like to correct a very demeaning untruth that has been perpetrated among Europeans by other Europeans, about us.' Peleiupu surveyed her listeners, who were surprised and impressed she could speak their language, and so fluently. 'According to the research of Professor Mardrek Freemeade, Professor of Anthropology at Harvard University and perhaps the most famous anthropologist in the world, and who lived in our district and studied our people and way of life, my ancestors were never cannibals.' Some of them nodded, sternly. 'You should read his third book, *Cannibalism and Love Among the Satoans*, which was published in 1921 . . .'

She went on to enlighten them about Freemeade's findings and Tavita revelled in what she was doing: she was making it all up and it sounded absolutely convincing, and they weren't going to admit their ignorance by challenging her. He glanced at Father Tomasi, who winked conspiratorially.

'. . . And more importantly, there is no evidence in our over-three-thousand-year occupation of our country that we *absorbed* ourselves.' She paused again, dramatically. Low, husky chortling from the depths of her belly. 'None whatsoever, Captain.'

'Wonderful, Mrs Barker, absolutely wonderful!' Father Tomasi exclaimed.

'Yes, thank you, Mrs Barker. I must apologise if tonight I have given you the impression I believed that your highly civilised people were . . . were . . .' Captain Trease struggled.

'Cannibals, man-eaters, absorbers?' Tavita heard his whisky-calm voice prompting.

'Let us now *absorb* this scrumptious-looking lamb!' Peter Fry spoke for the first time. 'And absorb into ourselves the essence of being New Zealanders!'

Bileen Griff looked so delicious, so scrumptious herself, that Tavita experienced no guilt as he absorbed her Aussie essence, in his imagination, under the captain's table.

The humid air felt like hot liquid as they strolled back to their cabin after dinner, so Tavita took off his jacket and tie and unbuttoned his shirt. 'It's strange how fiction shapes the way we see things, isn't it?' Peleiupu remarked. He looked at her but his attention was still with Bileen. 'Our dinner tonight was straight out of the stories by the young English writer, Fausett Malcolm. Or should I say: I saw our dinner tonight through Malcolm's stories. Malcolm's been travelling our islands on boats like this and writing about characters like Captain Trease and his dinner guests.' She tugged playfully at his elbow. 'We're not in the stories so we shouldn't be at Captain Trease's table, should we?' He didn't react so she added, 'Well, should we?'

'But we are coming into the story,' he quipped. 'Into their fiction!' She bumped her hip against his and laughed. 'And, boy, you really storied them tonight about Freemeade!' he added.

Over the years she had tried to interest him in reading fiction and poetry but he'd not taken to it, preferring to listen to her clever and gripping renditions of the stories and poems — and learning from them. 'I want my squat Samoan feet anchored firmly in the earth,' he'd once declared to her.

As they undressed for bed, he caught the concern in her eyes. 'You shouldn't drink so much, dear,' she said.

'I only had three drinks tonight,' he insisted.

She slipped into bed and turned off her bedside lamp. He got in beside her. She turned around and kissed him. 'Goodnight,' she murmured.

He couldn't sleep: the heat and the dark were saturated with Bileen Griff. Wildly saturated. Throughout their marriage he'd never been unfaithful to Peleiupu, even though he'd often been sorely tempted. Bileen as 'temptation' was the most overwhelming he'd experienced. Now his sinful lust and covetousness — yes, that was his description — were overpowering, but he resisted and resisted.

Arrival and Search

They couldn't sleep properly and were up and dressed and out on deck as dawn started radiating in a series of pale yellow waves across the sky and the entrance into what Iakopo told them was Waitemata Harbour. In their uncomfortable new clothes they watched the waves of light nosing back the darkness, expecting to see forests covering the headlands and hills, and long white clouds, the whole island. But there were no forests or clouds. 'It is all grass,' Maualuga remarked. An inane, innocent observation, Peleiupu thought, but as she concentrated on the landscape, she had to agree with her daughter.

'New Zealand is meat and grass,' Iakopo said.

'What does that mean?' Tavita asked.

'The palagi have turned the forests into grasslands . . .'

'Paddocks,' Maualuga interjected.

'. . . and now have millions of cows and sheep and cattle feeding on the grass . . .'

'And people feeding on the butter and mutton and beef and the wealth earned from those,' Maualuga completed it. 'I read that somewhere, Papa.' Maualuga was, academically, the brightest of their children. She consumed knowledge and information in huge, sometimes frenzied gulps.

Once through the heads, their ship slid neatly through an almost still sea that was luminous with dawn light. As the light intensified, it revealed Waiheke, Rangitoto and the other islands of the gulf. Peleiupu saw rivers of houses and buildings sweeping towards the centre of the magnificent city. Auckland. Larger even than she'd imagined. What a challenge! So much to learn and use . . . Her fears diminished.

They emerged from the ship and Peleiupu sucked in the air of the new country; it hurt her lungs with its unfamiliar coolness and weight, and its taste of smoke from numerous chimneys and towers. They said goodbye to Father Tomasi at the top of the gangway. Then the purser escorted them down ahead of the other passengers, and took them through Customs and Immigration. The children and Tavita refused to look at the faces of those around them. The unsmiling officials were curt and formal and so pink, Peleiupu thought.

They couldn't see any Polynesians in the crowd that was roped off from them, but out of it, just in front of them, stepped a small bespectacled man in a neat black suit. 'Mr Barker?' he asked. When Tavita nodded the man shook his hand. 'Welcome to Auckland and New Zealand, sir. I'm Matthew Service of your law firm Awrie and Service.' Peleiupu recognised his name from their correspondence.

After Tavita had introduced her and the children, a young blond man stepped forward and was introduced, by Mr Service, as Marcus Pierce, a junior partner in their firm. 'We have a company car and a coach-taxi waiting,' Mr Pierce said. 'We've arranged for your luggage to be taken to those vehicles. You just need to identify your suitcases.' Peleiupu asked Iakopo to go with Mr Pierce.

As they followed Mr Service through the crowded sheds Maualuga whispered to Peleiupu, 'Why are they staring at us?'

'They're not.' But she was feeling it too. She glanced at Tavita and Lefatu and knew they were feeling the same way.

Tavita and the girls got into the company car — a Studebaker — with Mr Service. Peleiupu insisted on accompanying Iakopo and Mr Pierce in one of the taxis. 'I hope you had an enjoyable voyage,' Mr Pierce said as they left the wharf area. She assured him they had — and marvelled that he had the greenest eyes she'd ever seen. 'Mrs Barker, we've booked you into the Reynold Storm, the best hotel in Auckland,' he informed them as they drove up Queen Street.

She trembled, every pore and cell totally alert to the fabulous world they were entering, wanting to understand and absorb it all: the tall buildings walling each side of the street, clock towers and spires pointing at the sky; shop after shop, business after business, any kind you wanted to imagine and learn the latest business methods and ideas from; the unbelievable stream of traffic — trams, horse-drawn carriages and coaches, carts and cars — the newly mass-produced model T-fords; and foot-paths alive with people sporting fedoras and cloches, furs and gloves. Though she'd read so much about that world out there, she could not now match the actual size and scope of it with what she'd read and imagined. And her ambitious heart and mind wanted to reach out and encompass it all, using it to shape her family's future in its image . . .

In front of the hotel, when Iakopo moved to unload their luggage, Mr Service told him to leave it to the hotel porters. 'One thing you must learn early, sir, is when you pay for service let the service do their work!' He grinned. 'The hotel staff will see to it that your luggage is delivered to your quarters.' With that he led them through the impressive marble and glass entrance, up a sea-green carpet that was so thick Peleiupu wanted to take off her shoes and walk barefoot but didn't because she was suddenly aware — and was immediately uncomfortable — that they were being observed by the many people in the lobby. Her daughters pressed closer to her.

They reached the massive front desk and the three male receptionists behind it. The most senior, a bald, stick-like man with large teeth, looked at Mr Service, who cleared his throat and said, 'These are Mr and Mrs Barker and their children.'

'Welcome, sir and madam, to our humble hotel,' the receptionist declared. 'Everything is ready. You're on the top floor, in our Majestic Suite, our Waitemata Suite, and our Governor's Suite. Your registration has all been completed by Mr Service. Just sign here, sir.' Tavita signed. 'Now I'll escort you to your quarters, sir.'

They tried to appear 'calm and collected' — Iakopo's description, later — as they got into their first lift. The girls clutched Peleiupu's hands behind her back. As the lift crunched upwards and sucked the solidity out of their bellies, Peleiupu swallowed her fear repeatedly and envied Tavita, who was again disguising his insecurity by talking confidently with Mr Service. We're not going to fall . . . not going to fall . . .

They kept pretending they were well used to such expensive surroundings as the man showed them around. Even in her reading, Peleiupu had not come across such wealth and splendid comfort. The children kept their hands pressed to their mouths, suppressing their cries of wonderment and surprise.

'How much is this going to cost us?' Tavita whispered as soon as the door had shut on Mr Service and the receptionist.

'We can afford it, *sir*!' she mimicked the receptionist. 'Who's being frugal now?'

'Do we need it?'

'Yes,' she said. 'Having money puts us out of the reach of much of the open racism, darling! Look how far up and away we are from the horse-shit on the mean streets of this fair city.'

'I'm a European, darling,' he joked. 'I look European. It's you and your native, sun-tanned children who'll be splattered by the shit!'

She hugged him and, pressing her mouth against his ear, whispered, 'Yes, but how do they view Europeans, their kind, who marry natives?'

'That's the problem with you blacks — you're too bloody perceptive!' They laughed and he lifted her up and carried her out onto the balcony overlooking the city.

Right after lunch their lawyers returned. Mr Service explained their business itinerary and the arrangements for the children's schooling, and then said, 'There is one unresolved matter: the matter of Mrs Barker's long-lost brother.' He went on to summarise the ways they'd used to try to find Arona and proving why it was so 'expensive'. 'And as I've written to you, we decided to hire the most respected firm of private investigators in the country — Bartholomew Brant . . .'

Mr Service appeared to have assumed that Peleiupu couldn't speak English: she was Samoan and female and the letters she'd sent previously had all been under Tavita's name. 'We would like to see Mr Brant tomorrow at two after we return from delivering our children to their schools,' she interrupted. An emphatic, utterly self-assured instruction in perfect English, an instruction that now put her firmly in her lawyers' reckoning.

'We will make sure Mr Brant is here on time, Mrs Barker,' Mr Service replied, bowing.

The school driveway was lined on both sides by newly planted rose-beds and single soldierly rows of pines. Ahead on both white walls of the impressive iron gates, in large bronze lettering, were signs announcing: ST MARGARET'S SCHOOL FOR GIRLS. Mr Pierce, who'd said very little as they'd driven through the wealthy suburb of Remuera, drove their car through the gates. The coach-taxi, with Tavita and Iakopo, followed them in.

It was the school holidays so there were no students about. Around them were neat sports fields centring on a large complex of buildings with a steepled, red-brick chapel in the middle. 'Looks very beautiful,' Peleiupu tried consoling her daughters, but they remained tense and fearful. Mr Pierce drove up to the administration building.

Peleiupu held her daughters' hands and pulled them in to her sides as they followed Mr Pierce up the wooden steps into the school reception room and office. Tavita and Iakopo followed.

The room had plush armchairs with school magazines and a vase of red roses on the coffee table. Framed photographs of previous headmistresses lined the walls, and a middle-aged woman at the counter greeted Mr Pierce, who introduced Peleiupu and Tavita. 'Yes, Miss Long, our headmistress, is expecting you,' the woman said. Opening the door behind her, she invited them to follow.

The three women in the headmistress' office got up and shook their hands, and Miss Long invited them to sit down.

As Peleiupu observed the three women their delicate slimness, ramrod-straight carriage and dress reminded her comfortingly of Misi Ioana. She warmed to them immediately — yes, they were women she wanted her daughters to model their lives on. Peleiupu anticipated that Miss Long would talk to Tavita instead of her, and pressed her foot down on his.

'We must thank our heavenly Father for bringing you safely to us, Mr Barker,' Miss Long greeted them.

'Yes, He has been kind,' Tavita responded. 'My wife will talk about our daughters.' Unwaveringly, Peleiupu gazed at Miss Long.

'So, Mrs Barker, are the girls fluent in English?'

'Perhaps you can ask them?' Peleiupu replied. The other two women, the matron and the housemistress, smiled.

'We find your beautiful names difficult to pronounce,' Miss Long said to the girls, who refused to come out of their wary silence. 'Perhaps you can teach us how to say them correctly?'

The girls maintained their silence. 'Answer Miss Long,' Peleiupu instructed them.

Maualuga glanced up at her. 'My name's Maualuga.' Then, looking at Miss Long, she pronounced, 'MA — UA — LU — GA! Maualuga.'

'Very good,' said Miss Long.

'Beautiful, what a beautiful name!' echoed the matron.

'Mar — uuuoloongar!' The housemistress tried it.

'Would you please say your name?' Miss Long asked Lefatu.

'Lefatu,' she mumbled, her top lip trembling.

'Speak up,' Peleiupu urged. Lefatu did.

As Miss Long, the matron and the housemistress detailed such matters as school organisation, rules, uniforms and pocket money, Peleiupu identified them as leading characters out of the romance novels of Janet Border — novels in which the heroines grew up in benevolent and inspiring Christian boarding schools, with keepers and teachers much like these three. She envied her daughters, who were now to enjoy and benefit from that life.

Later, when the matron took them to their dormitories and showed them their lockers and other dorm facilities, Mr Pierce and Iakopo dragged in the girls' massive trunks and placed them by their beds. 'You must've packed even the sand from Satoa!' Iakopo joked in Samoan.

'You're just weak,' Maualuga said.

They then toured the whole school, with Tavita and Iakopo growing more silent, and Peleiupu growing more loquacious in her praise of the school's impressive facilities. They were going through the chapel when the matron said, 'We don't have other Saymoans in our school. And only three Meeori girls, from good aristocratic families.' Peleiupu felt privileged, chosen, proud that they were the only Samoans who could afford such a school.

She sensed that her daughters were on the verge of tears as they returned to the headmistress' office.

Soon it was time to take Iakopo to his school.

'We'll see you tomorrow,' she said to her daughters, who just stood there, silent tears sliding down their cheeks. She gathered them into her arms. 'Don't worry, you'll be fine!' she whispered in Samoan.

Tavita behaved in a very un-Samoan father's way: he embraced each of his daughters, tears brimming out of his eyes, while Peleiupu and Iakopo and Mr Pierce and the three Misses tried not to watch.

Soundlessly Peleiupu cried into Tavita's shoulder as they drove to Iakopo's school. Soundlessly she sobbed into her son's shoulder an hour later after they'd met the headmaster and housemaster, inspected Iakopo's school and taken him to his dormitory where she'd tried to unpack his trunk and he'd ordered her not to. Soundlessly she sobbed in the corner of the back seat of the car, refusing to let Tavita console her, all the way back to their hotel and up the lift into their suite, where she locked herself in the luxurious bathroom and, at last, sobbed loudly and heart-rendingly into the marble walls, gold taps and ornate mirrors.

When she refused to come out, Tavita called, 'It wasn't my decision to lock them up in boarding schools!' He waited until her sobbing subsided to a pitiful whimpering. 'And don't forget that that detective is coming this afternoon to talk about your long-lost brother.' Still no reply. 'Anyway, why are you crying? We're seeing them tomorrow and the next day and the next . . .'

'Shut up! Shut up!' she shouted.

Unlike their lawyers and her children's teachers, Mr Bartholomew Brant didn't bother to hide his New Zealand accent, and she liked the fact that as soon as he walked in, he included her in his reality. 'Good afternoon, Mrs Barker,' he greeted her, shaking her hand before he turned to Tavita.

They sat down and she noticed that he was holding a large file. He looked nothing like the detectives she'd met in her books. Slightly untidy, with unkempt black hair, no moustache — she'd expected one — inquisitive brown eyes, round face with a few pockmarks on his cheeks, absolutely no freckles, thick neck on hefty shoulders, large hairless hands with thick fingers, and a powerful body that he was trying to hide in a loose-fitting suit. 'You're busy people so I don't want to take up too much of your time. You ask me questions and I'll try to answer them fully. That way you won't get information you already know or don't want to know. Is that all right?'

Tavita nodded. 'To do that we'll have to ask you the right questions, won't we, sir?'

Grinning widely, he replied, 'Too right, Mr Barker. After all, you've paid good money for the information!' They laughed together.

'So here's the first question, Bart. May we call you that?' she asked.

'Yes, please. I like informality — it's the New Zealand way.'

'Ever since Arona left Samoa years ago we've had to learn to live with his absence and the whole collection of stories about him, known in our village as *The Tales of Arona the Sailor*. So here's my first question: have you located my *real* brother?' she asked.

'As you know, your brother has been missing for almost thirty years. There was no systematic search in twenty-five years of that time. You asked your lawyers to look for Arona four years ago, and through their agents in New Zealand, Australia, England, Europe and America they compiled this hefty file. Like the tales you've inherited, this file is rich with stories about possible Aronas. But all fiction — or possible fictions. I understand you're a great reader of novels, Mrs Barker, so you'll probably find this collection enthralling reading.'

He went on to itemise two possible real Aronas who were in the file. 'Aaron Sailor' had come into the investigators' reality in 1918, as a Samoan who'd fought in the British Army and had returned to Auckland with shrapnel-riddled lungs and a melancholy he couldn't recover from. They'd traced his grave to Waiuku Cemetery, here in Auckland.

'Aaron Navigator' was first mate on the Blaste Shipping Line ships trading between Auckland, Sydney, London and Paris. He'd disappeared from the records in 1909. No one was sure whether he'd been a Samoan or not. His employers kept describing him as 'a very reliable, intelligent, trustworthy member of the Polynesian race'.

'So when they hired me a year ago and gave me Aaron's file, I decided, on a hunch, to do something different.' He waited — he clearly enjoyed the suspense, so Peleiupu indulged him.

'And what was that, sir?'

'Simple. Restart here in Auckland. Assume Arona was now twenty years older, wiser, and, disillusioned with adventuring the Seven Seas and surviving the tough life of a sailor, had returned to Auckland. Imagine him wanting to settle down with a missus and kids. What bloke wouldn't want that . . .'

'But why settle here? Why not return to his true home and family?' Tavita interrupted.

'We were all waiting for him, yearning for him to come home,' Peleiupu added.

'Again, we can only speculate about his reasons.' He pondered and then said he'd posed himself the question: where would a thirty-five-year-old Samoan on his return to a very intimidating Auckland have gone if he'd needed help? He and his staff had done a thorough search of all the possible records. They had even advertised for information in the papers and over the wireless. 'Not one bloody clue,' he said. 'Just more fictional possibilities. Then bang: my bigoted cousin visited. And over numerous beers while he tried to con money from me, he suggested that — and please forgive me — "Boongs in trouble seek safety with other Boongs". I could've strangled him. When I calmed down, I went into the Auckland Maori community, with Arona's photo — the one of the fifteen-year-old you sent to Service — and a reward for any information about him.'

'What did you find?' Peleiupu continued to play his game.

'A lot of Samoans and other Pacific Islanders, some with ancestry going back to the middle of the last century, many married to Maori, and all part of the close-knit Maori community . . .'

'But aue, no Arona?' Tavita chorused.

'Alas, no Arona. None of them had heard of Arona — or wanted to admit to his existence.'

'What do you mean?' Peleiupu asked.

'Perhaps your elusive brother does not want to be found.'

'Or he may have died in another country not long after he left home, or he may not have returned to New Zealand,' she admitted finally, her voice breaking.

'That may have happened, Peleiupu, but' — his eyes were alertly bright — 'two weeks ago I got a phone call from a man who refused to identify himself, who said he was replying to my ad. This is exactly what he said: "The Aaron you're looking for is history and does not want to be found."' Peleiupu's heart was beating in her gullet: hope was alive again.

'Does that mean he's still alive?' Tavita beat her to it.

'Which Arona is alive? Did the caller mean, the Arona you knew and loved is dead, or that Arona — all that he is — is dead?'

'Perhaps Arona is frightened that we may not like the Arona he has become?'

Peleiupu offered. 'Remember when he left, he was going to be a great discoverer and adventurer like your father, his hero and mentor, David.'

'And he doesn't want you to find out he's failed to achieve that?' Bart suggested.

'Yes,' she said hopefully. Bart kept looking at her. 'Well?' she had to ask.

'I need your permission to keep looking for him.'

'Why?' was her automatic response. 'I promised my parents before they died that we'd find him.' Bart glanced at Tavita.

'Pele, he said he doesn't want to be found,' Tavita reminded her.

'You don't have to decide right now,' Bart said. 'Study this file tonight, then decide and let me know. I'll be disappointed if I'm not allowed to solve the mystery that is your brother, but you've already paid me plenty to endure that disappointment!' Deep-throated chuckling. 'Perhaps it is best to live the rest of your life with an Arona you knew and loved.'

She couldn't wait. As soon as Brant left she cleared the large dining-room table, opened the file out on it, beckoned Tavita over and, after studying the first page, handed it to him.

Whenever she wanted to learn, understand, plan or untangle a problem, her attention to the task was total, undivertable. Tavita knew that, so two hours later he ordered dinner through room service. He ate his, then showered in the luxurious white-tiled bathroom, and went to bed, while she continued to absorb the information in the file.

In the early hours of the morning she fell asleep on the sofa. She woke at 6.30 am, showered and dressed quietly so as not to wake Tavita, ordered their breakfast and, when that arrived, she woke him. As they ate, she told him Pierce was taking her and the children shopping for the children's uniforms and other things, and Mr Service was taking him to meet the company that was going to help them plan and build their picture theatre, the first one in Samoa.

'What about the file?' he had to ask.

'Fascinating,' she replied, cutting her piece of toast into quarters. 'Good material for a novel.'

'But you're not a novelist, darling! You're a realist who'll do anything realistic to fish Arona out of whatever is real in that file.'

'We're playing Bart's reality games, aren't we?' she laughed.

'I like him. He's real and he likes us, treats us without condescension . . .'

'And he's a very handsome detective!'

'Watch it: he's obviously a bloody neat detective of the heart,' he imitated Brant's way of speaking. 'Have ya decided what ya're goin' ta do, baby?'

'Yeah, I wanna find me brother, mate!' she too assumed a New Zealand accent. 'Dead or alive, mate! Ar'm ringin' the Brant after breakfast ta tell him we wan'ta be interviewed in the paper, with a family photo, saying we came specially ta Kiwiland ta find our long-lost brother and prodigal son.'

Their family photograph, taken in the suite sitting room, appeared with an inset of Arona's photo, under the headline: ALL THE WAY FROM SAMOA TO SEARCH FOR LONG-LOST BROTHER, on the bottom half of the front page of the *Morning Star* the next morning. The article that accompanied it spoke movingly of a family who'd spent thirty lonely years searching for a son. 'Please, Arona, or anyone out there who knows him or where he is, contact us at the Reynold Storm Hotel or through this paper. Please!' Peleiupu was quoted in the article. A sizeable reward for information was also offered.

Mr Brant arrived with Cynthia Waters, his assistant, who revealed stockinged legs beneath a low-waisted dress that barely reached to below her knees. Her hair was short, too, having been cut off at the shoulders and straight across the forehead in bangs. Very stylish, thought Peleiupu. A phone had been extended into their dining room so Miss Waters could answer the calls they hoped would result from the newspaper article. Mr Brant wanted Peleiupu to stay in case callers wanted to speak to her, so Tavita and their children, accompanied by the ever-obliging Pierce, went shopping on their own.

'I accept your hunch that my brother is still alive,' Peleiupu told Bart.

'Is that based on what you read in the file?'

'No, it's motivated more by faith and hope and that phone call.'

The phone started ringing. Three calls later, Miss Waters provided them with a summary: two anonymous callers who were interested only in how much the reward was; and a woman conveying her sympathies to the Barkers — she too had lost a son twenty years before. A steady stream of calls then filled the rest of the morning. What Brant considered useful leads were given to their main office to follow up.

Peleiupu found two of them fascinating stories in themselves. A man informed them that his neighbour, a John Tapu, was a Samoan posing as a Maori so as not to be deported; he looked like the Arona in the photograph, and also had a traditional Samoan tattoo from his knees to his navel. 'Bloody primitive but handsome!' the man said.

The other was from a woman with a wheeze, who, after being told the size of the reward, said she'd lived with a Fred Diaz for eleven years, believing he was Brazilian. When he'd disappeared mysteriously she'd found that his birth certificate had his name as Malcolm Stull and his place of birth as Apia, Western Samoa. Further inquiries had revealed he'd fled Samoa and a murder. The police were still looking for him and she hoped they'd find him and 'put him away for life for breaking my heart and trust'!

Just before midday, Miss Waters called Peleiupu to the phone. 'The caller insists on speaking to you.'

'Hello, this is Mrs Barker,' she said into the phone.

There was a heavy pause at the other end, then a thin, papery voice said, 'We hope your black brother is dead, Mrs Barker. We don't want fucking darkies in *our* country!' Clunk. For an incredible moment she couldn't believe what she'd heard.

From then on, Mr Brant insisted on Miss Waters vetting all the calls.

After breakfast the next morning a female caller wanted to speak to 'Peleiupu and only Peleiupu'. They were surprised the caller knew her full name. 'Talofa, o Peleiupu lenei e tautala,' Peleiupu tested the caller. There was an off-balanced pause at the other end.

'I'm sorry but I don't understand Samoan,' the woman said. 'Pele, I'm asking you to stop looking for Arona.' Almost a plea.

'What happened to my brother?' Peleiupu insisted. The woman replaced the phone quietly.

For three days, there were no useful leads, and they kept hoping the woman would ring again. Then a telegram arrived.

> Dear Mrs Barker,
>   Saw photo of your brother in paper stop An Aaaron Maunga and wife worked for me in 1920 stop He looked like your brother stop They disappeared six months later leaving no forwarding address stop I have farm on Bludredd Road just outside Stratford stop Come and see me stop
>   Ron Hunder

Bart got a map and showed them where Stratford was. 'In the wop-wops in the shadow of the great mountain,' he said. 'Only dairy cows and cow cockies.'

'Don't ask me how I know, but I think this is the start of the true unravelling,' Peleiupu said.

They agreed that Bart and one of his assistants would go to Stratford to visit the Hunders. They left by train that evening.

To distract themselves while the detectives were away, Peleiupu and Tavita, escorted by Pierce, carried on with their business transactions. The name Awrie and

Service opened all the doors, rolled out the first-class treatment, and helped seal the deals and contracts, the main one being the building of the first picture theatre in Samoa. One evening, escorted by Miss Waters, they and their children went to see the latest Charlie Chaplin film and loved it, and knew the people at home would too.

On Saturday, an hour before the train was due in, they were waiting impatiently at the railway station. Peleiupu tried not to run to Bart when he emerged from the train, tried not to snatch the photograph from his extended hand, tried not to choke when she recognised the man in the photo. Mautu. Uncanny, but physically Arona looked just like their father at that age. This man, though, had wary, sad eyes, streaks of grey, and emanated an undeniable feeling of not trusting anyone. Dressed in an oilskin and gumboots, he was standing beside a line of steaming cows in a muddy milking shed. Beside him, trying not to look at the camera, was a slim, tall Maori woman. Peleiupu kept wiping her tears off the photo as Tavita steered her back to their taxi.

'Tell us,' Tavita asked Bart as soon as they were in the taxi.

According to Hunder, Aaron and Areta Maunga and their five-year-old daughter Naomi and their one suitcase had appeared at their farm two years earlier, claiming they were from Wanganui and looking for work. Hunder hired them and gave them the small house at the back of the farm. They said little, kept to themselves, never spoke of relatives or friends or their past. Always locked their house securely at night even though Hunder told them there was no need to. Never went into town — Hunder got them their supplies. Areta was obviously a teacher — she taught their daughter at home.

He was the best worker Hunder had ever had — could fix anything, and learned about farming pretty quickly. Must've been a sailor. How did Hunder know that? Easy, mate. Would you believe it, the bloke used a bloody compass to find his way around the farm; used nautical lingo also to talk about speed and weather and wind and was a bloody wizard at predicting the blooming weather! He also knew a lot about the world, though he tried to hide that too.

Wouldn't dare tangle with him, Hunder claimed. There was something about him — a controlled watchful silence — that made you want to steer clear of him. Too right, Hunder and his missus and their kids respected Aaron and Areta. Not many Meeorees and darkies they respected, but they sure respected the Maungas. He was bloody sorry to lose them. Jus' upped and left six months later, without telling anyone.

Peleiupu and Tavita agreed with Bart that they should try to trace Areta.

Nursing the photograph in her hands, Peleiupu said to Tavita, 'It's wonderful — we have a sister-in-law and a niece and we're going to see Arona soon.'

'Let's not hope too much,' Tavita cautioned. 'And don't forget we're returning home next Wednesday.'

'I'll change our bookings. I'm sure Mikaele and Siniva are managing things well,' she declared.

He hesitated and then said, gently, 'Darling, we don't want this search to become an obsession.'

'Obsession?' she protested. 'I promised my parents on their deathbeds I'd find Arona!'

'You know what you're like.'

'What am I like?'

'Darling, once you're committed to achieving something, you never relent!'

'Well, isn't that a good thing? Where would our business and family be if I wasn't like that?'

'You mean I don't feature in any of that success?'

'I didn't mean it that way!'

Tavita grabbed his overcoat and hat and stormed out of their suite, slamming the door after him.

Bart appeared for afternoon tea with the exciting information that Areta Waihiri was from Bluff. She had left Bluff — 'last port of call before the South Pole' — years before, spending most of her life in Christchurch, then Wellington, as a primary school teacher. She'd married one Toby Curtain and they'd run a two-teacher country school in Matangi, a small settlement in the Wairarapa. He'd died in 1913. No children. She'd returned to Wellington but had then disappeared from there. No one seemed to know where she was.

'Seven years later she appears with Arona and a child in Stratford,' Peleiupu added. 'What happened in those seven years?'

'My men have located a sister in Dunedin and another in Hamilton, not far from here.'

After Bart left, promising he'd have more information that evening, she visited some bookshops along Queen Street. Luxuriating in the rich world of books, she bought stacks of them and got the shops to pack and send them to Apia. At the last shop, while she was bending down to pull a book out of the bottom shelf, she was suddenly aware that someone was watching her. She swivelled around. A few paces away, two red-haired young women were looking through a thick book of photographs. To their left some men in plus-fours were browsing through the magazine rack. No one — not even the shop assistants behind the counters — was looking at her.

At dinner that night Bart informed them that the Waihiri family had not been close-knit. The father had been strict and sometimes cruel, and the four sisters couldn't wait to leave home. After Toby's death from cancer they'd not heard from Areta again. Peleiupu asked Bart about the fourth sister. He consulted his notes and told her the youngest sister's name was Miriama. She'd been Areta's bridesmaid and had stayed on in Matangi with Areta and Toby, working as a farmhand. But before Toby's death she'd shifted to Auckland to find work. That was the last the others had heard from her.

'We must find her,' Peleiupu urged. 'She's the one who rang.'

'Your evidence?' Tavita asked.

'Intuition. A hunch, Bart would call it,' she replied.

The following day, just before noon, Bart returned. 'I think we've found Miriama Waihiri,' he beamed, handing Peleiupu a sheet of notes. 'Or should I say, Miriam Mary Waterbeast alias Mary Marian Watercat alias Miri Hotu. She has a criminal record stretching back to 1911 when she moved to Auckland. Mainly for petty theft, then for impersonation and fraud. She's been inside three times. In recent years she's had convictions for drunkenness and prostitution. Now she's living on her own in a small scungy room in a large scungy boarding house in Freeman's Bay, five minutes from here.'

'Terrific, mate!' Tavita exclaimed.

'We want to meet her,' Peleiupu demanded. 'If she knows anything, she'll probably open up to us rather than others.'

'I suggest we arrange a meeting away from her place and this hotel, and controlled by us,' Bart said.

'That's what I want,' she said. 'And I want it arranged immediately.'

'What do I tell her?' Bart asked.

'Pretend you're a rich client wanting her services,' she replied, and was surprised at her own bold callousness.

'I'll tell her a car is picking her up,' Bart said. 'Then we'll bring her to a safe place where you'll be waiting.'

The place he arranged was a large modern home with low-pitched roof, spreading on the slopes of Mt Eden: a friend's home, Bart told them. 'They're away on holiday.' It was spacious and expensively furnished, with huge chimney-breasts and built-in inglenooks. It had magnificent views of the harbour and Rangitoto from its sweeping bay windows and from the deep-set veranda.

A car door slammed and she heard the sound of two people coming up the front stairs and into the house. The sitting-room door opening and Miss Waters and a short, compact woman with heavy make-up and dressed in a white blouse and long black skirt appeared.

Peleiupu caught the startled look of recognition on the woman's face as soon as she saw her, but the woman regained her composure quickly. 'What the hell is this?' she demanded of Miss Waters. 'I'm not into sheilas or threesomes!' She started to leave.

'Good afternoon, Miss Waihiri,' Bart greeted her. She turned around. Her short frizzy hair sparkled in the afternoon light. 'We know who you are.' Miss Waters left.

'Am I supposed to know who you and your two mates are?' she asked.

'I'm sorry we brought you here under false pretences — you'll get your money for that, but Mr and Mrs Barker want to talk to you,' Bart said.

'And for that you'll be paid as well,' Tavita interjected.

'What do you wanta talk about?' she asked, scrutinising him intensely.

'My brother Arona and your sister Areta,' Peleiupu said. 'Please sit down, Miriama,' Peleiupu invited her.

Miriama sat in the armchair opposite, crossed her legs and, holding on to the chair's arms, stilled her trembling. Bart left.

'I don't know the people you've just mentioned,' Miriama said.

'Would you like a drink?' Tavita asked, indicating the trolley of liquor and crystal glasses behind him.

'Don't touch the stuff,' she replied. 'Not at this time'a day.' Leaning forward, she smiled and said to Peleiupu, 'Now I know who you are. You're that Samoan woman in the paper. You're here looking for ya brother. Right?' Peleiupu nodded. 'Boy, the reward you're offering is a lot of money. I'd like to claim it but I don't know anything about your brother.'

'We know that Arona and your sister and their daughter were working on a farm just outside Stratford in 1920 and left in a hurry,' Peleiupu began. Miriama refused to react, so Peleiupu gave her the information Bart and his staff had collected about her and her sisters.

'Okay, I was the one who phoned you and told you to stop your search,' she admitted. 'I'd like that drink now,' she said to Tavita. 'Whisky.'

Tavita handed her the drink, and they avoided looking at her as she delivered the glass to her trembling mouth, took a long, hard swallow, sighed and wiped her mouth. 'I needed that — and this one.' She handed him the empty glass. He refilled it. She drank that quickly too. 'Yeah, bloody good whisky, good for the nerves.' She smiled for the first time. 'Aaron and Areta and Naomi don't want to be found by you. Aaron gets in touch with me now and then. The last time was when you appeared in the paper. He told me to ring you — he even gave me the wording to use.'

For the next half hour or so she talked about Aaron's and Areta's life together. After Toby died, Areta had moved in with her in Sandringham, wearing her grief like a birthsac, thriving and growing in it. Then Aaron came out of the blessed blue and helped her get reborn. He and Areta started as 'born-agains' the day they met and fell in love. Miriama had never seen such love before.

'The joy of it, the good of it spread to me and made me feel good about myself and the shitty world. And when Naomi was born, we had a wonderful family,' she continued. Arona was generous and considerate but he was also secretive and played his cards close to his chest. He rarely talked of his past life. For instance, Miriama didn't know much about his Samoan side until Peleiupu's photo appeared in the paper; she knew little about his travels but he'd obviously been everywhere and knew about world affairs. And money. He could get hold of lots of it whenever they needed it. He never divulged his sources, though. It was strange, but money and material things didn't seem to matter to him. He lived frugally and Areta liked that, though they tended to indulge Naomi.

'Then it happened — just like that,' she said. 'I came home one morning after some wild partying and they were gone.' She stopped and pondered. 'Just a note: *We'll get in touch soon. Ring this bank number and ask for your new account. Please don't go to the police. We are safe. Arohanui, Areta.'*

Tavita poured another whisky for Miriama, one for himself and a gin and tonic for Peleiupu. Handing them out he proposed a toast, 'To Arona and Areta — may we find them soon.'

'Now, can we ladies have a little talk?' Miriama asked. Tavita left. Reaching forward, Miriama held Peleiupu's hand between hers. 'Apart from Arona and Areta, I'm the only other person who knows where Naomi is. They told me in case something happens to them. Now do you want me to tell you, Pele?'

Peleiupu hesitated, then she nodded.

Miriama gave her the name of a boarding school, and the name Naomi was registered under. 'Don't tell anyone else — not even your husband.'

'How do you and Arona get in touch with each other?'

'I was going to tell you that. We put a small message in the personal columns of the *Morning Post*, saying, "Happy birthday, Captain Ahab, the *Moby Dick* is docking at . . . " wherever and at whatever time you want to meet. You're dying to find out where Arona and Areta are, aren't you?' she went on. Peleiupu nodded, eagerly. 'Well, I'm sorry ta disappoint you, love, but I really don't know.' She bent forward and embraced Peleiupu. 'I love him and Areta so much. Who knows, when this is over, we may meet again some sweet day, in Auckland!' She pulled back from Peleiupu.

After she left, Peleiupu arranged with Bart to have half the reward money given to Miriama, with one more request for her to contact Arona to see them.

Two mornings later Tavita was the first to the dining table after the waiter wheeled in their breakfast. 'A note for Mrs Barker,' the waiter said, handing it to him. He hurried back into their bedroom with it.

'Miriama has contacted me about your meeting,' Peleiupu read aloud, her voice trembling wildly. 'She pleaded with me to see you. I also can't deny my desperate need to find out what has happened to our family, especially our parents, Pele.'

Blinded by tears, hands shaking, she handed Tavita the note.

'So after talking with Areta, I've decided I have to see you, Pele and Tavita, at 12.15 tomorrow. Walk up Grey's Avenue towards Pitt Street. Make sure you're not followed.'

'He's alive, he's alive, my beloved brother's alive!' she cried. She hugged Tavita and turned him over onto the bed, and she laughed and cried and laughed.

They rang Bart, who came quickly.

According to Bart, Grey's Avenue was the heart of Chinatown, a ramshackle maze of restaurants, shops, opium dens, overcrowded houses and flats just behind the Town Hall. Not always safe, but he'd arranged security for them.

A light drizzle started sweeping across the area as they entered the avenue at lunchtime. They slipped on their light raincoats. The restaurants were crowded; lines of traffic splashed up and down the street under large sprawling maple trees, dray-horses huffed and stamped between the vehicles. She put her arm through Tavita's and pressed against him.

Near the top of the street, their hair drenched with rain, a dark blue car — its canopy raised — backed out of a driveway immediately in front of them, blocking their way. The car's back door swung open. 'Inside!' a male voice called. Tavita pulled Peleiupu in after him. The car backed swiftly onto the road and started following the traffic. The car smelled of mildew.

Because the driver was wearing a thick cap and the collar of his overcoat was pulled up to cover the back of his neck and head, they couldn't tell who it was. Peleiupu reached over the front seat and, touching the driver's shoulder, said, 'Did Aaron send you?' The driver shrugged off her hand and maintained his silence.

They were expecting a lengthy ride but the car turned onto Pitt Street, then left again and up a narrow unsealed driveway between two high buildings, and stopped in front of a small villa with creepers all over the roof of its front veranda. 'Out here,' the driver instructed, pointing at the door of the villa.

As soon as they were out, the car backed down the driveway; they watched it cutting through the puddles as it sped down towards the centre of the city.

The front door opened, but there was no one there. Peleiupu held Tavita's hand as they approached.

A sharp smell of mould and they were up the dark uncarpeted corridor and through another open door, into the mellow light of a clean, well-furnished sitting room. The door closed almost noiselessly behind them. They stood surveying the large room.

They heard footsteps to their right. Peleiupu sucked in her breath and held it. It was uncanny how the man who now filled the doorway into the dining room resembled Mautu, Peleiupu realised. The same large and bulky head and torso; the squat, heavily muscled body and legs that anchored him close to the earth; and, when he started towards them, the same ponderous gait; the same deceptive, winning smile; the same slow, hooded, penetrating eyes. It was as if their father had risen from the grave. She started weeping. 'Aue, aue, my beloved brother! Our parents are with God; they waited and waited for you, Arona!' She rushed headlong into his arms and he held her tightly. 'Why, Arona, why didn't you ever get in touch with them?' She pushed him away. Her hand swept across his left cheek in a snapping slap. Then again and again. He made no attempt to evade her blows. 'Not even a letter, Arona! Nothing!' She arched back to hit him again. Tavita trapped her in his arms from behind.

'That's enough, Pele!' he ordered. She turned and sobbed into his chest.

'I wanted to come back, Pele. God knows I wanted to. But . . . '

'But what? You have no love for your family!' she accused him.

'That's enough, Pele!' Tavita intervened. 'You should be happy we've found him.' He turned. 'It's been a long time,' he greeted Arona. They embraced.

'Yes, across a terrible stretch of the world and an ocean of time we can't recross,' Arona said. Tavita sat Peleiupu down on the sofa. Arona sat down beside her.

'I should've come with you,' Tavita said.

Arona shook his head and said, 'No, you're lucky you didn't. Your father was a great, persuasive storyteller. I believed him. He even shaped pain and suffering into spellbinding adventures and tales of good triumphing over evil.'

'But you also wanted to find out about the world, Arona?'

'Yeah, mate. I saw myself on that alia our dads built — what was the name of it?'

'*Le Sa-o-le-Sauali'i-Pa'epa'e*,' Peleiupu replied. 'The Ship of the White Phantom.'

'I saw myself captaining that marvellous craft and sailing all over the Seven Seas adventuring with all manner of people and creatures.' He stopped and then, almost in

398

a whisper, added, 'But I soon wished I hadn't started on that journey.' For a moment he withdrew into his memories.

'Where's Areta?' Peleiupu asked. He looked surprised. 'Yes, we know about Areta and Naomi. Our investigator is quite efficient.'

'You mean, Mr Brant?' Arona asked. 'Yeah, he's good.' He paused and then added, 'Areta will be here soon. She's been wanting to meet you ever since we saw you in the paper. My own need to see you was so painful I sometimes followed you and my nephew and nieces . . .'

'So you've been the one . . . ' Peleiupu interrupted him.

'At that bookshop you almost caught me out, Pele. Almost!' They laughed. 'Living at the edge, outside respectable people's reality, in the shadows and dark, teaches you how to be invisible . . .' His gestures, mannerisms, speech, even the way he leaned his head forward to the left and studied you from that angle, were their father's. But as he talked she began noticing the scars on his face, arms and hands. None were recent ones. The scars belonged to another man — a stranger she was apprehensive about knowing. And under all that shine of strength was a deep pallor — a fear? — Arona was trying to disguise.

'She's here!' Tavita said.

Peleiupu recognised her from the photograph but was shocked by how thin she was. Areta was walking in from the dining room, dressed in a simple, flowing black dress, red silk scarf tied around her head, no makeup or jewellery, and smiling. Arona started introducing her but Peleiupu rushed forward and embraced her. 'Now, no bloody crying!' Arona joked, throwing his arms around them both.

For a moment Tavita felt awkward, alone and watching them, so he pushed up against Peleiupu's back and put his arms around the women too. 'We are family, we are whanau!' Areta declared. 'It's beautiful! It's wonderful!'

A short while later Areta gestured towards the dining room and said, 'I've made some lunch. It's not much but I hope it's a good enough welcome for you. I hope you like seafood.'

Arona told them the house belonged to a friend who spent most of the year travelling around the country selling farm implements. This was only the second time they'd ever used it.

At the centre of the table were a large baked fish and two grayfish with sliced tomatoes and lemons. Around those were set bowls of raw oysters and mussels, a platter of thinly sliced fried paua, sliced bread and butter and a lettuce-cucumber salad. 'Looks wonderful!' Tavita exclaimed in Samoan. Seafood was his favourite fare.

'All of it is from the bay where we live,' Areta said. They took their seats. 'It is good that God has brought us together at last,' she began, taking Arona's hand. They all held hands around the table while Areta closed her eyes, bowed her head and prayed in Maori. Then, smiling, she invited Tavita and Peleiupu to start.

Tavita filled a small bowl with raw mussels and another with oysters. They all watched him squeezing lemon into the bowls and then noisily sucking a fat oyster off the end of his fork, chewing slowly and then sighing, 'It's the best!'

'So you're still a seafood fanatic, eh?' Arona laughed. 'Remember that first time we were allowed to go fishing on our own?'.

Tavita, mouth bulging with food, nodded. 'Yeah, and you caught our first fish, bit its kicking head to kill it, and then, after dipping it back into the water, started ripping at its flesh with your hungry teeth!'

'And you were so hungry you snatched it away from me and decapitated it with your teeth . . .'

'I can't remember that! I've never been *that* hungry!'

And so from these boyhood reminiscences and anecdotes and with Arona's encouragement, Tavita and Peleiupu began to give Arona and Areta the history of their aiga since Arona had left. They joked, they laughed, they cried, they ate with their tears falling into their food. Areta and Peleiupu held hands throughout.

After a time Arona grew more silent. 'We don't have much time left today,' he said, 'so I can only give you a brief story of the life I've led since I left home. Whenever I run out of story, please ask me questions about things you want to know. All right?' Areta held on to his arm, encouraging him.

Peleiupu nodded, reached over and touched his shoulder.

Arona's Story

Not many of us ever end up where we intend our selves to be at any given stage in our miserable lives. Look at me: when I left Samoa I intended to explore the Seven Seas and the papalagi world, becoming a devout Christian captain commanding my own defiant ship and returning triumphant to my loving aiga. An alcoholic Dutchman in one of my crews once said that we are our circumstances and the choices we made — or should've made but didn't. Where does God come into that? I've asked often. Most of us end up where we are and who we are without meaning to. Profound, eh? Are some of us born evil — born with a love of evil?

The two inescapable memories I've carried from the day I left Satoa are to do with our parents, the time I went to say goodbye to them without them knowing I was leaving. Lalaga — and I can see her so vividly even now — in her ragged working tiputa, sitting on the fale floor, weaving a sleeping mat, her expert fingers and hands performing to that rhythm and pattern of generations of weavers; within that, she had her own beat — quick, methodical, relentless, a reflection of her personality. For a while I just sat near her, watching. Her rhythm lulled me into a hypnotic peace that almost made me change my mind about leaving. When she became aware of me she glanced over. I've never forgotten the quick light in her loving eyes and her smile, which said I was her son and she loved me and expected me to fulfil her plans for me. I got up and scampered away. I'm still running away from her expectations and dreams, and now she's not here to forgive me.

I found Mautu soon after, out the back feeding the pigs. The place stank of mud and stale food. He was calling the animals and scattering the food scraps, mainly bread-fruit, among them. He was obviously enjoying it — fooling the pigs, making them rush in the directions of his scattering. His face was alight with a childlike radiance. That's the Mautu I've carried around the world and will carry to my grave: Mautu, the dreamer, feeding the grateful swine.

He didn't see me standing there; he didn't see me sneaking away into the evening that stretched away over the planet. If I'd had some inkling then of what was ahead in the darkness, I wouldn't have left. But the branch of the British company in Apia, Sharply and Sons, which owned the cargo vessel *The Forsic*, was pleased to sign me on. I was told by their recruiting officer that they'd not met such an enthusiastic native who spoke fluent English and already knew much about the geography of the world. I hid the fact I was a pastor's son. But my enthusiasm waned when I saw our cramped, smelly quarters and met Captain Merton McNaught and some of his palagi officers. They were polite and welcoming but their 'emanations' told me I was the lowest of the low. That afternoon when I met the other three Pacific Islanders, who were much older than me and who'd travelled the world, I felt safer, more worthy.

Sitiveni, the Tongan, was in charge of the laundry and cleaning; Maika, a Fijian firewalker, was an oiler in the dark bowels of the ship; and Mala, a Samoan from Poutasi, was a cook. I was the youngest of the crew, I found out later.

Captain McNaught decided, after listening to me read from Stenson's *Islands of Treasure* and testing my mathematics and writing skills, that I was the first native he'd met who was capable of becoming an officer, so I was to undergo a thorough appren-ticeship in all the activities and duties on a ship, starting with laundering and cleaning, under Sitiveni's supervision.

Our first mate was Jim Mullheath, from Auckland — a stocky, burly man who was respected and feared by most of us. 'Watch him,' Mala warned me about him. So I did. The first time I met him he shook my hand furiously, saying I reminded him of his son who was my age. He said, 'Big diff is, he's as white as stale milk and you're as rich brown as royal excrement!' His laughter was as threatening as the sea before a storm — loud, not caring whether anyone would dare object. But he liked me and took me under his wing, especially after he found out I was better educated than most Pakeha. 'I admire that, Aaron, yeah, a fucking Boong who reads and speaks our lingo better than us!' Soon after that, when he discovered I played chess, he bought me my first chessboard and insisted that we play at least once a week. He hated losing, though he never showed it too openly, so I let him win most times.

I worked with Sitiveni and two other cleaners, and no one paid us much attention as long as we did our work. So I was able to observe everything on that ship without being noticed. I soon found out that Mullheath controlled a gang spread throughout the ship, who peddled cigarettes, drugs, sex and anything else the crew craved; they also smuggled opium and other illicit drugs and goods between the countries our ship visited. Captain McNaught seemed unaware of all this. I was surprised to find I wasn't shocked by those illicit, illegal, immoral activities. In fact I was fascinated and attracted to them, encouraged by my Pacific Island friends and Mullheath.

The route from Apia to Auckland to Sydney to Singapore to Hong Kong was one of pleasure in the flesh, in drink, food, drugs, in behaviour deviant from all that our parents raised us on. 'You have an appetite as huge as your body, Aaron,' Mullheath kept telling me. Not that I took to it all immediately. No. I watched some of it, and condemned it as evil, but I knew I was lying to myself. Where was the conscience I was raised with? you may ask. With Mullheath's enticement I discovered I had a lust for living through my body and nerve-ends. A boundless, shameless capacity for that — and also the hypnotic compulsion to find out where my limits lay. 'It's all body and flesh,' Mullheath said. 'There're no such beasts as the soul and the spirit. Our purpose is to investigate the limits of the nerves and the flesh. Our only morality is that. May the fittest continue to survive. And you're young and fit — very fit, Aaron.'

Imagine it: I was destined by our mother to be a minister of the church, and here I was wallowing in the sins of the flesh. But I couldn't stop. My appetites seemed rooted in the Devil. I wanted to try out even the most forbidden of temptations. I also found I had a mind described by Mullheath as one 'inclined towards criminality'. 'You're like me, Aaron,' he said. 'You're gifted at profiting from the weaknesses and vices of others.'

The hierarchical structure of *The Forsic* reflected the power structure of the papalagi-dominated world at large. If I worked hard and pleased my white masters, I'd be made an officer one day, but that was it — that would be my limit. I would never be a captain. That was confirmed in my travels to other colonised countries. This is my convenient rationalisation for why I became 'an evil criminal and sinner'. But I didn't realise this until I was much older.

At our first ports of call, Auckland and Sydney, I observed that Sitiveni and Maika who, while on board were anonymous crew members, accompanied Mullheath and his two most trusted palagi gang members everywhere. At the second pub, when Mullheath was confronted by an angry man accusing him of betraying a deal, Sitiveni and Maika steered the man into the back alley and pulverised him. They also delivered some of the illicit wares to contacts in the city. Back on board I asked them about it. They admitted, with pride, that they were Mullheath's 'bodyguards and enforcers'. For that they received, at the end of each trip, a good percentage of the take. If I played it right, they told me, I too could make a 'good living' to send home to my family.

What about Mala? I asked. Odd looks and smiles, then Maika said, 'Mala is with us for other activities you're still too young to know about.' I played the innocent cleaning apprentice and went straight to Mala and asked him. 'I'm the captain's cook,' he replied. 'I cook for and serve Captain McNaught.' When I told Sitiveni I thought Mala was very privileged, he smirked in a strange mocking way. That was the reaction of the others as well. I was so naive. I soon found out that Mala's role was to keep Captain McNaught happy and ignorant of our illegal activities.

Like good God-fearing Islanders, we kept our Christian life and illegal activities separate. We held a lotu every Sunday. Sitiveni loved delivering fiery sermons about evil and eternal damnation; Maika loved praying his long, basso prayers asking our wrathful God to forgive us for our 'evil, palagi-inspired wrongdoings and crimes'; and Mala, in his beautiful falsetto, loved singing the hymns of his boyhood.

Because I was so young and the son of a pastor, my three mentors protected me on board. That and Mullheath's paternalism deterred anyone from trying to harm me. Captain McNaught also kept praising me to the crew and the company as 'the cleverest, most civilised darkie to have come out of the savage South Seas'. I learned to play to that stereotype.

Lalaga's capacity for hard work, her wizardry with language and accounting, and her frugality with money, which I had hated but inherited, stood me in good stead. Sitiveni and the others were illiterate so within a short time I was their letter-writer and accountant. Mullheath was very literate. Like you, Pele, he loved reading fiction, especially novels about crime and exploration and conquering the unknown. His favourite book was *Moby Dick* and he compared himself to Captain Ahab. But he was intellectually lazy and depended on his innate cunning and ruthlessness to control and exploit others. He loved the grand design of things but hated doing the detailed work to realise that. He left that to others — to his lieutenants, Keith 'Flash' Renolds, an ex-cook and ex-boxer, and Steve 'Lick-Me' Johnson, an Aussie burglar and thief. They were loquacious flatterers of their boss and knew how to make easy money, but they couldn't read a full sentence of the Queen's English or organise anything. So within four years I became their indispensable reader of anything to do with writing and accounting. I bought business books in our ports of call and studied them.

I cultivated invisibility and used that to control things. I got Mullheath to believe that my ideas were his when he conveyed them to our gang. 'We are a business,' he lectured them. 'So we should behave like one and introduce better business methods and systems. Get me?' Everyone nodded enthusiastically. 'So I've asked our Black Brain here' — meaning me — 'to do that'. From then on the 'non-savage' members of our gang referred to me as the Black Brain. I hated it but I'd learned that one can't afford such emotions in business — not at the lowly level I was at at that time.

We set up accounts under the company name, Frigate Enterprises, in Auckland, Sydney and London, the most stable economies on our route. Over time we also rationalised and strengthened our buying, smuggling, distribution and selling systems and mechanisms. Instead of competing with other gangs, we forged alliances.

Of course none of this was as orderly as it sounds. Violence is an inevitable part of the business I was in, and when it was unavoidable Mullheath, through Flash and Lick-Me and our three savages, carried it out, quietly and efficiently. Mala, to my surprise, was the best and he seemed to enjoy it.

At the end of my fourth year, during our Christmas leave, we held our first real annual meeting at a posh tourist resort in Sydney and I recommended that we should invest in legitimate business. Mullheath turned it down. While the others were enjoying the lavish Christmas party I'd organised, I retreated to the squalid affluence of my room and drank myself stupid, trying to defeat my homesickness. I cried my heart out for you and our parents. How could a pastor's son, raised on God and Christian love and honesty, find himself in the excrement of evil? And so early in his exploration of the world and the geography of being human? But there was no way back.

In January the following year, outwardly innocent, bumbling, naive, obedient Samoan that I was, I was awarded my seaman's ticket, to the loud congratulations of Captain McNaught and company and crew. 'The maritime world is now your oyster, young man,' Captain McNaught said. 'Stay with me and you'll soon be a first mate.' Mullheath gave me a miniature ivory walking stick that he said he'd found in a myster- ious cave in Zanzibar. The carvings on it were of African gods of crime, he said.

My future as seaman (and criminal) felt utterly limitless. But I should've continued heeding Mala's advice and kept a vigilant eye on Mullheath, our illustrious leader. Needless to say, as I grew in influence and started believing I was outsmarting Mullheath, I neglected that advice. It was also difficult not to trust him: he was genuine in treating me like a son, I believed.

Back in Auckland he said he was taking a few weeks off and would rejoin our ship in Hong Kong. He left Flash and me in charge. Alas, he didn't show up in Hong Kong and on our return to Auckland our leader was nowhere to be found. Our people in Auckland said Mullheath had vanished. Rumour had it that he'd shipped out under another name. Worse news was to come. Our Auckland bank balance had been reduced to an up-you-too £100! I guessed that our accounts in the other ports would also be empty. It was then I knew hatred — real, naked hatred. He'd betrayed me, his son. I could taste his blood. Our white master was laughing all the way to the bank at our expense. But I recalled — and consoled myself with — Barker's advice: Don't turn the other cheek, get even!

Flash Renolds and Lick-Me Johnson, once Mullheath's sycophantic mates, now wanted his blood. But Flash made a fatal error. While we were still in Auckland he called a meeting and, with Lick-Me's support, declared that he was now leader. Then on our way to Sydney, Flash disappeared overboard in a midnight tropical storm. Lick-Me signed off at Sydney, saying his wife was very ill and he needed to get home.

I was twenty-three and had the profound loyalty and support of my fellow Islanders and Captain McNaught who, with Mala's advice and influence, promoted me to first mate to replace Mullheath. I was respected and knew I could easily assume Mullheath's leadership but I didn't. Not openly, anyway. Being young and a native, a black, a darkie — call it what you will — I wouldn't be trusted by the palagi we had to deal with. I had to have a palagi front.

For the next three years I limited our illegal activities and consolidated my position as first mate. Through Mala I controlled Captain McNaught. Then God, in His usual way, intervened. Captain McNaught died of a massive heart attack in the middle of a raging storm, mid-Pacific. I had to save our damaged ship and steer it to Honolulu. On our way there we buried our beloved captain at sea. I conducted the service, and an inconsolable Mala sang Captain McNaught's favourite hymn, *Oh God our captain save us from the storm*. I remember the magnificent sun surfacing from the depths of the Pacific, like a fearless white shark, to claim his body, as Mala's voice reached up to God.

I anticipated that the company would not appoint me captain of *The Forsic*, and it was also time to move to a more favourable location. So, with my fellow Islanders' agreement, I negotiated with Captain Robert Hamer of *The Fuameet*, a bigger ship in our fleet. In previous years we'd had dealings with him — he ran a similar operation to ours. He was English, about thirty, loved himself blindly, was ruthlessly ambitious and greedy and cunning and racist and would therefore underestimate us 'savages'. It was also known that Sharply and Sons was grooming him for an important managerial position. He was supposedly happily married with three beautiful daughters and no vices, but we knew he liked young girls — preferably under fourteen — and, like Mullheath, was lazy, leaving the detailed work to others. His two officers and henchmen were Daniel Lions, a compulsive gambler, and Ben Tested, who loved being *tested* with whips and other torture instruments.

We, the darkies, the savages, would rise to power and wealth with Captain Hamer and his henchmen.

It's hard to believe now how calculating and without conscience I was but I *loved* the planning and manipulation. I thrived on it.

Anyway, Captain Hamer hired me as first mate, Sitiveni as head of laundry and cleaning services, Maika as assistant engineer, and Mala as second cook. What Captain Hamer and his henchmen didn't know was that their crew already respected our reputation as 'the black savages from the blue lagoon', and fell into line behind us as soon as we came aboard. What the henchmen and his crew didn't know was that I'd paid £1000 to their honest captain as our stake in the operation.

We soon became indispensable to Captain Hamer and his henchmen. I kept them happy, catering extravagantly to their vices, greed and weaknesses while I consolidated and expanded our illegal activities throughout the fleet and in our various ports. I encouraged Captain Hamer's reputation for leadership and brilliant management and eventually he was appointed manager of the Asia-Pacific section of Sharply and Sons and stationed in London. He agreed with me that we needed someone in the heart of the company to protect, promote and advance the interests of *our* company. I was to continue as manager on the shop floor, as it were. He promoted Lions to captain of *The Fuameet*, on my recommendation.

In those years I lost my adopted family. Mala decided to give up the sea and died of VD three years later. Sometimes, especially during the still nights, I can still hear his melodious singing skimming over the lulling sea.

In a sleazy brothel in Hong Kong, when we moved in to collect overdue debts from its owners, we were attacked. Before I knew it, Sitiveni, who'd tried to shield me from a knife from behind, was on the floor, bleeding. We managed to get him back to the ship. That night he died in my arms. We buried him at sea. I collected his personal belongings and when we next called into Nuku'alofa I took them to his wife and family. He had four beautiful children — the oldest son was studying to be a pastor as his father had wanted. I gave his wife some of his share of our profits, and told her more money would be sent to her every six months. I have kept that promise to this day.

After his friends' deaths, Maika decided to retire to his village on the island of Beqa. He used his share to open a store and copra trading business. He married the widowed daughter of the Ratu of Beqa and was made leader of the famous Beqa Firewalkers. He named his oldest son Arona.

I still miss them, and their love and unquestioning loyalty.

I replaced them with Lefefe, No-Fear, a Samoan from Manono. I found him in Liverpool: he'd deserted his ship for a buxom blonde. He'd left Samoa when he was about fifteen and, over the years, had acquired an enviable reputation as a highly skilled and courageous navigator and fighter. God again intervened on my behalf. The woman he was crazy about had deserted him, so when I met him he was suicidal and depressed and homesick for Samoa: ready for my rescuing.

Jake Sacred-Water was a Maori I recruited in Boston of all places. He didn't tell anyone what his Maori name was. You asked at your peril. In public he always wore clothes from neck to ankle to cover what some people claimed were 'ugly pagan tattoos'. Again, no one dared ask to see those. When I met him he'd been at sea for six years, and was an expert reader of complex maps, charts, weather, accounts and people with 'a criminal bent' — his description.

Tom Quitnott was (and still is) the only palagi I've ever loved, respected and trusted fully. Jake and I saved him while he was being attacked by a gang on the Melbourne wharf, smuggled him aboard and signed him on as crew. All I know about his life is a rumour that he was born in Bluff of a mother he never knew and an Irish butcher who'd died in prison two years into serving a life sentence for murder. Tom still refuses to talk about his life. Once he said, 'I was born in the present, live in the present, and will die in the present.' He was about twenty-five when we took him in and was the fittest person I've ever known, following the most disciplined and austere routines. He was a strict vegetarian, trained two hours daily, didn't touch alcohol or tobacco or any other drug, and abstained from sex except on his birthday, when it was a twenty-four-hour celebration. I soon discovered he was an expert in weapons and explosives.

I'm again talking as if everything were a breeze. It wasn't. My life was always at risk. I suppose that's why I was fascinated by the criminal life: you had to put up your life as collateral. And when you're existing at that ultimate level of risk, life tastes and feels exquisite. Living at sea you're also risking your life, against the elements. Only the sea, in its size and depth and power and rage and forgiveness and indifference, can match the challenge to risk everything.

Four attempts that I know of were made on my life. The fourth one cost Sitiveni his. I was nearly swept overboard three times. Maika saved me twice. I began to wonder if God was saving me for a particular mission. I've never been seriously ill, though our ship sailed to and through ports and countries that suffered frequent epidemics and terrible diseases such as beriberi, influenza, mumps, measles, smallpox, venereal disease. Every port, every on-ship inspection, was fraught with customs and immigration regulations and officials, but I was never caught. Even when deals went awry and enemies betrayed us, I was never charged or tried by the authorities. I was leading a charmed life! I was accumulating money easily and in large amounts but, apart from sex, I had little else I wanted to spend it on. I found I didn't crave material possessions. I could've lived ashore in palatial circumstances, but I wasn't interested.

I loved the sea, I loved being a sailor, I loved running our operations and making deals and making sure they worked out. And I kept dreaming of that day when I'd return home to our parents' alofa and forgiveness.

God may have meant me for special things but He also punished me with loneliness. I couldn't trust anyone, I couldn't come home, I couldn't find love beyond the flesh, I was without wife and children. In Sydney I believed I was in love with Sophia, a marvellous Aboriginal woman. She became my family whenever our ship called in. I wanted her to have our children but she refused, saying Australia was too dangerous for black children. Then a deal with some Sydney clients went wrong and they had her killed. For the first time in my life I thought I was going mad with grief and guilt. I was to blame for her death. The people I loved were risking their lives just being associated with me. Lefefe, Jake and Tom took over my ship duties and responsibilities while I tried to recover. God again chose to heal and save me.

On our return to Sydney a few months later I left Tom and Jake there. Four weeks later, when they caught up with our ship in Los Angeles, all Tom said was, 'It's done, boss.' The sweet taste of revenge was exhilarating but brief. I was left with Sophia's death and her huge, crying absence. Until I met Areta, I avoided permanent relationships with women. It was very difficult, for the heart and genitals in passion observe no rules and compel you to risk everything.

Over the years while travelling to and through Europe I got to admire the Germans and Bismarck's remarkable achievements in unifying Germany. I even took a few weeks' break and travelled in style through Germany, courtesy of Captain Hamer and Sharply and Sons. Jake, who I was training for the leadership, came with me. Sharply and Sons were great admirers of German industry and government. But as I visited the factories and was feted by their owners and absorbed the nationalistic euphoria that was sweeping the country, I became uncomfortable and then alarmed. German industrialisation was remarkable but it was for war and conquest.

Back in London Jake and I met secretly with Hamer, Lions and Tested. 'There's going to be war,' I informed Hamer. He looked shocked then he started laughing — and his henchmen joined him — in that loud, abandoned, arrogant manner reserved for dismissing and demeaning colonials and menials. 'Bullshit, Aaron!' he declared. 'And if war did occur it'll be great for our shipping company and *our* business.'

'How is it going to be beneficial?' a brave Jake asked. You could've heard a pin drop. How dare an ignorant, tattooed savage challenge their observation? 'War may disrupt the shipping routes and trade,' Jake refused to be intimidated. 'It may even sink many of our ships.'

'We need peace and fat, wealthy citizens with money to spend on their needs, vice, and weaknesses,' I said.

'I understand your ship is leaving tomorrow night.' Hamer cut the conversation short. 'We've enjoyed hosting you here and in Germany. I hope you've enjoyed and learned something worthwhile from your tour.' He got up and left.

'It is best that you leave our civilised continent to our civilised understanding,' said Lions.

'We know best what is happening here,' chorused Tested. He and Lions then left.

Without their civilised knowledge, before we left their civilised London I shifted all the unofficial accounts of our company and half the official accounts — my share — to Switzerland, Sydney and Auckland — places that would be safe from a European war. It was time to break away on our own, so when we got back to Auckland Jake, Lefefe, Tom and I signed off. Jake and Lefefe were to run our Australian branch.

When the war erupted and started devastating much of Europe and world trade and commerce, land and property prices and shares started tumbling. So through certain property firms and lawyers, we stared investing in those commodities. We were going legitimate. Sharply and Sons lost many vessels and much trade and almost went bankrupt. Because Hamer and his henchmen had been influential and vocal promoters of the benefits of war within management they lost their jobs in the company reorganisation and, enraged that 'the blacks from the blue lagoon' had outsmarted them, came after us immediately after the war ended.

Power and debauched living had softened them, made them reckless and overconfident. Lions and Tested were recklessly daring when they personally came to Sydney looking for us. They contracted some local professionals, who they were told were the best, to help them. But I knew they'd be no match for Jake and Lefefe and their men.

I sensed that whatever the outcome of the encounter in Sydney, Hamer would come after me when he heard I was still breathing. So Tom and I, with British passports, sailed to London on a freighter controlled by our men. On the evening of our third day at sea our radio operator reported that Jake had sent a message: 'Our civilised Pommie guests are happy to be cruising the bottom of Sydney Harbour. Our friend No-Fear was wounded by an Aussie swordfish but is recovering quickly.' In London it was easy to arrange a similar fate for Hamer. He didn't know that we'd saved from debt and penury the high-class madam who was arranging his liaisons with young girls. She enticed him with a fourteen-year old virgin. He couldn't resist. I left the rest to Tom.

The media spun into wild speculation, reporting Hamer's bizarre suicide: he was found hanging from the rafters of his master bedroom. Some papers argued that he'd been driven to it by bankruptcy; they all exposed (and exaggerated) his sordid, sleazy history of frequenting expensive brothels and hiring under-age prostitutes.

Why did I go to such ends? Because I wanted to eliminate all threats to the woman and child who were now my family, the centre of my life. I'd met Areta a few years before the war.

Not long after I returned from London I had this dream that was so real I still believe I — or my soul — actually returned to Satoa in the form of a frigate bird. I found myself with Lalaga and Mautu in that home we grew up in, alone and walled in by impenetrable darkness, which clogged every gap between the fale posts. I was so happy to be home, I wept. They were old and frail and wept as they welcomed me 'back from the dead'. I confessed to them my terrible crimes and sins, and Lalaga said, 'Son, we can't forgive you, only God can do that, and because He has a magnificent capacity for forgiveness, He may forgive you.'

'But you must promise your mother and me that you'll never again take the life of another human being,' Mautu said, holding out our family Bible. Without hesitation, I placed my right hand on it. 'Swear on God's book and the honour of our atua, Fatutapu!' And I did — I did, and with that, I felt my fears and guilt melt away. I was free, free at last.

But look where we are now. In hiding, on the run. Why? Because some of the fearful skeletons in my past have walked back into the present. Yes, as Mautu would've declared, 'Our sins are revisited on our children and those we love.' You can't rewrite the sins and violence out of your history. And sometimes they return as deadly surprises.

We'd erased Hamer, Lions and Tested, but our problems were not over. A few days after my dream a frantic Lefefe contacted me to say Jake's body had been found floating in Sydney Harbour: he'd been tortured and then killed. Before we could even mourn Jake, the police raided Lefefe's apartment and, claiming they'd found evidence Lefefe had killed Jake, arrested him. While his trial was on, I tried through our Sydney lawyers to seal off the tracks connecting me to Jake and Lefefe. We also managed to save some of our Australian investments and property before the police embargoed them.

Someone knew a lot about us, but who? I checked with sources and contacts in Australia, London and New Zealand. Nothing. Even our police informants were too afraid to talk. Then my Auckland lawyers and business associates informed me that the police were sniffing around some of our shareholdings and property investments in New Zealand. Someone was interested in cutting me down to size.

For the first time in my life I hesitated to act decisively. There were dangerous moments when I even wanted to be caught so that my family would be safe. That's when I took Areta and Naomi and disappeared into the landscape, leaving Tom and others to look after our business.

Some decisive revelations just happen, don't they? I was sitting on the Stratford railway platform, in the blustery cold, waiting for the train and flicking through the morning paper. In the business section there was a photograph of a new board of directors for a company that owned a chain of freezing works. The man on the left of

411

the chairman was James B. Blundell. I examined him closely, my heart racing. He certainly looked different: an obese, jowly, moustached creature threatening to burst the seams of his expensive three-piece suit, but his eyes still had that cocky, arrogant, sneering gleam; and his smile, that haughty, up-you-too twist. Gotcha, Mr Mullheath! I almost yelled on that cold railway platform in that small, anonymous dairy town.

I collected my family and returned to Auckland, where I quickly checked Mr Blundell's official curriculum vitae. Very impressive. He owns a large investment and property firm and other companies, and is a director on many company boards. He made his initial wealth dealing in Maori land and is a well-known philanthropist, his favourite charities being the Christian missions among Maori and in the Pacific Islands. He has given some public parks and buildings to the city. He is married to the daughter of one of the leading merchant families of Auckland and lives in a palatial home in Remuera. The more I found out about Mr Blundell, the more impressed I was. Mullheath had come a long, long way! My excitement also threatened to blow my skull open as I devised scenarios for Mr Blundell's comeuppance.

I gave Tom the information about Blundell and how he was behind No-Fear's and Jake's killings and we discussed the options. In his usual austere, understated manner he said, 'Let's go. I want to pay him for No-Fear's and Jake's lives.'

I told him it wasn't going to be easy. 'He's a very powerful and public figure, with power and influence in the police and government.' Then it hit me like a ton of guilt-filled bricks — my night-time promise to my parents. When I told Tom about it, he said, 'It was only a dream, mate. This is real — Blundell can kill us. Besides, we don't have to do it. Just expose his criminal past to the press and the cops, and the law'll take care of the bastard.'

I knew it was a mistake but it was the only option open to me.

Through several sources I leaked that information, in the form of copies of documents I'd kept from our *Forsic* days, to the police and the leading papers. We waited, and started panicking when nothing appeared in the media and my contacts told me the police knew nothing about the evidence I'd sent. Of course the media are owned by powerful people and special interests that can be influenced, intimidated and corrupted. The police are the same.

The reaction when it came was chilling. 'No one believes your shit, Nigger, and we're coming after you,' the man whispered over the phone. Once again I took Areta and Naomi out of circulation.

Then out of the beautiful tropics and the heart of Samoa, you came looking for me. And here we are.

Accidents

'What about the parcels?' Peleiupu asked, immediately after he finished speaking. Arona looked puzzled. 'We received a big black parcel every so often, and we assumed it was from you.'

'I forgot about those.' His eyes lit up with mirth. 'Yes, whenever my guilt became almost unbearable, I wrapped one up and sent it, and I never knew whether any of them got to you. It was like sending out a plea for forgiveness and praying it got through to our parents and their generosity of heart.'

'Yes, we got them — or some of them. And Lalaga and Mautu and all of us looked forward to getting them. The parcels became part of *The Tales of Arona the Sailor*!' Peleiupu and Tavita laughed.

'You didn't come home but the rumours and stories and the parcels did,' Tavita added. 'Arona the sailor became a living, fabulous person in Satoa, even though you stayed away.'

'But he wasn't enough for our parents, eh?' Arona asked, sadly. Peleiupu and Tavita looked away. 'I can never make up for that.' For a while they sat in silence.

'What are you planning to do now?' Peleiupu interrupted.

'I don't know,' Arona replied. 'I can't break my promise to our parents.'

'No, you can't,' Areta emphasised.

Right then a short, compact papalagi man in a grey woollen shirt and black jacket slid silently into their midst. He waited politely until he caught Arona's attention and then said, 'It's time.'

'This is my friend Tom Quitnott,' Arona introduced him. The man stepped forward and shook hands with Tavita and then Peleiupu, who was surprised to find that the mythical Quitnott was quite small.

Areta got up. Peleiupu moved over and held her. 'Do you have to go now?' she asked Areta.

'Yes,' Arona said. 'We'll get together again soon. Tom will contact you. By that time you'll have decided whether I'm still worthy of being your brother. I have so much death with me.'

'You had to do what you had to do,' she said. 'God understands.'

'We're so happy meeting you today,' Areta whispered. 'Arona has yearned for this all his life away from Samoa.' Arona bent down, kissed Peleiupu's forehead and pulled away. Tom started heading for the door. 'We'll meet again.' Areta kissed Tavita and then followed Arona.

'Someone will come and take you back to your hotel,' Arona said. He put his arm around Areta and steered her out the door. Areta turned, waved, and was gone.

Ten minutes later they had to run through the dark, cold rain to the car that was waiting for them.

In silence the driver drove slowly through the thick deluge, with the windscreen wiper barely able to keep the windscreen clear. Tavita reached over and held Peleiupu's hand. 'They'll be all right,' he tried consoling her. She shook her head.

Back in their suite, she spent a long time under the hot shower, then dressed in her thick woollen dressing gown and slippers and joined Tavita for the hot tea and biscuits he'd ordered. Her hand shook as she raised the cup to her mouth.

'Did you believe his story?' she asked after her third sip.

'What do you mean?'

'Just that: did you believe him?'

'Of course I believed him! Are you crazy? He's your brother and my friend!'

'We believed *your* father's stories and look how true they turned out to be.' She was deliberately hurting him. 'Look what they did to Arona. Even Arona's way of storytelling is like your father's.'

'Pele, my father may have embellished a little . . . '

'A *little*. Huhh!'

'Why are you doing this? Why are you deliberately hurting me — and Arona and Areta?'

'Because it was your storytelling father who led him astray.'

'Astray? What do you mean, astray?'

She placed her cup firmly in the saucer and then, gazing into his eyes, said, 'You know much of your father's version of his life was a lie, admit it.' He looked away.

'Don't forget your father bequeathed his official version to Mautu and me, so I know.' Not long after they'd married, and she could no longer bear his intense curiosity about his father's life, she'd told him what Barker had written.

'How do you know that written version is the truth?' He had her and felt good about it. 'Because it's written down? Because in that written version he swears it is the truth?'

'Bugger you!' she snapped.

'Anyway, why would Arona lie to us?'

'Shut up!' Trembling and pale with anger, she jumped to her feet.

While she stood there on the verge of tears, he poured her a gin and tonic and whisky for himself. She tried to push the drink away but he opened her fingers, wrapped them around the glass and raised the drink to her mouth. 'Cheers,' he said. Reluctantly she took a sip. 'If Arona is lying, then Blundell doesn't exist and we're not in danger. So we don't need to be afraid,' he added. She drained her glass and extended it to him. He went to refill it.

Peleiupu mellowed. 'As I listened to him I had to try to rid myself of all the exaggerated stories, tales, rumours — in fact all the fiction and mythology that he'd become for us over the years, and I tried to see the Arona and Mautu I knew but I couldn't. And today what he told us about his life is even larger than the fiction we'd inherited. But is it any truer? And I'm trying to believe this Arona doesn't enjoy manipulating and killing people — that he's had to do it to survive.'

'Hold on, darling. Think of some of the methods we've used to build up our business and protect our interests and family.'

'We've always stayed within the law.'

'Are you sure?'

'We've never killed anyone.'

'We've destroyed some people.'

The phone rang. Tavita picked it up. 'It's Bart,' he mouthed. After the call he reported the news to Peleiupu. ' Like you instructed, Bart and his crew followed Arona and Areta as far as Warkworth. No one was tailing them.' He came and sat down beside her on the sofa.

'I'm glad they're safe,' she said. She buried her face in his neck. 'I want to love the Arona we met today. But I'm frightened for them.' She opened her dressing gown and he nuzzled into the soft, warmth of her breasts and body. 'They're family, Tavita. We've got to save them.' He started kissing her breasts. She held his face and, turning it up, she licked at his eyes and mouth. 'Make love to me, Tavita. I'm afraid!' she whispered.

They made love, wildly, frantically, wanting to bury their fears in each other.

She couldn't sleep for a long time, disturbed deeply by the realisation that the history of her aiga, from the first Atua Fatutapu and Sina's vengeance exercised through the frigate to subsequent Tuifolau, was a story of exacting revenge for any wrongs committed against them. And though she tried, she couldn't convince herself she wasn't following that tradition herself. She remembered how she had helped her brother Iakopo die, and she couldn't dispel the thought. To add to that pain, she couldn't make herself believe Arona's story, and that hurt more because her love for him was her life itself.

Tavita was pleasantly surprised when he woke the next morning and heard her humming as she dressed. 'Hurry up, we have so much to do,' she urged. 'I've rung Bart about Mr James Blundell. I told him we want to do business with him. That way, we can get close to him.'

When he joined her in the dining room, after a quick shave and shower, she hugged and kissed him, and he recognised she was back to the Peleiupu who knew what she wanted and how to achieve it. 'It was great last night,' she grinned.

'Respectable daughters of respected pastors are *not* supposed to talk about sex and brag about their multiple orgasms!'

'You must've woken up the whole hotel with your one long, long, long, loud coming!' she laughed.

When Bart arrived an hour later he confirmed much of what Arona had said about Blundell, and then warned them that Blundell, in his early rise to power in Auckland, had been suspected of having links with criminal gangs in Australia and Asia; even now it was rumoured that his legitimate companies were being used to launder the money from his criminal activities. 'Why are you interested in him?' Bart asked.

Peleiupu didn't hesitate. 'Mr Service has asked if we're interested in buying into some of Blundell's businesses and acting as his agents in Samoa for importing and selling his products.' Tavita never ceased to be amazed at how easily she could lie. But was it a lie? Or was this the way she was going to approach Blundell?

'He's a very scary man, Pele,' Bart said. 'A pillar of respectable Auckland society, but scary. You don't cross him.'

'You don't think an innocent, naive, sultry South Seas maiden can do business with him, mate?' she said, smiling.

Was it jealousy Tavita was feeling as he looked at Bart and recognised admiration and infatuation as he gazed at Peleiupu? He'd seen it before — in nearly all the men who worked closely with her. They all fell under her spell eventually.

She wasn't in bed. Half-past-one, his watch said. He slid out of from under the sheets, went into the sitting room and switched on the light. The balcony doors were open and he found her in the cane chair, wrapped in a sheet, gazing out at the dark city. The light wind smelled of high tide, and the city rolled away from them towards the gulf in waves of orange, yellow, red and blue lights. Above them, the heavens were a fathomless black silence. Standing behind her, holding her shoulders, he asked, 'What's the matter?'

'I couldn't sleep. I'm too scared about our inability to protect Arona and Areta. And then the bird visited me.'

'What bird?'

'*Our* bird. You know — the frigate. It flew in from the east through the black sky and over the city and perched on this railing. I came out to it. It was as real as you are now.' She paused and caressed his hands. 'It dripped black water and stank of decaying coral, and just stood there staring at me with those fierce, haughty, female eyes. I kept asking it why it had come but it refused to answer, so I said, "Bugger off then. Go on. If you're not going to be civil, bugger off!" Then the bird said, "It hasn't taken you long to learn New Zealand English, eh, mate?"' Tavita smiled.

'"You're not supposed to know any English!" I heard myself carrying on that ridiculous conversation.

'"Ha, I'm not just your kuaback, from-the-bush bird!" it said, puffing up its chest. "I'm sophisticated, highly educated, intellectual, well-read, well-travelled, ageless, and multi-lingual, mate!"

'"And you're immortal and an atua, I suppose."

'"Too right, bitch!" It flapped its threatening wings and thrust its head and beak at me, its eyes blood-red with anger. "I'm your atua. I know what's happened, is happening, and is going to happen. Ha!"

'So I asked it what was going to happen.'

'"If I told you, you'd almost die with grief!" Then it must have been scared it had said something it shouldn't have, because it covered its face with its wing and started scuttling along this railing.'

'I pleaded with it not to go and woke up to find myself in this chair.'

Tavita came around and, kneeling before her, rubbed her cold hands.

'Why did the bird come?' she whispered.

He helped her up and they returned to bed.

Except for the receptionist at the desk, the hotel lobby was still empty of people. Tavita stopped and looked again and saw Bart in the armchair at the far side. Bart had rung him to come down. Tavita hurried over. Bart held his arm and steered him away from the reception area.

'Did you listen to the news this morning?' Bart asked. Tavita shook his head. 'There's been an accident.' Stopped. 'Up North, near Kaikohe — a car went off the road into a gorge.'

'And?'

'They were killed.'

'Who?'

'The couple in it . . .'

'Do we know them?'

'It just said they were Maori, and the police are trying to contact their relatives.'

'It's not them — it can't be them!'

'I'm going to Kaikohe to check.'

'Who's going to tell Pele?' Tavita heard himself pleading.

'Better wait until we know for sure,' Bart said, avoiding the responsibility.

Once Tavita was back in the suite he downed two quick whiskies and then ordered breakfast. When he went into the bedroom she was at the dressing table putting on her make-up. 'Do I look devastating?'

'Yes, darling, absolutely killing!'

'Enough to melt the hard hearts of hard-hearted palagi lawyers and gangster businessmen?'

He tried to laugh. 'Yeah, but what about the ones without hearts?'

She got up and, straightening her dress, said, 'I never thought of those.'

'Pele, they have other organs you can melt!' She hurried over and they held each other for a long time, laughing intermittently.

At breakfast he suggested that their programme for the day should include a meeting with Mr Service to arrange a meeting with Blundell — perhaps in the following week; finalising the contracts for their cinema in Apia; booking their return fares on the *Matai* — perhaps in a fortnight's time; having afternoon tea with their copra agents, and signing contracts; telegramming Mikaele about the shipments of goods to Apia for their stores; and having dinner with their children. He was surprised when she agreed to all of it. He rang Pierce to come and pick them up.

Before they left the hotel he sneaked another whisky. Throughout the day, while fulfilling their schedule, he would continue drinking without her knowing, and keep hoping and praying for good news from Bart.

Next morning, Tavita woke for the early news. Nothing about the accident.

418

Anxiously he continued waiting for Bart's call. He paced the room and finally relented and took his first whisky for the day — and hated himself for being so weak.

At first he didn't hear the cautious knocking. Then when he heard the distinct rap-rap-rap he rushed to the door and pulled it open. An unshaven, tense Bart stood in the doorway. Behind him, avoiding his eyes, was Tom Quitnott; he too looked as if he'd been up all night.

'We tried to get here as soon as possible,' Bart said. Tavita stepped aside and the two men came into the room. 'I'm afraid it's bad news,' Bart said. 'Arona and Areta were the couple in that accident.' Tavita wanted another drink to still the shuddering that was surging from his belly and radiating out to the rest of his body. 'It looks like an accident and the police believe it was.'

'But I *know* it wasn't,' Tom said quietly. 'Arona told me it was going to be this way.'

'Do you want me to tell Pele?' Bart asked.

Tavita shook his head furiously. 'I can do it.' Bart poured him a whisky. Tavita declined it. 'I'll wake her up.' He started for the bedroom. But Peleiupu, in her white dressing gown, was already emerging. Tavita looked at the other two.

'It's bad news, isn't it?' Peleiupu asked, looking at Bart.

'Yes, it's bad news,' Bart replied, avoiding her eyes. 'They've been killed.'

What she did next would stay with Tavita for a long long time. There was no visible sign of shock, horror, grief or anger. 'Sit down, gentlemen,' she said matter-of-factly. She sat down on the sofa and patted the space beside her. Tom sat there. 'I expected it,' she said. 'The bird came and told me the other night.' When she saw Bart's puzzled look, she added, 'The frigate bird is our family's god.'

'It was my fault, Mrs Barker,' Tom said. 'I allowed him to hesitate, I offered him the wrong option, I allowed him to see you and thereby come out of hiding, and I didn't provide them enough security and protection . . .'

'It was also our fault,' Pele interrupted. 'By insisting that we meet them, we forced them out of hiding.' She paused and then, touching Tom's arm, added, 'It couldn't have ended any other way, eh?'

'Arona was the only human being I trusted with my life. He and Areta and Naomi are my family, the only one I've ever known,' Tom said. Tavita noticed there were tears in his eyes.

Peleiupu straightened up, smoothed her hair, clasped her hands in her lap and, face utterly composed, declared, 'We must observe a time of mourning, and make sure they have a proper funeral and cremation.'

'But we can't wait,' Tom said urgently. 'Blundell may act now — against us!'

'It is our way,' she ordered. Again she touched Tom's shoulder, gently. 'We've arranged to meet Blundell next week. I'm sure he's curious about us. Let them suffer, too, worrying about what we're going to do.' Tom bowed his head. 'Bart, I want you to take some of your staff and make sure all the funeral arrangements are done properly. Don't be extravagant — we don't want public attention. Tavita will come with you.' She turned to Tavita. 'I know, darling, it is not our way to have cremations, but it is the only way we can take Arona and Areta to Samoa and home.'

'What about Naomi?' Tom reminded them. 'I want to take her to her parents and their funeral.'

Peleiupu was now in full command. 'No, you will stay with me. We have many things to do. Tavita will take Naomi.'

'But they're after her too — she's not safe!' Tavita protested.

'We want them to know where she is, just as they know where you and I and our children are. With us and our loved ones in their full view, they know we can't retaliate against them because they can see what we're doing.'

'What if the press gets hold of Arona's real identity?' Bart asked.

'I'm sure Mr Mullheath won't want that,' Tom replied. 'Not yet, anyway. The press may trace Arona back to him and his dirtier earlier life.'

'Areta and Arona should be cremated under their present identities,' Peleiupu said. 'By the way, encourage the police to believe it was an accident.'

Tom rang Naomi's school and, after talking to the matron, told Tavita Naomi would be waiting for them when they got there. 'When we get there her name is Naomi Waihiri. That's her mother's maiden name.'

Quickly, Peleiupu packed a bag for Tavita and one for herself — she was to spend two days with Tom.

No one said anything as Tom drove them to the school. They all expected a long trip into the country but at the bottom of Queen Street, Tom headed up through the university to Parnell and St Stephen's Avenue. Queen Mary's School for Maori Girls was down a driveway lined by flax and shrubs.

'Is this it?' Tavita asked. Tom nodded.

'Right under their noses: good move,' Bart said. 'I thought you had her hidden in the wop-wops!'

'She's waiting in the matron's office,' Tom said.

When they got out of the car Tavita glanced up at Peleiupu. She looked tense and upset. He held her hand. 'I'm sure she's a strong child,' he said in Samoan.

They followed the other two down a long corridor that smelled of long wet days. Some of the students smiled and nodded as they passed. At the door of the office Peleiupu stopped, turned and started retreating. 'It'll be all right, I'll handle it,' Tavita said, releasing her hand. He followed Tom and Bart into the office.

He stopped as soon as he saw the teenage girl Tom was embracing and kissing on the cheek. When she turned and looked at him, he almost gasped. Lalaga. The same prominent forehead and deep-set, alert eyes; the same slow, winning smile; the same long torso and short limbs. 'This is your Uncle David,' Tom introduced him. 'You know, the one your dad keeps talking about?'

She stepped towards Tavita. 'Kia ora, Uncle,' she said. 'Did you come all the way from Samoa?' He nodded, unable to speak. 'Did Aunt Pele come with you?'

'Yes, I did,' Peleiupu's voice rescued him from tears. Peleiupu stepped past him and swept Naomi into her large embrace. 'You look just like Lalaga, your grandmother. We're happy, so happy to meet you at last.'

Tavita bent down and kissed Naomi on the cheek. 'Your grandmother was a very strong woman,' Tavita said. 'Your aiga has always had exceptional women.'

'And a few exceptional men,' Peleiupu added. She sat down with Naomi, holding her hand.

'Like your dad and your grandfather Mautu.'

'Are you strong too?' Peleiupu asked. 'Your Uncle Tom tells me you *are* strong.' Naomi nodded hesitantly, and waited. 'Because you've had to help your parents and protect yourself, eh?' Naomi nodded again, this time more resolutely. 'You'll be able to meet your cousins Lefatu, Maualuga and Iakopo very soon. They're going to boarding schools right here in Auckland. You want that?' Naomi nodded again and waited. They suddenly didn't know how to go on; they couldn't look at one another.

'You know your mum and dad and I have been preparing you for this, eh?' Tom found another way, finally. She nodded and continued waiting. 'So you know what has happened?' She winced and nodded and waited, her grip around Peleiupu's hand tightening. 'Is your bag ready?' She nodded and rose to her feet.

They watched her as she walked across the floor and picked up her black bag, which was lying by the matron's desk. 'I'm ready,' she declared.

She refused to let anyone touch her as they hurried to the car.

They stopped beside a burgundy car parked by the wharf. Peleiupu hugged and kissed Naomi. 'Be brave,' she whispered. She kissed Tavita and got out hurriedly with Tom. They waited until they saw them disappearing around the corner, heading north; they were to return in two or three days' time.

'Some of my men are up there already,' Tom informed her. 'They'll work with Bart, and they'll make sure nothing happens to Naomi.' He opened the door and she got into his car. 'You're too trusting, Mrs Barker,' he said when he was seated behind the wheel.

'And you don't know much about me, Mr Quitnott,' she countered. But for the first time she was wary of him.

'I have a letter that Arona left for you,' he said as they drove into Freeman's Bay, a run-down, shabby neighbourhood in the centre of the city.

'We don't have much time to prepare,' she said.

'For Blundell and his crew?' he asked. She nodded. 'We don't need much time. Arona has already prepared me and some of our blokes for that purpose. Just tell us when, Mrs Barker.'

'Don't tell me *that* part. Just let me know about his other activities and what he and Areta wanted for Naomi's future.' She paused, and looking cautiously at him, added, 'I'll let you know about that other move before we leave for Samoa.'

'When do you meet *Mister* Blundell?'

'Next Friday, mid-morning.'

He drove the car into a small garage in front of a villa that was wedged in between two others in a narrow street of villas. He took her bag and she followed him through the tar-smelling garage and along a path around to the back of the house and a small vegetable garden bordered by what she thought were papaya trees. 'A couple use the house as if it's their home. They won't be in while we're using it.' He unlocked the back door and she followed him into the neat, warm, well-lit kitchen and dining room. 'Apart from a few trusted people I'm going to bring to meet you, no one else will know we're here.'

'I like it,' she said. Family photographs, comfortable sofas and chairs, trophies, ornaments on every surface as if it were still Victorian times, a wood fire in the fire-place ready to be lit, and above the mantelpiece a framed photograph of a majestic Mt Everest.

'The house is always fully provisioned. I'm not much of a cook, though.' When she didn't offer to do the cooking, he said, 'Your brother was a bloody good cook. I loved all the island dishes he made.'

'I don't want any tears or sorrow,' she heard herself saying.

'Sorry,' he murmured. 'I'll show you your bedroom.'

A few minutes later, back in the sitting room, he asked if she wanted to see Arona's letter. She hesitated and then said yes. He handed it to her. 'I'll leave you alone. Call me when you're ready to start work,' he said.

The small white envelope had only one sheet of paper in it, she figured. She fingered her name on the envelope. *Pele*, was all it said, yet she was afraid to open it, for with it would come a responsibility she believed she wasn't ready or able to assume. She wandered over to the glass doors, which opened out to a garden that smelt of ripe compost. A flash

— a white cat scuttled through the vegetables and up into the shrubbery.

She sat down at the hefty rimu dining table and didn't falter as she peeled up the back flap, pulled out the folded sheet of paper and spread it out in her hands. His handwriting hadn't changed much — it was still ornate, with wild flourishes and large rounded letters:

Pele, lo'u tuafafine pele,

In the time I've been away from our beloved Samoa I've lost most of the Samoan language I knew. I want so much to talk to you in the language of our childhood and growing up, but I can't.

You are reading this short letter because Areta and I are dead. (I instructed Tom to give it to you only if that happened.) I hope with all my heart that Naomi is alive and with you. If she isn't then I've wasted my miserable life.

I have set up the Satoa Trust with you as its sole trustee. It is to be used to care for, protect and help Naomi and our aiga. My lawyers and Tom will give you all the details. All my legal businesses are in that trust.

My 'other' businesses and investments I leave to Tom and to you to do with as you wish.

Areta and I want you to care for Naomi as one of your own children. We want you to take her to Samoa with you and raise her in the life I chose to leave. I want her to grow up and be like you and Aunt Lefatu and Ruta and Naomi in that long genealogical line of the Atua Fatutapu and the frigate bird.

I chose to explore the world, and look what I found. Areta and Naomi and my own sister and aiga again. I'm also proud that I've kept my final promise to our parents.

I hope my beloved Areta and Naomi can forgive me.

My alofa to you and Tavita and our sisters and aiga.

Arona.

She refolded the letter and slid it into her pocket. While the afternoon shadows lengthened across the garden and started crawling up the houses behind them, she stood at the glass doors, gazing out and recalling the life she'd enjoyed with her brother and sisters and parents, and what it could've been if Arona hadn't left home.

They worked deep into the night, with Tom detailing the structures and personnel and connections in and of all their organisations and activities. Every time he stopped, she prompted him with questions. She came to admire his memory and ability to shift and connect and relate the important details and themes and people. She kept notes on this information. He complained of a headache finally and staggered off to bed. She showered, had a cup of tea and, though fearful and anxious about Tavita and Naomi, fell asleep quickly.

He had a simple breakfast of toast, tea and marmalade ready when she woke. During breakfast he declared he was 'full of beans, ready ta eat up the whole planet and the evil Blundell monster!' There was a cunning, intelligent, calculating, better-be-careful-of-me Tom who, once committed, wouldn't quit, but there was also a childlike Tom who didn't seem to understand the simple, ordinary things of the everyday world, she observed.

During that day Tom brought to her Arona's lawyer and other people. From them she collected detailed information about the trust and Arona's other businesses.

For a frightened while she didn't understand why she was sitting up in bed drenched with sweat and crying and shivering. She stripped off her nightie and, while drying herself, remembered her dream, full of ominous one-eyed creatures with steel scales and long talons who, as she approached them, turned into fiery missiles that shot at her, zinging violently past her ducking head. When she couldn't shake off her fears she hurried out to the back veranda and watched the dawn spilling across the city.

Later Tom walked onto the back veranda and found her praying. Politely he sat down and waited for her to finish. 'Do you do that often?' he asked.

She gazed at him in disbelief. 'Yes, I do it regularly. Our family is of the church. We are staunch Christians.'

'Yeah, Arona and Areta used to have — what do you call it in Samoan?'

'Lotu?'

'Yeah, that, every Sunday evening.' He pondered for a while. How could a man who had killed and destroyed others be such an innocent? she thought. 'I don't know much about religion,' he said. 'There wasn't any of that in the foster homes I was in.'

'The Bible is a very beautiful book,' she tried to encourage him.

He got up and retreated into the house. When she went in a few minutes later, he was cleaning the kitchen and stoking the coal range.

'All right, mate, seeing you've been good, I'll cook us a Samoan lunch.'

'Just give me a list of the stuff and I'll go and get it.'

'It's Sunday, no shops are open.'

'Hell, what's the bloody use of having connections if ya can't get groceries and food on Sundays!' She slapped him on the shoulder, playfully.

When he returned, he boasted he was an expert table-setter — Areta had taught him. That had been his contribution to their meals. So while she cooked, he set the table. The food was ready within two hours and she carried it out to a perfectly set table: white linen tablecloth and serviettes in real silver rings, silver cutlery and expensive crockery and glasses, Samoan pandanus tablemats, and a vase of tiger lilies, 'Areta's favourite flowers'.

'You do know how to set a table!' she congratulated him.

'Jesus, I'm as hungry as an empty dunny!' he said to cover up his embarrassment at her compliment. Such a colourful but inappropriate remark, she thought.

They sat down. He immediately started dishing out the food but stopped when he noticed she was looking at him. 'Let us pray,' she said, bowing her head.

After grace he waited for her to start. 'I know all the dishes you've cooked,' he said. 'That's sapasui, that's oka, fa'alifu fa'i, and of course cucumber and vinegar salad, and whole baked snapper.'

Surprised at his correct pronunciation, she asked, 'Who taught you the language of the civilised?'

'Arona. Cunning bugger refused to let me taste any of the food until I could say the names correctly. Boy, did I learn fast!'

She started heaping food on to his plate. 'Your reward.'

He was a neat but fast eater. She tried not to look at him as he ate. Every time his plate was half empty she heaped more food onto it. 'Will you be able to find the people who were hired to do it?' she asked.

He nodded. 'When I find them, what do you want done with them? Remember they were just doing a job they were paid to do.'

'Are you saying they bear no share of the responsibility for it?' He refused to answer. 'Nothing will be done with them until I say so,' she instructed.

'Okay, boss,' he said, and then started digging into the side of the snapper.

'Please don't call me that again. I'm not part of . . . ' She couldn't say it.

He paused in his eating and looked unwaveringly at her. 'Are you sure, Mrs Barker? Arona was your brother, family, blood. And that blood is pumping wildly 'cause you're enjoying the game, the hunt, eh?'

It was early Tuesday afternoon when Tavita, Naomi and Bart returned. After Peleiupu brought Naomi into the suite and they embraced and cried together, Peleiupu said, 'You're staying with us now. You don't have to go back to school.'

'She was very strong and brave up there, but it's been hard for her,' Tavita said. 'She should try and sleep.' He handed Peleiupu Naomi's bag.

As she steered Naomi to her bedroom Peleiupu said, 'We've prepared this room for you, and tomorrow you'll meet your cousins.'

Tavita went to the bar, and got a beer for Bart and a whisky for himself. 'Where shall I put this?' Bart asked about the large carton he'd brought in. Tavita indicated the side-table by the mantelpiece.

'It's so bloody sad,' Tavita sighed, sinking into the armchair. 'All her short life she's had to learn to live under another name and help protect her parents.'

'Kids usually find it difficult to keep secrets, but she has. She coped hell of a well up there.'

'Yes, but how do you live with the pain of your parents' death?' Tavita murmured.

Peleiupu returned, saw the carton and went to it. 'Is this it?' she asked.

'The urns are in it,' Bart replied.

She caressed the top of the carton. 'How was it in Kaikohe?'

Bart glanced at Tavita, who appeared to have withdrawn into himself, so he told Peleiupu about what had happened: how when they'd reached Kaikohe the police had released the bodies to them with the official verdict of death by accident; how they'd hired funeral directors and the bodies were prepared and laid out in their coffins in the funeral parlour; how they had then taken Naomi — poor, poor kid — in to be with her parents, and she'd tried not to break down. 'But when she got to her mother, she . . .' Bart stopped, unable to go on.

'She cried, but there was no sound,' Tavita continued in Samoan. They remained silent for a while. 'You should've been there, Pele.' She didn't react and that annoyed him more. 'Naomi didn't want to leave her parents.'

'We managed to get her to our hotel and got a doctor to see her, give her a sedative . . .' Bart said.

'Yeah, you should've been there,' Tavita insisted.

'I had other things to attend to,' she stopped him.

When Bart saw the anger in Tavita he said, 'We had a service at midday the next day. The funeral directors provided a minister. He was Maori: a wonderful man who befriended Naomi immediately.' He paused. 'Apart from us and two of Tom's men and the local police sergeant there was no one else at the service. It was obvious Areta and Arona had kept very much to themselves. Tavita said a short eulogy in Samoan. The minister prayed for their souls . . .'

'And that was it before the flames turned them into ash,' Tavita interrupted. 'A convenient form for us to carry to Samoa.'

'Were *they* there?' Peleiupu ignored Tavita and asked Bart.

'They probably were but I didn't care if they were. As you've said, it's best that you're out in the open, in their full view,' Bart replied.

'I've arranged a family service for Arona and Areta tomorrow evening at the Catholic seminary in Ponsonby,' she told Tavita.

'We're not Catholics!'

Again ignoring his anger, she said, 'Father Tomasi, your friend, is staying at the seminary and he's agreed to conduct a simple family service.' Tavita drained his glass. 'I thought it'd be appropriate for Naomi and our children and us to be there as an aiga.' He remained silent as he held his empty glass out to Bart. 'We'll have a full, proper service for them when we get to Samoa.' She stopped and then asked, 'Is that all right?' He started on his third drink. 'Have I done something wrong?'

Tavita shook his head. 'No, Pele, you never do anything wrong. Everything you do is perfect. You always decide everything, you . . . ' He jumped up and stormed away into the bedroom.

'He's very tired,' Bart said. 'He's been through a hell of a lot.'

'So have we all.'

'I'm going home to get some rest. Is there anything you want me to do before I go?'

She shook her head. 'I've talked to Mr Quitnott about things. There are matters I'd like your advice on but they can wait.'

'Pele, I'm sorry about your brother and Areta.'

'Thank you for all your help since we got here.' He turned to leave. 'By the way, do you have a family?'

He nodded. 'A wife and two daughters.'

'Would you like to bring them to the service tomorrow night? We'd love to meet them.'

He hesitated. 'My wife and I are separated. She's got the girls in Wellington.'

She didn't know what to say. He left quickly.

The west was aflame with the colour of blood and rich sea-egg roe as Pierce drove Tavita and Naomi and Peleiupu through the arched gateway of the seminary. Bart had gone to pick up the children.

At the bottom of the chapel steps stood Father Tomasi. His white mane and black soutane glittered in the sunset light and made him appear to be floating.

Father Tomasi stood on the running board and opened the car door. Tavita stepped out and they kissed each other on the cheek. 'I'm sorry, so sorry about your brother and his wife,' Father Tomasi said to Peleiupu as he embraced her. 'And who is this beautiful young woman?' Father Tomasi greeted Naomi.

'Naomi, my niece,' Tavita replied. Father Tomasi embraced Naomi.

The other children arrived with Bart, and Father Tomasi greeted them enthusiastically. Then Peleiupu introduced them to Naomi. Looking solid and formidable in their school uniforms, Lefatu and Maualuga hugged and kissed Naomi and then held on to her arms.

Pierce got the carton out of the car boot. Tavita took it from him and followed the others up the steps.

The small chapel with the high dome was austere and bare. Its only extravagance was the five stained-glass windows through which the sunset was now pushing a slowly moving, psychedelic light. The altar was covered with a shimmering ie toga; on it was a stand of burning candles. The combination of lights made them appear unreal, without form.

As the others took their seats in the front pews Father Tomasi took the carton from Tavita, opened it, wiped the urns with a white silk cloth and and placed them at the centre of the altar. Tavita turned to see who was behind them. Bart sat at the end of the back pew. Out of the darkening doorway stepped Tom, who acknowledged him with a nod and walked right up the aisle to sit down beside Naomi, who immediately held on to his arm.

Father Tomasi cleared his throat, then welcomed them in Samoan oratory. Not once did he make a mistake in the genealogies of the Aiga Sa-Sao and the Aiga Sa-Tuifolau, or in the appropriate oratorical language. 'On behalf of our spiritual family here in Ponsonby, I welcome you this evening,' he switched to English. 'I greet you in the name of our Lord and Saviour. We are gathered here as an aiga to welcome back to our midst our beloved Arona and Areta . . .' Tavita heard a muted sobbing; he refused to look at the children. When he remembered that, as head of their aiga, he had to speak later on, the tension in his chest and belly worsened. All he'd intended was to bring his family on a holiday, put the kids into school, do some business, and look for and find Arona. End of story. But look where they were now.

He surfaced from his fears when Peleiupu and Iakopo started singing Arona's favourite Samoan hymn.

He joined in, and so did his daughters.

After the hymn, Iakopo went up and read from Ecclesiastes, a passage that Peleiupu had chosen. Tavita's anger at Peleiupu mounted again as he listened to his son's reading. She controlled everything, even this service was hers, part of the dangerous game she thrived on, risking even their children's lives.

'Papa, they're waiting for you,' Maualuga whispered. He stood up and hurried to the front.

In formal Samoan oratory he greeted Father Tomasi and the other visitors, describing Tom Quitnott as 'Arona's true friend and brother'. He avoided looking at Naomi as he spoke. '. . . We came to New Zealand to look for Arona. God was kind. He led us to Arona and to the magnificent lady he chose to love and marry, Areta, and to their wonderful daughter, Naomi.' He was weakening, but he held on. 'Tragically, Arona and Areta were killed in a motor accident.' He paused, swallowed. 'We can never read God's way; we can't always hold on to the people we love . . .'

He felt weak and drained when he returned to his seat. Maualuga moved up against him and held on to his arm. He would avoid Peleiupu for the rest of that evening.

After the service, Iakopo and Lefatu picked up the urns. Peleiupu invited everyone to their hotel for dinner. Tom declined and left. Once outside in the falling dark, all the children chose to go in the car with the urns, with Bart as their driver.

During dessert, Peleiupu announced that after it, all the young people were going to bed. They didn't object. 'May I sleep with Fatu and Maua?' Naomi asked.

'Of course you can,' Peleiupu replied. 'Iakopo can shift into our suite.' She'd booked the adjoining suite for the children.

A few rushed minutes later Peleiupu thanked Father Tomasi, said goodnight, and left with the children.

Tavita didn't want to be alone with Peleiupu. Not yet. So he offered his guests port, liqueurs and cigars. Bart and Pierce declined and left. After the service, Tavita had been hanging out for his first drink, and he hadn't cared who noticed how greedily his mouth had grabbed at the glass, hadn't cared if they'd heard his relieved sigh as the first sip had slipped smoothly down his throat and chest, warming him through. But after that first drink — and he'd really looked forward to a night of heavy drinking with Father Tomasi — his thirst had vanished. He'd tried enticing it back with the second drink, but it had refused to be enticed. During the meal, he'd noticed that Father Tomasi wasn't drinking much either.

While they lingered over their cigars, Father Tomasi told him he'd run into Bernie Griff and his wife Bileen in Wellington. Immediately Tavita's thoughts moved to Bileen. How he wished he was with her, away from this pain and trouble, immersed mindlessly in the ecstasy and voluptuous heat of sex . . . He stopped that interior surge of euphoric escape: it was inappropriate, callous, sinful at this time of mourning and sorrow.

Peleiupu's bedside lamp was still on and she was lying with her back to him. He undressed quickly and slipped into bed.

'What was that all about?' she accused him over her shoulder.

He deliberately took his time. 'What are you talking about?'

'Don't play games with me, David!' She called him David whenever she was angry with him. He felt her turning around. 'You've been angry with me ever since you got back from Kaikohe.'

He turned his back to her. 'I'm tired.'

She scrambled up and knelt behind him. 'Do you think it's been easy for me?' He refused to reply. She grabbed his shoulder. 'I'm trying to organise things so it'll be easier for you and every one else!'

'Bullshit!' he snapped, rolling onto his back. 'It's all for you, Pele. You're obsessed with controlling everyone and everything!'

'God, you're stupid!' She drove her fist into his chest. He caught her hands and held them.

'You enjoy controlling and manipulating the people around you — me, your kids, Bart, all your hapless servants. You didn't even love your brother deeply enough to take his daughter to his funeral.'

'That's not true!'

'You don't like what Arona became, darling? Just take a good look at yourself!'

'You're just jealous!'

'You're not doing this out of genuine love for your brother, but because you're enjoying avenging his death — you don't like losing to anyone, ever.'

'Does that mean you're not going to help me?' She was now astride him, trapping his hips between her thighs.

'Too right I am, but it's not going to be good for us.'

'You're just scared of . . . ' She tried to free herself as he wrapped his arms around her and pulled her down towards him, and started kissing her breasts. 'That hurts!' she cried as he sucked her left nipple. When he refused to release it she reached down, grabbed his genitals and squeezed. He tried to wrench his hips away but she held on. The cutting pain shot up into his belly. He released her nipple.

'Fuck you, fuck you,' he murmured.

'Fuck you too, fuck you!' She wrapped her arms around his neck, pressed her forehead hard down on his, raised her hips and then came down and around him. And held him and held him.

The Meeting

The meeting with Blundell, in Mr Service's office, was scheduled for 10.30 am the next day. So when the children left with Pierce after breakfast to play tennis at the Services' home, Peleiupu asked Tavita how he thought they should handle the meeting.

He looked at her. 'Are you trying to make me feel good by asking for my advice?' She shook her head. 'You don't have to cajole me, Pele. I know you're the brains in our partnership, so you'll have to do most of the negotiating. I'm no good at it.'

'Blundell is going to assume that, being the man in our partnership, you're the boss.' She smiled.

'Are you going to play to their stereotype of you as the dumb, obedient wife who knows nothing about business?'

'He'll also be assuming we're naive, gullible, easily intimidated darkies.'

'And we should encourage that. Pele, as you well know, I don't have the confidence or nerve to carry it through.' For the first time in their marriage he didn't mind pleading: there was too much at risk.

She leaned forward and, pressing her forehead against his and breathing in his breath, said, 'I love you. All the people in Satoa and Apia have enormous admiration and respect for you. Without you we wouldn't be where we are now.'

'Yeah, in the shit, our lives and everything we own at stake. I'm so scared I'm getting fear-diarrhoea like Mautu used to.' He tried to laugh.

'I'm afraid too, but we can't get out of this one,' she whispered. 'He won't let us.'

'So, as you've said in the past, we just have to prepare well?'

She nodded and kissed him. 'Your father and Sao, my parents and Fatutapu are with us.'

For most of that day they prepared in great detail, trying to cover all the options. They called in Bart for his advice and to finalise protection for them and their children; they called in Tom to recheck some of the information about Blundell — especially on his weaknesses, and to hear Tom's planned measures to counteract any violent moves by Blundell.

The children were tired from tennis, so straight after dinner the girls kissed them goodnight and retreated to their bedrooms. Peleiupu asked Iakopo if Naomi was all right. 'She says she's looking forward to going to Samoa,' he told her. 'We love her.' When Tavita asked him about school, Iakopo explained he quite liked it but was finding the papalagi students disobedient and ignorant. 'Shall I get you a drink, Papa?'

'No, I have to think straight tomorrow,' Tavita replied.

Iakopo headed for his bedroom, stopped and asked, 'Uncle Arona and Aunt Areta didn't die in an accident, eh?' Tavita looked at Peleiupu. 'Naomi told us they were killed.'

'It's best you don't know too much about it, son,' Tavita said finally. 'We want you to look after Naomi and your sisters.'

'What if something happens to you too?' Iakopo asked.

'Nothing will happen,' Peleiupu insisted. 'Mr Brant and others will make sure we're safe.'

'He's so much like his grandfather,' Tavita said as Iakopo left.

'Which one?'

'Mautu.'

A short while later they got into bed but couldn't sleep. They held each other, got too hot and decided to sit on the balcony.

The slow wind from the harbour wrapped itself around them lazily, cooling them. From the dark streets below rose the dumb noise of traffic and, as they gazed up, they allowed the upward-swirling movement of the star-seeded heavens to grip their fears and whoosh them away. 'Perhaps the bird will visit us tonight,' she remarked.

It didn't.

They were dressed and had breakfast ready when the children joined them. They tried not to appear tense but sensed, from the children's subdued and careful behaviour, that they knew. 'I want to say the karakia this morning,' Naomi offered. They held hands around the table and bowed their heads. First she prayed in Maori then in English, her fervour and commitment reminding Peleiupu of the way Arona had told his story.

'. . . Our Father, please protect us today. Take special care of our parents, Pele and Tavita, who continue to face threats from our enemies. Make them strong, give them the courage and determination . . .' As Naomi prayed, they grew stronger in their resolve.

Shortly after breakfast, which they had forced themselves to eat, Cynthia Waters arrived to take their children to a South Auckland farm and horse-riding — Bart had arranged protection for them while they were there. The children embraced them. Tears welled in Iakopo's eyes. 'We'll be all right,' Tavita assured him.

While they waited for Bart, they checked — again —that they had all the papers they needed for the meeting, and then sat in silence trying to still their fears. 'You look really in control,' she complimented him. She straightened his tie and waistcoat and readjusted his watch-chain.

He brushed bits of fluff off her suit. 'Yeah, a real businessman. And you look the really supportive, loyal, obedient businessman's wife.' She flicked his chin.

Not long after, they were in Bart's car, heading down Queen Street to the impressive Service Building, nursing their fears. 'Don't worry about the children,' Bart said. 'My people will protect them with their lives.'

They stopped at the entrance. 'Good luck,' Bart said. Peleiupu avoided looking at him. Tavita nodded, got out and held the door open for Peleiupu, who handed him his briefcase.

They strode into the building, their shadows leading them.

Mrs Twobells, Service's grey-haired secretary who'd looked after them on their previous visits, met them in front of Service's office and took them down the empty corridor to the board room. She opened the door and led them in. 'I have got morning tea ready if you'd like some.' They accepted her offer. In the scent of gardenia that filled the room, Peleiupu caught the whiff of dampness and mould.

It was a large, oak-panelled room, with a massive kauri table and padded chairs around it. Portraits of stern-looking men — previous partners? — lined the walls.

Just as Mrs Twobells was handing them their cups of tea Service strode in, smiling, hand extended. 'Good morning, David,' he said, shaking Tavita's hand. 'Beautiful day. Reminds me of what it'll be like on Judgement Day.' Tavita recalled that Service was a senior Methodist deacon. 'Mr Blundell and his team will be slightly late.' No apology — powerful and important people didn't need to.

'I'm sure Mr Blundell is the busiest man in the country,' Tavita said, smiling wryly.

While they waited, they discussed other business opportunities, with Service addressing most of his advice to Tavita. Peleiupu listened and looked attentive, smiled and nodded at the appropriate moments.

Half an hour later Mrs Twobells returned with two expensively suited middle-aged men, who bowed once and stepped aside. Through the gap between them lumbered Mr James Blundell, leaning on his intricately carved ivory walking stick. Long white hair and tidy beard, round rosy-cheeked face sprinkled with age spots, thin red lips, pale white skin that emphasised the blackness of his suit, which had been tailored to try to disguise his weight. It was the piercing blue eyes that held Tavita. His heart started racing and his breathlessness returned. He steadied a little when he felt Peleiupu's firm grip on his arm.

'Mr Blundell, I'd like you to meet my friends from Seemore, Mr and Mrs David Barker,' Service said. Blundell waited. Tavita took a step forward. Blundell stretched out a hand and Tavita gripped it.

'How do you do, young man?' Blundell said. 'I've heard good things about you and your beautiful wife and children.' He deliberately slowed down his English. 'You're the first Seemoeans I've had the pleasure to meet.' Tavita stepped aside. Peleiupu came forward. 'And you, Mrs Barker, are even more beautiful than Mr Service has described you.' She showed no fear or distaste. She smiled, eyes lowered appropriately. Turning to his companions, Blundell introduced them as the managers of the companies in which the Barkers were interested in investing. Tavita didn't catch their names.

They took their seats at opposite sides of the table, with Service sitting with Tavita and Peleiupu. Blundell and his managers declined Mrs Twobell's offer of morning tea. In the presence of Blundell, the usually in-command and forceful Service was subdued and ingratiating, Peleiupu observed.

'I've studied your requests, Mr Barker, and I see no problems,' Blundell began. 'In fact, I welcome your interest in my company, which always *needs* new investors!' He guffawed, tiny flecks of spittle scattering into the air. 'But even more important, I need intelligent, savvy, up-and-coming investors like you, Mr Barker.' He nodded towards his managers.

'We understand, Mr Barker, you want to invest in our meat operation?' the first manager with the round bald head asked.

'Yes, sir, that is correct,' Tavita replied. Then he added apologetically that he wanted to double the amount he'd asked for earlier. The manager glanced at Blundell. 'Is that all right?' Tavita asked.

'I can vouch for Mr Barker,' Service said. 'He's made and is still making a fortune in copra. He also owns about twenty stores in Seemore.'

'I like that, like that!' Blundell exclaimed. 'Good on ya, young man. I like to see Meorees and others like that succeeding.'

'We're still a modest company, but, like you, sir, we want to grow and become immoderately wealthy!' Tavita said.

'Yeah, beautiful: grow with me, boy, and be immoderately wealthy. I like that!' He guffawed again; this time the spittle was thicker. Tavita kept beaming; Peleiupu kept smiling. 'So be it, Mr Barker. A very generous sum of trust in me. Anything else?'

'We also want to invest more in your property company, sir,' Tavita continued.

'You don't mind my calling you David?' Blundell asked. Tavita shook his head. 'Welcome aboard, David, to *your* company. You're the first native shareholder I've allowed in.'

His second manager then took over. 'At the moment, Mr Barker, Morric Heedstead, a very successful Australian company, handles all our business in the Pacific,' he explained. 'Why should we give that to you, sir?'

'As you know, sir, we don't want and can't handle the whole Pacific operation. We just want Samoa, our little country. We can handle that.'

'What can you provide that's better than Heedstead's?'

'We know the country better; we're influential there. Besides, in exchange, we want your company to handle our copra in New Zealand and Australia. That's worth quite a bit now.'

'Great move, son!' Blundell exclaimed. 'Welcome aboard again. I don't know shit from copra but they tell me it's good money!' When he guffawed this time, the spittle sprayed across the table and over Service's papers. They pretended not to notice. 'David, you've thought of everything, and I love and admire that!'

'Anything else, Mr Barker?' asked the second manager, with the ill-fitting plate of false teeth.

'Perhaps you can suggest other ways we can benefit from our new relationship, sir?' Tavita ventured.

The managers glanced at Blundell, who laughed and said, 'Good move again, son. We're a very large and varied company. We've got our sexy fingers in just about every juicy business orifice in this voluptuous country, and Aussie. You're welcome to put your delicate fingers in some of those!' He started guffawing again, coughed and, thumping his massive chest loudly, stopped.

'Thank you for the offer, sir,' Tavita said in the voice he'd used whenever he'd wanted a favour from his father.

'We can discuss those orifices later, David,' Blundell said. 'Meanwhile, Mr Service, who I'm sure you're paying extra well, and my overpaid jokers will go away and draw up the appropriate papers to clinch our new relationship.'

Service and the managers got up and left.

'Don't know about you, Mrs Barker, but whenever I finalise a lucrative deal, I get unusually thirsty and hungry!' He guffawed again but averted his face from Peleiupu's direction.

'I'll get you a cup of tea and some cakes, sir,' she offered. As she moved to the tea tray she could feel Blundell's gaze exploring her body, but she kept smiling.

After she served them tea she deliberately sat beside Blundell and opposite Tavita. She served Blundell biscuits and cake. He obviously liked being fussed over, so she even put sugar in his tea and stirred it.

It came unexpectedly; they'd planned for it but hadn't expected it then. 'By the way, Mrs Barker, how successful have you been in tracing your brother?' Blundell asked, his voice heavy with concern as he dunked his biscuit in his tea.

Lowering her gaze, her stance emanating sadness, she said, 'We have found him.'

'That's wonderful, Mrs Barker.'

'He died with his wife in a motor accident near Kaikohe.' She emphasised each word. Tavita caught a look of suspicion in Blundell's eyes.

'I'm sorry, so sorry,' he said. 'I didn't mean to be nosy.'

Peleiupu bowed her head, hands clutched to her face. 'That's all right, Mr Blundell.'

Tavita took over. 'Arona didn't exactly lead an honest, sin-free, Christian life. No, sir! The police said he and his wife had been drinking a lot.' Then, gazing directly at Blundell, he said, 'But of course you knew about Arona's accident, sir.'

An amazed blink, then the haughty, arrogant blue eyes were upon him. 'How do I know about it?'

Control yourself, no anger. 'You had them killed, sir, and we know you know we know.'

Chuckling softly, Blundell said, 'Why would I want your brother dead?'

'Because he was an old business acquaintance who knew too much about your past, sir.'

'He also wanted to settle scores. Against me!' They could hear his heavy, menacing breathing. 'Why are you buying into my business?' he demanded, cold suddenly.

'Because it is a profitable investment,' Tavita replied. 'Your companies rate in the top ten in Australasia, sir.' He paused and then, smiling, he said, 'And as part of our insurance policy.'

'Meaning what, boy? I don't like clever half-castes!' That dug in painfully but Tavita didn't show it.

'We're now at your mercy. You know that, sir. We're in *your* city, where we're unfamiliar with the rules; our children are in *your* boarding schools . . .'

'We warned you, David. We told you not to keep looking for Arona.' His voice had softened again, his gaze was less menacing. 'You're very perceptive, son, but your wayward brother wasn't. He tried to fight me in my own patch. Foolish, very foolish.' He sighed. 'David, what guarantee do I have you won't turn against me like your brother-in-law did?'

Trying to sound ingratiating, Tavita replied, 'We are leaving our children in your schools as your hostages, as a guarantee that we'll always be your obedient business partners, sir.'

'My brother lied because of the nature of the business and life he'd chosen, sir,' Peleiupu helped. 'His life couldn't have ended any other way. As devout, God-fearing Christians, like you, Mr Blundell, we condemn the sinful, vengeful criminal life that he led.'

'You don't love him enough to seek vengeance, in an Old Testament sense, Mrs Barker?' Blundell asked, carefully.

'We didn't see Arona for thirty years, sir. We met him recently and we were shocked because he was not only a total stranger but a violent, unrepentant criminal. He'd trampled on the whole Christian traditions of our family. My parents would've rejected him as their son. We reject him too.'

'Besides, what's vengeance got to do with doing business and making money, sir?' Tavita asked.

'Shit, son, I like that. I like that!'

'As my husband has told you, sir, we're just a simple Samoan family who're at your mercy because of our brother and not through any fault of our own.' She bowed her head and wept silently into her handkerchief. Tavita reached over and held her arm.

'Your brother, Mrs Barker, was a beautiful and very bright young man when I first met him.' Blundell sounded sad. 'Yeah, as quick as the flash of a white shark's hungry teeth. Bloody quick. Great brain, quick learner. I taught him a hell of a lot.' He smiled. 'Introduced him to the pleasures of the world and to his own enormous appetites and hungers and abilities.' He laughed softly. 'I did love him, treated him like a younger brother. Yeah, and he returned that with his growing knowledge of business, which came in useful in expanding our business. But he was too trusting. Underneath that brain, that cunning criminal inclination and ability, he was still the honest pastor's son. Yeah, he trusted me. Or should I say, the pastor's son trusted the crude and violent, devious Mullheath I was then.' He continued laughing. 'He built our business, modernised it. You could say, he became a large shareholder in my business. You could also say he still is a shareholder, because he's never withdrawn his investment. And you're only adding to that.'

Were those tears in Blundell's eyes? Tavita wondered.

'Mr and Mrs Barker, I'm very pleased that you're being realistic and sensible. This is business, strictly business. Your brother ended up mixing business with a suicidal desire to destroy me.' Tavita tried to look grateful as Blundell reached over and clutched his shoulder. 'Son, you and your beautiful family are not going to regret investing your money and loyalty in me. You'll receive huge dividends in money, patronage and protection.' He reached down and grasped Peleiupu's hand. 'You and your children are safe with me. You have my word on that, Mrs Barker. You are family.'

Still holding her hand, Blundell struggled to his feet. 'Getting too old and fat,' he sighed. He bent down and kissed Peleiupu's hand; his lips and breath were warm on her skin. 'You're very beautiful, like Arona was beautiful.' Peleiupu lowered her eyes. 'David, you and I are going to go a long way together.' Tavita tried not to wince as Blundell's heavy grip tightened around his hand.

They watched him picking up his walking stick. 'I don't have to stay for the signing of our agreements, David,' he said. 'I'm bloody glad I came today to meet you.' He turned, stopped and, gazing back at Peleiupu over his shoulder, said, 'I did love Arona.' He rolled the name over his tongue lovingly. 'I did.'

Almost an hour later, as they left the board room and started hurrying down the corridor, Peleiupu began shaking. Tavita put his arm around her and gathered her to his side. She put an arm around his hips. They steadied each other as they fled.

'Arrogant bastard!' he snapped as they broke out of the building into the hot summer light.

'Who the hell does he think he is?'

'God — a white god who thinks he can stomp on us black ants.'

Bart opened the car door. They slid into the back seat and Bart drove off quickly. She reached up and kissed the side of Tavita's face. 'You were good, bloody good!' she whispered in Samoan.

'So were you, darling,' he replied, caressing the inside of her thigh.

'How did it go?' Bart intruded.

'Well, I think,' Tavita replied. Peleiupu helped him take off his sweat-drenched coat. 'I was so afraid I sweated through my every pore!'

'He's a frightening man,' Bart said.

'But I think we did quite well.'

'How much time do you think we've bought?' Bart asked.

'I don't know,' she said.

'I don't think he'll break his word,' said Tavita. 'Not yet, anyway. After all, he's got our kids and a large hunk of our money.'

'That's a hell of a lot of trust!' Bart said.

'Perhaps too much,' Peleiupu said.

'I think he actually liked us. I almost felt sorry for him,' Tavita said. 'So sorry for him I wanted to kill him.'

'Especially when he called you a clever half-caste?' she said.

'Yeah, especially for that!'

She remained silent the rest of the way, caressing his hands. How she loved and admired him! He'd conquered his fears and had performed superbly. And now that she'd decided on their next move, she felt at peace with herself and God. Tavita need never know. Blundell at their meeting had decided his own fate, without being aware of it.

On Saturday afternoon she rang Bart to come and take her and the children back to their schools. The children objected and complained, but she promised to let them return on Thursday, the day before they left for Samoa.

When they reached the girls' school Naomi asked to spend until dinner time with Maualuga and Lefatu. Peleiupu agreed readily; they'd pick her up at seven that evening.

As they drove back Bart described the day as one of those Auckland summer days in which the sky stretched up to the gods in a clear fathomless blue, and the crisp heat was a gentle touch all over your skin — all you wanted to do was lie on the beach and sleep and dream of a world without winter or rancour or . . .

In the time she'd known him, she'd sensed that under the businesslike, fearless male front, Bart possessed a gentle, poetic way of viewing things and people. She avoided observing him as he drove. Yes, she was attracted to him; she'd admitted that to herself the week before when he'd advised them on how to handle Blundell and revealed a genuine concern for her safety. That admission made her feel awkward whenever he was near. He wasn't the first man she'd felt that way about, but none had ever become serious; she'd always managed to suppress it before it had reached that stage. But with Bart, the more she tried to rid herself of if, the more it persisted.

'There's a proposal Tom and I would like to make to you, Bart,' she heard herself saying. She felt him looking at her. 'Could we stop somewhere and talk?'

They parked at the end of a no-exit street beside a small park that sloped down to the beach only fifty paces away. He asked if she wanted to sit on the bench or the sea wall. She shook her head and tried to steady herself by gazing into the shimmering noonday light reflecting on the sea's surface.

'So what is this offer?' Bart asked.

'You're not helping us just because of what we pay you, eh?' she asked.

'At first, yes: you're the best-paying clients I've ever had.' He paused and then, looking at her, added, 'But I've become part of your fight.'

'Fight?'

'To find Arona, then his killing, and now your struggle to stay alive against Blundell.'

'But it's not your fight.'

'It is. As I've worked for you, I've realised it's my fight too. He is the brutality, greed, arrogance and cynicism of power. And I don't like seeing unequal contests: the underdog getting clobbered by obese and arrogant blokes! Everything was stacked against you very naive, very innocent, very dumb noble savages. But look where you are now.'

'Yeah, in the shit, so David said today. In the shit and at Blundell's mercy.'

'You've changed the odds a little, though, haven't you?'

'Thanks to you and others. We'll always remember that.' She brushed back her hair. Yachts with white sails were racing from east to west across the harbour. A black dog ambled across the beach, tongue hanging out, pulling a frail-looking man bundled up in a shabby overcoat past the changing-sheds.

'So here's the offer, Bart,' she said. 'I've tried and am still trying to love the man Arona became. If not love him, feel some empathy for him. It's bloody difficult. He must've been quite monstrous — without conscience. Like Blundell. But he was aiga, blood, family, and I love Naomi. I also promised our parents I'd find him and bring him home. Well, I've found him, and with Blundell's permission I'll be able to take him home.' His profile glowed in the white light of the car window. 'Being the brilliant sleuth that you are, you know that Arona was involved in a lot of criminal activities. Apart from the trust set up for Naomi and our aiga, he left behind other lucrative but illegal sources of income. I'm starting to talk like Blundell! Tom wants those to continue but I don't want to be involved in them.'

'What do you mean?'

She fought the compelling temptation she felt to take the control on offer. 'I don't want to. I can't, anyway, because I'll be in Samoa.'

'So?'

'Tom knows this. And he says he's a good lieutenant but he needs someone else to replace Arona.'

'You don't want to do that?'

'I'm tempted, I may as well admit that.'

'It's dangerous, dirty, risky. You're a mother and respected businesswoman. And I guess you don't need the wealth because you're making enough of that legally.'

'You're not tempted?' she changed tactics.

Smiling, he kept gazing at her. 'Of course I'm tempted — by the power and the money and the risk . . .' He started laughing. 'Tom and I have talked about it while we've been working together to help you.'

She raised her eyebrows. 'I'll still have a share in it, though!' Her breath checked in her throat as she watched his long-fingered hand move to caress the back of her own. She welcomed the sharp, tingling that his touch sent through her.

'No, it can't be, Bart,' she heard her frightened voice declaring. 'I have a husband, children, aiga.' What a stupid thing to say, she realised.

'And at the moment we need to deal with a deadly threat to all that, eh?' he said, withdrawing his hand and looking away.

'Yes. That's more important than anything else.'

'So the possibility of us . . . us . . . '

'I think we should go back now.'

He started the car and backed out onto the road.

She hugged her corner in silence, too afraid to look at him, too afraid of her true feelings.

Just before she got out of the car in front of the hotel she said, 'Tom will be very pleased with your decision.' She paused and then added, 'So am I, Bart. Thank you.'

On Sunday morning she kept the curtains closed and dressed quietly so as not to wake Tavita. She scribbled a note saying she was off to church and left it on his bedside table.

It was as if a soft transparent yellow tide of light had surged in from the harbour and flooded the empty streets up to the tops of the tallest buildings. She whistled in her head as she thought about her parents, and danced through the streets.

As arranged, Tom was waiting in his car at the bottom of Albert Park. She got in and they drove off to the safe-house where she'd been before. They sat on the back veranda, sipping lemonade. Curious, she asked, 'Haven't you ever touched alcohol?'

'Nope!' he said, shaking his head. 'Never liked the taste of it.' She'd expected a complex reason and was surprised at the simplicity, the innocence of his answer.

As she briefed him about their meeting with Blundell, he listened intently, nodding his head.

'What do you think?' she asked at the end.

He sucked in air and said, 'The bugger, the creepy bugger, actually likes you and David!'

'Nonsense! He was only pretending.'

'No, he does; he feels he owes you because, despite everything else, he *did* love your handsome brother. And because you've thrown yourselves at his mercy. He also admires talent, savvy, hard work and guts. And you and David have all those . . .'

'Thank you!'

'. . . Besides, there are too many of you to get rid of without attracting attention.'

'And he doesn't yet know how much dirt we have on him, or where we keep the evidence.'

'You're learning fast, Pele.'

'Will he let us go home next week?'

'Why not? He can still get to you in Samoa. He can buy jokers there to do the job. Every two-legged creature has a price.' Soft chuckling.

His remark offended her and made her feel vulnerable. 'I've talked to Bart and he wants to join you.'

'Great. He's strong and straight. But does he have the stomach for the other side of it? I have to train him: he's spent too many years as a cop with a conscience.'

'I've told him, and I'm telling you: I want a share of the business.'

'Jesus, Pele, you're starting to talk like Arona! See, I told you: once you get a taste for it, it's like an aphrodisiac — better than sex!'

Annoyed and unsettled by the frankness and truth of his perceptions, she changed the subject. 'Have you found out who carried out the killing?'

He nodded. 'Easy, Pele. There aren't many pros of that calibre and price in God's Own Country.'

She waited but he wasn't telling. 'Well, who was it?'

'You don't want to know, Pele.'

'Why not?'

'You're slow on this one. You don't *need* to know. It'll get you into more hot water with Blundell.' She felt stupid; she was so naive. 'What do you want done with them?' he asked. 'You're the boss, Pele.'

'What do you advise?'

'Do nothing. Let Blundell take care of his own. There's talk around — and I'll make sure Blundell hears it — that the two of them are talking too much. I'm sure they'll disappear shortly.'

'When is Blundell going to move against us? You're the pro, Tom. What do you think?'

'I don't know when, Pele, but he will, he has to. You know too much.'

Fear was again surging through her. 'So what do we do? Just sit around and wait?' When she glanced at him, he was gazing straight into her heart. It was chilling. 'What?'

'You know the answer, boss. I only carry out orders.'

Even though she'd decided Blundell's fate during the meeting, she hesitated, knowing, with an enormous but exhilarating fear, that this was the decision that would either stop her at the border between good and evil and return her to God's magnificent and forgiving grace, or take her over that border into power-without-conscience, and without God, for the rest of her life.

She leapt. Into the way of Fatutapu and the frigate.

When she told Tom what she wanted done, she did so calmly, with a salving serenity permeating her every cell — the same serenity she'd experienced when she'd decided, as a child, to help end her baby brother's suffering from the Satoan Disease.

After two hectic days of shopping and packing and finalising their business affairs and dealing with matters to do with their children, and preparing Naomi for their trip to Samoa, they were exhausted and stressed and ready for a long afternoon sleep before a farewell dinner. Someone rapped briskly on their suite door. Tavita swore as he dragged himself up.

It was Blundell's second manager: bespectacled, smiling, holding two parcels with red ribbons around them. Behind him was a young woman carrying two large bouquets of flowers. Tavita shook the man's hand and invited them in. Peleiupu hurried from the bedroom.

'These are from Mr and Mrs Blundell, sir,' the manager said. Tavita smiled as he accepted the parcels. The woman gave the flowers to Peleiupu. They both thanked them. 'He also asked me to give you this.' He gave Tavita a letter in a blue envelope edged with gold. Tavita invited them to stay for a drink but the manager apologised — they had to be at another function. He bowed and shook Tavita's hand. 'Mr and Mrs Blundell wish you a very enjoyable and safe trip home,' he said. 'Personally, I'm very pleased that you're now an important part of our company. You're one of a few non-family people he's allowed into our organisation.'

'Please thank Mr and Mrs Blundell for these beautiful gifts,' Peleiupu said.

As soon as Tavita had shut the door behind their unexpected visitors, Peleiupu started cutting the ribbons and opening the parcels. He held up the letter. 'Open it!' she urged.

He slit it open with his forefinger and read it out loud.

Dear Mr and Mrs Barker,

We wish you a safe trip to Samoa with Naomi, Arona's beautiful daughter. If there is anything we can do for your children or to improve our business dealings, please let me know.

I am extremely grateful that you have invested in my company and family.

We all loved Arona, but he is now in our past. Let us keep him there, and begin anew.

God bless you.

Yours sincerely,

Jack Blundell

The smaller of the two parcels contained an old, wooden, much-used chess set, which had been cleaned and restored with great care. In the box was this handwritten note:

This was Arona's first chess set. I bought it for him and used it to teach him how to play better. A few months later he was beating me consistently. It now belongs to you and Naomi.

In the larger parcel was a beautifully finished rimu box with a greenstone kiwi inside. Tavita whistled as Peleiupu lifted it out. The bird had diamond-studded talons and beak, and red sapphire eyes. Peleiupu stood it on the coffee table, where it sparkled in the afternoon light. 'Bloody expensive!' Tavita exclaimed.

Peleiupu ran her fingers over the bird. 'Kiwis can't fly,' she joked.

'No, and they're not as cunning as your frigate!'

'Nor as ruthless.'

They stood back and looked at the letter and gifts. 'What do you think?' Tavita asked.

'Cunning old bugger's weakening.'

'Getting sentimental in his fat, rich, old age?'

'And he's sure we're too afraid to cross him.'

They slept easily, heavily, that afternoon.

Their ship was to leave in two hours, and visitors were being called ashore. Naomi had withdrawn into a sorrowful silence, wedged in between a protective Lefatu and Maualuga on the sofa in their cabin. Iakopo sat on the sofa arm, sipping a lemonade. Tavita, Bart and Pierce were drinking and talking at the other end of the cabin. The reality of farewell had closed in.

'You know what they call Lefatu at school, Mum?' Maualuga asked. Lefatu pinched her but didn't stop her. 'Because they can't pronounce her name, they call her Heart.'

'Do you mind that?' Peleiupu asked Lefatu.

'I mind but I can't stop it, so I have to live with it. The teachers too are starting to call me that.'

'I'll write to the headmistress,' Peleiupu said.

'No, Mum!' Lefatu objected. 'I can take care of it.'

'They call me Catch — you know, Maua, meaning caught?' Maualuga laughed. 'Good name and they know I can *catch* any of them.'

'Do they have a palagi name for you?' Peleiupu asked Iakopo.

'Jake — short for Jacob,' he replied. 'I don't mind; it's not worth worrying about.'

It was her fault her children were now caught in the deadly struggle with Blundell — she'd been the one who'd wanted to give them a papalagi education. Her fault too that they were being subjected to this hurtful racism.

The men came up and stood around them. 'Did Uncle Tom say goodbye to you?' Peleiupu asked Naomi, who nodded.

'I saw him yesterday,' she said. 'He gave me this.' She held up her left hand. A silver bracelet. 'Got my name on it. He had it made for me.' She started crying. The girls hugged her. 'Uncle Tom said I'll be all right in Samoa.'

'What does he do?' Iakopo asked. Peleiupu glanced at Naomi, who appeared too preoccupied with crying to have heard him.

'Bart can tell you,' she said.

'Your Uncle Tom runs a security business,' Bart offered. 'He provides people to protect your property or business.'

'And he and Bart have decided to merge their companies,' Peleiupu said.

'That's great news!' Tavita said. 'They're going to be difficult to beat.'

'I think we should leave the ship now,' Bart advised. Tavita stood his daughters up. Peleiupu held Naomi's shoulders and helped her to her feet.

'We'll come out to the deck and wave goodbye to you,' Tavita told his daughters. 'Stop crying,' he added in Samoan. 'It's not far to go now before you come home for Christmas.' At the cabin door he stopped everyone. 'Now,' he said to his children, 'you have to look after one another. You, Iakopo, must look after your sisters. If you need help, you get in touch with Mr Brant or Mr Service. Understand? Trust no one else.' They nodded through their tears.

'What about Uncle Tom?' Naomi prompted.

'Yes, trust Uncle Tom too,' Peleiupu replied.

'Now go down to the wharf with Mr Brant,' Tavita instructed them.

Peleiupu insisted on accompanying the children and the two men down the gangway onto the crowded wharf. The sun was sinking swiftly over the gulf and sending a thickening darkness, like a steady wave, over the harbour, wharves, the city.

Tavita and Naomi stood at the deck railing, watching them. They saw Peleiupu and her children hugging as a group, then she broke away and started backing onto the gangway. They saw Bart hurrying to her; they saw her hesitate, then she kissed him on the cheek. Tavita's belly clutched momentarily. Jealousy? Suspicion? And he thought he heard Bart calling, 'Don't worry, it will be done properly.'

On their second morning out of Auckland, their ship caught in the still, humid heat of the tropics, Naomi woke them up and got them to follow her into the sitting room. There, on the side-table in front of the urns, was a chocolate cake with one white candle burning in the middle. The urns shimmered in the candlelight. 'It's Dad's birthday today,' she told them. 'I got the chef to make this.'

'I'm sorry we forgot,' Peleiupu said, hugging her. 'He was away for so long . . . '

'He said Samoans don't celebrate birthdays but Mum and me always insisted on a chocolate cake — his favourite — and one candle,' Naomi explained.

'Naomi, I'm glad you remembered.' Tavita kissed her on the cheek.

'May I say a karakia?' Naomi asked. Tavita nodded. They bowed their heads, their reflections swimming on the casings of the urns. 'Te Atua, as you know this is Dad's birthday. I know he was not a righteous man, that he did things that were sinful and evil, but when he met Mum he tried, he really tried, to follow Your ways . . .'

That evening, while they were dressed in their best clothes and enjoying the special birthday dinner that Peleiupu had arranged with the dining room, their waiter brought them a telegram for Naomi. She read it aloud to them:

MY BELOVED NAOMI STOP BART AND I AND SOME OF YOUR DAD'S MATES HAD A BIG PARTY TODAY TO CELEBRATE YOUR DAD'S BIRTHDAY STOP WE MISSED YOU VERY MUCH BUT KNOW YOU ARE SAFE WITH YOUR AUNT AND UNCLE STOP SOMEDAY SOON WE'LL MEET AGAIN STOP TELL YOUR AUNT AND UNCLE THAT WE DID EVERYTHING ACCORDING TO YOUR DAD'S PLAN FOR HIS BIRTHDAY STOP HE WOULD'VE BEEN PROUD OF US STOP IT WORKED LIKE A CHARM STOP BART SAYS JAKE HEART AND CATCH ARE FINE AND SEND THEIR LOVE STOP SEE YA SOON STOP TOM

'What was Dad's plan for his birthday?' Naomi asked.

'For Tom and some of his friends to go out to their favourite pub and celebrate,' Peleiupu lied.

Tavita glanced at Peleiupu. She was pale, trembling visibly; her face shining — with relief? Happiness? But why tears? She reached over and grasped Naomi's hand.

Return to Niuafei

It hadn't rained in the three weeks since they had returned, but clouds were now sliding in from the horizon and massing on the mountain range. Peleiupu's throat and body tingled with the expectation of the cool, quenching feel and taste of it. Yes. She waited for the rain, for Apia now felt small, oppressive and unimportant compared with Auckland. The mail she'd been expecting hadn't arrived either, and her life was standing still because of it. She was pleased with most other things. Naomi still woke at dawn, crying for her parents, but she was fitting into their aiga and the sisters' school well. Their aiga and community and Pili were healing her with their boundless love. Naomi loved Pili, her 'orphan', and took care of him whenever she was home. Poto, Semisi and their other Satoa relatives had come to welcome them back and took Naomi into their hearts. They believed Arona had been a successful sea captain who'd traded and travelled to the four corners of the earth, and had died, tragically, with his proud and regal Maori wife, in a car accident. Their sacred ashes were now in urns made of real gold, in a special shrine in Peleiupu's sitting room. Many had visited to pay their respects and marvel at the sight of all that gold. Some had asked if the ashes were going to be buried or scattered. Peleiupu had avoided answering.

Their business was doing exceptionally well under Siniva's and Mikaele's management, so Peleiupu was leaving it to them while she waited. Tavita was now too busy in the newly formed Citizens' Association, which was leading the opposition to Governor Dickinson and the New Zealand administration and fighting for self-government. As more and more people joined that opposition, it was not going to be good for business. She had told Tavita that but he'd refused to drop it. He argued that he was fighting for Sao and all the people killed in the New Zealand-introduced epidemic, and against racism. And had she forgotten how they called them half-castes — 'the dregs of civilisation'? She couldn't argue against that because she knew he'd accuse her of selling out to papalagi rule. So she was leaving him to it. He came home late and was sometimes quite drunk. She refused to believe the rumours that he was also having affairs — she couldn't conceive of it.

She had agreed with Tavita, Lefatu and Ruta to take the ashes to Satoa to Lalaga's grave and then to the sacred palm grove, Niuafei, in Fagaloto, to be buried with Mautu. But she kept delaying . . . She continued to wait for the mail and, as she waited, her hunger for mangoes turned into a craving. She went to the market with Pili early in the morning and picked out the fattest, juiciest, sweetest ones, filled a large basket and brought them home where, while the other members of her family ate their usual fare, she and her son gorged themselves on the ripe fruit until she was almost bursting with the richness of it.

Are you pregnant? some of the women asked. She was highly offended but they reminded her that only pregnant women got intense cravings for particular foods. No, I'm not pregnant, she told them, but she was empty — yes, utterly empty — and wanted to fill that emptiness with the sweetest, smoothest taste on earth . . . fill it until she was almost choking and drowning in it.

'How come you're crazy on mangoes?' asked Naomi who wasn't fond of the fruit. 'It's terrible — like dead, sweetened porridge,' she claimed.

Peleiupu told her the story of her first mango pressed against her cheek by her father so long ago. 'I'm a descendant of the mango,' she told Naomi. When Naomi raised her eyebrows in disbelief Peleiupu laughed. 'It gives me the runs,' Naomi said. She was right, but what was a little dose of the runs compared with the enjoyment of a splendid addiction? Besides, it kept you 'filled' while you waited for the mail.

It was Friday lunchtime, Peleiupu was belching and round-bellied with mango when her secretary brought in the box of mail and placed it on her desk. Her heart quickened; her hands shook with anticipation. The secretary rushed off for her lunch. She waited, afraid yet dying to rip into the mail. Quickly her fingers scrambled through the letters, searching for it. Three letters from her children — she'd read those later. Bills and more bills. Business letters and useless advertisements. Near the bottom of the box was a large brown envelope, fat with papers. Up and out and she was tearing it open. The contents tumbled out and spilled across her desk. Newspaper clippings. Large black headlines and photographs, demanding her attention. Her hands were shaking uncontrollably; she wanted to know and she hoped and hoped.

A note in Bart's handwriting:

> Dear Mr and Mrs Barker,
>
> Tom and I thought you'd be interested in these. Please let us know
> if you want us to do anything further.
>
> Arohanui, Bart.

It was front-page news in nearly all the main New Zealand papers.

PHILANTHROPIST BUSINESS LEADER AND WIFE DIE IN FREAK MOTOR ACCIDENT.

There were photographs of Blundell and his wife at a recent fundraising function, and two photos of the smashed car lying among thick bush in a ravine . . .

SLIPPERY ROAD CLAIMS LIVES OF BLUNDELL FAMILY

More photos showed police examining the badly smashed vehicle; the car being winched from the ravine; the Blundells with their two grandchildren . . .

She flicked through the rest of the clippings, her heart singing. Went to her door and locked it. Returned to her desk and started reading the articles. Even her eyesight was heightened, magnifying every word, every picture. Most of the articles said that the Blundells, one of the first families to own cars in the country, had been on their way to their holiday house in the Coromandel when the accident occurred. Passing motorists had noticed the break in the roadside fence and had stopped and found the vehicle at the bottom of the ravine. It had been a very wet and windy Saturday morning. Difficult driving conditions. Some articles were short histories of Blundell's life: all were tributes that presented him as a dynamic, generous, patriotic Christian father, husband, business leader, who'd risen from poverty-stricken circumstances on a small Waikato farm to be a sailor and captain and then an import-exporter . . .

One of his 'dearest and closest friends' described him as 'a fair dinkum, unassuming New Zealand bloke who loved God, king, and country, and who gave to all those in need . . .'

Only two articles, one in the scandal-mongering *True* and one in the Communist Party paper the *Red Flag,* challenged that saintly image. Both papers claimed Blundell had been twice under investigation, early in his career, for tax fraud and the illegal importation of drugs but said the investigations had been terminated because of Blundell's influence. *True* hinted that Blundell had led a double life, secretly consorting with young prostitutes of both sexes, and using drugs and alcohol. The *Red Flag* accused him of being 'a capitalist roader whose companies exploited their workers, heartlessly and unscrupulously'. He was also alleged to have been involved with hiring thugs to break up any strikes in his businesses.

Peleiupu learned from the clippings that the Blundells' only child, a son, had been killed in a skiing accident ten years previously. That son's children — a boy and two girls — had become 'the centre of their grandparents' life and love'. They must have been about the ages of her own children, Peleiupu speculated.

She folded the clippings, pushed them back into the envelope, resealed it and locked it in the office safe. She decided Tavita should not see the information. Not yet. Though Naomi knew her parents were killed, she didn't know anything about the Blundells, so she needn't see the clippings either. Not until she was older and stronger.

There was no one in the sitting room when she entered. She moved up to the small shrine — a teak table covered with a white silk cloth. The two urns on it were adorned with six sea-shell ula that Ruta had made specially for Arona. She reached out and straightened the ula and smoothed down the tablecloth. Then she stepped back and sat down on the sofa to contemplate the shrine, the urns. She drifted into the swimming gold of the urns . . .

The *Lady Poto* turned into the entrance into Fagaloto Bay and was soon free of the turbulence of the open sea. Naomi and Pili were in the pilot's cabin, with Mikaele teaching them how to steer. A few Satoa relatives were playing suipi on the deck. Peleiupu was feeling more hemmed in — even the sea seemed a wall to her desire to be out there in the wider world. She'd spent yesterday and the previous night in Satoa. She'd taken the urns to Lalaga's and Mautu's graves by the church, and, in a service conducted by the pastor, had celebrated Arona's (and Areta's) final return to their parents. Most of Satoa had turned up, many weeping and congratulating Peleiupu on fulfilling her promise to her parents of bringing home the beloved prodigal son.

Now it was the final phase of Arona's return. Peleiupu walked up to the prow of the boat. The slight chill in the wind penetrated to her bones but she let it, for the discomforting cold distracted her attention from Tavita's inexplicable refusal to accompany her. He had claimed he had to be at the trial of two Mau leaders, but she suspected it was more than that.

'Look, look!' Pili called to Peleiupu, pointing at the sky ahead. There, hovering over the centre of the village, were three frigate birds, glistening black M-shapes. Peleiupu recalled the story of Ume and how he was killed by their ancestral frigate, in revenge for betraying his sister. She persuaded herself that, in a profound way, her revenge for Arona was that of the frigate. And now she was bringing Arona back to Niuafei, the heart and shrine of Fatutapu and the frigate. One day she too would be returned to Niuafei and buried beside their father. 'Are we going to see Lefatu and

Ruta?' Pili interrupted Peleiupu's thoughts. 'Naomi'll love them.' He came with Naomi and stood beside her.

'Your father used to love coming here,' Peleiupu told Naomi. 'This is where our Aiga Sa-Tuifolau began, hundreds of years ago, and where the guardians of our aiga still live today.'

'Is this where Fatutapu lives?' Naomi asked. Peleiupu couldn't believe Naomi knew that name. 'Dad used to tell me about Fatutapu, our aiga's atua.'

'What else did your father tell you?'

'That one of the reasons he left Samoa was because he didn't want to be a pastor and he couldn't say no to your parents.'

'What's that got to do with Fatutapu?'

'He said he always felt that Grandad Mautu became a pastor because his mum and dad wanted him to.'

'And?'

'If Mautu had had his way, he would've been Fatutapu's guardian. But they chose Aunt Lefatu for that.'

'So some of this is not new to you?'

She shook her head. 'My dad told me lots of other things too. I loved his stories but I didn't think the stuff in them was important to me.'

'Now it is?'

She nodded. 'Yes, because I'm in Samoa now, with my aiga.'

'How come you don't tell us stories like that?' Pili interjected.

'I will soon,' Peleiupu promised.

'What about now?' he demanded.

So as their boat headed across the bay to Fagaloto in the healing, welcoming shadow and gaze of the frigates, she started telling them about the atua who took the form of the frigate to come to earth and court beautiful Sina . . .

Lefatu and the elders of their aiga and all the matai of Fagaloto were waiting in the faletele to welcome them. Lefatu insisted that Peleiupu come and sit beside her, and then pulled Naomi into her lap and, in greeting her, wept silently. She took Pili and cuddled him to her side. Peleiupu couldn't see Ruta anywhere. Later Lefatu told her that Ruta had gone to prepare Niuafei. Mikaele brought the urns through the solemn silence and placed them at the foot of the fale's centre post. The ava ceremony of welcome began . . .

Peleiupu had once believed Lefatu would never age. Now as she observed her she had to admit she was old: long wispy white hair; her body, with ill-fitting skin and muscle, a bundle of folds and wrinkles; rheumy, cataracted eyes; her whole weight anchoring her to the floor as if she'd not be able to stand again.

As the ava ceremony ended, Lefatu called, 'He's come home. Arona, our child, has come home at last. Bring him to me!' Peleiupu bowed her head, took the urn and presented it to her. Kissing and caressing it, Lefatu raised it to her forehead, crying, 'My beloved, my beloved!'

Most of the women joined the muted wailing. 'We want to greet him!' some of them called. So Peleiupu passed it to the woman next to Lefatu.

'Bring me Arona's beloved wife,' Lefatu said. Peleiupu did so. And Areta, too, was greeted and passed from elder to elder.

Peleiupu noticed that many of them touched it briefly, warily, and then passed it on: it was not the Satoan way to cremate people and put them in small containers. Areta was also a stranger and you did not 'handle' strangers' spirits in a familiar manner — it wasn't safe.

'We had them cremated because it was the only way we could bring them home,' Peleiupu said, trying to allay their fears. 'Otherwise Arona would've been buried in foreign soil.'

'You did the correct thing, Pele,' Lefatu ruled. 'Foreign burial practices have also become part of our way. Remember we didn't bury people in boxes before the palagi came. And I like this practice because it has allowed Arona, our prodigal son, to return to us.' The elders agreed with her.

'Where are Arona and his beloved wife to be buried?' one of the elders asked. Peleiupu looked at Lefatu, who ignored the question and told her to tell them about Arona's life away from Samoa.

So, as the afternoon aged, Peleiupu gave them a laundered version. She had never considered herself a good storyteller but, as she spoke, more and more people were drawn into the fale. Their rapt attention held her, made her realise that perhaps she had inherited the gift from her parents and Barker and Stenson and all those books that had enriched her imagination. Through her telling, Arona and Areta would become rich, fabulous strands in the ie toga of life that was their aiga, Fagaloto, and the ever-moving present.

Suddenly she felt an intense cold spot on her right cheek. It radiated out until the skin of her whole face was a thick mask of cold and, in trying to peel it off, she woke gasping. 'It's me!' Ruta whispered into her ear. 'It's only a mango — your favourite.' In the pale dawn light Ruta thrust the wet mango into Peleiupu's hand. 'I collected a basketful on my way back.'

'From Niuafei?'

'Yes, I tidied it up and got it ready for Arona and Areta.'

The mango fitted perfectly into Peleiupu's hand; she dried it with her sleeping sheet. 'Has Lefatu decided when?'

Ruta nodded. 'She wants us to go now. She's awake with the children, and ready.'

'Who's going?'

'Only the old lady, you, me, Naomi and Pili.'

'No one else?'

'No, that's what Lefatu wants. Besides, many of the new Samoans wouldn't understand.'

Peleiupu realised as she dressed, quickly and quietly so as not to wake the others, that her craving for mangoes was gone. Just like that. She hurried with Ruta to Lefatu's fale. Pili started to talk but Peleiupu distracted his attention to the mango, which she put into his eager hands. Ruta handed Naomi the small basket of mangoes to carry. Peleiupu gathered up the urns and held them against her chest.

Lefatu staggered to her feet. Ruta steadied her. 'You'll have to help me through the dark,' she told Ruta. 'Have you told Naomi about Niuafei?' she asked Peleiupu, who told her that Arona had already done that. 'Good, very good,' she whispered.

The eastern light was seeping quickly into the dark sky as they hurried through the sleeping village, leaving their footprints in the dew-covered ground. With Lefatu and Ruta beside her, Peleiupu once again felt safe in the heart of their aiga, walking towards Niuafei and Fatutapu and her father, glad to be away from the individualistic, viciously competitive life of Apia and business. She was walking with her ancestors and all her memories to do with them . . .

By the time they were through the thick vegetation of Totoume Peninsula to the edge of Niuafei they were wet through with dew, and their feet and legs were covered with mud. Not even the children were complaining, though.

The shrine's circle of flat boulder seats and its floor of pebbles, broken shells and coral glowed in the early morning light. Peleiupu handed the urns to Lefatu who, unaided, shuffled across the circle, her shadow preceding her like a guide, and placed the urns on the central boulder. She turned and, beckoning to Naomi and Pili, called, 'Come across now.' Naomi took Pili's hand and they walked to Lefatu and the healing centre of the shrine. Lefatu sat them down beside her on the second boulder seat.

Peleiupu suddenly needed to hold Ruta's hand. Ruta smiled at her and led her across to the third boulder seat. Just before she sat down, Peleiupu felt a sharp sliver of shell cut into her little toe. Using her nails, she picked it out. A spot of blood filled the tiny hole. She looked up. Ruta had taken the next seat.

In respectful silence and awe they watched the sun rising, its rays cutting through the gaps in the canopy, the palms and the other vegetation, and flooding the shrine with a luminous white light. Its heat turned the dew into light steam, which wove up into the canopy and sky. They watched as the presence of Fatutapu and the ancestors wove around and into them . . .

There was a rattling on the broken shells and they broke from the spell. Lefatu was starting to cross the shrine to the entrance of the path to Mautu's grave. Ruta and the children followed her. Peleiupu gathered the urns.

When she arrived, she found the others around Mautu's grave, which Ruta had weeded and cleaned the previous day. 'Mautu, my beloved brother, we've come to bring you Arona and his wife Areta,' Lefatu said. 'You've been waiting for them for such a long time. You can thank your daughter Pele for keeping her promise to you. We have also brought Naomi, Arona's daughter, for you to bless and welcome into our aiga . . .'

As Lefatu's voice, like fine sinnet, bound everything in equilibrium, Peleiupu, in her thoughts, talked to Mautu, 'Papa, I've kept my promise but I've done so at an enormous cost of sin and evil to myself and Tavita. You raised us not to take an eye for an eye, a life for a life, which was the way of Fatutapu and our bird before the Light of Jesus Christ reached us. But I have. My anger, my hatred, my arrogance, my pain made me follow our way of the frigate and avenge my beloved brother's death at the hands of evil men. I need your forgiveness and help . . .'

Later when she surfaced from her thoughts, she heard Lefatu saying, 'Mautu, this is probably my last visit to see you. My bones are weighing me down as if I'm carrying all the ancestors. Ruta and Pele are now doing the work I was doing, so it is almost my time . . .'

Ruta pulled a bushknife from under a boulder and started using it to dig a small square hole beside the head of Mautu's grave. Peleiupu squatted down and scooped the soil out of it with her hands. Naomi helped. Ruta lined the small grave with a piece of tapa. Then they each kissed the urns, and Lefatu asked Naomi to place her parents 'into their home'. Tears streamed down the girl's face but, boldly and in silence, she laid her parents down. Then she knelt and, with Pili, pushed the soil into the grave over the urns. Ruta and Peleiupu knelt beside them and, together, they pounded the soil down with their hands. 'We will try to visit them often,' Peleiupu promised Naomi.

'I'll take good care of them,' Ruta said. Naomi went over to Lefatu, who got up. Naomi held her hand and led her down the path.

A while later, as they headed back, eating the remaining mangoes, Peleiupu asked Ruta if she could remember if Arona had liked mangoes. Ruta pondered for a moment and then replied, 'I don't think so. Remember? He used to collect them and give them to us to eat.'

The Future

A strong smell of alcohol was coming through their bedroom door. She sat up in bed, knowing he was entering. He was a black, unsteady shadow swaying through the darkness. She sucked in desperate air as the bitter revelation and truth clutched at her breath; sucked it in through her mouth until the air was clear again and her pain was replaced by the most savage fury she'd ever experienced. She turned up her bedside lamp. The light ballooned out and netted him bending down, trying to take off his shoes.

'Turn id off!' he insisted, pulling off his left shoe. He staggered as he stood up and threw his shoe at the cupboard, where it thumped and clattered to the floor. 'Why didya have ta waidup for me?' His vision, as he tried to see her, was in fragments he couldn't stitch together. He bent down to take off his other shoe and stumbled over. 'Shhiittt!' he cursed. He rolled onto his side and tried to get up. He had to get up — stand up to her!

She was looming above him — she wouldn't remember how she got there. He wasn't the Tavita she loved, the man she'd devoted her life to. With both hands she grabbed his side and pushed him over. He crashed onto the floor and rolled over, laughing and pedalling his feet in the air. 'So it's true, eh?' she demanded.

'Whad's true?' he started taunting her. He didn't care any more if she knew, he just wanted to hurt her. He tried to regain his feet but she pushed him over again. 'Now that's enough, Pele!' he muttered. Placing her foot on the back of his shoulder, she pushed him face down onto the floor. 'Ya can't do that ta me!'

his body was a massive bag of liquid he couldn't control. 'No, Pele, who the hell da ya think ya are?' He reached up; she slapped his hands away.

'I can smell her all over you!' she said accusingly. Since their return from New Zealand, she'd refused to believe the rumours about his affair with Bileen Griff.

He was bloody well going to give it to her. 'So whad? At least she cares for me; she doesn't treat me like a hopeless weakling.'

He grabbed her ankles and didn't understand why, though he tried with all his might, he couldn't lift her, topple her.

'Again the whimpering, pathetic Tavita who can't cope!'

'See whad I mean? Pele, ya love ta control everything, everybody: your children, me, our aiga!' He thought he was shouting but she could barely hear him. 'But, ya Mighty Majesty, ya can't control my cock. No, ya can't!'

That remark was the bushknife blade that slit into her moa. 'Yeah, I can't control it because that's all you are — you want to fuck everything in sight. That's all you're good at!' She drove her knee into his ribs and he toppled to the floor again, with a winded gasp.

He had her. 'So you admid, your majesty, that my cock is good enough for you, eh?'

He believed he was laughing as she locked her arm around his neck and, lifting him up, dragged him out of their bedroom and across the corridor into Iakopo's empty room, where she dumped him onto the bed.

Later, much later, she'd forgive herself for what she did next. He rolled onto his back and, in the shadows, she glimpsed him trying to unbutton his fly. 'I'll help you!' she shouted. Shoving her hands in, she clutched both sides of his fly and, in one violent motion, ripped the buttons apart.

He thrust his hips up towards her. Her arm arched back, her furious shadow danced on the walls and then her unforgiving hand cut down swiftly, hard. 'Sshhiiitt!' he cried, choking, the pain bursting up from his groin into the pit of his head. He grasped his genitals with his hands.

'No one betrays me, nobody!' she shouted. She wheeled and stormed back into their bedroom, slamming the door behind her.

He knew even before he was fully awake he was suffering yet another relentless attack of remorse and guilt. It now happened after every bout of drinking, and this time it was doubly tenacious because adultery was mixed in. He couldn't remember much of what had happened with Peleiupu that night, only that she knew about his adultery and her fury had known no limit. He struggled out of bed, shielding his eyes from the blaring morning light. The quick sharp pain between his legs reminded him of her unforgiving slap, right there.

Staggering to the bathroom, he stripped off his clothes and shoved his head under the cold tap. The cold soaked into his hair and into his skull. He couldn't face her. But he dried his hair and face furiously with the towel and hurried over to their bedroom. He was going to apologise, admit everything. No, it wasn't his fault! Their marriage had started going wrong long before their trip to New Zealand. He turned the doorknob quietly, opened the door and peeked in. The bed was made. She wasn't there. He slid in, got a clean shirt and pair of trousers from his cupboard, dressed, shoved on a pair of sandals, and turned to leave. Naomi was in the doorway, uniformed and ready for school.

'Morning, Uncle,' she said cheerfully. 'Are you all right?' He nodded, his insides and hands trembling, shaking. 'I brought you this.' She extended the glass of whisky to him. He hesitated — what was the child going to think? His right hand acted against his wishes — it stretched out and took the glass. Then his two disobedient hands raised it to his thirsty mouth. She looked away as he sucked back the drink. 'Did you and Auntie have a scrap last night?' she asked, after he'd returned the empty glass to her. He nodded; the warmth of the whisky was permeating his throat and chest and the insecure rest of him. 'Mum and Dad had a couple of fights when Dad got sozzled,' she said, eyes twinkling. 'He came off second best and he never took Mum on again. He also made sure he never got drunk while Mum was around.' Wise advice but he didn't welcome it.

When they got to the dining room the women serving the breakfast greeted him respectfully, with eyes lowered, and hurried away. 'Where's Pili?' he asked.

'Pele's taken him to school,' replied Naomi.

'Are you going to eat with me?'

'No, I've had mine. Had it with Pili and Pele.' He sat down.

She handed him his serviette. 'I've got to go to school now,' she said. But she lingered. 'You're my parents now,' she added. It was a plea. Before he could speak, she ran out of the room. He started shaking again.

Two more quick whiskies eroded the relentless sharp edge of his guilt, made him feel more anchored. He'd disappear before Peleiupu returned, avoid further confrontation for the sake of their children, family, and Naomi. However, after his fourth consoling drink, he decided not to be a coward and face the consequences of his betraying her, take his just punishment. A fifth drink. Yes, he'd face her — after all, it wasn't all his fault.

Just then she entered and, with the luminous light from the windows armouring her, glided into the centre of his vision. Challenging him. He continued eating. She poured herself a cup of tea and sat down opposite him. He wasn't going to apologise, he wasn't going to grovel: he'd done enough of both in their relationship. She was also deliberately daring him — her whole silent, accusing, defiant presence told him that. 'Did you take Pili to school?' he heard his voice asking. What a bloody stupid question. He glanced up.

'Are you going to use alcohol as your excuse?' she asked in English. No way was she going to back off: he'd treated her like shit.

'See, there you go again!' he retorted in Samoan. 'You don't even want to use our language in our relationship!'

'I'm not going to be distracted,' she countered in English.

'You're so taken with palagi ways, you use English all the time now.'

'You are not going to get me to argue about other things!'

'I don't have a hope of doing that. Pele, you're the cleverest, most perceptive person in Samoa and in our family.' He couldn't stop himself. 'You're so perceptive you've always been able to read me like the kids' faitaupi, eh.'

She was determined not to be diverted. 'Have you been unfaithful?' A direct, clean move which, as it penetrated his defences, made her feel braver, angrier. He stabbed his fork into his bacon and looked away. 'That's all I want to know. Have you?'

It was unfair, unwarranted, it wasn't his fault. He looked up at her. He couldn't escape those fierce, truth-seeking eyes. 'No!' he lied. Even as he said it, he regretted it. But 'No!' he repeated.

'So not only are you a slave to your genitals, you're a liar too.' She said it slowly, digging it in.

The plate broke in a loud metallic clack as he slammed his knife and fork down on it; his chair screeched as he pushed it back and jumped to his feet. 'So I'm a liar, eh? And you, what are you?'

'You've been unfaithful, Tavita. I know that. Don't try to . . .'

'What about Bart?' He enjoyed that.

She couldn't believe he could be so devious. 'What about him?'

He smiled, deliberately. 'Well, what about the thing between you two?'

'What *thing*? I can't believe you're capable of such lies!' Don't get angry, she told herself. That's what he wants.

'Admit it — you were attracted to him.'

She was losing control again. 'Yes, I was attracted to him, but that's all!'

'Keep your voice down,' he cautioned. 'The whole bloody family and neighbourhood can hear you.'

'I don't care!' she was not going to play his game.

'What about the lies you've been living?' He ventured into his real pain. 'What about those?'

She knew what he was referring to but wasn't going to admit it. 'What lies?'

Knowing she was unprepared, he went on the offensive. 'Firstly, the whole noble, censored life of your *noble* brother that you've given to our family and people to swallow.'

'I'll deal with that later,' she countered. 'What other lies were you referring to?'

'You gave the order, didn't you?' He watched his question triggering anguish in her quick mind. 'Didn't you?'

'What order?' She tried to regain her composure.

There was no going back: let it all out and let her experience some of the guilt and pain. 'Darling, you gave Tom, your noble brother's assassin, the okay to go ahead with Blundell's execution.' She cringed, tightening herself protectively around her vulnerable centre. He enjoyed it. But when he saw her tears, some part of him wanted to protect her. He reached out. She slapped his hand away.

'Someone had to do it.' She paused. 'I had to do it because, as usual, you didn't have the guts!' There, she stabbed him right where he lived.

'You don't mind having people killed?'

'It was them or us. He killed Arona and you know the police weren't going to do anything about it.'

'The Arona we found was a thief, a liar, a murderer and a bloody gangster. You didn't like him and don't lie to me about that!'

'But he had honour and courage!' She got him again. 'Besides, Blundell was going to kill us and the kids.'

'Pele, I've watched you being corrupted by wealth and power. You love it!'

'It's not true!' She tried to persuade herself. 'Blundell wouldn't have left us alone.'

'And, you hid it from me and that's as good as lying to me.' Keep weaving, keep putting her on the defensive.

'Look at your own noble family,' she continued her attack. 'I learned from your *beloved* father.'

'What did you learn?' he asked warily, sensing she was changing tactics.

'Remember? Your dad didn't tell you very much about his early life, eh? Or about anything else, did he?' Smile, stick it to him. 'No, your talkative, soulful dad preferred to confide in me and my dad. And I was the one who filled you in on your father's life.' She could feel his anger — and pain. 'So let me remind you of your heritage, darling.' She paused again. Let him wait in trepidation. 'Your noble father was not a lord or an earl or anybody. He was a poverty-stricken abandoned orphan who, like Arona, went to sea and had many noble adventures. To save some orphans and avenge his abuse by a ruthless, heartless villain, much like Blundell, he plotted and captured the abuser and, after torturing him, with pleasure, stabbed him to death. The villain, like Blundell, deserved his execution. And your father, like me, felt no guilt about it.'

'My father exaggerated . . .'

'You mean he made up adventurously heroic stories? Like the ones I've made up about Arona and his adventurous, honourable, courageous life and rebellion against monsters like Blundell?'

Tavita grew paler. Peleiupu stepped back and steadied herself.

'You're just like the rest of them,' he snapped. 'You all think my father was a strange, hopeless palagi: a braggart, a good-for-nothing! But he loved you, Pele. He loved you and Arona and your father. He loved you more than my mother and his own children!'

She hadn't expected this: he was confessing some of his deepest, most secret fears. Her love for him surged; she suddenly wanted his forgiveness.

'You can go to hell, Pele. I didn't need my father's love, and I don't need yours. Besides, you're so in love with money and power you're betraying your own parents, Sao, our dead son, and all our dead.'

There was some truth in his accusation but she couldn't stop herself. 'At least I'm not — I'm not fucking a papalagi!'

Time stopped still, gasping in fright; it didn't want either of them to make another move in this moment of truth, this threatened breach of the faith and alofa that had bound them together for so long. But the future was inevitable.

Desperately she wanted to take back her insult, her truth. She stepped towards him. He moved towards her but it wasn't in forgiveness and alofa. He would later tell the elders of their aiga that he'd done it because she'd trampled on his mamalu, honour and mana as their ali'i and head of their aiga.

The incredible shock of his fist in the centre of her face reverberated beyond physical pain and forgiveness. It was the first time he'd ever hit her. The second blow punched into the core of her being and as she tumbled away from him into the darkness flooding her eyes, she cried, 'Tavita, Tavita!' knowing that when she surfaced from that dark they would be beyond trust and forgiveness and they'd not meant it to be that way, that future . . .

Epilogue

'Let's go, let's go!' Arona whispered urgently into her ear, and Peleiupu was awake and hitching on her ie lavalava and shaking Ruta awake, and they were rolling out of their mosquito net, with Naomi mumbling, 'Wait for me, wait for me!'

Arona was already over the front paepae and jumping down onto the wet grass and rushing into the wet dawn towards the church when Naomi caught up with Peleiupu and Ruta. Peleiupu grabbed her hand and pulled her after them into the incoming tide of ripe mango scent . . .

The sky was overcast and wild with the promise of more heavy rain. Their skins started goose-pimpling in the sharp cold, and the water-soaked ground wrapped its wetness around their bare feet as they ran squishily through it. 'Hurry! Or we'll be late!' Peleiupu urged her sisters as the hungry ripe mango smell continued weaving into her nostrils and down into her eager lungs.

The large stand of mango trees behind the church loomed up over it, and even in the dark she could see that the trees were still laden with ripe fruit. She imagined other children scurrying around under the trees collecting the fruit that had fallen during the night.

Dragging the empty basket, Arona disappeared into the darkness under the mangoes. No others yet! she thought gladly, then she saw two other children running into the mango stand from the opposite direction.

She dropped Naomi's hand as Arona pushed the basket to her and started selecting the best mangoes from the ground and dropping them into the basket. 'Quick, quick!'

he kept urging his sisters, who scrambled around picking up the fruit. Across the stand she recognised Tavita and his brother Mikaele — as usual they were trying to out-race them, their pale white skins red from the cold. From behind them other children were joining the scramble, the race, which, since the mangoes had started ripening a few weeks before, occurred every morning at dawn.

As she watched her brother she marvelled at his skill and speed; they all called him the Mango King because he out-raced even Tavita, his main rival and best friend. They couldn't understand Arona's mad enthusiasm to be the Mango King — he didn't even like mangoes that much. After each race — and he'd always collected the most and the best — he simply took one or two bites out of one, gave it to Naomi or Ruta, and then talked to his friends while the others gorged themselves on the succulent fruit, with the thick golden juice dribbling-dribbling-dribbling out of the corners of their insatiable mouths. He always made sure there were enough mangoes left for the people at home, and picked out the fattest for their mother.

Because these trees had grown from mango stones an American sailor had given the then pastor years before, everyone referred to them as Mago Amelika, and they were special. Satoa had one rule about them: no one was allowed to climb them or throw sticks or stones up at them to knock down the fruit. No one.

So why did Arona do what he did next? Had some evil aitu entered him suddenly and driven him to it? Was it a mad daring that blinded him to the consequences of his actions? For years they would ponder that question. For now the only real thing was the mad act. He peered up into the dripping darkness of the mango foliage, seemed to catch sight of a hypnotically yellow fruit — a small brilliant sun, he'd later describe it — and before he or they knew it, he was jumping up and catching hold, with both hands, of a low branch. Before they could stop him — they were too afraid to think about it — he had swung his legs up over the branch and was standing on the junction of the branch and the trunk of the tree.

'It's not allowed!' Tavita was the first to call.

'Come down!' Peleiupu called. 'Has your head gone mad?' But he didn't seem to hear, not even when the other children called as a chorus. He appeared absolutely beyond their hearing and their fear of what the elders were going to do to him.

'I'll going to tell Mautu!' Naomi threatened.

'We're going to tell, Arona!' chorused Ruta.

Immediately, the other children started to scatter home and away from being caught and associated with Arona's action. Mikaele was trying to pull Tavita away but he refused to move. 'We're all going to be beaten by Mautu!' Mikaele cautioned.

'Let's go!' Ruta said to Peleiupu, who was transfixed as she watched her brother climbing confidently from branch to branch.

'Hurry, hurry!' Peleiupu heard her frightened voice pleading.

They stood still, all of them, as if they were going to remain in that position and moment forever, witnessing, with fear and huge admiration, Arona's mad act, his right arm reaching up cautiously, up through the dripping leaves, his hand opening to cup the glistening, golden fruit, his fingers closing around it until it was secure in his grip . . .

'And he doesn't even like mangoes,' Tavita said. Peleiupu turned to him and caught him securely in the centre of her sight, as she was caught in his.

At that moment Arona's familiar laughter started falling down from the mango tree, and they gazed up and saw him, face round and bright with joy, as he held up the golden fruit and showed it to them . . . Such daring, such beautiful madness.